THE SHIFT

GEORGE FOY

BANTAM BOOKS
NEW YORK TORONTO LONDON SYDNEY AUCKLAND

THE SHIFT

A Bantam Spectra Book

PUBLISHING HISTORY

Bantam trade paperback edition published July 1996
Bantam mass market edition / April 1997

SPECTRA and the portrayal of a boxed ''s'' are trademarks of Bantam
Books, a division of Bantam Doubleday Dell Publishing Group, Inc.

Excerpts from *Archy and Mehitabel* by Don Marquis. Copyright 1927 by
Doubleday, a division of Bantam Doubleday Dell, Inc. Used by permission
of the publisher.

ISBN 0-553-57471-X
Published simultaneously in the United States and Canada

Bantam Books are published by Bantam Books, a division of Bantam
Doubleday Dell Publishing Group, Inc. Its trademark, consisting of the words
''Bantam Books'' and the portrayal of a rooster, is Registered in U.S. Patent
and Trademark Office and in other countries. Marca Registrada. Bantam
Books, 1540 Broadway, New York, New York 10036.

PRINTED IN THE UNITED STATES OF AMERICA

RAD 10 9 8 7 6 5 4 3 2 1

Praise for
THE SHIFT

"This is what both SF and the hard-boiled mystery were born to do, and Foy has done it well. . . . THE SHIFT is so near-future you might find yourself surfing your cable system for the *Tonya Harding Show* or looking up the Marla Maples High School in the New York City phone directory."
—*Locus*

"Solid entertainment and an enjoyable read . . . Imagine Michael Crichton crossed with Robert Ludlum and you get the idea."
—*Cape Cod Times*

"A compelling noir mix of science-fiction thrills, virtual-reality wonders and 19th-century horror."
—*Publishers Weekly*

"Tautly plotted, highly colored . . . Grimly effective New York scenes—both old and new—blend with convincingly extrapolated virtual realities."
—*Kirkus Reviews*

"Stunningly vivid, all-too-plausible . . . [a] fresh and powerfully imagined new take on the coming video revolution."
—*Booklist*

"A hip, scintillating, futuristic thriller; a blend of virtual reality and real horror. When the killers in VR and the assassins in the 'real' world start to exchange rolodexes, you know you're in for a wild time, greased by writing as fast and cool as a roller-coaster ride in Greenland."
—Janet Morris

AUTHOR'S NOTE

This is a work of fiction, but fiction is only elevated facts, and I like to get the facts straight. Although the virtual reality setup described in these pages does not exist per se, all the technology—from the haptic suits to the fiber-optic cable networks—*is* around, ready for someone to put together enough money and computer time to turn it into a real system. The New York City of the present is real. The Riker's Island section is very close to real, given the paranoid refusal of the Department of Corrections Public Affairs Bureau to let me visit the place in depth. The 1850s version of New York is as close to historical reality as a stack of research could make it. One detail had to be bent: Pfaff's Saloon did not actually open on Broadway until the mid-, as opposed to the early, 1850s.

Several people and two institutions helped in the writing. My friends Peter and Lynn Dervis, Peter B. Sessa, Doree Duncan Seligmann, and Jane Waisman gave unselfishly of their time and advice. Roger Randall, Rena Down, Ghotam Chaudry, Bevia Rosten, and Chris Safran helped with specific details. The archives of Dervis Historical Resources provided vital background. The Writers Room in Manhattan furnished companionship as well as more prosaic resources. Jonathan Matson was unstinting and wise in his counsel. My daughter, Emilie, cheerfully put up with the habitual abstraction of the working writer. My wife, Liz, provided unfailing support through a long, cold, and lonely winter. To her the following pages are dedicated.

THE SHIFT

ONE

You know the street well enough you get to recognize how people are going to cap you.

The Asians use autos like modified Tech-9s or Bullpups and they'll smoke the guy next door and miss you and have to clean up with blades later. The Rastas use cheap trey-eights with generic soft-nosed slugs but they'll off both of you the first time with no mistakes given the size and quantity of the holes.

The Colombians take out the neighborhood in a happy carnival of Uzis. The Albanians carve your brother's throat with a carpet-cutter. The Italians smoke you with a .22 caliber and precision, mostly because they don't pull the trigger on the jammy till it's touching the back of your neck.

The Asians tend to stalk you first; which is why I have a feeling the guy behind me might be Asian.

It isn't a great piece of turf, from a victim's point of view; a frost-humped string of subgrade asphalt lined with cattails and trashed Plymouths and the kind of smell you get only after twenty years of burying with a front-end loader some of the nastier chemicals known to man.

In the distance you can see the burn of cars as they rush the long iron leapfrog of the Pulaski Skyway, honking and backfiring in their anxiety to get across, like nervous schoolgirls trying not to trail the hem of their dress in the shit of the Jersey marshes.

In the distance, behind me, you can see the spotlit bulk of a video-server, not one of XTV's. To my right, the sullen Gothic piles of the few corporations remaining in Newark quail under the flight paths of 777s; to my left, the icy moneyspires of Manhattan glint against the smoky night.

That's the trouble with this road. Everything is farther in the distance and in different directions except the bullrushes and the stink of organo-chlorines and the black mobsterridden depths of the Hackensack River to one side.

That, and the mincing, feminine trip of footsteps behind me; footsteps that sound softly whenever I move, and stop whenever I do, and retreat when I come after.

I walk faster. I think I hear the footsteps speeding up but I can't be sure because of the noise of my own feet. Behind me it's a strange soft rhythm, a silky "slip-*slap*," feminine as I said because it's light and quick; binary in the sense that there's two sounds in each step, like you'd get from platform heels and leather soles and the way a city woman leans forward from the hip as she walks, holding off the jackals with momentum.

Slip-*slap* . . . slip-*slap*.

Despite the feminine undertone I have no doubt it's a man shadowing me. Maybe it's the weight of the tread.

I stop abruptly, turn around. The footsteps continue for a pace, and halt in turn. For an instant, against the horizon of cattails, through the darkness that seems to rise like a lousy dream from the mud and water around, I think I can make out a tall figure, its outlines blurred by something long and black like a coat.

I blink, and the figure is gone. The rushes are blighted and dark and resemble men in the vertical. The temperature is just below freezing and sound travels well in the chilly air.

I walk back in the direction I came; the footsteps recede. Whoever's making those footsteps is staying behind that last bend in the road.

"Fuckin' idiot," I mutter to myself. I mean, this is not the city but it's only six miles in a straight line from Tenth Avenue and it's no trick at all for the violence to overflow that far.

My heart pumps so hard it hurts my ribs. I've had maybe one or two gin-and-tonics over the limit back at the Fish House Grill. If the booze boosts my confidence in one way, it also makes me more apt than usual to dream up horror stories.

I immediately start to visualize what might be trailing me. I mean, visualization is my specialty; and Asians seem too mundane, and I've never heard of the tongs venturing so far west of Mulberry Street. This abandoned ground, with its combination of mutated marine life and the vast vomit of the city, seems more apt to spawn something correspondingly huge and vicious out of the rats and PCBs that inhabit it. A dead Gambino *sottocapo* maybe, black water gurgling from the .22 hole in his spine, rotted flesh dripping off his bones but his brain sparking green as foxfire from the chemicals he was buried among—squelching through the swamp muck with both arms outstretched—

The hairs on the back of my neck take on ohms. I start walking again, faster. Behind me, ever faithful, my shadow starts up to follow.

And, this once, he gets the timing wrong. Now I can easily hear his feet in the clipped spaces between my own steps—like bad audio, echoes lagged behind the visual in one of the new productions I'm setting up for work.

I come to an abrupt halt, and hear one offset "slip-*slap*" before he mimics my stopping. This part of the road curves like a soap queen's curls but I think it straightens out beyond the next bend. A hundred yards after that there's another boatyard or marina similar to the one beside the bar I left behind me only fifteen minutes ago.

I start to run. I'm no jock but I am wearing my usual light Burmese hiking boots with star-cut Kevlar soles and they grip the cracked asphalt like the tigers in those old Goodyear commercials. Soon my breath is making storm noises in my windpipe and I don't hear anything behind me and I don't look. I can see the line of cattails and a black heap of something broken that marks the turn in the road.

I'm summoning new strength, new speed, and I pound around the tight curve like a Tanzanian hurdler five yards from the finish tape; and my heart, which I was sure couldn't

beat any rougher or faster, starts slamming triple time. I brake
so fast I nearly pitch forward on my nose, skidding like Moe
Howard avoiding the law. For a fraction of a second a sound
like crying squeaks out of my throat.

*Three black shapes in cheap jackets are filing out of the
rushes on one side, lining up across the road twenty feet
ahead of me.*

Behind, the footsteps slow to a walk, then—nothing.

The wind rattles the dead stalks of the marsh.

I turn around. The son of a bitch behind me still doesn't
show. I turn back.

They are men, not very tall. Besides the ersatz-leather jackets, two wear stonewashed shifta-rap trousers and the third has
a baseball cap. All three hold in one hand something that
glints in the meager light coming off the Pulaski a mile or so
away.

In panic, part of the human brain clicks into cliché and
refusal. At least that's what mine does now, making reassur-
ing noises like, this is all a mistake, something I made up.
This really ought to work since I spend my days imagining
problems much like this one, fake situations I put away and
forget about by logging off the terminal when I go home at
night.

The other lobe, the one where clichés don't work, can tell
exactly what's going on from the way these men move silently
and in coordination without even looking at each other. They
hold the weapons comfortably forward, and the opposite hand
is held ahead too in both protection and decoy. These are no
Five-ohs and they are not Jersey punks looking for beer
money and they *are* looking to put a real hurtin' on someone
and since no one else is around that someone has to be me.

And suddenly my brain pulls the switch on all the cool
analysis. It seems to both drop revs and speed up, like a sports
car reaching overdrive. I hurtle off the road into bullrushes on
the left with nothing in my head now but the deafening noise
of a mind screaming silently in panic.

I literally don't know how long I run like that. The cattails
are tall as buses; they are woody and you have to lean into
them until they snap to get through. My world is made up of
massive visual deprivation and the sound of breaking rushes
and crunching ice and the total effort necessary to keep from

snapping my fool ankles in the frozen mud and cattail stalks and junk metal.

I run. I slam into something hollow and tinny and fall elbows first into a thin scab of ice covering four inches of brackish water and rotted grass. Suddenly the smell is a thousand times more foul than before. My hands are lubricated with slime as I stumble to my feet again.

I run. I detect bulk ahead and scramble around the hulk of a car.

I run. High over the fractal horizon of cattails I see light, more to the left, and I turn in that direction. The mud gets softer. My lungs cannot feed enough oxygen to my legs and both bronchi and muscle tissues are screaming for air, lactic acid, a Funship Cruise, anything besides this kind of struggle. I have to slow down, there's no way not to, but I'm still moving at a fair pace when the footing grows hard and the sky opens up around me.

A road. Gravel, pitted, even in the chemical darkness of a New Jersey night I can see that, but it's still a road, and that means people built it to go places people go. I turn left instinctively, moving away from the men, jogging now because I can go no faster. Now I hear rushing and sloshing and the crunching of ice somewhere behind my left shoulder. A whistle sounds, so close and clear it forces my grudging muscles to haul out of the dregs of their reserves a shambling canter.

There's a telephone pole ahead. A bright arc-lamp shines over the rushes, illuminating a low breeze-block building with boarded-up windows, what looks like straight sparse trees growing out of the river; masts clinking aluminum, tied to rotten pilings stuck in the pitch-hued tide.

"EAST KEARNY MARINA," a sign reads. "PRIVATE. NO ADMISSION. BOAT OWNERS ONLY. DOGS."

The marsh falls off on either hand, giving way to a tired space littered with rusted cranes and junked Atomic-4s and old tires. A couple of sagging wooden cabin cruisers are propped on crooked jackstands. The light shines on vacant parking places, leaving the rest in shadow. Nothing moves.

The whistle comes again out of the bullrushes behind me. I work my legs into a trot, to my right, toward the docks. A quartet of sailboats of the pointed bathtub variety, along with an ancient patrol craft, lie leashed to a cockeyed pier. The boats are so tired and delaminated they seem not so much to float as to be accepting suicide Ophelia style in the turgid stream. Two of the patrol boat's portholes are lit with a yellow glow much friendlier than the blank bluff of the yard's arc-light.

Over the mount where the boat's radar scanner once turned I recognize the tall needle of the Kowloon Bankcorp Building downtown, as well as the huge "X" mounted on the X-Corp tower shining over the invisible shores of the city, but these symbols of my work and life seem even more remote and irrelevant to me now than usual.

I walk fast down the dock, holding the rail, for the boards are slick with frost. I step onto the vessel's deck.

I realize this boat is older than I thought; the shape of it against the Pulaski looks exactly like a navy torpedo boat, maybe not quite *McHale's Navy* vintage but close enough. The decks are of soft plywood, covered with decaying gear of a nautical nature. I stumble over a deflated life raft. The light thrown from the portholes disappears. Remembering the lay-out from *They Were Expendable,* I grope my way in the sudden obscurity to a door in the after bulkhead of the wheelhouse. I knock, not too loud.

"Hello," I call, trying to ration my scarce breath. "Hey, ah, can you let me in? I need help."

I hear metallic clicks from inside, as of padlock hasps being snapped home.

"Please, man, someone's trying to mug me, they're coming after—"

"You git off," a woman screeches, so close to my ear against the plywood door that I pull back. "You git off, motherfuckah, or I'll fuckin' drill ya, ya *bastahd*!"

"Please—look, I'll show you—"

The explosion is very loud. The blast lights up deadlights and portholes in many assorted parts of the old hull. She must have aimed a shotgun right through the cabin roof. Chunks of paint and rotten plywood patter around the sagging deck. I fall backward, banging my elbow against a cleat or something. I check my face but nothing is missing or hurt except that my ears ring and my heart is trying to leap off its mounts again. I should have known—this is not the kind of yacht club where they welcome all boat-lovers with sailing yarns and a martini.

I get off that tub as fast as I can, hunching low as I creep back down the dock. I jump off sideways at the end. I clamber backward so I can hide behind the mud and broken bricks of the embankment while watching the parking lot, and that is when he wraps his arm around my neck.

He must have hidden under the dock while I was trying to charm my way onto the PT boat. He wears cheap hair gel; the smell of it perfumes the air around me. He is very strong, his arm feels like a steel band trying to contract to zero around my spine. For a numbing second I know I'm about to die.

But the strength also gives him confidence; he thinks he can yank me easily back into him, into the comfortable arc of his knife.

My conscious brain doesn't live here anymore. My hands and balance centers react on auto, letting him haul me but twisting left as he does so. He's got his left hand around my neck, which means the knife is in his right. I spin around fast, off balance, my left hand chopping behind me and hitting his forearm in midswing while my right jabs into the windpipe; or that's the way it's supposed to work but my left arm catches the blade and I screech in pain. Also I can't see his neck and the slicing edge of my right hand glances off his shoulder into cold air.

He steps back into the shadow of the dock at the very moment my friend from the PT boat switches her cabin lights back on. I immediately spot two things: a foot laced into Flexator running shoes under a sweatsuited leg and, in a pool of broken light, an Ace Hardware carpet-cutter, with the blade extended three quarters of the way out, lying in the thick mud of low tide.

I take two short sideways steps, foot crossing foot, just like Sam Rodney taught me. My feet slip in the mud, but I keep my balance, and kick sideways into the exposed kneecap. He grunts, *"Doo meh,"* something of that order, and collapses on one knee under the dock.

I haul ass out of there. I'm up the mud bank like a goddam mountain goat. Halfway across the parking lot a sound starts, not so loud but weird and quick, it's like one long tearing of thick canvas recorded on a cheap boom box and I know exactly what it is. I start yelling again, without wanting to, pathetic clueless stuff as I throw myself behind a boat and scramble along the side of a breeze-block office into the shelter of cattails once more.

Machine-pistols, I think, and my thoughts are as trembly and weak as my voice would be if I could talk at this point. Fuckin' *machine-pistols*!

I've pretty much used up my strength here. The frozen ground is very rough and it takes all the juice left in my legs just to walk fast across the ruts and potholes. The leather jacket I'm wearing weighs my shoulders down. I hold my hands in front of my face to fend off the rushes and warm liquid trickles down into my left armpit.

The firing has stopped.

The whistle comes again, clear over my right shoulder this time. Much farther away, deep in the marsh, a coyote howls, lonely. The bullrushes are brittle silver stalks, the sky is orange, the thin crusted ice in the wet hollows is deep blue. It would all be pretty if I wasn't so likely to croak in it. And then I realize I am seeing *colors*. This means light has to be coming from somewhere. I look up.

A corner of something white and huge rises through the jagged horizon of swamp growth. Two lines of arc-lamps outline the perimeter surrounding.

The video-server. Typically it's a giant cube of armored plastic maybe fifty feet wide by forty high connected to big consumption areas by ten-inch pipes filled with fiber-optic cables. It's stuffed with millions of dollars' worth of computer equipment: transputers, boards for graphics and clipping-dividers and compression and reserve memory, all arranged in parallel and multiplexed to boot; a sort of relay station that stores and feeds back game options and menus to customers using the interactive video-nets.

And what this means, in turn, is that the cube is wired like a nuke base, full of sensors, on-line cameras, and direct radio links to police headquarters.

I jink left, toward the cube, burning pure adrenaline now, enough for a half trot. The rushes thin. The video-server is built on a manmade hillock in the swamp; miniature levees stretch out on either side. Two ten-foot-high Cyclone fences topped with outward thrusting spikes and big coils of razor-ribbon protect the knoll's perimeter.

I clamber across a dike and over a small aluminum fence. Up the hillock and I put my hands on the wire to shake it and the next thing I know I'm flat on my ass beside the secondary fence. My hands are on fire where they touched the live wire and my body generally feels like it's just shot up a case of powdered methedrine. A siren ululates like a Cold War nightmare from the top of the big white cube and I can see the housings of cameras on the roof swing around in my direction, sniffing for intruders. I get to my feet slowly and then drop down, my muscles crying "Uncle" as the suddenly familiar sound of soft rapid explosions shirttailing one on the other jitters from the marsh behind me.

I roll under aluminum fence and clean down the slope, into the shadow of the cattails. I'm beginning to love cattails. I crawl into the wet smelly stalks of the marsh growth.

I lie trembling in the icy mud, and press my face into it. The mud is cold and neutral. I'm so tired and so scared, its arctic touch feels kind. It does not want to kill me immediately and for this I am pathetically grateful.

The firing stops. There comes a beat or two of silence, under the breath of a growing breeze.

And then, soft but distinct, I hear it. Slip-*slap,* slip-*slap;* although now it's turned into more of a "slip-*splash*" as my pursuer minces toward me through the cattails only a dozen paces away.

I groan involuntarily, and press my forehead deeper into the hollow I'm making in the wetness. I hope that when it comes I won't sense it beforehand.

A whistle sounds, urgently, twice. The footsteps pause. And stop.

Over the whacko howling of the 'server alarm I can hear a different wail coming high on the wind, growing as it comes.

Sirens. The *yeow-yeow-yeow* of cruisers. Five-ohs, cops, and "Book 'em, Dano."

Ice crackles as he peers around. Cattails rustle.

The footsteps start up again. I can see him, almost dancing in my mind, the machine-pistol cradled on his forearm.

After three paces I'm certain the footsteps are growing softer, more distant.

Inside a minute I can hear nothing but the siren above me and the sirens approaching and, somewhere deep in the marsh, the cackle of a lone nightbird bitching loudly over its interrupted sleep.

I nod.

"Whaddya doin' aroun' here anyway?"

"I was getting a drink," I tell him, "I jiss took a walk."

"We ain't gonna book you for trespassin'," his partner offers magnanimously.

"Prob'ly seen some kids makin' trouble," the first one remarks, still staring at the Morgan.

"Whyn't you go on home," the second one adds wearily, "we'll follow you to the highway, so's you don't git scared."

I say okay. I don't mind admitting I get scared. I think they should be more concerned about four guys trucking around their beat with carpet-cutters and Tech-9s and negative attitudes but I'm whacked out with fear and shivering with cold. The gin wore off about an hour ago. Anyway, I don't argue with them.

I check the backseat before I climb in the Morgan—I've seen those flicks, too—but there's not much room there for assassins in the first place and nothing's on the bench except jumper cables and a safety helmet and a menu of graphics codes for a TV project I'm doing on my own account. I put in key and clutch, pull out the choke, and hit the starter button and the comforting roar of the hundred-bhp Triumph engine surges around me and I feel almost like I did eighty minutes ago when no one had tried to kill me and life was only as complicated and frustrating as it has been anyway for the last six months.

I don't put on the helmet; it's not the law yet, in New Jersey. The cops convoy me past black railroad drawbridges, a power plant, and darkened truck depots to the junction of Fish House Road and 280. With this escort I feel like the president; I wave imperially at them and miss the on-ramp. I need fuel anyway. I figure I'll follow the cruisers into the center of town and find a gas station. I keep an eye in my rearview but no headlights trouble the road behind. A dump truck rolls the other way, toward the marsh, probably hauling pirate waste, its company logo obscured by grease. The cruisers pull into a Dairy Donut. Soon I'm among the stucco corner shops and brick-face boardinghouses of Kearny. I gas up at a Getty. On my way back I fish the cellular phone out of its hiding place and try calling Larissa. Her machine answers. I miscount the stoplights and end up on a road of Scottish butchers and carpet outlets.

A small building shaped like a vinyl-sided shoebox carries a neon sign reading "McAndrew's Pub" over the usual Rolling Rock and Zero Cola displays. The great tremble of released nerves inside me needs filling, and booze will do that job as well as anything. A driveway leads around to the back. I steer the Morgan's long nose that way, and park in the dun shadow of a Dumpster.

Inside, the bar is a dim place deeply committed to no-frills drinking. It's so thick with cigarette smoke and long-nursed grudges you almost have to shove to get in the door. The kind of bar I'm used to, the kind I like. This joint serves no radicchio and you can smoke in every square foot in defiance of federal ordinance. I don't smoke but I figure drinking is a thoroughly self-destructive proposition and if you want to drink you should find a place that takes a truly no-holds-barred approach to fucking up your health.

The decor of McAndrew's, as you might expect, possesses a distinct Caledonian flavor. There's McEwan's on tap and tartans everywhere; Black Watch curtains, Henderson wallpaper, all ripped and dark with smoke. I figure the bar stools are Royal Stewart but since I'm color-blind to reds I can't be sure. A TV in the corner shows Rangers versus Celtics on cable. Postcards of Oban harbor and the Forth Bridge tacked behind the bar, large men with light eyebrows and a couple of women dressed badly enough to be native Scots. Well, I'm tall and gangly, I have orange hair and a chin that sticks out. My leather jacket and jeans also don't attract much attention, though a couple of people glance at the mud crusting on my neck, and look away quickly.

I sit on one of the Stewart stools and lean both elbows gratefully on the polished oak. The bartender, a guy the size of Ben Nevis with a bushy beard and a T-shirt that reads "We Do It Better in Dunoon," glances at my left hand, which has dried blood running in contour lines around the knuckles.

"Someone tried to kill me," I explain, "in the marsh."

"What'll ye have, lad," he replies too politely in an accent that owes everything to Edison Township and nothing at all to Edinburgh Castle.

"Gilbey's and tonic."

"We don't serve gin. Sassenach tipple," he adds, or at least that's what I *think* he says, it's hard to tell for the accent.

"Give me a Bruichladdich, then."

He shambles off, returns with the bottle, and fills a shot glass with it. I drink the first in two gulps and as the malt whisky slides down it seems to grind off the back of my throat the shameful gaseous flavor of panic, and then the metallic taste of fear, and under that the desiccation from physical effort and the stale indifference of exhaustion. I don't usually drink whisky but this stuff is alright. A couple of sips into the second glass and now I can feel a little distance between myself and the shock of almost seeing my unique and surprising life drained inside two minutes from a couple dozen bullet holes or a carpet-cutter slash across the jugular.

I understand, suddenly, that what I told the bartender was no exaggeration—someone *did* try to cap me back there. My heartbeat powers off suddenly like that Asian was mincing around behind me again. It takes the rest of that shot and most of the next to slow it down.

One good thing about McAndrew's, I think; this is definitely not the kind of joint Asians hang out in.

I mean, I didn't get a look at his face but the guy under the dock said something—*"Doo meh,"* or was it "Doo mah?"— and that sounded oriental. And I've done enough cop shows to know the sound of Tech-9s, which the buzz says Asian gangs are carrying now. Of course my friend in the plastic jacket was also sporting a carpet-cutter, like the Astoria Bad Boys, and *they're* Albanian—

I'm beginning to warm up. The heat melts some of the tension in my back and legs so that I sag harder against the good oak of the bar. Someone switches channels on the TV and a familiar jingle scratches itself onto my consciousness. I look up and catch the weird graphics for the *Real Life* house ad that are supposed to represent 3-D immersion on sets not designed for it.

"Enter the dimension of Virtix," the voice-over intones weightily. "An adventure more real than the room you're in. *Real Life;* it's a *whole new world.*"

The TV is zapped through a lofty documentary on the Manila node-rebels to settle finally on test cricket. I pop one of the pills Pentti prescribes for me, and wash it down with more single malt. The bartender looks at me suspiciously till a commotion in the corner claims his full attention.

One of the large men with light-colored eyebrows is wrestling something that looks like a sheep recently killed by an oboe. It resolves into a set of bagpipes. A smaller, darker man has already shouldered his pipes. They stand in the other corner, the one with no TV, glaring at each other. "I can't think of anyone who'd want to kill me," I tell the bartender, "except maybe my ex-wife."

This isn't true; it's just the kind of inane comment, angling for macho camaraderie, that you make to bartenders. Larissa doesn't want to kill me, most of the time. In fact, we still see each other once in a while outside of work, when we're feeling nostalgic.

And then a deep groan comes out of the corner, it sounds like a yak complaining of ulcers, followed by an atonal squeal that settles down into the measured paces of "Whack the Dildo," an old Clam Fetish song converted to a reel, and the other guy chimes in, and the way the notes miss each other, harmonies yanked half a note from true, seems to accentuate the feeling of unreality, of being out of synch with the kind of world that shows ads for Virtual TV while people are trying to trim other people's necks with carpet-cutters.

I walk unsteadily to the men's room.

THREE

I WAKE UP the next morning knowing exactly where I am and happy, for a change, with every goddam detail of it. The timing element of one of my terminals makes dog noises from the study and I don't scream at it to shut up the way I usually do, even though the Vox-recognition unit works, sometimes.

Outside the big factory window of my bedroom the gray light of November dismally drip-washes the colors of the warehouse across Hubert Street. The scene is all runny, grays, blacks, and browns, and the wind picks up old *Daily News*es and Denny's wrappers and kicks them like soccer balls into the air.

My head aches from the whisky and my arm hurts where the Asian-Albanian cut me. And I smile.

What the fuck, I think. They must have mistaken me for somebody else.

The memory of last night is there, unusually clear, and because its clarity is odd, and the events themselves are so strange, it all seems to lack reality for me now, like one of the plot lines I'm supposed to convert into scripts and scenes and graphic environments, stories that fade as soon as the work is done.

When I go into the main room I find the bulk of Lenny the Mooch sprawled snoring on the futon under mounded blankets. After Larissa and I parted company she kept the house in the Village and I moved down here, to Tribeca. This used to be a slum for the last English in New York. Over the years it became a neighborhood of factories, some of which were converted to lofts. Because I was used to living with somebody I bought a place that was much too big. When Lenny the Mooch saw it he decided his role in life was to fill that vacuum to the extent possible.

Lenny and I went to college together. He's doing a PhD in drama theory on the ten-year plan and has goofy ideas that correlate sometimes with my work. So I don't kick him out except when I have female company. Usually I just ignore him and that's what I do this morning as I grab a shower and ladle French Roast into the coffeemaker and swallow Advils and try to collect some of the notes I write to remind myself of what I have to do at work.

I check the living-room workstation; it includes phone and fax as well as the usual computer facilities and B-Net connection hardware. No e-mail and two hang-ups on the voice. Halfway through my first coffee I draw a complete blank on what I did with the Morgan and the sweat starts up, familiar, inside my palms and on the back of my neck. The headache pounds my skull like that janissary hitting the gong in the Lew Grade films intro. Then I get an image of a Dumpster, a Jersey cab, that Scottish joint with the big bartender. "Kearny," I mutter, "*Jesus*."

I'm pretty sure I slipped the bartender a Franklin to look after the wheels while I took a hack home and slept off the Bruichladdich he'd been pouring down my gullet all night.

It's at this point I realize that I was the victim of no dreams last night, none at all. That's the golden lining to booze overdose and it makes me happy all over again, since my dreams tend to be weird and leave me feeling like I ate ashes for a week. The headache fades under the magic massage of ibuprofen. The lilt of "Whack the Dildo," Glasgow style, seeps into my mind and I mutter "Jesus" again. Thinking of how much Louise, whose parents were born in Glasgow, would have detested that joint.

Louise is my mother. She lives with my sister in New

Jersey, in a big house full of crystals and tarot decks and self-help manuals. I don't see them very often.

The notes tell me I have an urgent troubleshooting meeting with the full production team for *Real Life* at 9 A.M. It's 8:40 so I take a cab to work.

Work is uptown in the new "Television City" the mayor and his developer buddies cooked up to build over the old Bermuda Lines and Swedish-American Line steamer piers so they could all legally get rich, the developers now and the mayor later. The X-Corp tower and the two big studio buildings on either side were designed by the architect Linda Woo, a woman everybody who works there has decided is certifiable. Woo believes strongly in curved lozenge shapes, and all three buildings were built in the shape of curved lozenges, which of course also resemble TV screens. This is fine as far as it goes except that Woo went on to make *everything* in the complex a curved lozenge, windows, chairs, tables, walls, the works, so that after three hours in there you begin to feel soft and round in the edges yourself, longing for the hard lines of the rest of Manhattan.

Only the eighty-foot-high, neon-illuminated, electroplated "X" on top of the tower is straight. Woo is a refugee from Hong Kong and so is a lot of the money in X-Corp and it all makes a kind of circular, oriental sense, organic vectors and everything. Then you remember it all cost so much, even allowing for the mayor's tax breaks, that we have to work twice as hard so X-Corp doesn't fall on its ass financially.

I pay off the cab at Studio A and take the freight elevator up to the sixth floor. I've got a nice big corner office as befits my semigalactic importance as Chief of New Projects/Entertainment.

Rob, my secretary, points at his watch and sighs. I grab my Shemp mug and the files I'll need and duck into the lounge to score a cup of coffee for the meeting. Amy Dillon is in there with a couple of other actors from XTV's big soap opera. The soap's called *Pain in the Afternoon,* usually known, simply, as *Pain,* and it's been living up to its title, week in, week out, for six years. Amy is tall and dark; she has thick curly hair and is lovely as an Irish lament. She and I have been going out a bit, except when we've decided to call it off, which is usually every three days or so.

I fill my mug and she frowns at me, wondering where I spent the night probably. I give her a stage wink, then slosh hot coffee over my cut as a voice yells, "Munn, you *cocksucker*!"

"*Yow!*"

I drop the files and dry my wound with Marcal napkins.

"You're twelve minutes late, asshole."

I don't have to turn around. Joel Kamm, the executive producer for *Real Life,* possesses the foulest mouth in New York. I refill the mug. Amy's frown has deepened. I pick my files off the floor and go to the Foodcar.

The Foodcar is the production conference room. It's called the Foodcar because it's long and it's got these aluminum-framed, lozenge-shaped windows down the length of it so that it looks exactly like the late unlamented Amtrak's excuse for a dining car. Blue upholstery on silver furniture, to match the X-Corp livery. When I cruise in, still licking my forearm, I see everybody's there, even Stefan Zeng who makes a point of never being on time for anything.

I sit down between Vivian Moos, the head writer, and Zeng, who's the de facto head of the software working group and probably my best pal in New York. Kamm sits down at the head, like the jerk he is, although if you want to get technical about it, *I'm* the boss in this room. He puts his cellphone within easy reach; he knows I don't allow calls during meetings.

"Okay, if we can get started now," he begins, with a nasty look in my direction, "we got a motherfuck of a problem coming out of the number-one pile of shit around here, in other words graphics."

Stefan closes his eyes, which is his Chinese way of coping when he gets pissed off.

"Before we do that—" Shelley Doyle, across the table, looks directly at me, not Kamm, for which I am grateful in a bureaucratic sort of way. "I've got a cattle call for the new Alexis at ten, I want to make sure we want a tough-but-vulnerable, like it says in the bible? I mean, there were last-minute changes last time."

Shelley is head of talent for both the *Real Life* video unit and for *Pain in the Afternoon.* There's a lot of overlap in this group. The bible is the plot book that tells the long-run story of *Pain.* Shelley looks at Vivian Moos now, because she's head writer for *Pain,* and also because everyone knows I forget the plot stuff as soon as it's finished; the *Real Life* episodes I write, for instance, float out of my mind like dandelion chaff. This, some would say, is an indication of how much I adore the stuff we're putting out.

Joel Kamm interrupts at this point, saying there are no changes in the bible that he knows of.

Vivian ignores him. "T-B-V is fine, Shel."

"Then if there's nothing else—" Shelley starts to her feet.

"This is a fuckin' production meeting," Kamm snarls, "you can't just leave."

"Stick it up your ass, Joel," Shelley tells him.

"Why don't you stay, this time," I advise mildly, "let's hear the problem out."

"It's software," Shelley objects.

"It's a new game," I tell her, gritting my teeth through the headache. "You know that. We need to be familiar with the problems, even if they're not our territory, know what I mean?"

"Et's a new vuhrld, okay," Ved Chakrapani mutters, quoting the ad slogan for *Real Life.*

In fact, Shelley does not have any direct involvement with software but she's been getting kind of wrapped up in acting problems of late, to the point where, on one occasion, she's taken SAG's side against XTV even, and I want to remind her that actors are only a tiny part of this production.

"Yay, Wildman," Stefan says sarcastically, under his breath so only I can hear. "Wildman" is his nickname for me; I have no idea how he came up with it.

Kamm gets to his feet, trailing a long sheaf of printouts. He's short and dark and quite good-looking in a belligerent sort of way, what you'd get if you bred Tony Curtis with a weimaraner. He wears dark blue wool suits from Barney's. He stabs a finger at sections of the printout, saying "Point-two-eight. Point-two-four. Point-three-one. Point-two-two . . . An' we're already a week behind schedule."

"Lag," Stefan whispers to me, "time shift."

I nod, carefully.

"It's unacceptable," Kamm continues. "I talked to Obregon and she says, any shift more than point-two-oh will drop the Nielsens twenty percent over two months. You're messing with *immersion* here."

"No *shit*?" Shelley comments.

"Why don't we look at it," I say quickly, before Joel and Shelley start barking at each other again. "Can we get a segment up right now?"

Ved Chakrapani says, "Okay." Chakrapani is the head of the graphics software division. "Okay" is the only word he can pronounce without weaving half of Bombay through the middle of it.

"I don't see the point," Kamm begins, "we got the god-dam numbers," but I get up and start walking down the hall to the *Real Life* screening room and they don't have any choice but to follow.

In the screening room we all speak into the Vox-box, the security device that keeps unauthorized employees from catching even the tiniest glimpse of *Real Life*. Then we climb up ladders to the three levels of seats. These are all placed far enough away from each other that the occupants can get a full 180-by-150-degree view of the huge concave screen curving above, below, and to each side of them. The screen glistens a little blue with the standby charge. I stop by the workstation to pick up a gel of filters that will compensate for my problems with the infrared end of the spectrum. I can hear Kamm's cellphone beeping.

Chakrapani rattles on a keyboard.

"Ve'll do it vit only vun agent first," he calls, and I nod. The lights dim. I pick up the shutter-glasses that are hooked on the armrest. I fit the gel in the relevant slot and put them on, and even though I've done this a thousand times before— even though I know the schlockiness of what we're cooking up for *Real Life* largely invalidates the elegance of this new medium—I can't stop myself from feeling that same kindle of excitement I felt when I first put on a face-sucker and dove into the wild world of Virtix.

FOUR

UNTIL TWO YEARS ago I'd never even heard of Virtix. When I got out of high school in New Jersey I wanted to be a playwright and basically I stuck to that rut of thinking for a good stretch of time and it did not include TV, not even the experimental fringes of it.

I went to Columbia and majored in English and creative writing and churned out short stories for Gordon Lish and avant-garde one-acts for anyone who would read them.

A couple of the plays were given staged readings in subterranean dives full of Barnard undergrads wearing men's T-shirts. One of the one-acts, a pretentious piece entitled *What Dogs Don't Smell,* got staged at a theater lab so far off-Broadway it was practically soaking in the North River. In fact its basement used to flood regularly during heavy rains, for it was built on one of the old streams of Hell's Kitchen and the ancient watercourse was still running under the cement. By one of those arbitrary flukes that wind up defining your life, a producer at XTV caught the show. He asked me to write, for a minimal fee, an episode for *Copkiller,* which was just starting; no one figured it was going to be a hit at the time.

Even then I debated whether I should do it—art versus money, the old conundrum—but rent had to be paid and I went the way of most artists. The episode was aired, and garnered good reviews, and the rest flowed the way these things flow; from freelance on *Copkiller* to staff writer on *Pain*. By the time I became head writer, of course, the salary had hooked me into doing the job the way good China White makes you put up with the shakes and vomiting. It became easier and easier for me to grind out the snappy plot twists and bitchy dialogue. The easier it got, the more bored and disconnected I felt.

Marrying Larissa, who was just being introduced in the role of Kirsten, *Pain*'s sexy foreign manipulatrix, did not help.

I started seeing Pentti around that time—Pentti's my shrink —and I remember telling him that much as I loved Larissa, I would look at her sometimes and think, *That's* what she's going to do, that's the way she's going to react, based purely on what Kirsten was scheduled to do in the next script. I was *seeing* her as Kirsten, half the time. Pentti nodded seriously, the way he does; he knew what I was talking about, since he specializes in TV people. He even had a term for it, calling it the Century City Syndrome for some ex-Orion line producer who started thinking he was Luke Perry or something. The marriage really started to bust up when I figured out that half the time I was right; *Larissa was beginning to act exactly as Kirsten would.* The boredom with my job, the disconnection in my marriage, linked up with the peculiar disconnection I've always felt as a result of how I grew up. I had what used to be called a "breakdown," spending three weeks in an outrageously expensive funny farm for industry people in Wilton, Connecticut.

The day I got back to work Rose Obregon showed me Virtix.

This was before TV City was finished and the VR lab became a top-security tax write-off for XTV brass. At that time the lab lived in a clapped-out former theater behind the old McGraw-Hill Building. I remember walking into this dark cave of a place inhabited by stacks and stacks of mainframes, LCDs, video terminals, piling up to the dark roof of the old theater, all hooked up to each other by wires and co-ax. Everything winking and humming in phase while this young

black techie punched algorithms into a terminal and mur-
mured, very faintly and politely, "Douchebag, douchebag,
douchebag."

The techie was sick-and-tired of demo-ing this stuff but he
did what Rose asked. He had me put on a light nylon body-
suit with gloves attached and wires that he hooked up to one
of the blinking black boxes. He made me stand on a round
platform maybe five feet in width. The platform was a mul-
tidirectional treadmill covered with rubberized material that
moved away from your feet as the ground would whenever
you took a step. The difference here was, the ground moved
but you didn't actually go anywhere. He fitted a parachute
harness around me and fastened that to a nylon cable so I
couldn't walk off the platform. Finally he strapped what
looked like a black plastic dog-mask with headphones included over my head. I saw nothing and heard little. His voice
came thin as the squeak of a bat.

"You're going to feel a little disoriented at first," he said.

"Hit me," I told him, "I work for *Pain*. I *can't* feel more
disoriented than I do already."

Obregon said, "He's achromatic in the red band," and the
techie said, "Okay," and I heard him punch the keyboard
again.

"Roll Virtix," the techie announced.

And I was in a clearing in the mountains of Idaho.

There's no other way to describe it. I *was* there. The headset contained eyepieces that exactly duplicated the field of
human vision. I didn't know then that the goggles were state-
of-the-art VPL stereoscopic high-resolution liquid-crystal
with ultrasound gaze-tracking—all I knew was, every damn
detail of the scene in front of me was three-dimensional and
perfect. The snow-tipped peaks were of that very deep shade
of blue they get when the sun dips toward evening. The wild
grass was a thousand separate kinds of yellow, the needles of
the chaparral pine possessed the thick resinous green you only
achieve with shade and altitude. The sense of depth, of objects
being separated by a distance you could touch and walk, was
so great that I was forced at once to treat that world, in all the
brain areas that mattered, as a place of actual geodesics.

I found out later that the perfection was illusory. The nature of digitalization in those days rendered the image closer

to the detail of, say, a photo-realist painting by Scott Pryor than to an Edward Weston photograph. But the Lanier Effect took care of any discrepancy so that for me what I saw seemed absolutely real. And "perfect" was how I thought of it.

Not only was it perfect—it was *moving*. The trees and grass do-si-doed in the breeze. A butterfly bumbled from a sprig of clover to a dandelion. I gasped, and wiggled in my harness; the scene shifted to the right because I had stepped leftward. The Virtix research guys had succeeded in compressing a digitalized video image to the point where they could play it through a basic Fujitsu fmTONES workstation to my face helmet. They had wired it up to ultrasound transponders in the body-suit that in turn were wired to clipping-dividers and a standard Polhemus Navigator that figured out where I would be standing in the scene, what I could see from that angle, what I would see if I moved.

Of course that wasn't a tenth of Virtix, even then, but it was enough to make me breathe like I was on my third orgasm. I realized in an instant that no matter what I'd said to Pentti, what was wrong with me and *Pain,* what was screwed up with me and Larissa, was not the sense of living an illusion —it was simply this: *the illusion wasn't good enough.*

Here, on the other hand, was an illusion so good you could live in it.

And if this was so good now, soon you'd be able to create worlds you preferred, and those worlds would be as complex and mind-fuckingly rich as you wanted them to be—as large and weird, even, as a human life.

I was hooked.

And the next second a Percheron warhorse with a knight in full armor sitting on its back trotted out of a stand of aspen into the Idaho meadow.

I noticed, for a split second there, some flaw in graphics; it was like a shift, but it had nothing to do with lag or timing, it was locked into the quality of image. It looked like a scaly disease, a virus made of lack of focus, that crawled around the skin of both horse and rider.

I forgot it immediately as the knight glanced right and spotted me. He kicked his mount, lowered the lance, and began trotting in my direction. The huge horse lumbered closer, faster, growing taller with every second. Mount and rider seemed to take up the whole Idaho sky. They jerked into a canter; I could hear the hoofbeats coming loud as kettledrums in front of me, the ground was shaking with their bass concussion. Reflexively I moved my legs to push myself away, moving backward in the meadow as well.

I was practically pissing myself, mumbling "shit-shit-shit" in the strange tension between knowing, with each cell of my short-term memory, that this was fake, a video put-on, while every cell in my long-term recall told me to get the fuck *out of the way* before this Ketchum Lancelot skewered me like a shish-kabob or trampled me under the tea tray–sized hooves of that animal. I must have tripped sideways, for the whole scene tilted as I fell, the horse was about to mash me underfoot, I screamed, *"Stop it!"*—and the scene froze at once.

The shift scaled back and forth like a bad case of crabs on the cuirass of the giant, motionless rider.

Rose Obregon was chuckling happily as they lifted the face-sucker off; even the techie was smiling.

"What do you think?" she asked me, but she could tell by my eyes, even through the embarrassment of panic, what I thought.

"Douchebag," the techie commented softly.

Later on, in her office, she told me about *Real Life*.

"You know about B-Net?" she said by way of prologue.

I nodded. B-Net was the broad-spectrum digitalized fiber-optic cable network X-Corp was installing in heavy traffic areas like New York.

A couple of other cable companies also were putting in digitalized fiber-optic at the time, but B-Net was a lot broader in spectrum and a shitload more expensive and everybody thought X-Corp's boss, Jack Tyrone, was crazy to pump up his debt ratio like that. Everybody except the consortium of Hong Kong banks that were trying to get their bucks out of Kowloon before the Provisional Working Committee froze their assets. These guys, especially the Kowloon and Singapore Banking Corporation, thought B-Net was a swell idea and floated the junk bonds to pay for it.

"You ever wonder what B-Net's for?" Rose asked me.

"The usual," I said. "Interactive cable, home shopping,

make a dentist's appointment 'n pay your bill 'n watch *Pain* at the same time and from the same terminal?''

"You flunk." Rose picked up a small European-looking Buddha she always kept on her desk in those days. "That's just the nachos and hot sauce. The *real* enchilada is what you just saw down there. It's called *Real Life*, and it needs a show-runner."

I looked at her carefully.

"I know what that is, down there. That's virtual reality. You're saying you can broadcast—*that*—through B-Net?"

She nodded. She put down the Buddha.

"An' people will have helmets, like that, and suits and treadmills?"

"Not necessarily. We'll offer a cheap version, just 3-D glasses and a mouse. Or, for a price, they can go the whole way. But either way, they'll be *in the show*. They can change the story; they can shoot, or run or fuck if it's in the option package—all in their own living room."

I thought about that for a minute.

"Why me?" I asked at length.

"You're the best writer we've got."

I picked at the skin of my forehead. It's a stupid habit I have when I'm figuring something out.

"Don't bullshit me, Rose," I said.

She looked at me levelly. She put her hands together, like a nun praying—that's the thing *she* does. Her fingers bore a lot of opals stuck to silver settings.

"Maybe we need somebody young—this is going to take a lot of energy."

"Uh-huh," I said. She stopped smiling.

"Or maybe—just maybe—I wanna give you a break?"

"A break."

"You don't want it," she said, gazing at the Buddha, "someone else will."

"I didn't say that," I told her quickly, "I didn't say that."

Now, almost two years and many Virtix demos later, I hear a faint buzz and suddenly I am *in* another place, another world, as immediately and totally relocated as the first time. The scalelike shift has long ago been debugged. The inevitable drag of familiarity has been balanced by the heightened precision of both sight and sound.

And I'm *on* a street in some crumbling industrial town in Central Europe. Up ahead a signpost reads "Posen/Poznan" so it must be Poland, or what used to be western Poland. In my ears the bass thunders as a column of huge Bundeswehr Leopard III tanks squeak-roar twenty feet away. It has to be cold, for bare trees sway in an invisible wind, and the noises are crisp as they would be in cold air. I can *feel* that cold in my bones. House gossip says that when they get the Flexator body-suit ready, the one they're working on in the VR lab, you won't have to imagine the temperature—the suit will chill your ass down as far as the story calls for.

I want to walk fast in this weather, or maybe I want to move quickly because without really recognizing it this reminds me a little of what happened last night, that sense of crisp contact between the hard world and myself. People walk by in bright U.S.-designed, Rangoon-made clothes. *Real Life* is going to be marketed as "Tales of the Cool and Powerful" and it centers around a bunch of American MTV groupies functioning as a copyright-infringement task force that works for an independent information-rights institute in Santa Monica. Somehow, copyright enforcement always takes these guys into much deeper zones of skulduggery. I seem to remember vaguely that this episode concerns a turncoat in the U.S. Senate who wants to sabotage the southern Californian alliance with free-market warlords in Norilsk.

Chakrapani, sitting at the workstation on the second deck, is the "agent" in this case, the one who walks, the man who reacts. There are ways of generating up to five characters in the scene for multiple participation but we're not set up for that option. He moves the joystick and although the rest of us haven't budged a toe muscle we all boogie forward down the street and cross, running, between two tanks. The noise of the tracks grows threatening in its volume and I feel my breathing speed up as we jump out of the way of the huge armor. *"Pass' auf, Kerl,"* a soldier shouts from behind us.

There's a man in a blue anorak up ahead now crossing Breslauer Platz toward St. Vaclav Church. Our mission, the mission of the Tunes Task Force agent, is to follow him. Chakrapani moves us in and out of crowds of pasty, sullen people shambling off to work and market. I see a pretty girl among the crowds, wearing an old kaftan-style coat; I want to turn to look at her as I could if I were working my own set, but Chakrapani won't let me, and I feel an automatic piss-off at this loss of my habitual control.

Instead, we're catching up with the blue anorak; he has stopped by the door of the church to speak to someone. Suddenly a clank of bells, a squeal of brakes, a scream; we've been hit. The scarred aluminum coachwork of a tram fills the screen and we fall backward, out of the way. Nothing but the bell tower, the dreary sky, people bending over us, mumbling in Polish (is Chakrapani having fun with this?). The hot woman in the kaftan is staring at me, her eyes widening in shock, her hand going to her mouth—

But her hand moves too slowly, her words are delayed somehow. There's a frequency-shift here, a drop in the rate of things. "I" try to get to my feet (Chakrapani moves the mouse forward), I try to talk (Chakrapani). There's a jerk as someone helps us to a sitting position—and the scene freezes.

For security reasons, only the actual writer of the segment and Rose Obregon are allowed to watch more than five minutes of *any Real Life* episode.

"Okay," Chakrapani says. "You ohl saw diss."

We fill up with coffee and head back to the Foodcar. Watching *Real Life* always makes me feel tired and beaten and I pop a couple of Pentti's pills along with another Advil. Even Kamm doesn't say much. That's one of the aftereffects of Virtix; words seem somehow less useful when you could, with Virtix, bodily kick someone into the world you want to show him, or her.

Zeng scratches his left butt, which is easy because he always wears shorts, even in November. His long shiny ponytail jerks as he rattle-fingers across a turbo-laptop. He is very thin and the oversize Indian shirts and basketball sneakers he wears serve to emphasize his lack of mass.

"That's the 'shift' you were talking about?" Shelley asks at length.

"I bet that streetcar was Random-generated," Vivian Moos puts in.

Zeng smiles. It's impossible to tell what question he's grinning at. Still looking at his laptop screen he says, "I've been working on that lag for three weeks."

"Three fuckin' weeks!" Kamm shrieks. He stares at Zeng's shirt as if the real problem here were a fashion offense. "Whyn't you fuckin' tell us?"

Zeng ignores him.

"The problem, as usual, is Grafix allocation." Grafix is the image generator in the Virtix system—what Zeng means is that at certain points in time there's too little computer power available to keep the image running. "I'm getting a focus group together, I wanna run that shift through a bunch—"

"Why?" Kamm interrupts. Zeng looks at me, or rather under my eyes, which is his way of looking directly.

"I think I can deal with this in another week," he tells me. "I don't want to go into it now."

"I got to do that cattle call," Shelley Doyle reminds us.

"Wildman," Zeng insists softly. He's staring right at me now. Zeng hates to have Kamm, or anyone else, breathing down his neck, fingering his antiseptic algorithms with clumsy layman's digits. Zeng is conscientious; if he says one week, it will get done in seven days.

At length I nod.

"One week," I say. "If it's not solved then, the whole issue goes Code Red. Agreed?"

Zeng says okay. Kamm starts to object and I say quickly, "What's the next item?"

Doyle and Zeng leave together and the rest of us run through some smaller glitches for half an hour. At the end of the meeting I hold Kamm back till the others have left.

"Don't do that again," I tell him.

"What?" Kamm stands so straight he's almost bending backward. His cellfax, suspended from his left shoulder, knocks against the aluminum doorjamb.

"Throw your weight around. Give people orders, in a meeting like this."

"It's the only way," Kamm says. "First motherfuckin' episode's goin' out December third, those cocksuckers won't jump unless—"

"It's an informal group, Joel," I tell him. "It's my show. You're just coordinating producer. If you can't cool it, I'll find you some other job."

He should be worried, because XTV is pretty hierarchical and I could get him reassigned if I wanted. Instead he says, "Yeah, try it, Munn, jiss try it," like I was threatening to punch him over a borrowed squirt gun in the schoolyard. He stalks out.

I look out the window. It feels warmer today, there's a skimmed-milk sunshine building weak shadows against barges. Across the river, faux-Miesian condos being built by a cat food conglomerate over the former NordDeutscher-Lloyd piers obscure the granite cliffs of Hoboken.

I feel stale and sort of layered, as if different parts of me were separating from each other. Part of that I guess is Kamm, and part of it is the jaded feeling I always get from *Real Life.* But the sensation seems stronger than those two factors together would account for.

"The shift," I mutter darkly, like Brando maundering on at the end of *Apocalypse Now,* "the *shift.*"

I get a sudden impression of black mud, cattails, and a tall shape with a sharp carpet-cutter mincing around in the darkness.

A tremor of reflex jerks my body. The memory image is maybe eighty percent less real than Virtix but because it's more personal it hits me with a wallop like a Leopard III tank.

Back in my office. The damn place, of course, is a Woo special, curved-lozenge-shaped workbenches and coffee table, an enormous glass lozenge-shaped desk, a lozenge-y, blue-silver couch, and one long lozenge for a window.

I do most of my work on the benches, which carry the three different workstations and the various connection boxes needed to hook into the computer core in the central tower of the complex.

When I really need to think I use the small, plain, Federal-style wooden desk I bought two years ago on a foray with Larissa into Bucks County.

I sit down at the B workstation, key in my password, and call up *Real Death 1.* XTV is a wilderness of nicknames; *Real Life,* among many of its minions, became *Real Death* because of the large number of murders, assassinations, and suicides salting its various plot lines.

Real Death 1 is the pilot, the first episode, the one I wrote myself. I move through it fast, clicking the mouse like a machine-gun. As usual, the plot mechanics seem dull, hard-to-believe, utterly unmemorable. I keep having to call up the locale index from the World Generator to remember where the fuck I am.

I trim a couple of scenes, change a name here or there. I summon up videos of different character actors whom I can electronically cut and paste into some of the editing slots, but none of them strike me as likely to alleviate the clichés or the essential dullness of the story line. Sex and intrigue, money and mayhem, run through this show like hydrocarbons in the Hudson. Sex and intrigue are not exactly rare on prime-time cable.

I would have liked to change the format but this was established early on by Tyrone and Obregon and the money mavens on the thirty-fifth floor.

What Jack Tyrone is betting on, what everyone is praying for, is that the medium will make the story largely irrelevant. "The first Virtual Reality serial; it gives you a world you can control," one of the ads says.

I edit for an hour or so, then break for lunch.

On the way to the lounge I stop by the *Pain* studios to look for Larissa. A costume designer tells me she's not on the schedule for today. "I happen to know," the woman says, watching me with that assessing look people get when they're figuring out if this is a romantic query, "she's going to the Thanksgiving party tomorrow."

Amy of course is in the lounge but I sneak off into a corner to eat the Salisbury Steak Special and she doesn't spot me. Ivan Gaynor, the vice president in charge of production, is slumming in the other corner with Ned Reynolds, the XTV news anchor. Reynolds last had an original idea when he fixed his skateboard with baling wire at age nine. He is known to his loving colleagues as "Braindead." Reynolds and Gaynor are joking and yukking it up. Larissa has been hanging out with Braindead recently and I wonder, sourly, how anyone can hold a conversation with that face for more than two minutes without falling into a sympathetic coma.

When I get back to my office I call Larissa's number and get her machine. Larissa, I know from long experience, likes to screen her messages, answering only the calls she welcomes. Rather than be screened out I hang up before I'm supposed to leave a message.

FIVE

I HEAD HOME on the dot of five, like any man too deadened by his job to summon one extra second's worth of energy.

I know I should go pick up the Morgan but I just don't have the jizz.

As I wait for the elevator in my lobby I hear the front door open. The elevator bank is hidden from the front by a dogleg of hallway. Footsteps come slowly, uncertainly, across the dirty tiles. I can feel my skin go cool and my heart whams easily into overdrive.

"Slip-*slap*. Slip-*slap*," the footsteps come, mincing, effeminate. I hear a clink of metal and a sinister whisper; most likely the killer is communicating with an accomplice outside. There is no other exit from this part of the lobby. I freeze for a second then, blood rushing wildly, click around into the Sam Rodney defensive mode, sideways to the perceived attack, weight on the back leg, right hand raised to chop, and a whole hell of a lot of good that's going to do if my pal from last night is paying a call with his Tech-9, like trying to stop a tornado by farting at it.

A shadow grows, huge and black, against the wall. In my fear I breathe in saliva and almost choke.

And Mrs. Dominguez, who cleans the hallways, waddles around the corner, her house shoes going "Slip-*slap!*" against the tiles, muttering to herself in Dominican Spanish.

My head still hurts. So does the cut. When I get upstairs I peel the Band-Aids off. The skin looks gray and putrescent. The palms of my hands are dark and sore and I remember the stench and the slime I fell into while haring around that swamp. They must have burned, too, when they touched the electric fence. I lather bacitracin over everything and re-bandage the cut. My heart still aches from the scare down-stairs. My brain feels merely embarrassed.

Thank the gods Lenny is not around so I don't have to deal with his cheerfulness. I take off my hiking shoes and look in the fridge. There's nothing edible except boiled meat dump-lings and chicken with cashew nuts from the Chinese on Varick Street.

I decide to fix myself an abs'ini.

Way too much ink and paper, far too many polygons of graphic space have been wasted on making variations of the martini. I mean, there's a craft to it but it's not so goddam complicated, especially if you have a friend like Lenny the Mooch, who loves martinis of whatever stripe and has nothing to do but fuck around and design martini-makers and con-vince Stefan Zeng's techies to build one for him at X-Corp's expense.

The Zeng-Lenny abs'ini device (patent forever pending) consists of a supercooled stainless-steel flask, an insulated box holding a crystal absinthe snifter also chilled to twenty degrees Fahrenheit, a room-temp vial full of Martini and Rossi vermouth *bianco,* and an aquarium pump with capacitor and spray nozzle attached. When you hit the switch the minia-ture pump spits a micron-thin layer of vermouth around the glass, which is then filled exactly to the brim with arctic "Snake Pit" absinthe distilled by the Zippy Collective at MIT's media lab in Cambridge, Mass. No more, no less.

I add a Kalamata olive and sip slowly at the liquid. I know this is not fashionable. I'm aware I use booze as a crutch and of course I shouldn't drink while taking the Prodex Pentti prescribes for me—but goddam, that chill drink tastes for a minute like you wanted the whole of your life to believe in angels and all of a sudden you spotted a neon flit of wings from an androgynous being warbling "Swing Low Sweet Chariot" behind that soot-smeared New York window.

I moon around my crib for a while, munching Lenny's smoked Muenster cheese crackers. Night has fallen and the former bread factory across the way looks like it has receded from the lights of almost the third millennium A.D. into the darkness of an earlier, slower time. I check the voicemail component of the workstation. No Larissa. Another hang-up. The fax whirs, a message from Lenny; Black 47 is playing at Paddy Reilly's, do I want to meet him there? I hit the code number that dials Larissa's number, hang up before her machine can answer.

I moon into my workroom, not really meaning to do anything. Still I suppose the distaste that's been stacking up inside me—distaste for the hollowness of *Real Death,* for the waste of time involved in dealing with its politics, for my selling out to the money of TV, the glitz of it, now and seven years ago when I went to work for *Copkiller*—well, it kind of gets too much on a day like today.

So that it's normal, when I come back here, I should at least two or three times a week zoom like a homing pigeon to the antidote.

My study is almost empty. The far wall has a bench built along its breadth, with two terminals hooked up to a couple of B-Net connection units and color-compensators under shelves sagging with reference books and maps. A row of hooks holds one full Pop Optix face-sucker, a lighter Zeng-made goggles-and-earphones unit, one ultralight pair of shutter-glasses with earphones such as we use in the screening room, and a cheap, early model body-harness with Polhemus transponders. You can pull a sliding screen across that portion of the room.

The other walls are covered with cork sheets painted matte black. A dozen maps and etchings are tacked to the cork. A large poster of Larry, Curly, and Moe miscarving a turkey is stapled to the ceiling. The floor is thickly covered with an assortment of rugs from the eight or nine apartment changes that I, like most New Yorkers, have survived.

From a large hook in the ceiling beam hangs a length of half-inch nylon. The carabiner shackle spliced to its end dangles at waist height.

I close the door and sit down at the left-hand terminal. I

take another sip of abs'ini and call up the B-Net menu. I click through the maze, streaking commands back and forth down the piped fiber-optic cables under the New York asphalt till I access the Virtix files back at TV City. I type in the passwords and pause. Do I want to go in full metal jacket here, or less encumbered? The way my head feels, I should put on the shutter-glasses, just dick around with the mouse tonight.

On the other hand, that's what I do, mostly, on *Real Life*. Dick around.

I kill off the abs'ini. I get up slowly and step into the nylon body-harness and zip it up. There's a switch on the left sleeve that activates both a battery pack and transponders in the knees and heels, elbows and hands. I flick that to "On."

I lift down the Zeng set. On the workstation screen I move the cursor to an unobtrusive box way down the list of Virtix menus. It's labeled "*MUNNWORLD*/MSTR/Clearance Code Required." I punch in my code, type "1" for the first episode, then "Enter." I check that the color-box, an old-fashioned servo-unit that compensates for my partial color-blindness, is hooked up—Lenny sometimes disconnects it. I turn off the lights, walk out to the middle of the room, fit the Zeng set over my head and face. I always meant to get a treadmill for my home unit, but soon learned how to walk in place. With Virtix, it's almost as effective.

I feel around for the rope with one hand, and hook the shackle to a ring on the body-harness.

The darkness is total. I can hear nothing. I don't feel so tired now. The absinthe has kicked in, the preparatory excitement of Virtix has grabbed me. On top of this I'm about to enter a place that is entirely mine, a world I researched, built, peopled—a place that existed once but now lives only for the man who brought it out of the rot and pus of the past into the artificial semiconducted life of my study.

Of course I feel like a god. It's a cliché, but what the hell. Virtix hath made it real. There is no god but Virtix, and Alex Munn is his prophet.

I wait for the fifteen-second switch-on delay to elapse.

And *Munn's World* opens before me in all its color and music.

———

It's late afternoon, I'm walking down Centre Street in the middle of Lower Manhattan but boy, oh, boy, this is no Centre Street you've ever known.

The buildings are short and haphazardly built of brick and timber, with porches and pointed roofs. The sky is smoky with wood fires and the street is crammed to overflowing with horses and carriages and pigs and goats and people.

The horse-drawn coaches and carts of course clue you right away you're not in the same time zone you thought you were, but it's the people who are a real shock. I mean, they look the same, their faces are like ours, but the men mostly wear very narrow drainpipe trousers and boots and either short jerseys or long jackets. The women, under short coats and wide bonnets, swish around in skirts that fall straight to the ground.

This whole scene, should *Munn's World* ever become a legit production, would hold titles and credits, so the detail here is not meant to be total. And of course I remember how I had to pay a fortune to a group of stage actors to model those costumes for video so Zeng could digitalize them into D-grade characters. And I know I spent months collecting lithographs and Matthew Bradys so he could scan them into his World library and fractalize the spaces between to generate more carriages and houses and so on. But I've found, all the time I've looked at *Munn's World,* that knowing all of this is beside the point—the clarity and depth and immediacy of the Virtix are so fantastic that my body *believes,* in some dimension both shallower and deeper than logic, it is actually standing in New York in 1850, and that's what gets my blood running faster once more, and sparks the quick electricity in my head.

Vendors sell oysters, gingerbread, baked pears. A hot-corn girl yells, "Hot corn, here's your lily-white hot corn; hot corn, nice 'n hot, oh, wot beauties I have got." Down the street a clam-seller tries to drown her out with "Here's clams, here's clams, nice clams today; hot clams, nice clams from Jamaica Bay."

A couple of toughs from the Daybreak gang swagger down the street sniffing for trouble. This is my first decision, as agent and lead character. I choose to step left, avoiding a confrontation.

At a street corner a pair of horse-drawn fire engines have

collided and the two teams of firemen are noisily slugging at each other with fists and ax handles. I walk carefully, lifting my feet up and setting them down—in my workroom I'm walking in place, taking high steps so the Polhemus system will know I'm walking forward, holding on to the dangling rope so I don't stray from the room's center.

Men play quoit games and strain at lung-testers. As always I find myself weaving S-shapes around the fickle crowds, the rooting pigs, the piles of dung. I can tell it's cold because plumes of vapor rise from the nostrils of horses as well as from the mouths of people queuing up outside the precinct house.

Turning left, I go inside the cop shop, walk up the stairs. The movement is not perfect, it's a little jerky and uneven in the climbs and tumbles but I have other problems to worry about. "Captain's waitin' for you," the desk-roundsman shouts. I put my hand out, it sticks into my field of vision and pushes open a door marked "CAPTAIN."

Captain Blake is portly and choleric. None of us wear uniforms, except for varnished leather helmets, day-sticks, and the copper stars that constitute our badge of office, but Blake likes to sport a navy-style coat with brass buttons. He holds a pipe and the room is gray-blue with the smoke. Outside the thick windowpanes I can make out the royals and t'gallant spars of ships docked on the East River, reaching high over the massed roofs of the city.

" 'Nother dead mick," Blake grunts, "in Coulter's." He takes his pipe from his mouth and spits in the corner. "Fuckin' slag. You think anyone cares? But someone upstairs—" He pauses.

"It's that 'Fishman,' " he continues. Blake's fingernails are filthy and grime has collected in the thick folds of his neck. "I need volunteers. Collect five men and reconnoiter the situation."

I turn to go.

"Hey!" he calls.

I turn back.

"I know about you, boyo," he says. "Your father's a Scot, that's bad enough—but your mother's a bloody mackerel-snappin' mick."

"Sir," I say.

"All I want is a report."

I have an option built into the show at this point. I could refuse to "volunteer." I've never taken that option and all that would happen if I did is that the plot would loop around to a different incident.

Five more "volunteers" are waiting for me beside the roundsman's desk. We troop into the street. It's gotten darker; candles touch windows with an egg-yolk glow. Outdoor fires emphasize the smoke and confusion of the street. We march to Centre, and left on Leonard. Someone shouts "Leatherheads!" and a rotten pumpkin splats on the stinking cobbles before us. A group of Bowery Bhoys spill out of a grog shop, all duded up in their rig; they wear plug hats of varnished leather, blue frock coats with brass fire-company medallions, plaid bell-bottoms, and thick heavy boots crusted with shit and the blood of Dead Rabbits—or so they would have you believe.

Their hair is plastered artfully over the forehead in the style called "soap locks."

"Blakie's girls!" one of them crows, and the others laugh. Some smoke thick cigars and spit the juice in our direction. Two of my men turn to bust into the Bhoys and I say, "No"; another option not taken, the Vox-recognition working fast on the simple negative.

In a commercial version of *Munn's World* the options would come spoken off a soundtrack hooked to your audio, murmuring advice from a mythical "angel" into your earlobe, but since I know the plot twists by heart I never click in that in.

We're well into the Five Points district by now. People no longer walk around us, they stoop and shuffle. Roughly half the faces are bog-Irish, blotchy with cold, thin with want. The rest are black, either the coffee color of those whose families have lived this side for a while, or the anthracite hue of slaves newly brought from Africa, and either freed or escaped. Kids from the junior gangs flit like emaciated moths, carrying messages and policy numbers between grogshops.

I look back and spot the Bowery Bhoys tailing us. There's a feel of snow in the air. People scream and laugh in the side streets. From the busted windows of a rotten stable a woman cries out, in passion or grief.

A tall, crumbling bulk rises between a grogshop and the charred remains of a wooden cottage. It's five stories high and built of moldy brick. Windows gape like black wounds where they're not covered by a patchwork of boards and rotten canvas sails.

This is the old Coulter's Brewery building.

The street narrows near the entrance and in the greater gloom we can hear a combination of growing silence and increasing noise. I turn around (*turning in the room*). I see a crowd of sullen men, women, and kids spearheaded by the Bhoys we saw earlier. They're holding scraps of wood now, and pieces of brick or stone.

"Get outta here!" somebody shouts, and the crowd rumbles agreement, a sound rough in power and rage. "We got a job to do," I mutter; I'm not sure the Vox gets it. Anyway, nobody reacts.

Once inside the doorway of the Old Brewery we can barely see each other. One of the men carries a bull's-eye lantern and by its anemic light we pick out people lying and squatting on a filthy stone floor. Most of them are asleep; some are drinking from bottles. A scrawny goat chews rags in the corner. A couple scrape food with their fingers from broken tin kettles simmering on campfires. They shrink away in apprehension or disgust as we move among them.

"We're looking fer a dead mick," one of my men, a fat guy with a sharp upstate accent, calls out.

Silence greets this effort.

"They put 'em down cellar," the same cop comments, and shrugs. I know, from the storyboard, that I was promoted over him, and he resents the hell out of it.

If the ground floor is scary, the stairway to the cellar is like a descent into the Last Judgment, some Boschian vision of Sodom and the Black Hole of Calcutta mixed, looped, remastered in your face. A couple are fucking, grunting like dogs under a torn coat on one landing. A girl pukes obsessively upstairs, into the stairwell. Rats squeak and bite for lebensraum. Some of them chew on an old man lying dead, apparently of natural causes, in a shallow grave scraped at the foot, and I wonder what they're waiting for to cover him up. Someone shits noisily in a corner. When we get down all the way we see it's a vast basement with a beaten dirt floor, thick with brick columns and broken machinery.

The bull's-eye barely penetrates one other space uncovered by people, in a nook protected by the gutted barrel of a disused bran-cooker.

"That's her."

She hangs from the bran-cooker, her left arm jammed between the body of the apparatus and a twisted steam pipe, the remains of her coat hooked on a spear of ripped tin. Even though I've seen this a hundred times, though I scanned the images and photo-shopped the wounds, I recoil at the sight as I always do, taking small steps now, and the scene retreats a few inches away as I move back.

The men, uncertain, group around me.

Then, following both the line of plot and the draw of whatever fate has made us cops in this time and story, we walk over to the bran-cooker.

She's an old woman, maybe forty-five, white, blue-eyed. Her grizzled hair is matted and filthy. Her mouth is open and crusted chocolate with blood. She was wearing two stained, ripped calico dresses, one on top of the other, and a woolen shift when she died. All three garments have been sliced open from neck to hem.

In the expanse of flesh thus exposed, the bleach-white skin glows with its own unutterable lack of life. And in that sorry field the killer carved five deep gashes diagonally across her body, from shoulder to left breast, from right rib to left kidney, from liver to thigh, and twice across the intestines and pudenda.

Her breast hangs from a ribbon of skin, and foot-long tubes of greenish-gray intestines have escaped from the last two cuts. Blood has flowed and clotted everywhere but what always touches me most is the dirt on her face and hands. For she was dirty in life, unable or unwilling to clean, deprived of water; far from the kind of world where mothers wash the faces of babies and have people who care if they are soiled or not.

"It *was* the Fishman," one of my men whispers. This one sounds like he's from southern New England. He also sounds thoroughly spooked. "That's how they cut floundah, when they salt an' flake 'em, back home."

A cheaply printed political flyer reading "Flynn for Council" lies at her feet. Beside it, someone has drawn crosses in the dirt, and shreds of dried henbane are sprinkled around the bran-cooker. Henbane wards off sorcery, and the evil of necromancers; superstition accounts for the woman being left like this, instead of buried with the rest in the cellar floor.

"Whyn't ya *kiss* her," someone shrieks from the darkness around us, "ya love her so much!"

"Did anybody see this," the cop with the upstate accent yells. "You filthy louts, did anybody see who done this?"

"You bastords done it!" a woman's voice screams. "*You* killed poor Maggie!"

"You'll kill all of us," a man wails, "all the sons of Erin."

"They killed Maggie Hernon," a boy yells up the stairwell, and the name seems to resonate around the molding, rotten walls: "Maggie Hernon . . . Maggie Hernon."

Jesus, Maggie, I think, looking at her eyeballs, which have frozen and then dusted over in the cold mustiness of this place.

The leatherhead who knows about salting fish is dark-complexioned but his face is dead pale in the lamplight. He walks around to one side of the bran-cooker and points. Behind the apparatus a hole has been dug out of the bricks and earth of the cellar wall. A tunnel, braced on scrounged lumber, runs out of sight into darkness.

To one side of the tunnel, on a few feet of whitewashed plaster, someone has scrawled "SQUATTER" with a thick, brushlike implement in large, angry gray letters.

When we get back to the entrance of Coulter's Brewery night has annexed the city. In its blue shadows the crowd has swollen into a black beast that completely covers the street for twenty paces in both directions. I see what I think is a Chinese face, but that can't be right because the first Asian didn't come to live in the city for another two years; anyway, he wouldn't have owned a carpet-cutter. Obviously it's a trick of perception, my brain filling in the spaces Virtix does not cover, in line with the Lanier Effect. I move my legs forward to see anyway. As I step out onto the steps a brick is hurled in my direction, and I duck. The Brewery's tenants crowd behind us now. Their mouths gape; their clothes are black; their hands stretch toward us in anger or pain, like crowds of the dead come forward, accusing, let loose by the vicious translation of Maggie Hernon from the death-in-life of the Brewery to the more permanent status she now inhabits.

One of my men takes a swipe at a Bowery Bhoy. The crowd surges back and then snaps toward us in response, shrieking, cursing, lobbing filth. I wait for a Bhoy to swipe at me with a fireman's ax, then parry easily with my day-stick. I can't help thinking, God help us if they bring touch into this; a Flexator suit would damn well put a hurtin' on you if that ax connected.

Obviously there's nothing we can do with that crowd. They just don't like us. My men are blowing their whistles but probably we're the only cops within six blocks. We fall back into the Brewery, shoving against the dead. "Back into the tunnel!" the fellow from upstate commands. We clatter clumsily into the vomitorious confusion of the stairwell, kicking at residents, pursued by brickbats and flung shit. The noise is constant now, a long ululation of "Maggie Hernon" and "Leatherheads" and "Stick 'em!" The upstate man clambers around the bran-cooker. He shines his bull's-eye down the adit and enters, gingerly. We follow, balancing fear against what agility we can muster, walking bent over, even crawling when the tunnel roof dips.

Twenty yards away, past a brief arc of boulder, we stumble groaning upright in a tiny cellar full of plump, grunting pigs.

No one comes after us at first. We stand, panting, listening to shouts echo from the tunnel entrance around the ragged wall of this cramped basement. The man with the lantern flashes its beam around, looking for stairs. He finds only a ladder and beyond that, crouched on an earthen shelf above the brown-black pigs, a small boy dressed in a rough smock and pantaloons.

" 'E were really tall, sorr," the boy squeaks in a thick Colchie accent. "Oi seen 'im, loik a mountain 'e were."

"You seen who," one of the men snarls at him.

" 'E 'ad a long black coat, like the very devil, sorr, oi tink 'e were the devil."

"Who?" The cop tries to grab him. "Come here, guttersnipe!"

"The cove what done Maggie in," the boy whispers. Then

he scampers up the ladder, twisting backward around the top
and out of sight before any of us can stop him.

And a hand comes out of the tunnel we just left, and then a
face, filthy, scarred, snarling.

" 'Ere they are!" the face shouts. "This way, lads!"

We clamber up the rickety ladder behind the boy. We bust
into a grogshop on the ground floor, gone empty with the
excitement burning around the block. A slattern behind the
bar yells "Oy!" indignantly; she pulls out an enormous pistol, fires it, and misses, the way she always does. The bullet
smashes a bottle of Monongahela whiskey that gurgles into a
hand of cards left unattended on the bar. My men take off
their helmets and we slope into the blackened alley and find
ourselves on Mulberry Street, just across from Pell.

We tiptoe our way out of Five Points, as we always do,
while the riot thickens and assorted members and hangers-on
of the Bowery Bhoys gang and the Dead Rabbits and
Daybreakers and Plug Uglies haul ass toward the scene; while
flames start from impromptu bonfires built by junior gang
members.

I follow my men, of course. Like every good leader. But to
my left, under a gaslight set in a small house of thick wood
and deep side porches, on the corner of Bayard and Baxter, a
door opens and a woman whispers, to me and me only.

"Are ye truly lookin' to find who cut Maggie Hernon?"

"Yes," I whisper. The Vox's convolvotron does not pick
this up. Something odd is happening. I get a weird feeling, not
unlike the sensation I had on the marsh, that every hair on my
neck is standing up and doing the Mashed Potato. It's happening, I hear myself think, it's really happening. *"Yes?"* I repeat
loudly.

"The unicorn," she says. Her voice is low, and she speaks
slowly. "Watch out for the *u-ni-corn.*"

She is slim, and dressed in overlapping frocks of worn
calico decorated with yellow roses, and cracked lace-up boots.
She has deep black hair and eyes that catch the gaslight and
bounce it back.

"But what—"

The door shuts, firmly. A dead bolt slams home. I lift my
hand and push the door but it won't open. "Jesus Christ," I
mutter, "Jesus Christ!"

The gaslight above my head clearly illuminates my varnished leather helmet, my thick day-stick. In the street, a junior Dead Rabbit stops. He grins happily and points at me.

I hurry after my men. I'm curious about the woman and the unicorn. Most of all, I'm curious about the fact that while there have been a few changes in the plot of the scenes surrounding Maggie Hernon's death, they've always been tiny and apparently of no significance.

Except for that woman. In the dozens of times I've run through the established plot, in the scores of times I've gone through the Old Brewery and escaped through that tunnel, *I have never seen that woman, nor heard any mention of a unicorn.*

I stop at the junction of Bayard and Centre. The same boy has followed me, and he has summoned a couple of his friends. A group of men cruises over, hefting cudgels. It could all be dangerous and I need to think and I don't want to go through the routine of running back to the precinct house and hearing Blake bitch about how he doesn't care about witnesses and rumors, just file the bloody report and close the case, so I take off my helmet—

—and I'm standing in the middle of my study, the Zeng headset in one hand, the rope in the other.

I'm blinking in the gloom and the silence in the middle of America's largest city while my head reels from the din and anger of what might or might not have been happening in the same town 150 years before.

SIX

BACK IN THE living room I push the button on the abs'ini-maker and take the resultant drink to one of the big windows overlooking the bread factory.

In the time of *Munn's World* this street was lined with crappy two-floor wooden houses set among larger concerns like a bakery hauling in flour and other produce from the big market where the bread riot of 1836 occurred, and where the World Trade Center now stands.

I sip at the freezing liquid. I'm half in the time of Munn the Cop and half in a definite excitement of the present. I walk over to the workstation and punch Zeng's phone code. His machine comes on, crashing music from the Punk era of which Zeng fancies himself a historian. Sid Vicious scream-ing

"God save the Queen."

It's the tape Zeng puts on to tell those in the know he is, in fact, at home. It's hard to get hold of Zeng sometimes, be-cause for some twisted cyber-anarchist reason he won't use a cellphone or a portafax or voicemail.

"Come on, Zeng," I tell the machine, "it's me."

A click as he picks up.

"Wildman?"

"I just went into *Munn's World.*"

"How's 1850?"

"Cold," I say. "But there's something else." I swallow gin. "You know a girl with black hair and dark eyes and a calico dress?"

"Lara Love?"

Lara Love is my wife's stage name. Her full moniker is Larissa Leonora Antonova, but she shortened the name for showbiz.

"I'm serious, Zeng. Her dress had yellow roses on it. Did you scan anybody like that?"

"Sounds like Amy's keeping her knees together again—"

"Zeng—"

"Sure. Probably. I don't know. We scanned a horde of people, if you recall."

I knock back a deep draft of abs'ini and breathe harshly through my nose.

"The point *is,* Zeng. You know, when we choose the tunnel option, we're moving out of Five Points? She came out of nowhere on Bayard Street and told me, 'If you want to find out what happened to Maggie Hernon, look out for the unicorn.' Something like that."

"Say that again?"

I know Zeng. He always keeps an amused, polite polish on his words until his brain kicks in active and then he gets serious as a Christian-Republican discussing tax loopholes. He sounds CR now. I repeat what I told him. He says nothing for a few seconds and then, "It's starting."

"That's what *I* thought."

"How many times?"

"Just the once."

"I'll go in," he offers, "see if it happens again."

"Shit," I say, "I didn't think it would ever do this."

"It's what I predicted," he says quietly, "it was only a matter of time."

I should explain what "it" is.

"It," seen in tight focus, is a combination of massively parallel hardware plus interactive software that Zeng calls a "Story Engine." Story Engines are not unknown; lots of people besides Zeng have built them. They exist to some extent in any interactive video environment, holding all the possible variations of plot that will happen to the player, or agent, who chooses option A or B or C. They are the machine that drives both *Real Life* and *Munn's World*.

What makes the Zeng Story Engine different is three new factors. First, it's much more complex; the roundsman, walking down the streets of *Munn's World,* is not restricted to set options. He's capable of busting up, down, and sideways at any time and screwing around with the plot and the story will follow him like a personal ecosystem, adjusting temperature and patching up holes in its historical ozone layer as it goes.

The second factor—what allows the first factor to happen—is this: Zeng's Engine is highly specialized. This specialization means the Story Engine contains *only* potential story possibilities; it can do this by relying on a different engine, called the "World Generator," as an encyclopedia of digitalized environments and characters from which to fish out the material it needs to cobble together its huge variety of plot options.

Thus the Story Engine, following the cop as he goes unexpectedly down, say, Beaver Street, instantaneously can fish out the buildings of Beaver Street, the people and animals that live in it, and draw conclusions from this environment that will feed back and affect the story line. For example, if the plot has taken us to where Beaver Street opens out onto the East River and its great bustle of traffic and cargo, it follows this confusion may put paid to the hero's chances of catching his quarry; and the fact that the fugitive has escaped is then fed back to the Story Engine, which automatically drops the quarry into the "future plot" file.

That's exactly how it happens in *Real Life* as well. Zeng made an okay Story Engine for *Real Life* but for *Munn's World* he really went hog-wild, adding super-deep life-boxes for different characters so the various convolutions of each personality could click in when certain conditions were met. This, too, will alter the contours of the plot.

The third factor, the icing on the cake, is the Random Motor, which is exactly what it sounds like, a bunch of non-linear iterations based on Blair's dramatic algorithms that create random, unexpected events in both the World environment and the story and character lines. And these events, like the tram in *Real Life,* like the various geographic facts flowing in from the World Generator, can materially affect the hero's options, and feed back changes into the story downstream.

In *Munn's World,* too, the Random Motor is highly souped-up compared to *Real Life.* But neither Zeng nor I have seen any big changes occur in the plot as a result of it.

Until tonight.

"It had to happen." I can tell Zeng is elated because he's repeating himself. "Was there an incidence of character?"

"Definitely."

"If the initial change is of that order of magnitude—" Now he's talking to himself, but he doesn't have to explain. I know his theory. He believes that if you make story and world sufficiently complex—if the life-boxes are sufficiently crammed with the peculiarities of a character's ego, if the details of the city are complex enough, if all those details and idiosyncracies act together with the random events by which any environment is affected—you'll end up with a *real* world on your hands in all important aspects.

If you let it run long enough, Zeng says, it will start to throw in strange attractors—patterns it chooses for itself and that will tend to deepen with use the way traffic will deepen ruts in a muddy road.

It will become a world so complex, and so textured, and so goddam active, that *it will make itself up* as it goes along, eventually becoming independent of its creator; unique in ways no one could possibly have imagined; living, in every vital sense of the term.

"Frankenstein," I mutter, draining the abs'ini.

"Yes, Igor," Zeng replies absentmindedly. "Did you notice anything particular," he continues, "when this happened?"

"Like what?"

"Like that shift. Did things slow down at all?"

"So that *is* it!" Munn can figure out anything if it smacks him in the face often enough. I scratch at my forehead. "That's what you were saying at the meeting. In *Real Life*—it's the Random Motor?"

"Ta-da!"

"The tram."

"Ta-da, again. You want randomness, you pay for it. Gigabytes, man, every time. Slows it down."

"But it's s'posed to be only three, four percent RAM use—the Random Motor?"

"Yeah. And who worked out the percentages?"

"You." I reach the obvious conclusion. "You *cooked the numbers?*"

"Sure." Zeng sounds utterly happy. "But it's not important."

"Prove it."

"I will."

I suddenly feel tired beyond the ken of previous fatigues. I think last night, the whisky, the chase of the carpet-cutters, took more out of me than I predicted. Which reminds me.

"Zeng," I say. *"Doo meh."*

"What?"

"Doo meh. Do you know what it means?"

"You think that's Cantonese, maybe? That's not Cantonese. That's gibberish, man—barbarian lingo."

"Zeng—"

"Maybe Thai, or Viet?"

"You know any Thai? I need to find out what it means."

"Why?"

"I'll tell you later. I don't have the energy now."

"All us Asians," he says, "we all same-same chop-chop talkie-talkie, huh?"

"Gimme a break."

"I'll ask around."

He hangs up. I've pissed him off. I'm too tired to care. I fall into bed without brushing my teeth. I leave my face unwashed, like Maggie Hernon. One of my last thoughts as I crash is, That's why Maggie was so dirty, she was as exhausted as I am tonight.

Unicorns are chasing me down Peacock Alley at the Waldorf Astoria. I know Larissa is at one of the tables, sipping tea out of thin lapis-colored china with someone I don't know, but I can't find her. I only see Joel Kamm and Amy Dillon, naked, making up dirty limericks for each other under an ormolu clock.

I run down a narrow flight of stairs that leads to a private railroad station under the hotel. The platform is dark but inside the shadows I make out great tigers and griffins carved in the stone pillars. A canal runs underground beside the railroad tracks. My bladder is full and I want to stop and piss but I have no time because the friends of the unicorn want to catch me and force me to recite all the lyrics of Johnny Rotten, otherwise they'll cut my stomach open with carpet-cutters. *"Doo meh!"* the unicorns holler. Their horns are scarred and their yellow teeth grin. *"Doo meh!"* I wake up gasping, my bladder taut as the Goodyear blimp.

The workstation utters shrieks like a peacock, which means it's Thursday, 7:30 A.M. I have to hustle for my weekly appointment with Pentti. I piss and shower. I put on jeans and a sweater and my fancy gaucho boots. I drink coffee. The wound is healing but my left arm hurts where the Thai or whatever he was cut it. The palms of my hands are still dark and sore. I smear on more bacitracin.

Lenny is not around. He left an *Economist* on the breakfast table and I suck in a couple of headlines with the El Pico brew. The Sonoran rebels have given up Huachinera to the *Federales*. The U.N. continues to protest. The Ukrainians make Cossack noises concerning the annexation of western Poland by the German Federation.

On page five Lenny has underlined a leader applauding the junior senator from New York, Henry Warren Powell, for "blasting" Federal limits on ownership of specific interactive cable markets. "You cannot build creativity on handcuffs!" Powell is quoted as saying. I don't like Powell—his campaign is built on ideas like you *need* steady fifteen percent unemployment to ensure a mobile labor pool for the service economy—but I have to agree with that last statement.

Lenny always thinks I'm fascinated by anything to do with interactive cable TV but I really couldn't care less about the finances.

It's the pretty pictures I like.

After a third coffee I walk over to the Broadway line station at Canal Street and head on uptown.

Pentti is compactly built, with a big tuft of gray-blond hair like a weathered haystack. He teases this up the back of his head to hide his bald spot, about which he is quite sensitive. He always hunches forward, or sideways on one elbow, to take in with maximum interest what you're saying; or else slumps backward, with fingers to chin, as if to invoke the spirits of Breuer and Lacan in the dispassionate dissection of the problem you represent.

He's the only man I know who still wears rollneck sweaters with jeans and running shoes. He plays tennis every day of the week. He has a pointy jaw and green eyes, which seem to grow closer together when he gets excited, taking on the predatory thrust of a fox. This usually happens after our sessions, when we gossip about TV and the industry in general; I think I mentioned a lot of Pentti's clients work in television. He's a camp follower in the army of showbiz and it has made him a well-informed and wealthy professional.

Our session begins, as usual, with what he calls a rundown. I start off with last night's dream, which is still fresh enough in my mind for me to remember well. He takes a note or two without great interest.

He asks me if I've talked to Louise and I tell him "no."

We shoot the shit about the divorce and, here and there, at what seem like random intervals, he calls up details of my growing up—my stepfather and his death; Montclair High School; the years Louise and I lived so far up the East Side of Manhattan that while the real estate people have taken to calling it "Carnegie Hill," it was actually the edge of Spanish Harlem. Remembering the scrapes I got into hanging around the *barrio* brings back the memory, never very far from my mind recently, of what happened in Kearny two nights ago. Pentti leans forward again and his features grow pointed; his patients tend to be rich and safe and few of them get shot at with Tech-9s or anything else.

Except on TV sound stages.

"They were Chinese?" he says.

"They sounded Asian."

"Why?"

"Well, it wasn't English."

"How do you feel about the attack?"

"Oh," I say, waving a hand around, "I'm against it."

"Answer the question."

I look at my fingers carefully.

"At first," I say truthfully, "it was just a shock, it made me feel—spacey, I guess, more than usual. But now"—I own ten fingers, just like last time. The palms still seem dark and odd-looking—"I guess I seem to mix it up with the other stuff. I mean, I know it was a coincidence, but now I feel like it was directed somehow, like karma—like it's my work that's trying to kill me, maybe even Larissa, in some way she wants me to be dead."

You go to shrinks long enough, you end up giving them the answers they want. He takes copious notes in a tiny cursive.

"D'you think you have a fear of Asians?"

"Only when they got Tech-9s," I reply.

Pentti's office has a lovely view of the Hudson that he hides behind drawn curtains. His collection of Gandhara artifacts lines what expensively strip-lit shelves are not occupied by volumes of JAPA. The desk is walnut; the paneling, cherry; the rugs are Kirghiz and Kazakh. He has a large marble-plinthed Empire clock that ticks very loudly. Now he dims the lights and switches on a single black Tensor lamp in the corner. He asks me to lie back in the teak-and-steel Danish divan he puts his clients in.

He pushes a button on his desk and tells me to focus on the sound of the ticking and the source of light. He sits in the shadows to my left. He talks, softly and monotonously, about will and lack of will. About eyes wet from straining.

About lifting that involves no force and a disconnection free of severing.

I'm used to this, and the calm I anticipate creates in great measure the calm I need to follow his directions.

When I wake up one of my hands is floating at nose level and I have to pull on it to bring it down.

"So?" I ask stupidly, as I always do.

"Nothing much." He snaps off the Notemaster, uncaps his Mont Blanc, writes a line. "You always ramble on about dark rivers; parts of the waterfront everybody else has forgotten about."

"So?"

"So it's boring. Clichéd."

"You mean—?"

"Sex, of course. The birth canal—"

"Please, Pentti."

"What every man really desires. Sex with his mother. Hey, you wanted a neo-Freudian, you got a neo-Freudian. But it's a dead end. Speaking of your mother—"

"Is there," I interrupt, "anything about—you know?"

He shakes his head.

"Can we listen to the tape?"

"It's not a good idea. You want to keep the tools clean," he adds vaguely. "I'll get Ruth to type up a transcript. Do you want me to talk to your mother?"

Pentti asks this same question every time and as ever I reply, "It won't do any good. Pastor Johnson says—"

"I know what Pastor Johnson says. But your mother holds vital information."

"Louise thinks shrinks are a crutch."

"Psychotherapists," Pentti corrects me, and closes his notebook. "Is it true Brooke Steele poisons Amy Dillon in the final episode of *Pain* this spring, so they can buy out her contract during reruns?"

We talk about the soap for a good fifteen minutes. This is on Pentti's time—he doesn't charge for gossip. He's not a bad shrink, or psychotherapist. In fact, he's the best I've had, although even he has not succeeded any more, in what I really want from him, than the four others I've seen, on and off, since I was seventeen.

I'm famished when I leave Pentti's office. I head east on Ninety-sixth and buy a hot dog from a Sabrett's cart. One hundred fifty years ago, I guess, the hot dog vendor would have been tending a charcoal fire and crying out "Hot sausage!" but in his basic function he is the same. It makes me feel good that the city, in important ways, seems to resemble itself across the spectrum of time. The vendor nods, recognizing me from previous visits.

Sabrett's is the best street dog for my money, better than Nathan's or Gray's Papaya. While the combo of nitrates, grease, and French's mustard likely will induce indigestion by noon, the first hit of that savory wiener and attendant steamed onions and sauerkraut gives my tastebuds the happy and excellent feeling of being fully alive for the first time today.

It's gotten a lot colder, and it's starting to rain. I eat contentedly, the freezing rain drooling down my face, watching a large black man scream "Oh, *God*!" and pretend to jump at passersby.

I have indigestion by lunchtime. I spend the afternoon doing paperwork, signing off on requests by the art department for everything from computer time to research photos. The Screen Actors Guild is pissed off at the deal we negotiated with them, whereby actors used for video-digitalization would receive bonuses in lieu of credit. A SAG supervisor calls me "a motherfucking blackleg fascist" and I hang up on her.

I call around, looking for Larissa. She has no scenes today and is neither in the Green Room nor home.

I spend a lot of time looking out the window at New Jersey. While I avoid thinking about carpet-cutters, I believe all my worries seek ways around the logjams and end up flowing where they meant to go in the first place, as Pentti says they do. It's two whole weeks before Thanksgiving but people are putting up memos and colorful cardboard turkeys to remind senior staff of the party this evening.

The way my unhappiness over the carpet-cutters comes back to me at this point is in the form of worrying over the Morgan. At three I tell Rob I'm taking a long lunch.

He reminds me about the Thanksgiving party.

I walk to Port Authority and catch the number 44 Descamp local to North Arlington and Kearny.

When I get there I cannot find the bar by walking. Everything is changed by direct light. Mount Trashmore squats to the north. The vinyl-sided streets resemble one another and I count half a dozen Scottish butchers, all advertising haggis. I call a cab and he drives me three blocks to McAndrew's.

The car is fine. Someone put a tarp over it to protect or hide its canvas top. There's a woman tending bar inside and I give her the tarp and another Franklin by way of thanks. "Well, fuck me pink," she says in a genuine Lowlands accent and stares at me as if I'd flown on silver wings down the kitchen vent; I guess since the shipyards closed no one hands out fifties in Kearny anymore.

I get back to 280 without mishap and shoot onto the turnpike. The TR4 engine roars happily and climbs to a loud eighty-five mph, leaving the juggernaut trucks and Greyhounds and production-line cars drearily fussing at each other in my wake. When I reach the 16-E exit I turn off and pay the toll but instead of heading to the Lincoln Tunnel I turn west on Route 3, watching the "X" on top of the X-Corp tower recede in my rearview over the Meadowlands.

Twelve minutes later I'm pulling into a curved pine-heavy drive on Midland Avenue in Montclair, looking up at the four-story shingled amalgamation of turrets, gambrels, mansards, porches, and heating oil bills that my mother and sister call home.

I grew up here, too, from the age of fourteen, when Louise met and married Seth Pastrich; but though I came to love Seth, and despite the many good times I enjoyed in this nonsensical house, Montclair never seemed like home to me the way the city did.

I climb through the storm door, which as usual has no glass in it. Inside, the hall is dark. The heat is going full blast, the ancient behemoth of a heating plant in the basement guzzling with abandon dollars and number-two oil, but that's no problem since Seth left Louise all of what he used to call his shekels, which came to a considerable sum. I can smell joss sticks. On the second floor someone is playing John Denver tunes on the Bechstein: "Sunshine on My Shoulder" and other crap of that nature.

Farther upstairs music is coming out of expensive speakers. As I climb the steps, calling, the electronic sound grows in volume and drowns out the piano. It sounds like amplified violins, Indian instruments, bells, voices chanting in a tone so mellifluous and slimy it almost makes the soles of my gaucho boots lose traction. It's heavy on the synthesizer, the kind of music you get watching full-busted Barnard undergrads combining "eclectic inspirations of East and West" in a new free-form version of modern dance—something with lots of smocks and diaphanous shawls. You get the picture.

They're on the third floor, in one of the sitting rooms. The weighty Edwardian furniture, the faded chintz and antimacassars from Seth's first wife, have been overlaid by Guatemalan *huipils,* posters of Nepal, rain forests, endangered crabs. Louise is sitting on the couch, talking to a portly fellow in a shiny suit with an ankh hanging around his neck.

"Alex!" she exclaims, getting to her feet and sweeping the long sleeves of her robe, Mrs. Pharaoh indicating her approval of a favorite courtier. She smiles her old smile, the one that warms stone at twenty paces, and I walk over and hug her with real strength.

It all goes downhill from there. I sit on an exercycle. Bumper stickers reading "Good Things Happen" and "Practice Random Acts of Kindness and Senseless Beauty" slug it out with more traditional Pastor Johnson gems like "Pay Off the Lord" and "Kickback to Jesus!" *Pain in the Afternoon* whines and bitches in the corner. Although Pastor Johnson prefers that the faithful tune exclusively to the Johnsonist cable channel, Louise and Sara have been loyal to me and Larissa in their own way by continuing to follow the lurid plot twists of the soap. The Pastor, it appears, allows them this one apostasy.

Louise points to her companion.

"This is Freesoul Mountainman."

I try not to crack up. The monikers these Johnsonists insist on adopting are as comic taken one way as they are sad taken in the obverse. Freesoul discreetly closes his briefcase and shakes my hand. I have to admit I say "Louise" here mostly to piss her off.

"Alex." Reproachfully touching my shoulder. Crystals jingle as heat escapes the mansard in room-sized drafts.

"I'm not going to call you 'Wilderness Starchild,' " I insist, a trifle desperately.

"You did at Christmas."

"For fuck's sake!"

"That language," my mother says, "is a product of blocking."

"I need to talk to you. It's important." I look at Freesoul, who nods reluctantly.

"There's echinacea tea in the pantry," Louise tells him, "whole-wheat brownies in the tin. I shan't be long."

"Look." When Freesoul has gone, I get off the exercycle and turn down the synthesizer music. "I don't want to argue. I wanted to ask you—"

"Yes?"

"You know."

"The usual?"

"I just realized—it's such a little thing, but it's really important to me."

"It's that *doctor* who says it's important." She says "Doctor" the way Baptists say "Catholic."

"Lou—I mean. Whatever, Starchild. Can I call you Wilderness?" She frowns. "Sorry." I'm twisting a finger around so hard I crack a knuckle. "I just need a little more information. Please, Mom? I can research the rest."

She gets off the couch and crosses to the window. She looks up at the sky—Cleopatra, I think, or maybe Anna Christie. Louise spent years of her life trying, unsuccessfully, to be an actress. She has a huge appetite for the dramatic; Pentti thinks, quite seriously, it's the deep reason I wanted to write plays. He says I wanted to buy the affection she withheld in a coin she would understand. I think the answer is simpler; with Louise around, you get a feel for the cheap drama of any situation. Once you have that feel, writing TV scenes is a piece of cake.

Outside, kids are playing in the yard. Followers of Pastor Johnson are always staying here, scarfing Louise's food, borrowing cash, letting their New Age offspring run wild in the rhodies where Sara and I played as kids.

"I made a decision, early on," she begins.

"I know."

"Then you know why it's *not* important, about your father. It was a—bad period, for me. Your father went away. He was Irish," she says, as if this were vital info. Maybe it is since it's the only thing she's ever told me about him. "I swore I would never curse you with the memory of a man you'd never met. But you *know* all this."

"Don't you think," I say softly, "I'm being cursed by the *non*memory?"

"There's no such thing as nonmemory."

"If a room already exists," I tell her, "even if there's no furniture in it, it's still a room."

"Carl Jung," she says. "I know the jargon."

"That's not Jung."

"It would make you unhappy, Alex." She has turned back to the television and her jaw is set straight and strong as that of a big herbivore. "Look," she says, pointing, "Larissa!"

"It makes me unhappy, not to know."

"Were you unhappy growing up?"

"That's got nothing to do—"

"It's got everything—"

Downstairs the piano stops. The synthesized music whines like opiated mosquitoes from the Bose speakers.

Suddenly and without warning the thought comes to me: I know how Zeng is going to argue away the lag problem in *Real Life*.

We both add our silence to the dying notes of the Bechstein.

"I love you, Alex," my mother says, walking over to me and hugging me tightly. "Accept my love."

"Aw, shit, Mom," I say.

Louise's eyes are light blue. They're watery, and look a little soft, as if the fibers of the retina had smudged a little. It's the way they look when she's eating Percoset.

My sister is waiting on the landing as I clump downstairs. She is very pale and thin but no thinner than usual. Sara has dark chestnut hair and the eyes and lips of Saint Catherine in some of the early illuminations. She gives me the Johnsonist hug, both mitts clutching the love handles. She sits with me on the steps and puts her arms around her legs and rests her chin on her knees.

Sara is twenty-three but she uses a lot of the mannerisms she had when she was ten, at least when I'm around.

"I heard you," she says.

"Uh-huh."

"Don't be angry at her."

"I can't help it."

"She just wants to help."

"Bullshit. She wants to keep a fuckin' rein on us—"

"That language," Sara says. "It's just blocking—"

"Don't you start," I growl at her. "Every time I spend ten minutes with you people it makes me want to blow crack, just to get the feel-good out."

She looks down. Her eyes are closed. I put a hand on her knee. Everybody protects Sara too much. Then again it's what she's always wanted, and maybe even what she needs.

"What are they giving you now?" I ask her.

"Prodex."

"That's what my shrink gives me, too."

Sara's adopted name is Willowbaby Moonhugs. She knows better than to ask me to call her that.

We talk for a little longer, then I get in the Morgan and split. The good feeling I had when I ate the hot dog after Pentti's is completely gone. I feel divided, as if a buffer existed that cut me off from the normal sensations of life. All I have is the Morgan to reaffirm the connection of gravity, of acceleration and inertia and solidity.

I use the car all the way, burning rubber through Montclair, hitting ninety mph on Route 3, trying to drive out the cloying taste in my mouth with the roar of the cylinders and the antiseptic flavor of speed.

SEVEN

THE STUDIO BUILDING is empty by the time I get back. I cross the walkway to the headquarters tower, the one with the "X"; the building that contains the financial system of both XTV and its parent corporation.

This is the tower of the bigwigs, the four-hundred-K-a-year execs, the office of Jack Tyrone himself under the giant buzzing symbol over the reefer units on the thirty-seventh floor, but the importance of the tower to X-Corp doesn't justify the number of security men who corral me and check my ID and tickle me with handheld metal detectors at the entrance to the executive dining room on the twentieth floor.

Some are normal X-Corp security geeks but others are pretty boys in suits like Freesoul Mountainman's. They wear shaded glasses and tiny white buttons on their lapels into which they murmur grim comments at set intervals.

"What's going on?" I ask one of the *Pain* writers heading out to the ladies' room.

She jerks a thumb behind her. "Henry Warren Powell."

I raise my eyebrows. Everybody knows Powell and Jack Tyrone agree on matters of regulatory philosophy—in fact, Powell was the chief sponsor of the deregulation bill that allowed X-Corp to buy majority cable coverage in big regional markets. Powell also uses Tyrone as an adviser on legislation but I didn't realize they were such asshole-buddies that Powell would come to our Thanksgiving party.

However, I welcome this friendship since it should mean they are serving real champagne instead of the cheap New York State or California variety they usually trot out in the interest of paying back Kowloon Bankcorp a little early.

The execs' nosh-room is an airy space upholstered in the corporate colors of blue and silver. It cuts right across the tower in the shape (*quelle* surprise) of a curved lozenge, with huge windows in the standard pattern on the east and west walls. A giant tapestry on the south end depicts, in a splotch of grayish color that's probably light red, an exploded human wired to city grids; Interactive Man hooked up to the World. On the other end a big abstract map of the globe shows in blue and silver relief the first B-Net webs in the greater conglomerations of Frankfurt-Nantes, Portland–Newport News, Indianapolis-Buffalo, Dallas-Atlanta, Santa Barbara–Marin, and Tokyokohama.

A thick crowd with men in double-knit facing *outward* marks where Henry Warren Powell holds court near the speaker's podium. I can make out his famous mane of sandy hair next to the grizzled crew cut of Jack Tyrone.

Good-looking extras in Pilgrim duds and tin-buckled shoes are wandering around with trays listing from the weight of champagne flutes and toast fingers lathered with smoked soy pâté. I take a glass and nod approvingly. Krug, possibly even Roederer. I finish it off fast and grab a couple more because you never know when they're going to pull the Cana trick on you, substituting Andre for the good stuff.

I meander over to the river window, nodding at people as the bubbly lightens the load in my head. The sun is going down in a thermonuclear blast of yellow; clouds like flying saucers contemplate the assault of Port Elizabeth. Kearny must lie behind the ridge with the church on it. Its frozen, dead marsh seems even less real now than it did yesterday, far less possible in fact than the strange new form of reality we're developing in this very complex. It's a measure of the champers's quality that I'm so sanguine all of a sudden about *Real Life*'s Value to Humanity.

I walk back toward the young people serving bubbly, threading my way through groups of investors, the recent exiles from Hong Kong—faces animated yet still, the forceful "ay-*ahs*" of Chinese. Zeng's right, I think. Those words from the carpet-cutter virtuoso did not really sound like the tones of a Son of Heaven.

Every corner holds someone in party clothes yawping into a cellphone or pulling hard copy from a portafax. I don't see Larissa anywhere, though other talent from *Pain* is in evidence. Amy talks to Brooke Steele, the man Pentti claims is going to poison her in the spring. She ignores me.

Joel Kamm schmoozes XTV's news director.

Rose Obregon is leaning against Antarctica on the north wall, talking to Ivan Gaynor and a Chinese suit. As I'm heading back to my window she waves me over. I carefully hold both glasses in one hand and press flesh with the other. The Chinese suit I don't recognize and have no reason to remember. Gaynor is an imposing-looking guy with a good head of tan hair and a laugh like a jackal. He is built in powerful horizontal planes, like a New Mexican mesa; broad basalt of forehead and gut, sandstone cheeks and shoulders, solid and strong. He wears a short monkey-jacket in the height of style and a thin bow tie, nicely selected to minimize his bulk. He has one of those ore-crusher handshakes you have to pretend to match while stifling moans of agony. He has a way of hooking his thoughts together, cause-effect, as if no other combination were possible. I like this.

When the chitchat is dispensed with Gaynor says, "Rose tells me you got a problem on *Real Life.*"

"Nothing big."

"The first episode airs in twenty days, and there are still two-point-three lags in the action sequences?"

Gaynor has a slight Midwestern accent. His "r"s are very sharp; I've never noticed this before.

"We're not sure it's a problem," I tell him. "It's very localized."

"Is that an answer?" He smiles at Rose and she smiles back and looks at me like I have dogshit on my face.

"We'll have a definite answer for you on Tuesday," I tell him.

"What about the SAG people?" he asks, to show he's on top of things.

"We're still talking, but basically, they signed a contract." He nods.

"I've only seen the demos," Gaynor says. "I should come down and watch a whole episode sometime. If Rose will let me." He has a way of looking at you with one hundred percent attention. He takes out a penknife, opens and closes the blades and gizmos on it. His eyes are shiny and blue as Swedish steel and they never leave mine. I know, now, what a bivalve feels like when it spots the clam knife. My palms start to tingle a little in reaction.

"It's really good." Rose is talking fast. She's jingling her key chain, something she does when she's nervous. I realize she's defending me, and herself. "I've seen the whole third episode and it's—it's just *dynamite*. I'll feed it to your workstation."

Gaynor says, "Good."

"They're all the same," I tell him. "Third episode, fifth episode, whatever—it's Virtix that's important, not the plot."

"First time I ever heard a writer admit that," Gaynor says, doing his jackal sound. The clam-opening gaze doesn't go away; he keeps looking at me as if he'd found a locked compartment inside my outer shell, and he's not the kind of man to leave anything unopened around.

I take advantage of the laughter to unstick myself. I should be more cozy with Gaynor, who is Rose's boss and therefore mine, but I cannot bring myself to pretend producing *Real Life* is my reason for living, which is the attitude our corporate mentality seems to require.

On my way back to the window a woman calls out "Munn!" and I turn to see Larissa in a tight, shiny, green-spangled dress that allows a view of the first swell of breast on the side. She's standing next to Ned Reynolds. She waves me over the way Rose did but I just grin and keep going and after five minutes or so she joins me, alone, by the window.

"Why didn't you come to talk to me?"

"I didn't want to talk to Braindead."

"Don't call him that."

"It's his nickname."

She looks over at Kearny without knowing it and I look at her face in profile. It's a big face—she's a big woman—and the rise and sweep of the nose and cheekbones and neck, together with the dark plummet of hair behind and the dramatic darkness of her irises, combine to give her a kind of military beauty, like a Spetsnaz brigade sweeping through a village of Yakut nationalists. She scares me, she attracts me still. Her fingers are long and graceful and they hold the champagne flute in intimate fashion. Her thumb rubs up and down the stem. I press hard on myself to keep the desire out of my voice.

"I been trying to call you."

"I have been out a lot." The Russian emphasis, never weeded out, still forcing itself through the "o"s.

"Uh-huh."

"Don't, Alex." She turns to face me. Her mouth is straight as a Kalashnikov barrel.

"I was being noncommittal. Independent."

"Bullshit."

"Really. You don't affect me any longer."

"I am delighted to hear it."

"So who've you been seeing? I'll *kill* the bastard."

She smiles at that. We look at each other for a fraction of a second, not long but it's enough for a little affection to seep through so of course I immediately grab that and try to build a bridgehead, mentally, thinking for the millionth time maybe there's some hope left in the corners of her smile from which to salvage a life together, when we're interrupted by the sound of clapping across the room.

Jack Tyrone and Henry Warren Powell have climbed to the small lozenge-shaped podium. XTV News cameras film from ten paces. I notice one of the shiny-suited pretty boys standing near us, gazing eagle-eyed at the writers.

Larissa turns to watch. She has always been fascinated by men of power. Tyrone's voice is gruff; although short in stature he grabs the lectern like a judo expert. The usual unfiltered butt smokes from between two thick fingers. Smoking is not allowed here but nobody seems to be calling him on it. He goes through the ritual CR hogwash about dynamic growth and brilliant breakthroughs and ground-breaking innovation and suddenly he's talking specifically about *Real Life*.

". . . most of us know will redefine how we see the world. In a real sense this party is also for *Real Life,* which airs for the first time just before Pearl Harbor Day . . ." He waits for the dutiful laughter to die down. "We owe a particular debt to Rose Obregon—" He looks for her in the crowd. She waves gaily from Antarctica and everybody claps. "Also"—he consults a plexiglass prompter in front of the rostrum—"uh, Alexander Munn, the producer."

My jaw hangs in surprise. My complexion is ruddy to begin with and I sense it turn the color of a sunset. People are looking around, trying to figure out who this guy is. Tyrone listens to Gaynor, who murmurs at him, looking at me from beside the podium—I can feel his gaze even at this range. *"Wave,"* Larissa hisses, and after a second I lift a hand half-heartedly and Tyrone bellows, "There's Alex!" and points at me and everybody claps again. Larissa chuckles deep in her throat—she is pleased for me. Tyrone mentions a few other names and then cuts to the chase.

"Ladies and gentlemen, colleagues—it is my great honor to introduce to you a warm personal friend, but more importantly a great friend of the free market—a staunch supporter of a free communications industry—the junior senator from New York, the next President of the United States, Henry Warren Powell!"

Powell steps to the lectern. He thanks Tyrone, thanks us all. He launches into a tirade, written by the clever young women and men who work for him, that hits all the usual bullshit keys. He has a voice that is strong and clear yet friendly with it.

He is tall, narrow-shouldered. He has big hands and a bony jaw and thick, Lincolnesque eyebrows and he leans forward kind of like Pentti and seems to draw you in, not so much to what he's saying as to *how* he's saying it, so that you feel you've got a friend, a big brother, a father, telling you that despite the steady unemployment and the murderous crime rate and the six-day internment-without-trial mandated by the AGATE laws he voted for, *everything's gonna be alright.*

I can see Larissa watching him so raptly she lets her champagne glass tilt. I rescue it before it spills.

After Powell steps down, and after the applause and approving whistles from the actors and shrieks of devotion from women have finally burbled away, she turns to me with eyes even more full of reflections than usual.

"He's wonderful," she tells me.

"I was having doubts about Santa Claus," I tell her. "Now I know I was wrong the whole time."

"Oh, Alex." She shakes her head, smiling.

"I want to talk to you."

That brings her up short.

"Now?"

"Later."

She cocks her head. She remembers that Tyrone singled me out for praise in front of the next President of the United States.

"As friends?"

"That's a cliché."

"No—it's a protection."

I nod.

"Okay. As 'friends.' I need to go over something with you."

"You drank my champagne." I nod again. "You're lonely, Alex."

Ned Reynolds strides up at that point and says something hearty and cheerful in that deep, exquisitely modulated voice of his. He puts a hand on her bare shoulder. There is not one strand out of place in the shiny mass of his hair. I want to whine something pointed to Larissa, on the order of "I can see loneliness is not a problem for *you*"; I turn away abruptly to cut myself off.

Drink another flute of champagne, and another. The noise in the big room is deafening. Amy is talking so intimately to her future assassin that their heads are touching. The champagne seems to have lost something, its airy quality replaced by bigger, harsher bubbles and a fake sweetness that leaves a rancid aftertaste. I walk around the bar. A lot of dead soldiers from the army of Roederer stand upended in the trash while the actors behind the counter unscrew the tops off Cordoniu bottles.

It's an old trick and it happens often, but this evening it seems particularly cheap. Maybe it's the sandwich effect; this company, built on the generation of appearances, throwing a bash for those who live by those appearances, and handing out good champagne for the sake of show. But now the show is over and the kliegs are dark and the reality is cheap and sweet in a way that is worse than sour.

I leave immediately.

Because the car park for TV City was subcontracted to very laid-back Calabrese chums of the mayor's and is not yet finished, I left the Morgan in a commercial garage near the entrance to the Lincoln Tunnel on Thirty-fifth Street.

Night has fallen as I reach Ninth Avenue and turn southward. The Korean and Vietnamese and Pakistani groceries guarded by Sonoran refugees spill fruit and newsprint into polythene-drawn perimeters. They alternate with the red flashing bulbs of strip clubs and porno triplexes and the strobing whizz-bang flash of robot-sumo and virtual reality parlors.

Between the shopfronts, in the India-ink doorways of turn-of-the-century tenements, the night fauna have ventured forth with the retreat of light. They lean into the neon in postures of seduction, of familiarity, of intimacy. They are thin and the night rises to the surface like bruises in the hollows of their cheeks and in concave planes drawn in their cheap rayon clothing by the reduction of flesh. They are Burmese and Rwandan, Guatemalan and Filipino, Chechen and Tamil, Yakut and Dinka and Xhosa. Many are refugees from bush conflicts in Sonora and Kashmir, Amuria and the Transvaal. There are many Cantonese, newly fled from Hong Kong. They whisper as I walk by, phrases that have a ring of poetry to them, as if the millstones of need and despair could grind a rhyme even from such poor corn as this.

"Smoke, sens'."

"Hey, missah, you wann."

"Ice, China."

"Ay cutie, you come?"

A prophet of Industrial Islam shouts from a Dumpster. Robes flowing, portafax bumping on his hip, he explains how the New Koran will reveal itself electronically to sort out information property rights once and for all.

Far over my head and to the left I can see the cranes and gantries of the Times Square/Forty-second Street Redevelopment project towering spindly beside the Paramount, the Disney-Versailles, the MTV Palace.

In a left-handed way the redevelopment of Forty-second Street is related to the presence of the fauna on a stretch of Ninth that used to be Hispanic, lower middle class, and safe. Before, Forty-second Street—"The Deuce"—was the traditional red-light district and that was where people went for what they found there, and the neighborhood was both defined and limited by this tautology.

Then the mayor and some of the same crew who built TV City decided to "clean out" the area. What this meant was, they gave away Godzilla-sized chunks of the street to Disney/ABC, with the tacit understanding that Disney would offer them lucrative boardroom positions once out of office.

But you don't clean out vice from a city worthy of the name. It's like trying to squeeze your colon away because you don't like the idea of shit. It just floats back in a different place, or a hundred different places, and in this case the shit flowed north and south along Ninth and Tenth, smothering the Hispanics toward Columbus Circle and the developing West African neighborhood downtown on Tenth, hooking east to link up with the new porn centers around Thirtieth and Fifth.

I slow down. The stale taste of the Spanish bubbly has faded a little, and so has the taint of seeing Larissa with Braindead. I refuse to ask myself if they're fucking. I watch the street, walking fast and alert like I grew up doing, hunching down inside my worn leather jacket, occasionally turning to check who's behind. Some of the hookers wear high heels and they sound a little like the footsteps in the marsh and then again they sound different.

After a while I don't worry about it so much.

Forty-second Street at this level now is all "family entertainment centers" selling *Barbie in Wonderland* paraphernalia, and wholesome, expensive vacation complexes based on *Snow White* themes. There's a tower that looks like a cartoon meteor crashing into an acre of flex-face billboards. The street is patrolled by teams dressed up as Goofy and Pocahontas, and they're always polite and helpful and smiling, even when they're zapping the fuck out of you with the fifteen-thousand-volt tazers they all carry.

Upscale *mate* bars, VR parlors, and Norwegian farm-salmon restaurants fill in the concessions Donald Duck left open.

It's drizzling now, without offense, and the humidity smears colors over the black asphalt of the Deuce. I cross quickly.

Tonight I honestly feel more at home in the bad districts. There's an honesty there, a frankness of attitude because nobody pretends to be something they're not.

There's an honesty of consistency, too, because this is the way it's always been: a culture of extremes. In New York the money always stayed uptown and down the center of the island in havens of insulting luxury built as far as possible from the docks and airports by people trying to forget they came over on a boat or plane just like everybody else. And everybody else—the people who got off the Airbus yesterday, the ones who don't have money or much of anything but the need to survive and keep their families alive—they swim if they can and live near the rotten water and the avgas smell of runways—and if they start sinking they end up on streets like this, hustling for a buck or a quarter even, sleeping under cardboard, spending the nickel on a cellophane bag of optimism when they can't survive any other way.

Knightsbridge over there, Port Said here. The way it's always been.

It was like this in the early 1850s. Tenth Avenue at this level was still farmland, with a few streets pulling themselves out of the manure. The true equivalent of this district then was the waterfront, maybe Cherry and Water streets between Corlear's Hook and South Ferry, or downtown on Centre Street, or parts of the Bowery.

I step around a beautiful transvestite. He's over six feet three inches tall and has legs that would make any woman jealous. An emaciated Matadi-14 victim cowers in a disused doorway, shitting his brains out. A gaggle of Kashmiri boys zip south in a flash of robes and a whine of motorized roller-blades. Young homegirls run numbers on nineteen-hundred-dollar speed-bikes, their Flexator shoes flashing as they pump.

The sounds of the street drown out the echo of people like Powell, Tyrone, Braindead.

"Oye, puta, mira-me."

"Live nude show, beautiful girls."

"Boys, video, boys, video."

"Ven' a ver mi chicas."

"Shashlik, hot dog, chimichanga."

"Hot chestnuts."

Christ yes, there *is* a hot chestnut seller. I haven't seen one of them in years and I stop to buy a bag. It's gotten a lot colder and the glowing pan of the pushcart warms my hands. The sharp smell of charcoal and carbonizing shells reminds me of when I was a kid and Louise used to bring me and Sara downtown to watch the tree go up at Rockefeller Center around this time of year. I get chestnut shell up my thumbnails and burn my tongue on the meats exactly as I used to do. These chestnuts taste better than any filet of Trondheim salmon steamed in dill aquavit or whatever over-sauced rubbish they're serving in the Disney-Versailles.

In fact, I'd take anything this street offers over the Unimondo culture, that travel-section eclecticism, that package-tour internationalism of decaf espresso and low-salt sushi marketed as high esthetics. The truth of the matter remains, Unimondo is aimed solely at making bucks and perpetuating the illusions of people who think they're different from the hustlers and johns darting or waiting around the cold gritty pavement of Thirty-seventh and Ninth.

Still nibbling the chestnuts I stop at the window of a robot-sumo parlor and watch the video footage of what's happening inside. Beside me a tall Jamaican in dreadlocks and a yellow jumpsuit bobs to the beat of his Discman. A thin woman, probably sick with TDF, clicks a dead channel selector at the screens in the window.

TeleDysFunction does that to people.

The videos show two machines—one looks like a vacuum cleaner crossed with a Bradley armored vehicle, the other like a dog on pistons—swerving, jinking, and tackling each other on a cement floor. Their hydraulic claws rip at the other's vulnerable cables, their minicams swivel as operators in darkened booths upstairs seek out the advantage, the plastic underbelly. People shout and cheer around the runway.

The vacuum cleaner topples the dog. It snips a plastic pipe in its victim that gushes out blue hydraulic fluid.

Illegal money changes hands.

And then the bells and applause are drowned out by a deeper, harsher sound that comes from outside and to my left. People scream, in challenge and then in fear.

A subtle, swift *pop-pop-pop* noise seems to grab me in the gut and freeze what vague thoughts were running through my brain at that moment. The tall Rasta presses himself into the robot-sumo glass beside me. I cannot move, except to stare down the street the same place he's looking.

Outside the VR parlor people are running like squirrels. Some hurl themselves to the ground. A bunch of small men, or boys perhaps, are backing out of the parlor. They hold black-snouted metal objects with folding stocks, not Tech-9s, maybe Skorpions.

The *pop-pop* noise starts again. Two people fall. They drop casually, not very fast, and lie still without fuss on the pavement. *"Buyaka-buyaka,"* the Jamaican says in satisfaction, imitating the sound of the guns. The small men get into a Vietnamese Honda. They, too, seem to move very slowly.

The car takes off, leaving a long screech of rubber in the aftermath.

Buyaka.

A crowd builds itself around the bodies. Sirens whoop and converge. I dropped my chestnuts, and I feel vaguely sorry about that. My stomach has gone very cold and all the angry self-righteous theories I had built on my way down the avenue have dissolved like helium from a ruptured tank.

The Rasta remains beside me, rolling a joint, shaking in grass from one bag and gray powder from another, both bags pinched expertly in the fingers of one hand.

"Wha' the fuck was that?" I ask him at length.

"Green Dragon, man," he says. "New ee-Asian gang, ronnin' the show.

"Or mebbe Chechen. Or Ahm of Allah; Tadzhik *bah-stahd*." He licks the joint, expertly. He has a big tongue, like a gray pillow. "Look like ee-Asian, though."

"Was it protection," I ask him, "or drugs maybe?"

"Buyaka," the Rasta replies. "It all *buyaka*, man." He lopes off down the street, away from the crowd. I lean against

the plate glass, watching the faces, amazed, excited even by the sex of death, go past.

Finally I continue on my way, but I cross the avenue first, keeping the wilderness of police tape and blood and *buyaka* as far from the crumbling frontiers of my walk as humanly feasible.

EIGHT

I GET HOME early that night.

Signs of Lenny are everywhere: the MSG-glued plates in the sink, empty chicken-cashew cartons in the garbage, a book on Sumerian theater theory, and a scribble of notes addressed to me beside the living-room workstation. But no Lenny.

I go down to Hamid's and buy half a roasted chicken with hummus sauce and bring it home to eat. I switch the living-room terminal to TV and read idly through Lenny's notes. The chicken is salty, bad for you, and delicious. I eat half. The notes read "New possibilities of virtual reality theater; total immersion creates new dilemmas." That it does, I think. "Theater Dionysian rite to initiate into cosmology, guild of toolmakers. What is point today?"

And here I thought Lenny was specializing in the Slang of Prostitution in O'Neill. I'm wondering to what extent his living here has affected his PhD status when from the TV I hear a familiar voice intoning ". . . great honor to introduce to you a warm personal friend, but more importantly a great friend of the free market . . ." I look up at the VDT screen and see Jack Tyrone and Henry Warren Powell and the grinning crowd of which, somewhere, I form a part.

It all glows in high-resolution hues corrected by a color box on the monitor. I watch the sound-byte—it's XTV News, of course. The piece flips to Ned Reynolds yakking about the latest car bomb in Laredo.

Then Braindead's pretty features wipe to a house ad for *Real Life*.

"Coming December third," a deep voice, which I recognize as belonging to *Copkiller* lead Deke Ballou, announces, "an experience so real it will scare you; so intense it will change your life. Order your Virtix connector now! *Real Life*, it's a whole new world."

I cut out TV mode in disgust. Tyrone and Obregon, Henry Warren Powell and the White House, Reynolds and my ex-wife—none of them seem real to me tonight in any sense of the term.

What's real is *buyaka*. The shock of what happened on Ninth has brought back to the soft marrow of me what it felt like to have *buyaka* coming at you for no reason at all through the poisoned grasses of New Jersey.

I pop a Prodex. I leave the rest of the chicken for Lenny and go to bed. For some reason I fall asleep almost immediately.

When I go to work the next morning I find the air has gone colder overnight, freezing the earlier rain. People and cars are sliding around like hockey pucks.

I arrive at my office early for a change. I have a headache, not a bad one, it merely feels like one of the bagpipers from McAndrew's has been miniaturized and injected in a couple of blood vessels in my left frontal lobe, there to skirl "Annie Laurie" till Yuletide.

Three Advils later and the piper has throttled down to "Skye Boat Song" on a teamster's schedule. Despite this handicap I manage to get to the bottom of the paperwork by ten.

The *buyaka* is still floating in the back of my mind but the mushy edges of everything else don't bother me at first. SAG complaints and in-house negotiations on computer-time allocation never had anything but abstract value to begin with, and I can handle them automatically and in a state of partial shock.

Joel Kamm drops in and casually calls me a "tight wad dick-breath asslicker." Rob brings me letters to sign. I meet briefly with Moos.

I call Larissa and by some lapse of fate she is in. I ask her if we can get together and she says sure, six o'clock tonight should be okay unless she gets a call from her producer, in which case she'll phone.

Finally I key up the pilot, the one I both wrote and produced for *Real Life*. Nothing shows on the screen. I check the menus and get a warning box saying "CLEARANCE UNAVAILABLE" with a code that means core malfunction.

I call up the fourth episode, the other one I did—I mean, they're not so different that it matters—and this one comes up without delay or problem. I watch it cold in 2-D.

I follow the digitalized actors moving among digitalized renditions of Santa Monica and Palm Springs. The morning starts to crumble around me.

Rob comes in forty-five minutes later.

"What's the slug on RL-Seven?"

"Huh?" I save the file automatically.

"The seventh *Real Death* file. What's the title of it?"

"I don't remember."

"You know, the one in D.C.?"

"I don't remember, Rob."

"Where they find the Texas crime cartel has infiltrated the shifta-rap CD-ROM conglomerate—"

"I don't remember!" I yell at him.

"Christ," he says, *"sorry."* He sulks back to his desk. I dig out a Prodex and swallow it with cold coffee. I look out the window for a few minutes. Then I call Rose Obregon. "I want to see you," I tell her.

"When?"

"How 'bout now?"

"So where's the fire?"

"It's important, Rose."

I can hear her sigh. We're all hooked up to video-phone at X-Corp. Nobody uses it, either because they're nervous the person they're talking to is not alone as advertised, or because they want to be able to scratch their crotch or make faces while they're on the phone. But I can see Rose's expression as if I'm standing there. Her eyes flip skyward, the fingers play with the key chain.

"I'm going to Heartland in ten minutes," she says. "Meet me there, we'll get a cup o' coffee."

Heartland occupies the fifth floor of the main tower. It's the complex of transmission studios and computer banks that control when, where, and how XTV's shows are broadcast through both B-Net and the older cable systems. The control mainframes for the Virtix system—the ones that tell the video-servers scattered around the country what to do—live there as well.

I don't have clearance for Heartland, which means the Vox-box, which checks my voiceprint against a list of people authorized to get in, won't open the automatic doors. I have to ring Security for admission.

Once inside it's like being in the corridors of some goddam alien spaceship. No outside windows, and everything is a kind of velvety gray. Bundles of B-Net fiber-optic lines snake around the fiberboard ceiling and up through the floor. White noise from fans and air-conditioning systems fills the cracks around the other sounds.

Big plate-glass windows allow views of various control rooms, where techies in white smocks alternately tap on keyboards and watch banked arrays of monitors each labeled with the call signs of different system subsidiaries.

In one of the control rooms two women wearing face-suckers are checking the resolution on a Virtix dummy of *Real Life*.

Rose is in there, talking to a man I recognize vaguely as Zeng's overlord, the Director of Broadcasting, the one Zeng calls "the Wizard of Wires." She motions me in while they finish their discussion. Everything is so hushed and solemn in here I want to pull a Moe Howard, punch some buttons at random, boink the Wizard of Wires in both eyes with stiff fingers: *"Nyuk-nyuk-nyuk-nyuk-nyuk."*

After five minutes the Wizard splits.

"So?" Rose asks.

"It's private."

Her eyes look heavenward. The key chain jangles. She

goes into the corridor, turns left, and speaks into a Vox-box down the hall. The door hisses shut behind us. I look around me in surprise.

We're in the central core of the main tower. This tier is maybe fifty feet by fifty and filled with plastic boxes ten feet long and as high as a man, lined up parallel to each other right across the room. The boxes read IBM-Nixdorf and Fujitsu-Cray, with various model codes. I see no tape reels and very few lights. Everything in here is run from outside. The sound of the air-conditioning unit is very loud.

"There it is," Rose says, pointing at the ranked mainframes. "That's Virtix. Seventeen neural networks, five hundred gigabytes per second 'n we still can't do better than a two-point-three lag."

"Only when the Random Motor kicks in."

She looks at me long and hard.

"So *that's* it?"

"That's part of it."

"You mean, the Random uses so much—"

"Yup."

"But I saw the time-charts. The Random's only s'posed to use four percent, tops."

"It's enough," I tell her. "Zeng's got an answer. It's not what I wanted to talk to you about."

"Zeng," she says thoughtfully. She leans against a mainframe. Rose is very sharp and I interrupt that line of thought before it gets started.

"Rose—"

She sighs, and taps the humming plastic she leans on. "Eight percent jump in lymphoma," she says, "working 'round these things. You worried about Larissa?"

"Larissa? What d'you mean?"

"Her contract."

I put two and two together.

"But I thought it was *Amy* who gets poisoned."

"You shouldn't believe everything you hear at the coffee machine." She chuckles. "Brooke *intends* to slip ricin in Amy's decaf mochaccino—but we decided Lara's gonna drink it by mistake."

I digest that for a second. On another day it would get me upset, but somehow today the fact seems without color.

What has weight is the compulsion in me to change what I'm doing for the better.

"I want to get off *Real Life,*" I tell her.

She looks away for a beat.

"Why?"

"I told you before. In fact, I told Gaynor. The plot's nothing. It's shit. It's a showcase for the technology, that's all."

"So?"

"So?" I stare at her. "Rose, you don't get it. The stories are crap. The characters are crap. Every episode is completely forgettable. I can't even remember what happens on my own episode two seconds after I look at it."

"The way you drink," she comments, and stretches her key chain between two fingers. The opal rings flash different fires.

"That's cheap, Rose. It's got nothing to do with drink. You *know* that material sucks."

"You want to quit?" She looks at me directly now and fishes in her skirt. I watch, fascinated, as she pulls out a single long cigarette and lights it with a miniature gold lighter that is one of the many objects hanging on her key chain.

"No Smoking" signs hang all around us. With the signal exception of Tyrone's office you cannot smoke anywhere in Television City and especially not in here.

Rose is dressed in a long tight gray skirt and a lacy blouse and a creamy silk jacket. She has skin the color of Mindanao teak, and a mouth and nose that look like they were cut by a diamond-tipped tool, and hair as long and dark as Larissa's. She wears very dark lipstick and eye shadow. In a funny way she's even prettier than Larissa, despite the good fifteen years of added mileage she has on my estranged wife.

"You know what I want," I tell her.

"Oh, no," she says. "Not whatchamacallit?"

"*Munn's World.* But it's far, far better than when you saw it—"

"Alex." She only took three puffs of the butt, just below the minimum needed to set off the smoke alarm. Now she crushes it carefully and wraps it in a Kleenex and drops it in a small chain purse she wears like a Sam Browne belt across her chest, under her cellphone.

She reaches for my right hand then and holds it with her

left and strokes it with one finger and on every stroke she makes a point.

"*Munn's World* is nice." (Stroke.) "It's not commercial." (Stroke.) "It's too depressing." (Stroke.) "I told you." (Stroke.) "You want off *Real Death,* that's fine." (Stroke.) "But *not* till the first season's finished."

I pull my hand away. The mad piper in my frontal lobe is doing the Highland fling now, nerves the melody, pain the drone. I can feel panic rising in my throat. This surprises me. I didn't realize till now how much *Real Life* was screwing with my head.

"I don't know if I can wait that long. I mean, it's no different, Rosie! Car chases and pretty chicks. It's a lie, 'cause it doesn't make us *understand* anything. It's wasted information."

"I wouldn't be too sure about that," Rose says absently. "Whyn't you wait till the ratings come in?"

"But I'm *drownin'* in this!"

She looks at the ceiling, and looks down, and then looks at me directly for the second time.

"Alex," she says. "I gave you a break once. You remember?"

"Yeah," I reply, adding quickly, before she can press this advantage, "and I did good by it."

"You did. So—"

"So now," I say, equally quickly, "I just want you to look at *Munn's World* again."

"No way."

"Please, Rose?"

"I tell you what I'll do," she says after a pause. "We get the first Nielsens back on *Real Death,* and they're outtasight, which they will be—I'll transfer you to Development. But there's no room for private projects at XTV."

"What if I go to Gaynor with it?" I say softly.

She stands up straighter. Her eyes, which can be quite warm sometimes, go several shades darker, and cold with that.

"You wanna go over my head?" Her voice, too, has lost temperature.

"I just—"

"Well, you go right ahead, honey. He'll jiss tell you the same damn thing."

She moves toward me quickly, even aggressively. I step back automatically—Sam Rodney says never let anyone get closer than three feet. My back bumps the wall.

Rose looks at me for a second, then, very hard and deliberately, kisses me on the mouth. I can feel the oil of her lipstick, and smell Narcisse.

"But next time you crack up, baby—you on your *own*."

The door hisses shut. There's nothing left in this room except the thrum of climate control and the scent of Narcisse that lasts about two seconds before it gets whisked away by the air conditioning.

I go straight up to the thirty-fifth floor and Gaynor's office. His personal assistant is polite but he doesn't like receiving people without appointments, even if they are Chief of New Projects/Entertainment.

He does not like chiefs of production if they're dressed in jeans and gaucho boots and cotton sweaters that hang almost to the knees and read "Clam Fetish" in big blue letters.

He does buzz Gaynor through the system and curdles his lips around the answer.

"He's very busy. He doesn't know when he can get to you."

"I'll wait."

"It must be urgent?"

"It is," I assure him.

I wait. I look out at Kearny; from this high in the tower you can see the railroad bridges and parts of the marsh.

I'm certain by now that attack was a freak incident, a *buyaka* chucked out of the city's rolling crap game of such incidents.

It doesn't interest me so much, not when compared to the slower kind of murder that comes stinking out of the funky carcass of *Real Death*.

I wait. I read the magazines in Gaynor's lobby. *Newsweek* claims Malaysia has built three H-bombs.

According to *Variety* the President is calling Powell a tool of the Megorg and predicting he'll go bust in the New Hampshire primary next year.

"Megorg" is a new buzzword for the financial web linking hyper-thyroid corporations like X-Corp.

I get coffee from a machine. *People* says "guerrilla bars" for smokers are springing up in the face of laws banning cigarettes in all public places nationwide. I think of McAndrew's.

The New York Times says monkey-jackets are in, gaucho boots are out.

I wait. Men and women with good tans show up, look at me with little curiosity, disappear past a walnut door. They wear three-piece Barney's suits or monkey-jackets or L.A.-style jumpsuits.

Nobody wears gaucho boots.

Finally at 2:40 there's a lull. The P.A. checks his makeup.

"Mr. Munn? You can go in for five minutes."

The walnut door hisses open.

You could play car-polo in Gaynor's office. You can see Sag Harbor from the window. I get winded crossing over end-to-end Isfahan to his desk. He gets up and mashes my hand and points to an armchair in the corner nearest Pennsylvania. He sits on a couch next to it, casual, buddylike. I check my knuckles for stress cracks.

He has a grin that makes you want to trade over some of your best baseball cards to him, the Pete Rose, maybe even the Hank "Bow-wow" Arft.

"Alex," he says, loosening his cravat. Through the Midwestern accent it comes out as "Elex." "It's been a hell of a day. With no appointment—I did the best I could."

"I appreciate it."

"Glad to do it." We're getting so friendly here I feel like we're related. He looks at me. The clam knife is in the background now, though I can still catch the wink of its blade. I also see good education in those baby-blues. It's the kind of learning that instills quicker moves than you get at Yale or Dartmouth.

I tell him what I told Rose. I start off like a cold V-8 in a blizzard but the valves warm up and I think I make a decent case.

"You have to challenge people," I say at the end. "They want some depth, they want to *learn* something, as long as there's a little sugar around it. My serial"—I'm talking about

Munn's World, of course—"it's got a lot of information but there's a heap of adventure around it. I think you'll like it," I add, to bring everything on home.

Gaynor may or may not be listening; he has that motionless glaze he uses when someone's making a pitch. He snaps out of it suddenly, rubs his jaw for a moment, looking over at the Atlantic.

"Two things, Elex," he says finally.

"The first is, I work by delegation here. Rosie Obregon is my proxy, and I don't countermand her decisions. I have better things to do than second-guess her.

"The second thing is, there are exceptions to that rule." I lean forward, suddenly tense. "In an emergency, I will reconsider the decisions of subordinates. This does not qualify as an emergency."

"But—"

Gaynor picks up a memo. "Rosie just faxed me this. It's a treatment for—*Munn's World,* right?" He smiles, not unkindly. "I have to say, Rosie is right. This is not what I'd call a 'challenge.' It's just depressing. This lone cop in 1850s New York. *Serpico* meets *Oliver Twist,* right? *Moby Dick* meets *Silence of the Lambs.* Come on, Elex. I mean, who d'you think you are? Conrad? Or Raymond fucking Chandler?"

The weird thing is, Gaynor keeps smiling as he says this. I'm convinced the guy is on my side somehow, even when he's stuffing my project into the toilet and flushing twice to make sure.

"But—"

"You think I don't understand you. Right?"

"It's not—"

"You're an *artist.*" Gaynor leans back and sticks out his arms. His arms are quite muscular, his pecs well rounded. He picks up his penknife with one hand and a number two Ticonderoga with the other, and starts to sharpen the pencil, peeling thin, curled yellow strips of wood onto his desk. In an age when all the real work is done on electronic screens, having a pencil on your desk is the ultimate status symbol. "You want to satisfy yourself. Make yourself worthy of all the bucks you're earning. I understand that, Elex." Gaynor drops the pencil.

"But you are not here to satisfy *you.* You are here to do a job. And by God, if you want art, it *is* an art. We give people something—an idea here, a scrap of the world there. *You* do that, Elex. And you're very goddam good at it.''

''I just—''

''Well, that may not be good enough for you.'' Gaynor folds the penknife and pockets it. He stands up, walks to my side, and leans over, kind of like a cobra hooding over a rat. The blade in his eyes is up front now; despite my best efforts, I look away. ''And in that case, you should look for something else. But I hope you'll stay, Elex. I *really* hope you will stay.''

''Couldn't you jiss look at it?'' I squeak finally.

''I'm sorry, Elex.''

I'm getting sick of him calling me ''Elex'' all the time.

''Look, Ivan—''

He walks back around the desk. It seems to take five minutes. He types something into the terminal.

''I'm raising you to a straight hundred and fifty grand. Elex?''

I stare at him. I've been checking out where the door is so I don't waste my strength in the wrong direction.

''It's not about money, Ivan.'' He ignores me.

''I'm really looking forward to *Real Life*. We all are.''

He's a very large dude but he seems much smaller against that window that takes in Long Island and Sandy Hook and Amish country, too, probably.

I feel a bubble in my throat, like when Louise used to scold me as a kid and I had to struggle to keep from squalling.

I turn and trek back out over the peacocks and arabesques of the fancy carpeting.

NINE

I CHECK WITH Rob when I get back to my office. Larissa has not called back.

I cannot work. I close the door and curtains and go through Sam Rodney exercises.

Two sideways steps—legs crossing like a dressage horse, kick with forward leg at opponent's knee, chop at throat with the edge of my forward hand; sideways step (chop), sideways step (chop).

One opponent down.

Deflect knife thrust with inward sweep of left arm, circling body right and kicking his knee out at same time; grab opponent's wrist with right hand, his elbow with left, forcing him, against the pressure on his joint, to the ground.

Bend wrist back, also against the joint.

Two opponents down.

I'm yelling and grunting as I do the exercises and Rob calls in to ask if everything is okay. I tell him yes, I'm working out.

I circle left, against an opponent grabbing from behind, like the guy under the dock. I stamp on his toes and punch his balls, but there's nothing in the Rodney exercises to beat the shit out of what's really affecting me.

Nothing against boredom. Nothing against prostitution of what crummy little talent I have.

Nothing against formula writing. Nothing against one long pornographic titilation of the easy under a camouflage of "contemporary drama."

Nothing against taking a soft shot in a society that desperately needs hard questions.

I'm not certain *Munn's World* poses the hard questions. But at least it shows something true. That *was* the city 150 years ago; those *were* the issues. That's what it looked and sounded like, and what they did to survive and change it. *Munn's World* does not indulge in the cult of sameness, of easy conspiracies and consumer luxuries. As a contrast, if nothing else, it deserves to be seen.

I sit down on the short couch they give us in case we need to screw any of the talent. I feel like an old rag that's starting to come apart after too many dish washings. I lie down and close my eyes.

The headache has slowed down once more, but the earlier brain reels and flings seem to have descended to my stomach now.

I breathe deeply, as a precaution against throwing up. Planets whirl, New Jersey sunsets, aliens with the face of Gaynor, of unicorns, of Rastamen. A tall guy in an old-fashioned dark cloak sits in my office, munching smoked Muenster crackers. He has a dead face, frozen in feature and expression. He stands up and opens a frayed carpetbag and pulls out a huge mint-green blender with stylized, braided waves engraved along the cowling. The mixer blades are sharp and shiny; they whir in vicious fashion. He swipes them at me and I retreat instinctively, springing across the dingy canal that divides my office into two equal parts. "Fishman," I say, "you're under arrest," but the words don't come out and I can't move. He swings again and the spinning blades chew across my wrist, spitting blood in a light gray cloud over the water—

I wake with a start. I have little sensation of having been asleep.

The headache is still there, maintenance level. My forearm feels sore. I'm sweating gently.

I get up, shaking my head carefully. I draw a couple of

deep breaths to drive away the dream. At least the bubble in my throat is gone.

The workstation clock reads 16:56:36. I ask Rob to come in. I apologize for snarling at him earlier.

"Sure," he says.

He tells me Larissa still hasn't called, which I guess means it's okay to see her. I'll be early if I leave now, but what the hell, I can walk in on her, we're still married.

Right?

When Larissa and I moved in together we sank all our savings into a small brick Federal-style town house that looks out on a yard full of locust trees and cedars and the back of a bunch of other Federal houses on Perry Street, in the West Village.

She takes a while to answer the buzzer and I resist the temptation to use the keys. She asked me to return all my house keys but I hung on to a set, just for luck.

Now she flicks on the security system and the camera swivels behind the fanlight. Her voice comes scratchy out of the speaker.

"Alex, you're early. I'm just taking a bath."

The door buzzes. I go in.

The townhouse was dark and cramped when we took it over. Our first move was to knock down some walls and cut away half the third floor to give the second a big cathedral ceiling. We hung a big mobile, a weird piece with plaster carrier pigeons perched on acrylic branches made by a Georgian chum of Larissa's, and repaneled the walls in lightly varnished birch. We put in enormous 1950s couches and folk art from Pennsylvania. An alcove holds icons and reliquaries from the area around Chudovo, in Russia, where she grew up.

I hear water running. The Yorkie, Pedro, snuffs and growls at my gaucho boots. I ignore him as I always do when our lives happen to cross paths. As a matter of policy I ignore all dogs smaller than Border collies.

I walk past her collection of Easter hats, the Azeri prayer rugs at the entrance. I amble around the second floor, trying not to notice the changes, avoiding photos most of all. The phone rings, and is cut off by her answering machine. "Hi, this is Lara, I can't come to the phone right now . . ." Chinese vases hold white roses; she always liked white roses. She has repainted the kitchen an antique sort of blue that isn't bad really.

Through a half-opened door upstairs I can see she has hung another bird mobile over the bed. The bedroom wall has gone a fuzzy shade of gray that is how red or pink usually comes across to my chromatically fucked-up visual centers.

The hooch is in the usual place and I mix a quick G&T. This seems to drive Pedro into a fury. Perhaps he's one of those PC dogs who turn rabid against male visitors drinking booze or smoking or saying "Sweetheart" or refusing to wear car helmets.

There's a Moira Dryer over the fireplace, a fine abstract with lots of greens and yellows. The remains of takeout from our usual Thai restaurant on the coffee table. Through the French windows of the living room I see that Mrs. Gewirtz, across the yard, has crammed yet more ficus into her kitchen. It must be like the Amazon in there by now. The gay couple next door to Mrs. Gewirtz have redecorated. Louis XV reigns in a domain once exclusively reserved for French Country.

The water stops. Larissa yells, "Why don't you come in, you are giving Pedro a thrombosis. It's a bubble bath," she adds, in case I've been getting shy in my old age.

It is, indeed, a bubble bath, of the kind featured in fifties films to convey the idea of a naked woman without showing anything. All I can see of Larissa is her two eyes and her hair pinned like a Kremlin tower over her scalp, so high I almost expect to see a red star glowing at the peak. The foam is spilling over the Siena tile. I shut the door on Pedro and his high-pitched yapping and sit on the rug-covered toilet lid.

Her eyes keep looking at me. They seem very dark, despite the bright makeup lights shining over her cosmetics counter.

"You devil, Alex," she says.

"Huh?"

"You *knew* I was going to take a bath."

I look at her. I take a swallow of gin.

"By the way," she adds, "why don't you fix yourself a drink?"

"Point taken," I tell her. "I was thirsty."

She says nothing further. The water spurgles. She jets columns of it through her fists; it's something she used to do in the days when we took baths together.

"You look tired."

"I am tired."

"Do you want to get in?"

The gin has been going down real easy until that point; now it sneaks back up and tries to drop into my windpipe. I cough heavily, trying to smother the sound at the same time because it sounds like a stage trick, a dramatic cliché.

My eyes water as I look at her.

"Well?"

"I came over to talk, Larissa. I honestly didn't know—"

"It's *okay*."

The dark in her eyes can take on a serious warmth of light, just as her hard practicality, her adamantine ambition, can without warning change to breathtaking, irrational generosity. It doesn't happen very often but when it does birds sing for her and lawyers give away money.

I pull off my boots, slowly, expecting her to laugh and change her mind. I shrug out of my sweater and T-shirt and drop my pants. I'm hard as Scottish charity by now but there's nothing I can do about that. In fact, like most guys, I'm somewhat proud of it.

I get in the near side of the tub, the ring of bubbles popping against my rib cage. The water is hot and oily, and for some reason it reminds me of the slime I fell into in the marsh at Kearny. I push that thought away, fast.

I try to keep to my end but although it's a big bath there's no way entirely to avoid contact. My feet touch hers and splay to gain room at the sides.

When I'm settled she lifts her left foot out of the bubbles and plants it on my chest. She has small feet, like a girl's, with tiny toenails that she has for some reason painted green. I touch her ankle, gently, with respect and admiration. I've always loved her joints.

"So talk, boychick."

"I'm worried about Poland."

"It belongs to Russia. It always did."

"What about the Germans?"

She waves her hand dismissively.

"Chopin? Paderewski?"

"Russians, all Russians. Poland was always a mistake."

She looks at me hard. Her foot slides down, very slowly, to my stomach. When her heel touches lower I gasp. She lets her foot slide till her heel rests on enamel, and works her toes.

"Jesus," I groan.

"What's the matter?"

The bubbles in her bath are matched by the bubbles in her throat. She is chuckling. "You were never so shy, before."

I'm wondering about the wisdom of this, about the long-term problems any intimacy today will undoubtedly raise in the future; but the nice thing as well as the dangerous thing about sex is, it makes you live for the moment. Specifically you put yourself temporarily under the control of your genitals, which are sending out subtle little commands, on the order of "touch her, kiss her, make love to her NOW!"

So I work my own foot east. Her thighs feel hard and smooth at the same time. My toes touch her pubic hair; it has softened in the water. I work my big toe lower, and the softening grows as I inveigle myself into the folds of her and feel a heat greater than the bath, a softening greater than the soap, a liquid wetter than the water.

She closes her eyes and sinks lower into the bubbles. Now nothing but that Spasskaya spire is visible over the mounded bath gel.

I can hear her breathing against a catch in her throat, quite deep. I'm trying not to lose control here, there's a peak to this wave and I'm already too goddam near it.

She may sense this—she was always good at figuring out where I was in the progression. In fact we were always very good at this activity, period.

She comes out of the cloud of bubbles, eyes, nose, throat rising like Aphrodite, and folds herself down over my end. As always, she weighs on me far lighter than you'd think. Her breasts sway a little. They're looser now than they were when we met but they look graceful as ever to me. She crushes their white slopes between us, squeezing out the water till nothing is left to separate the two skins.

My arms fold over her. They recognize her back, her waist, the curved muscles of her ass. My chest knows her breasts, the deep fullness of them, the exact weight they carry in this shape.

We kiss tongue to tongue. The taste of musty seashells. Her eyes are still closed. She lets herself slide where gravity will take her and my cock, as if radio-guided, follows the valley of her legs into the perfect softness at the apex of her walk.

She says, "Asha," almost as if she missed me.

I push gently.

I am not sure how long I can hold myself in.

Part of the problem is the perfection I am touching inside her and the feeling of great privilege all men must feel at the trust implied in such entry. Partly it's the unbelievable smoothness of her skin and the way the bubbles multiply and refract to different parts of my brain the complete softness of her.

Partly it's because I truly have missed our life together and the intimacy sex both symbolized and, in many ways, formed.

And partly I'm going too fast because I've not slept with anybody in a while. Not since a month ago, in fact, when something similar to this happened after a cast party for *Pain*.

I stop her, hugging her waist tightly, swallowing great gulps of air.

She starts up in a different way, more circular, very slow. Her head drops and her mouth opens. Her motion grows quicker against my arms, and that triggers a quickness in me, and a mounting rhythm that has the power of all rhythm, and she whispers, "Oohh, Asha," and moves violently sideways.

Light breaks, prisons open. In a small video mounted somewhere behind my headache I can see the wretched people of the Old Brewery spilling out of the broken walls of their hovel into a mountain prairie, their eyes blinking at the good sun, the clean green grass, the blue and distant snow, and there is no Idaho knight to scare or hurt them, nor will there ever be.

We lie like this till the water gets tepid. Finally I let go. My left hand has rested between her legs; when I lift it to turn on the hot faucet it drips water gone dark and gray. I look at it curiously, for it's the color blood appears to me.

"You got your period?"

"No." It seems to amuse her.

"Then—?"

"It happened last time, too. I'm just not used to it."

"I made you bleed?"

"Like a virgin. Men like that, don't they?"

"But—you're not sleeping with Braindead?"

She sits farther back. Her voice loses affection.

"I have slept with no one since you."

I shouldn't say it. I don't mean to but my controls have slipped with the near-total abrogation of tension in me. I slide forward, closer to her. The bubbles are dissolving and I can make out the curved symmetry of her waist through the pine-colored water. I touch her lips with one of my fingers. To the Inuit fucking is nothing, but to touch the lips of a woman not your wife is grounds for murder.

"Why don't we give it another try, Larissa?"

"Is *that* what you wanted to talk about?"

She is staring at the faucets now. She shuts off the hot, and tweaks the cold water quickly.

"No," I tell her. "I didn't expect this."

"I told you the last time. It changes nothing."

The bathwater makes *Poseidon Adventure* sounds as she gets up. Even in the aftermath I find myself torn by her departure. She takes a towel and rubs herself dry.

"We were both—horny. Yes? We are friends—that is all."

"What do you really mean—we're 'friends'?"

"That is *all*!" She drops the towel. Her body exposed is a miracle, a force. Real life, not some facsimile version thereof. She takes down a long flannel shift, a sort of extended night-gown, the kind she always used to wear around the house. She is going to leave this bathroom, this intimacy, me. The water is growing cooler and cooler around my thighs.

"Larissa," I say desperately, "what happened to us? We— well, we used to talk about kids, an' everything."

"Kids." She turns around so quickly the Kremlin totters. She catches the spire of hair and untwists it with fast, angry fingers. "Kids. The usual bourgeois rubbish." Her hair falls like a blown-up building. I recognize with little fondness the old speed in getting her dander up. She's almost spitting in rage.

"You Americans are all the same. *You* are always the same. You have no respect for my work—my career."

"That's not true. Nothing stops you from having both a husband and—"

"You were always in my way! I would come home late, you would cry about this."

I get out of the bath. I take a towel from the rack. The towel is new and very fluffy. Even as my gut sinks I can feel my skin rejoice in the pile.

"That wasn't the soap, you staying out late—"

"That was talking! Drinking and talking with directors, and actors. You don't think that is important?"

It's an ancient argument. We both know every line and dodge. We also know there's no way to get out of it once we start. Still I try to talk rationally, pulling on my T-shirt and Clam Fetish sweater.

"Nobody needs to go out and drink till three A.M. for work. I don't—"

"Your work is not art. Your work is like the men selling their bodies on Gansevoort Street. That is not art."

I stand straighter. My pants fall down again.

"Oh, and your work is? Kirsten, the foreign vamp on, on the schlockiest soap in the biz? That's *art*?"

"Fuck you. Get out."

"Well I guess you'll be able to find something better, next year."

It's mean and stupid and I wish I'd bit my tongue out as soon as I say it. I hope she won't pick up on it but of course she does—she can read what I leave out better than what I put in.

"What are you talking about?" She reaches for a brush and studies it closely.

"Nothing."

"You mean, my contract?"

So she knows.

"Your art," I tell her, and hate myself for what's in my voice, a poison far crueler than the ricin she will consume, by accident, when Brooke lays out the doctored drink for Amy Dillon.

"It does not matter," she says. "I am auditioning next week for Tarantino. Tarantino!"

"Larissa," I tell her, less gently. There's a lesson here I

think she needs to learn. "You always *audition* for everybody."

The brush takes flight and wings my shoulder. A jar full of cotton balls drops and smashes. She jumps across the tiles and pushes me backward. I'm still trying to pull on my gauchos. Her hair twists wildly and her fists pound at my collarbone.

"Get *out*!" she shouts. "Out out out!"

"I don't want to!" I yell.

"Out!"

"We have to talk!"

"Out!" She opens the bathroom door. Pedro jumps yapping three feet into the air and savages my sweater.

"Talk!"

("Yap!")

"Out!"

("Yap!")

She pushes me hard toward the stairs. Across the yard I can see Mrs. Gewirtz staring at us through the leaves of her jungle, her watering can dribbling from one hand. Pedro wrestles himself between my feet. I stumble, and fall down the first four steps, dropping one of the boots, catching myself with difficulty on the banister.

Together, Pedro and Larissa harry me to the front door. They shove me when I slow down. My ex-wife snaps the locks viciously behind me. Only when she switches on the intercom can I hear the tears piling up behind her voice.

"I don't want to see you again, Alex. Not in private. *Nikagda, nikagda, nikagda.*"

I don't know Russian but I do know that word. Larissa uses it a lot.

Nikagda.

It means "Never."

I sit on the stoop in the light of her barred windows. Passersby glance at me and then look away with the firm suppression of wonder that New Yorkers as a class all share. The bath has softened my back muscles and I slouch like a guilty kid.

The sobs have ganged up in my chest. I stand, and manage to keep them down. I pull on my other boot.

I walk off, down Perry Street. Some of the houses on this street were built in 1822, when the yellow fever epidemic drove people out of what was then the city. The rich folks escaped here, north of Canal Street, to the village of Greenwich, where the air was clean and free of what they thought must be poisonous clouds of pestilence.

My chest feels like it has yellow fever in it. Yellow fever of art, plague of the heart; the tissues of love, of need and passion, unglued by disease, flooding out with the treasonous seep of my body's fluids.

I walk south, down Greenwich Street, my hair still wet. Now it becomes a clumsy, half-solid mass as it slowly, in the cold air, freezes to ice.

TEN

ON MY WAY home I stop by Happy East, the Korean on Hudson Street, but by the time I'm halfway down the main aisle I've forgotten what the hell I came to buy.

I pick up a quart of milk, mostly because that's what you go to a Korean for. Security cameras follow me as I walk, strongly reminding me of Larissa's fanlight. At the counter Mr. Soong nods at me conspiratorially.

"Hi, Mist' Alex."

"Hi."

"You wan' see what I got yes'day?"

"What's that?" I say, wishing I could buy things here like a normal New Yorker, with a Jefferson, a grunt, and minimal contact. He bobs behind the counter, and surfaces, bearing a shiny plastic box covered with chromed gridwork on one side.

"Sonic assault weapon," he announces. "Nonletha'. Someone come in wit' a gun, sonic weapon goes off, high frequency, stop him completely. Then, I shoot." He grins happily. I nod. Mr. Soong, who has never been held up, lives in expectation of the inevitable. Already he has shown me a .22 sleeve derringer, a box of capsicum canisters, a .44 target pistol bigger than Harry Callaghan's, a sawed-off shotgun, a tazer, and a stun grenade. It must look like an AGATE armory, under his cash register.

Back in my loft I moon around for a while, picking up objects, putting them down. Lenny is not around and judging by the neatness has not been back since I left. Three faxes from the office lie beside the workstation.

One of them confirms my salary boost.

The city light has done its thing again, canceling sunset, summoning night like someone threw a switch.

I turn the workstation to XTV. It being news time, the screen flowers into a blown-up, blow-dried Braindead in moire monkey-jacket and green-starred tie, with a cute blue thumbnail of greater China blue-screened in behind him.

". . . by Suez-Thurn," he is saying. "The Beijing government today announced it has hired the Franco-German financial giant to oversee the transformation of China's various regional stock markets into one national system. The deal, with stock options, reportedly is worth over seven billion dollars. Meanwhile—"

I slap the channel zapper hard. Twelve square capsules line up across the screen, holding thumbnail versions of what corresponding channels are showing. I spot a familiar scene, loud in flashing lights, and my thumb instinctively pushes the cursor in that direction.

"No way you're gonna get her out alive."

"I gotta go in," the detective growls, "I don't care."

Captain Ramirez looks at him for a beat.

"Get me some backup here," he growls into his radio.

Copkiller. It's an episode I wrote, four or five years ago. The cheesy dialogue fits neatly into the box of contempt already formed in my brain to hold it.

I wonder how long it will take Larissa to sleep with Braindead.

I zap off the terminal, walk to the kitchen butcher block to push the button on the abs'ini-maker; but my hand stops in midair.

Somehow, I'm not ready for booze. Too much has happened today, the tissue is too recently torn; and alcohol, even sweet chilled absinthe ichor, so immediately communicated to the pericardium, like iodine on a napalm victim, would hurt more than heal. Good drinking is never medicine, but a more subtle art.

Also, I can hear, like a refrain of mockery, the facile lingo of Captain Ramirez declaiming; and behind that, a dubbed soundtrack, Rose Obregon commenting, "The way you drink."

I stand there for a moment, surprised by the novelty of this no-booze concept. Without either an abs'ini or the deadening effect of television, the silence rises around me louder than a siren.

It's mostly to fill that space that I turn on my heel, march into the studio, and lock the door. I take gear from the wall, type in the various passwords that summon *Munn's World* on the Virtix, suit up.

Snap onto the positioning cable in the room's center and wait for the delay to run its course.

Munn's World always starts black, a fade-in, while a woman's voice sings the theme a cappella.

> *"How comes this blood on thy shirtsleeve?*
> *Oh, dear love, tell me!*
> *It is the blood of my old gray mare,*
> *That plowed the field with me."*

The tune is "Cruel Edward," an ancient ballad repopularized in the late 1840s. As the haunting, minor-key melodic line runs its course, the details of the scene gradually appear out of the darkness, and I look around me curiously, like a man getting off a train at an unfamiliar station.

It has snowed in New York over the past seven days, and the city is covered with soft layers of white, over which the smoke of coal and wood fires deposited a thin edge of black, like the crosshatched shading on an old woodcut.

Horses slip on the grimy slush, the cargo on the carts they pull slipping dangerously. Drayers curse with deadly intensity. Boys from the gangs' farm leagues—junior Dead Rabbits, Daybreak Lads, Bowery Kids—forgetting for once the policy routes, the Fagin schools, the junior brothels and saloons where, apprenticing to pimps and hustlers at age eleven, they are learning to grime the childhood out of themselves—well, they turn back into boys all of a sudden; wing snowballs happily at the overstuffed men in stovepipe hats lifting their long fur coats out of shit-impregnated drifts.

I'm conscious for a few seconds of moving, stupidly alone, in my office; and then the environment takes control and I'm treading down a wooden sidewalk, not immediately sure of where the hell I've wound up.

One small problem with *Munn's World* is that while the Navigator keeps perfect track of where you are within the city it knows; and while you will always jack into the system more or less where you left off, or at time coordinates you choose; you can never be sure where exactly, in what street, what room or house, that will be. The story always drifts a little, as if the momentum of its depth and life kept the data disks spinning the teensiest bit after you logged off last time.

In this case I shoved the time ahead a week, to get past some of the cop defaults I'm less interested in right now, and I figure, looking around, the Polhemus carried me a ways up Centre Street, somewhat north of the precinct house. Newsboys hawk *Frank Leslie's Illustrated Newspaper,* whose front page displays, in greasy 36-point type, the words "SIXTH KILLING OF IRISH VAGRANT IN MANNER OF FISHCUTTER." One of the *Leslie*'s tame printmakers has created a romantic and wholly fictional representation of a sinister bearded fellow waving a scimitar in the general direction of a swooning woman.

I turn around carefully, for the snow conceals hillocks of rotten garbage that make the footing uncertain, and pick my way back to the Sixth Ward cop shop. The squadroom is crowded and warm, the coppers generally more interested in hanging around the cast-iron stove than doing patrol.

Taking a whale-oil lamp from the duty-roundsman's desk, I leave the squadroom without talking to anyone and climb, past Blake's office, up three flights of stairs to a storeroom under the eaves.

The space is cramped, full of tack: worn-out saddles, spare martingales, moth-eaten horse blankets. It stinks of manure and mildew—or would, if I could truly smell its aroma. The room's one advantage is privacy. Even roundsmen don't get their own office in this building. Since the fourth Fishman murder, the investigator in charge, which is me, has been coming here, drawing out lists and diagrams with steel pen and inkwell balanced on an upturned fire bucket, nailing the papers chronologically on the lathed wall.

I stand under the frost-starred eaves, looking around at the diagrams. An old man from Dunmanway, County Cork, slashed and left hanging by a bight of tarred line from the roof of the Jacob's Ladder tenement, around the corner from Coulter's. A Kilkenny child, disemboweled in the usual way, stuffed in the lazaret of a disused schooner serving as a coal barge at Walton's Wharf. Even if I'd not drawn the diagrams myself I could sense the sterility of this investigation from the empty spaces; the virgin column marked ''Witnesses,'' the excessive whiteness of the paragraphs in which evidence is numbered; the too-great pains I took to draw out the placement of the bodies, the angle they made with the words their killer painted, in the convenience of rage, close to hand.

On the rough laths I have pinned the five flyers, all urging you to choose ''Flynn'' in the coming council vote; each of them found, grimed with ink and blood, beside the victims' corpses.

Footsteps sound in the stairs. The door is thrown open. The voice of my leatherhead from upstate seems to bounce off the hard stereo air.

''I seen 'im coming up here, Cap'n. I wouldn't of said anything, but I figgered something was goin' on.''

Blake pushes his way past me, stumbling over a saddle, cursing. His pipe is dead but he sucks on it anyway, causing sick plumbing sounds to rise from the bowl. He takes my lamp and peers closely at the diagrams. The lamp makes yellow arcs over the list of names.

Joseph Stephen Gavin. Liam Shaughnessy. Bridget Marie Walsh.

Blakie stares at me as if my face were another diagram.

''My office,'' he snaps.

Downstairs he refires the pipe, then comes to stand a few inches away so that the burst vessels of his cheeks show like bloodflow charts, and the smoke from his nostrils looks like a steamer lighting off.

''Don't like it,'' he grunts. ''Beat cops welshing on

roundsmen. This whole business has got out of fucking hand.''

He stomps to the desk and picks up a piece of paper.

"Know who this is from?''

"No,'' I say clearly.

"You don't know.'' Blake nods. "It's from the chairman of the board of aldermen of the City of New York.'' The aldermen, known far and wide as "the Forty Thieves,'' appoint cops and supervise the police generally. The paper rustles as he unfolds it.

" 'The matter of the disemboweled Irishmen, known in the popular broadsheets as "The Fishman Case,'' is causing concern at all levels of city government. Truly it seems that an excess of zeal on the part of the investigator in charge is creating apprehension out of all proportion to the importance of this affair. Need we remind you that these victims without exception are wretched immigrants who choose to live among conditions where vice and intemperance are more likely than not to put an end at any time to their unhappy existence.' ''

Blakie folds the paper.

"You're off this case,'' he says.

I know all this by heart but it doesn't stop me feeling anger as it unfolds.

"But you tole me, before—someone *wants* to find the killer.''

"He's been overruled. The case is on the Second List.''

The Second List is where they sign up the stuff they can't figure out. It's a long goddam list. The smoke pumps solidly from Blakie's pipe. If I didn't know better I would say Captain Blake is embarrassed by what he has to do.

"You're on Bowery detail as of tomorrow,'' he continues. "*The Song of Pirate Mollie* is opening at the Alcazar, there's players with support from both Bhoys and Rabbits, gonna be trouble.''

When I push open the door out of Blakie's office a half-dozen patrolmen coincidentally are doing jobs that keep them within earshot of the door. I ignore my colleagues and walk downstairs and back into the colder chaos of the street.

There's one advantage in this development; so far, the pace of routine and the paper-load attendant upon the killings haven't given the cop time for real investigating, but now I'm on theater patrol I can go back on my tracks and try to find the evidence I missed.

I walk south down Centre. The melting snow rushes noisily down the gutters. It gurgles into the black culverts connecting it with Lispenard's stream, a waterway that used to drain the Collect Pond northwest into the Hudson. The stream still parallels Centre Street on the west side, only underground, in deep, rat-patrolled tunnels.

A street railway car thunders past, its six-horse team snorting, large hooves smashing up sheets of gray slush over the sidewalk. When that sound has faded I hear a short rhythm of footsteps running up behind me, splat-*splash!* splat-*splash!* A quick panic from 150 years in the future makes me spin around so fast that the background slows, just for an instant, and the detail seems to lose, for a fractured second, a micron of its depth.

One of my patrolmen, helmet and billy club half concealed under his short coat, skids to a stop as I turn around.

"Yeah?"

"I was tryin' to catch you." He looks at me without great friendliness. "They took you off the fishcutter, right?"

"Yes."

"The whole station house was listenin'. The thing is—"

His breath makes as much smoke from cold as Blakie's did from tobacco.

"Don't like micks," he says finally. "But I don't hold with the killing either. And the way he flaked out that woman —the thing is, I know he's from the island."

"How?" I shift on the slush (shifting on the carpet of my study). "What island?"

"They do it different. It's just a style. But the twin gashes, low down, by the tail—that's how they do it on Nantucket."

I shrug. "I'm off the case."

He ignores me. Perhaps the Vox is acting up again.

"If I wannit to find out anything"—he focuses on a hot corn girl across the street—"I'd go to the old fish docks. There's a man—Caleb Hallett. He auctions groundfish. He's from the island, too. Tell him Saul Coffin's son sent you."

He ducks awkwardly, and is lost behind a crowd of teamsters backing a cart toward a coal chute.

I continue down Centre Street, retracing the route I took

after our last foray into Five Points. New York being, then as always, New York, you see more African faces the closer you get to the slums. Black women stand behind the savory braziers of roast oyster stands; in the dark groceries, behind the counter where the Irish owner pours watered whiskey from stone jugs, black musicians holler out songs with a chantey beat, stamping the rhythms with bare heels.

I turn right at Baxter, then left down Bayard. The little wood-framed house with the deep side porch looks much poorer, more forlorn in daylight. A political poster has been glued on the clapboard wall. "ELECT FLYNN," it reads, "Candidate for the New Americans." I lift the cast-iron knocker and rap it hard, several times, against its base.

Stand back to watch the windows. No shadows disturb the cheap curtains. Snow has piled six inches high against the door's lower panels. No one has been in or out of this door in at least twenty-four hours.

I remember the woman's face. It was lovely, intent. A wave of disappointment washes over me.

I continue down Bayard. At Bowery I go right, avoiding a fire engine that bombs merrily around the corner, its occupants yelping loudly, a horde of mongrel hounds and boys in pursuit. The visuals of winter are enough to make my feet feel wet. There are young women on this part of the Bowery, waitresses in the German *biergartens* or would-be players hanging around the stage doors of the popular theaters, and they look at me with the devastating lack of interest of city women, no matter what the era; unimpressed by any man not rich or powerful enough to give them what they came to New York to get.

On one marquee I spot the words "The Song of Pirate Mollie" being nailed up by a pair of sixteen-year-old Bhoys; this is where I will stand watch tomorrow.

The Bowery blends imperceptibly with Park Row, but as soon as I turn left on Roosevelt it's as if something terrible and all-embracing has moved in, to press its fell imprint on every working part of this neighborhood.

Grim brick warehouses replace the columned houses. The sight of hemp and fish evokes the smells that must mingle here with the ever-present stench of human waste. The animal waterfront, looming in the crowded masts at the eastern foot of the street, seems to reach out with a growl to embrace you and take you in with its savage, tar-flavored love.

Bearded seamen in bell-bottoms, short jackets, and leather porkpie hats stroll around, looking for trouble, which is a waste of time because trouble is all around and looking for them. Bouncers call from saloons where the bartenders keep a bottle of spiked gin ready to knock them out so the pickpocket boys can roll them and the crimps can drag the sleeping bodies to a ship making up a crew for the Horn, and San Francisco.

Whores lift their rustling layers of skirt, trying to lure the sailors into panel joints where they'll get them out of their duds and into the sack while another girl, opening a secret panel under the bed, crawls into the room and rips off the entire wad the poor bastard earned over eight months of mind-blowingly dangerous toil on one of the tea-trade ships.

The screams of gulls compete with the thud of steam winches, the clang of forges, and the shouts of loading gangs working the wharves.

The ships themselves are watched intently by signalmen from the pirate gangs; for this is the Fourth Ward, which has to support over fifty associations of river pirates, not to mention the cutpurses, bunco men, con artists, pimps, assassins, and corrupt assistant aldermen that feed off the bloated mass of waterfront crime like sharks ripping gobs of fat off the back of a dead whale.

I hit the waterfront at the base of Dover Street and walk south under the massed bowsprits of moored ships. I go slowly, as I always do; I paid particular attention to the detail in this part of the city and I like to check it out.

South Street in the early 1850s was a strip of dusty wharf-front severely pinched between the warehouses on one side and the ranked ships on the other, as if the sea still retained its mastery over this part of the main, keeping it dry only as a convenience to itself.

A sharp-prowed ship rises, framed fresh and pungent in new oak, from the sawpits and builders' ramps of Webb's shipyard; a scrawled sign announces the construction of the *Celestial* for the A. A. Low & Bros. shipping line. Most of the ships docked, their bowsprits overhanging the roadway, are Blackwall frigates, fat merchantmen with fake gunports down their sides; or else the workhorse schooners that do the unromantic coasting work on which the port's wealth is really built. Occasionally you can spot the fancy brass and billowing smoke of a steamer or, rising from among the yardarms of lesser ships, the sky-reaching topmasts of an extreme clipper. For this is the heyday of the clippers, and the height of the San Francisco gold rush, and every free foot of wall space is plastered with garish posters advertising the departure of the fastest, cleanest, smallest (for small holds meant quick loading), biggest (for big ships moved quicker) clipper ship that ever sailed anywhere.

To Sail on or before Sunday, Dec. 3
A. A. Low clipper line to San Francisco
The Famous A No. 1 Extreme Clipper

ODYSSEY

P. G. Briggs, Commander
is now completing her loading at
Pier 26, East River, and will have

IMMEDIATE DISPATCH

Shippers will bear in mind the Odyssey
has made the voyage in 97 days, and
being of small capacity will probably
fill before her day.

The official fish market now does business out of a building the city has erected beside the Fulton Street ferry, but a number of the more conservative wholesalers have not yet moved from the old site at Coenties Slip. Because of the split market—and because fish is mostly sold between 1 and 4 A.M., before the retailers open—there is less chaos here than uptown; still the depth of detail is extraordinary. I have to search through the crush of horse drays and longshoremen and crimps for ten or fifteen seconds before I spot the small wooden office building on the slip's north side with the sign reading "Caleb Hallett & Sons; Fish Merchants/Salt/Provisions."

The downstairs is gloomy and crammed with boxes. Men haul blocks of ice the size of small horses into the cellar. The ice is wrapped in canvas and insulated with straw. A clerk leads me upstairs to a small room littered with scrawled yellow auction slips and filled, at the window end, by a desk. A fat fellow sits at the desk, doing long sums in a ledger.

"Two hundred and forty-eight, plus twelve, two hundred and sixty," he says. "And what can I do for thee?"

"I work with the son of Saul Coffin," I tell him.

"The po-lice." He says it in two words and his eyes are hard. "I suppose thee'll be wanting a contribution, but thee'll have to take up the matter with Mr. Sims, of the Tammany Wigwam, to whom I've already been more than generous."

"I don't want a gift." Hallett rubs his nose gently with his pen as I explain why I came.

"Saul Coffin's boy," he says finally. "Saul was a reformist in the Great Schism. His boy, Aaron, got a girl with child on the island, and left her to her shame and misery. It is odd that he should assume I would help a friend of his."

He looks out the frosted window, at a schooner with ice-coated shrouds warping into the slip, the boxes of equally frozen cod piled high at her waist; at a crowd of boys harrying a fruit vendor on Albany Dock.

"The city grows too fast," he murmurs, almost to himself. "Every day brings more wretched creatures from every corner of the earth, and nowhere to house them and nothing to feed them with. Over a hundred thousand, in ten years. If thee wishes to observe the old fish docks," he continues in a louder voice, "thee'll need a job; the river gangs will not tolerate onlookers. I'll not pay thee a farthing, understand?"

He leads me back downstairs. Within five minutes I'm dragging ice into his cellar.

I "work" for the rest of the day; in fact, with a couple of (shouted) commands to the Vox, I make the day pass in fifteen minutes, bringing the action to normal speed, here and there, to walk around the different wholesalers and examine the way they gut fish. Over half the houses are boarded up, the owners moved north to Fulton; most of the rest deal in salt flounder, and only two cut and dry the fish on their own, for the triangle trade, laying them out on wooden frames on the roof and in south-facing yards. I pretend to be a fellow fishcutter, an islander working for Hallett, looking for chums from home. The men are filthy, busy, tired. They respond with grunts or non-

committal shrugs. When they cut the flounder, flaying them to
the bone with long, crudely sharpened knives, they all put in
diagonal gashes, northwest to southeast, then northeast to
southwest, and no twin cuts near the tail at all. I suppose this
must be the New York style of filleting. These are regional
differences at their most basic; like children's rhymes, or
tradesmen's curses, they will not change with fad or history.

Night comes. The tide shifts, the schooners rise higher in
the docks. The ice team quits. Old man Hallett nods to me on
his way to the wharf to inspect a shipment of Montauk pollock.

The moon appears, curving over the sky. The market gets
very quiet around ten, just before the first customers show up
for the auction.

I'm sitting on an empty hogshead, watching the spotters
from the river gangs keep an eye on traffic—which schooner
anchors alone, how much of a watch they leave aboard, that
kind of thing—when I notice the ship easing gently past Governor's Island and into the reach opposite Coenties. It's of
moderate size, very low and narrow. It has the sharp bow and
tall masts of an extreme clipper, though it's small by clipper
standards; its unusual design made odder still by the dark
color of the topgallant, main, and mizzen sails, which are all
the skipper is using for maneuvers.

This is a pocket clipper, built to carry compact, valuable
cargoes at speed and in stealth. In the 1850s that means only
one thing: the ship is a blackbird; her only possible role, to
pick up slaves from the Portuguese ports of West Africa and
zip them past the Webster-Ashburton blockade to New Or-
leans or Charleston.

The blackbird swings abruptly, the forward topgallants
backed against the wind. I hear the rushing clatter of an anchor chain. The dark sails disappear, gathered up by invisible
crewmen on the footropes.

A jolly boat is lowered from the ship's counter. Oars flash
at the soft glow of the city behind me. The boat disappears in
the shadow between two Sandy Hook herring smacks moored
at Albany Pier, then reemerges, pulling back toward the
blackbird.

A tall man in a long black coat walks slowly from the

jumble of drays and fish crates, and pauses at the foot of the pier.

I've seen this before, of course, yet I cannot repress the familiar thrill of excitement and dread. I recall, as I'm supposed to, the words of the boy outside the tunnel from Coulter's.

" 'E 'ad a long black coat, like the very devil, sorr . . . loik a mountain, 'e were."

The man, abruptly, turns. He pulls the collar of the coat closely around his face, jams a short stovepipe hat deep over his brow. As he strides past where I sit beside Coffin's, I notice his coat has the ruffled back panel and deep flare of the fashion, newly imported from London, made famous by the Earl of Chesterfield. Otherwise I make out nothing but a deep blackness where his eye sockets should be, shadowed against the gaslight at the base of Coenties.

I slip off the hogshead and follow, keeping to the shadows between the lit windows of saloons.

I notice that the streetwalkers and hustlers, who would ordinarily hound a well-dressed man making his way up the harbor, stay clear of this one. He is tall, of course. Though he seems to have some stiffness in one knee he walks like a city dweller, fast and intent. I wonder if he's heading for Sweets' Refectory, the restaurant on Fulton and South that has always been the unofficial headquarters of blackbirders. Or maybe he's going to take the Fulton Street ferry to Brooklyn; but he turns left before Fulton, onto John Street, paying more attention to the buildings as they grow in style and substance. These houses are the granite and marble offices of the city's greatest merchants, and the banks they both finance and are funded by.

A short way up, at number 167, he stops and climbs a set of rose-granite stairs between two cast-iron piers with Corinthian capitals. A plaque bears a square insignia; a ship's flag, painted gray and yellow. Taking something thin from inside his coat he slips it into the mailbox, then continues up the street again, westward.

A rightward jink up Pearl, to Park Row. He turns left on Chatham Street. The big gaming houses concentrated in this part of town are starting to hum with noise and activity. Elegant carriage horses snort and stamp outside the gaslights and colonnades as broughams and sedans disgorge expensively attired patrons; and, just like that, in a section leading up to Barclay Street, where the houses are richest, where the tall windows squeeze out slim glimpses of red velvet and gilt mirrors and crystal chandeliers, and cries of joy and disappointment as the cards play out, I lose him.

I stand on the curb, away from the gaslight. I love the way it happens. A black carriage trots out of Barclay Street, oil lamps swaying like the running lights of a ship. There are a number of fellows in stovepipes and cloaks jostling to get into Frank Sears' faro house. The hack drivers yell at each other, lining up outside. He could be in Sears', or Bartolf's, or next door at Stuart's; or he could have sloped off down the dark side streets, for the gaslights and whale oil do not bathe the city in glare the way electricity will in forty years' time, and shadow reigns in this island town.

I notice, for the first time, a railway-type clock set in the lintel over the Stuart house. It's lit up from within, and its ornate hour hand points to a pearly, glowing XI as I stand, waiting for what I know will come, on the cold Russ pavement.

And it comes the way it always does, in a fast slap of boots, the dark wing of a long coat flung up to blind me, the wink of a knife as he lunges. The reflex, of course, is to step aside, and even if you don't the blade is programmed to hit the fleshy part of the shoulder, leaving our hero with a wound painful but not lethal, even given the minimal hygiene of the period.

Only this time the blade flashes past the shoulder and plummets, deliberately, into the left side of my stomach.

I look down in shock.

The Polhemus dutifully shows me what I should be seeing in that place; the hilt and part of the blade of a fancy knife sticking out to the left of the belt buckle.

In the instant I look down, my assailant abandons the shiv and strides off coolly, to disappear a second later into the indifferent crowds.

I grab the hilt. The knife comes out easily. A faint smear of light-gray spreads like a big spider across the linen front of my shirt.

Goddam, I think. That son of a bitch really tried to *kill* me this time!

And a light wash of real anger floods around the area where the pain would be, if it had been real pain, caused by a real knife in the stomach of a person made of flesh instead of the ghostly connections of circuitry.

ELEVEN

WHEN I LOG off *Munn's World* I go straight to the abs'ini-maker and this time I punch the button.

The resultant concoction is as cool and clear as ever. The odd thing is, the first gulp goes down the gullet like a cat chasing mice down a sewer pipe, but then the drink kind of avoids the left part of my stomach, flowing around where the "knife" would have connected, withholding numbness from that place, and I can feel a knot there—not pain from a wound, more like a burning area, as from a pulled muscle where the blade went in.

"That was a surprise," I say aloud to myself, but in a way I was looking for surprises so I'm not as shocked as I think, if you follow me.

Part of the shock, I guess, is related to the memory of the carpet-cutter, and that also helps explain things in my head.

I grope my arm again where the real blade sliced through, and find the cut pretty much healed.

Overall, with the exception of the clenched stomach muscle, I feel better. The story, as usual, imperceptibly wound its skein around me, drawing me in the way a man o' war jelly-fish hauls up the fish caught in its tentacles, anesthetizing it with slow venom, bringing it gently into the avid darkness of its mantle.

I know Larissa is still down there, the echo of her *nikagda* smoldering in the deepest part of my gut, well below the knife wound. But the depth of *Munn's World* deprived it of oxygen, reducing it to coal only, rather than flame; replaced it with the shock of attack, and the memory of the woman I looked for on Bayard Street.

That, and the overpowering presence of the long-ago city, still existing in my mind the way theoretical physicists believe parallel universes go on, after starting from the same event; perfect, equal, and largely impervious to the other world.

I drink a second abs'ini. The cold-licorice absinthe tastes better and better. My loft, big as it is, starts to feel smaller and smaller. I want to talk to somebody, to share my excitement about the way *Munn's World* is going.

I don't want to talk to Zeng, though. The excitement in me is not so specific. What I want is to sit and drink with people. I want to bust a move. I want to convert the energy in me into jokes, laughter, and the absorption of music.

So I put on my second-best leather jacket and go out into the hopeful night.

I keep the Morgan in a garage on Desbrosses. From there it's a ten-second drive to West Street. The traffic is sparse this time of night. The Morgan burbles at the Battery Park City lights. Ahead of me the harbor opens up, black by contrast with the fractal explosion of sodium-arc lights from the Unimondo condos a-building in Bayonne. The Irving Trust Building, the Bartholdi lady, seem outdated and lonely against the glare of construction lights.

The night feels oddly warm, though it's only thirty or thirty-five degrees out, and I open the windows halfway; then I realize it only seems warm to me because the 1850s city was so much colder, during my last visit.

The lights change. I roar around the tip of Manhattan—past the downtown heliport that marks the old Coenties Slip. On impulse, because the ramp is there, and empty, I turn onto the Brooklyn Bridge, pushing the car hard in second up the twisting, spiral roadway and onto the span. The giant steel struts rush past against the sky, the wind tugs at my hair. A huge sign flashes atop the new Holy Roller tower; "18 days,

23 hours, 11 minutes," it reads, "till your life changes." A hologram of a Mag-lev locomotive appears, 3-D, out of the sign, grows to terrifying detail, and jumps off into thin air in a way that seems to me kind of dangerous; I can imagine cabbies newly arrived from jungle villages up the Irrawaddy slamming on the brakes to avoid imminent disaster.

"Real Life," the hologram flashes, in blue-silver letters. *"It's a whole new world."*

I take the first exit, onto Cadman Plaza. The abs'inis are wearing off. Brooklyn Heights, to the south, is a wasteland of pretentious bars where the kind of people who either work for, or invest in, Bayonne harbor-front development come to show off their fake-silk monkey-jackets as they sip arak and tamarind juice.

I turn north, swerving randomly under the bridge approaches, where the Unimondos queue for daring theater experiences held in the old Roebling construction shops; past the plastic dorms and health clubs the Rollers have built for their crew-cut missionaries.

Working by feel I head downhill, toward the darker streets, the more dilapidated warehouses, sensing actual relief when the roads lose their scab of asphalt and revert to the rumble-jump of cobblestones.

On my left I catch a glimpse of rotten pilings standing like tombstones in an arc of river, surrounded by junked cars and "No Trespassing" signs. The black I-beams of another bridge fill the sky overhead. This is the area known as DUMBO: "Down Under the Manhattan Bridge Overpass."

Push the car up Jay Street and brake abruptly outside a stucco corner joint with metal siding, Budweiser signs, and four-leaf-clovers over the armored door.

I leave the Morgan right outside. Jay is a shitty street, mostly brick ex-factories full of start-up compression-graphics firms and the lofts of industrial action-artistes maybe three blocks from some of the nastier projects in New York. Half the streetlights are out and the gutters are dense with litter, but I have a theory about this. The worst places to leave a good set of wheels, I believe, are where the oncology specialists and Megorg lawyers hide out, on the Upper East and West sides of Manhattan, or in Brooklyn Heights and Prospect Park. The jimmy-artists *know* that's where the Swedish and Bavarian wheels live and they spend their nights over there looking for 'em, leaving their home streets relatively safe. I've parked my car in some bad places—Alphabet City and Red Hook, Mott Terminal and Hunts Point—and never had a problem.

I go inside.

It's a crummy bar, mostly Irish, all white. Fake gaslights, plastic leprechauns, green rayon rugs. A cheap counter of varnished veneer carries on each side fasciae of glass columns, bracketing the Wolfschmidt. The men are in their forties and fifties, lined up like cormorants on pea-colored Naugahyde stools in the illumination of a fiberglass wagon-wheel chandelier.

It's all goddam fake in here, except for the genuine cirrhosis and waste inherent in every booze-darkened nose and road-map cheek.

The clientele shuts up. I sit at the only stool available, behind the counterfeit Gay Nineties cash register that warbles a digital "I'm forever blowing bubbles" every time you call up the open-till code.

The bartender comes over, a dark-faced guy with small mean eyes wearing a "New York/It Ain't Kansas" T-shirt. I order a dry Gilbey's martini, always a gamble in a place like this but a martini's as close to an abs'ini as you legally can get and I don't want to break the rhythm yet.

After a while the conversation resumes. A sixty-year-old guy built cheaply over a giant gut picks up, "Anyway, that's not what I heard."

"Well, ya'd think whale tastes like fish," a forty-year-old in a plaid suit and no tie responds, "but in point o' fact it tastes more like a mammal. Like steak."

"It *is* a mammal."

"That's my *point.*"

Silence. My martini comes. It's awful. This ain't real gin and it must be twenty percent vermouth of the Zip-strip variety. I attack it, nonetheless.

"Ya see how that ostrich escaped, out West—Arizoner or someplace?" the bartender throws in.

"Afraid it wuz gonna go to Vegas."

"Lose its feathers on the craps."

Chuckles. Someone puts money in the juke. I gulp the drink fast, before the taste can catch up, and order straight gin with a Bud chaser. The talk washes over me, vapid but in a way it's good, it's what I want, the froth of companionship, superficial sure, meaningful of course not, but at a cell-and-hormone level it's satisfying; as if life, any life, rubbed off some of its marginal spark and warmth to heat up your own basic affinity for breath; meanwhile letting the other stuff percolate, the mental image of that froth in her bathtub, the *nikagdas*, come back up but gently, in a way I can digest without Bromo-Seltzer.

Suck the gin, down the Bud. And another. Clam Fetish sings "Octopus Blowjob" at low volume.

" 'S'things are big," plaid suit remarks. "Five feet tall, they hit you with their foot or their leg, you're dead."

"What?"

"Ostriches."

"Dolphins don't do that," the bartender observes.

"Dem fish go to schools."

"Like in theme parks you go to, see 'em kickin' basketballs. An' bears. You go through, they're wavin' an' everything."

"Take yer fuckin' arm off."

"Dolphins?"

"Broads like 'em."

"Hope that wa'n't your car."

"Bears?"

The bartender leans over the register at me.

"I said, I hope that wasn't your car!"

I look up.

"That car—that fuggin' sports car, or whatever. It's *outta* heah."

I get to my feet, walk over to the window. Nothing but cobbles, six-pack rings. No Morgan. I peer left and right, around the neon shamrock. The first tiny puddles of relaxation inside me vanish as if somebody opened the Holland Tunnel under them.

"It's gone!"

"Yup."

"But—did ya see what happened?"

The bartender shrugs. They're all looking at me now, the zoo conversation forgotten.

"Did it get towed?"

"I din *see* it," the bartender says. "I got other things to do."

"You left a car in the *street*?" the suit asks incredulously.

"Yeah, but it was only ten minutes ago!"

"They can jack it in a minute," gut tells me, nodding solemnly.

"Thirty seconds," suit contradicts him. "I seen 'em do it. Mebbe even twenny."

I stand at the window, rubbing the condensation away, feeling a new shock open up a little to the side of the ache where the knife went in.

Looking up and down the empty cobbles with a stupid but real feeling that comes from fooling around too much with VR that I can stop this whole scene, back it up, alter the Story Engine so my Morgan comes back to me, every calf-leathered, walnut-varnished, Lucas-shorted nineteen hundred pounds of her.

I call the cops, of course. They check to see it wasn't towed, then dispatch a blue-and-white. The patrolman sits me in front, motor running, and fills out forms in the blasting heat. He has no idea what a Morgan is, and looks at me with the same mixture of pity and contempt that the guys inside demonstrated for anyone nebbish enough to park on lower Jay Street.

When the cop leaves I thrust my fists into my jacket pockets, walk downhill toward the waterfront, then follow the curve of Wallabout Bay. Groups of homeboys hang and slang under the brick towers of the Farragut projects, deep in the turned shadows of the long, hooded sweatshirts they affect. They seem nervous about something, and ignore my presence.

I walk hard, stamping my heels onto the cold concrete. I'm furious about the Morgan. Like all good fury, this emotion is aimed mostly at myself, for leaving the car on that street; but there's a big shot of sadness in there, too, because I really liked that little machine. For all its bad ignition system and poor heat it was a game and rapid companion. I bought it when I was courting Larissa and partly *because* I was courting Larissa, and its aroma of oil and old hide always brings back the trips we made together: to Bucks County, to Cape Cod, all the way up to Vermont once so she could see birch trees and be reminded of Russia.

Around the corner of Navy and Nassau, following the old Navy Yard fence northward. To my left, a row of mansions rises behind razor-ribbon. They are of clapboard, with stucco trim. This is where the senior officers lived when the base was alive; the flag captains in ordnance and engineering. Even in the half dark of the city night you can see the eaves are sagging, the plaster peeling, the windows broken. Inside, the oak paneling will be warped. In the spring, daffodils grow out of the rampant ivy, the legacy of some green-thumbed navy wife.

It seems a crime that in a town where fifty thousand people don't have a roof over their heads, these houses should be allowed to rot; but the city has taken over the Navy Yard as an industrial park, and waste is, and always was, built into city government, an ineluctable percentage, like the kickbacks in a Bronx garbage-hauling contract.

My anger has a lot to do with the city, of course. Sometimes I can coast along, heated, insulated, cushioned by credit cards, a spacious apartment, taxi and limousine rides, impervious to the constant voltage of violence outside; but you still have to risk yourself, between the doorman and the limo, and inevitably something happens—somebody shoves you in the street, or pisses in your doorway, or leaves crack vials crumbled like snow under the mailboxes, or a bike messenger knocks you down and leaves you bleeding in the gutter, or the limo gets rammed by an insane Urdu-shrieking cabdriver—and you remember just how thin is the membrane separating you from that high ionic differential of misery crammed next to wealth; the millions of new immigrants, hungry for dignity and power, rubbing against the millions trying to preserve what dignity and power they've managed to acquire. And the shock makes you leap, and pounds your heart.

I keep walking, fast.

When I was a kid I used to walk all over the city and those leg muscles never went away. The gin is like a little blue bird singing in my head. Past the huge warehouses and engineering works. The air starts to smell like burned enamel as I approach the towering chimneys of the Navy Yard incinerator, raining its dioxin ash away from the rich neighborhoods, into the Bronx, in line with the prevailing winds. A sign reads "CMO CLUB," a line of mansions surround an overgrown parade ground. I remember Larissa's stories about her father, who was a colonel in the Soviet missile command; the back-biting among officers' wives, the competition for dishwashers while the hundred-kiloton warheads aimed at Brooklyn and Colorado Springs hunkered warm in their alveoles.

My walking has flattened the different angers in me. The memory of Larissa summons little irritation now. Though some sadness rises at the thought of what has occurred be-tween us, it mostly stems from a feeling of nostalgia, and wasted opportunity.

I think, maybe I'm finally getting over her. And in the excitement of that thought I walk even faster, the rhythm of my soles a fast merengue, while the blue bird sings more strongly and I wonder where the hell in this wasteland I can find a decent bar.

The Navy Yard ends, finally. I'm moving into Williams-burgh. Since I don't know this neighb so well I stick to the river. I pass a succession of discount houses with names like "Der Yid" and "House of Tiles." Across the river, the Em-pire State Building is lit for Christmas. Gawking at the island, I almost miss the bar; on my right, two mullioned windows in green frames, soft illumination, the hum of conversation. A sign reads "The Right Bank."

I walk in gratefully.

I recognize The Right Bank before the door swings shut behind me. Not specifically but generally; it's the kind of self-consciously avant-garde joint that used to produce my one-acts. The paintings on the walls are obscene, daring, bad. They serve Unimondo drinks like Olde Gansevoort and *sake;* there's an Alsatian hound and a pair of ski boots on the floor, evidence of eclectic eccentricity, a whiff of Duchamp. Hawk-ley-ite leaflets on the wall, Zippy tracts on the counter.

In the rear, I'll bet you anything, is a small room for "un-derground" theater. A railroad clock over the door reminds me for an instant of *Munn's World* and the odd, continuing numbness in my stomach. The martini, when it comes, is icy and dry and it makes the blue bird happy.

I amble through the crowd. They're mostly under forty, clad in dungarees, Yakut sweaters, a shockingly high percent-age of gaucho boots. A guy in a tuxedo, sweating hard, fum-bles with a half-dozen cellphones and portafaxes. A couple of women wear the green kerchiefs of the Manila node-rebels. I order a second martini. Carefully balancing the new drink I move with the flow of current toward the back of the bar.

Sure enough, there's a brick-walled, klieg-lit room where people stand, listening with rapt attention to a colorless young man on a gray stage cluttered with nondescript props, talking verse into a microphone.

I lean against the wall, sipping. The poem is about dingleberries and dirty underwear. It has a sort of manic interest, in that the writer obviously spent time researching his subject. "Dingleberries with tomato seeds," he says. "Fuck! Substance of our greenmarket loathing. Vegetable proscenium of the cloacal doorknob!"

The poem earns loud applause. A short, skinny girl, one of the Manila kerchief crowd, climbs up to the stage. Her blond hair is dread-braided back around her head in complex patterns. She wears glasses with dark blue lenses, and a cigarette dangles from her left hand despite, or maybe because of, the nation's ban on public smoking. There's something defensive and awkward about her, as if she'd just found out she wasn't supposed to be here; was breaking, by her presence, some stylistic ukase of which she'd never been informed.

"I'm going to read," she begins, and coughs. "This is the first in a series, called *Manhattan Trilogy*." She clears her throat again.

> *"Looking out the Halcyon window*
> *There, in the park,*
> *A baby naked in the dark*
> *The city crouched*
> *Needles scratch at her throat*
> *A spavined couch*
> *The blood congealed . . ."*

She reads badly, without conviction. She has a high voice, sanded, like an alto sax.

> *"In my own gaze smitten*
> *The primal void,*
> *The pain and tripes of*
> *A million lost kittens."*

She's getting more into the rhythm, but the audience hasn't got time for this. They're fidgeting, low conversations starting up. As she notices, she loses what rhythm she had; and the drop in energy and pattern increases the audience's impatience, spurring the process of entropy.

By the time it's over—and it's a long poem—her hands are visibly shaking. A couple of polite claps from friends. Some asshole from the corner calls, "Don't quit the bank job!" and people chuckle. She pushes her way through the group of people she knows, shaking her head vigorously, past me, into the bar proper.

I hesitate, then—maybe because of the gin; or maybe because of that quick sense I had earlier that the hold Larissa had on me is finally gone; or maybe it's just that the loneliness has built up to the point where I can do these things again—I follow.

She buys a brew, and makes her way to the door. She doesn't leave, however, but sits at one of the chairs in the window alcove, next to a thin, curly-haired guy with a bushy beard, and stares into the darkness of the river opposite.

The curly-haired guy makes a remark, and pats her dreadbraids with familiarity. She says something that makes him freeze. He gets up and walks into the poetry room.

I order another martini. After a while I walk over, plant the glass on her table, and sit one chair away. She sees my reflection in the window, and doesn't turn around.

"What exactly bothered you?" I ask.

Stupid line, Munn, my brain comments. My heart is beating fast. Man, it's been a long time.

"Fuck off," she tells my reflection.

Ordinarily I would, but the blood is making turbine howls in my ears, distorting my sense of reality, and the martini has given me the usual gin-ish arrogance.

"The asshole in the corner?" I continue in a calm voice.

She turns. Her mouth is very wide, and works in several sections, so that if she were to smile three sides of it would pull up, like an old-fashioned theater curtain. That's theory, of course; right now her lips are thin and drawn taut.

I notice, for the first time, the nose ring. A tiny snake, with yellow garnet eyes, hiding at the base of her left nostril.

"What the hell *you* think?" she answers finally.

"Well—Poe. Melville?"

She looks at me fixedly from behind the glinting Ray-Bans, trying to figure out just how loony I am.

"Well," I stammer, "they all got bad reviews, at first."

"So I gotta die to be appreciated?"

"Wouldn't hurt."

Her mouth loosens, a tiny bit.

"Hey," I add, "I get catcalls, too. And I don't even perform."

"You booed me."

"No I didn't." I finish the martini in one gulp. "I don't know enough. See, my idea of good poetry is Don Marquis."

"You're kidding."

"Well, no. I mean, *Archie and Mehitabel*—you know, Archie the cockroach?"

No response.

"He had kind of a cool attitude to life."

"I thought Archie was the *cat*."

"No, that was Mehitabel."

"It was Archie."

"You sure?"

"Well"—she looks less pissed-off, for a second—"I think so."

"Whatever," I say, though I know damn well the roach was Archie. "Anyway, I identified with him. Ever since I was a kid, every place I lived had roaches."

"You grew up in New York?" Her voice is bored now. She takes out a pack of Indian Camels, shakes a butt loose, sticks it in her mouth.

I nod. "I figured, if a roach could pound a typewriter like that, I could do a lot better, seeing as I didn't have to hop up an' down on the keys, worry 'bout Raid and Roach Motels and things like that."

Both sides of her mouth lift, for an instant. The cigarette falls out, she catches it in midair.

Encouraged, I offer her a drink. She shrugs, I order.

"Whaddya do," she asks in the same bored tone, "that you get bad reviews?"

"I write for TV."

"Jesus." She looks vaguely shocked, and I wince. "You work for a show?"

"Not one that's on."

"You used to?"

"Uh-huh."

"Well?"

"Copkiller."

"Not *that* shit?"

"Yeah." Kicking myself mentally for telling her. Because there's something about her mouth that has hooked me, a little; that, and the way she got hurt back there, and the way she won't admit it. She has a long neck that kind of undulates, like a swan's, when she bends her head to drink.

The tuxedoed fellow with the communications gear leans, trembling, over the bar, trying to send three faxes at once. His cellphones beep, out of rhythm.

"They shouldn't let him in," she murmurs.

I raise my eyebrows.

"Tee-dees. TeleDysFunction. Cops hate to mess with 'em."

"Oh," I say.

"The talk was right, though," she says.

"What?"

"The dialogue. In *Copkiller*. The way the cops talked. It was right." She looks at me carefully. "I gotta go."

"Where?"

"What's it to you?" The shades flash neon. Then, relenting—"Someplace I don't have to hear—that." She jerks her thumb toward the rear of the joint.

I notice a different accent coming out of the deliberate liberal-arts pronunciation, just vaguely, not enough to determine origins; like the top of ancient foundations showing under land being cleared for a strip mall.

"Can I come with you?" I ask her.

"What if I don't want you to?"

"Up to you."

The blue glasses shift again. I catch a quick darkness behind them as she observes me.

"Aright, then." She swiftly picks up the grimy printout of the poem she read, and crumples it in a pocket of her jacket. "Let's go."

She has a car, an old, black, battered Pontiac sedan slathered with odd cabalistic signs painted (she says) by an artist pal of hers. I think of the Morgan, and a wash of frustration runs through me. But abruptly that disappears, like runoff channeled away down storm drains, chased by the immediacy of the night and the front-end clarity of gin—and also by that quick freeing sensation I had earlier.

The energy of this woman has something to do with it also. She doesn't wear a driving helmet, doesn't ask me to, even though it's the law, in New York.

I sneak glances at her profile as she drives. She's not beautiful in the way the MTV channels teach us to expect; her nose and chin are both a bit snubbed for that; however, the size and darkness of her eyes, the bits I can see behind the shades, and the sharp angle of her cheekbones seem to cut deep enough into the topsoil of her physical appearance to let out a whiff of clear cold springwater, from places very deep underground, and that is more interesting than mere beauty.

She drives like shit, like somebody who didn't grow up driving and has no inclination to learn. She sucks on her unlit Camel and mutters something about trying not to smoke. She slows down outside a bar on North Sixth Street, mutters "Fuck, it's closed!" and pulls a 360 that knocks over three garbage cans.

"Wasn't that a red light?" I ask her, as she accelerates down Driggs.

"The light wasn't working. You blind?"

"I can't see reds," I explain.

"Seriously?" She glances at me.

"Seriously."

"Whaddya see, then?"

"For reds? Not much. Gray, mebbe."

"How can you drive?"

"You read which lights are which by where they are."

"You'd make a lousy bullfighter."

"Yeah," I tell her, "I'd make a lousier bull."

To the BQE, southbound. She turns off south of the Brooklyn Bridge. The Pontiac pokes its way to the waterfront, just where I would go; only she bears left, down Doughty Street, pulling into the eternal strung-lights and valet parking of the River Café, which I wouldn't do because it's always jammed with limos and attitude and TV writers; but in this, also, she's foiled in her intent.

A valet comes out of the shadows with hands up in deep denial.

"Sorry—private party."

The squeezed strains of a Strauss waltz shimmer from the converted barge upon which the restaurant is built. Waltzes, and fake fin de siècle Vienna costume balls, are big this year among gossip columnists and those who go to parties so they can be written about by gossip columnists.

She swings the big car and parks it illegally outside, under a tree drenched in Christmas lights. She fumbles in the back-seat and finds a half six-pack of Brooklyn lager. I'm beginning to like this woman.

Short on destinations, we get out of the car. Across the black and pulsing river, the city rises like a vast dynamo, its hundred million lights throbbing in the harbor humidity. We climb over the metal fence, onto a converted barge across the slip from the River Café. This one is used for classical music concerts. We clamber up a companionway to its roof. A thin sheen of ice gleams on the steel deck; we tread delicately, like dancers.

The waltz is still going on.

Without overthinking it—in this the gin remains useful—I quite naturally reach out and, taking her right hand in my left, lead her into the sweet three-quarter shuffle of the dance.

She follows for a couple of beats, then stops, holding herself very straight, searching my face in the dark.

"No."

"Why not?"

"Not with our clothes on."

"What?"

"You heard me."

I stand there for a moment, my heart trying to jam itself into my windpipe.

And then, partly because it makes no sense at all, and thus accords with a lot of other things that have happened in the past three days—partly because this show of defying convention, however facile, touches the same muscle in me that wants to get out of the schlock of XTV and B-Net and into something that defers only to my own sense of rightness—but mostly because I can imagine nothing nicer than to dance naked with this particular stranger, I shrug off my jacket and my shirt.

She watches me for a bit, checking to see if I'm really dumb enough to take the dare.

Then she slips off her jacket. In a minute we're standing on the chilblain deck of the barge, among the thrown question marks of our underwear, while the November river ties freezing lace of breeze around our corpse-white bodies.

A small coastal tanker rumbles by, southbound.

Across the strip of water, the band medleys into "Wienerblut." On the river's other side, the shadows of John Street, where only a few hours ago I followed a cloaked stranger into late-night ambush, lurk among the lights of the Seaport *WaBenzi*-bars.

Here, on this barge, I and a naked woman, whose name I don't even know, come together. Her skin, in the contrast of wind, is hot. Her hand touches me like a velvet steam pipe. Her ass is graceful as the music next door. She is still wearing her Ray×Bans.

I reach up and, delicately removing the glasses with the thumb and forefinger of one hand, drop them on her crumpled pants.

And we waltz.

TWELVE

SHADOWS—DOZENS, HUNDREDS of them—flit vaguely across a plaster ceiling so cracked and fissured it looks like the graph of a Richter-eight quake.

This is not my ceiling.

I'm aware of a slight thumping in my brain, a louder thumping next door, a deep unease in the digestive areas.

The smell of bizarre herbs. High shouting outside, heavy on the vowels. I turn my head slowly.

Stacked manuals. A Sears air conditioner. On the grimy wall-to-wall, two Fujitsu-Cray 4400 mainframes in parallel, with a metal teapot balanced on a stand on top. A poster announces "Black Flag at CBGB/OMFUG Sept. 14, 1979."

Zeng. Zeng's apartment.

I sit up slowly. The metal cot shrieks. I'm wearing only underpants.

I don't remember getting dressed after waltzing with that woman on the music barge in Brooklyn.

Her doubloon-colored, braided hair. Eyes large and dark.

My stomach doesn't like movement, but if I go slowly, for the present, it seems willing to hang on to the Buick.

I shuffle to the window. Dust billows as I pull aside one of the curtains.

I peer across a fire escape, through lines of stiff washing, to brightly colored signs in Cantonese, smoked ducks hanging in the window of a restaurant, a tea parlor filled with teenagers, a stationery store; a bodega selling bok choi and bamboo shoots, a hundred people in brightly dyed nylon moving around and shouting at each other.

Elizabeth Street.

The stationery store is a front for the Chinatown numbers racket; the tea parlor is the local HQ for the Ghost Shadows, under contract to the On Leung tong. There's a permanent high-stakes mah-jongg game in the restaurant's back room. The bright signs conceal garment sweatshops that employ fourteen-year-olds. The shoe store, so Zeng tells me, sells unnumbered pistols from a small safe under the plastic espadrilles.

I'm two blocks away from what, 150 years ago, was Coulter's Brewery. This area is no longer called the Five Points but in other ways it hasn't changed much.

I shuffle into the kitchen/living area. This apartment also was a sweatshop making knock-off jeans before Zeng took it over. It's long as a CR campaign speech. Every surface, excepting only stove and sink, is piled high with mainframes, VDTs, surge-protectors, manuals, scanners, haptic gloves, telephones, face-suckers, modems, all angled toward a trio of refectory tables in the kitchen.

The windows are obscured by stacked manuals and in the penumbra a half-dozen color monitors flash brightly.

A teapot set over a small camping stove vents perfumed steam into the atmosphere.

Zeng, sitting at the center table, rattles his fingers across two keyboards simultaneously, watching blue icons chase each other across the terminal screens.

"Wildman."

"Uh-huh."

Rattle, rattle. The Ramones sing "Sheena Is a Punk Rocker." Zeng, never taking his eyes from the screen, hands me a pair of shutter-glasses.

"Okay. I got something to show you. This"—rattle, rattle—"is a scan, using my old Z.40 fractal compression."

He picks up a couple of photographs and shows them to me. The first, an aged, black-and-white shot labeled "Dervis Historical Resources," shows a battleship crammed with cannon turrets, portholes, masts, its four smokestacks vomiting smoke into a clear day.

The second is a modern gas-turbine frigate with only radomes and missile launchers marring the Stealth angles of its deck. He feeds them sequentially into a scanner, and taps out a series of commands.

On top of the fridge, a large screen flickers into life. Graphics boxes contain options for the programmer; zoom, multiply, movement/detail, story vector. I put on the glasses.

A huge ship sporting thousands of portholes, hundreds of missiles, dozens of radomes and bridges and crow's nests, pounds out of the screen through a high sea 3-D in our direction. It's a mishmash of the two ships Zeng just scanned, obviously with tons of extra info thrown in. The fractal quotient is in the stratosphere; you can see every drop of the goddam spray, you can see fuckin' reflections in every drop. Zeng pounds a command; the screen hesitates for a nanosecond, then zooms in quickly to a close-up of the bridge, a man in a blue uniform staring anxiously through a clear view screen.

"Now watch with the Role-chopper."

"The what?"

"Watch."

Back to the ship. The bow is huge, gray, riveted; it plunges deep into a swell. A tiny fish leaps from the bow wave. My stomach heaves in sympathy. I turn away, knocking a Kevlar haptic-vest hung by its wires off a kitchen stool.

I've never seen this vest before. It's extremely light. I put it on, merely to do something with it, to get my mind off the nauseating sea, patting the Velcro shut, looking back at the screen just in time to see the portholes under the forward turret launchers glare yellow.

Three of the topmost bridges tilt, slowly at first, then faster as the deck beneath them ejects a column of black fire. Secondary explosions shake the great hull.

Zeng zooms in. Plates crack, melt under the heat.

Closer. Rivets pop, circuits turn into liquid silicon. High-pressure steam strips a finger of flesh till only white bone is left and the Annapolis ring circling the finger falls away. A single molecule of metal loses two electrons, gains one, loses it again.

"That's nice," I say when the show is over.

"Nice?"

"But you don't have any random input in there."

"Maybe not. But you know what the focus group said?"

"Sure," I tell him. "They said, they didn't notice that shift."

Zeng turns to stare at me.

"How did you know?"

"I'm not sure." I move closer to the sink. The haptic wires and the shutter-cord trail behind me. I'm not certain if I'm going to toss my cookies or not. My stomach feels like the sea in front of that ship. Zeng is staring at his screen again. In the cool blue shine of the VDT, in his loose black shirt and shorts, he looks like an ancient spirit tweaking the twisted potential of a Cabala program.

"You think Rosie will buy it?" His fingers rattling again, plastic locusts.

I shrug. Like an aroma reminds you of a certain food, just the mention of Obregon's name calls to mind the flavor of yesterday's debacle.

And then, traveling down the timeline, I remember the taste of talking about it to the bad-poetry woman—but the slot of memory where her name should be is empty.

I never got her name.

In the fog of hangover the rancid flavor of Rose, Gaynor, and *Real Death* fades, replaced with the cold cocaine high of dancing buck-naked on the frozen steel deck of a barge, the lights of the city dripping like liquid ice around us.

The soft heat of her against my hips; me bending to kiss her while my excitement rises against her stomach; and her pushing me, gently, away.

"You don't want to fuck me."

"No shit?"

"I fuck men I don't know."

Try to analyze *that* through the brain bubbles of booze; making the only sense of it I can.

The Plague, still rampant in the city, the number of tainted men and women skyrocketing; the touted vaccine delayed, so they say, for another year.

I stiffen, the upper part of me that is, the lower part being already fairly stiff, and she chuckles in my arms.

"No, not *that,* pal. I always use latex."

She is trembling gently against me.

"If I was more honest," she whispers, breaking out of my arms, reaching for her underwear, "I'd just stab 'em with a knife. Leave 'em bleeding on the linoleum."

The trouble is, I don't remember shit after that.

Zeng is muttering. *"Doo meh,"* he whispers darkly. I want to stop, ask him why, but in the greater heat of this recall I let it pass.

I don't have a clue how I left Brooklyn. All that remains is a hazy snapshot of her Pontiac, a black wave of uncertainty after the barge, the great lack of breath that came when she challenged me to take my clothes off, and I can still feel it, that pain in my chest, I still can't breathe—

And I *can't* breathe. I try to take a breath. My chest is sucked in tight by this vest, my stomach heaves wretchedly against the straps. In sudden panic I scrabble with my fingers at the Kevlar, trying to summon the breath to yell at Zeng, who shouts at me, triumphantly, *"Doo meh!"* and hits the keyboard. The pressure, abruptly, is gone.

I swivel, fast but not fast enough.

"Bad gin," I mumble, and barf helplessly all over a brand-new CD-ROM unit.

"You shouldna done that," I tell him later.

He cleaned up without complaint, guilt-driven; his family are mission Catholics. He found a small wooden box from which he took a thin gray root that he chipped into the teapot with an iron knife. He removes from an invisible shelf a bottle of liquor in the greenish depths of which I can see some sort of silver lizard crouched, drowned in alcohol.

"Please don't open that."

He shrugs.

The tea smells of mold and lilies. It's hot, and when it reaches my stomach it spreads out like a woolen blanket.

"So," I say, when my stomach has settled somewhat, *"doo meh?"*

"It's Viet," he replies. He lights a joss stick and places it on the ancestors' altar over the stove. This is the classic gray and blue niche, with the gold-leaf ideograms, that you find in all corners of Chinatown, Catholic or no.

Zeng has covered his with clipped pictures of Sid Vicious, Joey Ramone. G. G. Allen, taped behind Lao Tzu.

"But what does it mean?"

"You motherfucker."

"*What?* I only asked a simple—"

"No. That's what it means. It means 'motherfucker' in Vietnamese."

I sip at the tea.

Zeng sniffs delicately at the joss.

"Makes sense. Even the old tongs—Hip Sing, On Leung —they use street gangs. The Ghost Shadows, they hired Viets to do their real wet jobs. In the old days, they used frogmen from the ARVN navy. SEALs trained 'em—you know, U.S. Navy.

"Chinese are scared of the Viets," Zeng continues. He pinches out the joss stick. The smoke wisps into the apartment's corner murk. "We're smarter, we know the Viets *like* to kill. So when the new Asian gangs come out of Jackson Heights and Astoria—Green Dragons, Lizard Dancers, Spirit Knives—well, they're run by Cantonese, but they hire Viets. Only these are the *new* Viets, trained by Spetsnaz—the Russians."

"*Doo meh.*"

"*Desinformatsiya.* They put out flyers, with bad messages; pigs, if you're a Muslim. Swastikas, if they're after Jews."

"Real sophisticated."

"They use carpet-cutters," Zeng says, and bends over the keyboards again.

It's still early in the morning. I take a shower and, borrowing underwear from Zeng, get dressed.

I sit at one of the spare terminals. Clicking through B-Net windows, I call up the latest editions of the *News* and *Times*. The latter, resolutely pro-Polish, has a page full of another anti-German firebombing in Cracow, with the rest of the rag devoted to the favorite salads of soap stars (Amy Dillon, I note, "adores" cilantro-arugula). The back page of Section

One is devoted to the culinary specialties of Hawkley-ite node-rebels in Manila. Another moth of memory flits back to the light of consciousness; she wore a node-rebel kerchief.

My stomach settles down. I graduate to Lapsang Souchong, dug from another of Zeng's boxes. The *News* has a long piece, illustrated with lurid color photographs, on the Lizard Dancers gang. On page seven there's another color spread, and this one stops me dead; a green Morgan roadster lies across the top of the page, with a man sprawled backward across the leather seats, his eyes open in terminal surprise.

It's just like my car, and you don't see many of those.

It *is* my Morgan. I can see a corner of the *Munn's World* menu splayed behind the seat.

I knock over the cup of Lapsang, bending closer to the pixels. "THIEF TOOK LAST RIDE IN STYLE," the headline reads.

An anonymous call at 10:30 last night led police to South Boerum Street in Red Hook, where they found a man shot 17 times at point-blank range in the driver's seat of a Morgan roadster.

The victim, subsequently identified as Elwood Delgado, 27, of Farragut Estates, was taken to Brooklyn Hospital where he was pronounced DOA at 11:07. Police say he had six prior convictions including armed robbery and grand theft auto.

The Morgan, an expensive British antique, had been reported missing at 9:55 P.M. on Jay Street by Alexander P. Munn, of Manhattan.

"Son of a bitch," I whisper in wonder.

In the photo you can see five bullet holes puckering the driver's door.

My stomach isn't settled anymore; it's not actively rebelling, but I can feel magma down there, and thoughts of volcanoes.

I look up at Zeng; he's lost in the depths of the algorithms he's working up, and the Ramones are playing so loud he wouldn't hear me if I shouted.

I go into the spare room and shut the door. Look out into Elizabeth Street.

The little bugs crawling in my stomach again.

It has to be coincidence. Elwood Delgado drove my car into a part of the city even I wouldn't go to. Elwood pissed off another car thief, and got paid back in the kind of currency those guys use instead of greenbacks.

Buyaka, man.

I'm only half convinced. It's getting close to nine and I should be heading for work, but the combo of great fatigue and the resonance from only two days ago, when I was hung over like this and also recovering from *buyaka,* turns me all trembly again. On impulse more than anything I pick the receiver off a faxphone and punch Pentti's number. It's a good hour, just after he gets in and before his first patient; I can imagine him perusing *JAPA* as he answers.

"See the *News*?" I ask him.

"You in it?"

"Yeah. Page seven."

I can hear paper rustling. Pentti always buys the *News,* for the gossip columns.

"Jay Street." The concern sharp in his voice. "That's near the river, isn't it?"

"Yeah."

He sighs heavily.

"You keep doing that, you're gonna find what you're looking for. What did I tell you? Dark waters; eros, the womb. The mother who left you, going out to work. Black, dangerous water; *thanatos,* death. The *father* who rejected you, before you were born. The death impulse, *because* he rejected you, you're not worthy of living—"

"Isn't that all kind of old-fashioned?" I interrupt.

"You chose a neo-Freudian," he retorts, "you're going to get neo-Freud."

"What if I'm jiss sick of bullshit," I suggest. "All the hype and Christmas lights, you know? There's not a lot of bullshit, on streets like that."

"I can't treat you, if you get yourself shot," Pentti says. "Stay *away* from the waterfront. It's extremely dangerous for you, in more ways than one."

"Pentti—"

"I *mean* it." He hangs up. I look out the window for a few minutes, thinking. Then I put on my leather jacket and walk to the subway.

Work is work. Rob hands me a message from a Detective Mohammed at the 84th Precinct in Brooklyn. I call but he's not in. A desk sergeant informs me the Morgan is being held as evidence at the Red Hook pound.

A watery sun pole-vaults in slo-mo over the island, trying to chivvy its rays into my frontal lobes.

I ask Rob to go out and buy me a pair of Ray-Bans. I wear them at my desk, which for a while gives me the illusion of being Michael Eisner.

For lunch I down a Prodex and a bottle of Olde Gansevoort tamped down with all-natural granola-fruit mush from the canteen. At three I meet Vivian Moos at Studio 8 for auditions. Production is due to start next month on the second season of *Real Life;* this is a tangible sign of the vast corporate faith Gaynor and the bosses all profess in the show's future.

On a flat in one corner of the cavernous space an assistant producer has set up lights and a blue screen. The notes announce that, in this segment, our MTV-enforcers seek to stop the neuro-psychology department at a major university from trying genetically to clone a breed of super-killers whose sprees of mayhem are cybernetically triggered by lines from Clam Fetish songs.

Like I told Gaynor, it's the technology that's important in *Real Life*—not the plot.

Anyway, I don't remember the story details but I have to say the casting agencies have sent us some of the more bizarre-looking SAG members for this particular story.

One is six feet eight and has a neck like a Manhattan Bridge support with biceps big as my thigh and a face like a bullfrog with leprosy. A female "killer" takes off her leotard to show us a tattoo of a coelacanth right around her midriff that does the shimmy when she belly-dances.

A technician takes input straight off the cameras and plugs it into the Navigator, which automatically correlates it with the World and Story systems. The tattooed lady, watching the monitors through shutter-glasses, audibly gasps when she sees herself appear in the secret cellars of the neuro-psych department, pacing back and forth between the rubberized walls, snarling between the cell bars; her private, obedient body, shrunk by fractal compression, captured by the Story Engine, programmed to different rules—made to move and act, for the first time in her life, by an intelligence different from her own.

I can see the emotions playing across her face, and they're a perfect reflection of the reactions rationally to be expected from this new technology: shock, excitement, awe—and, finally, the first faint stirrings of fear.

We're halfway through the audition when the studio phone terminal blinks. A gaffer waves me over, hands me a receiver. Rose says, "Alex, dear?" The honey in her voice laid on in sarcasm, since we both know she doesn't talk like that.

"Uh-huh."

"I just saw Gaynor and Wimer." Wimer is the Wizard of Wires. "They have an idea about the lag problem."

"Uh-huh," I repeat, more warily this time.

Rose pauses. Thinking back, I can hear caution in her very first word tones; through the medium of the phone line we are circling each other like feral dogs, aware of preexisting tension, alert to what comes next.

"Basically, what they want to do is shallow out the Random Motor, twenty-five, thirty percent. They got numbers saying it'll cut that shift to below threshold—"

"No way."

"Way, Alex baby." I can hear, faintly, the jingle of her key chain. "You cut the random that much, it'll give enough computer use back to the rest—"

"But the whole point of this is to make it *real*! Real life, man! Rose, you cut even twenty percent of Random from the show, you *know* the loss is gonna be exponential, there'll be so much less input, you basically won't get that element; and without any Random, you got yourself just another fuckin' video game."

"You're exaggerating."

"Only some."

"Well, that's the way it's goin' down."

"Listen, Rose." I struggle, through the packing of tiredness, to get my thoughts in order. I pick at my forehead with stiff fingers. "Zeng did that focus group, ya know? He's got the results now. It says, the shift only happens when the Random Motor kicks in—that's always a surprise, and most of the time it's under a lotta stress—anyway, what the study shows is, *nobody notices*!''

"It doesn't matter."

"Exactly."

"No. I mean, Gaynor already made the decision. The show's eighteen days from broadcast today."

I can feel my face getting hot.

"But that's *my* decision. I got things under control."

"Alex—"

"I won't do it!"

"Alex—"

"No way!"

"Turn on the video."

"What?"

"You heard me."

Nobody turns on the video-phone screen, for reasons I've already gone into. The tiny screen to the left of the cradle flickers on, but I have to dick around with contrast before I can see Rose's face.

It's not her face she wants me to see, however. It's a cue card, printed in boldface caps, held in her left hand, that reads "IF YOU REFUSE GAYNOR WILL FIRE YOUR ASS *NOW*."

With her right hand she's fooling with the lighter on her key chain.

"And, Alex."

"I *see* it."

"No. I mean, those shades. Who you think you are—Michael fuckin' Eisner?"

I slam the phone down and the screen goes dark. I can hear the assistant line producer saying, "That's fine, sir. Please leave your name with the assistant. Next!"

By reflex, mostly, I punch the number of Larissa's studio. I have no idea what I'm going to say to her, or even if I really want to talk to her after last night.

In any case, the issue doesn't arise. The studio manager says she hasn't come in.

I return to my office and pop another Prodex. Rob brings me a sheet full of messages, mostly from the SAG woman. I have trouble thinking over the fury in me. The anger in DUMBO last night was aimed at my stupidity, because of the

Morgan; today, once again, it's my capacity for prostitution that really pisses me off.

"Gotta get out of this," I mumble aloud, "shouldna ever got into this." Over and over, in tones that vary in volume but not in intensity.

I waste my time and Jack Tyrone's money for the rest of the afternoon, signing papers and gazing through my dark glasses, through the lozenge-shaped windows, at the gray scaly back of the Hudson.

THIRTEEN

I DON'T GO home from work.

I don't feel like canteen food; nor do I want to sludge up my gut with hot dogs.

I take a cab to Aquavit and eat a Greenland herring with mesclun, alongside cattail-flour rolls and Sisu beer, in the back room. The healthy food doesn't waken the excitable gases in my stomach; the beer kind of mixes the cumulus of fatigue and the cirrus of anger, letting them crust around the sides of my brain a little.

The bartender at Aquavit is tall, blond, and lovely, but I don't look at her often, no more than once a minute anyway. Jumbled among the clouded thoughts of last night lies the faint outline of a woman with a short nose and chin, and eyes like a pool of darkness behind her shades, who reads poor poems in uncertain tones; even though she's only a fraction as pretty, the vague image of the poetess has about a thousand times more soul than the bartender, who knows from the corporate card that I'm at XTV and manages to look simultaneously mysterious and camera-friendly every time our gazes cross.

When I leave the restaurant I hail another cab and pay the driver thirty bucks up front to drive me to Brooklyn.

The Right Bank is right where I left it, on Kent Street; this shouldn't surprise me but the fact is, being drunk and being on the recovery side of a hangover are two different worlds. I'm irrationally relieved to find the two worlds still linked by the geodesics of the city.

There's another poetry reading scheduled for tonight; they run them five nights a week, a notice says. Also, it's a Friday, so the place is more crowded than last time. I spot no node-rebel kerchiefs. Most of the audience tonight wears black.

The first reader crawls on stage in pink pajamas, rolls on her back, and screams for a minute solid before wailing, in San Juan Spanish, verses that include a lot of *putamadre* and *chingon*.

She is soundly applauded. I think my woman might want to take tips from this one, but I don't see her anywhere, and when I ask the barman he says this is a completely different lineup from yesterday, pinch-hitting from the Nuyorican Poets Café on East Third Street.

I ask him if he knows the girl with braided hair and dark glasses from last night and he shrugs and says, "Far's I'm concerned, they're all fuckin' fruitcakes with bad teeth."

I order an Olde Gansevoort, and another.

Clam Fetish plays on the juke, electric violin and synthe-sized room-harps weaving in and out.

> *"At work on the blown hatches of your heart, the porno vampire sucks ink, your farts are dust."*

Schliemanning through the multiple-stapled announce-ments on the wall I find last night's schedule. "An Evening of Hawkley-ite Protest," it says, "Political Poetry from Lower Manhattan." The list of names contains five that are recogniz-ably female. I figure her moniker has to be either Rosalita Sanchez-Glantz, Carole Landesmann, Emilie Anne Freedom, Kaye Santangelo, or Maia Derzoglu.

I kind of hope it's not Maia Derzoglu.

Anyway, six more beers, a couple shots of gin, lots of illegal cigarette smoke, and a fair amount of strings of verse snipped off and drifted around to the front of the bar later, the woman has not shown up. It's eleven o'clock and I doubt she'll appear now so I pay the tab and leave.

The earlier clouds have disappeared. The night air is cold and dry, chillier than yesterday, and it cuts into my lungs and sinuses like an expert surgeon.

I figure I'll walk around the bridge, maybe over to Newtown Creek, find a café or diner or something. Newtown Creek was the staging area from which Howe's Hessians attacked when they took over Manhattan in 1777. From the highway it looks like mostly gas tanks and chemical companies, but I've never really explored around there and I figure the walk will do me good.

Down Bedford, Driggs, always heading north. My leg and thigh muscles warm up, the arms swing neatly. Twenty-five minutes later I've traversed Greenpoint, left the kielbasa butchers and the newer camp-tique shops behind. The onion domes of the Polish churches loom and vanish.

As I get near the BQE flyover the signs turn from Polish to Spanish and the streets lose their patina of care. At Greenpoint Avenue the ground slopes under the expressway to the creek.

It's not easy to find the water. I have to search among large deserted blocks of brick-faced warehouses. The signs advertise auto parts, wholesale Chinese food supplies, medical specialty gases.

At last, between the Peerless Importing Company, a truck depot, and a concrete pipe warehouse, I find a stretch of shoreline unprotected by fence or brick walls.

The creek itself lies black, hemmed in by rotting bulwarks, dead barges. Locusts and weeds die among the nameless tarry filth along its banks. Directly opposite, a graveyard fills the space between an old cement plant and a billboard advertising ear deodorant.

I try to imagine what it must have looked like when the British were here—a farmhouse on that hill, orchards and a small stream sloping down to a salt marsh, the marsh giving way to clean river. The beer is wearing off by now, and in the trenches it leaves undefined, the cold creeps in.

I turn south again, treading slower, less motivated now I found what I was looking for, moving toward the G subway line which I know cuts north-south across Greenpoint at Nassau Street.

I don't hear the footsteps for a while.

I've crossed Greenpoint Avenue, the signs gone back to Polish; though the area is quiet a few younger, professional types walk pedigreed dogs, or jog down the main drag. I don't see a subway stop and, wondering if I've gone too far east, take a left at Klub Sportowy onto Diamond Street heading west.

Halfway down the block a particularly sibilant scrape, as of one shoe being dragged to get the dogshit off, makes me turn around.

The street is empty.

The houses are unassuming two- or three-story buildings, faced with vinyl or aluminum siding whose counterfeit smoothness barely reflects the sparse illumination. For a number of seconds I hear nothing further. Then, just as I'm about to turn, it comes again.

Slap.

Slip—*slap;* slip—*slap.*

I'm desensitized, somewhat. It's been six days since Kearny; and there was Mrs. Dominguez, and thousands of other footsteps I've heard in the city since then, some of which, by the law of averages, had to resemble those of the man in the marsh.

But memory is a finer tool than we realize, and in this case it comes up with a preliminary match, the correlated patterns that trigger a loud "*it's him!*" in the chicken centers of the brain.

Also, I'm highly aware of the fact that the footsteps are real close, judging by their volume—but as in the Kearny marshes, I can't see who makes them.

There's something just plain *chronic* about that.

Slip—*slap.* Then silence again. I get a feeling I've been hearing them, in the back room of my mind, for several minutes. I watch the intersection by the Polish football club. A garish sign advertising cheap flights to the demilitarized zone of Warsaw creaks in the night wind.

Nothing.

I actually wonder if I imagined it.

I swivel, and continue in the direction I was going.

Walking somewhat faster. Behind me I hear the sharp shuffle-step begin again. When I get to the next corner, I turn abruptly left and stop with my back to the side of the corner building, listening.

To that mincing slip-*slap* getting closer, closer, down the street I just vacated.

My heart pounds as fast as if I'd been running. Abruptly I leap back into Diamond Street, and stare straight at where the sound of the limping man is coming from.

The street is still empty.

The footsteps cease. A brief echo subsides against the vinyl clapboard.

More than anything, I think, it's the timing; the quick lag between my stopping and his stopping, like the microsecond of shift in the rushes of *Real Life;* that's what convinces me.

For it really is *exactly* the same as in Kearny and in that precision lies no space for coincidence.

Which means, in turn—the beer-smoothed brain churning out the calculation quite neatly—that the carpet-cutters, and the *doo meh* bastards wielding Tech-9s, are somewhere very close.

Another night, I might be braver. Another night I might march out to confront the threat, trusting someone will be around to bear witness should I run straight into the carpet-cutters.

But I'm hungover, tired, and half drunk. I don't feel good about myself anyway; and I've got no illusions about how quickly a Tech-9 will chop anyone's chest into hamburger.

I turn and run.

This road—"Eckford Street," the sign reads—is what the real estate vampires call a "crease" territory; houses interspersed with garages, half-used redbrick workshops. The cars parked here are older, beat-up, the kind my poetess drives.

I wonder, as I sprint, if I'll ever see her again.

The street ends one block away against the six-story white-brick wall of an institutional building. By the time I get there I'm puffing and blowing and my body feels like all the beer in me sogged down to the thighs and calves.

Three-foot-high blue letters proclaim "Marla Maples High School." I look both ways. I can vaguely hear the slip-*slap!* behind the breath crashing in my ears.

The streets on either side are deserted.

I take off once more, at a trot, one thought fluttering like a trapped june bug around my skull; I am *completely* lost.

The school building is dark; no safety there.

Still, Brooklyn is a city; if you made it separate from the other boroughs, as it was until 1898, it would still be the fourth largest in America, after New York, Chicago, and L.A. And a city that size is not like a Jersey salt marsh; you run long enough you're bound to encounter people—even a cop.

So I keep running although, in another similarity with Kearny, my lungs are starting to seriously hurt, and the cold air feels like switchblades rushing into those seldom-used passages. I reach the corner of the high school and turn right, checking quickly ahead to make sure nobody waits for me.

Nothing. Risking a glance behind—

Nobody there, either.

A big yellow building with the words "Levy Bros. Bedframe Corp." rises ahead. To the right of that, darkness, space, and fencing, and a loom of sky that in the city means one thing only: a park. Behind a black web of trees, the onion domes of an Orthodox church, the twin towers of the World Trade Center, and the chimneys of the Fourteenth Street power plant, rise like details behind a stage set's scrim.

Movement comes at the far end of the street I'm on, at the corner of the bedframe plant.

Two compact figures in short black jackets separate themselves from the shadows. They move in synchrony, one to each sidewalk, and start loping in my direction.

Behind me now, in Eckford Street, the sound of footsteps stops.

Gutlessly, I turn back to look, certain I'll see nothing. But I'm wrong.

The orange cone of a streetlight outlines a tall man in a long coat and a dark hat with upturned brim. He stands still as a mime, maybe sixty feet away, next to the high school sign.

Between hat and cloak, in the space where his eyes should be, I see only a deep lack of light, as if he could track me with absence.

My body, if not my brain, has realized that running is the only thing left to do. I turn and run in the only direction possible, toward the park, sprinting faster than I did in Jersey, over the low iron-post fence the city puts around its parks for decoration, and then—breath crying under the rushing avalanche of fear—along the chainlink built to keep people out of the park's center. The chainlink is twisted and broken every thirty feet or so where people have rammed cars or pried up the metal mesh to get through. Against the frosted ground of a grassy verge I can see the two black figures ahead converge to cut me off at the end of the fence, where the park meets a broad avenue.

So, at the first negotiable gap in the chainlink, I twist and crawl through the broken grid and book right, slipping here and there on the shining frost, toward a tribe of buildings at the park's center.

Two high brick walls, with pavilions spaced at intervals, fade into the gloomy distance on both sides.

As I get closer I make out a series of pseudo-towers over an arched brick passage to the left. Grilled windows and boarded-up doorways punctuate its mass.

Between the two walls lies a deep, perfectly rectangular indentation, maybe two hundred feet long by eighty across. The tipped-over, burned-out carcasses of three automobiles lie in the middle.

A swimming pool. The dirty tiles shine with ice.

In front of me a smaller indentation is infested with cattails and dominated by a cracked cement diving board.

I hustle around the smaller pool, down the side of the big one, staying in the shadow of the left-hand wall.

What reason remains amid the white noise of fear and exertion insists that unless every gang in New York is trying to *buyaka* my ass, they *cannot* have covered every exit out of a park this size.

And right on cue I hear a whistle from ahead, where a third brick wall and chainlink fence, at ninety degrees to the other two, close off the vast rectangle of the pool.

"Jesus." I'm talking to myself again. "Jesus Christ." My knees and ankles feel all wobbly. The archway in the middle of the "towers" on my left opens on a courtyard with a boarded-up ticket booth in the middle. It's blocked by solid fencing.

A moronic, loud voice in my head says, "You're going to *die,* Munn, you asshole," and loops the words like a thirty-second cart. Spotting a corner of staircase behind one of the left-hand pseudo-towers, I dodge down the steps. Then I put on the brakes, flattening against a busted doorway under the staircase, and twist around, looking behind me.

Two figures move against the silvered stretch of park, splitting up, one to each side of the pool. Silhouetted as they are, I can just see their hands, and the vague shape of something clutched.

"Shit," I grunt.

The whistle sounds again, close now and off to the north—the direction I was running in.

I retreat backward, into the building. I don't want to go in there, the park outside is trap enough, but I'm running short on options, anyway my legs are in control now, they seem to be taking me deeper into the blackness and there's little I can do to resist.

I turn, scuffing junk accumulated on the floor. A wayward twig of streetlight illuminates rusted cans of Fancy Feast and Sundew Fruit Punch. A sign reads "EATING PROHIBITED."

The smell of human shit and piss and the mold of abandoned buildings invades my nose. I make out more light, very faint, coming from windows set high to my left, at a distance that could be half a mile for all I know the difference.

Beside me, what looks like a ticket counter. Presumably this is where you would get a towel and the key to a changing booth before going for a dip.

Then, a partition, a high room with lots of tall cement booths. Beyond that, to the left, lies what appears to be a vast hall, cut by a couple more sparkles of window, their light bouncing against a floor that looks like it was surfaced in polished steel.

I walk carefully into the hall, bracing myself against the wall. My steps echo, heavy on the treble, against the tiles.

When I stop, my feet simply slick away from me, and my ass hits the deck with a slam that vibrates right up my spinal column.

The slam kind of wakes my brain up. I crawl back out of there, as quietly as I can; then, getting to my feet, hustle through the partition room, parting a pile of old Sundew bottles behind the ticket counter. And there I squat, in the shadow of the old, peeling booth, waiting.

The wait lasts only twenty seconds or so. These guys are not hanging around with an eye for tourism. He comes in the doorway fast, kicking up litter. Hesitates, whistles softly.

After another twenty seconds I hear a second set of footsteps. These two don't limp; they move like hunters, with stealth and greed and running shoes. They pace along the wall, breathing softly, taking the corner into the partition room together.

Very, very slowly I raise my head over the counter. One of them has gone deep inside. The other stands at the entrance to the silver hall, covering his buddy like any good squaddie would.

His breath hangs solid in the freezing gloom.

My hand closes around one of the fruit punch bottles. No breathing now; I'm way too scared for that. I heft it carefully, because if I fuck up they'll be onto me within ten seconds and then I'll be in a situation I don't want to think about because then I'll be dead.

In total silence, I lob the soda bottle through the partition room, over the bulkhead, and into the dark depths of the silver hall.

The sound comes with the shock of all noise having no visible cause. In the peace of the frosted hall, the glass smashes like cannon fire. The black figure pushes himself violently sideways, away from the hall, and makes the discovery, as I did earlier, that friction is not a law you need worry about in a place whose floor is solid ice. I see him stretched out on the silvery surface, while something heavy and metallic skitters audibly out of reach. A voice grunts, alien words, sounds that make no sense.

I crawl carefully to my feet and tiptoe out of the reception area. I make some noise against the rusted cans but I doubt they can hear this.

At the top of the three stairs I look around the swimming pool for a long time, perhaps two seconds in all. Then I slide to my left again, the direction I was going in before. I heard a whistle from there earlier, but he must have moved on by now, and anyway this is the smallest stretch of open ground to cover; to the end of the building where a short gap exists between the brick wall and a spike fence that's supposed to keep bad elements out of this condemned recreation area.

So I run down this narrow alley, into the shadow of massed trees at the far end, blessing Brooklyn and all law-flouting elements not currently present because the iron spikes are twisted apart every fifteen feet and the chainlink ripped beyond that. Someone whistles again, it sounds like it's coming from one of the broken windows, high against the pseudo-towers' mass. I squeeze between two spikes, under the chainlink, jink left behind a couple of pines backing up against the building's main entrance.

Then, even more cautiously, I venture out of shadow, out of the park, onto the wide avenue I spotted earlier.

I'm shivering all over now. My legs have almost no strength left and every sinew in my knees feels like overcooked linguini. I cross the road and hunch behind a row of parked jalopies on the far side.

No sound at all, excepting a distant siren, a faint slish of wind.

Bending so low that my spine aches, I scuttle like a blue crab away from the bulk of the condemned buildings to where a line of normal Brooklyn row houses marks the end of open space.

A sign reads "Bedford Avenue." There's a G train stop down Bedford. I guess I was too far east, not west, of the line when I turned into Diamond Street.

I continue down Bedford, still hunching low from car to car. A bus roars up the avenue, heading toward the park. A woman walking an Irish wolfhound stares at me. Her dog growls.

I keep an eye out for cops; none show up. I spot the green globe of the subway station from two blocks away. I make it across the intervening sidewalk without mishap, then down the steps into the bright station. The token vendor glares at me from inside his armored booth, pissed off because I keep him from watching his portable TV. I exchange five bucks for two tokens.

Part of my mind, stupid, optimistic, already is composing victory songs to silence the overwhelming fear still buzzing around the rest of my skull.

I hang around the token booth, the way you're supposed to late at night.

A couple in vinyl coats walk down the steps to the "ALL TRAINS" stairway, arguing in Polish.

Five minutes pass. I interrupt the token vendor's viewing.

"This train running?"

He doesn't look up.

" 'Scuse me—" I rap on the bulletproof glass.

"What?" Exasperated.

"Are the trains running?"

He focuses on the TV again.

"Far's I know."

I stay by the booth. Even the token vendor is better than nothing.

Three and a half minutes later, a faint rush of air moseys up the "ALL TRAINS" staircase. Greatly relieved, I walk along the corridor, up and down the steps over the top of a tunnel that are a feature of these old train stops.

And freeze.

Mouth open, I draw in added oxygen, sliding on the railing for support as I stare at the wall that separates two bricked-up doors marked "MEN" and "WOMEN." The wall obscured from me till now by the exit turnstile.

A large yellow poster has been glued on this wall. It's the same format as Industrial Islam posters. Unlike the I.I. art, however, the detail has been lovingly etched out. It portrays a horse's head, with nostrils flaring, eyes staring, an air of gallop, mane flowing from the speed. But this is not a horse.

From the center of the creature's forehead rises a tall spiral tusk.

My hesitation is short-lived. I take the stairs three at a time. The train on the right, southbound side crashes into the station as I reach the platform.

I stand in the doorway of the second car, gulping air, watching the platform behind me till the doors close. No one follows me or gets on the train in that interval, and I sink down to the floor with my back against the door, too exhausted and trembly to step over to a seat.

I take the G train as far as it goes. At Smith and Ninth the loudspeakers squawk "Last stop, everybody off." I check the map quickly; you can change here for the F train back to Manhattan.

I peer carefully at the three people who get off with me but they're all brown of face and bright of clothes and not interested in me; they have their own problems to worry about, living in this part of Red Hook.

I walk down to the token area and hang around the lights. No one is on the elevated platforms.

A pair of Apache attack choppers swoop over the station, with "AGATE"—for "Anti-Gang And Terrorist Environment"—stenciled high on their armored sides. They chase their blazing searchlights into the depths of Brooklyn.

The idea of Manhattan, and home, suddenly feels like Nirvana to me, a safe harbor where there are always cabs and cappuccino bars; where tall, limping, cloaked men, and squat killers, never appear out of the asphalt shadows, not in this century at least.

But the goddamned Transit Authority seems to runs only one train every ninety minutes this time of night; and when the el starts trembling and swaying at the mastodont rush of metal wheels on the outbound F track I decide I've had enough of sitting around in empty places waiting for violent people to show up at their own convenience.

So I take the train, ride it away from the city, all the way to the terminus at West Eighth Street, Coney Island.

Despite my nerves, I figure that by now there's no way I'm being followed.

These people, whoever they are, are not supermen; they are Vietnamese kids who shop at Ace Hardware franchises and say "motherfucker" when kicked. Although the ramp to the boardwalk is deserted, I move down its length with some confidence.

I turn right, westward down the empty expanse of serried planks stretching between Brooklyn and the Atlantic.

Never mind Pentti and his neo-Freud; I've always felt calmer by harbors and beaches, more able to relax and sort out my thoughts. Water is calm and, unlike most people, knows where to flow to sort out its own balance.

Tonight, I have a great need to do my own sorting out.

Because what this attack means—so I argue to myself, stamping on the frozen boards, my leather jacket drawn tight against the bite of wind—what it means is, first, the attack in Kearny was no accident.

Behind a stripped concrete pavilion that reminds me of the abandoned swimming pool, a vast ship loaded with cars slowly slides across the night horizon.

Second—I'm mumbling against the wind—this means, for some reason, somebody either wants to kill me, or at least frighten the living bejesus out of me.

"Brilliant, Munn," I hiss sarcastically.

I keep walking. It's too goddam cold to scream and roll around the boardwalk, sobbing, which is what I really feel like doing.

To my right, the black twisted shape of the old Cyclone roller coaster rises like a nightmare construct, a kind of engineered evil, against the loom of city behind.

Farther down the boardwalk, a string of red and white lights illuminates a row of arcades facing the sea.

One of these, blocked with aluminum panels, projects a square of yellow light in the direction of the car-carrier. A large sign overhead promises "YES! We sell Pina Colada and Hygrade beef franks/cold beer/clams on the half shell." I push aside a tarp blocking the entrance and go inside.

Third, I think, rubbing my hands in the wash of a space-heater roaring through the depths of this arcade bar, if somebody wants to kill me, it has to be for a reason. Something I have done, something I do, maybe even something I know.

Though half its space is shut off with another tarp, the bar area remains vast. The concrete walls, painted a flaking, deep-sea blue, are covered with colored aquatints of Coney Island sixty or seventy years ago. In the center stands a red-painted square of counters, fryolators, and steam tables; to the left, a long bar, built of cheap wood, at one corner of which two men sit with beer bottles lined up for company beside them.

"You open?" I ask the fellow behind the bar.

"For 'nother three days," the man replies. "We're gonna

be open all da way, and den dey tear da whole fuggin' place down.''

"And me wit it," his friend vows, loyally.

I order one beer, and, immediately, two more. I'm unbelievably thirsty. Behind the counter, between the Don Q. strawholders and pictures of men with lobster claws instead of hands and tattooed ladies, six boxes of computerized toys are stacked.

"Enjoy the Frog Band's realistic stage show," the boxes read. "The Frog Band performs in synchronization with your favorite music."

Everybody wants a fake reality, I think, even if it's only a musical frog band.

Myself, all I desire at this point is reality; but one where nobody wishes to slice me up, or shoot me, or come after me with black coat and limping gait.

The wind gums the condemned arcade, the sea mumbles loudly at the beach, the men mumble softly to each other.

I don't think about that unicorn at all.

FOURTEEN

I STAY AT the bar till the two geezers decide to lock up, temporarily, at 4:30 A.M.

I've been drinking cheap beer steadily but the alcohol has no effect, it just gets burned up by anxiety.

"Come back aroun' nine, ten dis mornin'," the loyalist patron calls, recognizing no doubt a fellow diehard, "we ain't leavin' till dey *trow* us out."

I leave the bar carefully, checking up and down the prairie boardwalk, but the rows of planks stretch empty in either direction.

A deuce of cop cars are sixty-nined on the planks near the aquarium. Leaving the boardwalk, I cross the beach to the soughing water.

Here, beyond stone jetties, I can make out a couple of black figures, but as soon as I show up they move away, as wary of me as I am of them.

The regular wash of waves vaguely suggests the fact that there are other beats in this world, different explanations possible, other patterns to turn to.

I have no desire to go home. One thing is certain: if someone is deliberately targeting me, then he knows where I work, where I sleep.

I trudge back across the beach and then, carefully hunching, venture into the forest of thick concrete pillars that holds up the boardwalk.

It's very dark in here. The sand has mounded against the supports, creating gentle, junk-covered dunes. I lie down gingerly, shoving away refuse. I lay my head against my folded arm and pull the leather jacket tighter around me for protection. The boardwalk lamps make thin orange lines between the planks. The sea lisps to itself in bad, rhythmic verse.

And out of the stone revetments pushing back the sea, a tall man comes striding over the dark sand. He wears a long black chesterfield and his eyes, under the rim of his stovepipe hat, have no color or light. People clap, rapidly. I am absolutely immobilized; I cannot move from my prone position.

The Fishman stands over me, hefting a long blue knife, looking for the perfect place in my body to start the slice. I strain upward, trying to make out his features, for I know who it is, I only need to see his face to remember . . . The clapping accelerates. A lot of people are glad to see Munn die.

I wake up in the blue bruise of dawn, aware with maybe thirty percent of my returning consciousness that this was a dream, while seventy percent of me shrieks *"murder!"* and curls up in a tight ball.

I'm lying beside an empty bottle of St. Ives malt liquor, a used condom, and a pair of soiled, flowered boxer shorts; souvenirs of somebody's hot night on Coney Island. A loud rattle like clapping accelerates and dwindles overhead as a cop van cruises down the boardwalk. The sand is scored like sheet music with lines drawn by the wet snow dripping from cracks between the planks.

I get stiffly to my feet. My head pounds savagely.

Before me, the feckless snow falls like neutrino tracks against the black graph paper of sea. Behind me, a disused roller coaster rises, dark with rust, over abandoned arcades and the trestle of the elevated railroad.

I walk away from the sea.

On Stillwell Avenue I buy a coffee and a hot dog with everything at Nathan's. The sun, rising behind a scrim of sullen clouds, colors everything acid.

I take the F train to TV City. It's Saturday, but I figure I'll be safer behind the wall of X-Corp security than at home. Besides, with *Real Life* only seventeen days from transmission, everybody will be working anyway.

Upstairs in my prestigious corner office, I sit at my Federal desk, not doing much of anything.

Still feeling kind of trembly, I pop three Advils and a Prodex. While the headache dwindles perceptibly, I continue to feel like I'm sauntering among black wisps of nightmare.

I log in and call up the auditions, culled clips, and overall summaries from the video unit.

I find Moos has picked all the secondary characters for season two of *Real Life*. However, instead of paying attention to the thirty-second clips of each character, I find myself thinking that in the last fifteen hours my life has accelerated its downward slide to screaming hell faster than one of those black metal cars bucketing downhill on the Coney Island roller coasters.

I mean, I seriously cannot think of anything positive that's happened to me recently.

I tick off the fingers of one hand with the index of the other.

My job has moved in on me like the sides of a garbage crusher, ready to flatten my ass with iron absence; absence of creativity, of true people, of honest situations. Absence of courage, for not resisting Gaynor when he insisted on cutting the Random Motor.

I tick off a second finger.

My relationship with Larissa is irretrievably lost.

I'm being chased by Southeast Asian psychos led by a man in a long dark coat, all of whom want to slice me up with carpet-cutters for no reason I can conceive of.

Third finger.

The sense I had when the Morgan disappeared comes back now; that the city has turned on me, has directed all its ambient violence in my direction, the anger in the subway faces, the hidden shivs and zipguns all rotating slowly like the missiles of Zeng's battleship to point exclusively at my pale and scrawny gut; only the feeling is maybe twenty times more powerful than it was when the car was ripped off, because the memory of the Morgan brings to the surface what I've known, without thinking, all along; that whoever shot up my roadster was not settling scores with a fellow felon.

Whoever sprayed the Morgan with automatic fire, more than likely, was trying to snuff out *me*.

"Shit, shit, shit," I mumble, and even that snub-nosed expletive comes out kind of wimpy and tremolo.

The only faint glimmer of good in all of this comes from the woman at that poetry reading, but in my present mood I figure I'll never see her again.

I search the phone directory anyway. The performers were billed as "Manhattan" poets, but there are no listings for Rosalita Sanchez-Glantz, Kaye Santangelo, or Emilie Anne Freedom in Manhattan. Only Derzoglu, M., and Landesmann, C., show up on the screen, with addresses on East Eighty-fourth Street and West Twelfth, respectively. Landesmann's number doesn't respond. I call M. Derzoglu, and get an answering machine with a man's voice.

I leave no message.

I need to talk to somebody. Rob is off; anyway he's still treating me curtly because of when I yelled at him two days ago.

I call Zeng, and get the Ramones howling "I wanna be sedated."

It means he's out.

I phone the detective at the Brooklyn precinct who left me a message about the Morgan. The station operator transfers me to the squadroom. A man answers, "Levine."

"I'm looking for Detective Mohammed."

"He's out. Can I help you?"

"Well—it's Alexander Munn. He left a message for me yesterday, about my car."

No response.

"Uh, it got stolen and then the guy was shot—"

"The English car?"

"Welsh."

"Whatever. Call back tomorrow, 'round four P.M."

"Sure. I—"

"Yeah?"

"Well—" I take a deep breath. "Look, I think, maybe I need to explain to you guys—"

"Yeah."

He doesn't sound in the least interested. I stumble on anyway, fear triumphing over embarrassment.

"Well, maybe it wasn't a coincidence."

"What?"

"The shooting."

"Whaddya mean?"

"I mean—" The words are backed up inside me. Maybe this is the solution; maybe I should have gone straight to the cops in Greenpoint.

I tell him, quickly, about Kearny, and go on without intermission to the men in McCarren Park; that cold, condemned horror of a swimming pool. But before I get close to the end of it he stops me.

"Wait a minute—wait a minute. You think these guys—in Jersey, in Greenpernt—they were after *you,* both times?"

"They're the same guys."

"But you said you didn't see their faces."

"Not really, but—"

"So what makes you think they're the same?" His voice is satisfied, like he just brought to its conclusion a long and complicated *Go* strategy.

"There was one guy, in a long coat—"

"Did you see his face?"

"No. But he walked—"

I can hear Levine covering the receiver with one hand. "Just a second, Rich," he calls, "I'm almost finished here." The hand comes off.

"Mr. Munn. Is there anyone else who might of seen them, or recognized them? Either in Jersey or Brooklyn?"

I think back, but I already know the answer. Levine sighs.

"Look at it from my angle," he says. "You go walkin' in the marsh in Kearny, after dark. You leave yer fancy-ass car in DUMBO, at night. You walk aroun' Nootown Creek, almost at midnight. I mean, I wonder what you're lookin' for. Know whad I mean? Frankly, if you *didn't* get chased by somebody, now *that* would be goddam surprising."

I hang up the phone, muttering darkly to myself.

I go to the Foodcar to get coffee. Kamm sits in one of the couches, whispering to Ved Chakrapani.

"Fuckin' Obregon," he says when he sees me.

"What." I'm in no mood for idle discourse with Joel Kamm, even if we both have Rosie on the brain. I fill my Shemp mug to the rim, and turn to leave.

"Fuckin' did what I tole her to do, huh?"

"Whad'ya tell her, Joel," I say, going out the door.

"Cut the balls off the Random Motor."

I stop in the doorway. The hot coffee slurps over my hand, but I barely notice.

"That was *your* idea?"

"Yup. An' it's the motherfuckin' turning point."

"An' how's that?" Licking my scalded skin.

"Between the cocksuckin' asshole crazies, who been tryin' to keep this whole thing some dickless art-school experiment. And the *serious* people, tryin' to keep this a professional production."

Kamm has his chin thrust forward, his shoulders squared back, like an ump telling off the second-base man.

Ved is staring uncomfortably out the window; three millennia of Hinduism have made him uncomfortable with direct conflict.

"Joel," I say, softly. "Did you try clearin' that with me?"

"You weren't around."

I pause, one beat.

"You're off *Real Life*," I tell him, "as of now."

I can see Ved start to smile.

Kamm's mouth drops open. Then, for an instant, a flicker of pure hatred shows in his eyes, before he turns back to Chakrapani and starts whispering again.

I feel better for at least forty seconds. Never mind the lack of elegance, it feels good to lash out at someone, even if it's the wrong target. And Kamm, for going behind my back like that, richly deserved what I just dished out to him.

But the uneasiness floods back immediately. Kamm is an ace manipulator, and there's no doubt that by making the suggestion he did, about the Random Motor, he was saying what Gaynor, if not Obregon, wanted to hear.

In a big corporation like XTV, saying what the boss wants to hear is a serious talent. Kamm will be back, I warn myself;

far from dealing with a threat, I've created for myself a dangerous new enemy.

And it's not like I'm suffering from a lack of enemies, right now.

Up in my office again I sip coffee. My fingers, void of other tasks, find the phone. They punch Larissa's number as if they'd been thinking of nothing else all day.

"Hi, this is Lara. I can't come to the phone right now, but please leave your name, and number . . ."

Maybe she's screening again.

It's a Saturday, SAG doesn't let her work weekends, so she won't be in the studio. I lean back in my chair, swivel around to watch Jersey through the soft lozenge glass.

Kamm calls me a "crazy." The cop, Levine, obviously thinks I'm twisted. Now, for the first time, I allow my mind to touch, briefly, the memory of that unicorn pasted onto the tiles of the Nassau Street G train station.

"The u-ni-corn," the girl on Bayard Street said, 150 years ago. I can hear her voice as clearly as I just heard Kamm's.

"Beware the unicorn . . ."

I shake my head disgustedly. If I'm so crazy that I'm transferring imaginary clues from *Munn's World* into the subway tunnels of the modern Apple, or vice versa, then I'm far too whacko to make sense of it in any case.

And where the unicorn is concerned, at least, the odds are heavily in favor of coincidence.

With that, I go back to the terminal and write up a long memo to Obregon, begging her, if she truly has to shallow out the Random Motor, at least to keep the cuts below the twenty percent mark, so that something is salvaged of the independence of story; so something is saved of the show's initial philosophy.

And thus the day progresses, between occasional bursts of work and long stretches of depressed, exhausted inactivity.

At four I give up.

I grab my jacket, take the number 1 train uptown to Sam Rodney's.

The Rodney School of Self-Defense occupies an L-shaped room over a shoestore between Broadway and Columbus on Seventy-second Street. Sam is conducting a class as I come in. He's short, wiry, somewhere between fifty and ninety. He always smells of old semen. He looks like a cross between an aging hawk and an anorexic woodchuck. The walls of his dojo are pasted several inches thick with clippings from the *News* and *Newsday* and the now-defunct *Post,* depicting examples of the myriad ways in which death and violence come at you from the depths of the city.

Sam has devoted his life to studying that violence, and figuring out how to counteract it. I watch him now, demonstrating to a twenty-five-year-old paralegal how to move if she's standing at the door of her apartment with her shopping in one hand and her keys in the other when an assailant grabs her from behind.

"You should drop yer shopping. Right? But in dah real world, yer instinct is, what? Yah. Hang on to it. So my technique is dis—see, his arm comes around ya, acrosst da t'roat, left to right, so he's right-handed. Yah. He's holdin' da knife in his right hand. So whaddya do? . . . No. No, no, *no.*"

He stands behind her, demonstrates.

"Swivel. To da right, inside, yah, chop wit da right hand down, acrosst his knife arm. Yah!"

Sam waltzes and glides. The "mugger" goes down, is immobilized with a wrist hold.

As always I'm struck by Sam's grace. His technique, he boasts, combines tricks he learned as a Marine shore patrol sergeant with jujitsu he picked up on station in China; but most of it evolved out of thirties-style ballroom dancing. It relies on always knowing where your balance center is. Secure in that knowledge, you use, as in aikido, the force of your opponent against him, in a circle that comes out as a lean pattern of weight and turning, Fred Astaire leading Bruce Lee in the tight footwork of a waltz.

Sam Rodney must have been one hell of a dancer. I remember, suddenly, the girl on the barge, who knew how to waltz a lot better than I did.

"Den, ya kick him on da knee. Yah. Pivot yer thigh, like dis. Or between da legs. Knee's better. If ya drop yer shopping—turn, chop in da t'roat. Yah—keep on choppin'—yah, dat's right! Chop! Chop! Yah! Yah!"

I join the class. In Sam Rodney's dojo you always wear

street clothes. Because I'm fairly advanced in his technique, he works out with me separately. I circle, step, kick at knees, chop throats, poke eyes, parry bats, twist elbows, shove and trip and rabbit-punch.

But it's the dance rhythms that are paramount; it is they, rather than the violence implied in all of this, that soothe the body in the overall flow of exercise.

"Turn, yah. Now circle, dat's right, yah."

After the class I buy the *Times,* get back on the number 1 train, unfold the paper for the long ride back to Canal Street. A bomb has gone off in front of the Chinese embassy in Washington, injuring three; Tibetan nationalists held responsible. The news doesn't hold my interest. Reading about violence is real different from having it happen to you.

It's a lonely feeling, to be a target.

I get off at Fourteenth Street and walk downtown. The walk will be good exercise.

Also, I'm examining, very theoretically, this idea—that I should make sure she really meant it when she said she never wanted to see me again.

I'm talking about Larissa, natch, and when I get to Perry Street I turn right, as I knew, all the time, I would. Walk up the steps of Larissa's town house, and without allowing myself a second's hesitation ring the doorbell.

Jesus, I think suddenly, what if Braindead's here?

I don't need the rip of anger it would cause me to find her in bed with him.

I force myself to ring again. And again, holding the buzzer down with my thumb for five seconds. The camera behind the fanlight remains still.

I get out my keys and open the various locks. I won't go in all the way. I'll just leave her a message in the lobby, proposing peace, accepting new terms of friendship based on my recent insight that we've gone past the point of cure.

Better leave her the house keys, too, since she'll realize, by this note, that I kept a set.

With the door open I hustle through the dark lobby to the alarm controls, scuffing mail or something with my shoe; you've only got thirty seconds to punch the code before the sirens start up.

And stop, finger three inches from the keyboard, because the green light is on, indicating the alarm is switched *off*.

Which is unlike Larissa, who was always obsessed with security.

Realize my leg is instinctively thrust out to fend off the inevitable assault of Pedro. But Pedro is not here. She must be walking the dog, visiting familiar hydrants, gone out so briefly she didn't bother with the alarm. She'll be back in three minutes, back even now, full of fury at my presence. I'd better get that note writ and lam outta here. I turn on the hall light.

And go completely still.

Pedro is not out for a walk.

Pedro will never walk again.

The little Yorkie lies on his side on the polished oak floor, his white fur stained a light gray around the chest. His tongue hangs slightly out of his mouth, dabbing a grayish pool that has to be blood from the wide wound in his throat.

He is the epicenter of chaos.

Every drawer in the sideboard has been yanked out and upended. Back issues of *Krokodil,* dinner candles, dog leashes, lie over the Azeri rug.

A Victorian coatrack is broken in two and her collection of Easter hats lies like the remnants of invading spaceships around the little dog; as if Pedro had succumbed valiantly fighting tiny bug-eyed monsters from a grade-Z epic.

I feel a flash of pity for Pedro that is quickly swamped by a rising tsunami of panic.

I move, finally. My legs feel heavy as cast iron. I drag them up the stairs. The nerve channels that fear uses are still warm from last night but that doesn't lessen the sheer pain of racing heart and torn lungs.

"Larissa," I gasp, and bust into the second-floor living space.

The mind adapts fast, even to entropy. Everything in the second floor has had the obvious things done to it. If it was hung up, it was pulled down. If it can break, it was smashed. The mobile lies in a tangle of colored wire on the floor. The Russian icons have been pulled from their niche, thrown and broken; gold leaf is scattered in the wake of their destruction. The Pennsylvania naifs have been crushed to matchsticks. A photograph of cold birches and mountains ripped to shreds. A

Chinese vase lies broken in the hearth, the white roses it contained dying of thirst on the nain rug.

I catch all this with eyes that are focused on my path through the destruction, for my wife is not here.

I check the kitchen, turn away, already inured to breakage. Climb the stairs to the bedroom, more slowly, thinking about how Larissa will feel when she sees this.

It's not so bad in the bedroom. They threw things around, the walls are vaguely discolored. The TV lies on its side, VCR and B-Net boxes still attached, the volume low.

The screen shows XTV's Channel-141; Larissa always watches XTV, awaiting her own image.

"When we come back," a talk show host promises, "men who sleep with their dogs, and the bitches who love them."

The sheets torn off, tangled up. The mattress is wet, a large splotch of gray puddled in the center. I try, unsuccessfully, to avoid the thought that she had sex before she went out; but there's too much liquid there, someone must have poured a pitcher of something on the mattress, in the wasteful logic of his wish to sully and make useless.

I move closer, thinking to touch the puddle, to see what it is; not touching it for fear of what it might be.

Something drops on my head. Tepid liquid dripping on my scalp and neck and onto the sodden mattress. I look up.

She is hanging facedown from the new Georgian mobile.

Her body is twisted like a great white spider in the nylon cables, and her right leg has been wound around the load-bearing wire.

Larissa's neck is stretched out and the head hangs free. Her face is very dark, almost black, her eyes wide and fixed. Her mouth frozen open in a moronic question.

And the grayish liquid dripped, dripped from her mouth onto the mattress where we used to make love; dripped from the soaked, torn shift that hangs in ribbons from one shoulder; drips still, thick and gummy and slow, out of the deep, obscene slashes—from shoulder to breast, from breast to waist, from waist to hip, with two shorter slashes just above her pubis—that have been opened in the clean white field of Larissa's body.

I take her down from there.

That's the only way to describe what I do over the next five minutes. I know she has stopped living because she doesn't breathe and her dark eyes are motionless in a way they never were in life, even asleep; but her body is all that's left and because I loved it once and, to some extent, love it still, I can't leave it there untended where it was hung by whoever did this to her.

The mobile is hung so high I can't touch it when I stand on the mattress. I haul the chest of drawers to the bed, lever it on top, and stand unsteadily on top of that but I can only reach her waist. The smell from her stomach is bad. I don't react to it.

I pile her upholstered makeup bench on top of the chest and, teetering dangerously, hanging on the mobile almost as much as she does, haul at the wire around her leg—levering at the stiff muscle like I was lopping a tree branch. I fall once, and climb right back up.

Without warning the support-wire gives and we tumble together onto the bed and halfway onto a fur rug beside it. I slam my head against the bedframe. Scramble up to look at her now, lying with the terrible wounds even bigger because she's sprawled backward, things black and unnameable visible between the severed bands of muscle. Her legs are open.

The mobile's wire is tangled around my ankles and I trip again, wind up crawling over to her, covering her legs with the rug, touching her face.

I kiss her. My lips are repelled by the relative coolness of her skin.

I guess I've been shouting all this time; I can tell from the hoarseness in my throat and the ringing in my ears. No idea what I've been yelling. My chest heaves, my stomach bubbles and expands. I get to my feet and lurch to the nearest window, wrestling the curtains free. I open the locks and raise the storm sash.

I can hear myself now, back to sobbing "God, oh, *God*" like that fruitcake on Ninety-sixth Street. The cold air, rushing in, seems to trigger the pent-up reflexes in my abdomen. I lean over the sill, ready to be sick, as if I could get rid of the past ten minutes by retching out the half-digested coffee and the Nathan's wiener that are all I've eaten today. But nothing comes.

This window opens on the Perry Street side. A taxi passes, two floors below me, honking at a delivery truck. A woman pulls a grocery cart on the opposite sidewalk. A man stands on the corner, absently watching the sky. A boy walking a golden retriever kicks dead leaves down the gutter.

I feel like I'm outside an aquarium, looking in. Everyday street life suddenly has become as exotic to me as pink eels and transparent carp.

The man is not watching the sky.

My pupils, expanding in the relative darkness, pick out more details now.

His face is half hidden in the shadows of his collar. I can see his eyes; they seem to glow, actually *glow,* a strange phosphorescent green against the shadow.

He's leaning against the corner of a building, watching the upper floors of this house, watching me watch him from Larissa's window.

He wears a homburg, and a long, dark coat that hangs almost to his ankles. A snap of electricity travels down my spine.

I push myself away from the window. At the bottom of the bedroom stairs I trip and fall into the remains of an icon and roll to my feet and keep going. I explode out the front door, down the stoop, onto the sidewalk. No idea where the oxygen comes from. A suit hauling an attaché case takes one look at me and jumps into the street to get clear.

The watcher is gone from the corner, but I expected that. I sprint in front of a Swedish car, down the opposite sidewalk, skidding the corner; and stop, half doubled up over the bitter juices roiling in my gut.

He's gone.

A glossy issue of *American Naturalist* flaps on the pavement as the wind riffles its pages.

People are visible on Washington Street but the only figures nearby are a family getting out of a double-parked van with Jersey plates, a gay couple in casual clothes looking through the window of a curio shop, and a ten-year-old boy, holding tightly on to the leash of his retriever, with eyes wide as Ping-Pong balls.

The boy is frozen in panic; watching this stranger, his face and hands streaked in secondary blood, crouching in the flat street illumination, panting like a dog-run deer as he stares up and down the cracked asphalt.

FIFTEEN

I CALL THE cops from the downstairs phone and they're here within two minutes, sirens and lights striping the small street with the loud strobes of emergency.

Over the next quarter of an hour the cruisers and rescue vans pile up until Perry Street is blocked. I can hear the stunned silence as they recognize Larissa. For all they work in Manhattan, they're not used to seeing faces from TV sliced like pastrami on cold fur.

They move in and out, young men and women with the serious, patronizing attitude of all cops in any era of history. One by one they visit the bedroom and come downstairs and as they come they move in circles that get tighter and tighter around where I stand, still hunched over the nausea.

A photographer flashes silver light in wide, fast sheets. Patrolmen string yellow crime-scene tape across the stoop. I suddenly decide I have to see Larissa once more. A cop who looks about fifteen stops me as soon as I move.

"But I'm her husband!"

"Sorry, pal."

He doesn't look sorry. He snaps two fingers nervously, and turns up the volume on his radio.

A man in plainclothes walks in, goes upstairs, comes back down.

He checks some of the basic stuff the first squad asked me. He's maybe thirty-five, thin, with a short, narrow nose, fleshy cheeks, eyes ringed like a raccoon's with discolored skin. His hands move without cease, swinging, clasping, clutching at pens, rubbing each other. His name is Polletti. He asks me a lot of questions that like the movements of the crime-scene men start out concentrating on Larissa and end up focusing more and more on me. Finally he asks me to come to the station house.

I hesitate. I don't want to stay here, but now I have the choice I don't want to leave.

"What about the dog?" I ask finally.

He looks at Pedro.

"He'll be taken care of."

Suddenly I cannot take my eyes off Pedro. For all I disliked him alive, the little terrier reminds me of when things were normal, and I don't want him left like that. I take a prayer rug and cover him with it, and while the patrolman moves to stop me, Polletti waves him away and lets me do it.

The precinct headquarters is on West Tenth Street, only three blocks away. It's a modern, two-story building faced with cement columns between which a yellow, pebbly material has been glued. Indoors, cement breeze-blocks painted gray or light blue, steel city-issue desks. A blue gate with a "STOP" sign protects the reception desk. A long glass case inexplicably displays uniforms from different police forces around the world.

Polletti takes me past a breeze-block wall into a corner filled with computer terminals and out-trays. He gets me a cup of coffee and leaves me alone.

Phones ring, faxes whir. I stare at a couple of cork boards with maps of the precinct and colored pins stuck in them. One of the boards reads "Drug arrests" and the other, "Homicides." There are no pins in Perry Street yet but I become fixated on the idea of watching when they do put one in. I'm allowing loose thoughts to stray back and forth so I can keep out of my mind what I saw in the bedroom, but that's dangerous because automatically I find myself wondering what she's doing at this hour, ordering the Thai food she loves, having dinner with Braindead, walking Pedro, and then the images wash back in and it feels like my stomach was dug out like hers. Tears rise, floating my eyes briefly in salt water.

Polletti comes back with a uniformed cop and a tall black plainclothesman who wears a brown corduroy suit and scowls kind of furiously at everybody.

The detective sits down and flips through his notepad. The patrolman sits at a terminal. The black man leans against the wall, folds his arms, and pretends to go to sleep.

"How long were you separated?"

Great, I think. The tone of this is being established from the outset; but I learned early on, when I used to get into trouble on Ninety-sixth Street, that it pays to be civil to cops.

"About—eight months, I guess."

Polletti rubs his nose, his neck, cracks a knuckle.

"I got here—you work for XTV. She was on *Pain in the Afternoon.* She was 'Kirsten,' right?"

"Yeah."

"That's XTV, right? So you saw her at work."

Nod.

"You think of anybody woulda wanted to do this to her? Any, uh, actors or somebody? Somebody she was havin' an affair with?"

"Maybe it was Hartley," the uniformed cop comments, referring to one of Kirsten's enemies on *PITA,* and cracks up at his own joke, until Polletti gives him a look that makes him concentrate on his typing.

"No," I say. A trembling seems to have started in my stomach and worked down to my knees, up to my elbows. I watch my right hand curiously; it's shaking, gently, like the tracks of the el when a train is coming.

"She was being written out, anyway."

"Whaddya mean?"

It's getting harder and harder to summon the energy needed to frame answers for Polletti.

"In the show." I shake my head. *PITA* seems so surreal compared to this hard gray cop environment. "She was Kirsten; well, Kirsten was gonna be murdered, in the soap . . . Poisoned. That's one way to get rid of 'em, when they close a contract."

And at that the memory comes, without warning, because

it's the last time I talked about it, when in the fury of hurt I told her what she already knew. Her face is present in my mind, alive, wounded. "I am auditioning next week," she said, and the memory of my cruelty, my deep desire to cause her pain; and the memory of her own huge need to be loved and respected by those whom she considered artists, which never included me; burst through whatever membrane I stretched between the shock of discovery and the first realization of loss. A paralysis climbs from the muscles in my stomach to the neck and freezes the trembling. The tears burn again at the edges of my eyes. I grunt, "Fuck!"

Polletti ignores me. The black detective, who watches me even when he's pretending to look elsewhere, rolls his eyes in exasperation.

"The M.E.'s gang said she had to have been dead between thirty-five, forty hours. Forty-two, max. That's two nights ago. You see her, two nights ago?"

I shake my head. "Not the night. I saw her, late afternoon."

"Same day?"

"I guess." I nod, take a deep breath. "I stopped by"—fighting to move the throat muscles—"the house."

"So that's—the fourteenth?"

"I guess. Yeah."

"She let you in?"

"Obviously."

"And how'd you get in tonight?"

I reach into my pocket, wordlessly hold up the three Medecos. The black cop takes them and slips them off my key ring with powerful fingers. He chews gum that smells like sugared cherries. I can hear the saliva squirting as his jaw works.

"So what were you doing, that night? The fourteenth."

"I was in Brooklyn. A coupla bars. Talkin' to cops, as a matter o' fact. Now wait a minute." I put my hands to my face and rub, hard, trying to squeeze out the sense of a loss so great that it could destroy even the motivation needed to breathe.

Three, four breaths, not so deep as to push in the stomach; then I sit up straight.

"Look." I speak fast, while I have it together to do so. "I

know what's going on here. I been seein' it for the last hour, what you're tryin' to do. I mean, I used to *write* that shit."

"Whaddya mean?"

"I was head writer for *Copkillers*."

"Oh, an *ex*-pert," the black man remarks.

"No. But I did my research. I know what you're leadin' up to. I know how you guys think."

"*Real*-ly?"

"Yeah. I mean, you know the stats. Almost half of homicides're committed by somebody who knows the victim. Boyfriend, father, stepsister, whatever. So, first thing you do, you pick up the husband. Especially a case like this, Larissa's famous, so you're gonna get a lot of pressure from Police Plaza to wrap this one up quick, make everyone look good."

"So, what you're tellin' me is," Polletti says in a completely flat voice, "you didn't do it?"

I look at him for a beat. It's amazing, the chemical speed of the body, how hot grief can convert into an anger almost as boiling.

"I was tryin' to get *back* with her."

"An' she wouldn' have you?" The black man's tone has gone all buddy-buddy. "You got angry, you had a lil fight—"

"Fuck you," I tell him softly. "I'm telling you, dickhead, I didn't *see* her that night."

"Easy," Polletti says. But you can't just stop a chemical process.

"You want me as a suspect, pal, you gotta charge me."

"We can do that," Polletti says, tapping his teeth with a ballpoint.

"I was with somebody, later that night, in Brooklyn."

"Who?"

I stare at him.

"I don't know her name," I say finally.

"Uh-*huh*," says the black cop.

"I wanna talk to a lawyer, now."

Polletti nods.

"We'd prefer to jiss talk for now."

I lean back against the hard chair. "Well, that's too bad, 'cause I ain't gonna."

He shrugs. The patrolman, who has been tapping this stuff in at the terminal, whistles a Tory Amos tune. Polletti says,

"There's a phone in the lobby," and stands beside me while I call X-Corp and punch through the menu to legal affairs, and punch through again to the emergency number. This turns out to be a night operator, who tells me the lawyer on call is Paul Woczik, pronounced "Woh-zhuk," and he'll get back to me.

I've worked with Woczik before, on a *Real Life* contract. I leave the number and address of the cop shop.

Polletti escorts me back to the desk, then disappears. The black detective has taken over from the patrolman at the terminal. He flips screens, reviewing what I said. Somebody calls to him, "Mohammed?"

"Yeah."

"Call fer you, from the Eight-four."

He slouches off, sticking big hands in hip pockets. When he comes back I say, "The Eighty-fourth—that's DUMBO, right?"

"Uh-huh."

"*You're* the guy I was s'posed to talk to 'bout my car. I talked to a guy named Levine."

"Yeah, he tole me."

"So he tole you what I said? 'Bout bein' chased?"

"Uh-huh."

I stare at him for a moment. There's little overlap between precincts in New York; they must have sent for him specially, because of me. Mohammed's eyes are very brown and hard to read.

I'm talking easier now. It's scary how fast day-to-day survival can yank out the knots of what should be enough tangled sadness to kill me.

"You know," I say carefully, "I never thought they'd try to hurt Larissa. I mean, they keep goin' after me, for some reason, but she had nothin' to do with me anymore. An' it *could* jiss be one of those sick crazies, the kind that go after famous actresses, but"—I lean forward, urgently—"*what if it was the same guys?*"

Mohammed chews steadily.

"You tole Levine it was a gang, after you. Why would gangs wanna burn you? Or your wife?"

"I don't know," I admit.

"No eyewitnesses," he continues.

"*Jesus.*" I slump in my seat. The plaster carrier pigeons

rotate slowly around the edges of my brain; Larissa's face, upside down, drips gray blood from the corners of her lips.

There's more, too, a separate horror trying to push its way past the horror I'm wrestling with now; a skein of evil coming out of the bowels of this city that has to do with the slashes in my wife's stomach and a duplicate evil embracing Gotham 150 years ago; but it's way too much for me to figure out here, and it sure as shit isn't a good idea to tell the cops at this juncture.

Mohammed doesn't look at me, talks instead to his workstation screen. "Polletti, he's a big fan of *Pain in the Afternoon*. His wife loves Kirsten."

"Really."

"What he just tole me."

"Fascinating."

Mohammed takes the gum out of his mouth, wads it under the chair, opens another stick.

The stench of sugared cherries.

"Say, you ever read *Fatal Vision*?" he asks in a party tone. "Joe McGuinness?"

"No."

"That was 'bout a Green Beret. Found his whole family— File Thirteen. Knifed an' raped an' everything. He said a bunch of drug-crazed hippies and niggers was after his wife. But it turned out, it was him killed his whole family." He shifts the new gum to the front of his mouth, then continues, "Far as I'm concerned, that story you tole, it jiss makes me think you did it."

I stare at him. My hands are closed as tight as my eyes were a moment ago.

"Ya know," I tell him, "I used to think *Copkiller* was pretty accurate. I mean, the cops on it were just average joes, not too bright, a little screwed up like anyone else. But maybe I didn't write the detectives dumb enough."

Mohammed smiles, and makes a tiny bubble of his gum.

"Keep it up, Casper," he says. "We'll see yo' white ass in Riker's yet."

I know I would like to punch this cop in the face; I also realize this would be a bad, bad idea.

And for all my arrogant writer's invective, for all Mohammed doesn't have the facile patter down like I do, his last six words stop me dead.

Because if things go badly Mohammed could get me sent to jail, he could even get me strapped to the lethal-injection table at Sing Sing, and there's nothing whatsoever I can do to him in return.

Woczik arrives. He is thin and sharp. His chin and nose are pointed, his lips are tight as can lids, the part in his hair was cut with a razor, his silk slacks are ironed to a vicious crease.

He shakes my hand perfunctorily and takes me upstairs to a tiny room where he asks me the questions Polletti did. He orders me not to open my mouth again unless he's there to say it's okay.

He takes me back down, then disappears with Polletti. Mohammed closes his eyes, slides down in his seat, tapping the armrest to a tune in his head.

Half an hour later Woczik and Polletti come back and spread papers over the junk on the desk beside me.

"Okay," Woczik tells me briefly, "compromise time. Detective Polletti is liaison with the assistant D.A., and he represents their views in this matter. They would like to charge you, because they can't think of anyone else to charge." He hones his lips with the tip of his tongue. "With this kind of case, of course, the media will be paying very close attention. I've convinced Mr. Polletti that any charges at this point would be a bad idea. Instead, you're gonna wear a bracelet."

"A what?"

"It's a small transponder device. Very light, you don't notice it after five minutes. You lock it around your ankle and they keep track of you."

"No way." I shake my head, can't seem to stop it. The idea of wearing a radio bracelet like a dog feels as if the nightmare itself will have a physical hold over me. Once locked, it will never go away. In a sense, that's the truth of the matter.

"That's the deal." Polletti shrugs. "You wear the bracelet, you sign these forms, which agree you don't leave Manhattan."

"You might as well jiss put the cuffs on," I tell him fiercely, "or lock me up!"

"That's the alternative," Woczik says calmly, "they hold you till arraignment."

"That's only twenty-four hours," I say.

"You wanna do even twenty-four hours in a New York City jail?" Woczik asks.

"No." My voice is so pathetically weak, it comes out as a whisper.

"No way."

SIXTEEN

I WALK THROUGH the doorway of my loft like Ulysses hitting Ithaca after his yachting expedition, wanting nothing more than to close the palace gates and shut out the Cyclops; but kind of like Ulysses, home suddenly isn't all it was cracked up to be.

I mean, nothing has happened here (Lenny is still out), but the track lights shine harsh on the hard varnished floor. The very sparseness of the place seems alien, as if all along, without my realizing, it had belonged to a different life-form with inconceivable needs in nutrition, hygiene, and security.

The workstation with its stack of B-Net boxes, color compensators, and fax-printers looks like the cheap special effects on which a horror pilot would be based.

I shut all the locks but it's an automatic gesture. What happened to Larissa perversely has watered down the pathetic panic simmering in my brain since being chased around that abandoned swimming pool.

I can just hear Pentti prattling on about Thanatos, and in a sense I think part of me would welcome being killed the way she was, mostly because with oblivion would come a form of absolution.

I'm neither Catholic nor Jewish, but to be purged of guilt in one swift thrust would be clean.

Fill a cup at the springwater dispenser and pop a couple of Prodex.

I sit down on the couch and close my eyes but what's immediately projected on the back of my eyelids makes me jump up and pace around. The ring of tan plastic and semiconductor locked around my ankle is light and no more annoying than an ordinary ankle bracelet would be, I reckon, but the knowledge of its presence makes it hang on the bone like a bowling ball twisted on with barbed wire.

My books are old, tattered, predictable. *The Gangs of Old New York. Front Street.* Blair on drama algorithms. *Black Current: A History of Scuba Spelunking,* by Joe Amaral.

On one shelf of the bookcase stands the Emmy I got for *Copkiller,* glinting in the passé vanity of all such awards.

All the way to the left, a tiny picture of Larissa framed in ornate Edwardian silver. She stands next to a sign that reads "Cavendish, Vt." She is smiling, because this is the village where Solzhenitsyn used to live, and birches stripe the snow all around, just like in Russia. Her eyes are filled with reflections of the sun, and her lips seem swollen in both arousal and contentment, a trick she was uniquely good at, and used to advantage.

I pick up the picture, holding it under one elbow so I don't have to see it. I walk to the bedroom and try balancing it across my eyes to block what was playing there before. Which works, for the visuals; but lying there on the soft mattress, I start to feel like there's a great black bowl of nothing opening underneath me, and my stomach, which was quiet for a while there, heaves in reaction.

I swing to a sitting position and reach for the bedside phone. I have to make an effort to push Larissa's number out of my mind. I don't want to ring Pentti, though I probably should. I punch in Zeng's number and get the Sex Pistols, as usual.

Finally, because the void is creeping closer under my ass and I'm ready for desperate measures, like calling my mother, I dial Louise.

"Give fully and ye shall get back a percentage."

"What?"

"I said—"

"Never mind," I growl, "who the fuck is this?"

"No need to use words, my brother. Can I help you?"

"You can help me by getting the owner of that house you're freeloading in, *now*!"

"Wilderness Starchild is away for the moment," he says evenly. "Wilderness, by her hospitality, is doing the work of the Lord, and Pastor Johnson."

"Then get me Sara."

"I'm sorry?"

"Willowbaby, er, Moonhugs," I hiss. My teeth are gritted so tight I can't get the syllables out straight.

"Just a minute, please."

More like three minutes later, Sara comes on the line.

"Who was that asshole?" I yell.

"That was Brother Karmabucks." She giggles. I can tell by her voice she's zoned, on speed or Percoset or whatever. "He's kinda funny."

"It's not funny," I tell her. "Sara, Larissa's—" I have to hook around for the words, fish them out of my mouth one by one. "She's dead."

"Larissa?" My sister's voice goes small and low. "Larissa's *dead*?"

"She was killed. I found her. Sara—"

"Oh, no, Alex. Alex, I don't *believe* it!" Her tone has dropped to what it used to be like before Johnsonism came into her life—neurasthenic, upset, real—and I feel myself kind of breaking up in reaction, the pent-up emotions flooding too fast for me to control.

"I don't know what to do, Sara." I'm clutching the picture of my wife so hard I could break the glass. I can hear a deep, composing breath come from my sister over the phone.

"You have to come home, Alex."

"Not right now. I jiss need to—talk, a bit."

"I know. I understand."

As abruptly as it came, the old voice is gone and the strange, floating quality she gets on speed, or Johnsonism, or both, is back. "You have to share a meal with us. You have to *give* to us, so we can give to you."

"Don't, Sara," I tell her. "Please don't give me the party line, just this once?"

"I want to *help* you, Alex," she says. "You have to let us give, too. Only God can let us give that way—"

I slam the receiver down. Jump up from the bed, pace into the hallway. The door to my study is open.

Now, maybe because I've been shaken up a bit more by Sara, I feel the pull of the study, the old city reaching for me with all the sexy attraction of escape, of a different world where I can forget the pain of this town and find a new, if temporary, life; but this evening the attraction isn't strong enough. The sadness in me would slip into *Munn's World,* contraband smuggled through the false bottom of the brain, the joy of its fugitive status forever tainted, the purity tarnished by what the real, modern city has done to my wife.

Although the tarnish, I realize—staring through the door at the map of New York in 1850, with West Street still in the river, and the city built only up to Gramercy Park on the East Side—the tarnish has already started.

Because somebody used the Fishman's slash to carve up my wife's belly.

I think my brain was cruising along on the possibility that what I saw wasn't really there, or else, it was a coincidence; but I know, without trying to review the scene in my head, that I saw it for real.

And the matching was too close—one or two parallel gashes you could explain away but five in that sequence is a plan.

The enormity of this fact thrills across my body like the touch of a snake.

"Got to tell Polletti." I'm mumbling to myself now. I lurch for the bathroom. The feeling of vacuum has twisted through my gut to put the squeeze on my intestines and something has to give. Sitting on the john, the picture of Larissa still clutched in one slightly trembly hand, I keep repeating, like a mantra, *"Gotta tell Polletti."*

Because if there's one thing that's certain, it's that the whole cloud of *buyaka,* and knives, and long-coated figures hanging around the corner, has gotten way too much for me; it has surrounded my ass like a huge thunderstorm wrapped around one little human, to the point where I can see nothing but wind and lightning.

Only someone standing outside has any hope of making sense of the whole.

When I leave the bathroom, however, I don't beeline for the phone. I keep pacing; movement, at this stage, is all that keeps my stomach settled.

And finally it's this fact that clicks into a goal for me. A very small and limited action, but one including a direction nonetheless.

The goal adds up like this: one way to get Polletti's attention diverted to the attacks against me is to convince him I didn't do the killing.

And the only way to do that is, find the name of the woman I was with the night Larissa died.

I have not thought of her for hours already, but when I do remember I find a path already trampled in that direction, toward the poetry woman, the artiste bar.

And since I'm congenitally good at taking the path of least resistance, without further ado I lay down Larissa's picture, throw on my best leather jacket, and call a cab to take me to Brooklyn.

The taxi is already over the Manhattan Bridge when I remember the bracelet on my ankle. I touch it, gingerly; it doesn't seem to be warming up or anything, no red light flashing to indicate transmission. Not that it would light up, necessarily.

"Shoulda called Polletti," I whisper stupidly, modifying the mantra; but it's done now, and anyway The Right Bank is only just across the river from Manhattan, and it would be amazing if the NYPD had equipment to pinpoint anything that accurately.

Anyway, we pull up without incident outside the bar on Kent Street. The place is jammed. People's backs are pressed against the windows and illegal smoke bursts out when I open the inner door. Of course, it's Saturday.

The realization comes as a vague surprise, so much has happened in the last twenty-four hours. I feel for a second like I've fast-forwarded through days' worth of action; I recognize this as a half-conscious reflex from *Munn's World*.

And being back in the same avant-garde fug as last night resembles a discrete part of *Munn's World* technology, like I had rewound the action to twenty-four hours ago, ready to go out and be chased through Greenpoint again. My back feels soft and vulnerable to carpet-cutters as I kedge my way, using sharp elbows and shoes, through the crowd to the back room, from where I can hear the usual overworked verse scratched out of a bad mike to the hipster throng.

> *"My cunt is*
> *the festering vagina*
> *of Poland ten times raped, oozing*
> *stinking sperm of*
> *phallus leopards*
> *trundling toward Dobreczyn."*

This auteur, a woman, has pebble glasses and a shaved head, all of which shine puce in the spots. I peer around the faces, looking for the short nose, the long neck, the doubloon-colored braids I remember like a log-on code from two nights ago. I don't see her, even when I shift around.

I do spot a gangly fellow with curly hair and beard who resembles the guy she sat with after her stint on showcase. He stands near the front of the crowd, looking serious. This batch of poetry groupies is made of sterner stuff than the other night's Michelsonians. I get snapped at, hissed, mildly rabbit-punched as I move toward the stage. Finally I reach the curly-headed guy and tap him on the shoulder.

"Could you come into the hallway?" I whisper. "It's important."

"Shhhh," a Zippy beside me says fiercely.

He follows in the path I open up. The bald woman finishes to heavy applause. The hallway is of unfinished brick with bad 3-D montages in Day-Glo.

He has prissy lips, half-closed eyes. "What's the problem?" He peers closer in the better light. "Do I know you?"

"No. But I'm looking for someone you know. She read here, uh, two nights ago, now."

"I know a bunch of people who read."

"It was a poem about, ah, crushed kittens, I guess."

"Yeah?"

"She was, kinda, booed."

"Oh. Kaye."

The bearded one has a smile I find a trifle smug.

"Kaye tries too hard. But I rather doubt you're from the poetry police."

"No," I agree. "I jiss need to talk to her. It's very important." I'm already starting to repeat myself. The smug smile remains in place.

"Why?"

I take a deep breath. I can feel the bracelet transponder shifting around my ankle. I hope it isn't showing below my jeans.

"I'm in trouble about—something that happened that night. I was with her part of the night, I need her to tell that to the cops."

"You were with her part of that night," he repeats. He keeps the smile, but his tone has dropped. His eyes roam around the room. "Good ole Kaye. What did you do?"

"With Kaye?"

"No, *that* I can imagine. What did you do, that the cops are after you?"

"Nothing."

His eyes focus back. Though still half closed, they're not asleep. "Alright, what did they say you did?"

"My wife was killed that night. Someone broke into her apartment."

"Not you?"

"No."

He rubs his beard, making sure nothing got stuck in it. "I can't give you her number," he says finally.

"Fer chrissakes!" I burst out.

"I'll get in touch with her, though. See if she wants to see you. I happen to know where to reach her." The eyes droop a little more as he turns away toward the back of the bar. I wonder if he's one of the men she fucks, in her own words, instead of stabbing.

I'd forgotten that line; forgotten how prophetically, in a totally skewed way, you could read it now.

Larissa's shift, like a soaked sponge, slow-dripping gray blobs of blood on the mattress.

The fatigue is back with reinforcements. My legs feel like they can only hold me up another thirty seconds or so. I turn impatiently, trying to get the kinks out, seeking to avoid the image of Larissa, knocking a black-dressed woman into her companion's beer.

"Asshole!" she snarls. I shove back to the bar and buy a G&T. People growl at me for snagging a drink ahead of them; their eyes and teeth glint furiously, like the coyotes you see slinking around the Taconic Parkway, eyes ghoulish-yellow in the headlights.

I hold my gin with both hands as I drink, wondering, Is the whole city tilted now, through some weird process where geology is reflected in the mind, so that what would once have come out as passion or simple argument, lacking a magnetic pole, a horizon indicator, slides off into that void I sensed earlier, a place where killing is as easy as fucking; a black hole in which lovers, and the bleeding bodies of lovers, tumble around each other like burned-out comets?

And then she's standing in front of me. I first pick up on the dark glasses, then the stance, a little off balance, off the shoulder—her long neck, the tragedy of mouth.

"Cute," I tell the bearded guy, who's pointing at me like the ghost singling out Scrooge's grave. "She was there the whole time?"

He shrugs. She says, "Oh, yeah—Don Marquis."

"Who?" asks the bearded one.

"That's his idea of a good poet—Don Marquis."

"Saints preserve us," the man replies, genuinely shocked. "I guess maybe he *did* kill his wife."

The shades hide her feelings the way they're supposed to. Her stance is not off balance, it logically pulls away from the threat I may represent.

"Maybe I better stay." Her friend puts a familiar hand on her shoulder.

"It's all right."

"You sure?"

"Don't get protective, Hugo.

"I'll be next door. If you're sure." Another hard look under the droopy eyelids and he disappears in the sea of black jerseys. She sips at a bottle of Olde Gansevoort, looking sideways. She changed her nose ring; this one is a simple silver band.

"Your name is Kaye?" I ask finally.

"Uh-huh."

"That guy—told you?"

"Hugo." She nods, looks at me now. "I'm sorry about your wife."

"You know," I tell her, "you're the first person who's said that?"

"What?"

"That you're sorry. The cops think I did it. My sister—well, she didn't think about it at all, I guess."

The light from a juke-video reflects blue in her RayxBans.

"Anyway," I continue, "it's not just an emotional thing, it's—a practical problem, for me."

"I can only tell you the truth," she says quickly. "That I saw you, from when we left here, till I dropped you off on the L train, maybe twelve-thirty, one?"

So I took the subway to Zeng's.

"You were pretty drunk," she adds, unnecessarily.

"I guess."

Silence. The mouth is straight, with only a hint of humor folded into the potential dimples on each side. I'm cut off from her, too, I think sadly, whatever we might have had vanished forever in the complexities of timing, the shriek of sirens, the convenient algebra of the police.

And right at that point, she leans over quickly and squeezes my hand, spilling G&T over the sleeve of my leather jacket.

"You were nice," she said, "about my stuff." I guess I look confused. "The poems," she explains.

"Oh. Yeah."

Silence, again. She gulps a good three inches of the beer, looks away even as she starts talking again.

"I only wanna write—let me rephrase that. I only want to get across—*that* kind of stuff."

Now my confusion is real. I stare down at my drink. I have no idea what she's on about, and I'm not sure it matters. In this sudden breakup of communication the void has surged back, growing in substance so that I can sense it, even among the babble of art talk, the Johnnie Walker wisdom all around.

"Whatever that is, in your face," she continues suddenly, still not looking at it. "You're so fuckin' torn up, if I could jiss—"

But what she "could jiss," I never learn. The outside doors slam open and a sudden, hostile silence pervades The Right

Bank, broken only by the Alsatian's barking. Looking around I see flashes reflected on the ceiling and then the helmets of uniformed cops pushing through the sea of black.

"Shit," I say, "shit, shit, *shit.*"

"What is it?"

She's too short to see over the people around us.

"Cops. I wasn't s'posed to leave Manhattan."

"You gotta bracelet?"

"Yeah." I lift my jeans leg, and then stagger as a hand grabs my shoulder and pushes me into the back wall.

"Fuckin' pigs," one of the women says.

The smell of synthetic cherry chewing gum.

"*That's* the muh'fucker." Mohammed's voice. Powerful hands slapping my legs apart, feeling the ankle transponder, checking the pockets of my jacket. I can hear hoots, catcalls, the bartender mentioning lawyers. A cop tells him to save his breath, under the new AGATE statutes they can bust in anywhere, anytime if they're looking for violent felons, and anyway with the smoking violations going on in here, the cop finishes, he better not get too uppity. Mohammed yelling, again and again, "I said, 'Shut the fuck *up!*'" And I realize the voice he's trying to quiet belongs to Kaye.

"Because if you don't have probable cause," she's saying loudly, "they could throw out the whole case, 'cause of this collar."

Mohammed's arm rests neatly against the back of my neck.

"You some kinda lawyer?"

"No. My father's deputy chief of detectives, Detective-Bureau Bronx."

"Yeah, *right.*"

"His name's Art Santangelo. Wanna call him?"

Mohammed pauses.

"He ain't *my* boss."

"Maybe not." A lighter color in her voice. "Why you pullin' him in?"

All I'm getting is audio here. The only visual I have is brick with cement pointing and a graffito that reads "Jah may wobble, but I an' I stand up."

I try to move my head but somebody lays the tip of a nightstick against my temple. Mohammed speaks into the radio. "Yeah we got him, ninety-two-Charlie this location."

Then—"He violated an agreement with the ADA. Know'm sayin'? Signed a paper, says he leaves Manhattan, he gets busted."

"You can really figger out, if I jiss cross the river?" I ask the bricks.

"It's all satellite now, man," Mohammed says. "AGATE satellite, pinpoint you to three meters, take a picture, read what butts you're smoking, if it wants."

The nightstick is pulled away without warning. I turn my head, see a couple of cops clearing a path out of the bar, Mohammed taking handcuffs off his belt; and Kaye, with her shades in one hand, hipslung, flicking her braids back. I don't know if she's trying to vamp Mohammed but it works with me; through the noise of exhaustion and the roaring in my ears and the growing sense of panic the cuffs raise in me, I think she looks fuckin' amazing.

But Mohammed pays no attention. He disappears out of my line of sight, twists my arms back—he's a lot stronger than he looks—and immediately the freezing bite of cuffs ratchets around my wrists.

He pulls me backward, marches me out, past the pale-skinned, swart-clothed drinkers parting before the dark uniforms of the Man.

After the bar heat the air outside feels doubly cold, and a wind does the boogaloo off the river in front of us. I get yanked toward the blue-and-white parked in front of The Right Bank, then, abruptly abandoned, to teeter around the sidewalk beside the first squad car.

"*You* still here?"

Kaye and Mohammed, leaning into each other in the illumination of the bar windows. The black cop looks like he's about ready to cuff her and bring her along for the party.

"Let me jiss tell you somethin'," she says, "then you can decide, you wanna bring him in or not."

"Lady, 's nothin' you got to tell me."

"I was with him that night, when he was s'posed to have killed his ole lady. That's what he came here for, was to ask me to tell the D.A."

There's something different creeping up into her voice, something I can't place; I'm not sure if it's assurance or contempt.

"If the M.E. says, the hours he was with me was when the homicide occurred—well, you know, you give dis guy cause to file wrongful arrest, or harassment—you *know* how far you goin' to go up da gold badge ladder."

It's not·attitude I hear in her voice; it's accent. The "r"'s have softened to "a"'s and "u"'s, the "th"'s to "d"'s.

The fringe-European languages of the late nineteenth-century immigrants who peopled the boroughs did not include the soft "th" sound; and in Kaye's voice I can hear her carefully cultivated Unimondo blurring, like watercolors in the rain, into a brogue that has all of the Celtic, Italian, Scandinavian, and Yiddish history of Brooklyn behind it. She must hide it carefully in The Right Bank, which despite its Brooklyn location makes money off a crowd that grew up in New Canaan and was educated in small, ivy-stifled campuses well north of the Harlem River.

Kaye stands very still. Mohammed, too, does nothing except chew his gum for a second.

". . . makes you think I was gonna bust him?"

Kaye's neck relaxes a bit. She looks down at her shades. Mohammed turns around to check if anyone else is nearby, but the other cops are holding the perimeter, and I don't count.

"Procedure is," he says, "first time, we jiss drive his ass back home."

She nods.

"You got any info, Miss Santangelo, you better come down to the station house. Six Precinct."

"Of course, Detective," she says politely.

Mohammed turns toward me.

"Whachoo lookin' at?" he says. He places a thick hand on top of my head, opens the cruiser door, and bends me into the backseat like he was closing a pair of garden shears.

The last sight I have of Kaye, she's shaking a butt from a soft pack as she reenters the warmth of the bar.

SEVENTEEN

AFTER MOHAMMED DROPS me off home I don't screw around with pajamas, just pull off my clothes and stretch out on my unmade bed.

And wake up in the dark with no time, no direction, and no sense of having slept, yet with a dream of Larissa still occupying the hard steppes in my head.

She was warm and loving, the way she was for about ten months into our marriage. No *coups de théâtre* or big decisions; we were just back together, steaming fish for dinner, talking together at the table.

Except that the knives arranged beside our poached flounder were much too long and pointed for fish knives. They had been sharpened and sharpened till you could cut through anything.

Maybe it was the sight of those knives that woke me.

I look at my watch: 4:30 in the morning. Almost four hours in bed and I must have got twenty minutes of sleep. I can feel every fiber in my muscles pleading for more R-and-R. I close my eyes; my head stays awake. Good dream thoughts of Larissa latch on to real, bad images of her upside down. I open my eyes, groaning as I strive to shove the images clear.

No more Larissa thoughts, they eat up my courage and energy. Yet trying not to think of her is like digging a huge hole in the middle of the street and pretending it's not really there; you still have to plot a course around it, or fall in.

The reflection of city lights on the ceiling. A gnawing in my stomach that's probably starvation. I've eaten very little in the last two days. The numbness from the knife thrust in *Munn's World* is swallowed by the greater hunger.

I switch on a light, get up, pee, walk around the loft. Avoiding the big hole. Find a dozen Oreos in the kitchen and eat them all. Thinking, very abstractly, about the Random Motor in *Munn's World*. Wondering if I've got it right, if the degree and frequency of its intrusions mimics at all the way random events come slamming into you out of nowhere in the "normal" world.

My eyes burn with the nervous energy that is the product of a certain stage of extreme fatigue. Sleep seems farther away than ever. Abstract thought beating the hell out of the more bathetic maunderings of my limbic system.

"See if that Random thing still goin'," I mutter confusedly, and walk to the office, yawning shallowly as I go.

Hit "MUNNWORLD\MSTR\1.3," click about eight defaults and I'm walking down the Bowery to report to the Alcazar Theater for riot detail. I'm walking normally in my room, far as I can tell. However, down the Bowery, my footsteps seem very short and tentative, like those of an old man, and I progress very slowly. Something in the logic of *Munn's World* is telling me I can't move fast. I look down, the Polhemus showing me my feet—and a bulky cummerbund of linen wrapped around my midriff, under the wool coat, with a big stain where the knife went in.

Well, no wonder I'm walking slow. I feel concern for me, for this poor bumbling roundsman walking around the snow-glazed streets with a hole in his gut. I guess it can't be that deep a wound or I wouldn't be walking at all; the Story Engine is supposed to make these decisions as, without pause, it checks the details for consistency. But the mere thought of that wound makes me feel like collapsing in a comfy chair with a hot toddy.

I look around me, pondering the matter. This section, residentially speaking, was a little bit Irish but mostly German. Virtually every building that doesn't contain a theater holds a German bar, *delikatessen,* or *biergarten.*

There's a *biergarten* just this side of the Alcazar, a small building with lots of fake arbors and outside seats among which, in the cleared snow, people drink beer and dance to a flügelhorn band. But I realize that however tired I may be, in fact or in *Munn's World,* the one thing I did not come here to do was sit and think.

The crowds are building up under the Alcazar's gas-lit columns. Giant posters announce the famed actor James P. Walsh in the role of the Pirate Captain. Smaller posters pasted on the walls around proclaim "Re-elect Capt. Isaiah Rynders to Board of Aldermen: A True American." Someone has crossed out "American" and painted in "wanker" on most of the posters.

I show my copper star and the bouncers let me in.

The Alcazar is one of the bigger houses, not as huge as the Bowery Theater but big enough. It's built of intricately painted wood supported by scrolled cast-iron columns and hung, in the better seats, with thick burgundy drapes, giving the whole gloomy space a veneer of oriental splendor.

The orchestra pit is vast and filled with wooden benches and tables. A row of boxes and two ranks of galleries with high brass rails rise into the musty heights. Tonight all of the stage and part of the orchestra are taken up by a huge wooden tank, lined with oilskin and filled with water; although the tank is hidden by the curtain you can hear, behind an oboe doing scales, a liquid sloshing. *The Song of Pirate Mollie* is a "tank drama"; there will be singing and acting, of a sort, but the real stars, as in many American productions since, will be the special effects.

The place fills up. In the boxes, men in silk toppers and capes escort ladies in crinoline and lace. Whole families are lined up in the grimy galleries. The women wear calico dresses, the men an eclectic assortment of jackets and straight pants. The cracks between families are filled by clerks, shipyard apprentices, and sailors.

As for the orchestra section, it quickly becomes a shouting tapestry of gangbangers. Daybreak Boys and True Blue Americans hold the front, Swamp Angels, Bowery Bhoys, and Dead Rabbits, the back third.

I can see, in a knot of True Blue toughs, the leader of the Nativist clique within the Hardshell splinter group in Tammany Hall. He's the man on the posters, Isaiah Rynders; he throws his chest out and waves his arms, making some incendiary point across the pit to a tall, curly-haired fellow with the thin chest, exhausted face, and smoky eyes of a minor prophet, or a consumptive. Their exchange is lost in the wild noise of the place. Everyone is shouting. To one side, protected from the crowd by a dusty rood-screen, a small orchestra warms up. Everybody is eating, as well; roast chicken and apples and fried corn washed down with beer, whiskey, and hot tea. The gang boys hurl insults at each other. Amid cheerful cries of "Heads up!" the gallery crowd spits tobacco juice and drops chicken bones on the hats below. Children cry, teenagers bellow, but no serious fights have broken out by the time the manager makes his announcement, and I can see the other coppers relax a little and turn toward the stage.

The curtain draws back. The crowd oohs. A merchant ship, maybe twenty feet long, with twenty-foot masts and cotton sails set, moves slowly, drawn by invisible ropes, from one edge of the tank to the other. The ship is beautifully made, the details of each gunport, fife rail, and lifeboat painstakingly rendered. The musicians crash into four/five time. Mollie's father, the skipper, sings in a pleasing tenor about a life on the ocean wave, hi ho, while Mollie prettily twirls a parasol on the fo'c'sle. Then a backdrop is hoisted, revealing thunderclouds and rising seas; and a second ship, this one black and sporting the Jolly Roger, floats upstage on a collision course with the merchantman. Miniature cannons boom, creating vast clouds of smoke. James P. Walsh, sporting a huge beard, cutlass, and tricorn hat, emerges from the black ship's hull—and all hell breaks loose.

Rynders's voice pulses out of the mob: "Bloody Irish wastrel, are there not enough *Americans* for our playhouses?" And at the signal two thirds of the orchestra gets to its collective feet, throwing beer bottles, corncobs, and hoarded brickbats at the stage.

Whereupon the other third, in a roar of happy anger, jumps on the Rynders mob.

Fists and cudgels rise out of the seething crowd. A dozen Swamp Angels are chased into the tank and wade out to the merchant ship. They climb aboard one side, unbalancing the vessel. The ''ship'' immediately capsizes, sending Mollie, cursing like a soldier, into the drink with her parasol. Water slops over the tank's edge, soaking the first rows. The coppers push into the fray and are easily beaten back. A cadaverous figure with a big nose and sandy hair climbs to one of the boxes and shrieks, ''Fishman!''

A crowd of his cohorts pauses beneath him. ''Fishman!'' they call in angry approbation.

''Death to the Irish scum!'' the cadaverous one screams.

''Fishman! Fishman!'' his cohorts agree, adding ''Death!'' and ''Yah!'' as they punch and flail at anyone and everyone.

I watch as long as possible. Exhausted and emotionally beaten up as I am, I still recall the weeks, not to mention the shekels, spent having actors perform standard motions against a blue-screen for the scanner.

And then someone, hanging from a gas jet, breaks off the fixture. Yellow flame billows. A woman's dress catches fire and she screams horribly. Men run for water buckets, but too late; one of the drapes hanging from the fancy boxes goes up in a sheet of flame.

The crowd immediately panics and rushes the door. I wash out with them, onto the Bowery, into the frozen slush, walking backward. Watching as the windows of the Alcazar turn dull yellow.

The various gangs carry on brawling beneath the marquee. The crowds of unemployed men hanging around the *biergarten* are drawn eagerly into the melee. A bell tolls downtown, four strokes for Section Two of the Second Fire District. Soon a horse-drawn fire engine pulls up with a wheeze of coal-actioned steam pumps and a clang of bells, but instead of passing buckets the firemen jump on one of the gangboys, who must be a particularly virulent enemy, and start pounding the crap out of him.

The *biergarten* is empty now. Couples and pacifists drift away, uptown.

A vast cloud of steam billows through the Alcazar's windows into the night. Inside the theater, the tank has finally broken, dousing the flames but not the fight.

I walk uptown with the pacifists, welcoming the relative calm and darkness, the sense of knowing where the story is headed now, somewhere peaceful and predictable.

Up from Crosby Street, where disembodied white arms curve from barred windows, and lost wails rise toward the fingernail moon from the private asylum at the intersection with Prince.

A vendor cries,

> *"My hoss is blind, he got no tail,*
> *when he's put in prison I'll go his bail;*
> *Yeddy-yo,*
> *sweet potatoes oh,*
> *fi'penny bit a half peck!"*

Past the Thieves Market on Houston and Bowery, into the grimy, unlit portions of Bleecker Street, to the "dollar" side of Broadway between Bond and Bleecker.

The saloon isn't easy to find; all that's visible at street level is a faint glow from thick glass bull's-eyes set right into the sidewalk, and a set of stairs leading downward to the cellar, under a ship's light fired by whale oil.

When I push open the door, however, the noise and light of people spill out; lampshine reflects off pewter sconces, glass decanters, the painted oak of the bar's counter and chairs.

The counter stands in the cellar proper, but most of the saloon consists of a long room running under the sidewalk, under the glass bull's-eyes. There a long, scarred table has been set up. Every seat at the table is occupied; at the head sits a plump man with a stained mustache, extravagant white hair, and a frock coat, ranting loudly and insultingly on the subject of editors to his attentive audience.

A fire burns hard at the far end of the sidewalk room, beside a barrel-vaulted antechamber.

The clientele is ninety percent male, and varied. A few are dressed well, in silk cravats and beaver-pelt coats and fine riding boots. A number of capes are hung on the coatracks. One man wears a Chesterfield but he is rotund and short, very different from the guy I followed from the docks. A lot of men wear cheaper clothes, wool pants, black boots, jackets of canvas or cotton. The few women, dressed too well to be whores, nevertheless drink and smoke the way no lady should. This is unusual, but a New Yorker would understand it after only a few minutes of listening to the conversation eddying with the pipe smoke up and down the bar's long counter. For this is a place, not unlike The Right Bank, where people who imagine they are writers or artists or thinkers come to drink with people they think are like them.

People of that sort enjoy flouting convention, as long as it doesn't cost too much.

I make my way slowly toward the warmth of the fire.

"Nothing Tennyson has done is modern in the least. Everything he does was done better, and earlier, by Byron."

"He showed me the best little shop on Canal Street, sells French pigments made from alchemical compounds . . ."

The bartender is a large, bearded fellow with a high-pitched laugh. It's hard to stand without being jostled. The only place to sit is in the barrel-vaulted niche, on a stone bench.

"Horace Greeley," the white-maned man announces, "is a self-made man who worships his creator!"

I squeeze in beside the niche's sole occupant, a thin figure, dressed entirely in black: long black frock coat, black straight trousers, black boots, black cravat. A long wedge of ebony hair obscures the top part of his face and a jet-black shawl hides the lower portion. He rests his chin on the table as his eyes, with a superb show of ambivalence, contemplate the tall glass of clear spirit in front of him.

The man's skin is white as fresh Vermont snow. His eyes are bloodshot, his occasional coughs cause his head to jump a clear quarter inch off the tabletop.

"Where Claribel low-lieth, the breezes pause and dip," a poet at the long table hoots, "only R. H. Stoddard could love a line like that."

"That book went to fifteen printers," one of the group at the fire says. "The last one said, not only would he furnish me with an advance upon publication, but he would buy a notice in the *Knickerbocker*. And what came of his fine promises?" He tosses a half glass of brandy into the flame and the liquid flashes blue, causing the blackness to flee, for one instant, the dark sockets of the man I sit beside.

"Hot air, quick flame," the dark man mutters. His voice is a little blurred by the muffler. His fingers move; they are very long. "These men are, at best, theater dramatists of the most vulgar sort."

"I just saw what the theater can do" (Vox locking nicely onto "theater").

"He was right about Stoddard, though."

"Another riot," I insist. "Like the Astor. An *Irish* actor." Still cueing the Vox.

The man turns his head toward me. His eyes, though in shadow, seem very bright.

"Then it will have been the Daybreak Boys, bought with Hunker gold; the True Blues. Against them, the Dead Rabbits, the Bowerys? Tell me I'm right!"

"Yes."

"Rynders. A barking dog of a man. The Angel Gabriel, a shrieking harpy. And Flynn, with the face of a martyr . . ."

"All three were there," I confirm, though I hate the Dr. Watson trap of Vox dialogue, the "Good gracious, Holmes, how on earth did you know that?" aspect of it. The man in black lifts his elbows to the table, and adjusts the muffler. I catch a glimpse of a long nose, a thin mustache, feminine lips.

"Flynn may be a saint, at that," my companion mutters. "He truly believes the lowest orders of man—the Irish, the slaves—must be accorded rights due the highest. He sits on the Forty Thieves, and when he gets up to speak you'd say he'd been given his tongue by the divinity.

"And yet"—the man grasps his glass with both hands now, lowers the muffler just enough to drink, and sips it delicately—"he owns a saloon and bagnio, he allies himself with a gang of Hibernian murderers, and does all the buying and whoring and fighting that it takes to get his vote."

I need a drink. Obviously I can't truly drink or eat in the story but the desire is there.

I buy a hot toddy at the bar, just for the hell of it. I get a free dish of Pfannenküchen and roast oysters and I watch the savory steam waft off the sweetmeats.

The Flexator suit the VR lab is working on—so says the scuttlebutt—will provide you with smell as well as the sense of touch. They suspend you in an isolation tank, so you feel nothing but what is fed to you through the wires and hoses. I could smell these oysters, through such a system.

"Now Captain Rynders takes this murderer as his own," my companion whispers suddenly, "who cuts these miserable wretches like they were mackerel."

"Fishman?"

"The Fishman," my companion agrees, and leans forward, over the elbows, so that he rises a little over our table, gazing down at his glass as if it were all the audience that mattered.

"It grows," he whispers. "They speak his name in the open." The whisper rises, too. "It is like a force of darkness, as if something lived, in the deep liquid bowels of the city, a great black monster that, conjured by the right combination of elixirs, of foul poisons—" His muffler has slipped, he's turning toward me, dark eyes capturing light, his voice tending toward a shout. "Unspeakable ichors, a distillation of a closely timed darkness—crawling ghastly out of its underground sluices and canals to suffuse the very soul of man!"

His words have fashioned silence in the sidewalk room and in that pool of lesser noise a tall man with a huge, grizzled beard strides over, squats on the other side of him, and, taking both my companion's hands in his own, holds them tight as if to warm them.

"Dupin," he hisses urgently, "Dupin!"

"What."

My companion slumps back against the brick wall of the antechamber.

"You must stop this behavior," the grizzled man whispers. Glancing at me fiercely, he lowers his voice to continue. "You will be recognized."

"I need a drink, Walt."

"No, you don't. What you need is a walk in the good air."

He helps the thin man to his feet, rearranging the muffler. The thin man stands there, swaying slightly while his friend drapes a black cloak around his shoulders, takes him by the arm, and starts to drag him away.

"Wait," the thin man says. He turns around to look at me. Against the all-encompassing black of his togs, those black eyes still manage to shine with a peculiar illumination.

"Remember," he says, and points a long finger in my

direction. ''The city is a city of darkness. It's *light* that is a visitor here.

''It's light, that is a temporary grace.''

''Dupin—''

''Remember!''

The bearded man tugs at his arm and they are swallowed by the crowd at the bar, leaving me staring at the steam rising from this drink I cannot touch, shimmering in front of me like the echo of the thin man's words.

It's light that is a temporary grace.

EIGHTEEN

In the morning I decide to go to work.

I can't think of anything else to do. Maybe I should go to Larissa's and sort through her possessions and papers but I'm not sure what kind of status a separated husband is accorded at the best of times. One that is a suspect in her death will most likely be blocked from hanging around the crime scene at all.

I call Woczik's office. He's not in yet. The terminal blinks —four voicemails, seven e-mail—and I don't check any of them.

In any case, no way I can go back to Larissa's without losing it emotionally once more.

I don't think about it directly but always in the back of my head this thing exists, like the slimy creature the dark man in *Munn's World* described, sitting there in the absence of light, making everything cold and clammy around. The corpse of a concept with only a sheet to cover it, a parenthetical horror (Larissa's death).

I ride the number 1 train to Fifty-first Street. People pile in and pile out, read the *Times* and the *News,* shift, cough, complain, avoiding each other's eyes. They seem, in the normal cast of their preoccupation, quite different from me, an alien tribe, hostile if you don't know their codes and rites. My skin itches under the hard plastic seized around my ankle. Though I suppose this morning could have been worse; I could have woken up in a detention cell on West Tenth Street.

Kaye Santangelo. Her face is distant in my mind, like a cameo, too perfect and miniature to touch. The idea of Larissa, on the other hand, is accessible, if I were to let myself slide in that direction.

She hated the subway. The crowds lining up at token booths, the crowds pushing to get in the steel cars, reminded her of growing up. Even the families of Missile Command officers had to queue for bread and vegetables and soap. I can feel a lump hardening at the back of my throat.

The train is held at Fourteenth Street. The loudspeaker shrieks of "police activity" at Penn Station. I can tell by the way my body cringes at the noise that my fatigue is intense, despite the sleep I got after *Munn's World*.

At Twenty-third a man opens the *News* next to me. I glimpse a publicity shot of Larissa spread across six columns on page three or five. By the time I finally get to work I'm forty minutes late, and that fact seems as supremely irrelevant as the taste of dust on Pluto.

I can feel people's eyes as I wait for the twenty–thirty bank of elevators. They watch me like New Yorkers, flicking their gaze away when I look back. Lance Martin, who held one of the character roles on *Copkiller* and is doing a made-for-cable movie for Vivian Moos, comes up and takes my right hand in both of his, reminding me, in a weird spacey way, of the grizzled man comforting the black-clad poet in Pfaff's Saloon.

"Alex," Lance says, looking me, actorlike, in the eyes. "*Al*-ex."

"You heard?" I mumble, confusedly, feeling my face heat up because now everybody is staring at us, even the ones who don't know who I am.

Martin's eyes are welling with easy tears.

"She was a perfect lady," he says in a full, rich tone. "Like a butterfly, a monarch. So delicate. I know you loved her."

Thank the gods the elevator dings at that point. We ride up

in the silence of tightly restrained farts. I get out at twenty-three, walk down the hall, and see Rob, his back toward me, piling cardboard boxes on his desk.

I stand behind him for a second, wondering abstractedly what he's doing. Reflecting that maybe I shouldn't have come in after all because I'm going to have to talk to people, explain what's happened, what I need to do.

"Rob?" I say, finally.

He spins around as if I'd pinched his ass.

"Alex!" His eyes are wide. "Hi—I—uh."

I move toward the door to my office.

"Alex?" Rob repeats in a strained voice.

The first thing I see is the top part of my Federal desk taken off its base and swaddled in bubble wrap.

The next items I register are the stacks and stacks of files and video clips, the product of six years of work for XTV, arranged in lines on the floor; and Rosie Obregon, seated on a chair in the middle, counting off the files one by one while an assistant calls up reference numbers on a terminal.

I stand there with my mouth open. I know exactly what has happened, but there's a lag between knowledge and acceptance.

Rose looks up. Her features harden for a second, automatically preparing for her role in all of this. Then she shakes her head, the lines relaxing a bit, and gets slowly to her feet.

"I'm sorry," she says.

"I don't believe this," I whisper.

"I don't know what to say."

I look at her.

"You know Larissa—I mean, that she died?"

"Yes. I'm sorry—"

"Please don't say that again."

Her face lines freeze once more. The assistant has stopped typing in commands and is watching us with frank fascination, taking it all in for a screenplay she's writing in her spare time. I can feel Rob standing in the doorway.

"So, I'm being fired?"

"It was not my doing. Gaynor—"

"Say it. Just say it!"

"Yes." She reaches for her key chain, jingles it in one hand. "You're being let go, Alex. I tried to stop him."

"Gaynor."

"I don't think it's justified."

I look around me.

"But you're the one who's cleaning out my desk. You couldn't even wait, to do that?"

She puts her chain back in its pocket.

"I didn't have the choice."

"Just following orders, *Herr Kommissar*?"

"Alex—"

"You think I *care*?" I yell at her suddenly. "After what's happened, you really think I give a *fuck*?"

She looks away, out the lozenge window. New Jersey is still there, lying disinterested as a prostitute under the thick humping body of smog.

I storm out of the room and over to the elevators. Secretaries lean over desks, faces gape out of doors to each side of the corridor to follow me as I pass. Waiting for the lift I realize I never asked her why I was getting the bum's rush, but the coincidence in disasters is too obvious to ignore. I mean, if an avalanche crushes your house and shortly afterward, hunched under the dining-room table, you find the telephone doesn't work, it's not too farfetched to assume the two events are connected.

At the thirty-fifth floor the first perimeter of guards lets me through, based simply on the color of my ID card.

In the cold circle of magazines and coffee tables protecting Gaynor's sanctum, the P.A. gabs with a bunch of suntanned fellows in monkey-jackets and silk cravats. He moves aside to stop me as I dodge around the desk but I'm walking very fast. Before he can get close I have thrown open the walnut door and started my long march across Gaynor's acreage.

From a distance I can see Gaynor seated behind his desk, yakking with a suited figure in the less-important-person's armchair to one side. Another man sits in the VIP chair before him. The P.A. bursts in behind me, yelling.

"He just barged through, Mr. Gaynor! D'you want me to call security?"

Gaynor has good eyesight; he already has me pegged. The figure to one side turns his chair to watch. With a start of surprise I make out the brush-cut hair and mamba eyes of Joel Kamm, my former producer for *Real Life*.

Gaynor lifts one hand, a Hapsburg gesture, to reassure the P.A.

Finally, after a hard trek, I reach Gaynor's desk and put my hands on its shiny top.

You can judge a man's power, sometimes, by how much crap is cluttering up his desk. I've seen the president's workspace on the news and it's always totally empty, because everybody else keeps his files. Gaynor's desk is like that; the only objects marring the perfect expanse are his silver pocketknife, a line of yellow pencils, and a B-Net terminal on the left side. Because the terminal is angled in my direction I can see the screen, which shows page three of today's on-line edition of the *Daily News* with the six-column spread of my wife's face across it.

"What the *fuck* you think you're doing?" I ask hoarsely.

Gaynor looks at Kamm without expression. The man in the important seat is Chinese. He doesn't react either.

"You *fired* me," I remind him. "I want to know why!"

"You don't have to shout, Elex."

I stare at him.

"I don't have to do anything, asshole," I say, more quietly. "I mean"—I wave at the *News*—"you saw what happened to my wife. After that"—the stupid knot in my throat, which never quite went away after the train ride, tightens again—"I can't *begin* to tell you how little your dumb job means." I clear my throat. "I jiss don't give a shit! But I have the right to know why."

"I can let you go anytime," Gaynor replies softly, "it says so in your contract."

"You have to have grounds," I tell him, "I could sue your ass."

"But I *have* grounds." Gaynor stares at me intently.

"What?"

"Artistic differences."

"*What* artistic differences?"

"Just yesterday," he says, glancing at Kamm. "The Random Motor?"

Kamm is looking at me with a canary-fed kitty look to his mouth. I feel like kicking his teeth in. Gaynor shrugs his shoulders for the benefit of the Chinese guy. The Asian nods in embarrassment. He holds a folder marked with the tiger logo of Kowloon and Singapore Bankcorp. Gaynor twists his terminal all the way around and taps the View Options key twice, so that the article on Larissa is broken out and blown up, her eyes shining ocean blue under a fifty-six-point head that reads "SOAP QUEEN BRUTALLY SLAIN IN VILLAGE PAD."

"They buried the lead," Gaynor drawls. "Read the fifth graf." Watching my face now.

Sources at Police Plaza told the *News* that Love's estranged husband, Alexander Mund, was extensively questioned after the slaying. The sources said police wanted to hold Mund for further questioning last night. After talking with Mund's lawyer, however, they agreed to hold off while they gathered further information.

The same sources also stated that a neighbor of Love's told police she allegedly witnessed Mund and Love violently fighting in her elegant Perry Street town house the late afternoon before the killing. Mund, 33, an Emmy award-winning TV writer, is the Director of Special Projects at XTV, which produces *Pain in the Afternoon*.

"You know how much money we put into promotion for *Real Life*?" Gaynor asks softly.

"Who cares?"

Joel Kamm starts to get up. I put my hand on his forehead and push him back into the chair.

"Jesus," Kamm gasps nervously, "he's *crazy*!"

"Over six million," Gaynor says, ignoring Kamm. "Do you know what you've *caused*, Elex?"

"A lot of free publicity, Ivan."

"But the wrong kind." Gaynor relaxes in his seat. His big hands touch each other elegantly, like tame fencers. "Sixteen days before *Real Life* comes out, and the show's producer gets accused of killing his wife. D'you have any *idea* what the Jesus Caucus could do with that?"

"The Christian Republicans like XTV," I tell him, "our violence is clean, it doesn't target financial services."

"Lara Love wasn't a financial service."

"But I'm not *accused* of anything!" I counter, and despite

my best efforts a little whine creeps into my voice. "The cops'll figure it out, I didn't have anything to do with it!"

"Doesn't matter." Now Gaynor points to the P.A., who nods importantly and treks out of the office. "People don't think; they smell—they feel. The other networks'll link your name to the killing, play it up, because they're shit-scared of what *Real Life*'s about to do to their prime-time Nielsens—" He sighs. "Please leave, Elex. I have things to do. We have to scrub the episodes you wrote, and I need to talk to Joel about that."

I look at Kamm with a modicum more interest.

"I s'pose he gets my job?"

Kamm smiles. But then the rest of Gaynor's words sink in. I turn back to the big desk. "Wait," I say sharply. "You're gonna *scrub my episodes*?"

Gaynor lifts his eyebrows.

"But why?" I'm genuinely perplexed now. "What's the point of that?"

"You clean out a cowshed," Gaynor says, "you might as well get rid of the bullshit."

I stare at him.

"You'll get a nice severance," Gaynor reassures me, "long as you don't sue, of course."

"You don't give a fuck, do you," I tell him evenly. "One of your actresses has just been killed—my *wife* has just been killed—and all that bothers you is the spin the CRs might put on the show."

A distant thudding. I glance behind me, where three large X-Corp security guards are trotting across the carpets.

"Good-bye, Elex," Gaynor says.

I lean over his desk, thrusting my face close to his. He doesn't flinch; his eyes remain calm and cold. I am wrong about the clam-opener; his gaze is much sharper and more precise than that. Next to his knee, a wastebasket is filled to the brim with yellow number two pencils, or what once were pencils until he carved them into thin slivers of wood with the penknife.

One of the X-Corp guards touches my elbow and I jerk away violently. They grab my arms and haul me across the miles of Isfahan. I let myself go, there's nothing else worth doing, no dignity left worth fighting for, while the rug polishes the toes of my gaucho boots and aerial vistas of Pennsylvania, New Jersey, and Connecticut slide by the long, lozenge-shaped windows on either side.

It's weird to walk the streets in the middle of the day when you're used to working inside.

It's strange to follow the north-south avenues of Manhattan when the main poles of your life have been brutally amputated in the space of a New York night.

The sun beats down with no power, turning everything a morgue color. A cool wind picks up trash, tangoes it around your head, drops it dead at your feet.

I don't have the physical energy to walk far. I don't have the psychological jizz to zone out with walking till the traumas boil, letting off pressure as I pound the pavement.

I want to move fast, arrive somewhere different, leave immediately. The trouble is, I can't for the life of me think of a destination.

I board the number 1 train and get off at Canal Street because that's the stop for the loft and home is where you go when you can't think where else to end up.

Halfway down Varick I find myself slowing, reluctant to proceed. It seems uniquely false to go home, as if nothing had happened, as if my life was as unchanged as the furniture and other patterns of my apartment.

Even *Munn's World,* in the dead light of this milquetoast noon, seems to me a mistake; a pretentious, expensive piece of escapism as obvious and unproductive as the blackout that comes from gin.

I continue down Varick and West Broadway. The wind blows more strongly as I approach the tip of the island. At the junction of West Broadway and Thomas I spot a bar on the right where I used to go before I met Larissa. I walk in, blowing on hands gone red and cold with the walk.

McGovern's Bar is, basically, brown, with a few green-shaded lights on the walls, sawdust on the floor, and framed photos of racehorses over the bar. Cheap tan wainscoting, black Naugahyde booths, a varnished clock. A line of middle-aged men sit folded over their guts at the counter, watching college football on a big Sony perched atop an old-fashioned wooden phone booth at the end. They glance at me as I order a beer. Then their eyes are pulled back, as if by wires, to the screen.

The bartender is the same guy who was always there. As he serves me draft Guinness I get a strong flash to the nights, before I met Larissa, time spent hanging out in this joint and others with the marginal playwrights and the waitress-actresses, all dressed in black. And a terrible sense of remembered loneliness soars over me with big wings like a Boeing. The goddam lump swells my throat and I have to order another Guinness, quickly, to keep the windpipe open.

I'm halfway through the second Guinness when the men at the bar start to glance at me, and whisper, staring back at the TV and then back at me again.

The whispering wakes me out of my task, which was checking the tan froth of the Guinness for aeration. I stare back at the barflies, and slowly the newscaster's words filter through the haze of my thoughts.

". . . they are looking to pick him up for further questioning. The couple was married four years ago, and separated earlier this year. Entertainment experts have characterized their relationship as stormy."

I look up at the newscast. It's old *ET* footage from three years ago, Larissa's first season on *PITA;* she and I coming out of a party at the Hostage Grill. She has on violet lipstick and her professional smile, and looks as crisply lovely as she always did on such occasions. I'm dressed in a waistcoat painted with scenes from the Sistine Chapel. I wear a fatuous, possessive grin and my hair is longer, but the chin and freckles stand out and the old soaks at the bar have no trouble at all making the connection.

"A sordid end to a fairytale romance," the anchorwoman says. "And now we have a *feel-good* story."

"Good," her partner interjects.

"About the Keanu Reeves Home for Sonoran Orphans!"

I look at my drinking companions. They stare back, mouths slack, as if I'd suddenly grown into a hippopotamus and danced the cancan. This does nothing to improve my growing sense of utter separation.

"So, you gotta problem?" I ask the nearest brown man.

It doesn't faze him; he continues staring. I noticed this

with Larissa; most people—unless they're suffering from TeleDysFunction—know that TV-Land isn't real, but it's still the place they prefer, the planet on which they choose to spend their time. Thus when someone from TV-Land shows up in their home, or bar, the hypothesis instinctively crops up, If this actor is a real person, maybe TV-Land actually *exists;* and they stare at you with the possessive fascination of Lubavitchers spotting a candidate for Messiah.

I wonder what the first part of the newscast said. My heart, all of a sudden, is jamming heavy metal. I drop a ten on the counter, get up and split, and nobody says a word except for the anchorwoman, still prattling on about Keanu Reeves.

I walk down the block. The wind blows me northward, up Greenwich Street, toward my loft. My heart still rocks with amplified pump-and-thrust.

I could go into the Tribeca Grill, where I know they have no TV.

I keep hearing the words of the anchorwoman: "They are looking to pick him up for further questioning."

I could stay in the Tribeca Grill all day, drinking on plastic, watching the wind roll empty crack vials down Greenwich.

If I sat there all day, however, I'd inevitably have to think.

If I think, I'll remember. There are times when it's better to let yourself get swept up by events, even if the events are, possibly, bad; because when you sit around and wait for them they affect you anyway, if only by anticipation.

I stay on course for home. When I turn the corner at Hubert I immediately spot the little group of men and women huddled beside vans marked MTV, FOX-5, and XTV double-parked outside my door.

I stop in my tracks. The theory is all very well, but now the reality of pursuit is clear, I'm not sure I have the gumption to face it head-on, not immediately anyway, maybe I'll go back and have another couple of Guinnesses—

And then the option is gone. A firm hand grips my elbow. I recognize the movement, the hackneyed shove toward the wall, before I smell the cherry gum or hear Mohammed's pissed-off voice snarling "Spread yer legs, *spread 'em*" as he clicks the cuffs home.

Polletti in the background running fast through the Mi-

NINETEEN

NEW YORK COPS carry nine-millimeter Berettas. They usually keep pump-action twelve-gauge "Streetsweepers" handy; the new AGATE squads are equipped with Dragon antitank rockets and light armored cars; but over the next few hours I figure out that the heaviest weapon at the cops' disposal is reiteration, and the power to inflict boredom.

Polletti and Mohammed take me back to the Sixth. A fat black lady rolls my fingers on an infrared scanner.

They seat me in the same chair as before. This time they cuff me to an armrest. They switch on a tape recorder and line up another flatfoot to take computer notes. Polletti runs through the Miranda again, just to make sure. He sits very close, the way he did last time.

"Thought we'd give ya a break, first."

I just look at him. He stares back pleasantly.

"Let ya change yer statement," he explains.

"Just being nice," Mohammed offers sarcastically.

"Let me see," I tell Mohammed. My voice, too, is gooey with irony. "You guys work out a routine already? Polletti starts out real scientific. *You* act kinda slow. I'm scared of

Polletti, so I don't see the trick questions you pop. Come *on*, don't you guys ever get sick of the clichés?''

''He's right,'' Polletti says unexpectedly. ''Whyn't you go git some coffee, or sump'in?''

The black cop gets to his feet. His face shows no expression.

''*You* know you did it,'' Polletti continues when Mohammed has split. ''*I* know you did it. Your fingerprints are all over the bathroom.''

''How'd you get my prints?''

''From your coffee cup, last time you were here.''

''Another cliché.''

''Worked, though.''

''I wanna talk to Woczik.''

Polletti sits nearer still. His hands are laced together like two lovers, and like lovers they wrestle, pull at each other, trying all the different joints and angles.

''Yer pals at XTV tole us all about it. The historical cop, the serial killer in Olde New York.'' He pronounces it ''oldee''; his voice is as sarcastic as mine was a second ago. ''Tell me—was it just, you wannut to be like him?''

I stare at him. Until now the accumulation of bad events has determined my attitude, a relentless fatalism powered by the flood of what's been happening.

But this is a real surprise; it knocks me out of that gray acceptance for an instant.

''You know about—my show?''

''*Munn's World.*'' Polletti's face is ten inches from mine. His pupils are small under the neon, his striped shirt neatly ironed. He wears a dark blue tie and his breath is sick with onion. I have to force myself not to pull away.

''So what? I'm a writer. You gonna bust every TV writer who writes about killers? I mean, what's the idea—'cause I wrote about it, I did it?''

''There's worse theories,'' Polletti says.

''You won't have any writers left, buddy, they'll all be in jail.''

''You know what I'm talkin' about,'' Polletti says, and now one of his hands moves to my shoulder and squeezes. ''You tell me about it now, I can promise you murder two. Maybe even manslaughter.''

"You jiss wanna bust someone, 'cause of the publicity," I tell him.

"Nah," Polletti says, still rubbing my shoulder affectionately. "It's my wife. She *loves* Kirsten."

"I know," I tell him, trying to keep my voice from cracking. "I wanna talk to Woczik."

"He wants to talk to his lawyer," Polletti tells the patrolman in an indulgent tone. He gets to his feet, automatically adjusting the shoulder holster. "Let him call, then let's get this asshole downtown."

They let me use the desk phone. The secretary tells me Woczik is in a meeting.

I leave a message, saying I want to hire the lawyer on a private client basis. The secretary, who obviously knows what I'm supposed to have done, seems kind of awed to be speaking with me. She promises to beep him.

As soon as I hang up Polletti cuffs me again. Mohammed shows up and they walk me out of the reception area. I notice the cork board marked "Homicides" now has a bright red pin stuck into Perry Street between Greenwich and Washington.

Out the glass doors, past a staring sergeant, into a day whiter than day should be because of the flashpacks. At least six Digicams are lining the sidewalk behind a squad of cops. I recognize Mike Taibi, XTV's senior reporter, gesticulating frantically in his trench coat.

"Alex," he yells, "over here! Make a statement."

I shake my head. I'm not going to pull my face down under my jacket collar the way "drug kingpins" do in similar situations. The newscasters yell and elbow each other, like a pack of hyenas in pancake makeup, all excited by the mediatic equivalent of blood. I can understand the impulse to duck.

Polletti, for once, is on my side. He elbows a pushy Fox reporter as I crawl into the unmarked car. Mohammed gets behind the wheel and fries rubber.

"You coulda taken me out the back," I tell Polletti. "I s'pose this is good for yer career?"

No response. They go straight to West Street and turn south. At West and Leroy a constellation of flashing lights holds up traffic. Mohammed switches on his siren and dodges around firemen diverting cars from one of the old warehouses. As we pass I see the windows gushing solid columns of smoke and a dark crab-claw of flame underneath; and I'm reminded of the fire in the Alcazar Theater, in *Munn's World,* and the avidity with which that flame seemed to consume the entire building.

We get to the Tombs ten minutes later.

Mohammed hangs with the car. Polletti and I join a line of cops, prisoners, and secretaries at a row of metal detectors at the north entrance. Most of the people here, prisoners as well as guards, are black or Hispanic. A tray to one side holds an ice pick, two vials of crack, and a carpet-cutter. I strain around to see who got caught with the carpet-cutter but it could be anybody. Polletti talks to the man at the desk and shepherds me to a cargo elevator. A very thin black man is hopping on one foot in the corner. "Part A-one-twenty-one," Polletti tells the lift man, flipping the badge from his pocket.

We ride in the usual silence. The elevator man says, "One-twenty-one," and opens the door onto another door of blue-painted wire mesh. Polletti pushes me toward the mesh, announcing my name.

The door opens. Polletti gets back in the elevator.

Guards herd me and the black fellow down a narrow corridor lined on one side with more mesh. I realize this mesh covers cells filled with men. The place is bright with grunts, muffled talk, the slap of Nikes on concrete. The fourth door down stands open, and we're directed inside. The door is slammed shut.

I don't know how many times I wrote this kind of stuff for *Copkiller.* I even visited a tank once, in the old Midtown North precinct house. I know this is for holding only, to wait for arraignment. But let me tell you that an intellectual and artistic appreciation of slamming doors, steel mesh, and guards is a nano-speck of input compared to what it actually feels like to have the door slammed on *you.*

"Only a tank," I repeat to myself.

The cell is lined with fold-down steel racks for benches. A sallow white fellow is stretched out on one bench. Two kids in their late teens, an East Indian and a black, sit on the other. The man I came in with walks straight up to the boys.

"You got a radio?" he asks. "Pocket TV? Gotta watch the game, gotta watch the game."

The kids stare at him sullenly. The sallow guy opposite sits up and says, "Fock, another tee-dee."

"Don't got TDF." The thin black man flexes his knees, once, three times, ten times. "Need to watch it. The game. Don't got TDF!"

"Which game?" the sallow man asks.

"Celtics, man."

"Celtics 'n who?"

"Celtics 'n Clippers."

"Clippers not playin' today," the sallow man remarks.

I stand with my back against the mesh. The black kid looks at me with vague recognition; he's probably been watching the news. The tee-dee checks me out, and his gaze focuses on my left leg.

He smiles.

"Transponder," he breathes.

I say nothing.

"Can I see it?"

"Ignore him," the sallow man suggests. The tee-dee stares at my ankle, singing softly. His fingers curl and uncurl obsessively.

A half hour passes. The Indian and the young black man are called together. Then the TDF fellow, after that the sallow man. I am left alone, but I still don't sit down. Sitting feels like the first hint of accepting my presence here. I won't accept it. Someone in the next cell sings, repetitively, the same line: "Ooh, ooh, ah'm on fire."

Finally a guard unlocks the door and walks me down the corridor to a wooden gate into the hearing area.

The room is a wash of light and noise. It feels good to be out of the metal cell, good to see people moving and talking but my main impression is one of lost control; people waiting hours for something they're not sure about, and when that something comes, it happens so fast they have no way of choosing the direction.

Maybe that's the definition of going to court.

Anyway I sit at the end of a long wooden bench to one side, separated from the main room by high metal railings. All my cellmates are lined up beside me like cuffed starlings. A pretty, blondish woman in a yellow business dress sits at a tall desk at the head of the room, her face close to a microphone. Men in suits walk around and whisper to each other. A tall, thin male attorney with silver glasses and tan hair walks over to the blond woman, followed by a pair of assistants. He whispers and lifts his chin in my direction, brushing lint off his Kenzo duds. She looks at me, makes a note.

Another suit fetches the sallow man and they all whisper together. "Docket number five-oh-seven-oh, *cinco, zero, siete, zero,*" the blonde says. "*Pueblo de Nueva York contra Juan Luis Echevaria; tres accusaciones de poseción de contrabando,* organic microchips—how d'you say that in Spanish? Microchips is okay." She writes something down. "Remanded into custody, clerk will schedule a hearing." Pause. "People of New York versus Alexander Munn."

There's a stir in the room. A knot of men and women, dressed too oddly to be cops, pile through the door, no doubt alerted by one of their own. They lift tape recorders and notebooks. A woman flicks pastel crayons at a pad.

A guard leads me to a seat in the second row. Mohammed is seated in front of me. Polletti whispers to the blonde, who bends to the mike and says, "Mr. Munn, do you have counsel present?"

"No, I—"

"Do you wish to be represented by counsel?"

"Yes, I—"

"Where is your counsel?"

"I left a message with him."

"Is that Mr. Wo—I can't pronounce this. Woke-zick?"

"Woczik," I say with relief. "Yes."

She reads through a piece of paper, obviously a fax.

"Well, he doesn't want to represent you. He says, conflict of interest." She looks up at me. The neon shines off her bifocals.

"But—"

"Do you wish to have counsel appointed for you?"

"I want my own lawyer," I say, in a soft voice because the strength has suddenly leaked out of my chest.

"This is merely an arraignment, Mr. Munn. You can represent yourself. Or if you choose to accept a court-appointed lawyer, we can move you out of here in five minutes."

I don't even have to think. Just the sense that the holding tank is nearby chooses the words for me. I agree to a court-appointed lawyer, as long as I can change attorneys later, if I want. The blond judge whispers with Polletti, then calls another case. The tan-haired lawyer walks around, making media gestures with a gold pen. Polletti sits down beside Mohammed.

"Need a Seagram's after this," Mohammed comments.

"You shouldn't drink," Polletti tells him. "Saw that last night, you drink like a black."

"I *am* a black."

"That's what I'm sayin'."

Mohammed turns to stare at his partner. Polletti ignores him. Very slowly, Mohammed removes the chewing gum from his mouth.

After five minutes or so a man who is the opposite of the tan-haired lawyer bustles into the room, struggling to open a briefcase. He is short, plump; he has hair tonsured like a Franciscan, and a Robert Hall suit. He sucks on a pencil held in his teeth.

He shakes hands with the judge, loses some papers, picks them off the floor, and sits beside me. "My name is Stamas," he says, "I'm a public defender." He asks me a couple of questions, the same details Polletti wanted about the timing of my breakup with Larissa. He sucks at the pencil and frowns.

"This will be tough," he says. "Ravitch—that's the judge —she wants to run for ombudsman next year, an' she's big on the domestic violence angle. An' Coltrane"—he gestures at the tan-haired lawyer—"that's the ADA—he wants to be President."

I don't laugh.

"Or somethin'. Anyway, this is too high profile, they're gonna try to prove somethin' with you."

"What does that mean," I say, "whaddya tellin' me?"

"I'll do the best I can," Stamas promises. Relaxing beside me, he jams the briefcase shut, closes his eyes, and appears to go to sleep.

The judge has gone on to the TDF case from my cell. He's accused of stabbing a bodega owner, stealing 320 dollars, two televisions, a security camera, resisting arrest. Bail is set at ten thousand bucks cash, which he doesn't have. He disappears back through the door of the holding cells. The judge looks at Stamas. I poke him in the ribs.

"Mr. Stamas," the judge barks.

"Oh." He jerks, stands upright. "Sorry. Uh—Your Honor, this is not the forum for discussing the facts of this case—"

"I agree with that a hundred percent."

"—but I have to make this point regarding bail. First of all, the record; this man has no prior convictions on any felony. None at all."

"I have here, shoplifting, resisting arrest."

"Those were all juvenile, Yer Honor."

"Oh. Right."

"Second, Mr., ah, Munn is a very well-known, well-paid screenwriter. He has been on police watch for twenty-four hours with a radio device, and has not tried to escape. Third"—Stamas is warming to his work; his little flabby stomach jerks back and forth with each gesture—"third, even if he is guilty in this crime, which he in no way admits, still this would be a typical *crime passionnel,* a one-off act of an individual temporarily pushed beyond the limits of control, and the hypothetical perpetrator of such a crime would pose no menace to society at large."

"How does he intend to plead?"

Stamas looks at me. I stare at the judge.

"Not guilty," I croak. My throat is bare of saliva.

The tan-haired man flicks a finger at Polletti, who stands up.

As the cop rises, I notice a bolus of gray chewing gum stuck exactly on the back seam of his jacket.

"Yer Honor, the defendant was on electronic watch only four hours when he broke the agreement, he went to Brooklyn, where he was apprehended."

"But that's not true," I mutter, and stand up. "Your Honor, I did that, but—"

"Be quiet," the judge says.

"But I was only—"

"Be *quiet* or I'll have you removed!" She beckons to the ADA and Stamas. They stand and whisper.

I can see Stamas's belly wobbling faster as he talks quicker. I can hear in the back of my mind the little blue bird calling. "You need a drink," it warbles, "a nice cool dry abs'ini, maybe a G&T, take you away from all of this''; but there's no bar here and none accessible until this is all over.

Stamas sits down beside me. His face has gone quite shiny and he doesn't look me in the eye. The judge glances down at her papers and says, ''The crime in question is disgusting. The circumstances, ah, indicate a ferocity, a lack of moral compunction that is unusual, even with all the daily bloodshed we see in this court.''

Even the blue bird shuts up.

''Ah, also, the suspect is a good bet, from prosecution's point of view. He had motive and opportunity. He previously violated the trust of the police. His income level makes him liable to meet any bail that accords with state and city guidelines. Therefore, suspect is remanded, to be detained without bail in Riker's Island until a pretrial hearing.''

She turns and fires instructions at the court secretary. She seems to move rather slowly, and her words come out deliberately, like smoke rings, from her lipsticked mouth. I'm still standing up.

The fingers of my right hand twitch, wanting to tap at whatever keyboard controls this game. My mind insists loudly that this is fiction. Something as ludicrous as Riker's simply cannot happen to a well-paid middle-class professional like me. I mean, that's what it was for—the money, the education —so you would *not* end up like all the rest, on a downhill blade of risk that, like the Bey's torture machine in *The Vikings,* acquires sharpness as you pick up speed.

''Rewind,'' my mind mumbles urgently, ''hit *default,* punch the bail-out macros!'' But there are no keyboards and this is not a game any longer.

And suddenly, to the same extent that everything seemed to slow down, it all speeds up again.

The guards take me by the elbows and shepherd me to a holding cell, where I wait for twenty minutes while the cell fills up.

Then, with a dozen other detainees, we are shuffled into the cargo elevator and taken to a garage in the basement. A yellow school bus with wire mesh screwed over the windows and ''NYDOC'' stenciled on the side is parked between two concrete columns.

Behind a metal louver a machine works rhythmically, *suck-*

gush, suck-gush. I stare at it in passionless recognition. This building stands right in the middle of what used to be the biggest freshwater lake in Manhattan, the Collect Pond; and what this pump is doing, it's sucking the water that continues to collect here, to keep it from flooding the courthouse.

We're led to the bus in pairs and shackled to a long chain that runs down the central aisle. The diesel roars.

I stare straight ahead as we move into daylight. The tee-dee keeps twisting and exclaiming in the next seat as he glimpses televisions in shop windows and bars.

Up the FDR Drive, over the Triboro. The same part of my brain carries on shrieking "rewind," but there's no way to go back, no way to undo what's been done. And time proceeds in the same direction and at roughly the same pace as the bus crosses the bridge, under signs warning that this is a secure zone open only to those with business here; to the perimeter of razor-ribbon, chainlink, and glassed-in control points that marks the entrance to Riker's Island.

TWENTY

LET ME TELL you about Riker's.

It's a 415-acre island shaped like a crouching bullfrog stuck off the north shore of the borough of Queens between Hell Gate and La Guardia Airport. It's connected to the mainland by the one long bridge. It has over fifteen thousand inmates, eighty-two hundred guards, a power plant, a tank farm, maternity hospital, AIDS hospital, mental institution, TDF clinic, law library, warehouse, water tower, fire station; also *ten* large prisons, allocated to men, adolescents, women, and those suffering from the various communicable diseases.

Ninety-two percent of the inmates are black or Hispanic, ninety percent of them never finished high school. Twenty-five percent of the female inmates are HIV-positive. The majority of the inmates have not been convicted, but are awaiting trial or sentencing. Fifty-two percent of the guards are black. The number of high school graduates among the guards is not known.

Even if you're aware of these facts—which of course nobody is, since the whole point of prison, society-wise, is to conceal and forget—you cannot prepare yourself for the impact of going to a place like Riker's the first time.

What happens is, you get stopped at bridge control. Big tinted windows glare down at the bus. Armed men in high walkways pace back and forth overhead. After the '96 riots the city got a federal grant to revamp the place so a lot of the hardware is gleaming and new. A guard checks the papers. The tall chainlink gates around you are encircled with shining razor-ribbon. That's one thing you'll always remember: the razor-ribbon. The whole island is laced with it. Every corner and perimeter of each structure and yard is amply festooned with the bright, lethal stuff. I want to know who got the razor-ribbon contract for Riker's; he must be one rich hombre.

A big gate trundles open, and shuts automatically behind us. Now you can see the buildings, of all different shapes and sizes. One reaches fifteen stories into the sky. It looks like a city that has grown up with intention but no plan, which is a pretty good description of how it happened. A system of two- or three-lane blacktops branches around brown lawns.

The bus stops beside a concrete building near bridge control. With a squad of guards looking on, we are unshackled from the chain and marched up a set of stairs to a wide, low-ceilinged room equipped with refectory tables, metal detectors, and thousands of gray lockers in tight rows.

We're told to drop all of our personal belongings on the tables. My credit and ID cards and Ray Bans are placed in a Tupperware-style box. A guard takes my leather jacket, belt, and gaucho boots and stashes those in a locker. Our cash is exchanged for scrip, pieces of official paper with the amount stamped on the face. In my case, because I usually rely on plastic, I receive just over thirty dollars' worth.

Then, one by one, we file through a metal detector, and get double-checked with a handheld unit. It's just like an airport.

What happens next is like no airport I've ever been to.

The guard says, "Drop your pants." I look at him, unwilling to understand. Two corrections officers stand ready to back him up. I drop my pants. "All of 'em," he says, "an' bend over." He doesn't smile at the corny line.

So, reluctantly, I pull down my underpants and lean over a table. "I can't believe this," I mumble to myself, "can't *believe* this!" One of the guards has on rubber gloves and a face mask. He squirts something on his right hand, pulls one cheek clear and, not gently, sticks a finger up my ass.

This is the point where the curtain of shock lifts; where I stop thinking in third-person abstractions. I yell in angry surprise.

"Nothin'," the guard says, stripping his glove off and throwing it into a pail.

"What th' fuck did ya expect?" I mumble at him. "Richard Gere?"

He ignores me.

The white flash of photo cubicles. We are given a bag with cheap gym shoes, white T-shirts and underwear, nylon sheets. Plastic bracelets with bar codes are snapped around our wrists. We're told to take a seat at the far end. When I sit down, my asshole hurts, and I feel sick. Nothing of the rush and humiliation of court and cops made me feel so helpless, so thoroughly invaded, as that rectal exam.

A man in civilian clothes tells us we're not yet convicted of any crime and won't be made to work. The bracelets serve as ID, and if we stick the laser bar code in the slot provided in public telephones, we'll get six minutes of free local phone time per day. Because of budget shortages, he says, no space is available in the regular dorms; we'll be sleeping and taking breakfast in something called an "MCHF." Daytime activities will be in a center known as "Bantum."

"Finally," he states, looking at us seriously, "Riker's is not a joke. Most of you are here because you did something wrong. This is a place full of dangerous people like yourselves. If you need help, the guards are here to protect you from one another."

Somebody behind me snickers, "Yeah, right."

We are shepherded back to the bus. No chain this time. The sun got scarfed by night since we came here but all of Riker's is lit with racks of white and orange lights on the various buildings and on poles where the buildings aren't. The bus rumbles down a highway between tall, razor-ribboned fences. Five- and six-story concrete complexes rise on both sides. Most of those have six to ten wings; each of the wings is as big as a whole apartment block in Manhattan. Every hundred yards or so we stop at a checkpoint. There are no humans at the checkpoints, only video cameras and speakerphones.

Every man on the bus is silent. The tee-dee stares at his laser bracelet, touches it reverently. Behind the chainlink and razor-ribbon fences I catch a glimpse of somber water, the bright multicolored shine of da Bronx.

Most of the buildings, as I said, are complexes with a bunch of different wings but the one our bus pulls up beside is monolithic and squat like a giant aircraft hangar.

The bus driver says, "This is gate C5. You report back here at seven P.M.; that's an hour an' a half. You a minute late, you get left behind in Bantum." He sniffs. "Believe me, you don' wanna do that."

Inside the Otis Bantum Correctional Facility guards funnel us into a central breezeway that intersects with a series of wide hallways. The hallways all end on steel-barred vertical gates that right now are slid in the open position. Against the cold metal, groups of men hang out, edging closer to watch as we walk toward the main recreation area. "Jiss down C corridor," the driver said, but it seems like a long way as the men crowd thicker in our path.

"Fresh fish," someone shouts, "come 'n git it."

"Look at dat one," another inmate yells, pointing at the Indian boy. "Ain't he cute, I be gettin' down wit him."

The Indian is walking beside his black pal. Then, abruptly, the black boy stops. *"Jacky,"* he calls desperately, and breaks from our group, running over to one of the many knots of blacks lining our route.

The Indian stops in turn, looking after his buddy, but the knot of men has taken in the black boy and he doesn't look back.

The Indian is visibly shaking. I realize, in surprise, that my own hands are trembling.

"Come on," I tell him through clamped teeth.

As we pass each corridor you can hear men laughing and arguing in the distance; so many men that it sounds like ambient noise, the breath of a huge, syncretic monster, a human slime mold in T-shirts and gym shoes.

Finally we reach the end of C corridor. The tee-dee is happy; he goes straight to one of the televisions hanging on high brackets around the vast rec room, and stands under the screen.

I sit at a table with the Indian boy, trying to get my bearings, ignoring the groups of men who walk by and make comments. When my hands have stopped shaking quite so

visibly I make for a bank of public phones against the far wall.
Before I get to within twenty feet of the phones a couple of
Hispanics block my way.

"Jiss makin' a phone call," I say.

"No, you ain't," one of them, a guy with round, pock-
marked cheeks and a bead necklace, replies.

"Why not?"

" 'Cause I said so, *maricon*."

I try walking around him. He moves sideways to block me.
I turn around to another bank of phones at the near end of B
corridor and before I can get near that one I am loosely surrounded by a group of blacks.

"What the fuck is goin' on here?" I ask, more of myself
than anyone.

"He's a fish," one of the black men says.

"*You* find out," another one agrees.

"But I got a bracelet," I say. "That implies I can use it."

"*Kiss* my ass."

The eyes of these people are different; they don't seek
communication, they don't give it out. The lingo is all body;
hips blocking, arms thrust out. This is a stance Sam Rodney
says is silly—it's all challenge and no balance, relative to the
source of potential attack—but it doesn't seem too smart to
get into a fight here.

A bell rings. The men start drifting, still in their schools
and groups, toward the refectory. I have absolutely zero appetite, but I would dearly love something to drink. Not absinthe,
for once; the blue singing bird of absinthe is a delicate creature built of casual free hours and I know it would be killed by
the deadly electricity of this place. I fetch the Indian boy and
we stand in line at steel steam tables that seem a mile long.
The men behind push and rib us when we hesitate. The Indian
gets a plate of vegetables. I choose a Salisbury steak with
spinach and a tall soda water.

The food is overcooked and hard to eat with the blunt
plastic utensils. I down the spinach and two bites of steak and
get refills on the soda. Coming back from my second refill I
am followed by two black men who sit down on either side of
us.

"You fellas need friends," one of them says. He has yellowish eyes and a big smile that reveals cracked teeth. "That's how it works, on the Rock."

"What's the Rock?" I ask.

"Riker's, man," the other guy answers. "You hep us, we'll hep you."

The Indian stares at his plate. I say, "How can you help us?"

"She-it." Yellow-eyes shakes his head.

"Cover your ass," the other one explains. "This a bitch-up place."

"Come on with us," Yellow-eyes says, "you wanna try some freaky jisi."

"Got it in our house."

"Rip off a piece of that white ass!" a man down the table calls, without even turning around.

"Mmm, *mm*!" someone else agrees.

"Shut the fuck up!" Yellow-eyes complains angrily.

"No thanks," I say, "some other time." I can feel my hands shaking harder than they were earlier.

"You better be sure," the other guy says, then stops.

Three other inmates have walked up quietly behind the Indian boy. I look up; they're all small, dark, obviously subcontinental. Two of them carry small black tattoos on their wrists.

I recognize the tattoos from research I did on *Copkiller*. Tiny green snakes, the symbol of the Memons' gang, in Bombay. It amazes me to see them in the flesh—as if *Copkiller*, catalyzed by this environment, had become as real as I tried to make it on TV.

The Indians say something quick and incomprehensible to the boy. He jumps up like he was injected with an ounce of synthetic adrenaline. Inside twenty seconds they've all disappeared in the greater mill of men. Yellow-eyes looks back at me.

A deuce of men, both black, crowd up behind him.

A half-dozen Tadzhiks squat in a circle nearby. Under their round Arm of Allah hats they watch us with intensity.

"Too bad," Yellow-eyes whispers, "no white gangs around."

"Hey, Kaymal," a man calls, "know who that is? That's the guy was married to Kirsten."

"That's the guy cap Kirsten?"

"Rip off the muh-fuck."

"Yeah, I *loved* that bitch."

Just sitting here over this bad food I have trouble breathing. My heart thuds at the same rate as it did in Greenpoint. With hindsight the danger I was in there seems so much lighter. Danger is always cool in a place where you can run.

"Bettah come with us, boy."

"You can't make me," I tell them, childishly, looking around for a guard.

"Bulls don' care."

Yellow-eyes leans close.

"You come wit us, fish, or you get *cut,* here 'n now."

I don't know why I respond the way I do. I'm not thinking by deduction and addition but in a wash of panic and straw-grabbing.

One of the straws is a quote I heard once, I think it was G. Gordon Liddy, a man jailed for a political crime many years ago; I don't even remember the exact words but what he said, in essence, was that the only way to survive in jail was to come off so crazy that nobody had any idea how you would react.

" 'Got his head into a pitcher of cream,' " I begin, desperately, quoting the only poem I know by heart, " 'and couldn't get it out,' um, 'he come up once before he drowned toujours gai, kid, he gurgled and then sank forever that was always his words—' "

"What da fuck," Yellow-eyes says. "Asshole."

"He jiss actin' crazy, Kaymal," another one says. "Everybody tries it once."

"I'll show him *crazy,*" Kaymal promises.

And then they all turn away from me and spread out, into the refectory. For a second I think, What the hell, it worked. And then I hear it, too.

It's more like a feeling, actually; like the electricity of the place, all the high tension of despair, arc lights, radio salsa, loneliness, and razor-ribbon, is swelling in a vast surge of lethal current. Two thousand voices hushed, two thousand voices tense and whispering, four thousand feet stirring very slightly. A bell starts clanging, loud.

A man screams. Another one shrieks, "Fuck you *up,*

moth'fuckah!'' The crowd draws tight around one of the telephones. A guard yells into his radio in the center of a twist of inmates. Metal flashes. A gate rumbles shut.

One of the protagonists bares his teeth like a leopard.

The crowd shifts at the refectory's north end. A wedge of guards thickened with riot helmets, bulletproof vests, and truncheons bursts into the room. The truncheons rise and fall, and the bass rhythm line of the crowd gets deeper and stronger.

Then, for no detectable reason, it stops.

I check my watch: 6:40. Twenty minutes to the time my bus leaves for the MCHF, whatever the hell that is, but it can't be worse than Bantum.

I exit unnoticed from the refectory. A line of guards blocks the gate to C corridor but when I explain where I'm going they let me through. My heart still rattles like a snare drum. I can't help thinking that if I spend more than a couple of days in here, the only way I'll come out is psychotic, or horizontal.

The bus stops under a rusted gantry. A plywood ramp leads to a tunnel of brightly lit razor-ribbon and aluminum sloping through the chainlink perimeter into night. I glimpse a dark spangle of water on each side. As we enter the tunnel a familiar shape looms through the sharp metal topiary. Carved bow and stern hidden under the flat sandwich of car and passenger decks; dark excrescence of pilothouse, radars still attached; lit portholes, heavily barred.

It's a Staten Island ferryboat, one of the older, orange models, the ones with names like "SGT. WILBUR T. TRAVECCHIO" after forgotten Stakhanovs of the fire or sanitation departments. The tunnel leads into a midships doorway that, in turn, opens onto a neon-crazed control area, with two passageways splitting off to the left and right. A guard station, replete with video screens, lies at the confluence. A lieutenant checks his list against our faces.

"You, Chavez," he says, "F-8. Sasi Mehta"—to the Indian boy, who looks more sullen now than scared—"A-2, with the other kid. Oakes—" But Oakes, the TDF victim, is stepping slowly toward the guard booth, staring at the massed screens. "Oakes!"

"He's tee-dee," one of our busload says.

"Whyn't he in the clinic?"

The lieutenant, hissing impatiently, makes a note on his pad. "Munn," he says. He looks at me and frowns. "Oh, *you*'re the celebrity. I'm putting you with Trelawney, in F-11."

"Cosmo gonna like *that,*" a guard comments sarcastically.

The guards peel us off one by one. I walk down one of the left-hand corridors. It's lined with doors painted blue, covered with mesh except for a narrow slot like a mailbox. The mesh is so tight all I can make out is a bare lightbulb, bunks, and dark shapes moving inside. Radios and boom boxes play soukous, shifta rap, salsa. Techno-reggae pulses from the door marked "11."

"Out, Rastaman," the guard calls, "we gonna do a switch here."

A loud shout of protest comes from inside the mesh. The guard unlocks the door and swings it wide. A black man in a green, black, and yellow snood is standing in the doorway.

"No, no, mahn. Me cannot *'andle* dees."

"Sorry, Cosmo."

The man is lean; clothes hang off him like sheets on a line. One of his eyes is bloodshot and a rough, mamba-shaped scar runs down his right arm. He has the kind of West Indian accent that turns all vowels into major chords.

" 'Oo's goin'? Me or Derek?"

"Derek."

"No, mahn." Cosmo shakes his head. "Why you *do*-in' this?"

The guard stares at him without affect.

"Lieutenant says, mebbe it'll slow down yer business, Cosmo."

"*What* business, mahn? What business? Me in *jee*-il!"

Cosmo is practically hopping in frustration. He keeps hopping while the cell's other occupant, a black man as squat as Cosmo is lean, silently gathers up his affairs and leaves. I have to push past Cosmo to get in. The door slams heavily behind me.

As soon as the guard is gone, Cosmo sits on his bunk and begins picking his teeth, muttering "Rasclout" repeatedly.

I look around. The cell is all steel: walls, floors, ceiling.

The bunks, one on each side, are of steel with welded supports. Against the bulkhead away from the door stands a stainless-steel toilet, with a sink built into the unit where the cistern would be on a normal crapper.

I put down my bag and sit on the bunk. There's nothing else to do, nowhere else to do it. The walls are hung with magazine pictures of Eek a Mouse, Nelson Mandela, and Halle Berry. A diskette marked "Dale Carnegie's Business Course" lies under Cosmo's bunk. Cockroaches streak across the deck, then pause in the shadows as they figure out how I fit into their cabin.

"Want some 'ash," Cosmo says, not looking at me.

I stare at him.

"Or moon-juice? Good stuff, lil cahbon-tetra, lil grapefruit. What de mattah, mahn, cat got you tongue?"

I shake my head.

"Shit," Cosmo mutters, "a fockin' ding, dem put me wit."

A sound comes from my right, from the inside of the cell. It sounds like voices, men's voices, but very faint; spirits trying to pierce the barrier between their world and ours.

I shift my gaze to the floor. Part of me felt interested when Cosmo mentioned juice and hash. In Riker's or outside, it's the same impulse, to let some slack into day-to-day tension, to turn a little inside that knot of worry.

At the same time, part of me feels sick. I'm beginning to realize it was the urge to booze that got me into this mess in the first place.

I mean, at least, it was the moronic need to get shit-faced that made me amble around Brooklyn instead of hanging out with Lenny at the time Larissa was getting hurt.

Now I'm going to have to jump through hoops to prove I didn't do it.

Apart from the cockroaches and a few ants now pursuing their bug routines, the steel deck is bare, its paint scratched with the stamps and tension of the men who've been locked up in here. If I put my mind to it I could see patterns in the thin paint—like the careful crosshatching of the unicorn in the G train stop—like the diagonal gashes in the belly of my wife.

I don't put my mind to it.

I lie back on the bunk, using my gear sack as a pillow. I close my eyes, to keep down the hot pressure of the darkness.

And as I push against the pressure inside me, it all comes together from the other direction; the miles of razor-ribbon, the hundreds of steel gates, the tons of concrete, the weight implicit in the twelve thousand men I'm locked in with.

And the push from outside meets the pressure coming from within, and they match each other; because there's a deep blackness there, knowing something in me is so dark and powerful that it could carve away whatever happened that night, and leave my brain in blackout.

"No, no, *no*," I mutter at the steel deckhead.

"Shut de fock op," says Cosmo.

TWENTY-ONE

I SLEEP OKAY. I wake up once in the middle of the night but some deep-seated survival reflex won't let me think about where I am or anything else.

I can hear voices inside the cell again, though neither I nor Cosmo is talking. I don't think about that either. When I drift back to sleep the same survival reflex shuts down dream formation, or at least locks it away from the areas that register.

When I wake the second time I jump bolt upright and almost take my head off against the welded bracket that supports the bunk. A bell is clanging right outside. I have to block my ears to dull the noise.

Through slitted eyes I make out the bright overhead light in its cage of mesh; the crack between two plates where a welder got lazy making room for electric fixtures; and Cosmo, sitting neatly on the edge of his bunk, stashing folded envelope corners in the pouch of his Y-fronts.

I stare at him. It's not that I don't know where I am; rather, sleep allowed my awareness of Riker's to evaporate, mostly, and it would be perilous in the extreme to let it all back in too quick.

"What the hell's that?" I ask finally.

"Breakfast bell." Cosmo finishes stashing his bags and puts his sweats on.

"What time is it?"

"Five A.M."

"Five *A.M.*?"

"Yah, mahn." He almost smiles. "You can wee-ait fuh second breakfast, like most de lee-azy bahstahd 'round heah. But deess one bettah—more quiet."

He tucks his dreadlocks delicately into the snood and stands up.

I get dressed quickly. The bell stops. The only thought I'm aware of is, I don't want to be alone this morning.

The refectory area lies on the deck below the main security area; a half-dozen Formica tables, a counter laid with coffee urns, paper cups and plates, doughnuts and cereal. A total of nine men from the ferry's complement of 124 has shown for first breakfast. Cosmo sits at the end of a corner table with his squat former cellmate. They huddle, whispering, turned away from the rest of the room. My social graces, to the extent they ever existed, kind of vanished when I passed into the country of razor-ribbon and I sit down right next to Cosmo as if we were old school chums.

He glares and hisses furiously at me through an aerosol of doughnut crumbs.

I don't give a shit. The canteen deck is warm. The TV plays the *Ollie North Show,* in which the former Marine officer turned impresario grills two Texan hermaphrodites living with transsexual parents. A radio plays 1010-WINS, telling us of an accident on the inbound Gowanus. The Hudson River crossings are all moving smoothly; normal people going to work early, all-night guards and wire-editors heading home. The coffee is acid but hot, and in the cold before dawn heat is most important. Through the barred porthole a tugboat butts a barge against the dark tide, its port light winking gray.

"Is it okay to stay on the ferry?" I ask Cosmo.

He twists around, grumpily.

"Yah. You can stee-ay here. Course you can't do nothin'."

"There phones here?"

Cosmo takes out a cigarette. "No Smoking" signs are pasted everywhere but the guard by the counter doesn't even look up from his *News*. The squat fellow glances at Cosmo for permission, then shakes his head.

"So I gotta go to Bantum?"

Nod.

"I tried to use the phones yesterday," I continue, "some guys said I couldn't."

Cosmo looks at me as if a cockroach had started singing "Many Rivers to Cross."

"Mahn, you don't know *nuttin'*."

"Got to pee-ay," the squat one agrees.

"But I thought"—I hold up my wrist—"the laser bracelet, you get free calls?"

Cosmo smiles. The smoke wisps between his brown teeth as he replies.

"Don' mattah, mahn. Got to pee-ay. You don'—or you try to go through a screw—dem lump you up *bahd*." Taking another drag, looking at me more closely. "You know, you white."

I wait. This doesn't seem like one of those existential insights that only incarceration, and the camaraderie of ruthless criminals, can reveal.

"You not very beeg, you not very ugly. An' you young."

"Him fee-amous, Cosmo," the squat one says. "Kill Kirsten, on *Pee-ain*."

"Trut'?"

"Trut'."

I sip my coffee. Cosmo still gazes at me kind of hard.

"You spend more dan tree, four days in heah, you mebbe get killed. You defin'ly get you ras messed up."

"I'm sorry?"

"You bunsah, you keister—you *ahss*-hole, mahn. Dem guys got no women, what you tink? Love Kirsten, too. So what you need"—he takes his cigarette, snubs it deftly on a paper plate, and drops the stub in his shirt pocket—"what you need is a bodygahd."

"Okay." I gulp the coffee in my mouth, it's nicely cooled. "I'll buy that. I need a bodyguard."

"What I'm see-ayin'," Cosmo continues, rolling his eyes a little. "You pee-ay me, I fin' a bodyguard for you. Dat wee-ay, you got a good chance o' walkin' outta here without HIV."

I take another swallow of coffee. I don't really have to

think about it. Quite apart from the violence of the place, I never disconnected from the jolt of bad energy I could sense running all through Bantum yesterday, that spiked like shorting wires during the fight. The truth of what he says, like a long sum worked through a computer over coffee break, has already established itself in my brain.

"Okay," I say finally, "but all I got is thirty bucks."

"Too bad," Cosmo says and, turning back to the squat one, starts running through a list of prices for jisi-yomo.

I leave the MCHF on the first bus out.

Part of me wants to stay there, in the relative warmth and safety of the converted ferryboat.

But I figure I have to get to a phone and at least hire a lawyer before I find a protected corner to go to ground in, like a mouse in a city of cats.

I count four crews mowing dead lawns on the way to Bantum. Inside, the building feels and sounds exactly the way it did yesterday evening. Here the lights scream white twenty-four hours a day, 365 days a year, and the jamboxes play shifta rap and preach Industrial Islam for all eternity and the men don't change in anything but names and numbers. I figure, even when they leave Riker's, their smell and desperation lingers on, in some gray karmic pall that taints the walls even over the massed graffiti.

The Indians are waiting for Sasi Mehta. The rest of us run what Cosmo refers to as the breezeway. Cosmo and the squat one are part of this load, but they stay away from me, and when we get to the rec area, lope off to their own pursuits and deals. I make for the phones and when I'm blocked by the two men—different guys from yesterday, but with the same warm and engaging attitude toward new acquaintances—I blurt out, "Look, I'll pay."

"Fuckin' right, fish," one of them says.

"Learn fast," the other one agrees. I wonder how they know I'm a fish.

"Sawbuck," the first one adds.

"Give you a freebie," the second one offers, "you come up to my house later?"

I hand over the scrip. They check the date carefully, point

to the nearest coinbox. I find a slot, not unlike a credit card port, to the side of the keypad. A plaque of instructions tells me, in English, Spanish, Cantonese, Creole, Hausa, Russian, and Hindi, to lift the receiver and slide the end of the bracelet through. At which point the little screen lights up, agrees that I am "Munn, A.P., 106722," with six minutes of telephone time in the 212-718 area codes.

I dial Zeng's number and get the goddam answering machine with the Ramones song. I leave a message asking him to hire me a criminal lawyer pronto.

The screen tells me I have 4.43 minutes left. Larissa's number hasn't quit my brain; it wiggles in the usual fashion, urging me to dial, see what she's up to.

I think, This is the definition of history, the sense that events that are finished still carry insight and momentum in the directions of my daily life.

With great mental effort I push Larissa from my head. I wish I knew Kaye Santangelo's number. Her face lies in my memory, too, a point of brightness and grace made lighter by the dark pole of Larissa.

Yet maybe it's good I can't reach her, for I was the one who brought the darkness that touched Larissa and carried her away.

I don't know how the darkness works, but I assume, were I to bring Kaye close to my own orbit, it could reach out and touch her, too.

On impulse, I dial Amy Dillon's number. She picks up on the second ring.

"Amy?"

"Who is this?"

"It's me—Alex."

"Alex? Alex *Munn*?"

"Yeah, I—"

Click.

I stand there, listening to the dial tone.

A hand grabs my shoulder roughly. I pull away, two steps, spin around, dropping the receiver, back to the wall with hands raised in defensive posture. The phone enforcers stand in front of me. Both keep their right hands in their pockets.

"You six minutes up."

"No way." I hold my stance. "The screen says four minutes an' forty seconds."

"It ain't screen time." One of them points to the fake Rolex on his wrist. "It's *our* time."

I open my mouth to argue. Then I shrug, and move around them to the center of the recreation area. It seems clear that if I'm going to fight on Riker's, I'd better pick my battles with care, and good timing.

I didn't have anyone to call, anyway.

I stay in the rec area most of the morning. There's always squads of guards here and I figure, if I stick to the crowded tables in the middle, I'll be fairly safe. A few inmates look me over and make some of the usual "Hail fellow fuck you" comments. Somebody yells, "Kirsten," in a salty tone of voice. I can see gangbangers, mostly blacks and Latinos with a number of Indians, Chechens, Tadzhiks, Hmongs, and Chinese thrown in, walking around in tight knots but they don't come too close. One faction of blacks obviously controls TV choices, including the screen near me. Somebody has the good taste to pay for the Three Stooges hour playing on Gotham Cable-148. Yet somehow the antics of Moe, Larry, and Shemp, instead of cheering me up, fill me with sadness because they belong to a time that I realize, in retrospect, was amazingly good and full of creative opportunity.

A crowd in the far corner bets on robot-sumo on channel 56.

Around eleven the loudspeaker announces exercise yard F is open. Enough men and guards move toward corridor F that I figure it will be safe to go along.

If it weren't safe, though, I'd go anyway. The windowless tiers of Bantum, the twenty-four-hour neon, and the cold cage life are turning me, somewhere deep, into a critter far more desperate than I was before. And that desperation repels me. I want to see light, I want to see outside to remember there's a world where once I functioned as a normal man.

The yard turns out to be the rectangular space between the bulk of Bantum and a low warehouse building to the north. It is, of course, entirely surrounded and roofed over by two perimeters of chainlink and razor-ribbon. The metal is so thick that it's hard to see through. Only in areas where sports equipment has been set up is the innermost fence, for safety reasons, free of razor-ribbon.

Still the air is fresh, or as fresh as it can be given that it had to wash over Newark, Manhattan, and most of Queens to get here.

You don't realize till you get outside how pervasive is the scent of Kool-Aid–flavored disinfectant, how strong the stench of hopelessness wound up in the molecules of sweat and jock-itch and gas from two thousand men confined with starchy food against their will.

The area is surfaced in asphalt. I walk around, keeping to the edge of the wire, moving fast.

A low-pressure front has come through since I was inside. The air is fairly warm, maybe forty degrees, so despite the fact that I'm not dressed for outdoors I work up a decent sweat. Six, seven times around the yard, driving the oxygen from my lungs, dodging the gang teams shooting hoop, playing handball.

Ten, eleven times, pounding hard at the pavement, my breath creating short wisps of white steam.

The basketball players are good. Most of the teams are divided naturally between Hispanics and blacks and they play seriously, coming out with short explosive comments: "*PASS* it!" "*DA*-melo!" "OFFSIDE, *putamadre*!" "Mo'fuckah, *foul*!"

Even though I'm no big hoop fan, as they dribble and shoot for the basket I feel a sort of abstract pleasure at the speed and coordination of these men. They leap three feet high and bounce happily off the chainlink.

One game involves two Hispanic teams, smallish agile fellows who crowd close in pursuit of the ball. Three of them, in a crescendo of synthetic squeaks and harsh breaths, drive it into a corner of the chainlink only six or seven feet away from me—then turn, inexplicably, away from the ball.

Other players take the pass, dribbling in place, making wide-armed blocking motions.

The three nearest me fan out, one on each side, one in the center. The guy in the middle pulls from the back of his pants a shiny, wickedly sharpened plexiglass shank, maybe eight inches long.

He holds it briefly next to his balance hand, as if in prayer, before walking in my direction.

It's a neat trap. The bunched wire at the corner of the yard effectively hides us from guards on patrol outside, while the ballplayers provide camouflage for the lunges and feints of knife play. I can't run in either direction because one of the flankmen would tackle me and then all the knife man has to do is step in and drive his blade home.

The shiv artist is a hefty Hispanic with lots of black hair combed over his forehead. He wears an ornate necklace of gray, black, and gold beads. He waves the shank slowly, professionally, then flips it fast to the other hand. I have to make an effort to keep my eyes off the plastic blade and look into his eyes. If there's any warning, it will come from that quarter.

"Gonna die now, mo'fucker," the shank man says. His eyes are the shade of slush.

Sam Rodney says, "A gang o' men come up on yah, yah got yer back to a wall, yah feint." My breath is rasping so hard it hurts and I feel a definite urge not to fight, to let it happen, because it would be fast and afterward I would never have to fight again.

But to give in would mean to give up, let the *vatos* win. And, as a native New Yorker, I hate to see anybody gain an advantage over me. I push off from the chainlink, feint a hand chop at the man on my right, then run fast at the shank man.

Except that I can't run fast; every step seems to take a full second.

Despite my slowness he doesn't run, just pulls back a bit from the chop of my right hand, which leaves him off balance. I turn, sidestep into him, kick at his left knee with my right foot. The kick connects, mostly; I can hear cartilage snap as the joint folds the wrong way. The shank man goes down, shrieking.

One of the guys still playing hoop yells, *"Andale, coño!"* Another fumbles the ball as he watches what's happening in the corner and I realize this one isn't Hispanic at all; he has the small, flat features of an Asian.

But the left-hand attacker is on me now and I don't have time to muse over the Riker's melting pot. I grab him by the shoulder as he charges, spin around with him, and drive him into the chainlink. The metal shivers with the impact. I immediately spin to meet the third man, and exactly at that point something hot and fierce invades my right side, just above the hipbone.

"Azul!" the cover team is yelling, *"azul!"*

Too slow, my brain comments, too goddam slow, but I turn around anyway, to face the rest of the attack.

The third man walks backward, staring at my stomach with the slight frown of a man examining a difficult job. I follow his gaze.

The clear plastic shank is sticking out of my shirt, and blood soaks the cloth just below the blade. When I grasp the weapon it falls easily out of the wound and hangs, heavy as uranium, in my palm.

I stare at the guy who did this to me. He wears the same style of beads as the other man. Abruptly he turns and sprints after his comrades, dodging a half-dozen guards barreling across the yard in my direction.

I lean back against the wire, put my hand over the wound. It doesn't hurt that much, but the amount of blood scares me. There's a din in my head.

I look up at the sky gridded through the razor-ribbon overhead. This is it, I think, it's the last time I'll see the sky, I'll really miss it, especially the sunsets over New Jersey, those weird yellow clouds.

The guards are lining up around me. One of them, lying prone, points a riot gun the size of a small cannon. The noise comes from them, they're all shouting the same words. "Drop it! *DROP* the shank, motherfucker!"

I wonder, if the word "motherfucker" was somehow eliminated from the vocabulary of prison, whether anyone would be able to communicate on Riker's Island.

I let the blade fall from my hands. Then I slide down the chainlink to the ground.

The whole thing washes by in a haze of light pain. The screws cuff me to a stretcher and whisk me to an ambulance and, in a flash of emergency lights, to an old gray building midway between Bantum and the MCHF.

The medics are young and fast. They probe at the pain,

x-ray it, numb it with needles, and stitch it up inside its own numbness. Afterward they write up reports by the yard and tell me nothing. Finally a nurse lets out the state secret; the shank missed the liver, not by much, sliced some tissue, nicked the bone. Assuming I escape lethal injection in Sing Sing, I will live to see another New Jersey sunrise.

I am shunted by wheelchair to a holding ward between the AIDS unit and the TDF clinic. This is great for morale, because for all I'm sick at heart and cut of stomach, the people roaming behind the bulletproof glass are worse off than I am. Some of the men, AIDS patients I guess, or those infected with Matadi-14, are so thin that the hollows in their cheeks seem to meet on the inside of their mouths. They shamble by, hairless and pale, in hospital johnnies. In the egalitarianism of disease, even black victims look white, or maybe it's the other way around.

The TDF patients, denied access to television, cluster at nodal points like the junctions of corridors, moving without cease. A number of them hang around the intercom leading to the holding corridor and I can hear the tee-dees hum theme songs and snatches of dialogue from the shows they're missing.

> *"Listen to the song*
> *of our castaways*
> *they're stuck here forevermore . . .*
> *Here on Finnegan's Reef!"*

> *"So long, Herald Square!*
> *Howdy, county fair!"*

> *"Though love will come,*
> *it's not too soon,*
> *for pain in the afternoon . . ."*

And even the minor-key Clam Fetish keening that accompanies the trailers for *Real Life.*

As I wait, I recall how TDF researchers have been belly-aching about the impact of *Real Life* on their patients. For people who, by reason of trauma or chemical imbalance, have flipped their concept of reality so that what they see on tube or hear on radio is true, and human life is fiction, the idea of a show that basically smokes the difference is disturbing, to say the least.

There have already been a handful of killings by tee-dees seeking cash to pay for a Virtix hookup.

I wonder what Joel Kamm will do to *Real Life*. The anger that thought brings is unexpected. I suppose even nasty children are loved by their parents; and *Real Life* was, for better or worse, my baby.

Then a trio of bulls in bulletproof vests marches up and without ceremony wheels me down an elevator and into a windowless van. After a short drive the doors open on Bantum's D gate, but they don't let me into a breezeway. Instead I get rolled to an elevator, taken to the third tier, led into a room where they tell me to take off my clothes.

"What're you talkin' about?"

"Don't make us do it for you."

"Just tell me why?"

"You're goin' to the Box."

The Box, I know from hearing Cosmo talk, is solitary confinement.

"But why?"

"You fuck aroun' wit shanks, man, you go to the Box."

"But that wasn't my shank!"

I don't want to go to the Box. The way Cosmo talks about it, it sounds worse than the rest of the Rock.

The guard who deigns to talk to me is chubby. He shrugs, not without sympathy.

"Deputy warden see you later, anyway. You explain it to him."

I remove my clothes. It takes me a long time and the guards make stupid comments. They take away the wheelchair and march me down a concrete corridor lined with doors of unbroken steel. My right side hurts so much now I have to lean forward and sideways to walk. The third door from the end is open. They shove me inside and slam the door.

The Box is well named. It's a concrete cube with absolutely nothing in it but the stainless john. No bunk, no chair, not even toilet paper. My "house" on the ferry feels like Club Med by comparison.

I sit down. It only takes me five minutes, trying to work out how to bend without breaking the stitches in my side. It's odd, but the pain feels familiar, as if I'd had it before, and then I remember: I was "stabbed," only six days ago, by the Fishman.

Gingerly I touch my stomach. The stitches feel raw, alien. The skin is rough to the touch.

Of course the Fishman's stab was not a real wound, and it was on the other side of my stomach. But I remember how I felt a real-live ache after it occurred. And now the memory of that ache seems to join up with the worse pain of my real wound, and the pain doubles and triples with that bond between memory and mayhem.

The novocaine must be wearing off.

The anesthetic is wearing off my brain, too. The adrenaline of attack kind of kept me from thinking much back there. I can look around at the tan-painted concrete and understand how perfectly the Box reflects developments in my life over the last few days.

"Larissa," I mumble hopelessly. "Larissa, what *happened*?"

It's not cold in here, yet I feel cold. Maybe it's the psychological effect of having no clothes on. My skin seems as pale to me as that of the AIDS patients. "Fish" is what they call new detainees at Riker's, and I look like a fish now, naked and gasping, removed from the water of my own life.

I can hear voices again, just like I did in Cosmo's cell. They're faint and indistinct; they remind me once more of ghosts yammering to each other through a thick but permeable membrane of fog.

The toilet drips.

I think, I must be going nuts. Abruptly I put my hands over my ears.

The voices stop.

I lift my hands; they resume.

Logically, that would imply the voices are not inside my head.

Now, listening harder, I can hear words, mostly "Yeah!" as if the ghosts of prison were agreeing with some brilliant point they themselves had made. Once in a while I catch a "Munn," but that has to be my brain screwing up again.

Gingerly, using the wall for support, I get to my feet. The

voices get louder at the cell's far end, next to the toilet. I bend, very slowly, holding my gut.

The voices are coming out of the toilet.

I get to my knees, like I was going to sell the Buick. The bowl is furry and stale-smelling. The sound comes from the hole. I stick my head halfway inside. This is what I hear, faint, distorted by echoes, made treble by the stainless steel, but recognizable nonetheless:

"Yeah!"

"Line?"

"Okay."

"Tregini bagini."

"Onway upway."

". . . mica."

"Line open!"

"Munn!"

"Unh, unh, unh."

"Pagini aygini nowgini."

"Yah!"

"Munn!"

"Hello?" I call stupidly, keeping my mouth disgustingly close to the gray water. Then, louder, "Hello!"

"Line open."

"Munn! Bail eet out!" ("Out-out-out," goes the echo.)

Bail out what? The water?

But it has to be the water. I look around reflexively, forgetting that the Box, by definition, contains nothing.

Finally, holding my nose at the gases I must liberate by my doing this, I cup one hand, trying unsuccessfully to keep it from touching the sides of the bowl, and scoop handfuls of water out of the craphole, onto the floor, until only an inch or so remains at the bottom.

"Line open!" The voice is much more distinct.

"Munn!"

"Yeah," I yell, "it's me."

"Jah, love," the answer comes, so I know it's Cosmo. "Munn, you heah 'bout dat contract?"

"Fuck off!"

"What?" I yell.

"Hagate los manes que me tumbàron lo tuyo," a voice cuts in.

"Contract, mahn. Money to keel you. You tink about dat offah now."

"Dìle a mi hermano, coño, que deja los chavos en casa."

"Cosmo?"

"Mai charras chaiyeh abi-abi," someone says, and *"Paissa deh-deh, bhan-chode,"* someone else replies. It's like trying to converse with a New York cabbie.

Someone flushes. Water jingles and flows and the level in my bowl shifts. The voices are more distant again, abstract. I wonder how many levels of Bantum communicate in this way. I assume the sound travels through half-full sewage pipes; I suppose they could transmit through empty vertical pipes as well, as long as the person you wanted was on the same vertical block as the Box.

After another fifty or a hundred minutes the door is unlocked and I'm led to the strip cell and allowed to put my duds back on.

The screws lead me with no explanation up three tiers, into a small office with a window. The light from outside stabs my eyes like a shank. I am cuffed to a chair bolted into the cement floor. The office contains dozens of framed photos, and books with titles like *State of New York Correction Code, Vol. XXII.* A sign on the desk reads "Thomas W. Fellowes, Asst. Deputy Warden." A neat, coffee-colored man comes in ten minutes later and sits at the desk with barely a glance in my direction.

"Mr. Munn?"

I say nothing.

"You'll be glad to know you're going back to normal housing."

"That wasn't my knife."

He folds his hands. "I know."

"There's a contract out on my life," I continue urgently.

He looks at me seriously.

"How do you know this?"

"Guy in my cell tole me."

He turns, taps at his terminal, and smiles.

"Cosmo Trelawney."

"Cosmo, that's right."

"He's a troublemaker. This is the third time he's been in

here, he does it on purpose. See, he runs a network; reefer, information mostly. I bet he offered you a bodyguard?''

No expression passes my face.

"Chances are, if there is a contract, which I doubt, he put it out himself.''

"But those guys weren't black,'' I object.

"African-American.''

"Whatever. I know enough about the Rock, the African-Americans don't hang out with the, uh, Hispanic-Americans. An' the guys that stabbed me spoke Spanish.''

Fellowes sits back in his comfortable chair. The photographs around him, I now realize, all show Fellowes shaking hands with recognizable people. Three city mayors, two governors of New York, a couple of congressmen, one movie star, and Senator Henry Warren Powell.

"Tell me,'' he says, "were any of them wearing beads?''

"Around their neck?'' He nods. "Yeah.''

"What color?''

I think back.

"Black, green. Red, maybe, I can't see red.''

Fellowes nods again. "Red. The Netas. They hang out with African-Americans, sometimes. Not with Rastas, though. Still, there's alluz a first time. I'll see the guards watch out for you,'' he adds, "that's all I can do.''

"Couldn't I get my own cell?'' I ask him. " 'N stay there, by myself?''

He frowns. "You mean, PC?''

"Whatever.'' "PC'' is protective custody.

"No.'' Shaking his head. "See, we can't do that every time someone says there's a contract. Everybody says that; we simply don't have the space.'' He sighs.

"Also, Mr. Munn, there's some publicity surrounding your case, an' frankly, with an election coming up, we can't be seen giving rich white males priority.''

"Caucasian-Americans,'' I correct him. He ignores the sally.

"My advice to you is—off the record''—folding his hands differently now—"hire Trelawney's 'bodyguard.' I guarantee you, the 'contract' will go away.''

He looks down at his papers. He must have pushed a button

or something because the guards walk in behind, uncuff me from the chair, and lead me out of the office of Thomas W. Fellowes, Assistant Deputy Warden of the Otis Bantum Correctional Facility at Riker's Island, and the color reproductions of all the famous people he ever met.

TWENTY-TWO

After my little chat with Fellowes I go straight to the guard station next to C gate and wait there, all the way through dinner hour, for the bus back to the MCHF.

The novocaine wears off by the time I get back to Cosmo's. The doctor gave me a paper envelope of Percosets and I swallow three and the pain is reduced by maybe point-two percent. I don't know which hurts worse, the cut tissue or the wide stitches. I've been walking slowly, doubled over a little to the right, pressing my right elbow into the bandage to soften the vibration of movement. Once in the cell I lower myself gingerly to my bunk and sit there, unwilling to move. The roaches run races around my sneakers. Cosmo comes in, sits opposite, takes contraband from his jockey shorts, and stashes it around the cell. He pulls out a shank, a metal blade, not as long as the one I got stabbed with, and stashes it under his mattress, along the frame of the bunk. Then he leans down to look at my face.

"You get my message?"

"Yeah." I can't talk very loud, either.

"So?"

"Deputy warden," I whisper. "He said, *you* put out that contract."

"What?"

I glance through my eyebrows. Cosmo's eyes are bugging; he looks genuinely surprised, though one side of his mouth curls up a bit, as if intrigued by the concept's elegance.

"Him cree-azy."

"Doesn't matter. If I agree—to hire you—you'll cancel it?"

"You don't understahnd." Cosmo stands up, paces back and forth twice. "I deedn't *do* dat beez-ness. Mahn, you get into da kee-llin'—you got no time fah real beez-ness." He sits down again.

"Why you tink me heah, on Riker's? Dat chahge a bum beef, girlfr'en mee-ake it op, me dohn put bee-ail so I get in heah. Distribu-shan, supply, all de ganj', it all de prison gangs, mahn, dem got it wrapped up tight on de street now. So I *need* to do a deal wit dem; Neta, Latin Kings. Ahm of Allah, Spirit Knife." He fires up a quarter cigarette with delicacy.

"Now de line say, some mahn pee-ayin ten tousan dallah see you iced 'fore you leave heah."

"I tole you," I say, "I'll take that bodyguard."

"You can hear it on de line," Cosmo adds, "don't rely on me."

"Okay," I whisper. "Okay."

"Tousan dallah a day, white money. You pee-ay my account, outside. Every ten day."

"That's a lotta dough." The Scots side coming out.

"You a rich mahn, Mistah Munn. You got a lawyah?"

"Yeah." I hope to Jah I do have a lawyer.

"Heem can handle it. Also"—using the cigarette as a pointer, stabbing at an imaginary blackboard—"you follow my rules."

"Okay."

"I mean it, mahn." Cosmo frowns fiercely, to show how serious he is. "Rock a wahr zone, mahn. Every plee-ace, every cornah like fockin' Sonora. You nevah know who you friend, nevah know you enemy. You only chance, mahn, you get a baby-sittah, right? A back-me-op. An' you get a weapon. You watch him back wit you weapon, him watch you back wit hees weapon. Got dat?"

"Got it," I whisper, and try to lie sideways on the bunk, which is a very bad idea, I can feel my side opening like the jaws of a grouper.

Cosmo, watching, shakes his head and pulls the last bit of smoke from his cigarette butt.

"Mahn," he says sadly, "me *worried* 'bout you."

Morning comes in the same cacophony of bells and lack of anything at all different.

I watch the roaches from my bunk. They seem to sense when we're asleep, which is when they come out to forage and party on the rusting planes of our cell world. When I open my eyes most of them run for cover, a phalanx of tiny legionnaires scurrying off under the shelter of shiny brown shields. One of them takes off vertically, up the bulkhead. It slips and falls into the square box that forms the socket for one end of the bunk support. Through the empty cotter pinhole I watch it struggle on its back.

I look around. Cosmo's Dale Carnegie diskette lies beside the November issue of *Wet and Pink*. I stretch out one arm, whimpering as this pulls the skin on my ribs, and cover the box so that the roach can't get out.

"There," I whisper. "See what it feels like?"

Over breakfast Cosmo and his squat pal indoctrinate me into the mysteries of being a protected person. They give me a nickel bag of pepper and an Old Spice aftershave squeeze bottle full of ammonia.

"Spray it into heem eyes, mahn," Cosmo urges, demonstrating while the squat one looks on with no expression showing. "Me get you shank soon." And, later: "You don't go *any-weah* witout Derek. You watch out every mee-nute. You don't tee-ake showah. You got to tee-ake Jimmy Brit, you got Derek wit you. Also, nevah leave you pants 'roun' you ankles, tee-akin a shit—you tee-ake one leg out *all de weeay,* so you can get op an' run, if you have to. You got dat?

"Don't go to exahcize yahd, chap-ell, movie theater. Dey wee-aitin for you all dem plee-aces, mahn.

"Dey wee-aitin."

The lieutenant who was there the day I arrived reads out the people getting mail, medicine, or visitors. My name is on the last two lists. The lieutenant is angry because the tee-dee is still on the ferry. A guard comes over to talk about *Copkiller*. He's a former flatfoot and wants to go over what he thought was accurate, or wrong, about the show; but I don't respond beyond polite monosyllables. One of Cosmo's rules was, don't cozy up to the bulls, because you will automatically be seen as a snitch and this will only turn other inmates against you—those, that is, who aren't already trying to stick me with their shanks.

I hang around the ferry with the squat man. We take the eight o'clock bus to Bantum. Still with Derek, I wait in line for the antibiotics I was prescribed for the shank wound, then queue up for the visiting-area bus.

The visiting area is under the new reception center. Cosmo replaces Derek, since the squat one has no visitors. Cosmo sees someone almost every day.

At the center, we're ordered to change into orange jump-suits—the idea is, we'll be too colorful to sneak out with the visitors—then we file through metal detectors. We're allowed through in groups, to a series of cubicles lined up in a long, low, neon-bright room. Guards sit on each side, carefully watching. This is the point, Cosmo said, where most of the smuggling into Riker's takes place. Through bulletproof glass I watch him kiss a plump girl, but his hands are held ostentatiously at his sides. At least three screws are giving themselves hernias trying to spy on him, and I have no idea how he plans to do it.

When my turn comes I find Zeng waiting in my cubicle, with another Chinese fellow behind. His companion is dressed in a clean suit and has crew-cut hair. Zeng looks exactly the same, complete with the two-foot ponytail, the long Indian shirt, the high-top sneakers; and suddenly my throat gets tight and I can't speak.

"Alex."

The grin is more pained than usual. He only calls me by my real name in times of great stress. He takes my hand in both of his and squeezes hard.

I look away, while the moisture recedes from my tear ducts. My chest feels small and prickly. We sit down opposite each other.

"You okay?"

I still can't look at him.

"Alex," he says. "I'm just gonna ask you one question, okay? I just wanna get it out of the way."

My eyes are dry now. My throat is hard, but it works.

"Don't," I tell him.

He shrugs. "Just for the record?"

"I don't believe this," I tell him.

"Listen, Wildman—"

"But you *know* me!"

"I'm sorry—"

My chest is screwed up again. I gaze down at the Formica on the cubicle counter. It looks like animals have scratched at it for five hundred years. I feel like an animal, a sick animal, a creature with tainted saliva and blood that kills. Unclean, shoot on sight.

It's bad enough to be threatened, jailed, in danger. It's far worse to feel that you deserve it, that you're so worthless even your best friend has to check on your level of moral hygiene.

It saps the survival instinct, because that instinct is based on the sense that you are worth preserving. If even your friends doubt you, then maybe you should die, or go to jail forever.

"I'm not gonna answer," I whisper at length. "If you've got to ask that question, it means it don't matter what I say now."

Zeng blinks several times. His eyes are like the "in use" light on a hard drive; the blinking indicates furious number-crunching.

"Okay, Alex." He holds up his hands. "I'm gonna take that as an answer." He turns to the other Asian.

"This is my cousin, Jack Wong. He's a criminal lawyer, he works for Legal Aid in Brooklyn." Zeng blinks again. "He'll talk to you now, I guess."

Jack Wong takes the seat. He opens his mouth to speak, and something buzzes on his belt. He whips out a cellphone, listens, snaps, "Tell him I'll call back in half an hour," hangs it on his belt again. Then he laces his fingers together and looks at me steadily.

"It looks bad," he begins. "The fingerprints in the bathroom don't help, although they can be explained by your visit two days before. The real bitch, I believe, is the tie-in with your virtual reality piece.''

"Munn's World," I croak. Wong nods.

"I don't understand," I continue, "how Polletti even knew about it."

"They had a warrant. They took the master disks from your apartment. It was done by the book—I checked."

"Yes, but how did they *know*?"

Wong shrugs. It doesn't interest him. "The big items, of course, are the graffiti, as well as—"

"What graffiti?"

My lawyer's eyes are very black and gentle, though the rest of his face betrays no sympathy at all.

"On the wall. The words there—didn't you find her?"

"Yes."

Something surfaces behind the gentleness, something rather harder.

"It read, and I quote, 'Squatter, squatter.' Just those two words. It was written in blood, presumably hers, over the bed."

"But that's from—"

"Munn's World, yes. Unfortunately, Detective Polletti already made that connection."

I've been leaning my left elbow on the counter so my right belly will suffer a minimum of strain. This of course puts stress on the left side, reminding me again of the stab I received in *Munn's World.* I feel like I want to puke, except that would make the ache worse. I clear my throat.

"The—the slashes. On her."

"That was the second point," Wong agrees.

"What the hell is going on?" I say in a light, polite tone. I'm not asking this of Wong, or Zeng, or even myself. I'm asking this of the world, which once seemed to possess structure and predictability and now seems to have shifted into a chaos whose few patterns appear dark and full of doom.

Wong takes out a cheap school notebook.

"The police interviewed a, uh, Caterina Magdalena Santangelo? The time she gives, when she saw you—unfortunately that does not exclude you getting to Perry Street in a time frame consistent with the M.E.'s report."

"You mean—"

"You could have done it after you saw Santangelo. You could even have done it before, the M.E. gets more vague after the body's been dead twenty-four hours. One good thing —you *couldn't* have done it in the afternoon, when you were actually seen with her." He closes the notebook, leans forward, and taps the book lightly on the Formica.

"You didn't want the baby?"

I'm staring at the notebook. It's black and white, marbleized, with a space for the student's name and class. The words sink in slowly.

"What did you say?"

"The baby."

"What're you talking about?" I look up at Zeng, who is staring at the inmates lining up behind the bulletproof.

"She was five weeks' pregnant."

I stand up, holding my stomach. The wound feels like it's tearing apart but I don't notice so much. Zeng glances at me now. Wong taps his notebook again.

I see her in the bath, with the thin shade of blood darkening the water. "I made you bleed?" I asked her.

"Like a virgin," she replied. "Men like that, don't they?"

I hunch over the counter, grim as Dracula, searching for words.

"I didn't know," I say finally. "But that's, kinda, what we fought about. Gettin' back together. Having kids." I look at Zeng. "I didn't want her to die."

"But?"

Wong has his head cocked, as if listening to faraway music.

"I remember"—whispering—"between losing the car, and seeing Kaye. But I don't remember, I jiss don't *remember* what happened after Brooklyn!"

Wong says, "The only people who knew about *Munn's World* were Stefan, and Rose Obregon—your boss at XTV?"

"Yes. Though anyone could have read the files, if they knew how."

"Anyone?"

"Well, anyone at X-Corp, who knew the basic codes. Especially if he had a hacking program. But—" I sit back slowly, talking more softly, trying to keep the stomach together. "No one woulda seen it. No reason to."

And I think, No one saw it who might want to hurt Larissa.

The only one who knew *Munn's World,* and who also was angry with Larissa, was me.

Alexander Munn, a.k.a. "Wildman" because of recurring drunken sorties he can't remember later.

Wong opens his notebook again.

"D'you wish to plead not guilty?"

I barely hear him.

"Mr. Munn?"

I don't look at him.

"I don't know."

"I shouldn't ask you this," Jack Wong says, "but—*did* you stab her?"

I hold my stomach tighter. I can feel liquid seeping; maybe one of the stitches has broken, or the wound is weeping, whether healthy fluids or infected matter I have no way of knowing.

"No. I can't believe that," I say finally. "I really—cared for her. I jiss don't *think* that way."

"But you were angry at her?"

"I guess."

Wong checks his notebook for cracks.

"The M.E. found traces of semen," he says.

"We made love." I speak without moving my jaw. "Before we fought."

The cellphone beeps again. Wong goes through the same routine as before, only this time he promises to call back in five so I know the interview is almost over.

"People are complicated," he tells me when it's finished. "If the trauma is deep enough, they can do things that are—foreign—to their personality."

"A goddam *Freud,*" I tell him.

"One other option," Wong says. He takes out a ballpoint and writes quickly in the notebook. "Plead not guilty by reason of insanity." He stops. I'm shaking my head, obsessively, like one of those Tourette people you see in the bus.

"It's just not possible. I don't believe it. I got angry? I jiss did something—like that—an' then I jiss wiped it out, without remembering? Without, even, like a feeling?"

Wong rips the page out of his notebook. He holds it up so the guards can see it, then passes it over. It reads "Dr. Wayne Malik, MD, DP, FACPT, MIIVT."

"I think you should talk to an expert. I've used this guy. New ideas—very effective. D'you know if you respond to hypnosis?"

"Yes."

"You already have a therapist?"

"Yes."

"It's better you use a new one. And Malik's good under cross. Real dramatic, you know?" Wong nods seriously, and I can see in that nod how he loves the whole theater of lawyering. "I'll arrange a session after the one-eighty-eighty." He pockets the notebook and stands up. "That's in three days, so we'll have to work fast." He sticks out his hand. After a beat, I shake it. Stefan stands aside to let him out, then stretches over the counter.

"Alex," he says. "Don't worry about the finances." He touches my shoulder, gently. Suddenly, though I'm sick of the questions I can't answer, I want with my whole being to keep him here.

"Zeng," I say.

"Yes?"

"I've been wanting to ask you. Did you scan Walt Whitman into the World Generator?"

Zeng's face creases into a smile.

"So he came out? At Pfaff's?"

"Yeah. And there was—something else." My stomach really is killing me now but I continue regardless. "The theater?"

"The Alcazar."

"Yeah. It burned."

"*Burned?*" Zeng's eyelids are blinking like navy signalers. He scratches his left butt, another sign of concentration.

"The brawl kinda got outta hand. One of the Daybreakers. Zeng—" I focus on his eyes, feeling vulnerable, despising that weakness. I can see the unicorn in the subway grinning nastily, as if he held the key to a door I'll never get through.

"It's as if *Munn's World* is coming alive. Somehow, it's coming apart. The different pieces are changing, you know? And there's something dark in there. Something weird—"

"Wildman—" Zeng sticks out his hand again.

"No. Listen. An' it's happening in tandem with my real life. *Mine,* I mean, not the show. And it's *coming apart!*"

"Easy," Zeng mutters, "easy." I lean back, putting my back to the cubicle wall. Someone on the other side says, "You tell the motherfucker he come aroun' again I cut his balls off." And a woman says, "Bobby, you ain't gonna git out for *twenny years*." Zeng asks me again if I'm going to be okay, but we both realize what a stupid question that is, and he takes his leave in a haze of embarrassment.

After another half hour or so I get shipped back to Bantum.

I spend most of the rest of the day with Derek, waiting for the infirmary to change my bandages.

When we all get back to the MCHF I'm totally burned out. The Percosets still don't work well, I can't fathom what Sara sees in them. It takes me twenty minutes to lie down on my bunk. Cosmo spends the time sitting on the toilet, one pant leg folded loose, grunting. A terrible stench takes over the cell, but on the list of my problems, that's fairly low.

I watch the cockroach in the bracket box. It's still struggling to lift Dale Carnegie so as to escape back to the warm bilge where its roach buddies hang. But the diskette is just too heavy.

I think of the Marquis poem—"i saw a kitchen/ worker killing/ water bugs with poison/ hunting pretty/ little roaches/ down to death/ it set my blood to/ boiling."

Cosmo sticks his free leg through the pant leg, pulls his pants up, but does not flush. He bends over the toilet and delicately, using a plastic fork, starts smooshing his shit around, isolating a number of slimy objects from the general mass. These he lifts into the sink, and rinses quickly with warm water.

"I don't wanna bodyguard anymore," I tell him.

Cosmo turns, and examines me.

"Can't jiss quit, mahn," he says at length. "You mee-ake a contract."

"No, I didn't."

"A *Riker's* contract. You ahsk for service, you got it. Now you pee-ay. Simple."

"Fuck off."

"You want to die?" Cosmo asks pleasantly.

I don't say anything.

I think, something exists inside me that makes the cannibal roach in my bunk-bracket seem benign by comparison. And if that force—I'm talking to myself now, the sibilants coming out like little spikes between my lips. "If it's so dark it could've killed Larissa—and then go on, with no memory, or shame . . ."

The talking, by the very power of words uttered, seems to connect to the force I'm describing, so that I feel it sloshing around inside, a hidden lake in a cave I thought I knew; a place, unfathomably deep, deadly cold, corrupt and without light. Water so foul that one touch of it will sully the purest of hands, follow the life-warmth to the ventricle, and cool it out completely.

"Yeah," I tell Cosmo. "I wouldn't mind dying."

The roach, still trying to climb the steel walls of its box, flips backward onto its brown shield.

Cosmo laughs. It's not a merry laugh, it has echoes of bad knowledge. The chain reaction carries him along for ten or fifteen seconds.

"Oh, mahn," he says when he's finished. "Dat's de trouble. You *cahn't* die, now."

He bends to look in the sink. The objects, clean, turn out to be condoms, with mounds and hard objects inside. He unrolls one carefully and takes out four little plastic bags full of black rocks and a small gearing mechanism.

"Rock's a complicated plee-ace, mahn," Cosmo continues. "Yestihday, you could have died like dat." He snaps his fingers.

Cosmo stashes everything in a clean sandwich bag, then fiddles under his bunk for a second, making the contraband disappear. He sits on the bunk, bouncing a couple of times as a test.

"Todee-ay, you *cahn't* die. You immortal. Till you pee-ay me dat green you owe me."

I don't answer. I can't think of anything to say.

The roach figures out how to right itself, and crawls up to the cotter hole once more.

TWENTY-THREE

I STAND ALONE by a dark river.

It's not a true river, though, it's too straight and stagnant. The poisonous colors from chemical reactions are trapped in the black water. The dead banks rise on each side, scarred with rotten structures and spirals of razor-ribbon. Everything around me is old and without life; the ruined buildings, the rusted cars, a half-sunken plywood motorboat.

Everything except what lies under that water. My gut lusts for what has gone forever beneath the surface. I lean toward the water, yearning; and as if in response the black canal shakes free of its own reflection, and a tiny fist the color of first light rises from the surface. Then comes an arm, a shoulder, and a baby's prunish face.

I can't go nearer, it's not allowed by the rules of this particular world. The baby is sucked back under, wailing, and the water goes silent and so still that you can make out every detail of the razor-ribbon in its polished surface.

I wake up crying. My face is slick with tears and the crappy nylon pillow is warm and wet. My chest is filled with the three-cylinder rhythm of my sobs, and there's enough combustion left to keep me stuttering and the water sliming out of my eyes for another three minutes.

Eventually the fuel runs out.

Cosmo snores contentedly.

And I understand, for the first time, that I killed Larissa.

The knowledge goes down easily enough, but it doesn't lie well in the stomach. I sit up, ignoring the pain. Stand, half doubled over, and limp to the sink. Holding it for support, I try to puke. If only the vomit would clean the darkness out of me, I think, the way spewing removed alcohol. If only it would make time slow, stop, reverse. I rock gently, against the sink. My eyes are closed.

After a while I become conscious of a different motion. My feet moving, one after the other. If I walk enough, into the darkness, maybe I can replay this whole episode. Choose different streets, use different options.

I open my eyes. The steel sink where Cosmo washed off his crappy contraband is still there. The overhead light cruelly examines the paint-covered rust of the old ferry.

This is life, not VR.

It will not run backward.

I get back in my bunk. The wound in my stomach is still sore, but for some reason it isn't quite as agonizing as before.

Not that it matters a damn. It's quite clear to me that I have to off myself, with or without Cosmo's help.

I just can't live with the guy who did that to Larissa.

I run through the list of options and equipment necessary. For hanging, I'll need a length of line. Poison—the ammonia Derek gave me, only more of it. To slit my wrists I've got to get hold of Cosmo's shank, and evade Derek for the time it will take. I'm halfway through electrocution when, to my slow surprise, I fall asleep again.

In the morning I feel calmer. The decision I made during the night is soothing as Valium. I can even summon some interest as I watch Cosmo stash the different packages his girlfriend brought in, consulting *Wet and Pink* as he does so.

"How'd she get 'em to you?"

"Kissing."

Cosmo opens his mouth and demonstrates, in disgusting

fashion, the art of prison-Frenching. He takes one of the little packets, wraps it in a fresh condom, and refers to *Wet and Pink* again.

"Whack-off magazines show you where to hide 'em?"

Cosmo's breath comes out explosively, a sign of irritation. He tosses *Wet and Pink* to my bunk. When I open it I find the first and last eight pages devoted to the usual minute anatomical detail. The magazine is well named.

The inside pages, however, are different. Dense text, printed on cheap newsprint, taped to the spine, open to page 134.

SLAMMING (CONT'D)

The volume of objects that can be fitted into the asshole obviously is constrained by the size of the ring muscle, which has nothing to do with the physical size of the dude or babe attempting it. With practice, greater volumes can be achieved. In one case, a woman was able to conceal a ¾ pound stash of Guajira basuco up her Khyber. Unfortunately, she made the fatal mistake of storing the snow in Trojan condoms—and then using Vaseline as a lubricant. When storing contraband in latex condoms, always use K-Y jelly, or vegetable oil if that's not around. They had to hose down the inside of the Avianca 707 the woman was riding in. Coat the hell out of the latex, and shove it no farther than four inches . . .

"What the fuck *is* this?" I mutter.
Twelve pages later:

The smuggling group is the A-1 expression of Hawkley-ite theory. It's flexible, perfectly suited to this environment. It creates and satisfies its own economy at the same time, setting up market nodes to balance supply and demand in a given area. It can never approach the threshold of scale, beyond which sheer size causes the institution to Godzilla—take control over the individual—because such a large-scale group would definitely attract the attention of the Man. Also, because of the environment of risk, it becomes vital to satisfy the needs of each smuggler so no one can snitch on the whole. For

these and other reasons, the smuggling node is almost perfectly democratic.

"This is Hawkley stuff," I say, peeking at the *Wet and
Pink* portion again before handing the volume back.

"Smuggler's Bible," Cosmo agrees. "Yah, mahn."

"You one of them? Hawkley-ites?"

"No wee-ay. Rasta wohk wit dem, in ganja tree-ade."

"But what've Hawkley-ites got to do with ganja?"

He looks at me, shakes his head in pitying fashion, says
nothing more.

I spend the day with Derek. The strange tranquillity that
came overnight only leaves me once. We go to the exercise
yard and walk around within ten feet of the bulls at the entrance. I'm a little nervous at first; I mean, even if you want to
die, it's kind of nerve-racking not to know when or how the
reaper's going to come at you; but nobody pays me the slight-
est attention. I'm no longer a vulnerable peon in the prison
wars; rather, I've become a spectator, under guard. And that is
how, pacing stupidly at the gate, I can watch it happen in
almost exactly the same way it engulfed me yesterday.

A crowd of handball players surrounds someone, masking
the move under the slam and rebound. This occurs at the very
end of the court, beyond the hoop and handball areas, where
the entire height of chainlink once more is festooned with
razor-ribbon.

And they don't stab this victim, simply throw him five feet
up, face first, into the wire.

There's an unbelievable scream. It echoes against the cell
blocks, tearing at the ears. Between one guy serving and another backhanding I catch a glimpse of three men throwing all
their weight on the legs of a man literally crucified on the tiny,
glinting, anvil-shaped blades.

I think, at first, they're trying to get him off. Then I understand, with a sickening jolt, that they're only impaling him
farther—that's *the whole point.* Every pun intended.

The men run off.

Sirens whoop, gates slam. Lockdown. I catch one glimpse
of the victim; his skin is entirely masked in blood. A para-
medic pushes at his neck, a sheet of warmed latex covering
hands and face. Another thumps on his chest.

Down the court, the other handball players resume their game, hard black ball making hard black sounds against the concrete.

In the evening, after Cosmo has gone to sleep, I stand on my bunk and examine the light fixture. Specifically I check out the crack I noticed earlier between two plates. This leaves a gap maybe half an inch wide between the protective wire mesh and the deckhead.

Then, very slowly and softly, I worm my hand under the mattress where Cosmo stashes his shank. I pull it out gently, and look at the weapon with admiration. It's an elegant piece of work, an iron brace painstakingly filed to a point like a stiletto. It has a handle made of two flat pieces of pine lovingly taped and bound with twine.

I take off my sneakers, run my feet under water in the sink for a couple of seconds. Stand on the metal bunk frame, and stick the shank into the crack, feeling around for a wire. I'm not sure this will kill me, but that's the idea, and I cast around for a good last thought to go on. The only sentiments I can summon are a vague regret, for Larissa and (for some strange reason) Pedro; and a surprisingly sharp sense of disappointment, that I'll never see the poetess again.

Kaye, for Caterina. The one who dislikes Don Marquis.

I'm searching back through my memories of Marquis, desirous of a good epitaph when, somewhere in the fixture's innards, the shank connects.

There's a huge blue flash, a smell of burning. Flash and smoke turn into a five-hundred-pound judo black belt who takes me by arm and back and legs and flips me across the cell into the corner by the can.

My chest hurts. My stomach hurts utterly, my lungs are completely locked. I wait for my heart to stop, but all that happens is a much less adept wrestler, yellow belt perhaps, hauls me by my T-shirt through the new darkness of the cell. The wrestler shoves me into my bunk, and stashes the shank somewhere; I can hear it clink.

The screws come around immediately, shining flashlights. Cosmo, lying peacefully in his own bunk, tells them the bulb blew. They either believe him or decide not to hassle with checking. When they've gone, Cosmo leans over and whispers fiercely, "*Don't* try dat again."

"What you gonna do," I ask him, through teeth gritted against my aching back and the tweaked wound in my stomach, "kill me?"

"No, mahn. When me get out, me get the money from you mothah."

I never told Cosmo about my mother; I'm positive this is just con talk. For a moment I think about Cosmo dealing with someone named Wilderness Starchild, and I almost smile.

Next morning I'm on the list for grand juries and the lieutenant comes around at six to lead me to a special bus. The stitches, by some miracle, are still intact after last night's electrolysis treatment. The wound hurts like crazy and the palm of my right hand is burned where it gripped the shank.

Cosmo tells me they deliberately keep the amperage low on Riker's, to prevent the kind of sideways exit I was attempting.

Within ten minutes we're off the Rock and on the BQE. The sight of Manhattan, through the heavily meshed windows, despite the pain, is truly wonderful. Every skyscraper and bridge rising to the sky feels like a clean abs'ini, its own blue steel bird, singing of space and the joy of having something to build, the time to fashion it.

I realize, with some surprise, that I haven't thought about abs'inis, or any other kind of booze, for at least three days.

We unload at the same underground parking lot. The pumps thud patiently in the background. Morning grand juries are held on a different floor from arraignments. The room I end up in fits more with my idea of a courtroom, with real mahogany benches for the jury. The wooden bench reserved for prisoners, though, is as hard as the last one I sat in. It reminds me of the cheap orchestra seats in the Alcazar Theater, in *Munn's World*.

I check out the jury—it's a goddam melting pot, a fourteen-person microcosm of the city, black, white, Hispanic, Thai, Chinese, Jewish, Ghanaian, man, woman, fat, thin. This 180-80 hearing is an open event and the public benches are full. Reporters jostle when they see me come in. Behind them a couple of spectators are waving. It actually takes me a second to recognize Louise, who is swathed in a turquoise silk shawl and wears huge sunglasses of the type long ago affected by Gina Lollobrigida. Beside her, looking terrified in a big sweater, is Sara, and the Johnsonist insurance salesman called Freesoul Mountainman.

And how can I remember that asshole's name, and not remember capping my wife?

Other faces leap out of different pews. Stefan Zeng, reading *Mondo 3000.* Lenny the Mooch, his fat bulk briefly blocking the entrance as he slopes out for a cigar. Vivian Moos. Ved Chakrapani.

I look from face to face, not waving back, partly because of the cuffs. And partly it's because with each face a layer of armor I didn't even know I'd acquired sloughs off, allowing actual feelings, real affection, to ooze out from wherever they were locked in. My goddam throat locks up again, my eye sockets grow hot.

I feel like an explorer lost in the Arctic, surrounded by orcas and ice, getting a glimpse of his ship hull-down on the horizon. It doesn't help, practically speaking, but God, it's good to know they're there.

So when Jack Wong pops up beside me, with Stamas in tow, and asks me if I want to change my plea or alter any details in the story he's going to present, I turn to him with more sand in me than I've had in a while and grunt, "No."

The ADA in the Kenzo suit walks in like God's chief minister, followed by four lightly pinstriped toadies. An overamped speaker announces that all the people in the whole state of New York are against me. The clerk rustles papers and summons both Wong and the Kenzo ADA. Wong comes back, sits beside me, and says in a low, conspiratorial voice, "Coltrane will make a deal."

"Who's Coltrane?"

"The ADA."

"Oh."

"So?"

"Whaddya mean, a deal?"

"He'll drop murder one."

"An'?"

"He's offering murder two, which means, since you don't

have an adult jacket, there's no mandatory life. You'll do fifteen years. He's looking for good publicity." Wong jerks a finger at the audience. "I mean, why do *you* think he allowed open hearing?"

I stare at my attorney. I wish something would show through his mask of legal efficiency. Stamas, at least, shows something, if only discomfort.

"You call that a deal?" I ask at length. "Fifteen years?"

"I'm just telling you."

"Are you advisin' me to take it?"

"That's your decision."

"Jesus," I say loudly. "I hire a lawyer, I get a New Age adviser. You gonna tell me how this makes *you* feel, next?"

"The evidence against you is very strong," Wong says calmly. "If you make them go all the way to nail you, they will ask for capital punishment."

Those two words again. You know, conceptually, the death machine is around, sitting in that concrete cellar in Sing Sing, its clear IV of Pentothal snaking to the belted, stainless table; but you lock that image away for the sake of staying sane.

Then you hear the words "capital punishment," and the chamber comes back to mind, numbing, like an idea of absolute cold.

I turn to the Legal Aid attorney.

"What do *you* think?"

"He's not in this," Wong says quickly.

"I'm just doing transition," Stamas mumbles. "I'm off it now."

"I still wanna know what you think."

Wong sighs in exasperation. Stamas looks even more uncomfortable. He pulls nervously at his double chin.

"I shouldn't say anything."

"So don't," Wong snaps.

A feather of irritation brushes Stamas's face.

"But I will say this. Speaking personally, not as an officer of the court. If you killed her, take the deal. If you didn't— fight it."

He picks up his attaché case, glares at my lawyer, and stomps off. I stare at his back. The trouble is, I believe I did kill Larissa. The idea of saying so, of opening the sluice of my own guilt, throbs with all the perverse lust of three hundred years of Scottish Presbyterianism. It would be so easy to accept.

But an equally perverse nub in me refuses to take that route; not, at least, until I understand exactly what happened to me on the night of 14 November when I apparently took a knife and hacked to death a woman I thought I loved.

"I still wanna see that shrink," I tell Wong.

"You want me to plead not guilty at trial? Let's get this straight. Not guilty, by reason of mental incompetence?"

"No."

"Straight not guilty?"

"Yeah. For now."

To give him his due, he doesn't seem annoyed. He walks back to the bench and yaks with the ADA, then returns.

"They still won't go for bail," he informs me. For the first time some sympathy cracks through his voice. "You'll be at Riker's till December second, at least."

I say nothing. There's nothing to say. To tell the truth, I never thought I could get bail at a grand jury hearing. The suggestion that I could surfaces briefly, throws a little disappointment around, sinks again.

"You've got an appointment here at eleven," he adds, "with Dr. Malik. I rented a conference room."

"The shrink?"

"Yes."

"Why'd ya make the appointment," I ask him curiously, "if you wanted me to cut a deal?"

Wong smiles briefly. "Please cooperate with Malik; as I said, he's used to courtroom testimony. And your mother asked me to give you these." He hands me two CDs. One of them is called *The Corruption of Grace: How to Shop Your Way to Heaven,* by Pastor D. B. Johnson.

The other is titled *Rocky Mountain Highs—the Greatest Hits of John Denver.*

As the guards lead me back to the holding cell, I wave the CDs at my mother and my friends where they sit, uncomprehending, in the twelfth row.

Dr. Malik is six feet five inches tall. He has a thin, dark face, a guardsman's mustache, and the vestiges of a cockney accent.

He looms over a VCR terminal in the tiny room, stacking cartridges. He asks the guard to remove my cuffs and stand outside. The guard pulls out a form and gets him to sign it. Malik sits me down, turns down the lights, runs a video.

Robert Conrad, dressed in dark cowboy gear, shoots a grappling iron from a derringer.

Robert Culp plays tennis with Bill Cosby.

Don Adams whispers to a secret agent hidden in a mailbox.

Cindy Brady steals a surf Barbie from Jan.

"What the fuck is this?" I ask.

"What are your first impressions of each clip?" Malik asks, switching on a palmcorder that he places on the table, lens pointed in my direction.

"You gonna figure out me killing my wife by showing reruns of *The Wild, Wild West*?"

"I'm a video therapist," Malik says patiently. Obviously he's used to questions like mine. "The primary relationship men and women tend to have is with stories, especially stories told on entertainment channels. It follows they will reveal the most about themselves by what they see in those stories. Do you feel threatened by Robert Culp?"

I sigh. And answer his questions. At least this beats the MCHF. We watch Andy Griffith consoling Ron Howard in *Andy of Mayberry;* Malik wants to know if I see any latent homosexual abuse here. He's very interested in how I perceive the relationship between Gilligan and the Skipper, and between the Professor and Mrs. Howell. After twenty minutes of similar questions he pulls out a flashlight and hypnotizes me. It takes a while—I suspect the Riker's armor slows things down—but eventually I go under. When I come to, he's packing his video gear.

"So?"

"Yes?" he replies.

"Did I do it?"

"The homicide?"

"Why is it," I ask him, "shrinks and lawyers always answer a question with another question?"

"Do we?"

"Oh, come off it."

He smiles, not warmly.

"You didn't relate the incident, if that's what you mean.

You fantasized at length about dancing with a naked woman on a boat in the East River. After that, I think, more images; castles surrounded by moats of black water. That sort of thing.''

"How frustrating for you."

"Actually," Malik says, flipping the tape from his palmcorder, "you are an extraordinarily apt subject for hypnosis. If Mr. Wong wishes to continue—" He leaves the sentence unfinished.

"D'you think I have TDF," I ask him, "some weird kinda form of it?"

"Do you feel as if you may?"

I ignore that question.

"I work in television. Or worked, I guess. I spent my days half in, half out of what's s'posed to be the real world. I mean, maybe I have a whole other world in me I don't know about! Maybe I have ten of them!"

Malik says nothing.

I put my arms on the table. I feel like my chronic depression just ratcheted up another ten notches. I suppose, without realizing it, I was hoping for certainty from this guy; the knowledge, one way or another, of what I really did, what I really am. Certainty, even the worst kind, would bring a peace of sorts. But a good shrink will tell you he's the last person to turn to for that kind of information.

Only one man has that knowledge and, apparently, he ain't talking.

The bus goes back over the Manhattan Bridge. Looking down on the dark flat river this time reminds me, not of the recurrent images in my head, nor of my dance with a stranger on a barge to the south, but of a story Larissa used to tell about her childhood.

She wanted to be a figure skater. The Soviet skaters were national heroes and she followed them the way kids in the States followed movie stars. Her father was stationed in a place where the rivers froze in October to black ice. She would go alone, after school, wearing warm underwear under a tangerine tutu, to practice on the river the spins and axels she saw on their black-and-white TV.

She realized, after her first disappointing rink performance, that she was not cut out to be Oksana Baiul. Larissa was incredibly hardheaded, so she decided at that point she would aim for less demanding arts to become the star she wanted to be. But she continued to skate. And in part of my memory I continued to see her as a slim blond girl gliding gracefully in the long twilight up the endless frozen river between the birches and the missile silos.

TWENTY-FOUR

THE NEXT MORNING I get up at five but I don't leave my cell. Derek comes in and watches me warily; Cosmo obviously clued him in to my botched electrocution.

I lie on my back and watch the roach in the bunk bracket. I think, He's probably hungry. He's like Archie, I speculate, a wisecracking New York cockroach. Only this time he got caught, for no good reason, in a square of steel he can't get out of because some asshole blocked the exit with a 3.5-inch floppy.

A wave of pity grows out of my chest. A sense of utter sadness blossoms out of that pity; sadness because of all the helpless insects hurt against their will. Sadness, because my wife was hurt; sadness, that she was hurt by me. Even my toes feel mushy. I start crying without sound, and I can't stop. This goes on for a couple of minutes. The salt of tears stings my burned right hand. Derek turns away in disgust and slots the nearest CD into Cosmo's ghetto blaster.

"Sunshine on my shoulder, makes me happy . . ."

"What de fock dees ras?" Derek roars, snapping out the disc and dropping it on the floor like a poisonous spider.

"John Denver," I tell him wearily, and bury my head in the pillow.

A guard comes by to tell me I have a visitor. Wong, without a doubt. I take the 8 A.M. bus to Bantum. Derek and I hang around the rec area until eleven.

Neither Derek nor Cosmo has visitors this morning so I have no bodyguard but I ride in the front of the bus, next to the guard, and nothing happens.

When I'm let into the cubicles area at the reception center I'm so sure Wong will be waiting in my carrel that my eyes pass right over her, automatically scanning for a small Asian in a dark suit.

Then something is triggered, a thread of memory in a nook of the brain that belongs to a wholly different place, a world before the Rock. Soft pale skin gleaming against the autumn night. My eyes track back along the cubicles.

"Kaye!" The name pulled from my mouth as if by a big wind blowing across my face.

She's wearing the Hawkley-ite kerchief, and a long black dress cut fairly low over her breasts. She has on tights with leopard spots under black combat boots. Her cornrows are braided up the same way but what really strikes me is how scrubbed her cheeks appear, like every freckle had been polished separately; and how her eyes look at you directly, without guile or warning. They are the eyes of someone who has never been badly damaged.

I know for a fact she never spent even one minute in a jail cell, unlike the Filipino heroes commemorated by her scarf.

"Hi," she says, too brightly. Not smiling.

"Hello."

Her gaze shifts lower.

"Why you walkin' like that?"

I look down. I still don't walk straight, because of the shank.

"Stomachache," I grunt.

She keeps glancing right and left. It's not the cons and detainees that bother her; she's looking at the gates.

"Claustrophobic?"

She smiles a little.

"Stupid, huh? Cop's daughter, 'n everything."

The smile leaves once more. Her eyes seek out mine.

I sit down, putting my burned right hand carefully over my left. "Could you not look at me like that?" I ask her.

"It's jiss—"

"I'm sick—"

"Sorry."

"I guess," I continue, "I'm sick of searching looks from friends; everybody tryin' so hard to believe I'm not a killer."

"I don't think you're a killer."

Her eyes are very calm and dark. Their darkness has different colors: gray, sable, paillettes of yellow.

"Yeah? An' what if *I* think I am?"

"But you don't remember."

"How do you know?" The same irritation is coming back; everyone wants to tell me what I did, what I thought, what I was reacting to. She reminds me of the girls in Montclair High, the ones who would lead you on, kiss you and touch you till you were practically coming in your pants—and then affirm that *you* didn't really want to go any further. So that, after all the daydreams you had of rescuing them from muggers, of marrying them in shady dells, in the frenzy of rejection you ended up almost hating them.

"The news said you had a blackout," she tells me.

"Well, it must be true then."

"I was with you." Her expression is puzzled. "You were drunk."

"I guess."

"I'm not tryin' to fuck you up," she says. The freckles on her cheeks lose color and her voice, pruned of its cheerfulness, has gone cold.

"What *are* you tryin' to do?"

She stares at me again; at the inmates kissing or cursing their girlfriends and mothers and mules; the fire-gates, ready to slam down at the first sign of human flame. She takes a deep breath, sits down, and puts her hands on the little counter.

"I'm sorry," she whispers. "This place gets to me. I can't imagine how you stand it." Another breath. Her hands pull at each other. "I asked my dad to pull the internal file on—your wife. I found something—it could help you."

"Uh-huh," I grunt, but what I'm thinking inside is, I should try the insanity defense, everybody wants me to plead crazy. It's getting so that even if I wasn't crazy, they would *drive* me nuts with their goddamned confidence that they can plot paths for me through the fog and void inside my brain.

So I stare back at her, tempted to slap her for what she's about to say.

She's leaning forward. Her freckles shining again.

"Ya remember the words written on the wall, in your wife's bedroom?"

Grunt.

"I mean, you remember *seein'* 'em?"

"The news said I had a blackout," I begin, but she shakes her head angrily.

"Stop it, please! I'm tryin' to help." And her face reads hurt and confusion, and I'm reminded of my cockroach, whom I've decided to name Archie. So I cut off the bitchy comment that was supposed to follow and say simply, "I don't remember anything."

"D'you remember seeing the words, when you found her?"

"No."

"Are ya sure? It's important."

" 'Squatter, squatter'?" She nods. "The first time I heard about 'em was from my lawyer, two days ago."

Kaye leans back and puts her hands in her lap.

"I know," she says triumphantly. "Ya wanna know *how* I know?"

I find I'm smiling, the tiniest bit. Her excitement is like a virus; you may not want to contract it but it reaches out and leaps your defenses and before you know it your blood is different.

"I give up."

" 'Cause they were written with a nightshift, dipped in blood." She is almost whispering. "An' the letters came out light red, almost pink. I saw the pictures. They weren't that distinct, 'cause her room was painted red, too."

I nod, thinking about what those pictures must be like. She has to have her share of guts, or maybe kinks, to talk to me after seeing them.

"Don't you get it?"

"Get what?"

"*You can't see red!* You tole me, remember? In the car."
She half stands, sits back down. "You can't see red, or shades
of red."

"I tole you that?"

"Yeah, the night we—danced."

I do smile at that, without planning to.

"If I go to the death chamber," I tell her, pretty calmly
considering, "the one thing I'll remember, that makes my life
seem okay to me, except for Larissa, is dancing with you on
that barge."

She nods. Then she takes an envelope from her jacket
pocket. It's stamped with a NYDOC stamp, which means it
was already searched. She pulls out three color glossies and
passes them over. I immediately recognize the fluffy pillow at
the head of Larissa's bed, and a large expanse of wall, and
nothing else.

"Is this—?"

"That's the words." She leans over and touches the top
glossy. With difficulty, as her finger traces the curve, I make
out a difference in grays that could be the top half of an "S."

"Can you read it?"

"No."

"Tole you."

"That don't mean anything," I say.

"Come off it!" she replies.

"I can write without seeing," I tell her, "anybody can."
She thinks about that.

"Yeah, but you wouldn't choose to. Whoever did this was
tryin' to tell us something, not hide it. If he was color-blind to
reds, he'd choose a different surface. The rug. A white wall.
You ever see someone spray graffiti?"

"I used to be a tagger," I tell her, "when I was a kid."

Her mouth pulls up on both the right and left sides. Her
teeth are white and clean. No one on Riker's has teeth like
that.

And that thought ricochets and whizzes around, because
for a second there I'd almost forgotten about the Rock; but
clothes are rustling, the tempo of people's talk speeding up,
which means this shift of visit is almost over.

The evidence she brought, though curious, doesn't even

convince me. It would stand no chance whatsoever against the Kenzo man or the blond, efficient judge.

"Thirty seconds!" a screw yells.

I stand up, using the counter for support.

"Really appreciate it," I tell her.

"You don't believe me," she says matter-of-factly.

I shrug.

"You don't even believe in yourself anymore."

"I guess that's right."

She hands me a slip of paper. A screw runs over, grabs the slip, hands it back. It has a phone number written on it. I stash it in my wallet without a word.

The guards round us up. I turn at the gate to watch her. She's walking away, through the other gate. She looks back once and our eyes meet. Then she follows the movement of the crowd and disappears behind the steel bars.

TWENTY-FIVE

WHEN I GET back to the ferryboat I go to Cosmo's and lie in my bunk in exactly the same position as before.

The memory of Kaye's face is clear. I especially remember the excitement in her, and the belief in me lying somewhere at the root of it.

But the trust of one person for another functions the way love does; it's a medium, which can only be as good as what's carried on that medium.

I mean, you can buy a top-class audio system, you can buy the Bose projection system that turns the whole room into an acoustically near-perfect speaker, but no matter how good the sound, it will still be worthless if you play bad music.

I am bad music. My tune is somber, roiled, evil in places.

Even the crystal humanity of someone like Kaye cannot change my music.

I remember when the bad music first came out, on Ninety-sixth Street and Third Avenue. Fighting with the Latino kids, beating up the sissy faggots from the French school on Ninety-fifth. We lumped up a Puerto Rican kid so bad he spent three weeks in the hospital. I learned to use a knife pretty good then, too. Ripping off the grocery store. Tagging our brash slogans on the walls. We'd spray subtle statements like *"Chinga tu madre"* and *"Puerto Rican fags suck cock"* down on 105th and First, where the Spanish kids had their headquarters.

Always picking black or dark blue spray cans to paint on white walls; or white and yellow paint on dark surfaces.

I put that out of my mind.

The issue is, my logical voice insists—the issue is, do I opt now for the loony defense? Or stick to a straight not-guilty plea and hope that, once the publicity wears down, Kenzo man will get sick of the whole business and cut a better deal?

I haven't heard Archie moving since I got back.

I sit up in my bunk, cry out sharply as the wound in my right stomach is compressed. Derek glances over from Cosmo's bunk.

I take the Dale Carnegie off the bunk bracket. The cockroach lies half on his side in the corner. When I prod him with one finger he jerks, and is still.

I cover him with the floppy and shuffle out to the refectory. With a sigh, Derek puts down a copy of *Hot Pussy* and follows. I pour a cup of coffee, palm a couple of ounces of sugar, and return to my bunk. I lift off the diskette again and spill a half ounce of pure cane crystals over the insect.

The roach stirs.

Derek opens *Hot Pussy* where he'd left off.

"Mahn, you ree-ly dinged-out," he comments.

"What everybody says." But I can feel something starting to tick inside me. It's like a tiny apparatus, somewhere under the heart, that I never knew existed until now. It is thin and powerless—certainly incapable of altering the course of major drives. But it feeds off unanswered questions the way my cockroach feeds on sugar. And the questions it chews on now are:

Would a skilled graffiti writer ever spray a wall with paint the same color as the wall?

Am I a skilled graffiti writer?

If the answer to questions one and two are no and yes, respectively, then—

Who wrote the words "Squatter, squatter" in blood in Larissa's bedroom?

"Listen," I tell Derek. "Nobody saw *Munn's World.*
Right?"

"Fuck off," Derek says.

"But someone wanted to kill me. Or stop me from doing
something. If they knew about *Munn's World,* they coulda
killed my wife, set me up?"

"Oh, mahn," Derek says in disgust, "me tryin' to read da
leetrature, leave me alone."

He flips *Hot Pussy* to the centerfold scratch-and-sniff.
Scrapes at it with a dirty thumbnail, then, sticking his nose
into the crack, inhales deeply from the page.

I sit on the side of the bunk. My stomach is hurting hard. I
down a couple of Percosets. I can't get away from the fact that
nobody was familiar with *Munn's World.* It's like an airtight
room to which only I had the key.

Although Stefan knew it backward; and Rosie Obregon
saw the pilot.

And anyone at XTV who knew my password, or how to
hack around it, could have gotten in.

Or even a hacker outside X-Corp who was familiar with
the way Virtix files work.

I walk into the refectory area. Pour another coffee and sit at
the corner table. Derek lumbers along behind and sits, facing
the other way so between us we cover 360 degrees of the
room.

Nobody pays us much attention. The usual glares from
PITA fans. A couple of Montserraters click dominoes at the
next table.

Al Roker doing the news, his big M&M's face under the
snowy hair filling the screen of the padlocked TV. Our personal tee-dee, the black man who came in on my chain, sits in
the spot he has dibs on, under the flickering pixels.

China, Russia boosting forces near the Amur. Senator
Powell calling for a "Berlin Wall" across the Mexican border. A big Johnsonist rally in Newark today.

The idea of Newark sends me back, synapse over synapse,
to Kearny and the Viet boys in short jackets and carpet-
cutters. It suddenly hits me, What a hell of a coincidence it
was for me to be chased down, once in Jersey and once in
Brooklyn, and then to wig out so far I would pop my old lady
in Greenwich Village a couple nights later.

Unless they were *trying* to ding me out, to the point of doing something so insane?

In the camera of my mind I watch the tall figure in his long dark coat standing on the corner outside Larissa's. The coat that looks so much like the chesterfield worn by the *Munn's World* killer.

I shake my head. I mean, no one can micro-manage a head trip like that; fine-tune it to the point where, by losing your hold on reality, you do what they were trying to make you do all along?

Just like in McGovern's bar, the first thing I hear is an absence of noise, before the words coming through the audio ports start to make any sense. ". . . protested in front of the Municipal Courts Building today as the case of murdered soap star Lara Love went to pretrial hearing."

Shot of twenty or thirty people, clustered behind police barricades under slate skies, with signs reading "We Love You, Lara," "Domestic Abuse Threatens All Women," "Kirsten Lives," and, most succinctly of all, "FRY MUNN!"

The reporter does his piece. A watery pastel shows a shovel-shaped chin topped with dim freckles and grayish hair in the defendant's area; Munn's face looking scared and guilty as fuck.

Al flips to a shooting in Flatbush that left four kids dead. The entire refectory stares at me, then goes back, without comment, to whatever they were doing before.

Cosmo walks into the refectory an hour later. He's accompanied by a round man dressed in gray sweats, with a black goatee and the tattoo of a large woman called "Concepción" on his left biceps. Cosmo tells the Montserraters to shove off and they comply. He leans over the table toward me, his thin features taut. His snood vibrates as he speaks.

"Trouble, mahn," he begins in a low voice, and jerks a thumb at the Hispanic. "Hector say we got trouble."

"Jeez," I say, "an' here I was jiss havin' a quiet vacation, like in Montego Bay or somethin'."

"Not funny," Cosmo replies. He leans even closer. His lips stay close together as he speaks. "Netas and Ahm of Allah comin' togethah to smoke you. Five nights from now.

Gonna be fee-ake fire alahm, cells open. Dem got ee-eight people on de ferry, gonna rush in heah—mee-ake a move when we sleepin'.''

"Damn," I say lightly, taking a sip of coffee.

"You doan believe me?"

I stare at the coffee. I'm not sure why I react like this to Cosmo. It's not that I don't believe him; it's that his words don't bother me so much.

Maybe it's because the tension on the Rock is so great—and so mind-fuckingly monotonous—that any event, however lethal, becomes something to look forward to, as long as it breaks the boredom.

Maybe it's because I want to croak.

Except that little ticking sound is still carrying on, deep in my rib cage. It's even clicking at a somewhat faster rate, like the old Lucas fuel pump in my Morgan whenever you went over ten miles an hour.

It feels like the first, faint hints of something I haven't felt in a long, long time.

It feels kinda like excitement.

I have to repress this. I've been on the Rock long enough to know that any excitement is deadly dangerous.

Because excitement implies passion, and passion implies something can make you happy.

And that makes you start to care about what happens to you. Once you start to care, you waste time dreaming about things being better.

You lose your edge.

So I push the ticking away. It subsides readily to idling levels. I'm still on the Rock, after all. *That* is the reality.

"An' what do you do," I say to Cosmo, "assuming you still wanna keep me alive? Tell the warden?"

Cosmo fishes out one of his mutilated cigarettes, holds it between two fingers but doesn't light it. He looks at me with pity.

"Mahn, sometime me tinkin' you reely lose you mahbles. Wahden doan believe you, an' if he do, he don' care. We all ice each othah, on da Rock, mee-ake his job easiah."

"Him on da news, mahn," Derek says in his basso growl. "Jus' now. Wahden care, if him on da news."

"Well, mee-aybe," Cosmo concedes, "but you go to

wahden, dem say you a snitch—den, when you come back, *every*-boddy out to ice you. Even me." He adds, "Contract got biggah, anyhow."

"Whaddya mean, bigger?"

Cosmo jerks his thumb toward the Latino again. This time he lets him talk.

The man shrugs. "Fifteen tosan," he says. He has a wicked Dominican accent. "German marks. Netas say, dis guy take out de contract, two, tree weeks ago. Mean *hijo,* mang; call 'im 'Drac.' "

"Drac," I repeat noncommittally.

"*Claro,* mang." Hector pulls up his sweatshirt sleeve and flexes a forearm. Concepción wiggles her bare ass as his muscles tighten and release.

"Beeg gringo, got a long black coat, like de vampire movies." Hector grins, suddenly, and opens his mouth. He only has three or four teeth. He points to the one incisor among them. "Dracoola. Choo get it?

"Netas don' like 'im," he adds, and the grin fades a little.

"I can get you out," Cosmo whispers, looking over his shoulder. He scrapes a match, lights the cigarette.

"Whaddya mean, out?"

"Out de back door." Cosmo takes a deep drag, and whistles smoke into my face. His breath is not pleasant.

I smile.

"What de fuck you laughin' at, mahn?"

"You're outta yer mind. You can't get me offa here. This is Riker's."

Cosmo straightens up. He puts his cigarette down. His eyes narrow. Derek glances around, briefly, from watchdog duty.

"You dissin' me, mahn?"

I hold up both hands.

"I'm not dissin' you, Cosmo. But no one gets off Riker's. Even I know that."

"I'm tellin' *you.* Dat right, Derek? I 'n I get you off, go togethah, me t'rough wid dis plee-ace, anyhow."

I glance toward the television. The tee-dee is staring at a colorful ad that would be in three dimensions if we had the right equipment. I realize why I looked up; the theme music is familiar. The same locomotive that leapt from the billboard over the Brooklyn Bridge tries to jump out of the two-dimensional screen in my direction, and fails miserably. The music swells; the voice intones, *"Real Life,* it's a *whole new world."*

"I thought you had your ticket out already, I thought your girlfriend was gonna drop charges—"

Cosmo's eyes narrow farther.

"Posse got to dat beetch."

"Ahm of Allah put Posse up to dat," Derek comments, "dem wantin' de territory."

"Shut up, Derek," Cosmo says. "Let's joss see-ay, ho'e chee-ange her mind."

I think, I wouldn't want to be Cosmo's old lady when he gets off the Rock.

"How do I know," I tell him, "you're not makin' this up?"

He doesn't loc-out; he says, quite calmly, "Don' believe me, mahn, it's up to you. You heah de fi-ah alahm, five night from now, remembah what I tole you."

"But why *you* wanna help me out?"

Cosmo takes a long drag from his cigarette, then crushes the butt carefully on the table and drops it in his shirt pocket.

"For fifteen tousan dallah an' expenses, mahn," he says. "Which you goin' to pee-ay I an' I, on top of dat two tousan you already owe. Mee-ake it twenty tousan, even."

I stare at him for a beat. I can feel the ticking speed up again, a little faster now than it was earlier.

I think, frankly, that Cosmo is crazy—chances are ninety-nine to one he'll get us smoked, or slammed in the bing for the duration.

But just the outside possibility, the one percent chance of getting off the Rock, triggers in me a yearning that's stronger than sex, and hunger, and thirst combined; that is independent of my desire to die, or my (possible) resurgence of hope; and that yearning is, for a week or a day, to be outside; even skulking around the sewers of the city, or prone in some wet Long Island potato field hiding from AGATE choppers, which is where escaped cons always ended up in *Copkiller.* To spend any time at all in the dirty air, unringed by walls, with a choice of roads not guarded by screws, or cut by the razor-ribbon of Riker's.

"Fuck it," I say. "How you gonna get us out?"

Cosmo looks at me with his usual lack of affect. His bones are tighter, his lips drawn as ever. Then, out of the blue, an eyelid drops over a bloodshot pupil, and rises once more.

Cosmo has winked.

TWENTY-SIX

THE HOURS PASS slowly at the best of times on the Rock. They drag twice as much over the next three days.

I don't shave anymore; Cosmo says the beard will help disguise my clock once I'm off Riker's.

He and Derek beef up security around my person.

Cosmo grills me carefully about my state of mind, and seems satisfied when I tell him that I wouldn't be hassling with escape if I was still interested in offing myself. He gives me a shank; it's a nine-inch piece of fairly soft aluminum, honed on both sides. The grip is made of toothbrush handles of different colors, yellow and blue and green, melted to the haft so it looks like a piece of gaudy Murano glassware.

Every morning Cosmo shuffles through the percentage of the whack library he hasn't rented out. He chooses the thickest issues and tapes them flat around my back and halfway up the chest until my abdominal cavity is entirely padded with copies of *Pussy Monthly, Wet and Pink, Juggs, High Society, East Coast Slave Girls*.

The color issues are best, he explains; the china clay glaze used to coat color pages, when sandwiched tight, makes them almost impenetrable to knife thrusts; the chapters of gaping sexual organs and Brobdingnagian mammaries in the annual roundup of *Union,* he claims, will stop a .22 short fired at point-blank range.

The two Rastamen make sure my schedule varies so that except for breakfast I'm never in a set place at a given hour. The squat man seldom leaves my side now. Cosmo, acting more and more like a harried staff officer, spends a lot of cash on the phones in Bantum, tells me nothing of his plans.

I watch a fair bit of television, something I don't do usually. One of the TVs in Bantum has a shutter-glass hookup, and among the stochastics built into Cosmo's schedule for me, I manage to catch the ''VR'' serial Fox slammed together to hitch a ride on *Real Life*'s publicity.

I'm perversely delighted to find it stinks. Some development hack put together a package of the parameters they wanted—CR values, fifteen products from major advertisers per episode, sanitized gunfire for family viewing, five interactive options between commercials—and eight episodes of *Frisco Fire* spewed out the other end.

Even *Real Life* will blow that out of the water, I figure. And as for *Munn's World*—well, if people could visit *Munn's World* just once, they would never watch ''normal'' television again.

Otherwise I don't think about *Munn's World* much. I never think about how it relates to Larissa's death. The small, ticking sense of excitement inside me wavers up and down but it must hook up to some last-ditch faith in myself because it never entirely vanishes.

Of course I can't be sure this excitement is not fake. The problem with being potentially cuckoo is, your ignorance of that fact is a given.

But I'm content, for now, to await Cosmo's actions. Once I get off the Rock, there's a couple of tricks I can try. Maybe I can trace who, if anybody, broke into *Munn's World* to rip off details, like the ''Squatter, squatter'' they later dummied up in Larissa's bedroom.

And if I find no one accessed it, no one but me—well, I can always show up at the Riker's bridge with my hands stuck out, ready for the cuffs.

So I watch TV and lie around my bunk. I spend quality time with Archie, the roach, who's responding well to a diet

of sugar and crumbled-up doughnuts. I trade three Percosets
for an equal number of phone calls in Bantum. My first call is
to Jack Wong, to tell him about Kaye's discovery—he's unimpressed, but promises to look into it. Then I call the number
Kaye gave me, and get her answering machine. Finally I ring
Zeng, who isn't in either.

I leave a message.

Zeng is going to be key in fingering whoever broke into
Munn's World.

Leaving the phone area, I reflect that I never once sus-
pected Zeng or Rose Obregon, the two people besides me who
know *Munn's World*.

I head automatically for C corridor, the squat man shambling faithfully behind, just to the side.

Stefan, of course, is a pal; but, more to the point, neither he
nor Rosie had any conceivable itch to scratch by hurting
Larissa or me. I'm still musing about it when out of a group of
mostly black inmates bursts a confusion of dirty hair and
dungarees, screaming "Kirsten!" and jumping at my face,
slashing a shank at my neck area—for which, despite the mad
noise and shock of violence, there's only one quick,
Rodneyesque riposte: to block the thrust, turn, spin him into
the circle of his own momentum.

Only he doesn't spin, but hooks my arm and holds on
tenaciously. And Derek moves in, solid, blocking the shank
with his mitt. The man is definitely a tee-dee. He has the tics,
the glazed eyes of TDF. As if that wasn't clue enough, he
continues to croak Larissa's stage name as he folds submis-
sively into Derek's arms.

The squat man grunts and looks confused for a moment.
Then he lets go of the tee-dee, who spins away, shrieking
"Kirsten!" in triumph, dropping the first shank while the
second, that he'd held concealed in his shirt, sucks blood from
just under Derek's sternum and funnels it all over the lino of
the rec center.

I hold on to Derek but I can't keep him upright. He sinks to
the floor. "Watch you *back,* rasclout," he whispers to me as
men make a circle around us.

The guards move in with stretchers and warm-latex dispensers. The bells clang.

They take Derek away, fast and smooth. The screws march

the tee-dee off. I stand in the middle of the rec center, amid the puddles of blood.

Feeling the men stare at me and whisper.

The blood on my shirt has turned it gray.

Finally I go back to the gate, and stay there till the bus comes.

Hector shows up on the ferry two hours later.

Derek died in the Northern Infirmary. Cosmo has assigned the Dominican to guard me from now on.

Hector is nervous and smells of cheap "Navy SEAL" aftershave.

I sit numbly on the bunk, watching Archie, wondering how I could possibly have grown fond of a two-hundred-pound guy who read *Wet and Pink* with his fingers and said nothing but "fock" on the rare occasions he said anything.

When Cosmo shows up he doesn't mention Derek. His features are more stretched than usual. When I try to say something, he tells me to "shot de fock up."

I obey.

The next day is when we're supposed to break out of here. I'm getting nervous now, so antsy I can't eat. I bum butts off the rotund Dominican, and cough on the acrid smoke. I ask him to fetch Cosmo for me—the Jamaican left on the first bus and hasn't been back. I'm sick of being deprived of info.

Hector just shakes his head, and lights another cigarette off the shag end of the first.

"Tranquilo, maricon," he growls, watching the corridor, fidgeting hopefully with the shank taped up his sleeve. "Slip 'n slide, mang."

The absence of Derek looms squat around both of us. He seems to have moved into the same closet in my mind that Larissa went into; the place where the dead live, where they cheat, for a while, the implications of their passing.

By late afternoon I become convinced that Derek's death has somehow screwed the escape plan. I tow Hector to the breakfast area, pour coffee, and sit listlessly, staring at the barred porthole.

I think it's possible, even probable, I will never see the world again except from behind steel bars.

And then I realize I won't even do that, because at five o'clock *today* the fire alarms will go off and a dozen men will race down the passageways of the MCHF with the sole intent of sticking me full of sharp bits of customized metal.

I finger my own shank, taped under *Pussy Monthly* in the small of my back.

Cosmo, without sound or much visual disturbance, slides onto the bench opposite.

Hector jumps.

"*Chingon,* mang, choo scare me!"

"Shaddup." Cosmo looks around carefully. He takes a wad of tinfoil out of his mouth, opens it deftly, extracts six capsules, and shoves three of them across the table in my direction.

"Eat deese now," he commands in a low voice. "Den go to dee house."

"Cosmo," I begin.

"*Now!*"

I shake my head. The guard at the end table looks up at us, folds his *News,* picks up a doughnut. He reminds me of one of the teamster electricians at Studio A.

"You gotta tell me what's goin' on," I whisper. "I'm not goin' into this blind."

Cosmo hisses. Saliva bubbles between his teeth, and his eyes burn.

"You don' trust me—"

"It's got nothin' to do with—"

"You got to follow ohders, or it won' wuhk."

"I'll follow 'em better," I tell him quietly, "if I know what I'm doin'."

He hisses again, rolling his eyes and opening his hands as if to ask Jah how he got saddled with this impertinent son of Babylon at such a chronic time.

Then he leans over and says, quite matter-of-factly, "Dees make you an' me seek as a dog. We trow up an' feel bad, de nurse-mahn come an' get us, tee-ek us to dee nurse-steeayshon on B deck."

"How d'you know that?" I am genuinely curious. "What if they send us to—"

"Nevah *mind,*" Cosmo grunts fiercely. "From deah, me have a route out. Me not tellin' you what. Now eat!"

I hold the capsules in my hands. They're half pink, half white, and IGF-Roche is printed on the side.

"Go on!"

I wash down the pills with coffee. Cosmo eats his dry. He points at Hector and says, "You on duty now." He grabs my arm firmly and leads me back to the cell.

For twenty minutes nothing much happens. I've got plenty of time to neaten up my affairs, since all I own is a wallet with two dollars in scrip inside, a NYDOC T-shirt, and underwear. I borrow a match from Cosmo, lift up the Dale Carnegie diskette, and watch as Archie crawls up the match and out of the steel box he's been confined in for the last four days.

"Good luck, buddy," I tell him.

He crawls away, down the matchstick, loses his footing, and falls on my bunk blanket. Takes off at a giddy pace, hurls himself off the bunk, wiggles on the deck, flips right side up, and scuttles for the darkness under Cosmo's bunk.

Cosmo's big high-top smashes down on top of him, leaving a brown smear on the steel.

"Why'd you do that?" I yell.

"Hate fockin' cockroach," Cosmo grunts.

"He was *my* cockroach!"

"Mahn, Rock really gettin' to you," Cosmo tells me in disgust. "You bettah hold you mud long enough to peay."

"Thought you weren't a killer," I reply, only half joking.

"I dohnt keel men, less I have to," Cosmo says. "But dere are two kind of people in da city—men, and cockroach." He points at me, the way he did at Hector. "You bettah mee-ake sure which one you ah."

Cosmo has no trouble filling the time. He must have eighty hiding places behind the shined steel mirror, in weighted bags down the toilet, in the crack over the light fixture. I'm watching him stash the contraband in his shorts—still fuming at the cold-blooded way in which he stamped out Archie—when the pill first bites at my stomach.

It's like an intestinal spasm, uncomfortable but mild. It releases slowly, then comes back double.

Then four times as painful.

Inside a minute I'm contorted on my mattress, groaning and retching. I lose the coffee, and all the food that came before spews over my pillow. I don't care about that, I don't care about hygiene, I don't care about anything except stopping this pain.

Cosmo, for all his toughness, is in no better shape. Froth bubbles around his mouth, and he screams louder than I do.

In the short silence between my own screams I realize what happened. Cosmo's contacts got bought off. They supplied cyanide instead of emetics, and now I'm going to die and someone will collect that fifteen grand put out for killing me.

I should be angry, but there's no room in me for anything except the monstrous pain in my gut.

"Shit!" I scream, "shit shit *fuck*!" Wishing only that oblivion would come at once.

Instead, the "nurse-mahn" shows up, with Hector and two guards. The Dominican wears techie's whites, which means he's a trusty. They lay out the latex, roll Cosmo onto a stretcher, and haul him off. They come back for me a few minutes later. I can't unknot my body so they carry me curled, a latex-wrapped inchworm, through two security gates, down a companionway to B deck. The neon flickers overhead. I find a little extra stomach foam to decorate the stretcher with. A barred gate slides open and my stretcher is deposited in a small compartment filled with bright metal shelves and the smell of camphor and Cosmo's puke.

One of the guards stands outside the gate, wrinkling his nose.

The male nurse pokes and prods and yells stupid questions at us. What was it? Was it needle? Was it China? Was it jisi? he shouts. He's a medium-sized balding gay man with a close-cropped beard. He keeps changing latex gloves and masks. He tells Hector to cut the editions of *Wet and Pink* and *Pussy Monthly* from my midriff.

I notice the Dominican flipping through *Pussy* when the nurse bends to check Cosmo's eyes for tracks.

That's when I realize the pills are wearing off a little. Some of the spasms are as intense as before, but the sequence is thinning out, and I can notice things.

I keep yelling and squirming nonetheless. So does Cosmo.

The nurse dials a number. The trusty puts down *Pussy*, reaches into the back of Cosmo's pants, pulls out a tiny, single-shot .22 pistol, and cocks it.

Lying on my side I have a perfect view. Hector appears to move slowly, I can almost predict each component of the motion he makes, as in a black-and-white movie classic where every frame is separate and you want to take a step yourself to complete the action.

He walks backward toward the doorway, toward the guard, as if to reach something on a shelf there. He turns and, in a movement that seems to take fifteen seconds but probably is accomplished at lightning speed, jams the pistol hard into the hollow at the base of the guard's jaw.

The guard, who is white, turns even whiter.

"Fuck," he whispers.

"Unlock de gate," Hector whispers.

"You can't."

"I blow choo fockin' head off," Hector continues calmly, "an' do eet mysef."

The nurse turns around, still talking into the phone.

Cosmo's leg scythes at the nurse's knees. The man jack-knifes, gasping. Cosmo, half sitting, grabs the phone, listens for a second, and mumbles, in a fair imitation of the nurse's voice, "Sorry, got to go, call you back?"

The screw, with the .22 still stuck in his face, unlocks the gate, slides it open, and, at the trusty's urging, joins the nurse on the deck.

I close my eyes. The cramps are less painful but they're still bad enough to make me fairly indifferent about what happens next.

What happens next is, not much, for five minutes or so. The screw and the male nurse squat uncomfortably against the shelves at the back while Hector points the .22 in their direction.

Cosmo, still groaning from the effect of the pills, retrieves keys from the screw's belt and unlocks our handcuffs. He cuffs both nurse and screw to one of the equipment stanchions, and covers their mouths with duct tape.

The trusty breaks open two of the locked drawers, sorts through a fistful of plastic hypodermics, then grunts in satisfaction. He shows one of the hypos to Cosmo.

"Stelazine," Cosmo says. "Right *on.*"

While Cosmo holds the derringer Hector shoots fifteen ccs of the drug into first the guard, then the nurse.

The spasms wear off almost as quickly as they came. Soon I can stand up almost straight.

Then the fire bells start to clang.

"Okee-ay," Cosmo yells. He sticks his head out the gate and looks carefully down the corridor. An alarm light is flashing at the base of the stairs. "Move."

Despite the bells I can hear feet pounding on the steel deck overhead. Cosmo sprints down the passageway, trying different doors. The fifth is unlocked. He switches on a light, motions us through.

It's a cramped locker, filled with cans of paint, acetone, rollers. The deck is of light steel with raised star shapes for footing. Cosmo bends over it, feeling at the edges. His action defines what it is, an emergency hatchway with an old-fashioned keyhole lock. He takes out one of the plastic bags he stashed behind our mirror. It's stuffed with familiar blue-white round objects, maybe a tenth of an inch in diameter.

Match heads. There must be several hundred of them. Cosmo works the bag into a sausage shape, then coaxes it through the wide keyhole. He's sweating like James Brown at the end of a set. He takes a whole match, pokes it into the bag, and lights it with another match. A drop of sweat snuffs the first match out. Cursing, he lights another, then jumps up, shoves us into the corner, and buries his face between me and the trusty.

Nothing.

Nothing.

A treble cracking; a "whang" that pops the air in our ears. The light goes out. A sickening, rancid odor of sulfur. A can of paint falls and spreads slime underfoot. The Dominican is mumbling "Come on, come on." I can feel Cosmo on his knees again, shoving us out of the way while he lifts the hatch underneath us. Suddenly he pauses.

"Shaddup!"

Hector shuts up.

There's been noise on other decks the whole time, muffled shouts, whistles, thumps.

This noise, however, is on B deck, and coming closer. The

low thudding of men running silently as possible on steel plates. The occasional squeak of athletic shoes.

"They ain't here!" a voice yells suddenly. It sounds like he's just outside the door.

"Modda*fuck*!" a voice with an odd accent says. "Dey s'pos' be in sick bay."

"Fly bastard, that Cosmo," a third voice comments admiringly.

"They aroun' somewhere," the first voice says. "They din get off."

"Spread aht," the second voice says.

"I tell homies what to do," first voice interrupts sharply.

"Don' tell Dragon wha to do," the second voice comes back.

"We all spread out," the first voice offers. "Okay? Only, you find him first, cut his neck vein *good* this time, make sure."

The shoes squeak. The bells stop clanging. In the sudden silence I can hear blood thumping in those neck veins, noisily taking advantage of what could be a very temporary seal.

Cosmo opens the hatch. It emits a creak like Yma Sumac in a bear trap. The musical sound of feet on steel rungs echoes in a hollow chamber. A damp whiff of old diesel fuel mixed with seaweed and rust rises from around my feet.

Light springs from the hatch, turning the thick smoke suffusing our compartment into bright yellow fog. Cosmo grabs my ankle and tugs downward. I get on my knees, poke my legs through the hole, my shoe is shoved onto a rung. I scramble downward, followed closely by the trusty.

I look around. We're in a narrow chamber shaped, saints preserve us, like a steel-braced lozenge, with one side of the lozenge curved upward toward us. In front, as you come down the ladder, is a workbench piled with bolts and brushings. A door-sized opening leads off to the left into a dark and cavernous space that probably once was the ferry's engine room. Our footsteps are muffled by rust. Buff paint drips from the hatch we came down, Pollocking our prison clothes.

The curved wall of the chamber, I figure, has to be the ship's hull. Cosmo is leaning against it, wrestling with a metal crab covering a circular plate flush with the corroded steel.

"Rasclout," he grunts, "focking *bah*-stahd! Why he no tellin' me?"

The crab has a screw fitting in the center that locks four arms on to a flange.

I know, without knowing how I know, that it's a porthole cover.

"Let me try," I offer.

"Arrr," Cosmo says, straining at the handle.

"Hurry," the trusty says, looking nervously at the hatch above us.

"Give me dat."

"What?"

"Dat—steeck!"

I pull a metal bar from the workbench.

"Yah." Cosmo whales on the screw handle. A third of it shears off.

"Lee-sen!" Hector commands.

We can hear it, even from here; a Doppler howl, like electric wolves.

The escape siren.

"Let me try," I repeat.

"Go *on,* then," Cosmo says furiously, backing away from the porthole. I lock my right hand around the fitting, which resembles a big steel tap handle. The burned skin where I played electrician hurts, but I've got too much adrenaline racing around my system to care. I wrap my left hand around my right, and twist viciously.

The handle squeaks.

"Alright!" Cosmo breathes.

Twist again. It feels stuck.

I can imagine the men in prison shoes smelling sulfur, finding the compartment. Opening the hatch, they draw their long shanks in triumph. I yank as hard as I can, and again, and then the rust gives and the claw loosens.

"Yah," Cosmo says, "*ras*clout," and hauls the cover all the way off.

Underneath is a big porthole of glass and green brass, secured by three eye rings.

Cosmo whips out his shank, threads it through each ring, leans his weight on them, and they come off smoothly.

Then the porthole is open. It's as if the sea crawled into the

MCHF. A freezing breath of salt, scum, and sewage washes into our nostrils.

Cosmo hangs a Maglite on a string around his neck. He clambers up the sloping wall, shoulders through the narrow opening, screws himself like a bolt until suddenly his legs kick and he disappears.

A distant splash.

The trusty does the same.

For a moment I hesitate. Every sane part of my brain insists this isn't a good plan, in fact this sucks. You cannot swim more than five minutes in the November Atlantic, and New York Harbor is, most definitely, an arm of the Atlantic. Not only that, this section of it is the anteroom to Hell Gate, a witches' brew of currents and rocks that scares the shit even out of people with big boats to float through it on.

The air, finally, decides me. It's cold, damp, and smelly.

It's the aroma of the East River, that I used to walk along with Louise when I was a kid.

It's the kind of air you can have as much as you want of when you're not in jail.

Anyway, I reason, if the gangs find the hatchway, I won't have those five leisurely minutes of drowning time; I'll be dead inside thirty seconds.

I scramble up to the porthole. The rim catches my gut wound as I worm around, and I cry out. It's very black out there, in the shadow cast by the hull under the arc-lamps.

The water seems very far away.

Then my hips slip over the flange, and before I can be sure of what's happening, I'm falling down, endlessly down, into the black water.

TWENTY-SEVEN

THE WATER WELCOMES me like death.

It folds right over my head, crashing loudly, and closes out all light.

It's so cold that it freezes my reflexes. I can't move, I can't even think as I arrow downward. There's peace here, a kind of fulfillment that comes with not doing anything more, allowing it to happen.

My lungs are first to protest. Then my heart which, after stopping for an instant, erupts into frenzied activity. Finally the brain kicks in, sending urgent messages to all limbs, crazed neuro-grams like move (stop) *breathe* (stop) *SWIM*!

Arms and legs flail. Before I know it I'm back on the surface, in air that feels like a shank edge because it's even colder than the water; splashing and retching, making "hoo-hoo" noises as I struggle.

A hand grabs my shirt and tugs. I kick in that direction. You wouldn't think there were waves in the East River but there are, sharp nasty things smelling of salty sink water, spraying into my mouth and eyes, making porno sounds against the overhang of the ferry's hull.

The water seems rougher here because the lights ashore

illuminate the waves. I'm paddling fast, trying to escape the cold gaining on my muscles. I figure I'd better get as much out of them as possible. Cosmo and the trusty pull themselves along a greasy rope. It tautens and sags alternately between thickets of something half submerged that shines cruelly in the sodium vapor.

Razor-ribbon. A tooth of it catches my pant leg. I rip it angrily free. I hate and despise razor-ribbon. The water seems to get blacker. Cosmo, treading in place, holds his flashlight overhead, cursing because it doesn't come on. Finally the ring switch connects. A finger of light stabs out once, twice, and dies.

"Rasclout!" Cosmo gasps.

A pair of searchlights switch on, spotting us. The screws have nailed us square. They dive out of the sky, making the waves silver. They have some kind of new siren that whistles so high and loud it hurts the ears, thunders so huge it covers the slurp of water.

Then the jet wings overhead, five hundred feet up, on course for runway 35N at La Guardia Airport. The lights on its tail spotlight the stripes of United Airlines. Behind that glow of portholes, passengers adjust seat belts, stow their copies of *Forbes,* safe and fed and warm.

As the jet fades I can hear the siren still yowling on the MCHF. A roaring much deeper though less pervasive than the Boeing now drowns out the bells. No searchlights are associated with this sound.

I think, at first, this is the noise of the death train, the black express come to collect anyone dumb enough to try swimming off the Rock in November.

The cold is so deep and basic that it blocks the marrow's connection with the blood, slows the blood's ferrying of oxygen to muscles—throws the switch on muscle, too. My legs are so exhausted they barely move. I swallow salt water, cough, swallow more. "Cosmo!" I gasp, panicking.

I see faces of women. Larissa, Sara. Louise. God, I think, it's all over, when you see the women.

The roaring is everywhere. It comes out of a dark wall that rolls a mass of froth into our faces. Someone jabs a long pole into my shirt, hauls me, coughing desperately, to the wall. My watch rips off, vanishing as I claw its smooth surface.

Hands grab my clothes, skyhook me into the air, drop me on something flat and throbbing. Cosmo lands on top of my legs. Still no lights, just the orange sky wheeling overhead. There's a stink of gas and herbs. My stomach tries to throw up. There's nothing left but a drool of seawater.

I'm aware of cold water pattering in droplets on my cheeks. It's drizzling.

The deck leaps and tilts. The roaring doubles, becomes a noise so all-encompassing it feels like the sound of the sun's creation. Cosmo and I are thrown into a tangle of wooden boxes and metal gas tanks as two huge outboard motors lift the plywood speedboat three quarters of the way out of the water. The boat begins to smack the waves, not hard because it's really more airborne than anything. Wind-driven sleet spins around our plywood pit.

I can hear, over the roar, a sound like a jackal, baying at the sliver of moon that dances behind the drizzle clouds in an off rhythm set by the transom of this dark boat.

It takes me thirty seconds to figure out what it is.

Cosmo is laughing.

Ten minutes later we're somewhere in the Bronx.

The boat comes to rest between two Bouchard trash barges moored to a smashed concrete dock beside a broken warehouse.

A black van waits among the shadows of the warehouse. We climb in and lie among piles of Burger King boxes. Brief snatches of sign or skyline through the windshield: Hunt's Point Avenue, a drawbridge, the Bruckner Expressway, exit for City Island. Men with island accents hand us oversize sweat clothes and sneakers, which we pull on, trembling. Manhattan pops up to the right, hypo towers mainlining the swollen clouds, as we swoop over the Whitestone. Then we subside into Queens.

The van is very warm. It feels oddly mythic to be moving like this, without chains holding me to the chassis. I've left the ferry that didn't go anywhere, maybe because it already was in hell. Now it's this van that feels like a ferry; the Rastaman in front is our dark boatman, taking us across the

Lethe—or Styx, I never could get 'em straight—back into the violent, technicolor life of the city.

I feel totally disconnected from normal living, as should a man who has just visited the underworld. Utterly open, a frozen, pill-scoured Orpheus, to be flitted around like a feather in whatever direction the wind chooses to blow.

I am more free, and more powerless, than I've ever been in my adult existence.

Time doesn't mean shit on the Styx Econovan. Space is open to question. I believe I recognize the Grand Central Parkway, but I'm not sure. The only solid impression I have is movement through different blurs, like when you swim through phosphorescence with your eyes open.

An undetermined amount of minutes later the van descends into streets where most of the lamps are broken. A dark mix of vacant lots, torched cars, vinyl-sided tenements, and the occasional city project rising like a blasted tree in the middle of a heath.

We pass one building, its windows glowing white with heat, ringed by Bradleys and fire trucks. A second fire blazes untended except for a crowd of kids. They dance in silhouette against the flames, chuck malt bottles through the windows of the house into the beautiful simplicity of conflagration.

A helicopter swoops low, spinning wheels of silver light around the surrounding lots, then rises, vanishing as suddenly as it came.

"AGATE," one of the Rastas comments.

"Babylon mothahfuckah," another agrees.

The van pulls up next to a tower built by the same sadistic moron who designed all the other city projects. A twelve-story building, a single-minded oblong of flesh-colored brick as bare and ominous as the slab in the old 2-D movie *2001;* and, like that slab, it's designed to awaken in men the instinct to create violence, and tools for mayhem. As if to magnify its dark power it lies next to three similar buildings. A sign reads "Seth Low Houses." A cheap logo underneath features a ship's flag with gray and yellow sections, and I shake my head, nervously certain that not all links between *Munn's World* and the real one are of my own manufacture.

A handful of men in Rasta snoods and jerseys lounge around the lobby entrance. Cosmo and Hector get out like presidential candidates and inspect the guard of men in the lobby. The walls are covered with graffiti that I read warily, half expecting to find "Squatter," or the nightmare unicorn; but these all say "Neta," "Victor," "Paco," and "Posse," scribbled and shadowed beside the ubiquitous "Fuck You"'s and "Chinga"'s.

The hallways are half-lit and smell of piss, shit, Decon. Every elevator stands blocked, bell ringing, on this level.

We ride up a lift to the eleventh floor where a Rasta with a trey-eight stands guard. The lights are out in these corridors. The Rastas produce flashlights and play them carefully up and down. The lino here is rotten and the concrete walls have holes and cracks along their length. Gray stains, from junkies wiping their arms dry after shooting up, run like decoration from one end to the other. A slogan reads "Celebrate the Industrial Allah; Share Software, not Needles." From various apartments I can hear boom boxes playing shifta rap, or the treble arguments of TV dramas. Not one door opens, not one head pokes out to check what's going on.

We enter the last door on the left. Sears furniture has been shoved against walls hung with posters of Jah Lion. Tangled bedding occupies the space left bare. In the cracks between mattresses dirty pots, paper plates, and half-empty cartons of jerk chicken are stacked. Cockroaches panic, like my friend Archie used to do, scuttling and popping toward safety. The windows are covered with Reynolds Wrap; I assume that's to foil infrared spying.

A big table in the center of the living room supports a line of plastic sandwich bags containing the soft yellow resin of jisi yomo, the green fibers of ganja.

The noise of the chopper grows, fades, grows again. I walk to a window from which a corner of tinfoil has come loose, and peer through.

My first thought is, Brooklyn has been destroyed. The streets below are laid out in a recognizable gridwork, but everything in the lots between is black and charred and dead. The few buildings still lit are last-chance refuge from the rage that must have taken over the neighborhood to make it go this bad.

And all around those islands, the city is burning. Well, maybe not the city, not even the whole neighborhood. Still, in each direction, I can see four or five buildings in flames, or starting to catch, sending white steam and dark fumes over the rest of the area, till it looks like every inch of the place is alight.

An AGATE Apache zooms past our project. It's joined by two more. In arrowhead formation they hover over a convoy of flashing fire department lights down a black avenue toward one of the torched structures.

Even over the whop of choppers and the sirens and horns, the peculiarly neat rattle of automatic fire sounds clearly.

One of the torched tenements falls into itself. A white spray of sparks and flame rushes up the ass of night, and collapses.

"Ahhh."

Cosmo breathes deep behind me. Satisfaction, contentment, are strong in his tone.

"Home."

Hector and I sleep on mattresses jammed against a smashed TV console in the far room.

I go to sleep fast, but the image of the city burning stays in my mind and keeps me from resting deeply. I wake at an undetermined hour, very aware of fire. My eyes open on dim cracked stucco, Jamaican graffiti. Someone screams sadly in the street.

A single shot rings in the distance.

My heart is pounding. For a second I don't know where I am. For a second, I *want* to be in my cell, a place where all coordinates and parameters are locked down solid.

The chubby Dominican sits at the window, peering through the exposed corner.

I walk to the main room. Roach brigades fall back, regroup. Cosmo sits at the table, a bottle of Red Stripe in his hand. A boom box plays Jah Modem, an electric heater blows on his sneakers.

"Well, eet's Cockroach mahn," Cosmo says cheerfully. "How you feel?"

"I'm not sure."

"Half joy, half pan-eec?"

I stare at him.

"Aluhs like dat, fuhst time."

I sit on a stool. A stripped-down Davis P-380, with cans of graphite oil and cleaning wads, lies on the table next to the beer. To the left of that, a fully rigged British Bullpup, its spare clip lined up beside a handheld radio. The base of my spine is sore and raw. I touch the shank still taped to the small of my back.

I rip the tape loose, grimacing, and slide the sharp aluminum across the table.

"Here."

"Keep it," Cosmo says magnanimously. "My geeft."

Electric marimba, synthesized steel drums boink in stretched rhythms.

Shots clap, far away.

A chopper hovers.

"Is it always like this?"

"Alluhs." Cosmo snaps a trigger mechanism home, screws it tight. "*Buyaka,* alla time in da 'ville. *Smuggler's Bible* say, Megorgs keep 'hood like dat, pool fuh labor when dey need it, don't give a damn if dem pop each otha rest of de time."

"You tole me you weren't a Hawkley-ite."

Cosmo pulls back the hammer slide, and sights along the barrel.

"Why you care?"

"Just curious, I guess. I—I know somebody, who's one of them."

Cosmo puts down the trey-eight, takes a sip of Red Stripe. He picks up the Bullpup, aims it between my eyes, lays that, too, on the table.

"Me tole you," he says, "I an' I in beez-ness, not politics. But me tell you someting else.

"Dat book see-ay, Babylon *is* Brownsville. Look aroun' you. Eighty pahcent of people wuhkin' McDonal to buy deir useless fashion jeans, perfumes, CD machine. Twenty pahcent starvin'."

A rip of auto fire.

"Beeg city," Cosmo says, almost dreamily. "Beeg organizay-shon. But at home, some Rasta mee-ake a node in my parish. Supply ganj' fah export. Set up e-mail fuh communicay-shon. Buy trucks fuh da mahket."

I shake my head. I've no idea what he's getting at.

"Down in Loisaida, not fah from heah," Cosmo adds. "Hawkleys mee-ake a node mahket, too. Hot cahs. Bread. B-Net link, even. Run dat neighbo'hood. Even clean da streets, trow dem pushahs out."

"I thought *you* were a pusher."

"Not skag, mahn." Cosmo looks hurt. "Not crack, eithah."

"But you need guns." I nod at the trey-eight.

"Time of transi-shon," Cosmo agrees. "Two tirds de world burnin'. New gangs now. Kashmiri, Tamil, Hakka. Armenian, Chechen, Hutu. Sea Dayak. Gorgeous focking mosaic." Cosmo spits at a cockroach ambling across the lino, misses.

"And?" I'm feeling sleepy again. I barely listen to him now.

"Dem nodes survive," Cosmo says. "Dose 'hoods wuhkin'. Asian, African, even white people like you wuhkin' in da mahket. Me not Hawkley-ite, Cockroach, but dem nodes sure good fah bees-ness."

I get off my chair, sprawl on a filthy mattress in the corner, and doze off immediately. I wake up with Cosmo shaking my shoulder.

"Cockroach."

"Wha—"

I was playing with Larissa's baby. Our baby. He was blond, and had Larissa's long fingers.

"You see heem?"

"Who?"

"You know. Hector. De trosty, come wit us."

"No. He isn't in that room?"

"No. Fock, mahn." Cosmo picks up the walkie-talkie. "Mike. Rattie. Dees base."

"Jah live."

"Jah live."

"Status?"

I roll to a sitting position. The shank lies beside me. Woozily I stash it inside my sweatshirt. Cosmo loads drug bags into a shopping bag.

"Cool ronnin'," the radio squawks.

"Cool heah, too."

Cosmo relaxes a tiny bit, but he holds himself tense, like a deer smelling hound on the wind. "Mongoose," he says into the radio, "you read me? Mongoose."

I hear nothing outside, no choppers, no *buyaka,* no cars or buses or neighbors. A dog howls in the distance, high and eerie. The wind warbles through a window crack. A small switch flips in my head; all of a sudden I couldn't sleep if I were in a warm soft bed, with a bowl of hot chocolate, reading *Swann's Way* in Latin.

Another howl sounds, closer, followed by a series of yips. It doesn't sound like a dog, it's too specific somehow. There's information being traded here.

"Is that—?"

"Coyote," Cosmo says. "Dem com' een, at night."

"Coyotes?" I repeat in a slightly tremolo voice. When I was a kid I was deathly afraid of wolves, for some reason probably having to do with German fairy tales; and, as far as I'm concerned, coyote is just wolf's short cousin. "Do they—" I begin, but Cosmo shakes his head.

"Time to go."

He walks carefully into the hall. I pick up my sweatshirt and follow. Cosmo hugs the left wall, the Bullpup cradled in one arm, the shopping bag in the other, moving toward the stairs. Our shoes crunch jisi bags, crack vials, the sharp plastic factories of smack.

One of the Rasta guards meets us at the elevator, another waits in the lobby. Cosmo eases a service door open. It's still night. The cruddy pavement glistens with fallen sleet.

"Cockroach," Cosmo says. "You walk fahst. Tee-ake dat street, Sackman, stree-ayt to Liberty." He points with the squat gun barrel. "Tee-ake a right, you see L train track, follow dat left on Van Sicklen to stee-ayshun, eet move you where you want to go."

He pauses, looks at me sharply.

"You doan fahget, now. Twenny tousan, cash. You lawyah John A. Wong, one-feefty-one Jay Street. You got tree days."

"Deal's a deal." My voice is hoarse. I'm still half in the dream.

"Yah. Well, you remembah dat." He fishes in his pocket, pulls out a subway token and a pair of cheap sunglasses. He grabs the snood off his head, and fifteen inches of dreadlocks burst joyfully into the poor light.

"Heah. Tee-ake dees." He hands me snood, token, and glasses. "Doan go *anywheh* you use to go."

I move through the door, and hesitate. I turn around, I'm not sure why, to check on direction, say good-bye even. The steel door is closed and no handle exists on this side to open it again.

The projects are deserted. The windows of the graffiti-hatched towers are mostly dark. I check my wrist automatically, and remember my watch is now at the bottom of the river.

I walk fast, following Cosmo's directions into a street where all the lampposts have been shot up.

Four explosions, exactly spaced, crack out somewhere far behind me.

Half the buildings here have burned or fallen into rubble. A small factory with its windows boarded up rises like a tombstone from the vacant lots. A large sign reads "Ethiopia Iron Works."

A tenement, blackened from smoke, vents steam from its roof. Most of this street—Sackman Street—is flooded with murky water over which a scab of ice is beginning to form. I recognize the site of one of the fires I spotted earlier from the top of Seth Low Houses.

My skin hairs prickle.

This place, with its blackened ruins, its ambient shadow, its abandoned cars, reeks of a terror so great no one wants to come within three miles of it.

I wonder what the fuck I'm doing promenading here in the wee hours.

A coyote howls, much closer than before. It sounds like he's eight or ten blocks away. I never realized they came so deep into Brooklyn. Panic burbles up in me, from the place all panic starts, and I have to grit my teeth and tighten my fists to quell it.

I walk faster.

On the horizon ahead of me, a black line runs across the jagged stumps of disused factories. The elevated railway.

The next block, approaching Liberty, actually has trees.

Maybe I'm lulled by the vegetable life. I don't notice the group of youths until I'm almost upon them.

They stare at me with faces that seem utterly impassive. Feeling is a function of hope and they have absolutely no hope or desires left.

They're all black, all lean. They wear sweatshirts and watch caps. Two of them have on motorized rollerblades, the kind with battery engines bolted on the heel. One of the rollerbladers holds back a thin, mean-looking dog on a tatty leash.

The dog stiffens. I can feel them examining me for twenty, thirty seconds after I have passed.

Then the thin, twin whine of the rollerblade motors starts up. Underneath, the footsteps of the rest of the gang.

I walk even faster, a kind of lope halfway to jogging.

They match my stride.

The electric whine rises in volume. Around the corner, at the end of a line of burned row houses, a bodega spills light and salsa into the night.

I run, hell for leather, down the ice-cracked pavement. When I reach the light of the bodega I turn around on my pursuers.

The street is empty.

A coyote yips in the distance, maybe at the moon, maybe not.

TWENTY-EIGHT

I TAKE THE train to Manhattan.

In a way that's a stupid move, because the island is where I'm known. It's where the cops expect me to go.

Still, it's *my* island. My expeditions to the outer boroughs were always just that—adventurous forays into the terra incognita of a decaying seaport. In Manhattan I know the staggered rhythms, the frontiers between neighborhoods, the schedule of light and dark.

I get off at First Avenue and Fourteenth Street. It must be around six or seven because knots of early workers ride the train, and when I come up the steps the tainted darkness is blueing toward dawn.

I catch a glimpse of myself in the window of May's noodle shop and my heart actually jumps, for I'm just the kind of weird bastard I would have crossed the street to avoid three weeks ago; a white boy with red-rimmed eyes, filthy hair, three days' growth of beard, and gangbanger's shades dressed in hip-hop sweats and sneakers with a Rasta snood to top it all off. Woof! A dangerous mix of styles and identities.

Nobody looks at me twice.

And I realize I made the right choice, after all. For the

boroughs are where territory and group identity are forged, the styles discrete and enforced with blood.

Manhattan, on the other hand—and especially the East Village—is where the groups come together, mingle, and adopt what they most like, or fear, about one another.

I'm hungry, and greatly spaced-out. In that space-out I visualize the boroughs as a sump for different acids and lead precipitated out of every corner of the world, building up, in their violent ionic difference, a charge; electricity focused through high-tension lines of bridges and subway and cable tunnels thrumming from the depths of each 'hood to Manhattan, where the pent-up juice regularly arcs in a blue flash of current between the poles of the Chrysler and Empire State buildings.

It's still drizzling, still chilly. My wound aches hard now. A scratchiness in throat and nose extends south into my lungs.

I walk down First Avenue, keeping a wary eye out for cops. The windows are dressed in multicolored lights, with fake frost, turkeys, visual platitudes of the Thanksmas season. Passing a Ukrainian butcher I lust briefly through the window at the smoked ham shoulders. The fumes from a shashlik vendor pull growls from my stomach. Wander up Eleventh Street, past Veniero's to smell the warm sweetness of baking pastries. In the doorway of a coffee shop on Second I take my wallet from the sweatshirt. It contains the same two bucks in Riker's scrip, the scrap of paper with Kaye's number on it, and Jack Wong's card. The paper is all soggy. Not even a nickel is caught in the folds.

My stomach is so empty there's no longer enough room for hunger. In my great fatigue thoughts grow vaguer and vaguer.

I want to call Stefan, or Kaye, but half the time the only number I'm sure of is Larissa's. Once, when Stefan's number does come back to mind, I borrow a pencil from a grudging news vendor and scrawl it on a scrap of *Village Voice*.

"Next step"—talking to myself—"get some dough." I've been at Riker's long enough, heard enough con-talk, to immediately start checking out banks, and the women hurrying to work with the fashionable Kazakh yak-herder bags precariously strapped.

However I realize just as fast that I don't have a clue how to proceed with a bank robbery, or a mugging even; I can't think of the first step. I mean, how do you silence a screaming, city-hardened woman without seriously hurting her?

There's a Banker's Federal branch on the southeast corner of St. Mark's and Second. The office part isn't open but the ATM does good business in the 7:30 rush.

I peer through the window at the bulletproof glass shielding the counter. I've heard that all you do is write a note reading "I have a gun" and the teller is trained to hand over the Dead Presidents while she presses a silent alarm. The trick is to get the hell out of there in the squeaky minute between cash and cops.

The precinct house is three blocks away, on Fifth Street.

I stand at the bank's door, watching people stash twenties in their billfolds. I take off the snood to finger-comb my hair in the reflection. A woman drops something in it and walks quickly away, without looking back.

I peer into the snood.

Twenty-five cents.

I squat, the way panhandlers do, taking care not to tweak my wound too hard. Slowly I lay the snood open on the pavement before me.

I think, Ten days ago I was a respected professional with some influence in a major industry, in charge of a production that would change the nature of communication, maybe even alter the way people looked at themselves. I had a big, warm apartment and I was earning 150 grand a year.

Today, I'm panhandling on St. Mark's Place.

I make two dollars and fifty-five cents in the first hour, and another dollar thirty-four in the half hour after that. Cops drive by and I put my hand over the lower part of my face but they seldom glance in my direction. Around a quarter to nine a black guy, maybe forty years old, comes up with a paper cup and attitude.

"This my corner," he says.

"You got a deed?" I ask him, which is a Riker's kind of response.

"I fuck you up," he offers.

"I fuck *you* up," I reply.

We stare at each other. His eyes are brown and hard. I know two things: first, this guy's done time; second, for whatever reason, probably because he's at least as hungry and ill as I am, he's not going to take this to the wall.

"Mothafuckin' jiveass moth'fuck," he grunts, and grabs the door when someone walks out. He stands as close to it as possible, opening it for customers, keeping his shoulder to me, proffering his cup.

The Riker's thing to do would be to whip the shank out of my sweatshirt pocket and stick him with it, but the Riker's way works off a big head of pressure due to being locked down and barred shut.

Already the gray light and freezing wind straggling in from the river, not to mention the sense of being able to move as far as I have the strength and desire to, have taken a lot of that pressure away.

I drag the snood back over my hair and walk down St. Mark's, jingling my change.

Halfway to First Avenue I step on something that bursts loudly into a nasal electric rendition of "Silent Night." I almost trip from shock.

Looking closer at the object, I see a thin, pancake-sized piece of green plastic, like an open butterfly wing, with "Infomart/King of Interactive Software" printed on the face. It reminds me of pictures of Russian antipersonnel mines. Fine print promises a nickel redemption fee if I return it to Infomart. I squeeze the two wings shut and it stops playing. I pocket the device and continue east.

Stromboli's pizza parlor is open. The scent of warm cheese and grease is absolutely irresistible. I buy a slice with my earnings, cover it with grated parmesan, garlic salt, and red pepper, and huddle in the warmth of the shop, by the big window, savoring the lukewarm pie.

There's a public phone outside the falafel shop next door. I dial Stefan's number. The machine is on. The song is the Sex Pistols version of "God Save the Queen," indicating he's in and probably asleep. In the space of the song a thought rushes in, like a draft from an open window.

They are bugging his phone.

Maybe they haven't done it yet, but they will soon. The new AGATE laws make approval of phone taps easy; and bugging, thanks to the digital grids, has become a matter of punching in a series of numbers.

I hang up, slowly. My eyes lock on to a familiar sign. "Chez Jules," it reads.

As effortlessly as the *Munn's World* face-sucker slips over the eyes to become your reality, I see Larissa and me walking down the steps of that restaurant.

It's New Year's Eve, two years ago. She just "found" the place, a little French joint in the cellar tarted up like the set for a Paris *guinguette*. A man walks around, dressed in a tutu and playing the accordion, a tiny capuchin monkey squatting on his shoulder. Muddy Waters's great-granddaughter sings Bayou work songs she learned from sheet music. Larissa's cheeks are dark with warmth and Moët and the owner keeps sending more free bubbly, and walking over to hug her as his reward. Larissa tries to pat the monkey, which bites her on the thumb.

The music stops, the whole place goes silent. The owner turns pale, because he knows who Larissa is, and knows she can afford any lawyer she wants; he's expecting to lose his restaurant in the inevitable lawsuit.

Larissa looks at the blood welling gray from her thumb. She splashes it with Moët, wraps a napkin around the cut, finishes her glass. Only I know how conscious she is of the dozens of eyes focusing entirely on her.

"Do you know 'Minnie the Moocher'?" she asks Muddy Waters's great-granddaughter, who nods. As the music resumes, she takes the owner in a stage embrace, and dances an ironic mambo.

Remembering that moment, recalling how I admired her then, I remember also how, during the whole performance, she never accorded me a role more important than that of audience.

I shake my head. The scene floats away like Moët bubbles at the surface of a glass. I look at the phone again.

Jack Wong will not be at work yet.

I examine the slip with Kaye's number. Her line may well be bugged also, but if I disguise my voice and speak elliptically I could get a message through without activating the trace.

Even if they have a voice-recognition unit hooked up, all they would find out is that I was in the East Village when I made the call. Of course, it's stupid to help them narrow the search even to that extent.

I drop the thirty-five cents and dial. I get the machine-that-stole-her-voice. I hang up in disgust.

Seventy cents gone, and I'm no closer to help than I was earlier.

I shamble down St. Mark's into Tompkins Square Park. Black-clad hipsters watch their funky-dressed kids swing and slide in the playground. I panhandle for a while by Leshko's with little success.

I trudge over to Broadway and Bond and sit outside the locksmith on the sidewalk that once sheltered Pfaff's Saloon. A Salvation Army Santa erects his tripod by the Atrium and jingles his bell. A lot of Christmas-carol mines have been salted around here, startling people with their tinny "Little Town of Bethlehem"'s and "Greensleeves." I pocket the ones I see.

The pickings here are better. More cop cars, but I'm getting used to the fact that because of the sheer numbers of homeless, the police don't notice panhandlers unless they create a nuisance. It was one of Henry Warren Powell's bills that cut support for noncitizens with disabilities, which accounts for the fact that there are so many people on the street.

Still, the sight of a cruiser continues to touch my heart with ice.

I buy a cilantro-gorgonzola bagel for lunch at a *mate* bar around the corner on Bleecker. Someone left a copy of the *News,* and without shock, I turn straight to a headline that reads "SOAP KILLING SUSPECT BUSTS OUT."

A picture of me fills three columns underneath. Staring at it, I start to smile.

It's the XTV pub shot. I was a little heavy, my hair was expensively cut, and I was wearing a garish seventeen-hundred-dollar silk jacket.

The Munn in that photo bears virtually no resemblance to the haggard, unshaven loser bent over his cinnamon mochaccino in the plate glass beside me.

Darkness creeps over the city, like a sheet being drawn over a corpse—and is rolled back, somewhat, by the counterpressure of windows and streetlamps; hovering, finally, at the orange-electric standoff New Yorkers call night.

At this point, when I count my change, my coins jingle like the Santa's bell, I'm trembling so. The drizzle has hardened into little pellets of sleet. Even the strings of holiday lights seem cold and heartless to me.

I'm too chilled to sit anymore. I need to find a place to crash for the night. With a grand total of six dollars and thirty-two cents and seven Christmas mines in my pockets, it's going to be outside. What I need now is a neighb with few people so that, in the corners I find to hide in, I can rest with minimum interruption.

I walk down Bond Street, then south down Bowery, retracing the route I took, as a cop, in *Munn's World*. The *bierhauses* and theaters are long gone. The cheap bars that once made the Bowery famous have been replaced by restaurant wholesalers and a couple of Tadzhik chophouses.

I could walk to Zeng's, I guess, but it's certain the cops will be staking out his apartment. I turn east down Houston, moving fast toward the FDR Drive. The exercise warms me, but not enough.

By the Red Square yuppie condo I kick up a bunch of flyers. They flip away in the north wind, dark shapes photocopied on yellow paper. I stumble after one, snatch it up. The head of a unicorn, neck arched prettily, mane flying in a different breeze, stands out clear enough in the streetlight.

I peer up and down Houston. A black couple kisses in a corner. A derivatives analyst hurries home with a video. No tall men in long coats, no Asians in short jackets.

Coincidence. It *has* to be coincidence. I can see yellow flyers up and down this block. No one could possibly have known I would come this way.

My breathing settles.

Anyway, I'm much too cold for pointless worry. I continue east, then south, following a path once called East Street through Corlear's Hook Park, along the river. The wind brings the scent and sound of the black water into my nostrils and forcefully reactivates the memory of the swim I took only twenty-four hours ago.

I check behind me, just in case whoever left those flyers picked up my scent.

Nobody.

Wander around an old playhouse, the condemned fireboat station. The first is caved in, the second ringed with razor-ribbon. Rats rustle nervously amid dead leaves. At the elbow of Corlear's, built right over the water, there's a venting station for Con Ed steam pipes. I can feel the sugary heat bead on my face as I approach. The space around the vents is covered with worn tarps and bits of cardboard. From the tents they've formed around the vents, like raccoons in a hollow tree, a crowd of men stare at me with nothing but challenge in their faces.

I keep on walking.

The FDR Drive rises to become an elevated highway just south of Corlear's. Here, though the wind roars unchecked through the I-beams, I can walk sheltered from the rain, under the rushing cars.

Still listening for the slip-*slap* of pursuit, still hearing nothing but traffic, and the sigh of wind.

It's the names of streets that finally save me from the terror of those photocopied unicorns.

For southwest of Jackson Street was the heart of the city's old waterfront district. On Clinton Street, between Cherry and Water, where the Twin Bridge Houses now stand, was the Brown and Bell shipyard that built the first clipper-style ship, the *Hou Qua,* for A. A. Low and the China tea trade.

In my mind I can make out, to my right, the yards down-river of Brown and Bell: Eckford and Beale on Jefferson, Foreman and Johnson on Rutgers. Between and to the southwest of them, rows of docks and floating wharves, thick with the rigging of coastal schooners and seagoing ships. Water Street, at this level, consisted of warehouses, the counting-houses of shipping firms, and bagnios like John Allen's Dance Hall at Number 304.

I can visualize the tapestry of it, the crowds of seamen, the whores in their taffeta, the glow of whale-oil lamps, the roaring fires in the grogshop hearths. The lust for *Munn's World* is so strong in me that I actually see flames dance in the dark shelter formed by the elevated highway and its forest of supports under the Manhattan Bridge.

The fires are real.

The realization sinks into me slowly. The way *Munn's*

World and my own life have started growing together, throwing tendrils of force and happenstance between imagination and reality, as morning glory vines will bridge the gap between two fire escapes—well, you can see why I'm unsure.

Also, portions of this street are surfaced with cobblestones, the way they would have been in the nineteenth century. Rats ripple back and forth, just beyond the lights, as they did then. The smell of the fires up ahead—burning plywood, paint, nameless chemicals—is different from the oak and pine aroma of a hearth. There's a strong smell of rotting cod, however, which would square with the herring smacks coming in every night to the fish markets, in the 1850s.

The fires, yellow and gray, swirl eight feet high out of old fuel barrels in the dead space under the highway, places that were navigable water 150 years ago.

And so, one foot in the present and one in the past, I walk into the village of the doomed.

I'm reminded here of those fourteenth-century paintings of towns decimated by the plague. The dark girders under the overarching span, the black bulk of water beyond, define a vast cave out of reach of streetlights, in which the dozens of flaming barrels both create and distort perspective.

Around the fires stand elaborate castles made from old pallets, crates, fish boxes, and Con Ed tarps. Some are built around trashed automobiles, the smashed windows covered with cardboard.

And, in the close space between the shacks and the fires, men driven by different epidemics—poverty, disease, mental illness, or all of them together—sit among the rusting I-beams. The fires make skull shapes of their strained features. They are clad in blankets, or a patchwork of Goodwill clothes that emphasize the emaciation beneath.

As I walk slowly through the crooked alleys defined by the DMZs around every campfire, each knot of the doomed stares at me until it's clear I'm not going to make a claim on their particular warmth and shelter.

Then, as one, they turn back to the heat.

The groups are all male, of different ages. A few are entirely black, or Hispanic, or Central European. Most are mixed. Racial differences tend to fade below a certain threshold of misery.

The northwest flank of the elevated highway, where the drainage pipes from the span splash water, is the strip of the tee-dees.

These groups have no fires; their shacks are poorly built and half-soaked. But their sites lie close to the streetlamps and every shack has hooked up a cable to the lamps' inspection ports. Each houses several much-battered televisions, radios, cellfaxes, telephones, and intercoms all going at once. Around these the tee-dees squat, humming as they stare and listen.

In one tee-dee castle I count eight different television sets piled up in a pyramid. Most of the screens show pure static, or rolling lines and bad color. Only two of the sets actually bring in a show. On one of these I see Braindead. Though he doesn't know it, he solemnly reads the news to a dozen men whistling in unison the theme from *Melrose Place*.

I move fast, away from that side. The sight of TDF victims brings back the image of that tee-dee who killed Derek, growling with his shank out of the knot of cons.

I stand by one of the normal fires, where only two or three men have laid claim to territory. The challenge is immediate and clear. One man takes out a baseball bat. Another whistles up a one-eared black dog, a close relative of the hound in the East New York Industrial Area. The dog snarls so hard that spittle flies from its muzzle.

I move to the riverside. There's room to make my own camp here, because, with all the rain coming in under the highway's eaves, this is not coveted real estate. I think I should look for a better place, but suddenly my energy is gone. A fit of coughing uses up all the juice I was saving for walking. My stitches burn.

Close to the river, separated from it only by the bulkhead, large craters appear. Here the waves ate at the soft fill used to claim this part of South Street from salt water, until finally the asphalt and cobbles collapsed. The craters are filled with trash. A junk car or two rears out of the holes.

A floating festoon of bright lights powers slowly up the river. As it approaches I make out the large glassed-in dining saloon, the "romantic" table candles, the ugly "Fun-ship" design of one of the World Yacht dinner scows. Synthesized Billy Joel wisps from the afterdeck. Inside, software salesmen from Quogue will be regaling lingerie importers from Hasbrouck Heights over a dangerous veal parmesan. Warm and dressed in their best sansabelt fashions, already a little high on that Modesto chablis.

Listlessly I pick up a large piece of cardboard and climb into one of the junk-car craters. I slip on wet bricks, soda cans, empty bottles of Night Train.

There's a strong smell of shit. The Olds lying nose-down in the hole has been stripped bare, even its roof was torched off.

The floor is intact, however, and in the angle the canted car makes against the rubble it was driven into, there's just enough room for a man to lie out of the sleet. I wedge the cardboard under the trannie and jam myself in the shelter of machinery, adjusting shank and wallet for comfort. One of the Christmas mines goes off, whining "We Three Kings of Orient Are" till I snap it shut. I position my head so I can watch, between the rear axle and the lip of the crater, an angle of the village of the doomed; enough for warning, should danger come from that direction.

And lie awake.

It's so goddam cold my muscles won't relax enough to let me sleep. The pain in my throat turns fiery and hard; my head slowly fills with mucus; the cut in my stomach throbs against its stitches. Every cough feels like another knife thrust.

A long, low gray shape scurries off the cobbles to the crater's edge. Another jumps into the pit, then stops halfway, glaring at me. The rats' eyes shine white, reflecting the World Yacht as it drifts back downriver to the tune of "Italian Restaurant."

The crater communicates, at its base, with the river. I can hear water gurgling intimately below my feet. I think, They tried to kill the waterfront, but it will always come back. They filled in the Collect Pond, dammed the marshes of Loisaida with refuse from Burnt Mill. They filled in the beaches south of Water Street and covered the old Ishpetenga that drains Washington Square into West Houston. *But the ponds and rivers, the marshes and beaches, are still there.* Under the cement and asphalt and B-Net cables, under the foundations and tunnels they lie, like ghosts unshriven, waiting for night to come. One good rainstorm and the streets around Houston and Avenue B clog up like the marsh they always were. Let the pumps under the Municipal Courts fail for three days straight and the Collect Pond will rise again, black and foul with the shades of all men hung on its shores. Lispenard's Stream, still flowing underground, worries patiently at the sewers and cables, causing the city thousands of bucks in repairs every year. And the fill over the East River is eaten by sea-tide, and collapses periodically, forming craters like the one I lie in.

My mind returns to *Munn's World*. If I was a roundsman now, I could walk down the pier, over the cobbles to Spruce Street, and Buttercake Dick's. The cherrywood tables would be crammed warm with hoarse *Herald* newsboys and the counter girl would fix me a hot biscuit with a pat of butter baked into the center, along with a cup of steaming sweet three-cents coffee. The woman from Bayard Street would be there, waiting for me, wearing a blue bonnet and a dress with many layers of petticoats. Her face would have a perky nose and angled cheekbones, like the face of Kaye Santangelo.

I want to go in there. I want to be in *Munn's World* so badly that if psychokinesis existed, it would create itself out of smoke and atoms just from the power of my thoughts.

Sirens yowl, and fade. The rats ripple around, sniffing for garbage.

"Shoulda called Kaye again," I mumble to myself. "Shoulda called Wong. *Gotta* call Zeng, whole pointa gettin' out."

Do it in the morning.

Shift for a comfortable position. Twist my head around to look for the rats.

The singing comes softly out of the wind, from the direction of the Brooklyn Bridge. It wavers as the wind blows and dies, but grows overall in volume. It's a man's voice, a decent baritone, throttled down somewhat. When the wind picks up again, I can make out the words.

> *"Let me tell you*
> *of a red-haired Mommy,*
> *and her sixteen sweet red-haired colleens;*
> *all goody-goodies,*
> *even Tammy,*
> *though she was in her teens."*

I twist around to peer under the rear axle. The singer is out of sight for the moment.

> *"And let me tell you,*
> *of this fellow Murphy,*
> *and his sixteen cute rambunctious boys;*
> *they were looking*
> *for some clean-cut action*
> *but they were sick of toys."*

He walks into my angle of sight. He's tall, and very thin. He wears three Walkman earphones propped over his ears; a number of broken radios hang on string from his shoulders. His torn jeans are held up by a rope on which are strung a number of pieces of raw circuitry. He is barefoot and wears a good, old-fashioned duffle coat with the hood drawn over his head. All I can make out in the shadow of the hood is a glint of teeth.

A tee-dee.

He approaches the nearest barrel fire. Two of the men have gone into their shacks. The last one was left to guard and stoke the fire, but assisted by a jug of Gallo, he has fallen asleep across a wooden pallet next to the barrel.

> *"And then Bingo! The Murphys*
> *met the colleens*
> *and their action, it happened*
> *with a Bang!"*

The tee-dee draws his hands from the ample pockets of the duffle coat. The right hand holds a fourteen-inch kitchen knife. The singing rises in volume.

> *"And all 34, would be known throughout hist'ry,*
> *they'd be known forever as The Murphy Gang!"*

He bends over the sleeping man, and slashes the knife across his throat, so hard and fast that the blade is almost buried in flesh.

"Christ!" I shriek.

The wounded man's hands reach up convulsively and claw

at his windpipe. I can see blood arcing like a rococo fountain against the dying fire.

The tee-dee calmly goes through his victim's pockets. He has changed his tune.

> *"Tiffany digs the fast stock cars,*
> *the monster trucks,*
> *the leather bars;*

I'm so shocked that, paradoxically, my trembling has stopped.

The tee-dee straightens up. His victim is still kicking and jerking pathetically. He looks down at the dying man, then turns and takes a couple of steps in my direction.

> *Brittany lusts for symphonies,*
> *and reading Rimbaud by the stars."*

He stares right into the angle between the Oldsmobile's gears and the lip of the crater.

I see, or imagine, his eyes glinting against the dark hood, staring into mine. The steak knife flashes as he waves it in front of him.

> *"Oh, those twin sis-ters!"*

the tee-dee croons, softly.

My lungs don't work anymore. Despite that fact, I manage to work my right hand down to the pocket of my sweatshirt. The shank catches against the lining, then pulls free. I hold it in front of me. Its rough aluminum looks short and dull against the evil shine of that kitchen knife.

> *"Yes, they're twin sis-ters . . ."*

The tee-dee turns. He wipes the kitchen knife carefully against the duffle coat and slips it into his pocket. He adjusts two of his radios, sets the earphones once more comfortably on his head, and strides off purposefully northward. I can hear the song diminishing as he walks:

*"You know they can
switch their clothes
switch their toys
and yes, they'll even switch their boys,
'cause when you're twins,
not one—
you have twice the fun!"*

The man in the firelight has gone quite still.

The "Suzy Prince" song is lost, finally, against the eternal background wash of the river.

TWENTY-NINE

THINKING THE VICTIM'S buddies may not be in a very sunny mood when they find him with no throat, I change craters as soon as I'm sure the tee-dee has left.

I spend the balance of the night neither asleep nor awake but in a sort of limbo punctuated by dreams or hallucinations. Many of them feature the broad features of Derek. All of them vibrate to the same frequency as my hypothermia.

By seven in the morning I'm back in the Unimondo *mate* bar on Bleecker Street, trying to warm myself with cinnamon latte and two sun-dried tomato bagels with tarragon cream cheese. My nose runs freely and I've developed a smoker's hack.

Also, looking at my wound in the men's room, I notice the skin around some of the stitches darkening, which is not a wonderful sign.

There's not much I can do about it. I go back to my pavement and lay out the snood. The money comes slower than yesterday. It has stopped drizzling and a weak sun shows up between puffball clouds. The air is full of a dry cold that keeps people's fingers tucked warm in their pockets.

At ten I walk over to Sixth Avenue, collecting a "Good

King Wenceslas'' mine on the way, and use a pay phone on the corner of Carmine. I figure, if the call is traced, it's far enough from Broadway not to affect my panhandling.

I dial Zeng. Still no reply. I wonder if he left town.

No answer, not even a machine, at Kaye's.

Wong, however, is in. The secretary asks my name. I say, ''Stefan Zeng.'' Wong comes on saying ''Stef'' in a friendly voice, and I interrupt.

''Sorry, it's not Stefan.''

''What? Who is this?''

''It's a—friend of his.''

''Oh. You.''

He doesn't sound very happy to hear from me.

''I jiss need to tell—''

''I can't talk to you,'' he interrupts quickly.

''I wanted to tell you why I got out of there, I'm trying—''

''Mr. Munn,'' he states, very clearly, I assume so the wire-tap picks this up without distortion, ''you are a fugitive from justice, therefore I cannot assist you until you have turned yourself in to the proper authorities, in this case the district attorney's office of the county of New York.''

''But I'm trying to find out who did that to Larissa—''

''I'm sorry,'' he says, ''I'm going to hang up now.''

''Wait!''

Silence.

''At least—listen, you still work for me, I need you to pay a friend of mine?''

''The Jamaican?'' Wong's voice is full of distaste. ''He already showed. I'm surprised at you, Mr. Munn—such a childish kind of trick.''

The line goes dead.

I slam the receiver in frustration, almost knocking off the sign that announces the next phone over is a B-Net unit allowing multiplexed fiber-optic communication with any other B-Net station in the world.

The level of police activity does not perceptibly change after my call.

I walk back to Broadway, and sit down on the freezing concrete.

Once, among the crowds, I spot a woman from the SAG negotiating team with whom I've had at least two business lunches, but though her gaze flicks over me, it doesn't take me in.

I'm in a different New York now, one as remote from the city I used to inhabit, in its own way, as *Munn's World*.

I find my thoughts drifting more and more back to *Munn's World*.

Sometimes I catch myself thinking like the roundsman. I wonder if the woman from Bayard Street will emerge, twirling a silk parasol, from Shakespeare & Co. up the block, or if that crowd of NYU juniors might not part to reveal the tall, cloaked shape of the Fishman watching me through the window of the Reebok store.

I wish desperately to go back to *Munn's World*. Blowing my nose into napkins filched from the *mate* bar, with the men and women who give me quarters struggling not to meet my eyes, the city in 1850 seems to me infinitely warmer, more humane than the pavement under my bony ass.

I realize this is pure escapism. I realize also the attraction, to someone finding himself somewhat beaten up by the real world, of entering a fictitious world, a place he can, more or less, control.

Still, my longing for the 1850s streets is so powerful that it starts to worry me. I wonder if—despite Dr. Malik's refusal to confirm it one way or another—I might not truly be developing the symptoms of TDF.

The thought is so mind-blowing that I gather up my snood, with the three dollars eighty-five cents in change it contains, and walk to the Infomart branch two blocks down Broadway, where tee-dees and teenagers always gather to watch the screens displaying interactive 3-D games, or shows like *Donna's Way* that were the precursors to Virtix.

Frisco Fire is playing in pastel colors in one corner. Horgon the Violator on a hologram platform appears to reach out for us from the other side of the armored window.

A tee-dee beside me hums "Petticoat Junction." I edge away, nervously. It's like the old conundrum of craziness; surely I can't have TDF if I'm so *worried* about having it?

Watching the big screens I feel nothing but utter disgust at the strong colors, the bad drama, the good software indentured to hack producers.

And a small, burgeoning interest in the Fujitsu-Cray 988

Turbo laptop with dual shutter-glasses and B-Net interface built in, sitting on the checkout counter.

I finger the fifteen Christmas mines distorting my sweat-shirt under the shank. Seventy-five cents' worth.

I know from past visits that shops like these always chain the hardware to the furniture with a combination lock and cable around the handle.

Plus, there's a burly Sikh screening customers through a metal detector at the door.

The Punjabi yuppie buying the Fujitsu-Cray, however, comes equipped with no such security devices. He's maybe thirty, and dressed in a slick, twenty-two-hundred-dollar Barney's three-piece, the kind Joel Kamm the asshole likes to wear, with Unimondo jodhpur boots of the slippery, leather-soled variety that probably cost close to a grand. He frowns as he inspects the 988's carrying case and start-up package. He frowns as he checks his credit cards for cracks. He frowns even as he smiles, the condescending smile Punjabis reserve for everyone else, and carries the package past the Sikh and out the door.

I follow him.

Part of my thought process does not quite grok the implications of my own movements. I dodge around the atoms of crowd, staying two or three pedestrians away.

"What you *doing,* Munn," the slow part of my brain mutters.

"Wait for it," the other part whispers tensely. "You don't have to do it, but if the occasion presents itself, don't fool around."

At the end, it's the Kamm suit that bridges the gap between the two brains. Anyone who wears a suit like that can afford to lose a little laptop.

Also, my mind reasons, if he looks anything like Joel Kamm, he *has* to be an asshole.

The ethics of it are tenuous, but I'm not trying to give Thomas Aquinas a run for his money. I'm just trying to survive.

With a 988, and a little luck, I may be able to hack into the access files at XTV and find out who else went into *Munn's World* to steal the details he added to Larissa's decor.

We cross Houston Street, still heading south. Halfway

down the block I become certain my mark is going to the
Dean & DeLuca Food Museum. D&D's is full of third-world
plutocrats like him; they're the only ones who can afford it. I
move up right behind him, ignoring snot in nose, scratch in
lungs, pain in gut. He stops on Prince, waiting for the light,
just beyond the surf of sleet pushed up against the curb by
traffic.

He's holding the bag with one hand.

Convulsively, I grab it with both mitts, and yank it from his
grasp.

It takes more strength than I anticipated and I drag him for
a second. A woman screams angrily. The Punjabi twists
around, his face a Shiva mask of fury. He skids and falls in
the slush. The bag slips from his hand.

Someone grasps my elbow, and I knock him aside and run,
uptown. Faces turn, contorted in consumer rage. People bay
like bloodhounds behind me.

The light changes. Vans surge down Broadway. I can hear
someone sprinting hard on my heels. I'm already winded and
my stomach suddenly feels like the shank was slicing it again.
I jink left, straight into the traffic, dodging wildly between a
cab and a FedEx truck. Honks, screeching rubber—a taxi,
swerving to avoid me, sideswipes a Red & Tan bus.

Then I'm across, and racing through the crowds of West
Prince Street. Slowing down as I take a left on Mercer.
Fanelli's windows are draped in fake snow and garlands of
pine boughs, making me wish, fiercely and incongruously, I
could just go into the bar and buy a half pint of Gansevoort
like any normal New Yorker. I'm almost doubled over by now,
breath dragging Freddy Kruger nails up and down my chest.

I make an effort to hold myself upright, then walk into
Broadway Lumber's garage.

The cashiers look at me suspiciously, but I have a new
Infomart bag in one hand and appear to know where I'm
going.

In fact, I do. Broadway Lumber cuts right through the
block from Mercer to Broadway. Hopefully, any pursuit will
be searching for me on Mercer, or points west. I walk through
the sweetness of pine and cedar, pausing at the eastern entrance.

A siren moans, and a cruiser pulls up at the northeast corner of Prince and Broadway.

I wait for a truck to obstruct the view from the corner, then walk slowly southward, out of immediate trouble.

It doesn't take long to realize that stealing the 988 wasn't the smartest stunt I ever pulled.

For one thing, it means that now the cops are going to be searching, not only for Alex Munn the screenwriter, who doesn't look much like me anymore, but also for a grimy hip-hop white streetperson who does.

I ditch the Infomart receptacle and put the gear in a couple of Red Apple shopping bags. I walk faster, eastward.

The pace wears me out. I feel as if I'm propelling myself, like a squid, with the explosive sniffing of my sinuses. I hold one arm pressed against my stomach to dull the throbbing there.

At Broome and Bowery I lean, sneezing, against a doorway. A pretty Asian woman comes out of the entrance and skitters fearfully around the bum sniffling snot against her doorjamb.

Right across the street, where lighting-fixture shops now stand, was the Bull's Head Tavern, which used to offer refreshment to the drayers and coachmen starting the week-long haul up muddy roads to Boston.

I need to find a B-Net phone, call up XTV files. Do what I busted out to do.

Much stronger in my mind than B-Net phones, however, is the Bull's Head, which was a low, white-painted wooden building always surrounded by horses and carts and men in tall leather boots stomping in and out and wiping off mud on a metal bar on the stoop. A wide chimney, perpetually smoking. They drank brandy with spices and ate hot roasted oysters in spicy horseradish sauce. The Bull's Head was thirty years gone by the time *Munn's World* happened; yet for me it's the same muscle at play here. The lust comes back twice as hard as before, so powerful it takes my breath away, strong as the accoutrements of passion, as when you open the blouse of a woman you're about to make love to, exposing the velvet shoulder.

Or, like when I came together with the bad poetess on that steel barge in Brooklyn.

I resume my walking. Grimacing as the load I carry forces me to tense my stomach, I now head south. There's a cluster of B-Net phones around Fulton Street, where the business district abuts the *WaBenzi* watering holes of the so-called South Street "Seaport."

By the time I get there the lunch crowds are gone. Only a few tourists remain, gawking at the mothballed sailing ships. The B-Net phones here are too exposed; a beat cop walks back and forth next to Abercrombie and Fitch, trying to keep warm.

I turn northeast, up Water Street, toward the fish market. A slow wine of interest spreads in my faded blood. Just as the city, in 1835, gained control of the rowdy and scattered market by building it a home on Fulton Street, so the current mayor has been trying for years to run the smelly market out of here, so his developer pals can get their paws on the real estate. He even started a new landfill project at the foot of Wagner Place; but the Mob holds the lease on the market area, and the Mob still has enough hold on the city to do what it wants.

And the Mob doesn't want to move.

It would make sense to enter *Munn's World* here, I think fuzzily; here where the cobbles and buildings still contain, locked in their rigid patterns, in the fixed markets, the vibes and noise of the time to which I soon will be returning.

A silver-blue B-Net sign stands out clearly between two boarded-up fish dealers, just off Dover Street, in the great shadow of the Brooklyn Bridge pylon.

The street is deserted. I take the laptop out of its bag, set it on the plastic shelf that is an excellent feature of these B-Net phones, and switch it on.

Run quickly through the setup procedures.

The Punjabi yuppie had the good sense to purchase MicroBee, the easiest B-Net interface available. I unspool the cable, hook it up to the shielded pay phone port. I type in the B-Net code, then the corporate access number, and then Larissa's phonecard number. Hoping belatedly no one will have thought to cancel it.

Welcome icons flash. "Standby; authorized; proceed."

I log on, coming very close to typing my own password into the appointed slot, which would be stupid; either it's been spiked, so it won't work, or it's been flagged, so they'll put me on an AGATE trace, automatically pinpointing this phone inside thirty seconds. My heart racing a little from that near screwup, I punch in Zeng's code instead, plus the "Johnny Rotten" password he uses when wearing his creative hat.

The screen wipes, displaying the next level of menu.

I call up the ACCESS files on *Munn's World* first; that should give me a list of everyone who pulled MUNNWORLD/MSTR files over the last year. Run easily through the first options on the housekeeping and security menus, until I'm brought up short by gray letters flashing "UNAUTHORIZED LEVEL."

I try a calendar command, looking for ACCESS by time and date. Finally I attempt a wild card search for the whole directory of MUNNWORLD entries. All I get is "extra verification required" icons.

It appears ACCESS records are way off-limits to the creative crowd at XTV.

I wish I knew Zeng's techie passwords, but I don't.

I take a fast look up and down Water Street, and hunker over the laptop. None of this really matters, because Stefan, with his technical rating, can dig into any file at X-Corp, almost.

With his hacking skills, he can break into the rest.

I take out the earphones and plug them in. Pulling my sweatshirt around me, I make a kind of tent shutting out everything but mouse, keyboard, and screen. I blow on my fingers and type in the control code for the MUNNWORLD files in the X-Corp computer core.

Finally, I pull one of the shutter-glasses from its recess and fit it over my eyes.

And realize, as the first plaintive notes of "Cruel Edward" swell in the 'phones, that the real reason I stole the laptop, the true direction I've been steering in for the last twelve hours, has been this: to call up *Munn's World,* default to the last point in the story line, and return to the familiar parameters of the old city.

THIRTY

THE GLASSES GO 3-D.

I can see, in excellent contrast, the poor furnishings of the roundsman's lodging house. The small sitting room contains a fireplace with glowing grate, a horsehair sofa, a table covered with oilcloth. The tall window is frosted in complex silver patterns that stand out clearly against the dark street behind. A whale-oil lamp draws a citron circle across a broadsheet spread on the oilcloth.

Immersion, without the isolation of a face-sucker and its 150×180 field, is not rapid. I'm aware of the screen's borders as I watch the action. The fact that I have to move and click the mouse to walk inside the world also adds distance.

I push the mouse and "move" closer to the newspaper. I've forgotten the click code for up and down; experimentation reveals that one click raises me to my feet, three leans me forward.

There's something to discover in this broadsheet. It's the *Herald,* and the date is December 10. Leaning forward to discern the fine print, I make out a "summary of intelligence" that excoriates the efforts of Ohio's Mr. Giddings and other "free-soilers, abolitionists, and humbugs," to "renew the slavery agitation'' in Congress. On the same page, there's a review of the Christy Minstrels concert at Mechanics Hall, and a Fourth Ward Police report about a sailor who died of ''apoplexy'' in a brothel at 58 Cherry Street. In the classified section, which takes up a healthy portion of the linen paper, I come across an ad, boxed in heavy rule, that proclaims:

NOTICE.—*AMERICAN JOURNEYMAN FISHCUTTERS*

lumpers and trimmers with no attachments desirous of engagement in ADVENTUROUS, REMUNERATIVE, AND PATRIOTIC EMPLOY will do well to attend a meeting *today* at 8 A.M. SHARP on the premises of *Thaddeus Ames & Sons,* 89 Water Street, where they will learn something to their

ADVANTAGE

I stand up. In other ways, the mouse makes it easier to move around. I don't have to worry about my coat and hat or picking up my feet.

Which is good because, outside, the snow has frozen the dirt roads into deep ruts and shit mountains and walking is difficult. The potholes of the 1850s would make the roadways of modern New York look smooth. A team of shaggy horses pulling a dray full of cabbages slips and snorts with effort on the ice.

My boardinghouse stands on Twenty-sixth Street and Fifth Avenue, an area, right on the northern edge of town, known for its hotels and fancy bordellos. The men coming out of anonymous brownstones farther west pull their silk toppers low against recognition as well as the wind arrowing crosstown from the Hudson. Across the street, wind has thrown waves of snow over the fields of a little potato farm, piling deep drifts against dead hedges.

One of the men catches my eye. He's tall, with sharp eyes and a bony chin and an air of authority about him. His clothes are beautifully made and his walking stick is of polished ebony. A black brougham drawn by two dappled geldings clatters down the street to pick him up. Flaps of leather have been pinned over the carriage's door but the wind is so strong it has unpinned one of the flaps, and I spot a symbol underneath, a ship's flag divided into yellow and gray fields, that strikes a clear chord in my memory.

As the carriage draws away a woman comes out of the brownstone he just vacated. Her right eye is swollen shut, and a bruise blues the skin around it. She is wearing only a house-coat, but does not appear to notice the cold. Her pretty, con-tused face seems to draw heat from some inner furnace of loathing as she stares after the black brougham.

All this is very interesting, for lots of reasons; but I, as the roundsman, have other fish to fry, other questions to pose.

For example, the meeting described in the ad, only forty minutes away.

"Default," I say loudly, and through a built-in mike the Vox neatly picks up the command. The scene melts, shifts—and in a sickening swoop I'm walking down Chatham Square, heading left into Pearl Street. The vendors are out in force this morning. It will have been freezing cold in the hovels they sleep in, and the prospect of working in fifteen-degree weather over a charcoal fire probably feels like luxury to them. As I walk, I watch the red-faced girls turning corn and hot oysters with wooden tongs. The clam vendors shout, "Clams, clams, good to fry, good to make a clam-pot pie." A match-girl cries, "Six fer a fip! Six fer a fip! Matches, matches!"

A pretty Irish girl, her cheeks gray under a nest of freckles, trembles violently as she offers hot spiced gingerbread from a broken-down cart. I "walk" over to her and say, "One, please." She scoops up the *reale* bit that appears on the plate and smiles at me gratefully before handing over a slice of the steaming brown cake.

Mind-food.

Thaddeus Ames & Sons turns out to be a long rickety wood-planked building, behind and over a bunch of coopers and ship chandlers, just south of Market Street. A group of men dressed in cheap jackets, low hats, and thick boots stomp around the frozen snow, making steam of their breath. I recog-nize a couple of guys I saw hanging around the fishcutting shops on Coenties Slip. In the distance, the bell of the New Lutheran Church tolls eight times. A door opens and a burly figure calls merrily, "In ye go, gentlemen!"

We climb, Indian file, up wooden stairs just as rickety as the rest of the place, and emerge into a dusty loft that takes up the entire top floor. A big lifting wheel stands by a freight door set in the wall. A space near the door has been cleared of equipment and furniture; beyond that, the planks are covered with huge pieces of canvas. Some of them must be sixty feet by eighty, laid on top of stenciled patterns.

Through dingy windows the morning sun rams square columns of light into the dust-ridden space, illuminating a dozen children between the ages of five and fifteen, hemming topsails with thick needles and leather sailmakers' palms.

The children wear thin jackets. The place is unheated except for a big stove glowing at our end. The burly fellow dips mugs of something hot and alcoholic from an iron pot on the stove. The crowd's mood improves perceptibly.

Conversation rises. Many of the men cut off plugs of tobacco and start spitting at the hot stove, which hisses and spits back. After a few minutes of this the jovial fellow climbs on a bale of canvas and shouts, "Gentlemen, your attention please!"

I notice a shift in shadow to one side. A figure has appeared at the top of the stairs, pausing at the entrance. He is fat, and quite pale. In the poor light his eyes appear black and shiny like a skunk's. He wears a blue coat of old-fashioned cut, drayer's boots, and a queer, rounded sort of top hat.

"Mr. John Glover," the jovial one announces, and steps off the bale.

Mr. John Glover doesn't bother mounting the bale. He walks to the stove, draws a mug of toddy, and downs it in one swallow. Then he looks hard around the crowd.

"Are ye all native born?"

A murmur of "Aye"s and "Yiss."

"Then we have good work for ye."

The fat man's voice is fairly low, and not all that strong. His manner, however, is so confident that the men crowd around a bit closer, looking over each other's shoulders to catch what's being said.

"Ye all know," Glover continues, "this country is being flooded with the dregs of Albion. The same tyrants we twice whipped in battle are opening the bilges of Ireland and letting the rats come here!"

The men grunt their agreement. A pitter-patter of tobacco juice hits the floor; nobody has aimed at the stove since the fat one came in.

"Ye know that. But did ye know that a treasonous faction among the Ancient Order of Tammany—even among the Board of Aldermen—want to *invite* those accursed rats to come live in New York?"

Relative silence. One of the children making sails starts to cough, pathetically. The real me, with my ass sticking chilly into Water Street, hacks in empathy.

Glover's voice climbs the scales, invoking all the dynamics of irony.

"And did ye know that this *honorable* faction, disdaining the recent compromise, also proposes to abolish the ancient tradition of *slavery* in the United States?"

The crowd voices a certain shock. Someone at the back shouts, "Flynn?"

"Aye, Flynn." The fat man lets his eyes pause on various faces in the crowd. God, he's good at this; I wonder which actor we scanned to get the seed performance. "The face of an angel, the soul of a devil. D'ye *know* what Flynn's faction would do if they won?"

No one knows.

"They would open the gates!" Glover announces. "Oh, aye, it would be like opening a sluice with the tide behind it. A tide of ignorant, filthy, plague-ridden, starving Papist Irish! And worse! A flood of Ethiopians, and freed slaves! Stealing your jobs! Taking your wives and daughters! Flooding this city until true Americans become the smallest fraction of the population! Do ye want"—Glover leans forward—"d'ye want to see the future?"

The men are silent and tense. A rat scurries among the canvas, as if to scram while the scramming's good.

"Go look at Doyers Street. Look at Mott, and Elizabeth. Irish men and escaped Negroes living and fornicating like animals in their own filth!"

"What can we do?" the same voice from the back calls out. I realize Glover planted a shill to prime him with the right questions. Glover reaches into his vest and fishes out a small silver piece such as the one I "gave" to the gingerbread girl.

"Ye can summon the men who will vote *against* that fac-

tion on election day. Ye can help us ferry real Americans
unjustly imprisoned on Blackwell's Island, and ensure they
come to cast their vote. Ye can help defend the native-born
from the gangs of Bowery Bhoys and other filth who come out
to stop ye! And for every dozen true Americans ye bring in,
ye'll get a *reale* bit.''

A few in the audience mumble. One man actually laughs,
and walks straight down the stairs. Glover smiles, points after
him.

''He missed the good part. I know it's not the best wages,
but I also know ye're not the kind of cowards who would
shrink from a good fight, and this fight will earn ye bread and
stew for a week. And at the end of those two days, we'll have
a feast the likes of which ye've only dreamed of, with all the
Monongahela ye can drink for every man jack who pulls his
weight!''

The shill starts to clap and yell, and most of the crowd
joins in. ''Mr. Sims will sign ye up,'' Glover shouts over the
applause, and the men form into a rough line that ends at a
hogshead where the jovial one has set up foolscap, ink, and
pen.

Glover steps off the bale, nodding happily at the crowd.
Then he turns and disappears down the stairs.

I edge around the crowd, and click downstairs in pursuit.

I can't move as fast as I'd like. The computer still has me
convalescing from the stab wound, and I can feel it dragging
me back. I manage to catch Glover turning the corner of Pike
Street, but when I reach the corner, he has disappeared.

I look around anxiously—and spot him, between a dray full
of tar barrels and a fruit cart, climbing into a battered, covered
trap pulled by a handsome roan mare. Though the trap sags
under his weight, the mare pulls it easily.

I look around for a hack. The truism applies in the 1850s:
there's never a cab when you need one.

Eventually I follow, on foot, as fast as my wound will
allow. Luckily Pike Street is jammed with pushcarts and vendors and for a while the trap advances at a walking pace.

At the corner of Madison Street the road clears, the roan
starts to trot, and Glover's carriage disappears from sight.

A couple of hacks are standing north of the intersection,

calling "Keb, keb!" as they wait for business from the ferry traffic.

I click into the lead carriage. The coachman scoops up the horse's nosebag. With a resigned shrug, he obeys my instructions.

This horse is no match for the roan but he trots along sturdily on his wide hooves, dodging pushcarts, the rooting pigs, the shit and piled snow with dexterity. We spot Glover's trap as soon as we turn into Madison. By the time he turns right into Frankfort we're not far behind. Soon after that the cabbie leans over and calls, "He shtop now."

I get out, pay the fare.

We're at the western end of Frankfort, a mixed zone of counting houses and various small industries: milliners, paint merchants, phrenology cabinets, and saloons. Signs advertising these and other businesses hang thick on every building save one—a triple-sized corner brownstone with tall windows and balconies and the calm detachment of a bank.

Inscribed under a Gothic clock over the main door are the words "Columbian Order of New York City."

Tammany Hall.

A group of Dead Rabbits lounge, smoking, to one side.

Glover walks up the broad steps and disappears into the wigwam.

I hang around the sidewalks for a little while. After the Rabbits notice me twice I cross the street to the nearest saloon, a place called "The Pewter Clock," that occupies the ground floor of a townhouse.

The joint is dim and crowded. Men dressed a lot like Glover cluster at the bar, smoking, downing glasses of whiskey, spitting tobacco juice onto the sawdust-strewn floor. I order Monongahela. The bartender looks amazingly like the barkeep at McGovern's. A guy next to me orders a meat pie Steam and brown gravy leak out of flaky pastry when he cuts it open, and my stomach rumbles. Someone going out shouts, "See yer at the meeting then, Tom!" and my neighbor nods, mouth full.

When he has swallowed his bite I ask him if he knows John Glover.

"What?"

"John Glover!" I yell.

He looks at me carefully.

"Sure."

"D'you work at Tammany?"

"Why you want to know?"

"He just offered me a job."

"An' you don't know who he is? Or who he works for?"

"He didn't say."

My drinking companion has a thick dark nose, and wears his top hat the way Glover did. Maybe it's a Tammany style. He turns to his whiskey, shrugs, and says, "He works for Ed Judson."

"Who?"

He swirls Monongahela around his mouth.

"What a lot of questions, friend. But it's no damn secret. Judson is Isaiah Rynders's fixit boy. If Rynders wants something fixed, Ed fixes it. Rynders wants something broke, Ed gets it broke."

I turn around and watch the men filing in and out of Tammany Hall. There are a lot of them; I must watch for over an hour, *Munn's World* time, and not a minute passes without ten people going up or down the steps. Some of them clutch parcels wrapped in bright paper for in *Munn's World,* too, we're not that far from Christmas. The sun slopes past mid-morning and folds shadows across the dirty granite steps.

He's just one of the men, at first. The only reason I pay any attention is because he has a woman on his elbow, and I haven't seen a woman go in or out of Tammany yet. She wears a worn, flowered dress whose multiple petticoats brush the dirt as she descends the steps; black coat, flowered bonnet, dark green shawl. I move to the window to watch her. She looks up at the man, smiling at something he said. She has deep black hair and dark eyes. My breath stops.

It's the woman from Bayard Street.

After my breath comes back, I take a closer look at her companion.

They're halfway down the steps at this point.

He is tall and wears a silk topper well down over his brow, tilted left so his face is in shadow. He has on a dark blue cloak whose collar wraps partway around his chin. His boots are supple, of Smithfield leather. But they can't disguise the slight defect in his stride, a minor letdown in muscle as he takes the strain on his left thigh; just as, from the shadow of his top hat, those eyes seem to project their deep lack of light all the way to where I'm standing.

"Fishman," I breathe happily, loving the instant of recognition.

At the bottom of the steps the woman hesitates. The man strides forward and waves.

The woman is looking through the warped glass of the saloon. For a moment our eyes lock, the darkness in hers seeming to connect with mine in that palpable electric shock of which such moments know the secret.

Then she turns aside, beckoning to one of the junior Rabbits. Abruptly she disappears behind traffic. It's no ordinary traffic, though; it's a complicated, gleaming smoking bulk of steam fire engine drawn by six huge black horses caparisoned with a network of polished harnesses that would make any twentieth-century West Village S&M shop owner flush with envy.

The brass pump valves shine bright; the firemen, all decked out in helmets, medallions, boots, and fire axes, hold themselves erect. Black smoke and golden sparks fly from the steam pump's chimney. Despite the trappings of modernity, it all looks oddly Arthurian, full of allusions to armored knights, daring quests, and alchemists' flames.

The cloaked man hands up the woman to the driver's bench. The driver cracks his whip, the hooves shake the ground, and the gleaming machine rolls east down Frankfort, leaving a trail of smog, panicked porkers, and admiring urchins in its wake.

Of course I should be running, hailing a cab to pursue the son of a bitch who stabbed me in the gut on Park Row.

Instead I stand outside, shivering in the filthy snow, watching the fire engine dwindle down the road; the engine with its bells, whistles, ladders—and its emblem, painted black on the side of a water tank, the head of a unicorn, horn carried proudly, the mane blown back as if by great speed over the words "True Blue Native, Fire Company 31."

Munn's World! I think hysterically.

It's gathering steam, like that engine.

It's burning down theaters and bringing fire companies into the plot without *any reference* to the original bible.

Someone bobs at the lower part of my field of vision.

"Sir, sir!"

It's a junior Dead Rabbit, the one the woman waved at.

"I got a message for you! Lady gave it." He proffers a slip of paper. This, too, was never in the bible. I click it up to read.

The cold has deepened as evening approaches, and my eyes water as I peer at the lovely copperplate script that seems to jump, so good is the 3-D, from the laptop's display.

"One who should be an ally fashions nightmares for your soul."

I blink, trying to keep the screen in focus. But the tears come from a real cold.

In the aftermath of shock, I become more aware of the link between the shivering body outside The Pewter Clock, and the trembling that same body is experiencing at the pay phone on Water. I hit the "End" command, and bail out of the X-Corp link.

Lift my head from the screen, dislodging the Red Apple bags. I remove the shutter-glasses.

It's like stepping into a cold shower.

The echoes and shadows of the modern city pour back like water into my overextended senses.

THIRTY-ONE

EXHAUSTION, HEAD COLD, and gut pain slow me down; the onset of hypothermia makes it vital that I walk as fast as possible to get the red corpuscles up and trudging around with their cargo of oxygen.

The 988 drags at my arms as I stagger north up Dover—past the corner of Dover and Water streets that used to be the Hole in the Wall bar, headquarters of the Daybreak Boys—then left again. I walk crooked, trying to keep strain off the muscles in my right side. My nose runs more profusely. I quickly use up the last of my napkins. The trembling is violent enough to jiggle my breath. I'm not sure if I have a fever or not.

The wind blows strongly off the river, driving the cold deeper into my pores.

People shimmer out of the faux port bearing parcels wrapped in shiny silver paper. Cabs rush by in a wash of yellow. Glancing down Peck Slip, I see the warm light in the second-floor windows of Sweets Restaurant, where slave traders dined in the 1850s, where derivatives analysts eat now.

Two AGATE Apaches thunder overhead toward Red Hook. I slouch down to Beekman, turn left again.

That unicorn on the fire engine bothers me more and more. It reminds me of something I'd put out of my mind.

(I have to take time off from thinking to shiver.)

The unicorn on the flyers in Houston Street. The one on the poster in the Nassau Street station. *They had exactly the same mane and air of gallop.*

"D-d-don't mean shit," I say aloud.

Only it does bring back other items.

Like the gashes in Larissa's stomach, and the graffiti over her bed.

"G-G-God," I moan.

Because I suddenly see, this is all about smuggling things from one world into another without your conscious self being aware.

And if, somehow, I'd already seen unicorns on the street before Larissa died, and stuck them all unknowing into *Munn's World*—then the reverse applies.

I could have taken things out of Munn's World, *and stuck them in Larissa's bedroom, without knowing I did it.*

I wonder if I ever brought home unicorn flyers. In my freeze and trembling this seems a totally essential avenue of research. Far more important than sensory studies based on the ability of men color-blind in the red spectrum to detect blood splashed on red paint.

"Larissa," I whisper, banking left to dodge groups of *WaBenzis* heading crowingly for the Harbor Lights saloon, "I never wanted to hurt you."

The street ahead and to the left looks familiar. It's Water Street, again.

My feet, like my thoughts, are going in circles.

I hate going back over old ground in any context, but I need to get out of this cold soon, and at least Water Street is free of crowds. Maybe I can sneak into one of the condemned buildings.

I shiver ridiculously northeastward. Halfway to Frankfort Street, one of the older fish houses has been converted to condos.

I peer inside the unlit lobby. A row of buzzers shines inside the outer door, which means that door is not locked. I walk up the steps, open the door, and lean gratefully against the wall,

into the wisps of heat coming out of the hallway, cupping my
right hand against the throb of scar.

The thought comes to me; maybe Fishman has taken control of *my* life. The blackness of that idea is indescribable.

It doesn't happen right at that moment—the real world is
not a TV scriptwriter.

I wallow in the warm blackness for a few minutes. A couple of more immediate thoughts intrude. I hope one of the
residents doesn't come back right now. I want to eat a meat
pie in The Pewter Clock. Failing that, I'd settle for a Sabrett's
hot dog.

And, slowly, the awareness of footsteps. Very rapid, extremely faint but with something, a tiny detail no more, that
matches up to a detail in my memory and clicks me, as if
working off some internal mouse, fully and instantly alert.

(Slip-*slap*.)

Everything is different about those footsteps. They're not
slow and ominous, as they were in Greenpoint; they're only a
quarter as loud. But, once again, the timing is the same, the
ratio of pause to beat; and, as before, it's this recognition that
causes my heart rate to bolt, and race crazily as the adrenaline
comes pumping in.

"What the *fuck* is going on?" I whisper.

What's going on is, he comes fast down Water Street. His
steps sound only a few yards away. The difference in speed
gives me a distinct, if not entirely rational, impression. Before, the footsteps were slow and loud for deliberate effect.

Now the man has decided to cut the show and concentrate
on getting a job done.

I press myself harder against the wall. I can hear a
whistling, the kind of tuneless, "yah-dee-dah" repetition a
man does when he thinks he's alone.

The spider of terror spreads its sticky paws around my
stomach.

> *How comes this blood on thy shirtsleeve?*
> *Oh, dear love, tell me!*

A shadow fingers quickly over the door of the house in
which I hide, preceding a tall figure in a dark coat that moves
past the glass portion of the outer door. The coat is not a

Chesterfield. It's beautifully cut of black wool and seems to flow around its owner as he moves. The generous collar is folded up and comes close to caressing the fancy charcoal homburg pulled down over the man's brow.

The difference in fashions doesn't change what my gut believes to be happening here.

I lower myself painfully so that only the top of my head will be visible should he decide to turn around.

But he doesn't look right or left. As distance starts to blur detail the tall black figure melds perfectly into the shape I remember from the corner of Perry and Washington, the night I found Larissa dead. He's heading for the B-Net phone I used earlier.

> *It is the blood of the old gray hound,*
> *that traced the fox for me.*

The tune he's whistling, the *Munn's World* version of "Cruel Edward," fades into the ambient wind.

When he comes level with the Net phone he checks around carefully. He looks like a predator sniffing for the scent of the prey that was just here.

He picks up the receiver, punches a long number. He listens for a moment, then hangs up. He looks back up the street and I bend farther down, although there's no way he can see me from that distance without supernatural powers. I shrink back farther, trying to stifle a cough; I certainly don't put serious psi capabilities past this fucker. I mean, he came on me out of nowhere, in Brooklyn, in Jersey. Maybe he has a sixth sense that vibrates when Munn is within range.

Maybe he's a goddam vampire.

Drac.

I peek over the bottom of the door glass again, my chest bursting with repressed coughs.

Now he stands on the curb, talking into something the size and shape of a cellphone. His shoulders swing impatiently.

A man turns the corner of Dover Street. He's of medium size, compactly built, and wears a short dark jacket of fake leather and stonewashed jeans. He's too distant to distinguish features. Yet he looks so much like my pals from Kearny that

I'd stake my entire current fortune of six bucks and thirty-four cents that the guy is a Viet.

The Asian, if that's what he is, says something quick to the tall man, nods twice, and disappears. A stronger gust of wind hurls old newspapers down the street. The tall man turns in my direction again, stows the cellphone in his coat. In the shadow of the homburg, his eyes glow green.

I'm not kidding. I mean, it's not very strong; it's like a pale reflection of headlights in a cat's eyes. But it's there.

Green. Like a wolf, like some weird goddam mutant from a Roger Corman flick.

I hear a low swish of tires, no sound of motor at all. A car glides by. The chassis seems to go on forever. It's a stretch limo, one of the long ones, with running lights on the side so you know it's all the same car. Room for cocktail bar, swimming pool, and helipad in back. The windows are smoked and the light over the license plate is out.

Brake lights flash. The limo stops next to the dark figure. He opens his own door and disappears into the glowing interior. The brake lights go off and the limo turns, to vanish around the corner of Dover and Water.

I squat against the wall for some time, wiping my nose with the sodden sleeve of my sweatshirt. I feel like I'm about to pass out.

Footsteps thump, inside the building, down the stairs behind me. A plump young man in a loud coat opens the inner door and literally recoils when he spots me.

When he recovers he starts to jabber about private property, investment values, and the police. I get to my feet, groaning, pick up the laptop, and go outside without answering.

Seeing the tall, cloaked man sucked the last dregs of courage and strength from my frame. I shuffle even more pathetically, bending over the warmth of my scar, heading down to South Street again. Sure, there's more cops and lights here, but all of a sudden that seems preferable to the dark corners and the kind of weird, wolf-eyed killers who lurk in them.

On South Street I walk uptown, past the silent fish market, till I hit the loom of the FDR.

I keep a very sharp eye out for black stretch limos. Unfortunately this part of the overpass is exactly where the limo drivers like to park to get a half hour of shut-eye, or a blowjob from a Fulton Street hooker, so I spend a lot of time ducking behind traffic.

In consequence, I don't notice what happened to the village of the doomed till I'm a mere ten or twelve pylons away.

When I do look up, I stop abruptly. The black cavern under the highway that normally holds only the flaming fires of the homeless now pulses with strobe lights and crime-scene spots.

The village is crawling with Five-ohs. They shine flashlights through the makeshift cabins and into the craters by the bulkhead. A bulldozer knocks down the shacks, one by one, smashing sparks out of the oil barrels.

A familiar yellow school bus with wire-meshed windows and the letters "NYDOC" stenciled on the side pulls into South Street as I watch, and heads uptown.

I shrink back into the Mob-run parking areas that lie between the encampment and the bridge.

And retrace my footsteps, keeping the stacked fish crates between myself and the strobing beacons of the Man.

The phone is not B-Net. It actually takes coins. It actually works. And, thank Edison, when the line opens, the voice on the other end is not a machine but a full set of human vocal cords, with all the hesitations and questions hardwired in the soft, wet circuitry of our species.

"Hello?"

"Kaye!"

"Yes? Who's this?"

"It's not your machine!"

"Who *is* this?"

"Well, uh—"

"Is this—"

"Uh-huh."

"Jee-sus."

"Nah, Pilate got his ass." I try to repress a cough, but it spills out anyway. When I've got over the fit I grunt, "Sorry."

"You *escaped*."

Her voice is not hostile exactly, but it's not friendly. It seems to hover halfway between the Kaye I remember, warm, leap-before-looking, and a woman at two or three removes of consideration.

"Listen," I say hurriedly, "I need to see you."

"You know they could be recording this?"

"Yeah."

"I don't think they are, though. We checked."

"Oh. Good." Thinking, How the hell did she do that?

"Why did you escape?"

"I had to. Someone—I know it sounds crazy—but they put out a contract on me. They tried to cap me, in Riker's."

Silence.

"Why d'you want to see me?"

I don't answer immediately.

"I guess—I don't have anyone else, to see," I admit finally. "I'm kinda—fucked up here, I guess."

More silence.

"What about your friend? The Chinese guy."

"He's not around. I don't know where he is, all I get is his machine."

"Your lawyer?"

"He won't have anything to do with me till I turn myself in. Look," I continue, "I'm sorry." The hint of self-pity in my voice is starting to make me feel ill. "I shouldn't try to drag you into this. I'll see you later."

"Wait!"

" . . . "

"Munn?"

"I'm waiting."

I can hear her sigh.

"I'm sorry," I repeat.

"No, *I'm* sorry. It's hard fuh me. My dad, 'n everything. I mean, you *do* know escape's a presumption of guilt?"

Another silence. When she talks next her voice, though not all the way rehabilitated, sounds more like the one I remember.

"I can't see you right now, I'm off to a concert. Maybe we could meet later?"

"Okay."

" 'Less, I guess, you wanna go, too?"

Another coughing fit.

"You okay?"

"Yeah. But I don't exactly have a shitload o' cash."

"Don't worry about that. It's the *Messiah,* at St. John the

Divine, eight o'clock. Meet me at the Hungarian Pastry Shop at—oh, seven-thirty. It's at 111th an'—''

"I know it."

When she hangs up, I dial Zeng's number once more. No human answers.

THIRTY-TWO

MAYBE IT'S THE contrast between the heat of the train and the growing wind. Whatever, when I get out of the subway at 110th and Broadway, the cold feels like nothing I've felt before; it's like stepping into the Arctic wearing nothing but boxer shorts; a wind so bitter it locks my hand joints around the Red Apple bags and burns my forehead under the snood.

I haven't been this far north of Ninety-sixth Street in years —only a couple of times since I left Columbia. The gaggles of students, dressed in jeans and parkas, coddled in spare time and Daddy's cash, remind me of how many miles I've traveled since then. Their wary appraisal of me—homeless, possibly sick, probably panhandling—their expert evasion, remind me of how deep I've sunk in the last week.

The HPS hasn't changed since the days I sat here for hours imbibing coffee and reading Bentley on Pinter, Meyer on Strindberg. The java's three bucks fifty now, but you still pour your own refills. The Hungarians look me over sharply when I come in. I plonk change quickly on the glass counter. I sit in my old alcove, between the day-care notices and the phone, blowing my nose on free napkins, wrapping my frozen hands around the warm mug.

She comes in fifteen minutes later. Her eyes are bright, her cheeks alight. She wears a floppy Russian paratrooper beret, pulled down on the left side, a long scarf, gaucho boots, pilot's jacket. She walks around the joint once before she catches me staring at her.

She leans over my table, nervously, like she's not sure it's me.

"Yeah," I mumble, "siddown," and blow my nose on a napkin.

"You look fuckin' terrible."

"You look fuckin' wonderful," I reply. I mean it, too. She seems to produce waves of vital energy so strong they hit the air like a piano hammer to give off clear notes. A-sharp, G-flat; Kaye-major. She takes her dark glasses from her jacket and puts them on, which means I see a blue reflection of a thin, unshaven, snooded weirdo when I look into her eyes.

"You up to this?"

"Sure." 'Long as you take my arm, I think, as you would your grandfather's. She changed her nose ring, again; this one is in the shape of a thin dolphin with tiny yellow eyes.

"Then we'd better go. I hope they're not sold out. Sorry I'm late," she adds, as an afterthought.

The ticket line stretches around and down the steps of the cathedral. The wind like a savage jackal chases fluffy rabbit clouds across the city glow. People laugh and make comments about the cold and other details. Their gaily colored scarves blow downtown. Their clothes are bright and their faces glow with health and an appetite for life that seems almost palpable.

"You sure you're okay?"

"I just gotta co'd."

"I noticed."

"Little tired, too."

"You look different." She hasn't touched me once. The frown remains. I feel the despair arch closer to the surface again. One touch from one finger of Kaye's would lull the cold in my head and give a measure of peace to my whirling brain. But her hands remain jammed firmly inside her jacket.

"I feel different," I mumble.

"I like the beard, though."

"Thanks."

Silence.

"Why'd you call?" She asks it almost angrily.

"I tole you."

"No—I mean, really."

Against the racing clouds the cathedral towers seem to fall, in a well-known trick of perspective, sickening and slowly onto my head.

" 'Cause you helped. 'Cause you're the only one who really helped." She says nothing. " 'Cause I'm a lil bit in love with you."

The Ray·Bans flash. "Don't give me that!"

"It's the truth." I look down at her, calmly. "I don't have the energy for bullshit." I blow my nose again. "Besides, it's only a little. Don't mean much."

She looks around at the people near us. The conversation, somewhat incredibly, links Matisse and shifta rap.

"Tell me the truth. Why didn't you stay on Riker's?" she asks in a low voice.

"I tole you. There was a contract—"

"I knew that."

I stare at her.

"You knew?"

"Mohammed tole me. You know, you're fuckin' lucky he got assigned to back up Polletti. They only did that 'cause the Eight-four wanted him outta there. Polletti thinks he'll get his promotion to second grade, 'cause he's got your case all wrapped; but Mohammed hates his guts."

"Why you tellin' me this? Why—" I wave my hands help-lessly.

The line starts to move forward.

"Because Mohammed hates Polletti's guts," Kaye repeats patiently. "He'll do anything to screw up that case against you."

"That makes me lucky? 'Cause I'm in some kinda cop-bureaucratic skirmish?"

"You don't understand. That's how the department works. It made Mohammed do his thing, anyway." She hesitates, shakes her head, knocking down one thought with the previ-ous one. "He talked to an art historian who lives behind your wife's building. He an' his boyfriend, they saw a couple Asian guys working on her fire escape that night, I mean, the night she was killed. Only, there's no record of her ordering any work."

"Two *Asians*? You're sure?"

"Yeah. But don't get your hopes up—Polletti says it doesn't mean shit. He's already tasting that grade-two pay-check."

Her face, in profile, is as radiant as I remember; far too pure to fit with this talk of clues and politics. As if she'd read my thoughts, she changes the subject to Handel, *stilo antico,* stuff I used to be able to bullshit about when I hung out at the HPS and read the *Times* Farts and Seizures section every Sunday. Stuff that, in my humble opinion, has zero relevance to my life at this moment.

I find myself staring around me while she talks. She buys my ticket and we walk with the crowd into the perfumed echo of the cathedral.

The dun columns rise into a haze of light. The transept is filled with candles and a green riot of poinsettia. I find myself looking mostly at the faces again. They're of all sizes, shapes, and colors. Some of them appear dumb, some smart. Some are ugly and not a few are lovely. All of them, perhaps because they're in a high pretty church about to listen to nice music, look serene and pleasant, even though I know that like most New Yorkers they would turn and savage my throat in a second if I stepped one inch inside their defensive perimeters.

"Hey," she whispers.

"What?"

"What're you thinking about?"

We're sitting in our allotted chairs now; these cheap tickets leave us outside the line of pews. The choir is filing in, dressed in surplices of a deep gray that must be scarlet.

I'm thinking, Everyone here is normal.

I have trouble summoning the energy to finish the thought. I lie slumped in my chair, both arms crossed over my belly.

"The audience." I wave vaguely. "I *like* normal people."

Kaye looks at me curiously. I realize I was mumbling incoherently. The music starts and swells.

Comfort Ye.

Every Valley shall be Exalted.

Kaye takes off her Ray Bans. I slump farther in my seat, so my head rests against the back of the chair.

It's warm in this cathedral, warm with the closeness of humans. The organ plays a solo, and a woman with a sweet high voice responds. The art historian opposite saw Asians on the fire escape, and Polletti says it means nothing, and it probably doesn't.

And yet, it's another crack in the dike of evidence that was walling me in with guilt for Larissa's murder.

It links up with what Kaye said about the red graffiti, and the men who've been hunting me for no apparent reason.

And out of that growing matrix of fissures in the guilt dike, lovely clear oxygen is beginning to seep.

Because, unicorns or no unicorns, one thing is becoming clear: *it's at least possible I did not kill Larissa.*

For the first time in days, my gut is saying, Easy on the self-destruction, babe; see what the morrow brings.

The massed voices surge into "How Beautiful Are the Feet."

My eyes close, and I'm conscious of nothing else till the crowd, rising to the Hallelujah Chorus, wakes me with the scuffle of their shoes.

THIRTY-THREE

THE FRAGRANCE OF the music-warmed cathedral follows me outside.

Kaye leads me to Riverside Drive. The pavement glistens like snow with the smashed window crystals of cars that have been broken into or stolen.

Her rusty, paint-daubed piece of Kenosha nostalgia, on the other hand, is intact. We get in. She takes off fast up 110th. The heat inches in, snatched breaths of warmed oil.

"Where we going?" I ask, after a while.

"I'm takin' you to my place."

"Why?"

"You got someplace else?"

No answer to that one. She enters the park at 106th and follows Park Drive like it was Daytona. The lovely peaks and mesas of midtown rise glittering over the x-ray trees. When the energy has accumulated enough to do so I ask, "Aren't you scared of me?"

"I guess." She hits sixty down the Sheep Meadow straightaway.

"So, why?"

" 'Cause you look sick."

"Is that all?"

With an exclamation of annoyance she slaloms around a couple of black, horse-drawn carriages. I stare right, wondering if they might not be holding Fishman, or A. A. Low, or people from that time; my thoughts, repetitive, marveling at how the boundaries between *Munn's World* and the present over the last two days on the streets seem to have got so much more brittle. But the carriage passengers are Porteño tourists in loud ski gear and 47th Street Photo bags, doing the circuit from the Plaza Hotel.

"You look different," Kaye says. I have to make an effort to remember what I asked her. "I mean, you don't look as—as clear—as you used to. That's prob'ly jail."

I clear my throat.

"Where you been living?"

"Under the FDR."

"Under the *highway*?"

"Uh-huh."

She digests that for a moment.

"You still don't look like a killer. I've seen 'em, you know."

"What?"

"Killers. Psychopaths. They have a Teflon feel to 'em. That's not really your problem."

She crosses to Second Avenue, then south all the way to Seventh Street, where she heads east again. To the south, gentrified tenements briefly swap places with low-rise city housing. An archway of strung lights precedes a block of crumbling nineteenth-century tenements interspersed with vacant lots, a sequence that echoes what I saw in Brownsville.

These vacant lots, however, are not dead. One holds a small village of shacks and tents, with black banners flying from makeshift poles. Another is set up with tables and canopies; a few people stand around oil-can fires, or run stalls, lit by storm lanterns, in which are piled a jumble of objects obviously meant to be sold. Some of the buildings glow soft yellow with kerosene lamps, bringing back again, quite strongly, the taste of confusion, of worlds blurring.

Others have electricity. On each of these, sparkly clouds of Woolworth's Christmas lights adorn the fire escapes.

The streets are busy, for midnight. Men and women,

maybe half of them Hispanic, the rest of assorted races, move from fire to fire or buy something fast at a stall. I catch a glimpse, in one of the unpowered buildings, of a Christmas tree covered in birthday candles.

"What is this place?" I ask. I'm too tired to talk loudly. I wave one hand at the surroundings.

"It's the node."

I look at her.

"That's right," she says, and smiling in a way that pokes fun at her own allegiances, pulls down her sweater just enough to reveal a corner of the Hawkley-ite bandanna. I remember Cosmo describing it; a market, he said, independent of the city.

Kaye's building is one of the electrified ones. Underneath the strung lights it's a forlorn brownstone with sub-code fire escapes. She leads me past a doorway entirely plastered with eviction notices, up stairs resurfaced with plywood. The walls and lintels sag pathetically and are propped with two-by-fours at strategic points. Roaches skibble into the cracks at our approach, reminding me, with a small pang, of Archie. Smells of garlic and boiled fish, the beat of shifta rap, follow us up. Someone plays Clam Fetish: "Throw me down your vortex, suck me with your cortex, I'll only treat you like a *Klingon* waitress anyway."

Kaye opens three locks on the top floor, flicks a switch, and disappears, presumably into the bathroom.

I step inside her apartment, gratefully putting down the laptop. It's a classic New York railroad arrangement laid out Victorian style, along a line of moral progression, from high social pursuits to baser instincts. A tiny living room leads to a kitchen with stove, sink, and bathtub laid serially. Following the flat to its logical conclusion you go through the bedroom and end up in the toilet.

The front door leads into the kitchen, painted green and covered with bright posters announcing the publication of poetry books. A kerosene lamp hangs from a nail.

Rickety bookshelves constructed of bricks and planking line the living room. Most of the books are thin, which likely means they're full of poems. A cheaply framed portrait of Edna St. Vincent Millay hangs over a tiny coal stove with a pipe leading up the fireplace. A large, mildly obsolescent

Nixdorf PC stands on an IKEA coffee table. The screen-saver shows big piranhas eating smaller piranhas. A gleaming, matte-black box sits beside the workstation. I move closer.

It's a B-Net hook-up, an A-30, the cheapest model. Disk files and cyber-rags, *Wired, M-3, Web-Yentl,* are stacked haphazardly around the Nixdorf. I'm still checking it out when the toilet flushes and she walks back into the kitchen.

"You wouldn't believe the trouble I had, getting that in here."

"How come?"

"B-Net in a squat?" She shakes her head. "Luckily, 'round here, there's always somebody to pay off. I bought the box, so I can get *Real Life* when it starts."

"You been reading the newspapers."

"You're a celebrity, Munn."

There's an office chair sagging sideways beside the coffee table. Suddenly I couldn't stand up another minute if you Krazy-Glued my vertebrae together. I sit carefully, groaning a little as the cut tissues bend and fold, and kind of subside against the cushion. She shovels coal into the stove, runs hot water in the sink, and says, "Let me see that now."

"Huh?"

She points to my midriff. I look down. There's a dark patch in the gray cloth of my sweatshirt.

"That," she repeats.

"Oh, that."

"Do me a favor—don't do the Schwarzenegger shit?"

She carries over a saucepan of soapy water, a roll of paper towels, latex gloves, scissors. Rolls up the sweatshirt and T-shirt, looks at the bandage for a few seconds. Puts on the gloves and snips, pulling carefully at the tapes.

The scissors feel like ice, the bandage, as she levers it away, like flame. She takes another look at the mess underneath. Her face grows a bit pale, her jaw sets firm, but otherwise she might be trying to figure out how to plug in the toaster.

"Knife?"

"Yeah."

"Riker's?"

"Uh-huh."

She glances up, maybe to check if I'm telling the truth. Her eyes are very light. The gray in them now reminds me of the East River.

She takes a wad of towels, soaks it in water, and cleans out the wound. My hands try to rip the stuffing off the chair. I yell, "Hah!" and wince away from her.

"Sissy."

"I thought," I whisper, "you jiss told me not to be macho?"

"Women. You just can't predict us, huh?"

"Why'd you really get B-Net?" I ask, to take my mind off what she's doing.

"My job."

"Which is?"

"I work for Ragnarok Press. They do a lot of on-line stuff."

"You mean, newsletters?"

"No. Hypertext. I'm the fiction editor."

"Really?"

The gray again, darker this time.

"What does *that* mean?"

"What?"

" 'Really.' "

"Nothing."

"Not, 'Your dad's a cop, how'd you get a fancy-sounding job like that?' "

"No." I think about it. "Well, maybe, a little. I mean—"

"Well, what did your father do?"

"I don't know."

"You don't *know*?"

"It's a long story."

She sits back on her heels and blows a stray hair out of her face, looking at me with the same expression, half challenge, half exuberance, that I first noticed in The Right Bank. "I'm sorry. You must be exhausted. A couple o' those stitches're septic." She shakes some powder over the wound, rips up a washcloth, and pins it over the area with duct tape. Then, shoveling through a kitchen drawer, she pulls out several pill bottles, selects one, and presents me with a glass of water.

"Erythromycin. Finish the bottle. One thing every cop's daughter knows is how to fix people up."

"Aren't you a little worried," I say slowly, " 'bout having me here?"

"Why?"

She strips off the rubber gloves.

"Because of—Larissa? Because of the blackouts. I mean, I don't even remember what happened that night!"

"You don't, huh?"

"Well—I remember the barge."

She doesn't smile. She's still looking at the bowl of gray, soapy water in which the rubber gloves lie like Harlem River trout.

Then she leans over, puts her arms on my knees, and rests her head on her arms so that I get a view I've never had before, the back of her head, with the doubloon-colored cornrows rolling down into fine hairs at the top of her neck.

I touch those hairs. Her skin is cool. Through all my exhaustion and physical discomfort the sensation of touching someone, and specifically a woman, comes through with locomotive power.

A tremendous sense of warmth floods through me. I close my eyes for a second.

When I look up, she has her arm under my left shoulder and is straining to keep me from falling into the stove.

"Time fer bed," she grunts.

I actually need her help to get up, and the effort required to stay on my feet seems about eight times what it used to be. She goes into the kitchen, picks up the storm lantern, and opens the bedroom door.

Her bedroom, as I said, is part of the usual Victorian railroad arrangement. All except for one detail: somebody knocked a six-by-four-foot hole through the outside wall and built a sleeping porch that sticks five feet into space. The walls and roof of the porch are of plexiglass screwed onto steel brackets. Quarter-inch support cables lead from the outside corners and upward out of sight. The floor is all mattress, quilts, and pillows. Beyond the grimy plexiglass, New York comes at you from above and below and sideways; black tar and broken aerials of tenements immediately to the north; then, in ascending visual arpeggio, the execrable orange pyramids of Zeckendorf, the clock of MetLife, the Krupp-steel eagles of the Chrysler Building perched in the heavens.

Lower, an old man pushes a shopping cart up Eighth
Street. A Hell's Angel sputters his hog south down Avenue B
toward the headquarters on Third.

Nice arrangement, with one problem. The five plexiglass
sides radiate cold. A breeze whistles around the porch from
cracks in the putty.

"Don't wanna go in there," I whisper.

"Come on, it'll be fine." She shuts off the light, fires up
the storm lantern. The sleeping porch goes orange like the
sky.

"Kaye," I insist, "can't I stay in the living room?"

She rearranges the quilts, folds back the coverings like a
maid at the Milford Plaza. Kicks off her boots, lines them up
neatly at the entrance, and gets in, pulling the quilts up to her
chin.

"It's warm."

I get in slowly. This bed isn't warm, it's bloody freezing.
All the cold from the streets and the FDR didn't go away, it
just hunkered like herpes in my bone marrow, waiting for me
to leave the coal stove. I huddle next to her. There's nothing
sexual about it, she has heat and I need it.

She puts an arm around me and rubs my back. The shivering doesn't diminish.

"Christ," she whispers, "you *are* cold," and pulls up my
sweatshirt at the waist.

"What're you *doing*?"

"Skin to skin," she mutters, "it's what the survival books
say."

"Oh, God," I moan, "I forgot you're a nudist."

She does it carefully. Within two minutes I am naked. My
muscles shake so hard they seem to lift me periodically clear
of the mattress. She wrestles out of her own clothes, presses
herself against me, gently at first, then with increasing
strength, as if to still my muscles with the power of her own.

We lie there for a long while. My shaking adopts pattern,
coming in fits, receding somewhat. The violence and period of
the fits diminishes. Whole patches of time occur when my
limbs are scarcely trembling.

I become aware of how warm it's growing in the cave
below our necks—how soft the curves and hummocks of her
body.

In my mind's eye, the softness of her turns into something visual, light as fog and of deep blue color, whose shape neutralizes the hard, short violence of Riker's the way smack exactly fits the dopamine receptors of the brain.

She kisses my throat, windpipe, arteries, line of jaw. Touches my thighs and finally my crotch, shyly, like a teenager playing doctor.

The fog lifts somewhat. A hardness is evoked in me that trembling no longer can subvert. She bends aside briefly, then unrolls something warm onto that hardness.

I know immediately what she's doing. Amy Dillon did the same thing, and I've seen a lot of EMTs recently employ a similar technique. The warmed-latex dispensers provide a barrier over the entire crotch area, or over the entire body if you want, preventing the passage of HIV or mutant Matadi-14 viruses; it's a wise precaution and something I would have asked for myself, were I a little more conscious.

She climbs on top of me, carefully avoiding the bandage, and gently kisses my mouth. I'm glad she didn't paste latex over her lips, as the manufacturers recommend.

Then, reaching behind her, she guides herself onto me.

We don't move at all now. Her breathing has gone trembly. I shiver, from cold or lust, I can't be sure which.

She raises herself, very slowly, lets herself down. I place one hand on the curve of each buttock.

My idea of what softness is has to be redesigned, razed to the ground, built again.

I can feel the warm liquid running out of her and sliding over the latex on my crotch hair.

She lets her weight fall on my pubic bone. Stops moving. Her breath catches in the throat. Her small hand clenches around my face, her body clenches around mine. The clenching movements paradoxically touch a lever in me that starts a process of unclenching. I rise against her, tearing at my stomach somewhat; the pain isn't great and I barely notice.

The blue fog is back, moving and alive the way fog always is. She says, "Look at me, Munn," and I open my eyes obediently. In the lantern's golden glow her pupils are black and her nostrils flare with the oxygen she must bring in to fuel this. The Chrysler Building rises to the left of her head, ithyphallic, an impossible rival to my own puny member trying to do to Kaye what the Chrysler does to the night.

I look at her eyes, shining in the lights of the city, the lantern and electricity, the 1890s tenements and the 1938 skyscraper. I want to say "I love you." I know, even then, that I'm not quite sure what I really love, Kaye, the city now, the city then, all of them together.

The fog turns into bridges, towers, birds so light they need their wings only for direction.

The secret of softness is, and must be, that hardness is evoked by it.

In some corner of my mind I'm aware, even in sleep, that my body is coddled and warm as the egg under a brooding hen.

And that brings out the hardness of the Fishman.

THIRTY-FOUR

I KNOW HE'S there, though I don't see him at first.

I'm enclosed in some kind of closet off a street I've never been on before, holding a stone figurine in one hand. I can hear him breathe outside the door, harsh wet breaths like those of a spiny sea creature cast upon the rocks. I'm so scared I'm shaking; my face is numb with fear.

Footsteps come down the street, light and fast.

As they pass, the Fishman's slip-*slap* starts up in pursuit.

I peer out of the closet, which opens directly on a cobble-stone street lit by numerous gas jets. In the soft light his shape is made vast by the black Chesterfield, the shadows of the homburg.

Maybe twenty paces in front of him, a woman walks in soft felt boots. She wears the bell-shaped dress and gloves and wrap of a fashionable 1850s woman. She walks slowly; her muscles are sore from making love. I don't need the glint on the cornrows of her hair to know that it's Kaye.

I slip out of the closet and follow but *Munn's World* won't let me move faster than a slow crawl. Ahead, Kaye comes level with a tall building. It has broad steps and a portico lifted on marble columns. Sea serpents, monstrous whales, and vampiric mermaids populate friezes above the columns. A leering Neptune holds a clock that reads "XI."

Kaye, climbing the steps, pulls a notebook from her reticule. I know it will tell her where to find, in that fancy house, the tablet that holds the secret of her father's hiding place; for the city has ordered that captains of detectives go undercover indefinitely, due to the Clock Wars.

Fishman pulls a shank, three feet long and gleaming, from his coat. My entire being seizes up in panic. I'm only at the foot of the steps when he catches up with her. Pulling the shank back, bending his shadowed face toward her neck, he winds his arm around her throat. Stop! I yell; no sound comes out. I hurl the figurine at Fishman and it bounces harmlessly against his shoulder blade, falling in petals to the marble.

Fishman turns and smiles. It's the first time I've ever seen his face. It's not a bad face, really; it's got gray eyes, freckles, a bony nose and chin. But the smile has no mercy in it, and I realize what I've known all along: that there's a spot in my own heart as cold and hard as marble.

For the face is my own, and Fishman is me, and Kaye is about to die, like Larissa, at the hands of a man who loves her.

My eyes fly open. The first thing I see is the Chrysler Building. The lights of an airliner cruise slowly overhead, powered by the rumble of sound behind. The city in its restless sleep breathes monoxide to itself.

My right hand gropes toward Kaye. I know for certain she's dead, that I killed her as she slept.

My insides slurp again with the dark, cold liquid that filled me at Riker's. I feel nothing but cold sheet.

I reach left and touch her ass, lying in a cold pool of blood. Ribs, cool skin; she's been dead for some time, then. No movement or heartbeat. I turn toward her; her profile is pure, white, still against the dying glow of the oil lamp.

"Kaye," I whisper. *"Kaye!"* Pushing her suddenly.

She doesn't move.

My hand, though, rises and falls, very slowly, over her right breast.

And between the breaths of the city, a small feather of

sound, as air moves quietly in and out of her nostrils to the same rhythm as her breast.

I fall back, trembling, against the pillow. The "blood," of course, was the liquid, hers and mine, leaked after lovemaking.

The exhaustion is still in me, like a stubborn jungle beast, but there's no goddam way I can get back to sleep now.

I roll over, favoring the wound, and kiss her gently on the temple. I scrabble around for my duds and clamber out of the sleeping porch.

The kitchen and living room, thanks to the coal stove, are hot enough to please a Yanomamo. I find a pan, tea, and matches and set water to boil on the range. A cockroach, narrowly avoiding immolation, leaps from the burner. A clock with no minute hand reads somewhere around four. When the tea is ready I go to the living-room window and look out at the night.

The teacup scalds the singed palm of my right hand. I shift it to the left. The windows of the city, holding the stored charge of all those hundreds of thousands of humans sleeping, dreaming, fucking, worrying, wraps another glow of energy around me.

The memory of Kaye, sighing in her dreams on the porch, draws a circle of warmth around the glow. *I didn't kill her;* in my head, that's what I tell the memory of Fishman. The warm feeling spreads a little further.

I don't know why, but the realization that my dream was wrong—inaccurate, goddammit!—seems to open the possibility that so much else in the past ten days that *seemed* one way may in fact have been quite different, all along.

They saw a couple of Asian guys working on Larissa's fire escape that night.

I finish the tea. The glows inside me don't go away once the tea is done. They subsist in the same places where the dark liquid of my guilt collected on the Rock.

I turn back into Kaye's apartment, trying to ignore the mariachi hope that follows from the shift inside me.

But the energy from that shift is too strong. Thoughts bounce wild around my pinball brain; and it strikes me that maybe the best way to deal with it is as pinball, a test of skill, no moral weight attached to the bounce and rebound.

So I sit on the edge of a busted couch and try to build a game from the rules I know.

The premise of this game is as follows: I didn't kill Larissa.

First (and obvious) consequence of that: someone else did. Who?

Other factors here: someone has tried to either kill me, or scare the piss out of me, three times, starting *before* Larissa died.

Again: who?

"Same question," I mumble, getting to my feet and walking around the tiny living room. Her bookcase, I notice, has a shelf like mine, devoted to odds and ends: ceramic tchotchkes, the photo of a guy with the face of a pissed-off camel in an NYPD uniform.

"They killed Larissa *only* to get me into trouble."

I'm talking to myself, the way I did at Riker's. But what I say is so interesting that I don't stop; I continue mumbling, like a tee-dee on a dead cellphone.

"Don't know who, or why. All I have is weird incidents. Like the Morgan. Or getting fired."

Getting fired wasn't so weird, I remind myself. It was cynical, but normal given how television works. And even Joel Kamm, who never liked me and, as it turns out, stood to profit from my demise, would not have killed Larissa to get at me; he just doesn't have the imagination.

Or the balls.

I shake my head and walk to the couch again. This game ain't easy, and the effort involved has ripped the thin skin of sleep to expose the accumulated fabrics of fatigue just underneath. The coffee table holding Kaye's B-Net box lies to one side of the couch. The proximity of the box, and the memory of getting canned, make contact, firing a tiny pinball light wired to that connection.

There *was* one strange aspect to getting fired. One silly detail.

They canceled the shows I wrote for *Real Life*.

Why?

People have been busted before without getting their shows scrapped. Deke Ballou molested a Cub Scout, it was in all the tabloids, and he's still on *PITA*. And *Real Life* is—I count it down—jee-zuss, *five* days from broadcast!

I frown, shake my head. This is a different problem; interesting but irrelevant to the real point of the game. Maybe killing your wife, for some arcane Nielsens reason, is anathema to programming executives.

I lie down on the couch but my eyes don't want to shut. Kaye's ceiling is so cracked it looks like it's about to collapse. I know the feeling.

I fetch my laptop and hook the 988 quickly to the B-Net box. And pause, remembering just in time that checking my personal files at XTV at this point would be as bright as walking around Police Plaza with a sign reading "Here's Munn!"

I pick up the September-October issue of *Mondo,* flip quickly to the classifieds, find what I want almost immediately.

Several years ago, when AGATE and the proliferation of digital nets made call-tracing and wiretapping a matter of routine, a passel of groups, mostly in survivalist territory, set out to commercialize secrecy.

For a small fee you could hook up to one of these switchboards, which would then route your call through a blocking program to prevent anyone from following the call electronically, or tracing it back to its source. Although, since the Zippy bombings, both the Christian-Republicans and the Center-Democrats have been trying to legislate these guys out of business, a bunch still exist, usually under the guise of "ethics hotlines," in places like Reno and Yakutat, Alaska.

The one I choose is called "Web Home Independence Society for Political and Economic Reform," a.k.a. WHISPER. I type the http address into the 988, arrange for home billing, and wait.

It takes about fifty seconds for them to hook me up to the X-Corp site. The screen clears and fills with the XTV menu. I go through the log-on routine once more, using Zeng's "Johnny Rotten" password. I click with no problem into the Special Projects area, and scroll manually into the *Real Life* menu.

The *Real Life* file names all bear the prefix "RL" with the episode number and the writer's name attached. The slug for

Vivian's episode, for example, reads "RL5-MOOS." The slugs for my episodes read "RL(number)-MUNN."

There is not one single "MUNN" file left in the *Real Life* menu.

I do a general search through Special Projects. No luck. Then a wild card command; this scrolls out the file names from my MUNNWORLD submenu, but finds nothing else in the rest of the system.

"Shit," I mumble, a little awed, "they zapped 'em *all*."

The screen abruptly clears. Visual noise for a few seconds. Then the WHISPER logo fills in the space where XTV's icons previously held sway.

The words "UPLINK INTERRUPTED" line up at the top of the screen. And then, flashing black and big in warning, "BACKTRACE ATTEMPT/BLOCKED" followed by "LOGOFF NOW!/LOGOFF NOW!/LOGOFF NOW!"

I log off fast. Even the secrecy switchboards can be circumvented, given enough time and computer power. And, of course, in criminal cases they can be forced by court order to reveal the source of transmissions; but that usually takes a week or so, and if I haven't sussed out who killed Larissa inside a week, it'll be too late anyway.

I sit back in the wingshot office chair, staring at the piranha screen-saver.

Zeng, I think. Zeng has a full set of master files, and he always backs those up. Also, as a techie, he can pull the ACCESS lists that will tell me who broke into *Munn's World*.

I lean over the 988 again, call up his Well number, and leave an innocuous message reminding him of a "meeting" tomorrow at his house. "12 noon," I type, arbitrarily, and log it "G. G. Allen."

G. G. was the name of one of the more obscure heroes of extreme punk. Zeng has expounded to me in the past on some of his more legendary feats of music and coprophilia. Even if Stefan doesn't grok the hint, the curiosity factor alone may keep him home for the appointment.

I lie down on the couch. I'm still watching the piranhas chewing when I fall asleep.

THIRTY-FIVE

I OPEN MY eyes on the zipper of an unfolded sleeping bag.

A bookcase with ceramic giraffes. A clock with no minute hand reads halfway between 9:30 and 10. The framed picture of a cop.

It's been a long time since I woke up in a woman's apartment. For a sleep-sodden moment I savor the taste of it; the details you expected, the things that surprise you. Little mysteries of perduring girlhood, reliquaries of a bizarre cult forever taboo to men. It's not surprising neither Amy Dillon nor Larissa let me stay in their places in recent months. Here are the clues to the heart of the temple, and few actresses are confident enough to give their men a peek.

Strange herbal soaps in the bathroom by the Tampax. A Kewpie doll in the same bookcase with the *Smuggler's Bible*.

I twist around in the couch. The light coming from Kaye's fire escape is gray and high. My laptop is still hooked to her B-Net box. At the sight of it all the gray-water memories come flooding back into my conscious brain.

Zeng, I think grimly. Where *is* that son of a bitch?

There's a note lying on the carpet beside me.

"Munn, Happy Thanksgiving! I'm off to Queens to see my

folks. Back around 5. Help yourself to what you need. Use the accompanying to buy what is not available. You can call me at 718 428-4096. *Don't* give them your name."

Two twenty-dollar bills are pinned to the note.

Thanksgiving, I think. Son of a bitch.

My wound is sore, but no worse. My head is still somewhat congested. Despite the snot in my sinuses I can smell my bad breath, the sour stink of a dirty body. I wonder how in hell Kaye could stand sleeping with me.

I get up, intending to pee, and stop at the bath. Because Cosmo would not allow me into the "carwash" at Riker's I haven't showered in five days. Forced by a compulsion as strong as hunger or desire I twist the taps and watch blue-green water fill the clawfoot tub.

Getting in, the hot water feels like a gift so precious you could not buy it at Tiffany's. I play with Kaye's rubber duck. I get a distinct flash of Seth and Louise and Sara, all sitting in the huge dark dining room in Montclair, candles burning, Seth clowning as he clumsily hacks up the bird. The house felt awfully empty after he died. Now, Johnsonists cluster around the table holding hands and singing "Country Roads."

Sacrilege.

I get out of the tub a half hour later. I'd like to shave, but at this point I'd better keep the beard.

I look in the bathroom mirror. The face that stares back at me is thinner, older. The eyes are the same color, but they seem to have acquired a subtle layer, something that reflects rather than accepts light, a shellac of hardness.

Riker's, I think. A coating of Riker's.

Kaye keeps a bottle of Clairol blond dye over her sink. I mix a cupful and wash my hair in it. When I look up, my hair has turned the color of cheap brass plate.

Seventh Street is quiet when I go outside. The wind has died down and a heavy cold has taken its place, lancing into my lungs like razor-ribbon, setting me ferociously to coughing.

The Christmas lights of the electrified rowhouses look weak and pathetic against the steel clouds. A few people wander around the market stalls, their breath trailing behind like occasional ghosts. I bumble in among them, keeping the Rasta snood low over my forehead. I buy coffee and a hot tortilla. Another of the stalls sells used clothing and I spend most of Kaye's forty bucks on an army-surplus parka, patched jeans one size too big, a purple ski cap, and a tattered blue scarf. The vendor, a Haitian with one tooth, laughs when I change in front of him. He refuses any trade-in value on the filthy sweats I hand in, and dumps them straight into his fire barrel.

With the parka buttoned high, Cosmo's gangbanger shades over my eyes, the ski hat replacing the snood, it would take Ray Milland in *Man with X-Ray Eyes* to recognize me.

The clean clothes on my washed body make me feel almost innocent. I walk west across Tompkins Square to First Avenue and then south, down Chrystie to Chinatown. The cold keeps itching my lungs and the streets' emptiness emphasizes my isolation. I think of Kaye, her dark eyes sparkling as she looks on the people she loves.

In contrast to the rest of the city, Elizabeth Street is busy as ever; the Cantonese don't have a whole lot of time for Miles Standish, especially when there's money to be made. The restaurants, groceries, fish markets, sweatshops, mah-jongg dens, and tea parlors are hopping with activity. I stand on the corner, looking up at Zeng's windows. Most of the shades are down, which is par for Stefan's lifestyle.

I call him again, from a corner phone, staring at his windows while the ring signal buzzes. The Sex Pistols come on, as always these days. I hang up the receiver, blowing on my hands. My stomach is queasy, my chest flutters with nerves. I know perfectly well that going to Zeng's is perilous, because the cops may have staked it out, but I see no other avenue open to me. Damn few people are going to want to help me at all. Of them, only Zeng has the know-how to get into the ACCESS records.

I hang around another three or four minutes, yakking to a dead line while people wanting the phone glare, curse, stomp away. I see no one sitting in parked cars or loitering.

Eventually, I take a deep breath, pull the scarf up around my nose, and hustle up his stoop into the lobby.

No cops come bounding out of the shadows as I hover in the dingy space. As is standard in tenements, the speakerphone hasn't worked for years.

After maybe ten minutes a dumpy woman comes in hauling a cart full of groceries. She looks at me suspiciously and mutters in Cantonese. I repeat, "Zeng, Zeng." She opens the inner door grudgingly. I haul her cart up the next two flights, which leaves her happy.

Zeng is two flights higher. Of course the doorbell is broken. I rap on the door hard, even kick at the battered metal, calling "Stefan!" A man peers up the stairwell at me, yells something, disappears.

The kicking has loosened one of my shoelaces. As I bend down to tie it I notice a small piece of wood crammed between door and jamb. There's another one wedged at sill level. I knot the lace carefully while questions rise around me like disturbed fruit flies.

If Zeng's door is wedged shut, maybe it's because his locks are malfunctioning.

But he has three locks, like most city residents. All wouldn't shit the bed at once.

Maybe he got my message and left the door open for me.

Abruptly I put my ass to the door and shove, and it flies open. I stagger sideways into Zeng's hallway.

The stacks of technical journals and software manuals tower darkly around me.

The air is musty, empty-smelling to the extent I can smell through my stuffy sinuses, normal for this apartment.

"Zeng," I call, not very loud. Quietly I walk along the hallway, and part the beaded curtain to the main section of loft.

My friend Stefan sits in a corner of the main room, watching me.

He looks at me with an oddly erotic expression; jaw slack as if in the grip of passion, eyes hooded and faraway, hands clenched against spiked sensation.

But the slackness of his jaw is due to the packing tape wadded into his mouth. The passion he experienced was the passion of absolutes, and the sensation was ultimate pain; from his collarbone down, his chest has been deeply opened, a slash to the right, two to the left, with parallel gashes in the lower stomach. Blood has flowed so thickly it looks like he's wearing a black shirt.

He's wedged against a row of three mainframes. The green

lights of disk drives, the white eyes of power indicators blink like seasonal decorations behind his head.

The cord of a surge-protector is wound around his wrists and knotted to a heat register behind the bookcase. The contents of the bookcase lie all over the floor, daubed profusely with dried-up blood. The smell in this room is half bad, half sweet, like manure with iron, or syrup with lye.

Stefan's face alters a little, and I recoil in pure horror as his mouth seems to shift, the corner moving up just the tiniest bit; it's as if he were saying, "Wildman, see how ironic this is; look at the computer man crucified on his own hardware."

Then I realize his face *is* moving. Four or five cockroaches are lying along the ridge of his mouth, hunkering into the depression the way roaches do.

Others work farther down. Their brown carapaces twist and bumble along the crusted carnage of my friend's chest. At that my stomach explodes. Partially digested tortilla and coffee as well as the strong acids accumulated from my recent way of life flood like a monsoon up the Yangtze esophagus. I've got no time for resistance or reflexes; I puke where I stand, doubling over the pain in my belly, retching without control on the cheap rug, the flung manuals, maybe three feet from where I barfed my guts out a couple of weeks ago.

Even as I retch I'm thinking, with disturbing clarity, about my next move. Not the door—stupid to go out the way you came in—someone in Riker's told me that.

Stupid, also, to leave empty-handed. Riker's thinking again.

I gag and spit out every drop of my stomach contents. I hold my gut till the pain there lessens.

Then, still bent over a little, and not looking at my friend, I walk over to the terminal on the kitchen table and call up his working files.

I could never have done this ten days ago. Not with Stefan dead in the same room. It's the hardness of the con that moves my fingers now. My mouth pulls downward, in mourning for Zeng, in grief for the ways I've changed; but I don't stop what I'm doing.

I can hear disk drives whir around the room. The menu comes up obediently. The mainframes, at least, are functional. The menu holds only three pages of files, every last one of them slugged with the gibberish codes of operating systems: VIRTIX\AT49:2, VIRTIX\TEST:BB, SCAN\FRCTL: CMPRSS—that sort of thing.

No MUNNWORLD, no *Real Life*. Not a trace.

A half-empty cup of tea lies next to his Filofax. The rattling of the keys under my fingers reminds me of the last time I saw Zeng, right in this room, conjuring impossible battleships from the complex spaces inside his mind and software, to the extent you could differentiate between the two; blowing them up again with the skill of a master and the bliss of a nine-year-old.

A hole for another absence forms in the spinning succession of caves inside me.

Then, with no warning the sadness vanishes, shoved out by an anger so powerful it makes my breath freeze and my eyes squinch shut for a second.

I log off the workstation, almost breaking the keys. Still avoiding Stefan's body, and breathing through my mouth so as not to smell him, I pick through the diskettes that were pulled from the bookcase and emptied around his feet.

His toes, in the usual sandals, are a little grimy.

"Didn't do it, Stefan," I gasp. "Didn't cap ya. Never even had a *drink,* since I saw ya in Riker's."

There are almost no floppies left. Whoever did this to my friend ripped off most of his files before splitting. I locate, in sequence, seven containers labeled "*Real Life*—master files," and another ten with *Munn's World* written on them.

Every goddam one is empty.

The smell is getting stronger; either that, or my nose is losing resistance. I bend over to retch, agonizingly. Nothing comes out but spit. And water, from my forehead; inside the furry parka, I'm sweating like a farm horse.

I look at Stefan one final time. His long ponytail hangs perfectly straight from the back of his head. I can almost hear his voice, precise, careful, nervous.

The roaches are still clustered around his mouth. Furiously I grab a floppy and brush them off.

Before I leave, I pick up the Filofax. I don't look at my friend again.

The fire escape lies outside the guest-room window, but the bars on the window, illegally, are locked shut, keys nowhere in sight. I guess they didn't come this way. I hustle back to the main door, still not looking at Zeng.

And recoil, just like when I saw Zeng's mouth, with something close to the same horror pronging into my throat.

On the back of the front door someone has pasted a unicorn poster. The long, flowing mane, the air of gallop—

Blood drains from my face into my chest. Then it rushes back upstairs, kicked by a greater fear.

Because if they went to all the trouble of killing my friend like Fishman, it was so they could add this murder to the already crowded docket of Fishman's creator.

Me.

And there's really no point in framing someone—*unless he's around to pin the frame on.*

I go out the door, pulling it quickly to. I take the uneven stairs as fast as my stomach will allow. When I get to the bottom I once more check out the street for surveillance. Again I don't see anybody; however, I realize now, with the borrowed acuity of danger, that the street is much too crowded to tell for sure.

The only way to find out is by doing it.

I open the door and step into the crisp air. My heart beats fast, sure, and under that, without a doubt, is a dark mass of horror; but deeper still lies a burgeoning joy that I'm at a loss to explain.

Anyway, nobody shouts or points in my direction. I turn right, south toward Fulton Street. The Cantonese haggle and laugh over raw pork and diapers. A few *gwailo* tourists meander through the crowds like chickens in a flock of starlings, point-and-shoots bobbing over down vests. A gaggle of Asian kids bursts from under my feet like flushed partridges. One of them, a boy, streaks excitedly into a tea parlor across the way.

It's the speed of him that catches my eye, not any sensation of danger. Which is stupid, because if there's one thing the history of New York teaches, it's that things don't change as much as they seem to; the Five Points is still the Five Points, and gangs still have junior members and hang out in grogshops, playing games of chance; and danger is always all around, lying in wait, as if the city, under all the pavement and lights, remained the same, sleepy carnivore on whose back you walked at your constant peril.

The tea shop door opens. The kid bounces back outside, pointing at me. He's cute, with blue-black hair and candy-crusted cheeks.

A squat Southeast Asian in a fake-leather jacket and stonewashed jeans stands beside him, flipping off his shades to see better.

He spots me. I'm not looking directly at him, I don't want to be obvious, but I sense him stiffen.

He turns and barks an order into the dark interior.

The carnivore is awake.

I start to run. On Elizabeth Street, that's not as easy as it sounds. Every six feet a knot of people, a stack of crates full of tangerines, or a rack of cheap clothes blocks the sidewalk. I have to jump, twist, and brake in ways painful for my scars. I veer left, off the sidewalk, trying to keep double-parked cars between me and the first vague resonance of running feet behind.

At the corner of Mott and Pell I dodge behind a newsstand and risk a backward glance. And take off immediately, left down Pell, the image fear-etched behind my eyes—three guys, I swear to God they're the same I saw in Kearny, in Greenpoint, that way of moving so typical of their kind of violence; as if, should you stand in their way, they would crush you and your family the way a normal man would rub out a cigarette butt.

That same glint of plastic and metal in the business hand.

Carpet-cutters. Jesus Christ almighty, fucking *carpet-cutters* again! My feet switch on the afterburners automatically, taking me diagonally across traffic. A van swerves, tires shriek. Chinese voices flute angrily in my wake.

Don't give a shit. On the opposite sidewalk one of the Viets has drawn level. He hip-checks people out of his way, right and left like a hockey forward, glancing at me between cars, waiting for a clear shot.

Another intersection, another right. This is Doyers Street, a small lane that curves around into Park Row and St. James Place.

The buildings are higher here, the traffic less dense, which sucks because it turns this into more of a straight footrace, and I don't have even the minimal speed and stamina I had in the Jersey marshes. I'm old now; tired, blond, and sick, and my stomach hurts and my lungs ache and my feet are sore and clumsy.

Con Ed's working the bend of Doyers Street, tearing up some of the old cobbles to repair a water main. Dust lies thick on the roadway, clogging my harsh breath.

The feet pounding behind me are louder, only a couple yards away. I can almost feel the chill of the carpet-cutter on the tendons of my neck. People stand and stare. A woman huddles behind her shopping in my path. I bounce her aside, then streak into the covered arcade that opens left, slipping a little in the dust.

The arcade is full of sale signs and women with shopping bags. The combo of dust, strain, and incipient bronchitis finally blocks my lungs. The resultant coughs slow me down some. As I reach the level of a tourist restaurant the footsteps behind me crescendo, and a fist grabs my parka, swinging me half sideways so that I slam into the restaurant doorway, almost smashing the glass.

He's young, with a pleasant-looking face and longish hair. His jacket bears the decal of a green dragon on the front. My sudden stop loosened his grip but not his balance. He crouches theatrically, moving his right thumb, and the straight-angled point of a carpet-cutter slides three inches out of its orange plastic handle.

I yank the door open behind me. The sharp blade slices my army parka, then tangles in the rough cotton as I crash backward into the restaurant. For some reason he doesn't follow me in; the door swings shut on his blade as I scramble to my feet.

It's one of those modern-style Chinese joints, a fish restaurant catering mostly to tourists. Shining Formica, drinks with umbrellas, a line of woks on a range, bright plastic pictures overhead labeled "General Ho's Shrimp" and "Seafood Pu-Pu Platter."

A doorway to the right reads "FIRE." I'm about to dive in that direction, through a crowd of large fair people with KLM stickers on their bags, when the door opens by itself.

A Vietnamese in a plastic jacket glides gracefully through the fire exit, opening his jacket as he does so. He's wearing shades, so I can't see his eyes, but in the slowdown of terror I make out every detail of the green dragon on his jacket, and the high school ring on his third finger, and the blue steel milling on the boxlike armature of the Tech-9 machine-pistol he holds in his right hand.

Four or five people notice him. Two or three realize what's going on. One of the waiters drops a water pitcher. No one has time to shout a warning.

The gangbanger smiles; it's a surprisingly universal expression, not Asian, not American; simply the product of block, of stifled currents, of the need to anesthetize an abscess inside by blowing abscess into everything around.

He pulls the trigger.

Sixteen inches off the floor the water pitcher explodes into blue light. A tall Dutch woman coughs, folds in two beside me. Her husband reaches to catch her, and twists around, gray droplets spraying from his shoulder. The sound of the Tech-9 is very loud, like a jackhammer on amphetamines, but it's absorbed into the utter silence of the tiny restaurant as every person inside takes a deep gulp of air preparatory to dying.

I catch all this on my way down to the linoleum. At knee level the line of tables interferes with the Asian's aim. He takes his finger off the trigger, moving aside to find a better angle. A Chinese man seated behind tries to stop him, a feeble movement, his hand on the man's sleeve as if to ask him if he's sure about what he's doing. In the killer's hyped state it's enough to make him wheel and kick at the offender, giving me time to get to my feet and duck behind another set of tables.

The Tech-9 explodes once more. Trampling the squirming bodies of tourists I rocket through a curtain marked "REST ROOMS."

The machine-pistol falls silent. People are screaming now, long modulated wails almost as loud as the Tech-9. I'm in a corridor. "EXIT" glows ahead, above a door in the gloom.

Something brings me to a halt. I learn slowly, but my education is finally catching up. One tactic these guys have down is the flanking movement, the encirclement.

Without really thinking I back, fast, into a door to my right marked "Women." I close it quietly behind me. I crook my parka-ed elbow around my mouth, trying to stifle the sobbing coughs. My chest heaves in and out, my nose is plugged with snot. My visual centers are crowded with the mindless gray slaughter in the front room.

Flexator squeaks on painted concrete. Someone marches down the rest room corridor and kicks the exit open. It shuts behind him. A whistle sounds, piercing, from a small window over the john to my left. He's in some sort of passageway behind the restaurant.

Moving carefully, I climb onto the toilet. The window isn't barred, maybe because what lies outside is a closed concrete alley, lined with empty boxes and garbage Dumpsters. Turning my head a few seconds per movement, I peer left, and right, down the passage.

Below me, a blue Dumpster stands chained by the restaurant exit.

Far to the left, a gate cuts a wedge of gray-blue light out of shadow.

Otherwise, the passageway is empty.

In the restaurant behind me, against the wails and sobs, a man shouts a sharp command. More Viets behind; and the killer in the street will turn back any second when he sees I'm not out there.

I'm certain I will die here. I see absolutely no way out of this trap and frankly I'm so full of new horror that anything to stop it, even my own death, would be okay.

But I've survived enough over the last few weeks to build a kind of momentum for struggle. It's this momentum that pushes me to the ledge—balancing precariously as I push the window open—and flops me face first into the open Dumpster underneath.

I think I mentioned this was a fish restaurant. What I failed to point out, or remember, is that the Cantonese love fish, all kinds of fish, any sort of fish. They buy anything that swims or floats, every ugly, slimy, bony cartilaged critter that inhabits great Neptune's domain—much to the delight of New England fishermen who, as soon as they've wiped out the "normal" species like cod, fall back on fishing out the ugly spiky ones they can flog to the Asian market.

What I have fallen into, forehead first in the dumpster, is seven hundred pounds of slimy, worm-infested guts of skate, sculpin, goosefish, dogfish, minister fish, conger eel, and mudcrawler. Creatures of the sea, like humans and other bottom-feeders, carry mostly salt water in their abdomens, and sinking into that mess feels a lot like swimming in a cold, thick, slimy ocean. My hands bend against the bottom. My feet find the rusty side of the Dumpster and, through the power of friction, walk me back to the surface.

I take a fast breath—and the smell locks my throat. "Fishy" doesn't begin to describe it. All the blood and excrement and digestive juices of these ugliest of ocean reptiles have sedimented down into the dumpster and fermented there over at least two days. Slime blocks my nostrils, and a string of fish colon has wound its way into the corner of my mouth. I gag, painfully, for the second time in ten minutes.

And close my mouth, holding one hand over the fish colon, mouth half full of stomach acid.

The whistle sounds again.

They got me.

I find I don't really want to die. I want the horror to stop but not at the expense of blood and breath. I know this because, to postpone the final second, I take a last gulp of air and let myself sink into the rotting fish guts once more.

And sit there, in a cold stink of silence, fighting hard to keep the gag reflex in check, until I have absolutely no oxygen left.

And so I rise, back to the surface, into the bright carpet-cutters, the black muzzles of Tech-9s, the sunglasses of my executioners.

Except they're not there.

Footsteps, running, recede down the passageway. The exit door slams.

After that, nothing. Nothing but the endless, sobbing wails behind the ladies' room window.

I wipe fish gurry off my face and risk a glance over the edge of the Dumpster.

Nobody.

Some gifts you don't look at twice. Although these acrobatics cause my wound to scream I scissor over the side of the Dumpster, jump to the cement, clumsy, fast. I've lost my gangbanger shades, but my left hand still clutches Zeng's Filofax. The gag reflex activates again; I keep my hand over my mouth as I retch.

The passageway ends on the Bowery. People, normal people, walk back and forth across the opening. I edge close to the entrance gate and peer around.

Still nobody.

Sirens build across the sky. A blue-and-white, arrowing up Park Row with lights flashing, screeches left into Doyers Street. If I walk left now, and keep going up Bowery, I'll wind up at the Canal Street subway station.

I don't want to move. I don't want to stay either. My stomach heaves again, trying to rise above the stink wafting off my clothes. The need for fresh air drives me finally into the bright blue light and up the busy sidewalk.

My eyes dart back and forth like nervous minnows but I see few Viets and no one with the Green Dragon logo.

Within a few seconds I'm part of the crowd shopping restaurant supplies in the Bowery, and ten minutes later I'm sitting on the number 6 train, reading the latest "Subway Talk" posters while people clutching cans of cranberry jelly and bouquets of roses shift hurriedly to the other end of the car, holding their outraged nostrils.

THIRTY-SIX

KAYE COMES BACK a little before six.

"Sorry I'm late," she says, dumping bags on the floor and her jacket on the office chair. "Shit—you're *blond*!"

"Yeah."

"It's kinda cute."

"Uh-huh."

"Wooh! That smell!"

"My clothes. They're in a garbage bag." I point to the kitchen.

I'm sitting on the couch with a towel wrapped around my drawn-up knees. I've been sitting that way ever since I got out of my second bath of the day, maybe three hours ago.

Partly it's because my clothes have been annihilated by fish guts, and partly it's due to the fact that I keep seeing the Dutch woman doubling over, her husband twisting as he tries to help her, and the alligator smile on the killer's face as he sprays the restaurant with 9 mm.

Hunched like this, my legs warming the right side of my stomach, I can concentrate on other things. The ceramic giraffes on her shelf. The cracks on her walls. Anything besides the images that float in as soon as I stop concentrating.

She walks over, touches my knee gently.

"What's wrong? Did you see your friend?"

I shake my head. I can't seem to look at her.

"Munn, what is it?"

"He's dead. Killed."

Kaye takes a deep breath. She removes her Ray Bans and puts them neatly on the bookshelf.

After that, she goes into the kitchen and makes tea. Which reminds me immediately of Zeng, causing the corners of my mouth to dip. I resist that fiercely; softness doesn't get you anywhere, I learned that at Riker's. My armor was starting to flake off, because of Kaye, and look what happened.

If you keep up your hardness, you will not be cut so readily. And if you are cut it will not hurt so much.

She comes back with two mugs and sits on the floor beside me, leaning her head against my left ass.

We sip tea for a while. The pretty shape of her nose dives occasionally into the wisps of steam. Her hair shines like frayed wire.

"D'you want to tell me?" she asks at length.

I shrug.

But sitting like that makes it easy. I can look at the cracks, or Edna St. Vincent Millay, and keep things under control.

When I've finished she says nothing for a long time. Then she gets up, carefully shoves me over, and lies next to me with her left arm under my back, looking me seriously in the eyes.

"What," I ask finally.

"Just checking," she says.

"Checking what?"

"When I saw you in Riker's," she says, "your eyes had gone funny. Oh, I ain't being poetic, I know the eyes themselves don't change, but the way you looked—there was something in that. You'd put up obstacles; I could imagine you hiding something. Ya know, I almost didn't come to St. John the Divine yesterday?"

I grunt.

"But that changed," she continues. "I saw it change, making love with you."

"And now?"

"It's still kinda muddy," she admits, "but it's better than

Riker's.'' She lays her cheek on my chest. Her hand fiddles with my bandage.

''I feel numb,'' I tell her after a beat. ''I don't know what to feel now. It's like that smell—so strong you can't even absorb it.''

''Uh-huh.''

''But what makes it really hard—you're not gonna believe this. I mean, I love Stefan. But under all of it, I feel sort of happy.''

''Why?''

''Because it means I didn't do it. Not Stefan. Well, maybe the cops won't agree. But *I* know I didn't do it—'cause I didn't go out an' get drunk an' forget a whole stretch of time.''

''You coulda done it in your sleep''—she puts a little up-speak into her voice, to cushion what she's actually saying—''when you were on the street?''

I chuckle. It's not a funny-ha-ha kind of chuckle.

''You don't sleep. Not under the FDR. You doze, here 'n there. Even then, I never had enough time. But what I'm getting at—all the time I was in Stefan's apartment—that was in the back of my mind. Like a little brass band, celebrating.''

''It's called life, baby. Here.'' Her voice is more animated. She jumps up, pulls a ring folder from the bookshelf. ''Listen.'' She starts to read.

> *''We sat at the funeral*
> *lined up like crows.*
> *The priest was there to polish his prose*
> *the girlfriend had already polished her nose*
> *the wife was inventing her memory of him*
> *everyone was there but Tim.*
> *We had come to worship our perduring lives,*
> *We hadn't come for Tim . . .''*

She glances at my face, and slaps the folder shut. I continue to examine the cracks.

''Ya know,'' she says, ''I *know* it's not that good.''

''I didn't say that.''

''You didn't have to.''

''How could I know it was yours?''

"Are you hungry?" She goes into the kitchen. "I brought back food."

I get up stiffly. She's spooning gunk into a pot. I stand behind and put my arms around her waist.

"That's funny-lookin' turkey."

"It's lasagna. My dad hates turkey."

"I like—I like the *life* in your poems."

"Please, Munn—"

"They're not the best. But they try to explain things, more than a lot that are technically better."

"Don't," she says.

"If it doesn't *explain* something," I continue stubbornly, "it's just TV."

"Please." She brushes hair desperately from her eyes. "Let me cook. If you want clothes—I shoulda tole you—there might be some in that closet that'll fit you. In a gray box?"

I find a pair of running pants, a little too tight, a T-shirt, a little too big. Automatically I transfer the shank from my fish-killed parka to the windbreaker's pocket.

The smell of garlic wrestles with the lingering aroma of dead goosefish.

I don't think about who these clothes belonged to. I sit down at my laptop and open a line to WHISPER.

Leaf through Zeng's Filofax to the X-Corp listings, wiping fish scum off the cards as I flip. Zeng, like most people, had a vast address file in his system. Unlike most, however, he kept separate copies of everything he did, filing them with a commercial backup service on Sixteenth Street. He also kept hard copy in his Filofax of every important log-on, password, and ACCESS code.

Under X-Corp I find a list of passwords he used for different jobs. Under "X-Corp housekeeping" I find a series of ACCESS codes. Most don't mean much to me; one appears to be exactly what I'm looking for.

ACCESS/SP\FILEUSR:BUDGET
SZ pword BLACKFLAG

I type in the XTV system number, put "BLACKFLAG\" in the password prompt, and add the code for the directory I want. WHISPER makes the connection. "Working" blinks in a corner of the screen. I wait for the "UNAUTHORIZED" warning to flash in front of me.

Instead, a list of options riffles out below the command field.

I click to the "subject" budget and enter a wild card command for "Munn."

The words "No such file/check spelling" line up under the command field.

So they spiked the ACCESS files for *Munn's World.*

I cancel that program, call up my directory, and scroll down.

The MUNNWORLD/MSTR files take up two entire screens.

I slump back against the couch. Kaye, bringing over a bowl of food a few minutes later, finds me staring stupidly at the laptop's screen-saver.

" 'S up?"

"Not much."

"You find what you were looking for?" She points at the laptop.

I shrug. "There's an ACCESS list—it tells you who called up any file over the last six months. It would've tole me who got those details—you know, like 'Squatter,' and the slashes —the knife." I swallow. "The unicorn, too, at Stefan's. But they killed the files."

"You mean, at work?"

I nod.

"Does that mean, your show—*Munn's World*—is it destroyed?"

"No, those files are still there. But that's not the point."

"I know," she says, "I was just worried, all that work." She proffers the bowl. "Here, this'll help."

"I'm really not hungry."

"Eat."

"Kaye—"

"It's my genes. I'm Italian. If you don't eat, I'll have a stroke, or somethin'."

I take a bite. And another. The lasagna is savory, hot, full of juicy hamburger. It reminds my vagic nerve or whatever it is that my stomach is empty. She keeps talking as I snarf the food.

"What about *Real Life*?" she asks.

"Now that *is* gone." I'm talking with my mouth full. "I checked earlier. The episodes I wrote, I mean."

"They scrapped the show?"

I shake my head, swallow.

"Jiss the ones I did," I repeat.

"But why?"

"I don't know."

She fetches a bottle of Stoli from the freezer, and two glasses. I look at the liquor with combined longing and loathing. When I refuse the glass, she wrinkles her nose and examines the bottle. I get the feeling she knows exactly why I don't want to touch booze at this point.

"Are they completely gone? Or can you find them somewhere—the ones you did?" She dips her lips into the vodka, and licks them.

"Maybe."

"Let's try."

"Why?" I can feel a wave of fatigue creeping up on me. The last thing I want to do is see *Real Life* again.

" 'Cause it doesn't make sense—"

"If I was gonna check out everything that din make sense—"

"You know what I'm sayin', Munn," she tells me deliberately, and tops up her glass. "Anyway, I'm curious. Jiss think —I could go to work Monday, and I'd be the only person in the world, practically, who's seen a preview of *Real Life*!"

"Maybe tomorrow," I say, shifting on the couch.

She looks away. Her voice is even more careful.

"Tomorrow, you could be back in Riker's."

I suppose that's the magic word. It kicks the fatigue back a notch. I sit up, groaning, and move back to the laptop.

The WHISPER number is already in the modem directory. I consult the soggy filofax, blessing Zeng's thoroughness, his use of indelible ballpoint. Zeng's backup firm, DataSafe Ltd., is cross-referenced; his password for DataSafe, "OMFUG," is printed underneath in neat characters.

DataSafe's system turns out to be very simple and graphic. Once I've typed in the password and names I'm looking for, I can click around the windows calling up master files. The first *Real Life* episodes show up immediately, seeming to ask, by implication, What's all the fuss? I download all three of my episodes into X-Corp's database under the slug BACK-FILESXXX.

Then, it's just a matter of telling the *Real Life* Navigator to accept BACKFILESXXX as a valid input.

I wish I didn't have to go through XTV at all, but there's no PC on earth that can handle all the data and iterations involved in *Real Life*. The Navigator system alone would crash this 988 instantaneously. *Real Life* depends, like a junkie on his pusher, on the phenomenal power and speed of B-Net video-servers.

"This is gonna cost you some cash," I warn Kaye.

"Deal with that later."

I take both pairs of shutter-glasses from their carrying compartment, unspool the wires all the way.

We arrange cushions on the couch. Kaye places her glass within easy reach. A small blue bird sings in my head, a single note, clear, compelling—and is silent.

I've already broken the connection with DataSafe. We slip on the shutter-glasses. Still going through the blocking service, I click back into XTV's databanks and call up BACKFILESXXX. I keep expecting the "UNAUTHORIZED LEVEL" or "CLEARANCE UNAVAILABLE" warnings to blink on. However, no one is paying much attention to "backfiles" slugs and before I'm ready, or even comfortable, the familiar Clam Fetish tune cranks in, trembling on the soundboard. And in the tunnel vision of shutter-glasses, my episode, the former first episode of *Real Life,* comes surging in three dimensions out of the high-resolution LCD, in soakingly pure color and lovely contrast.

And so, with only a little brake from the half-assed immersion, we're moving inside the persona of a guy who must be a Tunes Task Force investigator, boarding a STOL commuter plane on a flight from Albany to La Guardia.

"Who's that?"

"Don't remember," I mutter, "I tole you, I was never interested in it."

"But you've got to—"

"Watch," I interrupt, closing my eyes for a second, "watch." I find her hand, pass her the mouse.

Click.

Opening my eyes once more. We're driving down a New York City highway. It's the Gowanus Expressway; off to my right I can see Coney Island, the distant spiderweb of the Cyclone outlined in a shimmer of sun. It seems like years since I was on Coney. I close my eyes again.

Beside me, Kaye squirms excitedly as she swerves around in traffic. A truck honks, and I jump. *Click.*

The next time I open my eyes we've slowed way down. I— we—*the investigator*—are peering back and forth as we enter a neighborhood that's very different from the city I'm used to. Yet we haven't been driving long enough to leave New York. Narrow asphalt streets, with grass growing in the frost cracks, wind between vinyl-sided ranch houses; bullrushes so high they remind me, a little, of Kearny.

It's later in the day and long shadows follow our Zaibatsu west. Out of nowhere, a 777-B lowers its fat silver gut out of the sky above our heads. Which makes sense; we must be near JFK, not far from Howard Beach.

This is a part of the city I've never been to.

We follow a canal, northerly now. Black stagnant water lurks, patches of ice forming around cattail stalks. A cement pedestrian bridge to the right. After the fast driving on the Gowanus, the investigator—Kaye—seems to hesitate a lot.

Around the base of one canal, up the edge of a second. The houses get smaller, shabbier until they're nothing more than shacks. Rotting four-by-fours hold up crooked beams jutting over the smelly water. Asphalt shingles, pieces of plywood, and tarpaper are tacked against the endless damp wind and polluted air. Wooden cabin cruisers, half covered with blue tarps, sit in the water as if planted in black cement; cheap speedboats hang on rotted lines off festering pilings. Old Chevies, rusted-out Japanese cars, fill the yards to overflow.

"Where the fuck *is* this," I mutter. The investigator is going dead slow now—or maybe it just feels that way to me.

I mean, I've been in some nasty parts of the waterfront, but the sense of dead-end hopelessness that rises out of this area like fog from a marsh makes me feel both squirmy and oddly ashamed.

I shift around on the couch. My face and beard are damp with sweat. I close my eyes, and my breathing settles down. I can hear the rumble of the Zaibatsu engine, the squish of tires. I hear the "Angel" prompting Kaye, who obediently asks a passerby for directions to a Mrs. Reardon's house. But now, without the visual, immersion is broken, the tension gone; this is nothing but television again, the idiot noise of a story I care nothing about. Through the tendrils of sound, the great desire to give up, curl inward like a fiddlehead, that has been pounding on my heels all day, can finally catch up with me, and take me down.

For some reason, the image of Stefan the way I last saw him can't penetrate this hard momentum toward sleep.

I come awake abruptly. Kaye, her face pointed with determination, is yanking me back and forth on the couch.

"Wha," I protest thickly, "what's goin' on?"

She stops yanking.

"Why din' you *tell* me?"

"What?"

"You know."

"No, I don't!"

"Jee-sus—it's why they're tryin' to *kill* ya!"

I lick sleep scum off my lips.

"What," I repeat stupidly. "Kaye, look, lemme just go back to sleep?"

"No."

"Oh. Well. What about the hot coffee, the fresh-squeezed o.j.—"

"I'm *serious,* damn you! You coulda tole me."

I note that her eyes go dark like harbor water when she's upset. Her mouth curves like the Ramapo Hills. I want desperately to take her in my arms and kiss her, but right now I'd probably get frostbite.

"Look, Kaye—jiss tell me what you're talking about?"

"*Real Life,* asshole! The episode *you* wrote."

"I tole you, those story lines go right outta my head—"

"You expect me to believe that?"

I stare at her.

"Yeah. Sure. I mean, I wrote it a good year ago."

"You wouldn't forget dis!"

The Brooklyn accent strong again; she must be really pissed off.

"Oh, yes, I would," I tell her.

She shakes her head, sits back on her haunches.

"Do me a favor," I continue softly.

"What?"

"Tell me what you saw."

She sucks her lips into her mouth, her eyes flicking from my left eye to my right, the way women do when they're trying, very hard, to determine just how full of shit you are.

"I saw Henry Warren Powell," she says finally.

"You did?" My surprise is real.

"Of *course* I did! You *put* him there!"

"Okay. Okay." I hold up my hands. "Pretend—jiss pretend, for the sake of argument—that I'm somebody who never saw this before in his life? Pretend you've got to explain it to me, like I was a kid."

"Munn—"

"Please?"

So she tells me the story, looking at me sideways now and then as the probability keeps coming back that I'm just some kinky bastard trying to head-trip her to Cleveland for some reason she can't fathom.

Telling me about Henry Warren Powell, who "Mrs. Reardon" said grew up in this area of New York City.

He's not called Henry Warren Powell in the story, though. His name is "John Henry Peters." His best friend was a boy named "Sammy Talbot."

But Kaye says it's clear who they are; and she says Powell, together with his buddy Jack Tyrone, roamed the marshes and streets of western Brooklyn, first as a duo, then as part of a gang called the Ozone Werewolves.

Kaye, following the story, clicked into the Forty-second Street research library, the Library of Congress, and NYPIRG files. The truly cool thing, she tells me excitedly—this I *do* remember, because it's something Stefan spent a lot of time on—is that *Real Life* actually consults the on-line records while you do the research. Gopher-ing up files right before your eyes as evidence. So there's no doubt in her mind about the accuracy of what follows.

Because Powell, as a Werewolf, shot a black kid named Vernon Mitchell, who belonged to a rival gang in Crown Heights. He also fathered an illegitimate child on a girl he ran with in his neighb.

She saw the clippings on the death. Though the Ozone Werewolves were questioned, no one was ever arrested for the murder.

Jack Tyrone, with an IQ of 154, scored 1595 on his SATs. He got a scholarship to Wharton, specialized in communications, started a cable TV company.

The paper trail is there; the publicity notices, the "Heard on the Street" column in the *Wall Street Journal:* and of course they're all listed under Jack Tyrone; just as the "Peters" documents all pop up, highlighted under the file name "Powell."

Powell, with the aid of Tyrone, who forged some of his high school transcripts, got a law degree at St. John's. He founded a network of advocacy groups, was elected to the borough council and then the state senate.

Tyrone—Kaye's voice grows softer, her tone more lyrical as she falls into the story's rhythm—Tyrone covertly funded Powell's campaigns. In return, Powell supported laws that made it easier for one cable company to acquire another.

Tyrone's cable empire set up the first fiber-optic network; his network endorsed Powell's candidacy for U.S. Senate.

I watch Kaye as she talks, which she does nicely, much better than when she reads poetry. The Brooklyn accent is still there, but not enough to caricaturize her, it's just a light shading, like paprika on chicken, to give it extra flavor. Her hands move as fast as I remember from The Right Bank. Her eyes have lost their anger and are full of light and motion. She seems weightless, unencumbered, and this puts huge distance between us; for with every word of the pattern she's piecing together—and especially every reference to that place of black water and rotting shacks where the whole filthy story began—she seems to add another ton of weight to the sump of angst sitting in my gut.

At length, she falls silent. She holds the glass to her lips and stares at the surface of the liquid. I know she's waiting for me to speak.

I clear my throat.

"So, Jack Tyrone, huh? An' Senator Powell."

She looks up. The half smile, casting light around the room. There's doubt there, fighting with approval—admiration, even.

"I'd like to know how you did it."

"I wish you'd stop saying that," I yell. "Goddammit, why don't you believe I'm telling you the truth? I don't remember that! *I don't believe it's my story!*"

She stares at me. Her cheeks pale. She puts her glass down and in a quiet voice says, "I wish ya'd just admit, ya can't tell me."

"Okay! I can't tell you! Because *I don't remember*!"

I swing off the couch, tweaking the stomach scar. I stand in the center of the little room, feeling the whole weight of things drag my ass: tiredness, discomfort, fish breath, and above all the sick feeling that something has gone wrong with my mind, and I don't know how or why it happened, or even how to measure what occurred.

I cover my eyes with the palms of my hands, then fetch my damp sneakers and lace them on. The stink of a hundred dead carp rises from the sodden vinyl.

"Where you going?"

"Out."

"Is dat how you deal with questions?"

I don't answer.

"Is dat how you deal with people who, who want to care for ya, but need ta—"

I don't look at her. I slam the front door behind me, and boogie down the stairs.

THIRTY-SEVEN

THE ARCTIC HIGH or whatever it is that socked the temperature so low two nights ago still locks the city in its grip. A westerly wind cuts down Seventh Street like a true diss. Kaye's castoffs protect me for roughly fifteen seconds.

I hunch against the cold, my fists burrowed in the folds of windbreaker. Make a beeline through the Christmas lights toward the brightly roaring trash fires of the node market.

Headlights catch me as I cross the street, a blue-and-white brakes to let me by; but the cops are examining truck license plates, and barely glance at my face. Heart beating faster, I move into the ring of men and women surrounding the nearest trash can. The fires are tended by stall owners, and no one seems to mind my intrusion. The flames churn and snap, lighting the faces of people like temple deities from below. Tinny radio music rises in our midst. I spread my hands toward the flames. The heat dries my eyeballs, the blasting breath of fire covers the stupid little breaths I make to cover the Maydays screaming in my head.

"Gaynor," I mumble, "it's *Gaynor*."

"*What* did you say?" the man beside me asks.

"Nothin'."

"You said I was *gay*?"

"No," I assure him. "Jiss talkin' to myself."

"*You* gay, buddy?"

"I wasn't talkin' to you," I insist, hunching closer to the fire.

I don't believe it was Jack Tyrone that started the whole chain of events. Tyrone didn't even know *Munn's World* existed.

Gaynor, on the other hand, did.

I'm quite certain now, on a gut level, it was Gaynor who took out the contract on my ass. Gaynor told Tyrone what was in that episode, and when Tyrone said, Do something, Gaynor complied.

I put a tentative notch next to that question mark. There's a small intellectual satisfaction in seeing one puzzle, most probably, solved.

The main turmoil, though, has nothing to do with Gaynor, or Tyrone or Powell.

It has to do with what Kaye will not believe; what I, also, have trouble imagining; the fact that I wrote a show like that, with all the research it must have taken, and then put it out of my mind so completely, I didn't even know I wrote it.

Of course, someone else could have done it, and replaced my show with his—or hers.

But that would have been tough to do, technically. In any case it doesn't explain why I still can't recall whatever *I* wrote to fill that slot.

The radio sounds come from my homophobic companion. Looking closer, I make out headphones, a mini-TV, and four Discman CD-players, dead and live, hanging inside his houndstooth monkey-jacket—even a satfax, sheltered protectively inside the tweed. He's white and, judging by the jacket and boots, middle class. Now, unshaven and smelly, his boots worn and his silk shirt crusty with dirt, he rocks back and forth, humming the theme to *Frisco Heat*.

And I see myself in him, mad in other ways, the insanity of not recalling *Real Life* latched on to my blackout after Brooklyn; the two insanities linking, reopening the dark tunnel to Larissa, and Stefan.

"*Goddammit, n-o-o-o!*" I moan, backing suddenly away from the fire, into the cold.

Crossing the street to Kaye's sidewalk, I look up in despair at the cheerful blink of Woolworth's lights.

The booze had nothing to do with it. I haven't had a drink in ten days, yet the memory of *Real Life* is as closed to me as ever; like a locked door, in my own apartment, to a room I've never visited.

Or have I?

I walk up the sidewalk, turning, walking down again. I suppose it's the rhythm of walking in place that reminds me of *Munn's World;* how I used to pace like that in my loft on Hubert Street.

The lust comes like all lust, a fast glandular discharge, hormonal in its power.

I want to see *Munn's World* again.

I stop and look up at Kaye's windows, aware of a sudden sense of loss.

I shake my head angrily. I'm sick to death of confusion. I want a story that's clear and predictable, whose parameters I can count on.

I walk back into Kaye's building. Going upstairs, a cockroach makes a break across a landing and I stamp on it, feeling it crunch against the plastic sneaker sole.

She left her door ajar, I suppose so I could get back in. Then I remember the other doors I've found open in the last couple of weeks, and I bust into her apartment, holding my breath, blood thumping in my ears.

The laptop screen is still on. The Christmas lights make garish patterns in the darkened sitting room. The lasagna dishes are washed.

I peek fearfully into her bedroom. She's lying on her back in the porch. The storm lantern illuminates her right thigh, a pile of manuscript pages, the shiny cornrows.

I can hear her breathe, like waves washing in and out on a distant beach.

I pull the blanket gently to her neck. Then I walk out to the living room and sit down at the laptop.

The process, via WHISPER, is exactly the same as for *Real Life.*

Blakie's office again. The black night of the old city crouches outside his frosted windows. The smoke of a whale-oil lamp adds to the shadows and the fumes from the captain's pipe.

"Dereliction of duty, the night of the Alcazar fire," he rumbles. "Illegal use of city property—I'm referring to that 'office' you set up on the fifth floor."

Blake has bronchitis. He keeps lobbing gobs of mucus toward the spittoon.

"Not reporting for work. Taking a side job. You got anything to say for yourself?"

Through the narrow field of the shutter-glasses, Blakie grins, and sucks on his briar. It must be my imagination, but I swear his nose glows a little each time he sucks.

"You're gonna say, how many coppers do the same every day? And you're right. But what they've all got is a hook. A friend upstairs to protect 'em. An alderman, maybe? An' yours just took a powder."

He gets up, coughing, and walks over to the window. A vague commotion from that direction; people yelling on the street outside.

"The 'Fishman' case is closed. And *you* are fired. Get outta here."

Double-click backward, out the door. My cop from out of state grinning at me from the duty-roundsman's desk.

I pause on the steps of the precinct house. (It's at this point, truly, that the immersion takes hold, and I stop seeing the borders of the glasses, or smelling the musty blanket I draped over my head.)

Although it's not snowing, it obviously came down some since I was last here. The drifts on the street are three or four feet high now. From where I stand, every surface of the city is covered with rime.

Between the drifts and the hard-packed street and the frozen housefronts and the load of icicles on windows and railings, each facet of the city seems to sparkle in the dark like it was carved out of a mineral softer yet shinier than diamond.

In this trembling crystal landscape a small, pathetic crowd has gathered in front of the cop shop. I think, at first, they are beggars. Their clothes are ragged and many have no coats. Some of them walk, not on shoes, but on chilblained feet swaddled in hay or newsprint, bound with strips of canvas.

When I walk down the steps they press closer, then pull back as the officer on door-duty swings his club at them.

"Where's Flynn?" an ancient woman screeches from their midst.

"What've ye *done* with 'im?" a man shouts.

A woman holding a child wrapped in stained petticoats elbows her way to the front.

" 'Oo's gonna protect us now?" she wails. " 'Oo's gonna protect my baby from the Fishman?"

"Leave him be," the officer snarls, swinging his club again. " 'S not his fault, he's a mick-fancier."

I walk around the little crowd. They fall silent as I pass. The mother is emaciated, her eyes bright with fever. I notice a couple of black men, shrinking toward the rear of the group.

I click on down the street. Even lying on Kaye's couch, my feet automatically make little stepping motions. It's hard going. Every few yards I have to dodge the blandishments of sausage sellers, organ-grinders, beggars pretending to be epileptics. Groups of people too cold to hawk huddle around the stall fires. Pungs, small passenger sleighs, full of bundled merchants, hiss prettily up and down, their bright lamps swaying, the horses' breath freezing into white cones. Snow wardens curse and holler, positioning their own teams to flatten the loose snow kicked up by other horses. The animals' droppings steam like fat cakes.

I'm going to Pfaff's; so, at any rate, runs the story line, and if it didn't I'd probably go there anyway. The thought of grog and a fire, even if I can't really drink the booze or feel the heat, holds enormous comfort for me tonight. So does the idea of men and women who will accept me without question, or threat of arrest, or anger at the failures of my memory.

Nor am I disappointed. The sidewalk-cellar is more crowded than the last time I was here. Even the alcove at the far end is plugged with customers. The fireplace is surrounded by a wall of journalists.

Pine and holly boughs decorate the sconces. A wide earthen punch bowl has been set up in the center of the room. Out of this a boy dips ladles of hot syllabub. I look for Whitman, who should be easy to spot, but he's not around. A plump man with a theatrical mane of silver-white hair passes me a steaming mug. It's the same fellow who presided over the sidewalk-cellar, slandering editors, last time I was here. Leaning over as he hands it to me he grunts, in a fairly loud voice, "Caleb says, 'Watch out for that black ship.'"

"What?"

"*Caleb.*" The plump man looks around, wiping his mustache with the back of a heavily frogged sleeve. "The men from the black ship have been at his fish house. Looking for *thee.*"

The man has clear blue eyes. His once-white mustache holds little crumbs of nutmeg and is stained brown from cheroots, one of which is stuck in his mouth like a pencil caught in a blackberry thicket. He nods, to signal the end of our conversation, and turns back toward the punch.

I push toward the fire. That was Henry Clapp. I know, because I scanned him in myself for the bar scenes at Pfaff's. He published the *Saturday Press,* the favorite journal of New York's Bohemians, but put the bulk of his energies into drinking, poker, and conversation. He was born and raised on Nantucket Island; and while I never wrote that part for him, it makes sense, in a crude sort of way, for the Story Engine to link up the two Nantucketers.

And the warning, of course, is logical, given what will happen later tonight.

I moon around for a while. No sign of Dupin, who was supposed to be here. Heading back to the punch bowl someone grabs my ankle, and I'm nearly pitched head first into a gaggle of poets surrounding Ada Mencken.

"Help," a voice whispers.

I look down. A pale hand shrouded in a tuft of lace stuffed into a jet-black shirt sticks out from under a pew. Black frock coat, black silk scarf, and a white wedge of face striated with ebony hair. A bloodshot eye becomes visible in the shadow.

"I am suffocated by pretense!"

I click downward toward him. He peers around melodramatically. His dark eyes shine out of the gloom. He closes them for a second.

"Tennyson has nothing to teach our native geniuses, like Halleck," one of the poets states.

"There!" Dupin whispers, opening his eyes again. "Did you hear *that*? Halleck! Oh, *God.*"

"You all right?" I ask him.

"I told you," he replies indignantly, "I am dying! Apart from that, I am tolerable." He hauls himself from under the pew. One of the poets steps back, laughing from his own pleasantry, trips over the prone form, and crashes helplessly to the bare planks, dowsing himself with syllabub. Amid the ensuing commotion Dupin rises to his feet, winding the scarf tighter around his face.

"The native genius," he tells the poets, "is to bring down the sublime to the level of mere commerce."

"Tory!" one of them replies.

"And Fitz-Greene Halleck," Poe adds, "is not fit to wipe Tennyson's arse."

Ada laughs.

"Come," Dupin says, taking me by the arms, "let us travel to some more salubrious place."

The freezing air outside seems to blow energy into my companion. His thin form stands straighter. He leaps wildly over a bank of filthy snow, bounces off a pig rooting on the other side, falls, jumps up, black clothes dusted with white ice, to wave his arms at cab lights approaching down Broadway.

The cab is a four-wheeler Dearborn, with wooden skids lashed under its rear wheels for snow work and two chestnut horses for traction. It stops in the middle of the street, blocking the dray behind it. Dupin shouts "Three-oh-four Water Street" as we climb in. The cabbie leans over, to peer through the cabin window.

"You are *sicher* on this, sorr?" he asks in a thick Hungarian accent.

"Yes, dammit!"

"So, iss two bits extra, for Water Street."

"Done!" Dupin shouts impatiently.

Grumbling, the cabbie makes a clucking sound, and we jounce off.

I click forward. At the corner of Houston and Crosby streets we hear the usual screaming and wailing from the private asylum—except that it's much louder than it usually is. Through the Dearborn's window I glimpse a group of barefoot women dressed in white smocks and shifts, rocking back and forth in the snow at the corner of Jersey Street, their mouths open like graves.

I wonder how they got out of the loony bin.

Dupin shrinks into his black clothes. Between the top hat and scarf all I see are his eyes, reflecting the coach light outside.

"It's the asylum," I reassure him.

"I don't like them," he whispers. "I always get the notion, perhaps it is I should be inside, and the madmen out."

The cabbie takes Norfolk Street, then Hester and Montgomery. The streets grow more narrow and dark, refuse is piled higher on the sidewalks. Still people throng the pavement. It reminds me, in an odd reversal of time's arrow, of Kaye's node market, the same feeling of people wanting, people selling, people coming together.

And then the usual shift downhill to the harbor, marked by the shipyards and warehouses, the forest of masts.

The cab pulls up beside a tall clapboard building on the East River side of Water Street. Its roof and walls are bowed inward as if from the weight of snow on top and the mass of cotton warehouses on each side.

The planks are cracked and the windows encrusted with filth; but light is visible behind the distorting glass, crooked chimneys pump gray smoke into the swollen night. You can hear shouts and applause from inside.

A sign under the brass lantern reads "John Allen's Concert Hall: Ale, Wines," with a little crucifix painted discreetly at the bottom. By the side of the Dutch stoop, a man lies half buried in a snowdrift.

The door opens, seemingly by itself. Dupin goes in. I follow more slowly, staring back at the motionless legs of the buried man.

Downstairs is one very long room, stretching in the direction of the river. The left-hand side, the one with the counter, stands three feet higher than the right. Down both sides of the room little alcoves and niches have been built from old ships' timbers. In those niches lurid purple candles illuminate religious statuary and icons of the most pathetic and awkward sort: highly stuck Sebastians, gore-caked Christs, Salomes serving platters of Baptist-special, all hanging among the curtains and couches that indicate the alcoves' real purpose.

The rest of the saloon hews to the same theme. A cardinal tends bar, nuns in wimples move through the crowd, dancing under trays heavy with beer and Monongahela. Incense rises into dark corners, where smoke-blackened beam-knees support the sagging strakes of the ceiling.

Only the right-hand side of the bar escapes a religious motif. There, a wooden pit has been built into the floor. As we enter, a crowd of trimmers, gangbangers, oyster sellers, ferrymen, and general waterfront layabouts are crowded around the pit. A boy upends a box full of cheeping Norway rats into the enclosure. A dog barks shrilly among the knot of people.

The cheeping crescendoes. A one-eared, nondescript terrier is thrown, still barking, into the pit. The crowd erupts into cheers. The cheeps and barks grow more frenzied as the rats muckle onto the dog.

A heavily jowled man dressed as a bishop escorts us through the gloom to the far end of the saloon and an alcove under a figurehead of Saint Joan, praying hopelessly upward as her feet are consumed by fire and dry rot.

"A fair treat for us, soors," the "bishop" intones, wiping the table, "two infloo-enshul gennuhmen such as yerselves."

Dupin asks him for a Tippe-na-pecco. I tell the Vox, "Monongahela." The drinks arrive, carried by a buxom mother superior and a novice with small breasts who hikes up her skirts to the knee as she sits on the couch beside me.

I hear a vague slosh of water around us that doesn't come from the short drinks. Water Street is aptly named; in the early 1850s many of its buildings still sit on piers over the harbor.

My novice has cornflower-blue eyes and a deep thirst, judging by the way she eyes the whiskey the bishop thoughtfully provided for her. She's also very young, and sits demurely next to me, playing with her crucifix in a curiously sensual way.

Dupin was going on about how he planted his clothes and papers on a dead man to get out of marrying his childhood sweetheart. Now he directs the burn of his conversation onto the women.

"It has seemed to me that the embrace of the church and the embrace of a demon have in common the abandonment of deductive reason," he remarks portentously. He sinks his cocktail in nothing flat and refills his glass from the flask of whiskey. "And that is the *point* of both."

" 'Ere, 'oo you callin' a demon?" the mother superior demands, pulling the scarf from his mouth.

A miniature doorway stands to the side of Saint Joan, and a small circular window next to that. Through the frost and icicles I can see straight to the East River. The Fulton steam ferry pumps sparks into the night as it pulls out from its berth. Toward Brooklyn, the poor man's sailing ferry is just now hoisting its jib and tacking for Catherine Street.

A graceful clipper lies moored the next dock over; the lights of her harbor watch move along the quarterdeck, guarding against pirates.

Another ship, anchored away from the docks, shows no lights at all. A pocket clipper. Her hull is jet-black. My heart bumps a little, and I lean closer to the window. Dupin notices the movement.

"A. A. Low," he comments, putting his arm gingerly around the mother superior, "wears two hats."

"What do you mean?"

He takes out a long pipe and points it through the window at the large clipper docked beside us.

"The *Samuel Russell*. Twelve hundred forty tons burthen. Note the narrow beam, the raked stem. She made San Francisco in a hundred-and-nine days, carrying general merchandise and flour for California gold-panners. Her profit for that trip was a hundred and eighty thousand dollars.

"Now that one—" He points at the smaller black clipper. "Note how closely she resembles the *Russell*. And yet she is smaller by four hundred tons, she carries nine-pounders, four on each side, and if you were to have the misfortune of sailing downwind of her, you would experience a stench to equal the worst flophouses in Five Points."

"A slaver," I agree.

The Vox does not pick it up.

"A blackbird," Dupin explains. He leans forward, pushing aside the mother superior, who's trying to open his shirt. "Carrying a cargo of humans packed in racks, chained three deep in the 'tween-decks. Five weeks in the tradewinds. If seven out of ten survive, it's an excellent trip, with profits of almost *five hundred thousand dollars* to be expected."

"I saw a man who fitted the description of the Fishman," I say. "He got off the blackbird."

"Ah-hah!" Dupin shouts. The mother superior grabs her hand back as if she'd been burned. In the front room a rat sails clear over the heads of the crowd, its neck broken. My novice sits up suddenly. "Got to powder me nose," she states plaintively, and disappears toward the bar.

"The 'Fishman' came off a Low Lines ship, you say?" Dupin's pipe burns more fiercely as he sucks at it. "But it adds up! You only have to apply the principles of deductive calculation, my friend."

"What?"

Dupin shakes his head impatiently. "Listen," he says, "Low is first among the merchants of New York. The merchants of New York are the world's most important financial backers of that damnable traffic. Where else can they obtain profits of five hundred percent? Together, they own a hundred ships like that one, although few ever make it this far north of Charleston Bay. I wonder—" He frowns, shakes his head, and continues.

"Now, the most important opponents of the slave trade also live in New York, or close at hand. I refer to the free-soilers, the abolitionist crowd—" He points his pipe toward Brooklyn where, if it were light, we could see the spire of Reverend Henry Ward Beecher's church on the Heights. "Note how my connections of logic turn solidly on each other, like a chain of rats biting each other's tail; for the *abolitionist* camp, in Tammany—the Softshells—is the same faction that *depends* on the ever-increasing Hibernian vote. Whereas there is a secret *slavery* faction that, while heartily approving the importation of enslaved Negroes, with equal fervor *opposes* the influx of free Irishmen into the city."

"Go on," I tell him, enjoying this, though Dupin is getting drunker by the minute, and his consonants are softening.

"Don't you see?" Dupin leans even farther forward. His dark forelock is like the lip of a cave from which the gleaming beasts of his eyes stare out in wonder. "Fishman is a *warning*." He thumps his pipe down, cracking the stem. "A warning to the Irish, of what will happen to them when the fight gets more intense. A warning to Ethiopians, as well, for there are thousands of escaped slaves living in close quarters with the Hibernians. Mark you how the abolitionist and Irishman, Flynn, has disappeared without a trace. Mark you also how that infernal rag, *Leslie's Illustrated*—recently purchased by A. A. Low's cousin!—endlessly trumpets the Fishman's abominations, at the expense of more worthy information.''

Dupin slumps backward. He picks up his cup and stares at the somber fluid. At the bar's far end, a man counts out bets for and against the dog.

''I have *seen* the Know-Nothings,'' Dupin mutters. ''They held me for five days in Baltimore and forced me to vote for their council candidate—and I tell you, Clay can do what he wants, this is an evil only blood will cleanse. This is an evil that reason—'' Dupin's mouth shuts with an audible snap. The mother superior wriggles out from under him and pushes herself off the couch.

I follow Dupin's gaze. A dozen men encircle our alcove. Almost all of them are short and sick-looking, but that doesn't dilute their general air of menace.

Three wear sailor's duds. Two bear the wide hats and macassar-curled locks of the True Blue American gang. A small guy in a fireman's oilskin has a face frozen on one side; the eyelid droops down and saliva shines that side of his chin. A baboonish-looking fellow beside him holds a straightedge razor in the tips of the fingers of one hand. I might well, in this time zone, know these last two by reputation: Slobbery Jim and Patsy the Barber, supremo leaders of New York's most chronic river-pirate gang, the Daybreak Boys.

''These ones?'' Patsy the Barber calls, and twists his razor so the candlelight flashes off it.

Behind the mob the scared face of our novice gulps ''Yes,'' then vanishes in the congregation of men drifting up from the ratpit to watch this far more interesting sport.

''You gentlemen have business with us?'' Dupin asks politely, and takes a delicate sip of his drink.

''Git 'im, boys,'' Slobbery Jim advises.

''Kill the ponces!'' someone in the crowd jeers.

Patsy, together with two sailors and a couple of Daybreakers, rushes the alcove. I click backward and find myself sitting on the couch's back.

Dupin jumps up and ducks a swipe of Patsy's razor, which puts him in direct line for the swing of a sailor's cudgel.

The cudgel lashes down, so fast I can almost hear it hiss. It smashes into Dupin's head with enormous force. His skull cracks, and pieces of blood and bone and soggy ivory goo fly around the alcove and are splattered liberally on my trousers.

Dupin slumps to the floor. He jerks briefly, and is still.

I stare at our attackers. Acid rises in my throat. In all the previous versions of this scene, Dupin is knocked out, barely hurt, free to crawl out later and die of cirrhosis at his own convenience.

Patsy the Barber looks up from the mess of Dupin's head. Patsy's face is misshapen, and a scar gives him three biceps on the right arm.

He gnaws on his cheroot, and steps toward me, slowly now, Random Motor congealing the action a bit; waving the straightedge the way a mating crab waves its bigger claw.

For some reason, I cannot budge. With all the weird attacks over the last few weeks, none has frozen me quite like the murder of my friend from Pfaff's.

"That wasn't s'posed to happen," I mumble in real shock. "That wasn't s'posed to happen!"

"Oh, yes," Patsy affirms, and begins a slow, graceful slash with the straightedge toward the arteries of my throat.

And the horror, swelling, turns into panic. Because if Dupin is dead, which wasn't supposed to happen, then they could kill me just as easily, although that's not supposed to happen either.

I remember the stab I got from Fishman on Park Row; how the blade, instead of scratching my arm, dove straight into my gut; and how, inexplicably, the ache of that wound stayed with my body, my *real* body, for days afterward.

I am suddenly convinced—though this makes no sense— that if they kill me in John Allen's saloon I will end up dead in my own, real, life.

I double-click the mouse, hard, throwing my body backward, behind the curtains. I press against the wall, next to the figurehead. Mouse to the right, deliberately—I can sense the Daybreakers clambering up the couch toward me. But the shift, slowing us all down, gives me time to think. I keep edging right, to the miniature door next to Saint Joan. I dive through it on hands and knees, clicking it shut behind me.

I find myself crouched in a tiny chamber built like a ship's stern gallery on the side of the building. A low bed covered with fancy draperies takes up most of the space. A pewter sconce full of votive candles flickers in one corner. The threadbare hooked rug is pulled aside, to reveal the ring of a trapdoor set in doweled planks.

I click the trapdoor open. The sound of water hisses hungrily into the room. In the square of open hatch, shadows of dock timbers stir the invisible blackness of the harbor below. This is where they dump the bodies: take them to bed, serve them Monongahela with a hefty spike of laudanum, grab their purse, down the hatch.

Neat, hygienic.

The door slams open behind me. I glower around; Slobbery Jim peers into the room, an ancient flintlock pistol wagging perilously in his free hand. Drool streams off his stubbly chin.

I stare at the water again. I've no idea how far down it is. It looks like poison, lightless, slimy—the river as undertaker, thick with the bodies of the men and women, rats and terriers, that have gone this way before; all reaching up with dead fingers and teeth to swallow me into the night.

But I've got no choice.

I click once and, as the deafening explosion of Slobbery Jim's pistol fills the badger room with light and sound, drop into the void.

And fall, and fall.

Suddenly water and brash ice rise in every direction, blocking out the after-image of gunpowder. The splash and gurgle are deafening, familiar. For what seems almost a minute, total darkness covers my field of view.

Then, in a burst of spray, I'm at the surface, more or less afloat.

Barnacle-encrusted timbers bounce me around. Pieces of saltwater ice scrape my shoulders. I fight clear of the pilings holding up John Allen's. The tide pulls me dangerously offshore, and a countercurrent, pushing west from Wallabout Bay, directs me back.

A tubby little sloop, oil lamps hung cheerfully in her rigging, lets out her mainsail for the westerly wind and lays a course toward Brooklyn that comes close to where I tread water, a hundred yards off Catherine Slip.

A man shouts. Sails slat, and many arms pull me aboard. Women in mobcaps, men in top hats, bend over me curiously.

"Ye took the hard way to Brooklyn, my friend," the mate growls. "That'll be two bits for the single fare."

"Brooklyn," I repeat, nodding to myself—

—and reach up, rip off the glasses, pull off the blanket. The outlines of Kaye's apartment take the place of *Munn's World;* obscure, yet familiar, and above all still.

I'm breathing heavily, and my hair is slicked over my forehead with sweat.

For the first time I can recall, the real world seems healthier, more comforting to me, than the story I conceived and produced.

I look down at the cheap nylon running pants Kaye gave me, half expecting them to be splattered with gore and gray matter from Dupin's shattered brainpan; but they're as untarnished as they were before I entered *Munn's World,* and for a minute, I stare at them, my heart slamming as I absorb the implications of fiction.

THIRTY-EIGHT

KAYE'S ALARM GOES off ninety minutes after I jack myself out of *Munn's World.*

She comes staggering out of the bedroom, dressed only in a T-shirt. The shirt reads *"7th Street Noda: Autonomia = Independencia"* in Day-Glo letters.

I'm lying wide awake on the couch with the unzipped sleeping bag over me. I've been awake ever since *Munn's World,* thinking over what happened at John Allen's Concert Hall, trying to understand it.

I haven't got anywhere.

She looks at me with an expression close to astonishment. Her eyelids are not all the way up, gold hair sprays out of her cornrows, and the lining of a pillow is clearly printed on her left cheek.

"Evening," I say.

"What time is it?"

"Nine o'clock."

"Omigod."

"You miss an appointment?"

"What? Oh—no."

She goes back into her bedroom. Water runs, the toilet

flushes. She reemerges and stands at the partition differentiating kitchen and living room, watching me intently.

"What's up?"

"Nothing." She continues to stare.

"There something you want me to say?"

She shakes her head. Looks away, looks back.

The phone rings. She doesn't move. The machine takes the call. I hear her message, well remembered: "Hi, this is Kaye, I'm busy right now—" The message clicks off, left hanging as the caller disconnects. She turns abruptly.

"We should go out for dinner. There's nothing here."

"But the lasagna—"

"No, no. I want to go out." Her voice is clipped, irritable. "There's a Ukrainian place." She disappears again, comes back two minutes later, fully dressed in gauchos, black jeans, her motorcycle jacket, the black paratrooper's beret. I stare at her, astonished; I've never seen a woman get dressed so fast, and with so little fuss. Larissa would still be at the makeup stage here.

Amy would have gone back to bed.

She hangs her shoulder bag over one collarbone, slips on her Ray·Bans, and says, "Let's go."

So we go out. For the first time since I've been here, which of course is not very long, the node market is deserted. A rusted pickup hauls vegetables out of the vacant lot, backfires eastward.

A guy with a Hawkley-ite kerchief peers after the pickup through a pair of Israeli Defence Force binoculars.

Kaye adjusts the windbreaker hood around my face, then heads west. She walks even faster and more efficiently than I remembered, which is fine with me since the wind hasn't gotten any balmier, and walking fast is the only way I can keep the chill at bay.

On Avenue A she heads for a tattered brown marquee that reads "Liliana's Restaurant/Ukraine Cooking." In the restaurant, a little joint with pressboard walls and pictures of Odessa behind the counter, a sullen boy slings hash on the grill and an absolutely stunning seventeen-year-old girl asks us what we want in an accent so thick you could pour it as gravy over stuffed cabbage. Kaye orders a coffee. I stare at her.

"I thought you were hungry?"

"Changed my mind."

I order steamed cheese pierogi and fried onions. I should feel bad, mooching off Kaye like this, but I haven't caught up on the backlog of starvation from living under the FDR, and hunger has a way of relegating your pride to bush leagues.

While we wait Kaye pulls out the Indian Camels, flicks the pack back and forth, her eyes invisible behind the shades.

I sit back in the cheap chair, enjoying the warmth of steam pipes beside me.

Her mouth, when tense, pulls downward as if she were sad. I'm beginning to recognize her expressions. She turns her head, listening. Then I, too, cock my head.

A chorus of sirens is surging fast down Seventh Street. A wave of NYPD cruisers and paddy wagons, followed by a mobile AGATE command center, breaks over Avenue A like surf and washes eastward.

Kaye, who has her back to the window, gets halfway to her feet, twisting to watch. The cruisers block off Seven between B and C. Loudspeakers squawk. People hang out of windows, pointing their noses in the direction of trouble. Men in blue bulletproof vests run in formation for the squatter buildings.

"They're busting the market," one of the smokers comments.

"Think the Hawkies put up a fight?" another asks.

"Like Tompkins Square," the first smoker replies happily.

"Dey arrest de squatters," the lady behind the cash register announces, with a glance at Kaye. "Goot."

"Vy goot?" the pretty waitress asks her. "Squatters leave goot tips."

Kaye sits back down. She takes out one of the Camels and lights it. Her fingers tremble slightly. I can't see her eyes; her nose angles toward the umber surface of her coffee.

"Kaye," I say gently.

She says nothing.

"Kaye?"

"What."

"The cops." I wave toward the window. "You knew about this?"

She picks up her spoon and stirs circles in the coffee. She adds sugar, undrinkable amounts.

I can see, in one closet of my brain, a note written in lovely copperplate script.

"One who should be an ally fashions nightmares for your soul."

Obviously there's no way the woman from Bayard Street could know how close Kaye and I have gotten; that's because, until this moment, even I wasn't aware of it. I mean, you can sleep with someone, fall in love with her a little; but it's not till you get hurt that you're able to measure the extent of the involvement; it's only when you're betrayed that you get the final bill.

I watch her take a very deep drag of the smoke. She starts coughing. When she has finished she grinds out the cigarette, violently, in a Zero Cola ashtray.

"Okay."

I watch her cigarette expire.

"I tole my father," she admits, and clears her throat. "I needed—some advice."

The Ray×Bans mirror Alexander Munn staring at her. My face, under the hood, behind the beard, looks bovine to me; unwell, astonished; the face of a victim.

"I *begged* him not to tell anyone." Her voice is rough with coughing and tension. "I really pleaded, ya know? But he said, he had to. He gave me—four hours—to convince you to turn yourself in." The shades flash reflections of police lights. "Den he was gonna call Polletti."

"I don't get it," I tell her finally. I clear my throat, to wash the shock from my voice. "Everything you said. You believed I didn't do any of that—"

"I believed that," she says. "I *still* believe it."

She takes off the Ray×Bans. The waitress brings over my pierogi. The steaming dumplings, onions, and gravy smell absolutely delicious, but my stomach is full now; replete with bitter disappointment, and the kind of fear that comes when, climbing a cliff, you rest your weight on a rock ledge and it cracks off and falls into the void beneath you.

"I think maybe I better go," I tell her.

"No!"

She stares at me, the dark gray irises unwavering. It's the look people adopt when they're telling you the absolute truth, and also when they're lying through their teeth.

"I wish I din't do it," she continues, "but I trusted him. I thought he was my dad first, a cop second. I was wrong. I mean, it's not his fault—"

She reaches over and grabs my right hand, clutching it fiercely. "Munn." Her voice is low, rough with tobacco. Her nose ring shines bright against her shadowed face. "Don't you see? I'm a liddle in love wit a guy people say *killed his wife*. I'm a liddle in love wit a guy who just wrote somethin' that could change history—literally. An' he says, he doesn't even *remember* it!"

I like the first part of what she said; I barely hear the second. My eyes focus on a man getting out of an unmarked Ford at the corner of Seventh and A. He's thin, with a short nose, skin smudged around the eyes. He stands on the corner, looking east as the driver enters the corner deli.

Polletti.

"Okay," Kaye is saying, "I can understan' that, but ya could at least *pretend* to listen!"

I'm shrinking back instinctively into the wall, into the floor.

"Look," I whisper, pointing out the window.

"What?" She turns.

"By the deli. Polletti!"

"Him?"

"Don't *point*!"

"Sorry." She stares for several seconds, turns back.

"Couldn't we jiss ask him—" She bites her lip. Her eyes are black now. "I'm thinking like a cop's daughter, again."

"Not very Hawkley-ite of you." I grin, asinine.

She gets up, fishes money out of her shoulder bag, and talks to the waitress. I don't listen; I'm trying to watch the detective without letting more than a fraction of my face into his field of vision.

He looks around once, a casual, cop 360; and though he's too far away to get any kind of look at me, I jump back as if I'd been raked by claws.

Polletti, to me, is Riker's. He's the dumb rage of a bureaucracy that likes to throw people into hell whether they're guilty or not; that would rather nail someone to satisfy its own pathology than find the real culprit.

When I look again, though the car is still there, Polletti has disappeared.

Kaye touches my shoulder. I jump. The waitress is going to let us out the back. Kaye spun them some story about a stalker, which they clearly don't believe, but she's a good enough tipper to expect favors.

The waitress leads us through a storeroom full of cabbage and egg cartons. She peers out, following Kaye's directions, and giggles.

"No *Cheka*," she tells Kaye, grinning.

A moment later we're hustling west up Seventh Street, away from the sirens and lights. The combination of cold and nerves does a number on me. By the time we reach Second Avenue I'm shivering harder than I have in twenty-four hours.

"I c-c-can't do this any-m-more," I whisper, more to me than to her. "I g-g-gotta *do* something."

"Okay. What?"

"I d-d-dunno."

We're heading south now, through the curry smell of Little Bombay.

"We need to chill somewhere."

"We?"

"Arright, Munn," she says crossly. The shades are back on. Her mouth, I notice, is set in that sad, determined way she has. "I fucked everybody over. I'm sorry, okay? But I warned my people. Also, in case you din' notice back there, I made damn sure you didn't get busted. And *now,* just in case you haven't figgered *that* out yet, I'm aiding an' abetting a fugitive. That's conspiracy, under AGATE; five years in Danbury."

"Okay." I throw my hands up. "Okay."

We walk for a while. At Second Street Kaye leads me toward her daubed Pontiac, angle-parked beside the Village View projects. She turns on the engine, then goes to a pirate coinbox on the corner of Second Street and First Avenue.

I suppose I ought to worry about this, who she's calling and so on. I don't have the energy. If Kaye can switch that fast from alliance to betrayal and back, then she's got more psychic resilience than I do, and I might as well give up. I sure as shit can't fight it.

After five minutes or so the heat starts to blast and my shivering diminishes. She comes back shortly thereafter.

"Jenny's not in. Neither is Sam."

"Who?"

"Friends of mine. 'N I can't get hold of Hugo . . ."

"I was thinking," I tell her, "we need a hiding place—"

"I already said that."

I ignore the remark. "A place that's out of the way, but not so far we can't do something, if we have to. Out of the city, but not all the way. A place no one will look fer us. That ring a bell?"

"The Upper West Side?"

"No."

"Upper East Side."

I shake my head.

"Staten Island."

"I was thinkin' of that place in *Real Life*."

"The canals." Kaye swings around to look at me. "Near JFK?"

"Yeah."

She punches the steering wheel. "A goal," she says, aping the tones of a Christian-Republican, that famous clip of Henry Warren Powell leading the filibuster against foodstamps for Chicanos.

"Thank you, Jesus, a goal!"

THIRTY-NINE

KAYE TAKES HOUSTON Street, switches southward on the FDR—rattling high over the craters I spent the night in—then finally swings up and over the industrial linguini of the Brooklyn Bridge approaches. The loose shocks rattle furiously on the gridded roadway. Looking down across the crinkled water at the lonely lights of a tug and barge, I reflect that only a few hours ago I was lying on the oaken floorboards of a wooden sloop, making the same trip.

The city looks very different than it did from the Catherine Slip ferry: the great faults and strikes of the Wall Street range, the volcanic plugs of the World Trade Center, the granite peaks midtown, all outlined and lit with a billion bulbs, physically change the shape of night from the low house-and-spire aspect of New York in the 1850s.

Another difference: in the 1850s, though columns of smoke rose from forges and chimneys, the sky between was filled with clouds and stars. The city possessed only the shy glow of its lamps and hearths, whereas modern New York has raped the sky in the orange glare of its streetlights and neon and wiped out the stars with that violation.

But, curiously, it doesn't *feel* so different. The black shape of the island, like a prow breaking into a narrow ocean, is more or less the same. The thrust of tide still carves the same channels in the riverbed, corpses still wash up in the tidal backflow of Wallabout Bay.

Blood and seawater have always been the aroma of the city, and a real New Yorker knows by instinct the taste of their salts, and relies on the pulse of both tide and heart to remind him he's alive.

On the Gowanus and then Shore Drive Kaye drives slower, so we can look for street signs. "I recognize that," she says, " 'n that." The joy that comes when a story matches well with life is quick in her voice.

We both spot the sign—"CONDUIT AVE/NASSAU EXPWY"—that marked where the investigator got off the highway in her Zaibatsu. I'm pleased that my memory works in this instance.

We get lost, of course, but even so it doesn't take that long; after all, Kaye "drove" this stretch of road only a few hours ago. We ride Bay Boulevard south, then turn, at a garish Italian seafood restaurant, into a neighborhood of large, cheesy stucco ranches. We skirt the end of a wide canal on our right. After that, the houses get smaller, the paint jobs old and flaky. Late-model Eagles and Zaibatsus are replaced by 1980s Dodges and Subarus, rust showing like eczema around their wheelwells.

We each see the concrete pedestrian bridge at the same instant. Now even I am affected by the strange way reality fits like a template over the preexisting landscape of fiction.

Except that it's not fiction. I have to keep reminding myself; someone took a video crew into this area and shot every road with a Fuji Digital Enviro-cam.

Someone found out where Henry Warren Powell grew up, and plugged the info into a VR serial.

We know where we're going now. The investigator got lost, and I'm unsure, but Kaye picks up landmarks quite easily, and she puts her hand over mine and squeezes when they move into the cone of headlights; a rotted house tilted at a thirty-degree angle into the stagnant canal; a giant patch of cattails rising out of the water; the row of shacks, each more dilapidated than the last, flying little Confederate flags and shamrocks; the "garage" made of a 1981 Chevy wagon lifted high on jacks to shelter the only-slightly-less-rusted hulk of a 1983 Olds.

Past a small brick fire station that reads "West Hamilton Beach Volunteer Fire Company" under the obligatory shamrock. We turn right up another lane.

"Reardon's up that road," Kaye mutters.

A 777, finally figuring out it is, in fact, a heavier-than-air machine, subsides massively over our windshield toward the airport.

"We prob'ly shouldn't get too close to the production," I tell her when the jetscream dwindles, "that musta caused a big stir around here."

Kaye swings the wheel right.

"Where you going?"

"I thought I saw—"

This lane was last paved under Mayor Impelliteri. In the interval, weeds have reclaimed the right-of-way. Two muddy ruts indicate where vehicles have passed.

She stops the car in a massive puddle. The headlights limn a vinyl-sided, two-story house. The trim is peeling and the Chevy Cavalier parked outside is as rusty as every other vehicle around here.

Kaye points to a hand-painted sign, mint-green and with pseudo-Runic lettering surrounded by Celtic braided-wave motifs that all leaves me feeling vaguely queasy. "Donegal Manor," it says, "Rooms for Rent O'nite."

"Here we are," Kaye says.

Donegal Manor belongs to a plump woman named Mrs. McCotter. She wears fake leather slacks and a garish yellow nylon sweater under an apron that reads "An Irish Blessing: May you get to Heaven a half hour before the Devil knows you're Dead." Her curled hair contains undertones of mauve. She stares at us suspiciously but my beard is quite full now and I see no spark of recognition behind her plastic glasses. She seems more interested in Kaye's nose ring.

I guess we do look a little odd for this part of town.

A television pumps out canned laughter. I spot a synthetic Christmas tree weighed down with improbable green ornaments. Kaye hands over the forty bucks in advance and our landlady leads us upstairs to a small room with a giant bed and a large dresser that looks like it was made of stained Lucite. The wall-to-wall carpeting is thick, and kelly-green. The room is extremely hot, and smells of cleaning fluids perfumed with Kool-Aid. It feels bad to me, a place built to trap and stifle, and then I realize why; it's the same brand of cleaning fluid they use at Riker's. I walk straight to the window, yank open casement and storm glass, and poke my head outside.

The room is part of an addition to the house's ass end. Right underneath me, the slimy pilings of a small dock lurch into the black, smooth surface of a canal.

A plywood cabin cruiser, water rising almost to the level of its gunwale, is tied by rotten lines to putrid cleats. The name "Maeve" adorns the flaking green paint on its bow.

Across the canal, a bevy of plaster leprechauns hide among overgrown weeds beside a shack built on stilts over the water.

Far away, very very faint, I hear the quavering, treble howl of a coyote.

I get an incredibly strong sense of déjà vu; that I've been in this neighborhood, stood in this room, looked over this bleak canal.

With no warning I remember the recurrent shamrocks in my more recent nightmares.

I think of Fishman, his long black shape tensed as he gazes down Water Street, sniffing for my scent. I shiver.

But I don't believe in second sight. The coincidences and events of real life are strange enough without dragging in vampires and premonitions.

I pull my head in as an airbus, flaps vibrating heavily, throttles down three hundred feet over the roof of Mrs. McCotter's lodging house.

FORTY

MOLLY MALONE IS evil. A weird light sparkles off her grinning mouth.

She's also plastic, three inches tall, frozen among a crowd of similar figurines on a plexiglass shelf that runs the length of our room in Donegal Manor.

The air is close and sweet with the Kool-Aid smell I noticed last night. The sheets are rayon, slippery. The mattress is way too soft. Kaye and I have collected like rainwater in the hollow we make in its center.

A plastic cat clock on the wall reads 10:41. The glint on Molly's mouth came from sunshine through the side window.

We've slept almost eleven hours.

I lie there for a few minutes, enjoying the warmth of Kaye's body against mine, savoring the luxury of being able to lie like this in a soft, sheltered spot while the tendrils of dreams slowly dissipate from the folds of my brain.

There was a dream in there featuring Ved Chakrapani; some mundane squabble about credits for the first show.

What they wanted, all along, was to prevent my segment from getting on the air.

The thought, pulled in by the dream of work, is so obvious

that I realize I had it all along, without ever verbalizing it. A classic case of woods-for-trees.

What's less obvious—though it's not exactly the lost equation for fusion energy, either—is the inference to build on that thought.

Which is this: *The only way to beat them*—and, incidentally, the only way to stop them from killing me, or framing me for the murder of someone else—*is to make sure it's my episode that gets broadcast over B-Net on the opening night of* Real Life.

"Shit," I whisper as a jet whistle-thunders over the roof above.

Like Patton putting flags on a map of the Ardennes I try to visualize faces now: Gaynor, his stainless stare, his flat vowels. Jack Tyrone, beefy, the yellow nicotine staining his fingertips.

Fishman. But that one is overload. Every time I see him, dark, with that green shine of eyes against the night, something inside goes cold and clammy, freezing my thought and motion.

I've only seen him after dark. I wonder if, like a vampire, he cannot go out during the day. His nickname, after all, is "Drac" . . .

I squirm against the rayon. Kaye mutters, "Keep yer hat on," and turns against me.

A language stronger than fear speaks out of the softness of her skin and the warmth of her under the blankets. Her face, half asleep, seems perfectly balanced to me.

If her mouth is too wide and tragic, that just means she's capable of a strength of feeling not accessible to lesser mouths. If her eyes, like a child's, are too big for her face, it's so she can see better with them, deeper, like a mutated being in a post-apocalypse flick, given laser peepers in compensation for atomic damage.

She opens those eyes. Their pattern of gray and blue-gray unlocks a need in both body and the complex source of memory.

She clears her throat, and puts her arms around me.

The spot that froze when I imagined Fishman shrinks, and dissolves in the perfect heat between us.

———

Mrs. McCotter cooks—for a price—if you can call canned Sloppy Joe with canned carrots and potato buds "cooking." She seats us in front of plastic mats with charts of Ireland and plates printed with "Murphy's Law" in a kitchen filled with other pseudo-Irish trinkets.

Kaye made me put on her shades before we came down. It's vital not to let down our guard, she said; Mrs. McCotter is as capable of turning me in as anyone. Unguarded by sunglasses, Kaye's eyes seem full of light, and softer than I remember, except maybe for the way they looked when we listened to Handel in St. John the Divine.

My cough is pretty much gone. It started tapering off yesterday.

I eat every scrap of the processed garbage Mrs. McCotter lays in front of me. Our landlady putters around, dusting figurines, polishing the antique Formica. The floor of this kitchen, warped by the marsh it's built on, sags to the south. Mrs. McCotter's hair has been chemically bleached and curled so many times that it could be a wig; today, it's arranged with bangs and a fall, like Elizabeth Montgomery in *Bewitched*. She makes little meaningless remarks: "Such a nice day." "Bought this one in Atlantic City." She tells us she thinks we're "romantic." Her sharp eyes dart from behind pink glasses, pricking into my own blue vision.

There's one other lodger here, a dark-haired thirtyish fellow named Brian who chain-smokes Merits and mostly lives in the armchair facing the TV. The television is on constantly. The canned laughter and applause constitute a background as sempiternal as the whistle of passenger jets above.

Finally Mrs. McCotter has nothing left to do in the kitchen. She makes one more vacuous statement and wanders off, clutching a polyester rag and a can of Pledge.

Kaye pulls out the pack of Camels and flicks them around her plate. I lean over and gently rub the curve of her nose.

She scratches her ass with no self-consciousness whatsoever. It reminds me of Zeng.

"So," she whispers, "what now?"

I shrug.

Finally—because, to paraphrase Conan Doyle, when the

subtle doesn't work, you have no choice but to resort to the obvious—I explain to her, in a low voice, the thought I got when I woke up.

Her eyes watch my mouth as I talk. When I finish she lines up the pack carefully with cracks in the urethaned tabletop, then takes out a cigarette.

"That's all theory," she whispers.

"I know."

"But there's gotta be a way to do it." She moves the pack at right angles to the crack. "I mean, how do *they* do it?"

I check the door to the living room. The Pat Buchanan show features a crowd of people who believe they recently have had sex with Elvis Presley. Brian guffaws, Merit smoke bursting from his mouth in little puffs.

"There's a place called 'Heartland,' " I tell her softly. "It's on the fifth floor of Television City—the X-Corp complex. That's where the transmission center is, you know, the digital machines, they're like VCRs, they actually play the master tapes to the B-Net lines."

"Heartland," Kaye repeats.

I take her pack of Camels and remove two more butts. "Here's the B-Net monitoring room. Here, if I remember right, is the digital studio, next door." I connect the ends of the two cigarettes. "And here"—I move the pack to the end of the line of butts—"that's the control room. It's a big place, because one whole wall of it is a bank of, I dunno, maybe fifteen hundred control tapes for different shows. There's a little robot, with a long hydraulic arm and a kind of vacuum attachment. It zips along the wall and sucks out the right tape for that time and spits it through the wall, into one of the players."

"Cool," Kaye says.

"If you wanted to change a tape, you'd have to physically get your own tape into the ARP room and substitute it for whatever's s'posed to play at that hour."

"So if you did that—"

"Yeah," I agree, "but obviously, the room is sealed."

"How does the robot know, like, which tape to pick?"

"The computer tells it. But that system is dedicated. It's not linked to any other computer or phone line or anything. See, last thing they want is some bozo hacking in and playing home porno flicks for a laugh, instead of *PITA* or something. So there's only one terminal that controls the ARP, and that's in the ARP room itself . . . Only techies can get in.''

"Your friend, Zeng, he could've?''

I look at her. I find that I'm proud of the way she listens, and how she absorbs information.

"I don't think he was cleared for ARP. He didn't work full-time.''

Mrs. McCotter bustles in. She's put on a green vinyl raincoat and a pink scarf, and has traded her pink glasses for giant movie-star UV shades.

"Gotta go to Key Foods,'' she announces. "Will you be wantin' dinner?''

"Yeah,'' I say. "No,'' Kaye says at the same time.

"We'll go out,'' Kaye adds, grinning.

Mrs. McCotter frowns. She calls for Brian, who follows her out. The front door slaps shut. The Cavalier's engine dwindles down the lane.

Silence, except for a jet circling. Kaye is still looking at me. Her grin grows broader every second. It reminds me of someone I can't quite place.

"Munn,'' she says.

"Yeah.''

"Take your clothes off.''

"What?''

"You heard me.''

I stare at her. Her freckles stand out very clearly now. I realize the someone she reminds me of is her, standing on the barge in Brooklyn while the cold wind whistled around us.

Yesterday, still snagged in the line of tension between Larissa's death and now, I would have refused.

Today, with the slack of sleep cozy in my muscles, it seems possible that I once again may have time for things like this; activities that make no sense, except in the exercise of intimacy.

"You're a fuckin' exhibitionist,'' I tell her.

"Yup,'' she agrees cheerfully.

My sport clothes peel off without trouble. She steps out of her jeans and leaves them deflated on the floor. She leads me into the living room. A commercial for Zero Cola flashes bright colors and music from the screen. I peer out the window, nervously naked, while she fiddles with Mrs. McCotter's archaic CD system. Drizzle bastes the cheap storm windows, a product of warmer air and a front from the southwest.

"Yecch," Kaye says, "show tunes." The violins of a Neanderthal musical rise turgidly from Pioneer speakers.

She walks back and hugs me. I kiss the rough furrows of her braided hair. We rock in circles, holding each other tighter and tighter. Mrs. McCotter's living room spins around us, a whirl of pastel-colored wallpaper, Lucite animals, the plastic Christmas tree with its tinsel harps and green Santas, ranks of scrapbooks labeled *Phantom of the Opera, Miss Saigon, Les Mis, Cats.* It gives me heartburn—or maybe it's just the food.

I start to chuckle. Kaye looks up at me.

"Nineties theater," I murmur.

"My favorite."

"Larissa was in that." I point to *Miss Saigon.* "She played the Vietnamese transvestite." That thought pulls up an association, but the link snaps and I lose it.

"D'you think Mrs. M. sees herself as Norma Desmond?"

"I'm still big," I misquote, "it's leprechauns that got small."

I look around, searching for the row of scrapbooks. The filaments of a second idea spring from their plastic spines, winding around two synapses, rubbing a little abstract heat.

That heat is nothing compared to the friction of our bodies.

I hold her tighter. She pulls herself up, locks her hips around my waist. I think, vaguely, of protection. She shakes her head. Mind reading works in some circumstances. With Fishman sniffing on our tail, the slow ways of death lose poignancy.

We both used latex, we didn't mainline.

The green and white lights of the plastic tree wink on, off, on, slower than our heartrate.

I'm still wearing her shades.

The way into her is as liquid and warm as a jungle stream. The scar over my right kidney twinges hardly at all.

Afterward she goes upstairs and showers.

I find the heartburn induced by Mrs. McCotter's cuisine has annexed my chest. I dry myself on paper towels in the kitchen and, not very enthusiastically, pull on my sport clothes again.

When she comes back downstairs her face is scrubbed but her cheeks are flushed and her eyes are brighter than the Christmas lights.

I grin. I can't help it. She just looks good to me.

"What're you smiling at?"

"Nothing." She grins, too.

"Anyway." I indicate my clothes with one hand. "I hate to mooch off you all the time. But maybe you could buy me jeans, an' a shirt, an' new sneakers?"

She nods.

"An' a 988 Fujitsu-Cray with B-Net modem and software, it's only thirty-seven hundred bucks."

She studies me seriously.

"Wasn't your laptop—?"

"Yup."

"Maybe I could—"

"Don't even think about it."

"You got an idea?" she says.

I point at the scrapbooks.

"They reminded me of Zeng. I wasn't sure why at first, but now I remembered. His backup files. He was always backing up everything, I told you. Anyway, there were some XTV things in his files he should never have in a million years. Which means—"

She picks up the Camels off the placemat.

"He was a hacker?"

I grin. "Sure. He even had a program called 'Hack,' or some such. If he knew how to break into security areas—"

She finds a lighter, takes a deep drag, coughs.

"Security," I go on, "they would arrange the lists of people who got in—"

"I got it," she interrupts impatiently, "I got it. It could get you into Heartland."

"I wish Zeng was alive," I say after a beat or two.

She walks behind me, and puts her arms around my chest.

"Munn," she says, "what if this doesn't work? What if you try to break into XTV's security computer, and they trace the call? What if that—'Fishman'—follows you, when you go to Heartland?"

"You can bail out," I tell her. "In fact"—I twist around to see her face—"maybe you should."

"It's too late," she says into my spine. "But I gotta tell you, I'm not sure my credit card limit is high enough for the laptop."

The shape of Fishman looms against the kitchen window. It's not really Fishman, it's a rotten gray tarp flapping over a gas barbecue grill in the next yard, but my brain, for a fraction of a second, is fooled.

And for that split second a revulsion uncoils in me, so strong, it's like an anaconda wrapping around my stomach.

"I will never let Fishman touch you," I tell her inside my head. "I'll never let that happen, while I'm alive."

Kaye's plastic is geared to the income of a fiction editor at a publishing house specializing in radical hypertext, but she figures the Hasidim at 47th Street Photo will have a layaway plan that fits her monthly account.

I drive her to the subway. She's gone for five hours. When she walks into our bedroom she takes one look at my face, drops her packages on the floor, sits at the foot of the bed where I'm lying against the green coverlet.

"Sorry," she says, "I'm sorry. You wouldn't believe the crowds. I forgot, this is the number-one motherfucker shopping day of the year."

"I thought—"

"I know. I tried to call you. She's not listed—*la* McCotter."

We can hear her downstairs, vacuuming. Brian snorts at a game show.

"I brought Zero Cola, 'n tuna sandwiches," she adds, "though I got such bad heartburn, I'm not sure I want to eat.

" 'N this, which I'm not sure you want to read."

"This" is a copy of the *Daily News*. We pick at the sandwiches while I read an article headlined "ESCAPED SOAP KILLER SOUGHT IN CHI'TOWN HIT."

The same picture of me as appeared with the Larissa piece is spread across the jump page.

Kaye pulls out Rolaids, a bottle of Advils. She points to a

graf way down the article where Mohammed is quoted as saying that at this point, I'm still "only a suspect."

Conflicting reports issue from the M.E.'s office.

I shrug. I don't see how the graf makes much difference, given that Polletti issues another warning about me in graf three, and the ADA, Coltrane, is quoted in the lead saying Munn is a sick psychopathic serial killer and everybody who knows him should move to Florida, where they legally can carry concealed Uzis for their own protection.

We unpack the laptop. While I boot the software Kaye goes downstairs and talks Mrs. McCotter into letting us use her phone. She returns to announce the conditions: local calls only, a dollar each, and Mrs. M. dials the numbers.

"It's not a B-Net line," Kaye adds doubtfully.

"Don't matter," I tell her, "we're not downloading."

The phone sits on a table next to the stairs. Mrs. McCotter fussily puts aside the plastic dwarves and lace doily covering its laminated top. I give Mrs. McCotter the number for DataSafe. It's in the Manhattan area code, which is local, and she nods in approval. She punches the digits, then leaves, ostentatiously, to sit with Brian in front of the *Ollie North Hour*.

I tap in Zeng's password. The DataSafe menus scroll, faster than you can read, down the green display.

Once in Zeng's files, I do a "search" command and find thirteen menus labeled "Hack," with different secondary slugs.

The first one consists of a list of Net addresses, most of them in D.C., none of them at X-Corp. The menus that follow are just as varied.

Zeng, to judge by these files, broke into systems as diverse as IBM-Nixdorf's French marketing office, the Disney-Viacom reservations network, the Minais Gerais Holding Company in Rio.

Apparently Zeng has constructed a graphic way of carrying out his cybernetic B&Es, prodding into the target network with a minimum of info, analyzing the cues he gets back, building, from that, a pattern of likely security systems, antiviral devices, deck mines, data links with other security systems, that all show up as abstract patterns of linear relationships on the screen.

I flick through the patterns. At the top of the screen a key explains the relationship of each pattern to types of security at the network in question.

Zero in on the center of the pattern, the heaviest concentration of relationships, and a number of windows emerge, outlining the different iterations the machine can work on: cypher, code word, and so forth. But the detail is irrelevant.

What matters is, only one of the hacker files contains anything to do with X-Corp.

I hit that command field. More designs appear—the shape of a violin, a rose, a spiral—and are matched by the pattern representing what Zeng's program is doing. It all leads me prettily, through a low-grade antiviral, to the accounting site where Zeng, it seems, regularly reauthorized his padded overtime checks.

Nothing else.

I go through the hacking file once more, hoping to catch something I missed. Kaye slouches against the shamrock wallpaper, manipulating the plastic dwarves so they perform unnatural acts on each other.

"Nothing," I grunt finally, rubbing my eyes to get the glare out. "Nothing, nothing, nothing."

She looks up, her eyes narrowed.

"Don't."

"Don't what?"

"Don't get that tone in your voice."

"Kaye, I don't know what to do now!"

"You've only been—"

"But I can't fight back," I interrupt her; and as the truth of what I'm saying sinks through the levels of my brain, my voice gets weak and bathetic. "Really, Kaye, they can jiss look fer us, an' look fer us, until—"

"Fuck, Munn," she tells me sharply, "pull yer shit together. Look, I saw something earlier."

She leans on my shoulder, peering at the screen. I can smell her, a combination of shampoo and milky skin that, even amid the growing depression, creates a tiny spark of appreciation in my chest. "There. That list." She points.

I hit the commands, wearily. The file names appear, reel in other names with ghostly lines. The patterns dissolve, regroup. I'm getting a headache.

"Dat one," she says. "Try it."

It's a file labeled "Raffles." When I enter, it reveals a stack of boxes full of French and German names. It appears to provide a path into the games computer of the European Defence Organization's Office of Strategic Planning.

"Cool," Kaye says. "Wonder what the security classification was on that? Try this."

"This" is labeled "Pflegenheimer." It has nothing to do with X-Corp either, but if you're interested in retargeting one of the National Ballistic Defense Agency's telemetry satellites, then that's the file for you.

"Shit," Kaye says excitedly, "I was right! He started using crooks, for code words, last year sometime. Pflegenheimer was Dutch Schultz's real name. Try that one—an' that."

The crook code words seem to denote the toughest nuts to crack, security-wise. My heart picks up the beat a little. X-Corp's high-grade security shell—as opposed to "soft" systems like accounting—has the reputation of being one of the hardest in the trade.

The ninth one down, labeled "Ronald Biggs," is all X-Corp.

Kaye's hand tightens on my shoulder. Neither of us says anything. Updated accounting codes, confidential budgetary directives, and, finally, a list of menus and addresses, all tied by straight yellow lines in spidery patterns.

```
XCORP-FINPROG
XTV/RLLIFE-ADBUDGET
XCORP/VRLAB-FANTASIA
XCORP-PLANTSECY\CLEARANCE
XTV-SYSTEMSECY\CLEARANCE
```

"That's it." As with most weak schmucks, the pathos disappears from my voice the minute the going eases up. I mouse the cursor over to plant security, and double-click.

A web of boxed options spreads immediately into the shape of a geranium. A flashing icon indicates the file will automatically dial the relevant B-Net number. I hit "Enter."

Two different flower patterns blossom. The petals on one all contain hard security devices like LOGS, CARDS, VOICEPRINTS. The other flower shows physical locations.

STUDIO 1, 6, 14. ADMIN BLOCK. VR LAB. EXEC
SUITE.

"There's no fifth floor," I whisper. "It doesn't make
sense."

Kaye moves the mouse.

"What's that?"

"What?"

"Sorry. It's in red. It says, 'Heartland.' "

As is often the case with computer systems, once you get
beyond a threshold level of information, everything seems to
fall into place. "Heartland" contains a list of employees
cleared to enter the different rooms on the fifth floor, with
voiceprint reference coordinates attached. I split-screen to
VOICEPRINTS and CARDS to check my own identity is still
listed in the X-Corp system—and heave a sigh of relief when
I find, like a tiny ghost still hiding in the vast machine,
"MUNN, Alexander P."

After that it's simply a matter of adding my number and
coordinates to the ARP room, Heartland, and main building
CLEARANCE lists. Then I click out of the program.

I sit back in the cheap chair. My hair is damp with sweat.
From the living room I can hear Ollie North yelping, "You
slept with an alien and the *dog* got pregnant?" as the audience
roars and Brian grunts and Mrs. McCotter sighs and says,
"That's not romantic, Brian. That's not romantic at all."

FORTY-ONE

THE DAY AFTER I hack into X-Corp's security system I e-mail DataSafe. Quoting Zeng's password, I ask them to make a hard tape of the control file for the first episode—"my" episode—of *Real Life*.

I also call up XTV, via WHISPER, and double-check the life-boxes, World data, and Story Engine for the first episode are still intact. That they are doesn't surprise me; it would be way too difficult and time-consuming to go in and individually pull out the first-episode details from the Sagans of characters and micro-files they share with the rest of *Real Life*.

Kaye rides with Mrs. McCotter to the Howard Beach Kmart, where she buys us anoraks and underwear. She also picks up a white technician's jumpsuit, more hair color, a rayon scarf, and clean sneakers.

Once these chores have been accomplished, however, there's nothing to do but wait.

It makes no sense to sleaze into Heartland and switch the tapes now, since every extra hour the outlaw tape hangs in position increases the risk it'll be checked for some routine purpose, and the deception discovered.

And the waiting, at least for the first couple of days, is not exactly unpleasant.

Kaye and I spend most of those first days pooled in the soft hollow in the middle of our bed. Naked in the Saharan heat of Donegal Manor, with our arms and legs and ankles and necks and hair all tangled up together; with our juices Waring-blended together in the hollow and our lips constantly tasting each other in the mixology of sex, and the sweat confused along the entire length of our flesh; we generate for a while a kind of intimacy that, like a dangerous addiction, needs greater and greater amounts of intimacy to satisfy the previous level of craving.

We make love with our mouths till our faces smell more like each other than each other does, sperm smelling musty in her cornrows and her juices perfuming my fledgling beard. We lie together with a finger tucked trustingly in each other's asshole and there's innocence as well as lust in that position.

Outside the cheap double-glaze, the jets run down their invisible radio highways into Kennedy.

At night they seem like great flying cities. Their running lights span Brooklyn, their flight is not based on airfoils but on the stately lift of antimatter; their thunder thermonuclear in dimension, their multicolored tails as exotic and distant as Martian Vogue music.

The second night, however, they are gone, diverted to a runway bearing north. The wind shifts as well, and of course the two events are related. The warm southerly drizzle disappears without a trace; in its place comes sharp air from the north and east.

For a while the clouds go, too. Lying in our funky hollow, we watch Venus subside yellow in the indigo sky over the three glittering mini-towers that are all that's visible of the city from here. The temperature outside drops steadily. Mrs. McCotter cranks the heat up.

With the northeasterly shift in wind we clearly hear the coyotes howling from their dens among the airport runways and the polluted marshes surrounding; or when they roam farther afield, patrolling for cats, and lonely children, down Lefferts Boulevard.

I remember the coyotes in East New York, stalking the abandoned industrial area while other predators watched from the shadows. My dislike of coyotes—the fear of all wolf-like critters that's lurked inside me ever since Louise read us *Little Red Riding Hood* when we were young—it's all still there; yet for some reason, lying half in, half out of Kaye, the fear can't reach me, the panic can't start, as long as we touch each other in this way, like talismans.

"It reminds me of Westerns," Kaye says, holding me harder in the middle of the second night. "We should be cringing around a campfire with our Winchesters, or some-thin'."

"They're coming closer every year. The coyotes. They're good at hiding, and preying on the weak. New York is perfect for them."

One of the coyotes has a broken, plaintive call that quavers in the chilly air among the flatter howls of his companions.

"You had a rap sheet," she says, as if this were the same topic. "I looked at it, when I looked at your file."

"Juvenile."

"Sure."

"You never got into trouble?" I ask defensively.

"I was charged once. Lewd and lascivious conduct." Her expression doesn't change. "Hugo and I took our clothes off in the Pompeian Hall at the Met." She rolls partway over, so she can get a better idea of my face in the half dark. "I hardly know you, Munn. Huh?"

"What difference does it make?"

"That I know you?"

"No. What I did as a kid."

"What you did as a kid is what you are now, only with sets 'n painted scenery nailed on top, to make you fit in the grown-up world."

"Jeez, you must be a poet or somethin'."

"Answer me."

I shift around to ease the kinks this bed puts in my back.

"Louise tried," I tell her. "Louise is my mom. My dad left when I was a baby. I never knew him."

She makes violin-sawing motions. I ignore her.

"We lived on East Ninety-sixth, three blocks from the park. It was a weird neighb, a third middle-class professional, a third Latino, a third black. I went to PS 198, on Third

Avenue. The usual scenario, Louise had to work, I started runnin' around after school, I joined a gang.''

"A gang," she sighs. "Which one?"

"Rats-96." I touch her cheek, and follow its pretty contour lines with one finger. "We had a lotta beefs; the Latinos, up Second and First; the rich kids, toward the park. With the blacks, we had a truce, usually."

"Graffiti. Shoplifting. Assault."

"I wear it with pride."

"It's nothing to be proud of."

"Maybe not. But it's what we did."

"How'd you get out of it?"

"Seth," I tell her. "My stepfather. He hauled us off to the burbs."

She thinks about that for a second or two.

"That's it?"

"Well, there was no Rats-96 in Montclair."

"My dad was on gang patrol."

"They had gangs in Woodside?"

"He was stationed in Jackson Heights."

"How'd you get out of it?" I mimic her tone.

"Whaddya mean?"

" 'Cop-World.' I mean, that's what it is—they all live in the same 'hood, all go to St. Pius X or whatever, same bars and childcare, the wives all hang out together—it's like gangbangin', only the other side."

"You're fulla shit, you know that?"

"No," I tell her. "You're jiss pissed off, 'cause you assume I'm doin' what you said I did before."

"Which is?"

"Being surprised, you did somethin' different."

"Different from what?"

"Marrying another cop. Or goin' to Fordham and majoring in criminology and becomin' a cop yourself."

She's trying to hold her breathing down.

"You think you got us all labeled so—so neatly, Munn."

"Aren't I right, though?"

"My sister went that route," she admits finally. "She got married when she was nineteen. He's a sergeant. She's got four kids now. I guess I'm scared, I could still do dat?"

"You're not nineteen."

"Fuck you. You know what I mean."

"So you went the other way?"

She rolls over fiercely, lying on top of me. She hasn't got enough breasts to cushion her bounce.

"Get this," she hisses. "I got a *scholarship*, Munn. I *liked* English. I got into Sarah Lawrence 'cause I was good at writing. I wasn't reactin' to *nothin'*."

I smile in the gloom.

"Wachoo laughin' at?"

"I'm not laughin'."

"You're smilin'."

"I'm smilin' 'cause I like you."

"Fuck you."

"Okay."

She rolls over on her back again, breathing fast.

"My dad believed the bad guys should be stopped from hurting people. Okay, so that's a lil simplistic. Okay, he doesn't have a clue about how da Megorg controls him. But *nobody* patronizes him, not to my face."

"I wasn't patronizing him."

"Sure."

"I'd like to meet him."

"He'd like to meet *you*."

"I jiss bet he would."

We stay in that position, shoulder to shoulder, like strangers compared to the way we're used to lying, as the half-moon comes up invisible over our heads, and bathes the canal and the lined-up shacks in front of us in light the color of stainless steel.

I get up to use the bathroom. When I come back I find Kaye asleep. Her face, lying against the damp pillow, is now devoid of anger and confrontation. The slackening of tension seems to allow the real personality to come out. The intelligence in her slightly slanted eyelids, the stubbornness in her strong cheekbones, the long mouth. The great gentleness in the curve of her neck.

Okay, so I'm prejudiced. But people's perceptions reflect their feelings, and that's the way I read Kaye.

A terrible fear rises in me. It's a sharpening of all the other terrors that have afflicted me over the past few weeks, and it focuses on this: that I could lose her, through misunderstanding, as easily as through the callous enmity of hard men; and in losing her, I could forgo that greatest quality of a measured life—to feel as deeply as it's possible to feel; to dilute the essential loneliness with a creature who accentuates, not the confusion, but the peace that I know *through looking at her* exists somewhere inside me.

I believe Kaye, in the honesty of her desires, represents the exact antithesis of Riker's Island.

As I get back in bed, she stirs.

"Coyotes," she murmurs, and rolls in my direction.

"I won't let 'em near you," I whisper, but she has sunk back into sleep and does not hear my vow.

That night I dream of Larissa again.

She skates toward me down a frozen river. The ice is so thick and deep it has the black, rocklike look of all such freezing. She moves with a rhythm and grace that are like dancing, her long hair waving back and forth a half beat behind her.

But this dream is full of objects that obey one set of rules and look like something else altogether. She wears skates that resemble the cowboy boots she loved to wear. The river is near her home in Chudovo, but behind the birches I can make out the Kowloon Bankcorp Tower, the Chrysler Building. She brakes to a stop, spraying me with shaved ice from her sharpened blades. She carries a package that is not a package.

"Hi, Alex," she says, "sorry I'm late."

Her eyes are uncomplicated, the way they were when matters between us stood that way.

"I missed you," she tells me.

I want to tell her the same thing. Just then Zeng ambles up and hands me a master tape. "This is yours," he says. The tape has a note pasted to it, written in the fancy script of the woman from Bayard Street. When I look up, Larissa has skated off, away from me, away from the city, toward a spot where the river, the trees, and dark shale cliffs all narrow into a single point of darkness; a spot where a tall figure in a Chesterfield coat waits, the hard nexus of his eyes neither transmitting nor receiving light.

In his hands, something shiny and sharp.

I wake up, gasping and sweating. Kaye mutters and grinds her teeth a little. She does this, in the wolf hours just before morning.

The room is hot as Florida. Naked, I walk over and sit on the arm of an ancient BarcaLounger next to the window. Icicles hang off the drip edge of Mrs. McCotter's roof. A tracery of ice is starting to form around the swamped cabin cruiser opposite.

The moon is throwing itself in slow motion on the sword spires of the city. I make out the Confederate flag flapping fitfully over the shack across the little canal.

The sense of déjà vu comes back, strong as a train. And hard on its heels, the memory of where I've seen this stuff before. I made this association the night we came here, then forgot it. Now the recurrence makes it more certain; the Irish motifs and the Southern, Confederate symbols in lock-step have been showing up in my dreams for months, to the puzzlement of my shrink and the confusion of his patient.

Celtic waves, Robert E. Lee.

"Hamilton Beach" blenders, for chrissakes.

West Hamilton Beach, whose Irish population tends to flaunt the icons of Johnny Rebel.

You'd think this discovery would give me a sense of accomplishment, or resolution, but all I do is keep staring across the dark canal.

As it turns out, this is a mistake—I should definitely keep pursuing the questions my dreams have raised—but at the time the taste of the Larissa dream is stronger than odd relationships from past nightmares.

Seeing her face like that, with no challenge or points to prove, brings back the warm river of emotion that once flowed from me to Larissa and back.

The only trouble is, now another warmth has pooled in my chest, begun flowing toward the small woman sleeping in the swaybacked bed behind me.

Okay, maybe I have heartburn, but it's not that. My feelings for Kaye are so close to those I held for Larissa that I worry I will blend them.

For some reason I can't fully fathom, it seems vital not to mix up the two streams.

The coyotes yip and yap. Then the crooner among them

gives his long, clear howl, ending in a quaver oddly like the vocal break Elvis used, the ''baa-*by,*'' in the refrain to ''Heartbreak Hotel.''

I'm still in the BarcaLounger when Kaye wakes up.

She yawns, knuckles her eyes, licks her lips. Then, as if becoming aware of peril, she sits halfway up, leaning backward on her elbows. Her breasts, flat and girlish, peek over the sheet.

''How long you been up?''

''Awhile,'' I tell her.

She peers through the window, clears her throat. The sky is an abstract white field across which march squads of gray scout clouds. The icicles are no longer dripping.

''It looks fuckin' cold.''

She kicks off the covers and lopes swiftly over. She sits on my lap, drawing her knees up and burying her face in my neck.

''Sorry,'' she says.

'' 'Bout what?''

''Last night. I was a bitch.''

''No, you weren't.''

''I can *feel* things—everything—pulling at me, pulling me back, tryin' to make me *normal.*''

''I don't think you're normal, sweetheart.''

''Say that again?''

''I don't think you're normal.''

''No—after.''

''Sweetheart?''

''Yeah.''

She pulls back her head, looks at me under lowered eyelids, then kisses me on the mouth. Her tongue finds mine, my tongue draws back.

I turn my head toward the window; I can feel the lean tension of her against my skin.

''Munn?''

''Yeah.''

Across the canal, a man dressed in army surplus comes out of a broken door and stands hopelessly over the open hood of a Camaro.

The slate in her eyes changes. I get the feeling I can keep track of how her emotions shift by checking out those grays.

She rubs the edge of her thumbnail along her lower lip.

"What is it?" she asks me quietly.

"I think we should, kinda, slow down here?"

The grays now are more somber than the high clouds coming at us from the north. Her mouth is neutral, straight.

"You mean—you 'n me?"

I nod.

"Why?"

I tell her why. I've been sitting here thinking about it for three hours and the words come out in some sort of order. I tell her about the dream of Larissa, and how I never used to dream of her when she was alive. I talk to her of Zeng, and of Derek.

"But what's dat got to do wit *us*?" Kaye asks.

"I don't know, exactly," I admit, looking over at the Stars and Bars. "I jiss know it's about remembering. You see that flag?"

She nods, a little sullenly.

"Well, it stands for a bunch o' things I find really sick. Like bigotry, isolationism. But, down South anyway, it means something more; it means, people remember."

"A parrot *remembers*."

"Okay," I say. "But memory is more than that. Here's what I'm getting at. At its best, it's who we are. It's all the things that made us. It's the only thing that gives us the chance to learn, to make ourselves better."

"Saroyan," she says.

"Alright," I concede, "but what I meant is more than just history. See, if there's one thing I'm learning from all of this it's that you have to respect the memory of the people you loved. The memory of the city. You have to remember all that, *or you'll forget who you are*. Maybe that's all I was really trying to do with *Munn's World*."

"I don't understand." Kaye leans back. Her mouth is stretched, the two peaks sunk into shallow valleys, the ends pulled down. "That all sounds to me like a lot of overintellectualized bullshit. Words. What we have"—she grabs my cock, which is hard because of her presence—"it's real. It's warm. It's not just sex, either. It's you an' me, because we could fit in maybe, I dunno, a thousand different ways. We feel *good* together, Munn! I know we do.''

''I never had time to think about Larissa,'' I say stubbornly. ''I need *time* to remember her. Because what I feel for you reminds me of what I felt for her. An' I don't want the two things to get confused.''

Kaye says nothing.

''I wanna know,'' I continue slowly, ''that what I feel for you is real, and not some reaction to losing her.''

''You tink dat's what it is?''

''No. But I wanna be sure.''

She looks out the window. The man pulls himself out of the Camaro's engine compartment, walks around to the driver's door, turns the key. Nothing happens.

''Okay,'' she says. ''It's beginning to make sense.''

''It would only be for a little while.''

''Sure.''

''Kaye.''

''What.''

She turns back. The man slams the door, kicks the car, and goes back inside the shack. Her eyes are deep with water, but she won't let it come.

''When this is over,'' I begin.

''Don't,'' she interrupts. ''If you're gonna do this, this—*theory*—then do it right. Which means, you can't set a time limit.''

I nod. She has a point.

''But lemme tell you, Munn''—she tries to smile, which only makes her mouth pull harder downward, making my chest feel like it's imploding—''I think it *sucks*. Because we could lose each other''—she snaps her fingers, not very successfully—''like *dat*.''

''Not if we remember—''

''Ah, *Jee*-zuss!'' she yells. Standing up abruptly, she stamps her feet. She goes to the bed, throws herself on it, and screams into the pillows. ''*Jee*-zuss! *Jee*-zuss! *Jee*-zuss!''

I get up and sit beside her, in the hollow.

I put my hand on the shaded dip between her shoulder blades. I want to make love to her now more urgently than I've ever wanted to make love to anyone. ''Kaye,'' I mutter, helplessly.

"I can't help it," she shouts into the pillows. "I'm Italian."

The clouds we saw scouting the sky in the morning are the advance party of a big cold front. The gray in the cumulus turns darker, exactly the way Kaye's eyes did when I told her about my Larissa dream.

As we sit poking at Radar-range meatloaf and Birdseye peas and onions, different voices on the TV talk, with increasing excitement due to the high ratings associated with such news, of snow in inches and feet, of airports shut in Minneapolis, Chicago, Cleveland.

"Huh," Brian grunts repeatedly. "Fuckin' shit."

"Brian *hates* snow," Mrs. McCotter explains, giggling. "I think it's *romantic*."

Today her hair has been teased into a beehive with a plastic flower pinched into the back. She wears a bouffant black lace blouse with tight purple slacks, a leopard belt, and fuck-me pumps.

Kaye doesn't talk much. She responds logically to what I say, but her voice and gestures are distant. I catch her looking at me when she thinks I'm busy.

When she uses our bathroom upstairs, she shuts the door.

It seems like every twenty minutes or so I hear the dangerous synthesizer, the portentous announcements for *Real Life*.

Waiting is, by definition, a vacuum of sorts, and only two events stand out from that void.

The first is a news program that has Brian chortling and cheering.

We're sitting in the living room then, the Christmas flashers tainting our skin green every ten seconds.

The announcer switches from a mopping-up operation the Philippines Army is conducting among the last node-rebel strongholds.

". . . latest in a series of incidents in which frustrated New Yorkers have taken matters into their own hands."

A shot of the Happy East Korean grocery on the corner of

Broome and Hudson. I stare at it, shocked; it's the Korean I used to go to, in my former life.

An EMS team is wheeling a sixteen-year-old black boy out of the shop. The paramedics have given up trying to resuscitate him. The reporter interviews Soong the grocer, who is clutching a bandage to his arm. "I *know* that guy!" I exclaim, then shut up. It's stupid to let Brian know where I used to live.

"He come in wit gun, I shoot him." It's all Soong can say. He repeats it several times before the editor cuts away. A cop examines the shiny sawed-off Soong showed me proudly a month or two ago.

The second event happens around four. I tell Kaye I'm going for a walk. She hesitates, then says she'll come.

Outside, the cold has made the air heavy and our breath hangs for a long while in the air around us. The gravel road crunches beneath our sneakers. The sun behind the clouds looks like bleeding beneath a skin of winter.

We stop on the cement bridge spanning the next canal to the west, and lean over, looking at the water. The layer of ice is thicker now; a herring gull, landing to examine a thrown pizza crust, walks on it for several seconds before it cracks, dumping his feathery ass in the water.

"What time you goin' tomorrow?" Kaye asks.

"Late morning. The techies usually break for lunch around twelve. I figger—"

"There anything I can do?" she interrupts roughly.

"I don't think so."

"Whatever happens between us," she says. "What you're doing is good. What you said about remembering—ya know, Megorgs have a vested interest in killing memory."

"I don't know—"

"It jiss means," she says impatiently, "X-Corp, big companies, government agencies. They're all life-forms, see? Dangerous, predatory . . . If they can keep people from remembering how things were different, keep 'em from remembering how things got this way—then no one realizes, *they're* the ones in control."

"*Now* who's spouting the intellectual bullshit? 'O-o-oh that Hawkley-ite rag, it's so furious, so delirious'—"

"Prufrock."

I clap. Her mouth straightens. I wrap my Kmart scarf tighter around my throat.

"So why you think they din' want your history series?"

"*Munn's World*? 'Cause it's not commercial."

"Okay." Her eyes are bright, hard. Her hand moves the way a good chef moves a knife. "But also, it's easier to sell the crap. Sanitized sex, violence without agony. So you don't think about why the cities are turning into war zones and the Filipino army is slaughtering node-people in Manila an' the fuckin' coyotes are eatin' babies in Canarsie an', an' kids are gettin' shot by deli owners . . ."

She starts to cry. Her mouth is twisted in a cartoon of tragedy that would look silly if it didn't make my throat close like a sphincter valve.

I put my arms around her and hug tightly.

"Nobody gives a shit," she sniffles. "They'll *kill* you if they catch you."

Another seagull lands near the pizza. There's a small, elastic crack, and he, too, is dumped into the odoriferous water.

FORTY-TWO

I DON'T SLEEP well that night.

Much of the time I lie awake in the BarcaLounger, watching dead trees stick-fight in the strengthening wind.

Kaye grits her teeth in her sleep. The first snowflakes fall, as predicted, around three in the morning. By seven, when she wakes up, the shacks across the canal have been transformed from crummy tarpaper into elves' houses from some Hallmark Xmas card; all their ugly holes and angles decorated like cookies with white. Snow lies thick and flat over the canal.

The seagulls now flock on the ice without having to swim.

Kaye opens her eyes. She walks naked to the window. The swirling blizzard outside sheaths her in blue tones. Her waist and hips look like a commercial for the slopes of Chamonix.

She turns and smiles at me, almost happily.

I shower carefully, adding more blond dye to my hair and beard. I put on the techie jumpsuit. We go down for breakfast. My heartburn is back, worse than ever. I chug a couple Advils to kill the central-heating headache. Neither of us eats much of the greasy Eggos on our plates. Mrs. McCotter has oppressed her hair into yellow French braids. "Look," she says, pointing at Kaye's cornrows, "we're twins!" Today she wears a loose smock with van Gogh's sunflowers silk-screened all over it. She keeps ooh-ing and ah-ing over the snow, while Brian grumbles ceaselessly at the XTV anchor presenting a "Winter Storm Watch."

Real Life ads still airing every twenty minutes on XTV.

Kaye doesn't meet my eyes. I've no great desire to look into hers. A curious bubbling sensation rises under the heartburn, and all my doubts and thoughts and other emotions have to operate, acid and insubstantial, over its glossy surface. The minutes ooze like cold Valvoline.

At 8:45 I put on the Kmart anorak, take cash and car keys from Kaye's wallet, and walk downstairs. Kaye is still in the kitchen, drinking coffee, watching Braindead through the living-room door.

"I'm off," I tell her.

"Yeah?" she says, still looking at the TV.

I can feel hurt swamping the nerve bubble. I turn and go out the front door.

She comes after me, as I'd hoped she would, and grabs me before I've gone down the front steps. Her arms lock tightly, but she says nothing and doesn't look at my face. She stuffs her Ray-Bans in my anorak, goes back inside, and shuts the door.

"Ah, fuck you, too," I mumble, not even meaning it.

The old Pontiac starts with no enthusiasm. Its tires spin in the half foot of snow already accumulated. The wind takes the fractal blues of the falling flakes and swirls them crazily between the gray canal and the beaten-down houses. West Hamilton Beach looks like photos of Leningrad during the Nazi siege. Once more, I think of Larissa.

I park the car near the Howard Beach subway station, and cake wet snow over the license plates. The original plan was for Kaye to drive me here. In the strange new limbo between us, however, I did not expect her to keep that promise, and she didn't volunteer.

The A train is late. The ride, slowed by track problems, takes a long time. I sit reading the forty-eighth installment of the tragic HIV-related tale of Julio and Marisol as displayed on the subway ads. I'm interested to note that Marisol is still in the hospital; to my certain knowledge she's been in the last throes of AIDS for longer than most ghetto kids get to live.

I detrain at Fourteenth Street and walk west to DataSafe. The wind has died down somewhat. The snow has settled into a steady, methodical dumping that spells trouble for the city's plowing budget. Cars are pulled slowly along white tunnels by the feeble yellow rope of their headlights. The Sanitation Department trucks jingle by on chained tires, burying parked vehicles in drifts taller than a man.

The DataSafe office is modern and white. They have the tape ready at the reception desk, and since (in theory) no one can download the data without a password command from the owner—and since the fee is already paid via Kaye's Visa—they hand it over without fuss. It's a standard model, same size and color as the tapes XTV uses. I'm back on the street inside five minutes.

A clock in the Tazza d'Oro coffee shop reads 10:53. Outside the Chembank I step on a Christmas mine that explodes into "God Rest Ye Merry, Gentlemen" and I recoil, skid, and fall on my knees in the slush. Heart pounding, I return to the A train.

Ten minutes later I'm walking across Twelfth Avenue toward Television City. The grand neon "X," thirty-eight floors above, is completely hidden, and the lowest floors show like hazy villages of curved-lozenge shapes above the snowy landscaping built on the old steamship piers.

There's a fair amount of traffic. Television doesn't stop just because a blizzard is howling. Quite the opposite, in fact.

On top of it all the biggest and most expensive new serial in the history of cable TV is premiering tonight. No weather excuses will be accepted from the publicity flacks, the people in affiliate-relations, the techies. They hurry in and out from meetings to breaks and back again, hunched against the bitter wind, seeking cabs, yelping on cellphones.

I walk up the forecourt to the main building. The entrance is set in the inverted bottom "V" of a giant brushed-aluminum "X" that dominates the first two floors in an incredibly subtle reflection of the roof.

I put on Kaye's Ray·Bans, stow the DataSafe tape in my anorak, and walk inside. The lobby is three stories high and silver. The rush of heated air is loud and strong as the blizzard. Concealed speakers hum "Rudolph the Red-Nosed Reindeer." An X-shaped desk, also in brushed aluminum, bars the way to visitors. A giant screen overhead shows, in small, shifting squares, all eighty-seven channels of the B-Net system. A rank of security guards mans two arms of the "X." Employees shunt obediently through a metal detector to a row of glass doors cordoning off four columns of elevators. Each of the doors is equipped with a keypad and Vox-box.

I pull the polyester scarf tighter around my chin and force myself to walk normally past the visitors' desk.

The atmosphere in here is really toasty. I can feel my pits already starting to lube up. The nearest guard glances at me where I stand in line for the employee doors. He keeps watching as the next person walks up to the panel, punches in his code number, and says "hello, hello," words of his own choice, words that don't count; all that matters is that the pattern of his voice match with seventy percent of the digital "points" linked to his code in the PLANTSECY/CLEARANCE file.

The lock clicks. The guy in front of me starts to move; but instead of walking through he holds the door wide for a woman in an extravagant fur coat coming the other way. She glances up at his face, smiling, and spots me standing behind him.

Her face is the color of oiled teak. A chainful of keys jangles against her breast, and her eyes shine with a kind of wise-ass humor.

It's Rosie Obregon.

I stand there like an idiot. Rosie looks down and pulls her coat quickly away from the locking mechanism, which is notorious for snagging hems.

Without another glance in my direction, she sails past me, waving to a limo driver.

I remain standing there. A hint of Narcisse lingers. My breathing doesn't work. Somebody in line behind me says, "Hey, pal, watcha waitin' for, Chanukkah?" I can feel the guard's eyes, they had moved away when Rosie sailed by but now they're back.

I walk up to the keypad. Christ, now I can't remember my own pass number. 070—and then it resurfaces as it should in a society where your bar code is what primarily identifies you.

"Err, yeah," I tell the Vox, " '*Toujours gai,* Archie, that's my motto.' "

Nothing happens. My breathing locks up again. The sweat pricks through pores in my brow. It *never* takes this long. Something has gone wrong, it was the wrong file, they had an alarm built in and now the guards—

The door buzzes, clicks, swings open.

The guard looks away.

I am *through.*

I float toward the elevator banks. When the car arrives I get pushed lightly by the crowd into its mirrored interior. Someone punches "5," so I don't have to do that. Canned trumpets blare "The Holly and the Ivy." Seconds later the doors open on the fifth floor, and using my elbows for propulsion, I emerge onto the blue carpeting of Heartland.

Well, not quite Heartland, not yet. Another barrier of blast-proof glass lies between me and the transmission center. I key in my number with more confidence this time, growl an assertive "identity check" to the Vox. The system, seeming to respond to my new forcefulness, buzzes me in after a shorter lag than previously.

A secretary walks by, and stops.

"Hi," he says brightly, "can I help you?"

Damn, is all I can think. Damn damn damn!

"Can I—" He's young, earnest, full of the mind-fucking importance of being involved in Broadcasting. He is also dangerous, because between his interest and his alertness he could nail me like a butterfly to corkboard.

"No!" Too brusque. "No—sorry, Bill Wimer's s'posed to be meeting me, but I'm early."

"He was down in the canteen."

"Huh!" Too forced. "No wonder. Half the ARP carts to check and the boss is eating Cap'n Crunch."

He laughs, and walks on.

I stare after him, in awe at myself. It's amazing what lies you can pull off as long as you talk the right language. All I had to do was mention ARP, and Wimer, and the secretary deduced I had a right to be there.

It's the basis of VR, I reflect as I speed away from the elevator bank. Get enough details right, and the subject *will* believe. Our brains are built to think in terms of stories; if you build a good enough story, you can get away with almost anything.

Even the presidency of the United States.

Thinking about Henry Warren Powell bows me down a bit. I don't want to meditate on the stakes here. The fear bubble balloons inside, and I'm breathing hard again.

I stop and look around me, but these corridors, upholstered in gray soundproofing, with thickly anaconda-ed B-Net wire bundles hanging out of ceiling panels, all resemble each other. I remove my anorak, hide the DataSafe tape inside the folded quilting, and start walking again, head down. As any New Yorker knows, the most suspicious thing you can do in a hostile environment is look like you're lost; you might as well hold a sign reading "Vulnerable."

Randomly, I choose the next corridor on my right, cross a bump in the floor. Immediately I recognize the blue doors leading to the main computer core where I talked with Rosie.

If I remember correctly, the ARP control room is off the next corridor, to the—*left*.

I turn left. My memory, for once, did not fail me. The long plate-glass windows of the first control room appear in the right-hand wall. In the silence behind glass, a woman in a face-sucker rattles commands on a keyboard, fine-tuning 3-D test patterns.

The studio next door is empty. The ranked monitors tamely show slices of the *Ollie North Hour,* a *Real Life* house ad, and eighty-five other capsules of hilarity, pain, mayhem, and bright packaging beaming out from this place at this particular instant.

I move to the next studio. This is empty as well.

Stare at the wide panels of sleek stainless holding up the thousands of videotapes ranked in vertical stacks.

Between the stacks, columns of VDTs and hardware controls stand all the way to the ceiling.

Hundreds of meter lights blinking yellow, gray, blue, white.

Dials, oscilloscopes, buttons; monitors watching monitors.

ARP.

I stare at the digital clocks prominently mounted by the control boards. They read 11:37:08. My original plan was to get here a little early and occupy a cubicle in the men's room until lunch break.

But the ARP control room is empty *right now*. My heart has speeded up to the point where it sounds like a Nigerian juju drummer on crack. The fear bubble has gone to max tautness. This would make breathing difficult, were I breathing.

If I wait another five minutes, I feel like I'll surely explode.

"Now," my brain whispers, "*now*."

I look up and down the corridor. I move slowly to the glass door. If someone showed up now, I'd have an excuse to abort.

No one shows up.

"O Come, All Ye Faithful," saccharine on the sound system.

I draw my first breath in a long while, and tap out my number on the keypad.

"Hello," I tell the Vox. "Hello?"

The door clicks open so fast that I get suspicious and stand there for a second or two, waiting for the sirens to start, the black AGATE squads to pop out of soundproofing panels.

Nothing.

I walk into ARP. The door shuts behind me.

Heartland in general always reminds me of those grim men in tights barking orders about "warp drive" and "dilithium crystals," and the ARP control room is like their starship bridge. The three command consoles are equipped with padded swivel seats, face-suckers, and dozens of fancy calibration screens filled with colored patterns like the ones in Zeng's hacker program.

The only sound in here is the beep of instruments, the rush of computer fans, the background noise of the scrubbed air pumped in by TV City's support systems.

As I stand by the door, a gray-painted metal gizmo—it looks like a vacuum cleaner with a tape deck bolted to one end—pops out of a recess, speeds across one of the ARP panels, sucks out a tape, races two stacks away, spits the tape into an empty slot, and zips back into its recess again.

A man walks by the control-room window without looking inside.

I shake myself, quite literally, like a dog. I walk weak-kneed to the first ARP panel.

The control tapes are numbered and carry narrow bar codes on adhesive strips across the exposed back. The bar codes, I know, enable the system to read the tapes and match them, both with the designated time slot and the machine that will actually feed them into one of the eight B-Net transmission ports.

There's also a tiny label to one side with the show's name in English.

I gaze at the ranked tapes in rapidly mounting despair. Eighty-seven cable channels to feed every hour or half hour means, theoretically, between 2,088 and 4,176 tapes a day. Realistically, of course, there's a lot of duplication, plus some of the time is reserved for local programming; but it's still an awful lot of tapes.

No way I'm going to have the time to read through this bunch before somebody who has the right to be here walks in and demands to know what the hell I'm doing.

I read down the line of tapes nearest me. These are daytime shows: *Divorce Videos, Coffee with the Carpenter.* I move to the left, and find an early afternoon news program.

At least I'm moving in the right direction.

Next panel. This starts with early afternoon. I rattle my fingers along the backs of the tapes, as if I could read the bar codes through my skin.

Pain in the Afternoon, WXTV/NY. So this is 4 P.M., weekdays.

Keep going. Early evening news, KNET/Dallas. What day is today? Monday. *The AGATE Files* runs Mondays, after the evening news. I skim through two more stacks. I pray to whatever gremlins are in control here the techies are taking a long break.

Car Polo Championships. Too far. *Courtney Love Presents* finishes at 10 P.M. EST. I pull back to the right, crouching to read the lower tapes.

It comes at me with no warning. *REALLIFE/EPISODE1-MASTER 8:00:15 P.M. EST 12/3,* followed by a long list of call signs.

"Son of a *bitch*," I mutter.

One final look around. Nobody in sight. I pull the tape. It resists at first, then slides out. My fingers are trembling so hard I almost drop it. I have to jam it between arm and chest and curl the fingers of my right hand like claws to get any purchase on the bar code label. It's some kind of goddam metal-plastic strip with a serious adhesive on the back. Just as my nails are about to come off, it gives, pulling away neatly.

The name label comes off easier. I rack the two tapes one on top of the other in my hands, then press both bar code and name label into place on my DataSafe tape.

I step to the panel and place the DataSafe tape into the 8 P.M. EST position. It slots in, catching on some sort of flange in the depths of the machinery. I fuss with it for a few seconds, making sure all is as it should be, and that's a big mistake. There's a clicking sound to my left, a recess in the side of the panel opens, and the robot zips out, vengeful as a Valkyrie, hurtling on its track, the tape deck snout extending on its eight-foot-long articulated arm.

No time to dodge. The arm hits me square on left elbow and shoulder. I get slammed sideways and backward so hard that I wind up on the far side of the control consoles, flat on my ass, with the wind knocked right out of my lungs.

I clutch my elbow, grunting at the pain.

The ARP robot whines high and to the right, pauses, picks out *B-Net Shopper,* moves that neatly into a 12:02 PCT position for San Diego.

Rapid knocks on the glass. I look up. A woman in a business suit stares down at me, a concerned expression on her face. I grin enthusiastically, though I feel more like sobbing. I point at the ARP robot, and roll my eyes graphically at my own stupidity. Look at Munn, ain't he dumb.

The woman, a true New Yorker, shakes her head in wry amazement that anyone as clueless as I was not euthanized at birth.

She disappears from the window.

I'm not sure if my elbow is broken. One-armed, I grab the purloined tape, unzip my jumpsuit, stuff the cassette inside. I pick up Kaye's RayۑBans, which fell off when the robot attacked, and put them back on. Grab my anorak, push the door's electronic release, and step out into the hallway.

A couple of men dressed in silk suits pass down the far corridor, talking softly. I wind the Kmart scarf around my lower face. I pause in front of the control-room glass.

The ARP room is quiet. Yellow lights blink serially; the

robot arm sleeps in its recess, waiting for the computer's next command. I can no longer distinguish, among the dozens of tapes in the 8 P.M. slot, which is the ringer I donated to to-night's lineup.

"It Came Upon a Midnight Clear" whines from hidden loudspeakers.

I turn right, toward the elevators.

FORTY-THREE

WHEN I GET off the train at the Howard Beach stop, a slight figure bundled in Kmart ski clothes is sitting on a bench near the token booth.

Kaye gets up stiffly as I approach. Her face is tired and pale and I feel a lurch in my innards at the thought of the shit I've dragged her through.

I put my hand to her forehead, and she leans against it.

"You made it."

"Yup."

"How'd it go?"

"Cool."

She smiles, and winds her arm around my elbow. I try not to wince; it's the elbow the ARP robot assaulted. We walk outside. The snow is falling more lightly now; the storm has a greater component of wind. I peer around for Kaye's heap.

"How'd you get here?"

"I walked."

"You *walked*?"

"I wanted to. I—felt bad, this morning." She stops, pulls me around to face her. "I mean, I just can't do it—those long good-byes, when there's a chance someone might, like, get hurt?

"Every morning," she continues, "my dad would walk out. We could hear gunshots, during the day sometimes." She looks down at the snow. "I guess there's more of my mom in me than I realized."

"Uh-huh."

"You're not listening."

"Yes, I am. But I'm wondering where the hell the car is."

"I'm telling you something important!"

"But how we gonna get home?"

I must be tired to refer to Donegal Manor as "home." I touch her cheek again, like I was touching a Fabergé egg. It seems that precious to me, and that fragile.

Kaye looks around.

"Where'd you park it?"

"Right here, I thought."

She points at a sign.

"You forget how to read?"

"Read what?" Snow is plastered on the windward side. We walk around to the other. "NO PARKING IN SNOW EMERGENCY."

"Oh, shit."

"Munn," she says, "you dodo-bird." She takes my arm again. I decide my elbow is not broken. The warmth of Kaye's body beside me seems to attenuate the bruising.

The far boroughs of New York are not set up for walking. We have to trudge north in soaked sneakers to get to an underpass that will take us under the train tracks. Then we strike out west, toward West Hamilton Beach. The road has been plowed although by the looks of it very few cars have taken advantage of this fact. The garages and depots dwindle, replaced by vacant lots, an occasional utility shed, cattails. We reach a sort of snow cliff where the plows stopped. Before us now lies a field of clean, unbroken powder. In the distance, the clumps of shacks and ranch houses of the Beach, their trashy protuberances hidden in a soft mounded whiteness, the occasional blur of wood smoke shading the blizzard.

"It looks like a village in the steppes," I say.

"They light fires, to keep the wolves away."

When we get back to the lodging house I run a bath in the

plastic tub and soak my frozen limbs. The fear bubble has shrunk in size, leaving acid in the space it once occupied. The hot water dulls the elbow ache. I look at the scar in my right side which, in healing, has gone rough and kind of liver-colored.

The line on my left wrist that marks where the carpet-cutter caught me in the Kearny marshes has almost disappeared.

The bruise on my elbow is turning yellow. I can time all the events in the past two weeks by what color my immune system is using to paint over the damage.

Kaye reads a trash novel, her feet warming on a heat vent. The snow slackens further. Another army of gray clouds is sneaking in behind.

At six we go downstairs for dinner. It's a "special" night, Mrs. McCotter tells us; she broke out her Swanson's emergency rations on account of the snow. Kaye gets Salisbury Steak with Creamed Corn and String Beans, while I am served Fried Chicken with Mashed Potatoes and Sweet Carrots. Compared to the usual fare at Donegal Manor, it's not bad.

Brian, still in a foul mood, eats Denny's burgers out of a bag in the living room.

"There's that new show on tonight," Mrs. McCotter says as she hooks up the dishwasher. "The 'real' one? You know they did some filming for that, right here in the Beach? I wisht I coulda got all the equipment you need for it."

"They get B-Net here?" I ask curiously.

"In the Beach?" Mrs. McCotter laughs. "We don't even have city water. We're not even," she adds proudly, "on city maps."

"If you had B-Net, though," I press her, "would you have bought it?"

"In a minute," Mrs. McCotter replies wistfully. "At least that headviewer thing, and the control, so you can change things."

I think that if people like Mrs. McCotter are ready to blow their month's budget on Virtix, the faith Tyrone had in *Real Life*'s ratings will have been justified.

The idea makes me even more nervous than Kaye's statement, earlier, about "my" episode changing history.

I mean, all those facts were on-line in the show; and I

rechecked the facts, staying up late that night at Kaye's, pulling down hypertext from the Washington Post/L.A. Times News Service, among others; but I still don't know who wrote that episode, or why.

I'm supposed to be a writer, and even a fiction writer makes sure his sources are accurate.

I shake myself. It's sure as hell too late now.

I watch Kaye pick at her Salisbury steak. Suddenly I'm happy that the episode is going to air, here and now, accurate or no. It's the only reason I can imagine for Fishman coming after me so hard and often; and I have to keep Kaye out of the Fishman's reach.

Nothing else matters. History's an abstraction, Nielsen ratings a sick joke. What matters is, I must keep Kaye from ever knowing that kind of violence.

I get up, fetch the laptop, and hook it to the phone. Summoning Mrs. McCotter, I dial the number for XTV. I don't need DataSafe, since I downloaded the hacker files into the 988 the last time I used them. I check the time—it's 7:50—and, delicately tuning Zeng's flower patterns, kill the entire "Heartland" file in the PLANTSECY/CLEARANCE directory.

With any luck, no one will be in Heartland this late. And from now on, no one, not even Jack Tyrone, will be able to get back in.

Those soundproof windows in Heartland look like any other plate glass, but you can't smash them with anything less than shaped Semtex.

Everybody's seated in the living room now. We watch the last minutes of *The AGATE Files,* real footage of the bomb squad disarming an Arm of Allah device in the Citibank Building last month. Mrs. McCotter zaps Jiffy Pop with a quarter pound of margarine and rat cheese and we munch the greasy snack, jaws working in unison.

Then the screen fades to black. The Clam Fetish theme booms. Constrained by the simple screen of Mrs. McCotter's TV, the investigator climbs into the De Havilland 686 that will carry him to La Guardia, and the beginning of his quest.

It's the basic show, since we don't have Virtix and thus lack the option of altering the plot.

The basic show, with two differences.

The first difference is, as soon as the inspector drives off the Shore Parkway into West Hamilton Beach, all of us in the living room are transmuted, from mute wondering observers of the usual fancy-ass L.A. studio environment, into, somehow, co-authors.

It's the same syndrome those guys in McGovern's Bar got, watching the TV picture of me, and seeing me in the bar at the same time.

Mrs. McCotter can hardly sit still. She keeps pointing out features—"That's Phil Ryan's, there; and the Sullivans' Ford Escort, with the rust, see the rust?" Brian keeps shushing her; his eyes never once quit the screen. He lights and stubs out his Merits without looking at them.

The second difference comes twelve and a half minutes before the end, right after the Tunes Trust investigator has found a witness to describe how Tyrone (alias Talbot) funneled cash to the aspiring senator's election bid.

The screen goes dark for a few seconds.

Mrs. McCotter gasps as if she herself had been switched off.

Then the opening scene of the colorized, 3-D version of *It's a Wonderful Life* rolls onto the screen, beneath a notice that reads "Due to transmission problems, the preceding show has been postponed to a later date. Please consult your local listings."

"Buffalo girls, won't ya come out tonight," Jimmy Stewart croons.

Kaye looks at me, frowning, concerned.

"It's okay," I tell her, "they showed more'n enough to get the picture, know what I mean?"

"*I* didn't get the picture," Mrs. McCotter mutters, crestfallen, "I din see the end!"

Brian lights a cigarette, watching the tip glow.

"I noo it was too complicated, all that interactive shit," he says.

FORTY-FOUR

WE GO TO bed early.

When I wake up the following morning, Kaye is curled like a hibernating woodchuck in the winter hollow of our bed.

She has a tiny snore, like a neutrino with a chainsaw, that summons, in my head, a sense of utter comfort.

My eyes are half stuck together with sleep gum. There's cotton in my head and a growling emptiness in my belly.

I check Kaye's watch. 8:42. I've been asleep for almost ten hours. Rubbing my eyes, I remember no dreams or interruptions. Donegal Manor is absolutely silent.

I crack open a shade. The snow is falling heavily again, the canal underneath us reduced to a soft indentation in a cotton landscape. No cars rev, no planes land. I wonder why I didn't sleep till noon.

Downstairs I dump Folgers Instant in a cup and zap it in the microwave. The kitchen table is thick with Swanson platters, account books, pencils, yellow pencil chips.

The chips remind me of Gaynor, his habit of carving up pencils. That association, working on form rather than content, reminds me of other memories summoned by the sight of the *Miss Saigon* tape in Mrs. McCotter's living room.

I'm starting, finally, to get a handle on the craziness.

Larissa in *Miss Saigon*. A made-for-TV movie. She was dead wrong for the role. We watched it together when it was broadcast, the way Kaye and I watched *Real Life* last night. Afterward Larissa turned to me and said, "What did you think?"

It was clear from the spark in her eyes what she thought; she thought she was wonderful. As a fiction writer I know that sometimes the greater truth is to lie a little. The point of writing is not to knock someone over the head with facts, but to make him see above them to the force that created the facts in the first place. I said, "You were wonderful"; and, looking back on it now, I realize that was, indeed, the greater truth.

Washing a mug, I look out the window to the yard. A big laundry van down the lane carries a wind-sculpted cap of snow. I like the way things as plain as a van, or a broken gas barbecue, when buried in chilly white powder take on an aura of mystery, even elegance. I like the way ordinary things like snow and barbecues are not affected by broadcasting a VR episode that will change history.

I like how my stomach isn't as tense as it usually is. Most days, when I wake up, it's as if, on some level, I were still expecting to see Cosmo sleeping in the next bunk. Or to confront the rat from the pit under the FDR, staring at me with those zinc eyes.

The tap gurgles. Brian whistles next door, a familiar tune. The water hiccups, and stops. "It was the blood of my brother-in-law, that went away with me," the tune goes. I think, The pipes must be frozen, wondering why all of a sudden this day has lost shine. The frozen canal before me still is hidden by its quilt of ice, yet I can *feel* the water hidden underneath, cold and rotten, darkening the scene, its shadow easily overpowering the flat light of the snowstorm.

> *And what did you fall out about,*
> *Oh, dear love, tell me!*
> *About a little bit of bush,*
> *That soon would have made a tree.*

It's "Cruel Edward," the song that introduces *Munn's World*.

And how the fuck would Brian know the theme to Munn's World?

All of a sudden every muscle in my body loses firmness. I take a step toward Brian's door, and my knee cartilage slips around the joint. Without breathing—though my heart is banging its emergency farrago—I ease open the door to his bedroom.

I stand quite still, amazingly calm.

Brian is not whistling.

His blood, like Zeng's, flew everywhere. Like Zeng, they gagged him before cutting him.

Like my friend, like my wife, they opened his gut like a flaked flounder. His chest is matted with dark liquid, the sausage intestines spill merrily over his crotch.

The blood shifts, oozes downward. Two fingers on Brian's left hand shake briefly. A couple of Merits soak in the thickening pool on the acrylic carpet. A noise comes from somewhere, not from Brian, a quick scrape transmitted by the "manor" 's rotting plywood.

Kaye.

I sprint through the door, up the uneven stairs, slipping on the runner, landing on my sternum four steps from the top. A whimper squeaks out of my locked throat.

Because she hangs there, her cornrows raked 'round by sleep and surprise.

Her eyes are closed. A narrow trickle of blood runs down the tendons of her throat, flowing around her collarbone and between her breasts.

I know, right away, she is dead.

Behind her, outlining in black every sweet corner of her small body, holding her up with one arm circled under her small breasts, stands the Fishman.

He's dressed in his usual coat. The charcoal homburg on his head is less fashionable than I remembered. His hands are covered in dark blue plastic gloves. Between the black collar of his coat and the brow of his hat, I recognize the eyes I saw on the corner of Water and Dover, neither giving nor receiving light. When the angle shifts just a little, I catch the faint greenish back-scatter I first spotted when he waited for me outside Larissa's.

He's wearing night goggles, Spetsnaz infrared made of

transparent plastic so tiny and miniaturized that from any distance they look like normal eyes, with maybe a case of exophthalmus.

In his right hand he holds a long, thin filleting knife. The blade, gloppy with grayness, rests against her neck, drawing a line across the slope of her windpipe.

"Kaye," I manage to whisper despite my absence of breath. "Oh, *Kaye.*"

Then her windpipe convulses, and she swallows.

The utter hopelessness that flooded me a second ago is instantaneously replaced with terror.

The fear is so huge it freezes my muscles. No direction I could go in is not blocked by the horror of what might happen to Kaye if I make the wrong move, say the wrong thing now.

I stare up at the Fishman, my mouth hanging open, a little drool hanging from the curve of my lip.

"So," Fishman says. "It's been a long, long journey. Eh, Mr. Munn?"

"Drac," a voice calls from downstairs.

"It's secure." Fishman's voice is quite pleasant. His sibilants are a little pronounced; the accent is educated, atonal. He could come from anywhere.

Footsteps sound below me.

"Let's move it, satellite window's gonna close."

I don't have to look to recognize that voice. Several pairs of feet trot up the stairs behind me. I smell hair gel, cheap cologne. I'm hauled roughly backward, down the stairs, and pinned on my back to the davenport.

The men who handle me are Southeast Asian. They're small, dressed in stonewashed jeans and plastic jackets of the type that look like leather. Two of the jackets have stylized green dragons sewn on one shoulder.

One of the men carries a Tech-9 slung around his neck; he whips the stock around and whacks me on the side of the head. My vision blurs.

A sharp jab in my arm. When my sight clears it reveals another Viet wrapping a hypo carefully in a piece of canvas and stowing it in a side pocket.

"*Doo meh,*" I hiss at him. His dark eyes flick at me, without emotion.

A truck diesel rumbles to life. No sign of Gaynor now. I

think of the whittled pencils I saw in the kitchen and wonder how long he was waiting downstairs. Passing the time as they hacked up Brian.

God, Brian—he will never more smoke Merits, or bitch about the snow.

The *finality* these people dispense, the casualness of it, still amazes me.

I wonder briefly what was in the hypo.

I turn to look for Kaye. Two of the Asians have dragged her down the stairs. One of them puts his hand over one tit and giggles. I want to get up and kill the guy, but my brain is starting to fill up with a smooth numb vapor that makes action difficult.

The Asians pick me up and stand me, more or less, on my feet. Fishman peers around outside, then waves. The cold air reaches in and slaps my face. The laundry truck has been reversed next to Brian's Cavalier. They hustle me straight up a loading ramp into the side entrance.

I stare around me. My eyes can move, even if the rest of my body seems to have lost contact with its bones and ligaments. There's much here that's familiar, for despite the laundry logos on the outside this is one of XTV's mobile studios, the all-terrain "Van-go" they send to earthquakes and Superbowls. The entire left side of the cargo compartment is filled with B-Net editing decks, workstations, and satellite controls. The dropped ceiling conceals antennas and transmission dishes. Comfortable leather pilot chairs are fastened beside the various instrument banks.

Ivan Gaynor leans on the back of one, talking into a cellphone.

I don't look at him; in fact, I barely notice him at all.

For seated the next chair over—her hands covering her mouth, her eyes wide in empathy, her long, theatrical gown sweeping to the floor on all sides—is my mother.

The Asians dump me roughly in the nearest pilot chair. Thoughtfully they fasten the seat belt, then leave me alone, and with no risk of escape; whatever they injected me with has so softened my muscles that I now list helplessly to port, sagging against the chest belt.

Louise gets halfway to her feet, then subsides.

I try to say, "Cut the cheap effects, Mom."

It comes out, "Gachefeum."

"Alex," she sighs.

Even in the drug haze, the poor quality of her acting gets through. She was always trying out for plays and commercials when we lived on Ninety-sixth Street. I wonder how much of her character was ground up by professional failure, to the point where she turned to Johnsonism to make up for it.

I wonder, What the hell is it in me that seeks out bad performers?

Pop psychology, I think, and giggle.

"An' what did you do to your *hair*?" Louise is saying. She shakes her head. "I'm so sorry, hon," she continues. "You must be really confused, but it's for the best, I promise you."

"What're you talking about?" I ask her. This my numbed mouth forms roughly into "Attao?"

A pair of legs wrapped in one of Mrs. McCotter's yellow bathrobes protrudes from a settee forward. The legs are too slim to be our landlady's.

"I always knew you'd figure it out eventually. When Henry called and said they'd found her car in Howard Beach, I knew —just like *that*."

She snaps her fingers. I still can't figure out what she's talking about. The diesel roars, the van lurches backward. The Asians pile in. Gaynor says something, pointing at the monitors. Fishman looms behind him, hanging on to the chair's back.

"Anybody see you?" Gaynor asks.

"Maybe. Maybe not." He shrugs. "There's a lot of snow."

"Someone will remember the van."

"So he stole it."

"It's got fake plates," Gaynor muses.

"Dragons'll repaint it." Fishman laughs. "Trust the Dragons to rig this as a laundry van. I mean, it's like a sick joke."

I start to giggle again, helplessly.

Gaynor growls something to an Asian I haven't seen before.

This one wears a smock and the perpetual, slightly contemptuous smirk of the total techie; it's an expression that reminds me, with a pang, of Zeng.

The techie pushes buttons. Twenty-six monitors overhead

fade and shift. One of the screens shows two sets of truck tracks receding down the white field of Mrs. McCotter's lane.

I feel unaccountably desolate, watching Donegal Manor dwindle in the distance.

That was home, for me and Kaye; the only home we've ever truly shared. It was safety, for a while. I wonder what they did to Mrs. McCotter. My compulsion to giggle is gone, replaced suddenly with an utter sadness that brings tears to my eyes and sends them spilling hot down my cheek.

Louise clicks her tongue, dabs the end of one long sleeve in her mouth, and leans over to wipe the tears away.

My drug-softened brain tries desperately to figure out how she fits into all this—and gives up at once. It's just too much to tackle right now.

Above my head, XTV News focuses on the snow to the exclusion of all else. Braindead, attired in a chartreuse monkey-jacket, says earnestly, "The worst blizzard in six years has shut down the New York area like a failed musical."

Three monitors down, however, the *Tonya Harding Show,* a Fox syndication, backdrops a promo clip for *Real Life.* The pasty face and green lipstick of the hostess fill the screen.

"Disturbing questions about just how much the Christian-Republican senator from New York revealed—or hid—from the voting public. An' we'll be talking with the L.A. police chief about last night's riot, as, in the aftermath of the *Real Life* broadcast, a mob of tee-dees looking for Virtix equipment looted over forty electronics outlets—"

Click. The monitors change colors. Giselle Fernandez, with a serious expression on her face.

". . . how fiction meddles with facts. A spokesperson for Senator Powell today stated that his lawyers would be filing a libel suit in New York courts against XTV. For perspective on this, we went to Dr. Giles Bang, a media expert at Columbia University."

The face of a scholarly-looking fellow in a striped cardigan fills the screen.

Gaynor has his jackknife out. Delicately, he reduces a Ticonderoga number two pencil to cat litter.

"First of all, how accurate are the allegations made by *Real Life*?"

Cutaway of fingers on a keyboard, a screen pulling up data.

"Here," Bang says, "is the *New York Post* article on the slaying of the young gang member, Vernon Mitchell, in Ozone Park on July 8, 1969. That was in the show. And here is a list of food stamp recipients, that's from the files of the former Housing and Urban Development Agency in Washington, this has Jessie Powell, who is also listed as Henry Warren Powell's mother, in West Hamilton Beach in 1970."

"Did you check these records yourself?" Giselle asks sharply.

"I have cross-checked about sixteen items so far," Bang replies calmly. "All of them are public record. All of them are accurate."

Gaynor snaps a command and all the screens go dark. He folds his knife and stalks forward into the accommodation, slamming the door behind him. The techie shrugs.

Fishman drops into Gaynor's seat and says something to the techie.

The Green Dragons crowd behind him, arguing in Vietnamese.

One row of screens comes to life. The VDTs, shining on his skin, make Fishman's face look even more unhealthy and dead than it appeared on Water Street. He pokes a button that changes channels, then sighs in contentment.

It's a nature program. A fawn nuzzles the clear surface of a stream. A doe looks up in alarm. Fishman relaxes in his chair. The Asians stalk off angrily. In the background I hear a woman crying. It's not Louise.

There's no way out now, I think desolately. Kaye is going to be killed because of my fuck-ups. I have royally bitched up on my vow to protect her.

My tears, flowing harder, are not entirely caused by the drugs.

Louise leans over with her damp sleeve and wipes them off once more.

Half an hour later the Van-go parks in a big garage. We are shepherded outside and pushed into a van bearing the normal XTV livery.

Ten minutes after that, this Van-go stops, and the engine is switched off. The gangbangers haul our asses off the van and into a small garage with a Vox-operated barrier next to an elevator at one end. A big sign reads "EXECUTIVE and VIP PARKING ONLY: All Others Will Be Towed IMMEDI-ATELY."

The walls are silver and blue. Although I've never been in the VIP parking area, I recognize the decorating motif.

X-Corp.

Four gangbangers drag me and Kaye into the elevator. The Asian techie, Louise, Gaynor, and Fishman follow. The doors sigh shut. Dim piped music and a choir of cybernetic sopranos tinkle "The Twelve Days of Christmas" as the elevator zips upward. After what seems like a half hour, but is probably only forty seconds, the lift stops and the doors open. A blind-ing white-yellow light beams into our eyes.

Gaynor steps out, blinking. Kaye and I are hauled in his wake. I'm getting used to being dragged around. My feet still make reflexive, spastic attempts at locomotion, but to tell the truth it's easier to be shlepped when you don't really want to go where you're going; it avoids moral struggle.

The light comes from floor-to-ceiling windows. They look like aquarium glass being nibbled by billions of tiny, white snow minnows. Then we're walking down a steppe of expen-sive silver-blue carpeting. This office doesn't just dick around with space like Gaynor's; it takes up every inch of the X-Corp tower at this level. Curved lozenges define the sky on all sides. At the far end, foreshortened by distance, a group of people cluster near a brushed-steel desk.

The Asians deposit Kaye and me on a leather couch. I'm still lolling, but Kaye has got back some muscle control. She hunches over her knees, protecting her breasts, for Mrs. Mc-Cotter's housecoat has fallen open. I try not to look at her, because every time I see her face the combination of sweet-ness and fear there makes my nose run in disgusting fashion. She stares with very dark eyes at the knot of people who are the focus of both geography and power in this room. The intensity of her gaze pulls my eyes in the same direction.

A squat man sits in a fancy orthopedic chair behind the gigantic desk as the snow minnows dance against the glass behind him. It's Jack Tyrone. He twirls a crystal flute glass in front of his eyes, looking through it to the windows. His other hand holds the usual Chesterfield.

A Chinese suit and a white-haired Eurasian woman leaf methodically through documents on one end of the desk.

A tall figure stands silhouetted against a window to the left, staring at a TV monitor with color-correction equipment hooked into it.

But it's the man seated to the monitor's other side who really holds my attention, when I can stop drooling long enough to focus.

He's around thirty-five, short, thin, with a narrow nose and eyes ringed like a raccoon's with darkened skin.

"Polletti," I grunt menacingly. It comes out "Pooey," with a little bubble of saliva attached.

Even in my zoned-out state, a few things are getting clearer.

FORTY-FIVE

LOUISE GOES TO the tall man at the window and puts an arm around his waist. He turns. The slight stoop, the Lincolnesque eyebrows, the bony jaw. In the middle of a preelection year, anyone in America would recognize Henry Warren Powell.

A chubby Caucasian stands at Powell's side, talking into a cellphone.

"The damage control is possible," Tyrone says suddenly. "Munn is mentally unstable."

"We're *all* unstable." Louise turns from her companion to address Tyrone. She walks to the couch, her face pulled in a Cordelia expression I've seen before. "It's in the *genes*." She pats my hair. She *knows* I hate this.

The tall man follows her. He stoops over me, examining my face. His own is creased with fatigue, but his eyes are sincere and concerned.

"We have *got* to get going, Senator." The chubby man folds his cellphone.

"I just wanted a look at him," Henry Warren Powell says, peering at me shortsightedly.

"It's in the genes," Louise repeats, as if no one else had

spoken. "We *all* need help, with reality. It's like John Denver says—"

Powell ignores her. He leans forward a little farther. "Can you hear me?" he asks. "Alex?"

I stare at him woozily.

"Jack is going to provide *care* for you, Alex," he continues earnestly. "At the clinic. It's only till the convention."

"I'm putting off the news conference till two," the chubby man interrupts. "I rescheduled a background-only with the *Ollie North* producers at twelve-forty."

Powell waves his hand tiredly. He straightens up, still looking at me, then turns away.

"You think the Secret Service doesn't talk to the press, when it suits 'em?" the chubby man asks of no one in particular, and helps Powell with his coat.

The white-haired woman says, "You can *admit* to confusion on your past. The biggest problem is coincidence in timing. The travel fund dips here, his reelection fund jumps there."

"The straw will not hold?" the Chinese man asks politely.

"He even listed *pages,* in the quarterly reports." She looks at me without expression.

Powell and the chubby man walk back across the steppes to the elevator. Gaynor pulls a box of number two pencils from his jacket.

"He's going to feed us to the wolves," he tells Tyrone, when Powell and his escort have disappeared.

"Not Henry."

"Maybe not. But the PAC-man will."

"Can I take him to the clinic now, Jack?" Louise asks suddenly.

Tyrone gets to his feet. It looks like this party's coming to an end. He walks over to my mother, puts his arms around her shoulders, and kisses her mouth. If my jaw weren't already hanging open, it would drop.

"I'll see ya, Louise," he says, and turns to Polletti. "Detective, why don't you help Mrs. Pastrich downstairs?"

The cop looks at him, then at me.

"We'll settle up when this is over," Tyrone tells him sharply, and turns back to his desk.

"We need to talk about the paperwork," the white-haired

woman says, "we need to deal with this." She lifts her chin toward me and Kaye.

The woman has very clear blue eyes. They are so clear and cold that I pull backward, away from them. That's how I figure out I'm finally regaining some use of my own muscles.

Polletti is still looking at me. There's a familiar expression on his face, and after a beat or two I figure out what it is. It's the look of somebody who has given up so much control, he doesn't have a clue how to get it back.

He shifts his gaze back to Tyrone, and nods doubtfully. He walks after my mother.

Louise is halfway across the rug. She never said good-bye. As I watch her walk, a half head taller than the cop behind her, I realize she's gone from me; was gone for years, kidnapped by a cloud of unreality, and self-obsession, that no pills possibly can rebalance.

What I felt in the TV van comes back to me, tracking on a little from there, as memories do; how many times have I seen her like that, going out the door to a job interview, an audition, a pep rally for another cult?

"He's crying," the white-haired woman remarks in disgust.

"It's the ketamine," the techie tells her, and unhooks the low-spectrum compensator from the workstation.

"I have to call Singapore," the Chinese announces, holding up his cellphone.

"So call," Tyrone sighs.

The blizzard holding the X-Corp tower in its grip relaxes for a second. The cloud tears, rags of vapor stream westward. Manhattan appears below, a complex gray plateau country full of mesas and ridges. Striated by the windblown snow, scarred by ice ditches, torn by the cold plow of the wind, it's a wilderness where only those with rocky hearts and ice-sharp claws can possibly live for long.

Then the blizzard closes in again. The schools of snowfish flock once more to the windows, as if attracted by the light inside.

The cyber-choir starts in on "Hark! The Herald Angels Sing."

Hauled once more.

My muscles may be coming back, but I still can't walk.

The elevator stops at the eighth floor. The techie Vox-es a soundproofed steel door next to the lift. A sign reads "EXPERIMENTAL ENVIRONMENT/RESTRICTED ADMISSION." Kaye and I are hauled through at the procession's head.

I've been in the new VR lab before, but only for brief demos. Ever since Virtix went into production it's been off-limits as R&D—another word for tax write-off.

I look around as much as my flaccid muscles will allow, but it's not that different from what I remember, not so different from the *Real Life* studios, for that matter. It has video-cams and lights set up for scanning, a big blue-screen, the rudiments of a set, banks of Virtix workstations and cables—cables everywhere, both fiber-optic and electrical, writhing like a herpetology exhibit.

The only odd features are a bunch of what looks like diving suits hanging from their own cable snakes in a self-contained workshop area near a rack of clear plastic sacs; and a fully enclosed, octagonal steel tank, maybe fifteen feet high and twenty in diameter, welded to stubby I-beams on the floor.

One quick glance takes all this in.

After that, events move more quickly.

The techie says, "Strip 'em," and walks over to a bank of monitors by the isolation tank.

Two of the Asians kneel me next to a cable bracket and tape my wrists to the metal with gaffer's tape.

Kaye shouts something. I twist to look at her. All four gangbangers cluster around her. One of them pulls off her housecoat. She has nothing on underneath. Two of them hold her, one on each arm as she writhes feebly. Yelling, I pull against the gaffer's tape and fall flat, mashing my nose on the concrete.

The gangbanger who looks like a high school sophomore puts his hand between her legs.

Kaye screams.

My tears are flowing again. My nose is bleeding. It's quite clear to me now that they can't keep witnesses around, and Kaye is going to die. I guess I'm going to get capped as well, but ever since Riker's, part of me has been ready for that. The magnitude of losing Kaye, on the other hand—for me, for every aspect of grace and precision that makes this planet worth living on—is so vast as to be unbearable.

Nothing will be left but black, rotten water.

"I love you!" I scream; it's melodramatic and overblown, and at the same time and given my utter helplessness, it's the only thing I can say that has any relevance. It comes out sounding like Marlon Brando in *Streetcar:* "E-l-l-a-a-o-o-u!"

The techie snaps an order. The gangbanger takes his hand away, licking his finger ostentatiously. They jab her again and drag her to the blue-screen. Weigh her on a scale, switch on lights and cameras, and scan her, front, back, and sides.

Her skin shines like ice in the T-22 exposure.

They dress her in one of the drysuits, pulling the Velcro tight, then lie her like a sack of apples on the edge of the set while they strip me and repeat the same process, *sans* handjob.

I've heard of the Flexator suits but never seen one made up like this. Obviously, it's based on scuba equipment. The material, molded of half-inch octagons, has the characteristic mauve gloss of piezoelectric fabric. Three tiny wires protrude from each patch, then gather in a great multicolored bunch around the back. Tiny bits of metal are molded inside the octagons, they prod my skin like a thousand tiny teeth.

The techie kneels over me. With great precision he inserts an IV, with tube attached, into the exposed patch on my wrist. He uses gaffer's tape to strap that securely into place, then goes to the controls and pecks at a keyboard.

And my body comes to life.

My left leg flexes, gently at first, then painfully—close to spraining point. My right arm snaps to a salute, punching my temple. Something pinches my right kidney hard. Both my legs spring downward, catapulting me up, and forward. I land face first on the concrete again.

The gangbangers crack up. They slap each other, shouting in glee. My nose bleeds more copiously than before. With difficulty, I roll sideways.

Kaye's knee comes up and hits her chin. Both her arms bend. Her eyes are quite black with fright. She looks like the marionette victim in a sadistic Punch and Judy show.

I laugh. I don't know why. The black sump of despair still laps at the pit of me, but Kaye in a diving suit is droll.

As for my earlier worries, they now seem unfounded. Nothing bad or final can happen to a man in this mood.

Kaye is laughing as well. Her mouth does that pretty triple-valley trick. Her limbs are now at rest. The techie continues to work at the controls. He's going to die, I reflect; we're all going to die. None of this technology is any damn use, none of our efforts are worth shit. The sun will nova and the universe drift apart, approaching absolute darkness and cold, and the fact that Kaye and I once, in Donegal Manor, possessed intimacy will make as much difference as one plankton pissing in the Pacific.

The tears dribble down my cheeks. Kaye is sniffling.

The light blue liquid flows slowly down her IV tube.

One after the other, the gangbangers haul Kaye and me up the stairs and onto a platform that overhangs the tank's top.

The techie fits webbed belts laden with weights and bottles around our waists. We are surrounded by men, holding us, adjusting Velcro and gaffer's tape. When they clear a bit I see Gaynor and the Fishman, gazing up at us curiously from floor level.

Gaynor's eyes are cold as ever, but he punches little affect through the chemical hardening in my receptor sites. The sight of Fishman, on the other hand, really cracks the armor, pulling out a worm of revulsion to wriggle around briefly in the glare of kliegs.

"So, you decided?" the techie calls down.

"Get rid of the problem," Gaynor says. "That's all."

"Problem?" the techie repeats contemptuously. "Be accurate, please? This ain't no Thomas à Becket."

"Make 'em *different*," Gaynor says impatiently. "Fucked in the head. If you can't do that, then whack 'em. Long as they can't testify."

"*Jawohl,*" the techie replies coldly, causing me to go off in a rumble of giggles again. "Only thing"—he jerks a thumb at me—"I thought Powell wanted him—"

"You don't work for Powell," Gaynor replies grimly, through a cloud of Chesterfield smoke. "You never did."

"And the—shall we say—vehicle?"

"Catatonic state," Gaynor says. His tone is so indifferent,

so devoid of emotion, that it comes across as pale green, like ice talking. "Aneurism, massive infarction. I leave it up to you." He turns to leave.

"Hey, Gaynor?" I call. It comes out, "Ah Gayno." It's the first time I've talked anywhere near straight in a while. Something the techie fed us must have counteracted the ketamine.

He glances up.

"Wachoo allus sharpenin' pencil fuh," I continue. "Still in third grade? Still tryin' to impress Mommie?"

I crack up at my own joke. Gaynor stares at me for a second.

"Hey, Elex," he replies.

"Wha?" I'm still giggling.

"You wanted to see *Munn's World* produced. Well, you'll be getting your wish—in a manner of speaking. I hope you like it."

He turns away. Fishman lifts his hat in a gesture that has a lot of nineteenth century to it. I think, he's a failed actor, too —or maybe it's just Spetsnaz training, the *desinformatsiya* Zeng talked about. The unicorn flyers, the black coat, the loudspeakered footsteps, all part of a way-off-Broadway production to scare Munn the way you wanted him to go. And Munn, being a not-too-swift, highly neurotic asshole, obediently trotted down the appointed path.

They leave through the same door we came in. Gaynor's gait is fast and clipped against the concrete.

Fishman's footsteps pause in their rhythm, making the "slip-*slap*" sound, but very gently, until they're swallowed in the ringing iron clang of the door.

There's a hatch in the top of the isolation tank, which the gangbangers now unscrew. Underneath, a steel hydraulic arm sticks out of a dark and complex resonance. They lower a large helmet over Kaye's head, and zip it to the drysuit collar. It's a diving helmet, wired for sound. A Pop Optix full 3-D viewscreen is fitted inside the faceplate.

Kaye panics for a second. The Asians hold her tight. Slowly, she relaxes.

The techie gathers up the slack in her suit wires and air hoses. He hooks them to the end of the hydraulic arm, then stands back and jabs a finger downward. With an overdue gentleness the gangbangers guide her to the hatch and push her off the top of the tank so she's hanging, twisting slowly, from the steel arm.

Kaye's helmet peers round for a second, hesitant like a blind animal.

The techie moves a lever forward. An engine whirs. She sinks slowly into the darkness.

I don't feel so good now. Seeing Kaye disappear into the water counters the happy chemicals. Something down there is going to hurt her so badly that her mind, or her body, will shut down rather than put up with it.

Then the techie drops a helmet over my head, and I see nothing whatsoever anymore.

Meekly I follow the hands that lead me to the edge of the hatch. It's okay with me; I want to be where Kaye is.

I let go of the hands and hang for a second, suspended by the hydraulic arm. Then I start to drop.

The downward motion is smooth. The Flexator material is so thin I can feel the body-temperature water on the other side.

The ride lasts half a minute. Finally I touch something rubbery, bumpy on the tank floor.

And stand, legs spread to hold my balance in a place with no up or down or sides to ward off the unknown.

For a long time nothing happens. Nothing happens, in a big way. I see absolutely nothing. I hear nada. Except for the soles of my feet on the ''floor'' I feel nothing, for there's no difference in temperature between the liquid and me. Nothing exists in all directions, and through the dregs of the happy drugs, the snake of terror squirms once more.

For nothing is the place all monsters live; and my own particular monsters always come from a nothing made of black, stagnant water such as this.

Out of the nothing, something touches my arm. It feels up and down its length. The something has thick fingers that strongly grip my gloved thumb.

Kaye.

One thing exists.

Then, the nightmare begins.

FORTY-SIX

It begins as something, the way all primary consciousness must; a thing undefined, except that it's different from Kaye's hand; a not-Kaye's-hand, slow, growing out of perfect darkness into a dim yellowish glow.

Square outline surrounding the glow. Chimney pots.

Housefronts.

Black movement of animals, a distant thud of hooves on snow as a cart draws across an intersection. Dim white dots float groundward, then sideways as the wind kicks in.

Munn's World.

It's like being born; like coming out of the uterus straight into a city street. Only not as warm as birth. In fact, suddenly it's goddam freezing. The icicles I saw last time have multiplied; ice and frozen snow cover every facet of architecture. Kaye's hand trembles in mine. I glance where my hand leads.

She is stark naked. Naked in a frozen winter. Of course, I think, she was scanned that way, which means I'm birthday-suited, too. The Story Engine, aware of our lack of clothes, feeds back those parameters to the Flexator, which cools our skin.

Even at that point, even in these straits, I can find time to appreciate the clean lines of her body, the way her ass mirrors the curve of a racing hull, how her neck arches fine like the bow of a clipper. Her nipples are blue and erect.

"Munn," she says. The audio is awesome; her voice is built of awe and apprehension; her lips move stiffly, though this may stem from the lack of facial sensors in our masks.

For a second or two there I'm set to answer. Then something else happens. It, too, only registers as "something," because it doesn't occur anyplace I can see or hear; it's like a prickling of skin, a ruffling of body-grass by a psychic wind.

New drugs are on their way.

I can sense the happy drugs ebb, and my intelligence with them. From a certain perverse curiosity, my mood dives like someone hooked it to a down-stroking piston.

I feel, at first, tremendously depressed. And then my heart begins to beat wildly. A gigantic sensation of terror floods me. My muscles start to shake so hard I have trouble keeping hold of Kaye's fingers.

Briefly, I'm conscious enough of the other reality to wonder what chemical cocktail they pumped into us, methamphetamines, mescaline, PCP, scopolamine maybe—

And then I'm screaming at Kaye: *"Run!"* Taking off full tilt down the street, for no reason other than the massive synthetic urge that's telling my brain it's gonna blow up if it doesn't move.

It's not so easy to run. Most VR treadmills are made of many small spheres under a movable, sensitized envelope.

This one, obviously, can be programmed to reflect conditions of terrain—and the conditions currently suck. We slip and slide on "ice," the balls jerk over "ruts" in the snow. The "air" around us is thick and liquid, slowing our movements, buoying us at odd intervals.

I lose Kaye's hand, find it again.

"Wait!" Kaye gasps.

My feet are numb with cold, which doesn't help, footing-wise.

"Stop! Please."

The terror in her voice gets through. I skid in the snow, stopping.

Kaye is bent over, compressing her diaphragm to make the breathing easier. I look around us. The snow has thickened, the white flakes coming in heavy clouds. Despite the snow I can see better; I suppose my eyes are adjusting to the night.

A trio of pigs roots and snorts at something at the foot of a snowdrift. Above them, the tall windows of a brownstone townhouse shine from the myriad tapers inside. Faint plinks of music press through the glass. A Christmas tree covered with German ornaments and candles makes its own shine in the corner. A girl in taffeta so heavy it looks like she's suspended in pink clouds sits at a fortepiano, playing *"Stück im Volk-ston."*

One of the pigs gets a good hold of its dinner and drags most of a horse's head from the drift. A couple of large dogs materialize casually out of the falling snow and stand, very still, their snouts pointing at the dead horse, white powder piling on their fur.

Kaye yanks at my hand. I yank back, making her stumble. Despite the drugs pounding at my heart, despite my overwhelming need to move, I can't stop staring at the dogs.

Have you ever walked into your house and realized that a thief has entered in your absence? Ever heard your lover tell a fib out of the blue, something inconsequential, except that the fact it's told at all indicates a greater betrayal?

That's a Milquetoast approximation of the feeling I get now.

I mean, I know things are terminally screwed up in the "real" world. But this is *Munn's World,* a place I built from the ground up, character by character, detail by period detail; and despite Gaynor's remark I never seriously believed he could have altered it, in all its sweet complexity, in the time he had.

And yet something is very wrong here.

Because those are not dogs.

Those are *wolves.*

I pull Kaye slowly until we're both edging away from the tinkle of fortepiano.

A third wolf lopes down the street. There's nothing doglike about the way it moves. It seems to flow, graceful, languid. It doesn't look at the frozen horse or the pigs. It stares at us, ears perked. Light from a deep glow in the sky echoes the yellow in its eyes.

The last wolf in New York City was shot in the seventeenth

century. There are no wolves in the World Generator. It's conceivable, barely, that a pack roamed down from Quebec, crossing the frozen river to the north . . .

But the drugs don't have patience for this kind of speculation. Kaye has speeded up, she's moving faster than I am ("catatonic state . . ." I hear Gaynor's voice—"massive infarction . . ."). I galumph beside her, because what's surging through our bloodstream hurts us the slower we go, the only relief lies in increments of speed and the only way we can attain speed is by kicking that treadmill as fast as possible.

I skid left, into a tight road that might be Oak Street. Ahead of us, to one side, clouds of whitish sparks reel into the sky, then recede into the turning wheel of darkness and wind. Something big is burning down there. When the sparks jump, they thicken the falling snow around us, injecting a million shadows behind the piled billboards, the glued posters, the porches of brick and wood lining this street.

"FIGHTING FOR THE RIGHTS OF TRUE AMERICANS," one poster reads. "ISAIAH RYNDERS FOR FOURTH WARD ALDERMAN."

What's burning is the next street. To our right, behind a wooden stable, a building crumbles. A cloud of sparks far more spectacular than what came previously shoots out of a brick wall. Then flame pukes greedily out of the windows across an alley, to lick at a house on this street, three buildings down.

A gaggle of children pelts out of the house, harassed by adults. Leaving the door open, they drag out wooden boxes, then stand arguing in the snow.

Two figures show at the far eastern end of the street, moving in our direction. Their dark jackets and hats, their black drainpipe trousers, stand out clearly against the gray drifts.

One of them, spotting us, exclaims loudly.

This one I can figure out. The Daybreak gang, at least, makes sense in this world. They may be deadly, but they belong here.

I look behind me.

The three wolves stand, very still, at the western entrance to the street. Watching us.

"Shit," I tell Kaye, "come on," and run toward the open door of the newly abandoned house.

"My toes," Kaye complains, but she moves eagerly. Her feet trip, her hands wring each other. This is easy for me, because I made this world; but I realize that, to her, it must be a nightmare of alienation and distress. My heart still races at the same unnatural speed as before. I wonder how long our cardiac tissue can sustain this.

The gangbangers see us run, white skin against the dark city. They advance to block us against the left-hand buildings —then stop, mouths open. They're young, sixteen at the most, they can't quite believe we have no clothes on. One of them stares at Kaye with lust plain in his face. As we climb the wooden porch the other sticks his fingers in his mouth and whistles.

A few seconds into the house and the temperature shifts upward forty degrees. I realize we're in a cigar-maker's shop. Sheets of pressed tobacco hang in wooden tubs full of rum, molasses, and brine. The floor is rough with leaf trimmings, which roaches, fleeing the fire, hurdle like Bruce Jenner. Treadle-operated cutting machines display long, gleaming blades. Sponges lie nearby in bowls of rum for cleanup.

I point toward the back room. The alley behind can't be blocked as yet. Kaye opens the door and stops, confused.

The room is full of tobacco.

I glance behind me; a half-dozen Daybreakers now stand among the cigar-maker's apprentices in the street. Putting my hand in the small of her back I shove her rudely through the door. The tobacco isn't solid; the weight of her body pushes aside a series of racks on which hang, doubled-over, sheets of cured leaves.

The tobacco is sticky and rough with tar. A low, cracking noise runs like a bad soundtrack under the room. It smells of cigarettes and booze in here, like a crowded saloon. The tobacco and rum stockpiled upstairs are on fire.

Kaye hesitates, and I push past her into the back room, scratching my shoulder on the Virginia leaf.

"Come on," I hiss urgently, turning. "Kaye—"

She's plastered, rigid, to the jamb of the door, staring back through the workshop junk at the animal that has padded in from the night.

Its paws are the size of small dinner plates. Its eyes are beautiful, almond-shaped, pale yellow. Its fur is silver and fine, except for a weird, crawly rash like a patch of vagueness that runs, repetitive, up and down the animal's flank.

The hairs on my neck crackle with dread.

A sound comes, so low-frequency it seems to resonate from everywhere. For a second I don't recognize it as the deep, considered growl of a predator eyeing the prey toward whose throat it's about to leap.

I haul Kaye backward and shove the door to. My hand actually *touches* the wood, imparting thrust, as the animal crouches on its hind legs. The door slams, and then shudders violently from the impact of the wolf's body.

A howl rises, inexpressibly alien, unbearably loud, from the other room.

We shoulder bodily through the tobacco sheets to the back door. When we open the door, the front of my body begins to bake. The crackling sound I heard earlier is all around us.

The alley has been invaded by fire. Pieces of building and charred wood patter into the snow. A mule, crazed with fear, pulls insanely at its tether, its neck rubbed bloody by the rope. Water hisses.

I think, They must have set loose the Random Motor, given it eighty or ninety percent input, more even than I wanted. For I never planned this fire, or the wolves, or anything remotely like them.

This time it's Kaye who moves first. Whatever shock she was in has dissipated. She pulls me sideways, along a porch. To our left, a man hangs, shouting, from a burning ridgepole until it collapses under him and he vanishes with a scream into the well of flames.

The alley is cut and obstructed by wooden palings and lean-to stables. With real agility Kaye dodges and climbs ahead of me. Touch and sight are oddly polarized; extreme light from the flaming buildings lies sandwiched against jet-black shadows; the fires' huge heat, falling across our naked shoulders, provokes almost the same numbness as the melted ice we splash through.

The noise increases. Kaye stops. A tangle of collapsed and smoking joists has blocked the way we are going. The air is filled with terrified snorts and whinnies; most of these yards contain pigs, horses, and other animals, all trapped now by the advancing conflagration.

I look left, then right. My vision is slow, it feels like the scene takes a microsecond to catch up, it blurs briefly, then focuses. The shift, I think, the Random Motor again; and I remember the compression scale I saw crawling around the wolf's fur.

Now every house in the alley is afire. Pieces of beam hang, then fall in a storm of sparks, cutting off long tracts of livable room. The smoke, coiling in thick banks, sets us to coughing painfully.

I grope for Kaye's hand, wishing fiercely I could live, wishing Kaye could survive. But there's nothing I can do anymore, not when *Munn's World* has turned so sick and vicious—not when the city itself is trying to wipe us out.

A couple of beams let go in the retaining wall of a three-story stone house twenty feet up the alley.

The wall falls outward, imperceptibly at first, then accelerating, smashing into the poor fences and palings and mud. We crouch to avoid chunks of flaming debris.

When we can stand safely, we find the smashed facade has opened a crater under its mangled beams.

Looking closer, I notice the hole actually is formed by the stoved-in roof of a tunnel whose shaft is made of open barrels buried end to end. Four or five inches of fetid water flow listlessly between the exposed vaults. I realize this was indeed Oak Street; here is the stream that used to drain the marshes on either side. They covered it over, but still it flows, patiently, only four feet below the surface of the alley.

Kaye scrambles into the crater. Without comment I follow. I have little interest in grappling with a story this nasty, but I find I'm still dedicated to keeping Kaye alive in the midst of it.

We crawl down the tunnel. Four feet overhead the whole goddam neighborhood is aflame, but here the darkness is cool and complete. Our knees slip in refuse and the ancient staves slime our backs and elbows. Angry squeaks signal the disapproval of the tunnel's usual tenants. The water is freezing and soon my knees are as numb as my hands. The tunnel stinks. I guess they rigged an odor synthesizer to the World system, and the thing is going balls-to-the-wall on the shit-and-rot command.

All in all, though, it beats being barbecued to death in a haptic oven. Eventually we see the round indigo of the tunnel outlet. We come out in a small ravine that runs through the center of an alley not unlike the one we just left.

I peer around. Piles of old hides and diverse refuse rise high around us. The stench here, amazingly, is worse than in the tunnel. Tall brick buildings on each side. Kaye scrambles up the sides of the ravine and darts through an opening between two of the buildings. I follow.

Catherine Street. This was all tanneries until late in the nineteenth century. I think, This is one sick and depressing drag. Then again, everything seems sick and depressing right now, I can almost taste the hopelessness in me; it sits like a black toad in my stomach and consumes all need for movement.

Now, for the first time, I realize they can program Kaye's IV to carry a different drug cocktail than mine. Because Kaye isn't acting hopeless, she's half crazy with terror; and terror implies a continuing attachment to life. She presses her back theatrically against the loading dock of the nearest tannery, her face stretched by the depth of her panic. Then she jumps into the center of the street, waving urgently at me.

I jog exhaustedly after her. A sharp pain spears suddenly down my left side. We're heading east now, toward Catherine Market. Behind and southward, pillars of fire have blossomed out of the inferno on Oak Street.

The street grows darker as it descends toward the south piers. It's too cold even for the hustlers. A man selling hot chestnuts stares as we limp by. I grab Kaye's hand, mostly for balance, and just then she stops so suddenly that I bump into her cold ass.

The road is blocked. In the shadows a crowd of men and women stand silently between a capsized cart and a timber dray. Some of the men wear the black drainpipes and low hats of Daybreakers; here and there, I spot a sailor's peacoat. Most of the crowd, though, wears the cheap patched clothing of the poor.

In the middle of the crowd, a child wails piteously.

I watch Kaye's face. Her eyes are mostly white. Her left

hand grabs her chest, under the left nipple. Her mouth hangs open as she pants. Perhaps there are lip sensors in there, after all.

The child screams again. The scream is not terror, but something far worse: utter agony, and the incomprehension that goes with it. I put my hands over my ears, just as Kaye whirls abruptly and plunges into the crowd. The spectators, amazed at her nakedness, part before her like the Red Sea before Charlton Heston.

I follow. I don't know what else to do.

As I move toward the front of the mob I pass more and more Daybreakers. Here and there people stand in odd poses, giggling or engaged in loony dialectic, dressed in torn white smocks.

A harsh, high voice carries, like an incantation, words whose tone is familiar.

"Less than human—spawn of Hibernian *dogs*! Slaughter them, every last one, yea, even to the women and *children,* that the sons of *America* may survive and prosper!"

Whatever brew is being slipped into my veins now must be full of bad speed. My jaw works and my veins pop. The pain in my chest is like red-hot wire. I can feel every millimeter of skin where fire baked the epidermal tissue. I draw level with Kaye as she reaches the hub of the crowd.

A half-dozen Daybreakers are tearing a child to pieces.

The kid is dressed in rags. He made a pathetic attempt at greasing his hair into a Bowery Bhoy's fancy-ass soap locks, and I suppose that was his undoing; this is not Bhoy territory. A woman leans over him screaming, "Thief, *yarrr*!" Three adults sit on his chest while another four pull savagely at his left arm.

The right sleeve of his jacket is torn off, and dark liquid spurts from the shoulder onto the cobblestones.

To one side a loony licks at the dangling arteries of what appears to be an oversize white chicken wing with a small hand attached.

Even through the savage speed the kid's agony does something weird to my stomach.

But Kaye—Kaye goes nuts. She leaps like a Fury into the group of men. The audience mutters. I skitter after her; with all my muscles shaking violently from cold and speed and nausea, skittering is the best I can manage.

The kid-rippers turn from the boy. Without pausing to think, they tackle Kaye. They may be surprised by her lack of clothes, but they're not the kind of guys to be long slowed by speculation over it. This is a puzzle they can handle.

They flip Kaye to the ground. Two of them pin her shoulders, and two grab her ankles and yank her legs open. "Get *off*! Leave me *alone,* you *fuckers*!" she shrieks. The other three spot me skittering; they tackle me fast, bringing me down hard on my back in the boy's blood.

Men laugh and howl encouragement. The skull-like face of the Angel Gabriel bounces up and down. "*Ravage* the mick slattern!" he howls. Only one fellow cries out in protest. His hoarse screams come at exactly the same time as I empty my lungs. Made strong by anger, I struggle to my hands and knees, with two toughs clamped on my back. A woman kneels in front of me between the cannibal loony and a Black Ball Line bosun. She is slim, dressed in overlapping frocks of worn calico over lace-up boots. She has deep black hair and eyes that catch the glow of fire.

It's the woman from Bayard Street.

She holds a hawthorn cane in one hand, and shoves it in my direction.

"I *told* you," she whispers harshly, "the *Unicorn* is in port," and puts the stick into my hand. I can feel its varnished smoothness, and a round button set in the hard wood.

"Use it!" she commands, and vanishes into the crowd.

With difficulty, for my attackers' hands dig deeply into my well-done shoulders, I bring my other hand over, and work the catch. The drugs help; I move three times quicker than normal, or maybe it's that everything else is moving slower, because of the high percentage of random input in this whacked-out scenario. Anyway, the cane starts to separate in two. I drop one shoulder, unbalancing my attackers, then pull it completely apart. I find myself holding a very long, narrow blade, worked with gold filigree and indented along its length by a blood-gutter.

Rolling all the way over on my back, I poke the tip deliberately into the shoulder of one of my attackers. He shouts, grabs the wound. Both men pull back, leaving my blade free again.

I roll to my feet and advance on the men holding Kaye. One of them shouts a warning. A second whirls, pulling out a long knife, but my blade is longer than his and I poke him easily in the forearm.

Then I turn and run the blade halfway through the gut of the man fumbling at his belt, with one knee between Kaye's legs, an expression of indecision still on his face.

I pull the blade out and stare at the tip, which drips dark liquid onto the snow. My stomach burbles and swells.

The other men fall back, eyeing my sword. Kaye lies in the slush, her eyes closed, arms wrapped tight around her drawn-up knees.

The kid beside her has stopped shaking. He can't be over eight years old.

I reach down, grab one of Kaye's hands, and pull her up-right.

The crowd behind me has gone quiet.

I turn fast, blade at the ready, and gaze straight into the eyes of the Fishman.

Close up, he's not as tall as I remembered; but that doesn't matter. Some feral quality, a constant readiness, creates a ring of power around him. His long black Chesterfield sweeps around a pair of fancy soft-leather riding boots. His collar is swept up, and the brim of his short top hat tilts down. The paleness of skin and a hint of teeth shine in the shadow between hat and collar, but what slams my throat shut over my breath is his eyes.

They shine soft green, powered by the gallium arsenide photo-cathode built into all Spetsnaz night goggles.

"Drac," I whisper, "you fuckin' son of a bitch. You scanned *yourself* in!" And the anger, that someone would fuck with my program like that—transplant a device from 150 years in the future into this city, this time—burns my gut worse than the fire did.

A sound comes out of him, a slow hiss like a snake's. His hands emerge from the folds of his coat. A man shouts, "Aye, Fishman!" A woman screams, "Carve him *up*!" The mob steps back to give him room for butchery.

He's wearing dark gauntlets. The right hand now holds a thin knife with a honed edge and no hand guard.

With no hesitation, he wings the knife in my direction. It flips end over end, coming straight at my throat, but in the same syrupy time spectrum as before—so that even in the slush and float of this environment, I dodge it easily. I look back after the spent shiv, starting to smile.

He almost gets me.

Despite the slow shift, he almost gets me.

He whips a *second* knife from his belt and dives almost horizontally, aiming the blade at my midriff.

The first inkling I get, he's in midair, a huge black bird tipped with steel, and if Kaye didn't hook a leg into his boots, unbalancing him, the lunge would sock that thin sharp blade all the way into my naked back, and Fujitsu-Cray only knows what the haptic suit could do with input like *that*.

As it is, he falls short. Pain like a thread of flame arcs across my right buttock.

Kaye scrambles to her feet. The Fishman lies winded by his fall. I slash the sword cane at the crowd. They fall back, muttering, griping, pulling the Fishman with them, out of reach of my blade.

Once more, we turn and run.

We run toward the water. I don't think this is a coincidence; the instinct to seek harbor is too basic in me for that. The whole time I was sparring with Fishman, my brain kept track of where east stood, where the docks lay.

I've lost touch with my feet. They thud like dead meat on the packed slush, the frozen garbage. Both Kaye and I stumble frequently. When I glance behind I see the black mass of crowd following, filling Catherine Street. The growing conflagration behind them beats light on their ragged shoulders. They move slowly, deliberately, as if they knew something I didn't.

It turns out, they do.

This street, like all streets in the port area, grows dense with parked wagons and piled barrels as you get nearer the docks.

There's something else down there, too; South Street is supposed to be the main waterfront road, but it's shut on each side by heaps of rocks and massive pilings.

Some of the pilings are already in place, stuck upright thirty feet into the harbor mud, measuring out the squares of water someone is about to fill with garbage and rock to create dry land.

We run like lemmings to the pier's edge. The blackbird, still anchored at the foot of Roosevelt Street, fades in and out of view as the wind rises and falls. A schooner loaded with pilings lies at the edge of the old docks. Now that I can see over the bulkhead, I notice ice has frozen the schooner in place; its solid white surface extends past the docks. A couple hundred feet out, it breaks up into dark channels and floes, then abruptly falls off into snow and dark free water.

I turn around, hoping against hope that the crowd will have stopped or dissipated, but it's twenty yards away now, filling up the entire gap between the barricades.

No time to climb, no way to swim.

I look at Kaye. She's hopping up and down. Her fists are clenched. She's panting so fast and hard she can barely get the words out.

"We got—to g-g-go!"

"There's no p-p-point!"

"I know. But we—c-c-can do it—ourselves. We can g-go —in our own way!"

Already Kaye is balanced on the icy tarred timber that marks the rim of the dock. I turn around and face the crowd.

They are ten feet away now. Fishman walks in the center. His face once more is steeped in shadow. The others stop when he stops.

He lifts one hand, his knife pointed at me in a gesture that smacks of religion and other blocked forces.

As I watch his hand it hits me again that a strong current will never turn to poison; what grows septic, in landscapes as in people, is stagnant liquid, blocked swamps, dammed rivers.

But the harbor will continue, on each side, underground, and the pus people make, the abscess they create, will be washed eventually to the salt and fragrant ocean.

I turn back to the harbor, and jump.

Beneath my feet, the treadmill vanishes.

For the better part of a second only the snowflakes, falling beside me, seem stationary.

FORTY-SEVEN

I PASS KAYE on the way down.

She's hanging on to a ladder, halfway between the top of the bulkhead and the harbor ice.

Ah yes, the ice. In my freaked-out ravings I'd forgotten that little detail. Its white flatness rushes up at me. Despite the cushion of snow it's hard as concrete. When I hit, it scrunches me up like a pathetic rag dummy. My forehead bounces a little, my left elbow gets a nasty little reminder of the ARP robot; but what takes the brunt of the fall is my left leg, which folds under my body and snaps with the brittle ease of a stick of linguine.

The agony is amazing. It's so far up the sensation scale that I can feel myself crossing the border of unconsciousness. I scream, loud and stupid. Kaye bends over me, yelling. Blood washes warmly where bone has broken through the skin. I roll over to get my leg out, and this hurts so much that for a while I think I *do* pass out.

When I open my eyes and catch a breath between screams, however, the scene hasn't changed much. Kaye still crouches, shivering and gasping, beside me. The black mass of crowd has stopped at the bulkhead above us. I can hear the Angel Gabriel's voice skirling wildly above the keen of wind.

The black pocket clipper seems a little closer than earlier.

The blackbird carries no lights. Even its figurehead is ebony; from this perspective I can clearly see the tusk of the rearing unicorn fixed under its bowsprit.

The wind increases, spraying us with particles of sea ice.

Kaye hunches over, wrapping her arms around herself to keep from shaking to pieces. Her dreadlock braids are frozen. Her skin is so blue with cold that some of the pain I feel seems to go out to her, in empathy; in remorse for causing her to die like this, freezing and afraid.

She stiffens her neck. I crane my own head around slightly to look where she's looking—back toward the docks.

Fishman.

Of course.

He is blackness against the dark structure of piers and bulkheads. He takes a couple of steps onto the ice, and waits. It's clear that he has all the time in the world. I lost the sword cane in the tumble, and anyway I can't fence with a broken leg. The snow, falling hard, outlines the dark shape of his shoulders. It limns the giant pilings, the barnacles and seaweed under the piers, as well as something soft, half-eaten, hung by its long black scarf on a timber.

Around the corpse, darkness shifts.

A dark shape the size of a small cat runs onto the ice, and pauses. It sits on its haunches and sniffs around; it's joined by another shape, and three more. For a minute Kaye and I and the rats watch each other in the sigh of wind and the hush of falling snow.

Then the rats—and the Fishman—start to move.

The animals don't rush us; they reconnoiter and circle, positions clear against the snow. Kaye groans, grabs me around the waist, and slides me across the ice, toward the edge of water. My leg bone grates every time she pushes. "I'm sorry—M-M-Munn," she gasps as she pushes, "I'm sorry."

She's going to shove us both into the freezing water.

I want to tell her I agree, that in fact I welcome such a finish because the horror in this world I created is so deep as to make death seem a warm and peaceful destination. But my teeth are clamped over my lips to keep the moaning low.

The waves of the East River lap close now. I can sense the snow build against my shoulders as she pushes me, and just once before the end, I let myself admire the power of this world, that it allows a detail as small as this to show.

Kaye's face is calm and pure above me. The last time I saw her from this angle was when we were making love. Her breath comes harshly. Whenever she takes a breather she clutches her left side with her right hand. I put a hand on her wrist for comfort. I don't feel so bad anymore, and at first I think the music is a signal of this change in mood, a tiny side hallucination that foretells peace.

But the strings and voices grow clearer. Kaye hesitates, then stops. Chest heaving furiously, she gazes over me across the river.

Behind her, the Fishman looms taller against the snowbound city.

The pain in my chest spasms again, numbing my left arm. Despite this, I move my shoulders, trying to look around. The shift in weight sets the ice cracking sharply. Suddenly the cold surface rocks, settles. Freezing water runs under my ass, turning the snow to slush.

But I can see across the river now. A scow is moored beside the pier of the Brookland ferry. It shines with torches and lanterns. Tiny figures seated under a canopy move in a rhythm that matches, after a microsecond delay, the music reaching us. A soprano voice rises, clear and delicate as a tendril of lily; it seems to clutch at my exhausted pericardium, bringing it warmth.

> *"And in despair, I bowed my head;*
> *'There is no peace on earth,' I said,*
> *'For hate is strong, and mocks the song,*
> *of peace on earth, goodwill to men.'"*

I lay my head back in the snow, watching a rat the size of a woodchuck lope to within an inch of the place where my tibia pokes wetly through the calf muscle. It has long, greenish fangs. I listen more closely to the music. I feel the heat of a fireplace, the smell of the Christmas tree, the soft caress of pajamas as we came downstairs and saw the presents for the first time . . .

The Fishman is only twenty feet away.

Kaye looks down. There's nothing left to do.

The rat peers around, whiskers twitching in agitation.

Suddenly it turns and hops across the black crack of water that now separates our floe from the island of ice surrounding Manhattan. The floe rocks again.

The vision of Christmas breaks up and vanishes as suddenly as it came.

But the gap is steadily widening—the river has removed our floe from the main body of ice.

The Fishman takes three fast steps, then comes to a halt.

He takes off his stovepipe hat and bows, ironically, across the six feet of water now separating us. His Chesterfield flaps like black wings in the wind.

He watches us as we drift away, a dark figure against the shining blizzard, growing shorter with every minute that passes.

The wind has veered northerly. The tide ebbs steadily toward the Narrows. The lights of the city fade with the rhythm of wind and snow and music.

Fishman's silhouette is swallowed by the complex shadow of Manhattan, the fractal scrim of blizzard. I can see the sparks and bulk of the Fulton ferry churning across the river, but already we've drifted so far south that they'll never spot us, amid the snow.

I realize we're going to drift right past Governor's Island and out to sea, and that's fine with me. I feel less and less pain or regret and I assume this trend will continue until I simply feel nothing.

The floe rocks, the wind lullabies our ears. The waves wash the windward side of this piece of ice, building a short revetment of rime.

I clutch at Kaye's wrist. She doesn't look at me; her head is poised to seaward. A sound happens, different from wind or ice, but familiar enough that I know I heard it a few seconds ago, though I did not pick up on it then.

Wood creaking against wood, a plash of water. She murmurs something I don't catch.

"Loom starboard oars," a voice commands loudly from

out of nowhere. I jump, and my broken limb seizes up again. A white boat surges out of the night beside our floe. Men in rough jackets and flat hats help Kaye swiftly aboard.

Then they haul me into the whaleboat. They are strong and sympathetic, but they can't keep my leg from bending over the gunwale, and this time I have no doubt at all about my losing consciousness.

When next I become aware of my surroundings I'm propped against a thwart while the sailors rhythmically pull the boat through the blizzard toward the accommodation lights of an anchored ship.

It's a barkentine, as white as the *Unicorn* was black. The upperworks shine with ice and varnish, the frozen rigging is caked with snow, the white-painted hull is hung with frozen seawater. It's very hard to see against the snow.

The officer in charge of the whaleboat steers us beside a sloping gangway. Kaye, wrapped in a jacket now, watches from the entry port as the men lift me across the snowy deck to a doorway spilling light from under the poop.

The passageways of this ship are of deep varnished wood hung with golden instruments. I am carried to a cabin in the ship's stern. Brass lamps hang on gimbals, brass clocks tick on the forward bulkhead. A large bed is built into another bulkhead. A porcelain stove painted with green and yellow flowers pumps heat around the cabin.

Through a porthole, the lantern on top of Trinity Church shines through the salvos of blizzard.

They lay me in the bed and cover me with quilts. My leg aches savagely. My toes and fingers, just starting to thaw, shoot long blue spears of pain toward my abdomen. The hot wire in my chest has cooled some, but it glows enough to hurt.

And yet, incredibly, I feel pretty good.

I look at Kaye, who stands, first on one foot, then on the other to spread the agony of defrosting toes. Someone knocks and she says, "Yes?"

The door opens, and Zeng walks in.

He carries a tray with a crystal decanter full of clear liquor.

He crosses to a chart table and pours the cocktail into crystal glasses. He's dressed in steward's whites; his ponytail is oiled and tied with tarry twine. His face is so familiar, so normal, that it immediately breaks up the memory of my last view of him, gagged and twisted and rigid in the terror of his dying.

And I realize, none of this surprises me in the least.

"I figured it out, Wildman," he says as he bends over the glasses. "I figured out a lot of things since you've been in jail."

"Who is he?" Kaye whispers.

"Stefan," I whisper back. "Shhh."

"Like, Polletti is crooked. Like, they're planning to use *Munn's World* on you, with the VR-lab stuff—so I changed the ending around, just in case."

He stirs the liquid with a silver stick.

"What you're feeling now is Ecstasy, 'stead of the scopolamine and methamphetamine compound they programmed with the rats. They put coke in there, too, and thorazine? Crazy mixture.

"And now"—he sets the glasses on the chart table and bows, ironically, much as Fishman did—"this program will automatically fax my cousin. Fuzz should be around in twenty minutes.

" 'Case you're wondering," he adds, "the action is looping 'round on their control screens—far as they're concerned, you're still being chewed on by furry critters."

"But you're dead!" I burst out. It's a stupid comment, but stupid is the way I feel, along with helpless, naive, inarticulate, and physically fucked-up.

"Shit, Wildman, I'm not dead," Zeng answers. He smiles that old, slow smile of his, so that under the mellow satisfaction of the Ecs', part of my heart slowly breaks off and shatters.

"Anyway, even if I was, I put in a real deep life-box for my character here." He takes a sip from one of the glasses and lifts his eyebrows approvingly. "Immortality, man."

I look at him in awe. I realize Zeng, like Gaynor's techie, broke my number-one rule in programming *Munn's World*: he included a character who has knowledge of both the past and the present, making himself, in the context of the story, a god.

There are not supposed to be any gods in *Munn's World*. Still, I can forgive Stefan, given the circumstances.

"You put in a Blair algorithm?"

"Tension-default," Zeng agrees. "I cued the music to the ice. Did it scare you?"

"It scared us," I admit. "It was *s'posed* to scare us to death."

Kaye, still huddled in the sailor's jacket, sits on the side of the bed.

"Was he always in here?" she asks.

"He scanned himself in," I tell her, "put himself in the story." I add, "We found the hacking program."

Zeng nods. I'm not sure if the Vox got that. Then I remember something else. I try to sit up. It's pretty painful, despite the Ecs', and I lie back down again.

I'm feeling tired, more tired than Hercules after his labors, more exhausted than Robert Falcon Scott at the tail end of his polar tourism.

"Only one problem, Zeng," I tell him, trying to enunciate well so the Vox picks it up. "You can't be here. The first Chinese didn't get to New York till 1858."

"Ah Ken," Zeng agrees. "But what was his job?"

"He was a steward," I reply softly, "on a ship."

"So he visited New York before he settled down. Okay?"

"Okay," I whisper.

I close my eyes. Against my eyelids patterns swirl, different colors. One of those colors is sadness, because although he's real enough in this program, my friend Zeng will never really talk to me the way he appears to talk to me now.

And another of those colors, a thin green, is a logical excitement, for if he did put a deep enough life-box in *Munn's World*—if enough of the details and complexities of his history were downloaded into the Story Engine—then in a real sense what he says is true, and he will always be here, iterating and active, changing the program he lives in just as he affected me, and the people of our city, in minute but measurable ways while he was alive.

Most of the warm colors, though, have to do with Kaye. She lies down beside me in the bunk. We hold hands, our shoulders and thighs touching.

My leg continues to bleed and I wonder if I'm going to hemorrhage to death, lying like this.

The issue seems of little importance.

A tune rises against the whisper of snow outside. A sailor is singing on deck. The song is the theme of *Munn's World:*

> *"And where will you go now, my love,*
> *Oh, where will you go now?*
> *I'll set my foot in yonder ship*
> *and I'll sail across the sea."*

The barkentine rolls gentle and slow against the little rip that always surfaces on the ebb at the southern tip of Manhattan island, near the Battery.

FORTY-EIGHT

TIME SHIFTS. SO does space.

I wake up to movement and darkness. The pain in my leg is as violent as it ever was. I don't know if I'm upside down or sideways. My breath stinks of conflicted chemicals.

The darkness is absolute. I feel no temperature, just a vague resistance of atmosphere. I'm aware of a certainty; this, at last, is death.

I vomit helplessly, and choke. When the helmet is ripped off a wash of half-digested TV dinner splats onto the steel platform over the isolation tank.

The cold, real air feels like acid on my cheeks.

Cops in uniform. Detective Mohammed, yelling into a radio. The colors of these men are strong, the 3-D excellent.

They lay me in a hard stretcher. One cop pulls out the IV. Another slices open the Flexator suit. He uses a carpet-cutter and I shudder, involuntarily. A third sticks a plastic tube into my air passages. It hurts, but I breathe easier.

Still mouthing the plastic I look around for Kaye. I don't see her. I kick in panic, and the agony bearing down on me as a result is hard as a Mack truck.

"Kaye!" I yell into the sterile tube. It comes out, "Knhhh."

Then I spot her. They peel her out of the haptic suit and hold her upright. A policewoman wraps a space blanket around her shoulders. She can't walk.

She sees me. In the amazing depth of this real atmosphere the gray in her eyes is very clear. Like cold seas, I think, like crystallized sky.

They carry us in stretchers down the steps of the isolation tank. EMTs show up and put an IV in my other arm. There're groups of cops everywhere, just like after Larissa died. Some of them shoot Polaroids, some fill out forms, some eat bagels and hand around polystyrene cups of coffee.

I start, very vaguely, to get the feeling this is what people call "reality." At any rate, it didn't pass through a video-server to get to my five senses.

The Vietnamese techie and two of the Green Dragons sit hunched against the blue-board, surrounded by uniforms.

Time passes. Nobody seems to do much of anything. The tan-haired ADA, the one with the Kenzo suits and silver glasses, walks in, barking at his cellphone.

A plainclothes cop follows him in and goes straight to Kaye's stretcher. He's very broad, white-haired. He has a face like a pissed-off camel. He bends over her, muttering, and strokes her cheek.

He walks over to me and looks at my face with cop eyes. I recognize him from the picture in Kaye's apartment.

Arturo Santangelo, Deputy Chief of Detectives for Detective-Bureau Bronx.

He doesn't smile or say anything to me. After a while he goes to talk to the ADA. A patrolman comes over, takes my untubed hand, and cuffs it to the stretcher. Not a very encouraging development, I suppose, but my sense of what is real, and what ain't, is so thoroughly altered by now that it affects me not one whit. In a world where carnivorous rats can advance on you across the frozen river while, outside, a killer techie fine-tunes the drugs that will cut the link between your brain and reality—if they don't cause your heart to explode first—well, in that "world," Riker's is only one hazard among many.

It's not even the worst.

The EMTs pick up my stretcher. As they move out, a commotion slowly arises. I am ferried past the control consoles. One screen is frozen on the shot of a Norway rat with his snout well dug into a bloody human thigh.

Another screen shows baby cheetahs following their mother, single file, across the Ngorongoro Crater.

I turn my head, feeling the vomit crawl back up my throat.

Somebody calls, "Wait!"

Another voice calls, "Hold on, Karim."

Murmurs of argument. One of my EMTs says, "We're Fire, we don't take orders from you."

A second EMT says, "Fuck it, we can ride both of 'em."

"Charge 'em double," the first EMT adds.

A couple more EMTs haul Kaye over on her stretcher. Her face is turned toward mine; her hands are folded around a chemical heating pad. Her skin white as processed flour.

"I'm fuckin' comin' wit you," she whispers.

The Ecstasy has worn off by now, and though the IV is dripping in some form of painkiller the input from my leg is bad enough to cut through metal, let alone liquid Valium.

Still, her words light something in my stomach, and it's warm and comforting as that stove in the cabin of the white ship.

"Riker's," I grunt weakly, "here we come."

I try to reach across to her stretcher, but the cuff holds me back.

FORTY-NINE

WE DON'T GO to Riker's, though.

We end up, under police guard, in separate private rooms in the quarantine ward at St. Vincent's.

Between the chemical cocktail the techie was feeding me, and the serial drugs they drip into my body to cope with frostbite, and the anesthetic administered before and during surgery, I suppose it doesn't make a hell of a lot of difference.

Still, wounds get better, anesthetics wear off.

Twenty-four hours after we arrive at the quarantine ward, a police source leaks to *The New York Times* testimony from one of the Green Dragons who was busted in the VR lab; stuff about the Fishman, the killings, the iso-tank. The cable networks, anxious to draw back the Nielsens *Real Life* was stealing from them, jump on the *Times* story.

In my locked, pastel-colored room the EKGs, the blood-pressure monitors, don't talk. There is no radio and the TV hasn't been switched on, but I can sense things happening outside. The public-address system shrieks "Security" as camera crews try to break into the ward. The orthopedic surgeons lose arrogance.

Mohammed and his rough questions and cherry gum are replaced by an assistant D.A., not Coltrane. He sucks Hall's cough drops and focuses on what he calls Gaynor's ''command and control'' of the Asian gangs. Three FBI suits want me to swear out a sheaf of statements on Tyrone and Powell, but Jack Wong won't let me sign anything yet.

A friendly Haitian nurse named Yvonne smuggles me a clipping from the *Daily News*. It's the first time I see the term ''Reality-Gate.''

Late at night Yvonne wheels me, with two cops in tow, to Kaye's room, but we're both so tired from the various drugs that all we can do is sort of drool vaguely at one another.

Three days after we get to St. Vincent's Kaye leaves, and two days after that I get sprung as well. Jack Wong and I need a five-man cop escort to get through the TV crews massed on Greenwich Avenue. More cops are called to get us through the crush at Police Plaza.

Wong tells me Kaye has already gone back to her job; when she's not working, she's holed up at her parents' in Woodside.

The new ADA tells Wong that as long as I wear another ankle bracelet, they won't keep me in custody. Although I didn't really think I'd go back to Riker's, that news seems to flood my stomach with July sunshine.

I ask Ved Chakrapani, my former director of software on *Real Life,* if I can stay in his spare room. An unmarked police car sneaks me from One Police Plaza to Ved's without any reporters following.

A week after I check out of the hospital, I'm keeping my ass dry on a piece of granite on a hillock deep in melting snow in North Elizabeth, New Jersey.

Wrapped in a borrowed coat with a bag of pretzels and a copy of the *Village Voice* spread out on the rock beside me.

The hillock is set in the undeveloped quadrant of a Russian Orthodox Cemetery. It's thick with the tombstones of vanished Slavs, surrounded by chainlink and brick-faced ranch houses. Above a new mini-mall and a line of elms to the northwest, through a squall line of sleet, I dimly make out the World Trade Center, the Kowloon Bankcorp Building, the Empire State.

The "X" on top of TV City is invisible.

The stone I sit on isn't fancy; it has no lettering carved in it, though someone scrawled "Larissa Leonora Munn" in chalk on one side. Frankly, I'm sort of pissed no one asked me my opinion on where Larissa should be buried.

Then again, given that they thought I killed her, why should they ask me my preference? And at least you can see Manhattan from here. She would want to see Manhattan, I think; she always spoke of the "Bridge and Tunnel crowd" the way people from Moscow refer to Yakuts.

Four bouquets of white roses, ranging from stale to fresh, lie on the granite; one for every day I've come here.

I munch a pretzel, looking at the World Trade Center, not thinking much. When events happen as fast as they have recently, it becomes all you can do to file and index what's going on. Understanding everything, for now, is way beyond reach.

I swallow the remains of the pretzel, and pick up the newspaper.

The *Voice* does not understand everything. Despite the fact that there's no gay Village angle to the story, however, they put a lot of time and energy into the reporting. I skim the lengthy piece.

> The glamrock whiz kid of the D.A.'s office, Coltrane, was highly reluctant to abandon what he considered his ironclad case against Munn, according to sources in the Manhattan office. It had all the ingredients—star appeal, quick wrap-up —to boost his career in a hurry. Three pieces of real life, no upper case, convinced him otherwise. The first was the testimony of Love's neighbors that Asian "workmen" were seen in her house around the time the killing of the soap queen occurred. The second was the autopsy on Stefan Chin Zeng, the virtual reality consultant slaughtered Nov. 28 in the by-now-notorious "Fishman" style from Munn's secret historical VR thriller. Test results showed that the murder happened between five and ten hours after Munn's Hollywood-style escape from Riker's Island. However, evidence from a Riker's

inmate, Hector "Lobo" Vasquez, who was picked up after participating in the escape, indicates that Munn was holed up in a project in Brownsville at that time.

The third piece of evidence, of course, was provided by Eddy "Weasel" Truong, a Green Dragon gang member who turned state's evidence after Munn and Santangelo were discovered undergoing high-tech brainwashing in XTV's virtual-reality lab . . .

Reading farther down, I smile.

Rose Obregon, now acting president of XTV, did not return phone calls but her secretary, Rob Adams, who used to work for Munn, stated that "He was always working on secret stuff." "The show came together despite him," Joel Kamm, who replaced Munn as head of special projects, commented. "He was an incompetent, arrogant cocksucker. It's a complete mystery to me how he could put together something like the Reality-Gate show."

I flip toward the end of the article. For once I agree with Joel Kamm.

Although since our first day in Donegal Manor, I've been catching the odd glimmer of illumination in this particular cave.

A synthetic beeping interrupts my ruminations. I pull Chakrapani's cellphone out of my Kmart ski jacket, flip it open. His voice comes clearly through.

"Munn?"

"Ved."

"Lunch today, okay?"

I close the phone slowly.

I look around the cemetery, thinking, I've spent enough time looking at this sad place, trying to understand things no cemetery, no gravestone nor remembrance, have ever been able to explain.

It's time to do, not think.

Abruptly I reopen Ved's cellphone and dial a set of numbers. A woman announces, "Dr. Pentti's office." I ask her to put me through on an emergency basis, and after a minute or so Pentti gets on the line.

"Alex," he says, "I'm so flattered. The whole world wants to interview you, and you call *me*."

"I'd like to see you today," I tell him, "jiss ten, fifteen minutes? I need to air out some things in my head."

I can hear him tapping at his keyboard, calling up the appointments file.

"I can make time between three and three-fifteen—"

"It's kinda urgent," I tell him, "I was hoping we could do it just before lunch."

He sighs.

"For you," he says, "alright. Twelve-thirty to twelve-forty. Ten minutes. Not one second longer."

One more call to make.

Another secretary announces "Ragnarok Press." She puts me through to Kaye, who gives me attitude the same way Pentti did. Her voice is wary since, for all the shit we've been through together, the exact nature of our relationship remains as undefined as it was when we talked over the canal in West Hamilton Beach.

"You in Jersey?" she asks, although she knows exactly where I am, and what I'm doing there.

"I'm leaving now."

She sighs, much as my shrink did.

I flip the cellphone closed and slide it in my pocket. Pick up my crutches, plant them in the mud, and climb to a standing position. This is no easy matter; the fall from the wharf in *Munn's World* fractured my left tibia in fact as well as fiction, and Fishman's knife put a real, if shallow, slice in my lower back.

I lost a toe, and Kaye nearly lost one, to hypothermia.

A team of Justice Department software experts is interviewing the Asian techie and his minions in the VR lab, trying to figure out how the Flexator suit can both channel water chilly enough to cause frostbite, and exert pressure in the exact spot and in the precise way a ten-foot fall on ice would work on the shinbone.

The FBI also would like to interview Fishman—it turns out he's a half Cuban named Antonio Macy, wanted for racketeering and murder in Florida and California—but he's disappeared without a trace.

Polletti has been suspended pending internal investigation,

but the Kenzo ADA isn't sure he has enough evidence to convict him of anything.

In any truly complex world, you can never tie up all the loose ends.

I turn around to look at the slab of Ramapo granite. The four bunches of white roses rustle pathetically in the wet wind.

They don't look like much, a mess of flaking, browning petals to sum up my poor loyalty; cheap fragments of symbols to shore against the ruins of a life I once held fully as precious as my own.

And yet, I've achieved a peace of sorts here. Because now I know that despite what I said to Kaye, I'll never come to terms with Larissa's death, the same way that you can never fully accept the absence of anyone you've ever loved.

The fact of the matter is, they all, like Stefan Zeng, programmed life-boxes deep in the dark channels of my memory; and those life-boxes are like homunculi, miniaturized versions of themselves that subsist, fully alive, as long as the host exists.

Knowing that, accepting it, enables the living to continue. I will always have a tiny Larissa fixing her hair under the left corner of my hypothalamus.

Yelling *Nikagda!* as I munch my Cheerios.

I turn and swing carefully back to the waiting radio cab.

A nervous, attractive woman in a Fendi frock reads *Variety,* tearing out audition notices, in Pentti's waiting room.

The receptionist treats me with great courtesy, and buzzes me in ahead of the Fendi woman, whose voice I can hear rising in argument before the soundproofed door shuts solidly behind.

Pentti springs up as I come in, shakes my hand, brushes his hair back over his bald spot. He's dressed in his usual rollneck, jeans, running shoes. The Buddhas with Attic faces line up sagely beside the issues of *JAPA;* the Empire clock tick-tocks, tick-tocks, loud and metallic behind him.

I perch on the edge of the Danish divan, taking care not to tweak my scars. I straighten my pants to cover the transponder on my ankle. Pentti leans forward on the desk, his "interested" attitude, and says, "Well, well, well."

"Well, well," I repeat.

"How's the broken leg? I read about it, of course."

"It's okay. They put a coupla pins in it—I should be walking in two weeks, hopefully."

"Good."

"Yeah."

He picks up a clipping from the *Voice,* brushes his hair back again.

"Is this what you wanted to talk about?"

It's the article that includes an interview with my mother. He points out a boxed section:

> VV—You had an affair with Henry Warren Powell, thirty-two years ago?
>
> LP—We were kids. So young—
>
> VV—But you slept together; in fact, he got you pregnant.
>
> LP—I bore his child—yes.
>
> VV—Alexander Patrick Munn.
>
> LP—My son.
>
> VV—And then he dumped you?
>
> LP—No. Henry wanted to marry me. I know he did, but times were different then. He was so ambitious. But he always helped us, he sent us money, when I was working as an actress on Broadway. Well, off-Broadway. I was in *Anna Christie—*
>
> VV—He sent you money? How?
>
> LP—I got postal orders. Every three or four months, sometimes. I knew they were from him.

"Is this what you wanted to talk about?" Pentti repeats, a tad impatiently.

"No," I tell my shrink.

"So?" He leans back and joins fingers under his chin.

"I want to know how you did it."

"I'm sorry?"

I wave my hand impatiently. "Let's please not beat around the bush over this?"

"I honestly don't understand. You said it was urgent—"

"You must think I'm a fucking idiot," I interrupt him. I

get to my feet, or foot. He watches me without any trace of nerves as I jam a crutch under my left shoulder, swing to the side of his desk, and pick up one of the little Buddhas. I turn the head back and forth in the light. "Maybe I *am* stupid. It took me a long time to figger out."

"Figure out what?" Pentti asks. "You're hiding behind a lot of vague statements."

The Buddha is as calm as Pentti.

"You know, whenever I watched *Munn's World*—my historical serial? I kept seeing these old-fashioned clocks, ticking, ticking." I hold the Buddha next to the marble plinth of the Empire clock. The brass hands tremble and flick as the escapements catch. "I put those clocks *everywhere,* it must have been some kind of subconscious safety valve. The way you made me listen to this clock, when you put me under hypnosis."

"My dear Alex," Pentti begins.

"How did you know all that about Powell? How did you figger out, we all lived in West Hamilton Beach?" I slam the statue on the clock, denting the armature. The second hand shudders, and stops. "It *had* to be under hypnosis. All that time, when I was asking you what I said when I was hypnotized, you were fuckin' *lying* to me!"

"Don't be ridiculous." He's looking at the clock. Irritation flowers in his voice.

"Faking the transcripts."

Pentti leans forward again, swiveling his chair a little to face me better.

"These questions are interesting," he says, "there's real projective identification here. How do you feel, when you say—"

"It was *me,* who told you the whole thing," I interrupt, crutching back to the divan. "It *had* to be. I told you the basics, when I was under. About Powell, and my mother, and Tyrone. I had no idea it was there, none at all . . . God, you must be good at what you do!

"You realized Powell was my father," I continue. "You saw you'd dug up a real smoking gun here. You thought you could affect who would be president—so you did some research. And then you tamped all that information back into my brain, with some kind of trigger, so I'd puke it all back out in the *Real Life* script?''

''I could write a paper about this.'' Pentti puts both hands under his chin.

''An', an' you put in a block, so I wouldn't remember what you just fished out of me.''

''Six minutes,'' Pentti sighs, looking at the clock. ''You have four left.''

''I don't need four minutes. I don't even need one. There's nothing I can do to you; the info you put in here''—I point a finger to my head—''it can't be traced. It won't hold up in court.''

''Of course not,'' he agrees. ''As the saying goes, this is all in your mind.''

''So why don't you tell me the truth?'' I yell. ''All I want to know is, why? *Why* did you go to those lengths? What was the *point*? What was your *percentage*?''

''You *do* need help.'' Pentti pulls a prescription pad from his drawer. ''I had you on nine milligrams of Prodex, correct?'' He writes something on the pad.

''And that's another thing,'' I tell him. ''Those pills had a few side effects on the memory centers, right? So that when I drank, I couldn't remember anything?''

''Maybe we're beyond the Prodex stage now,'' Pentti murmurs, still writing. ''There's a clinic in Pound Ridge that specializes in this sort of trauma. I could probably get you in tomorrow—even tonight?'' He watches me speculatively.

''You must be outta your fuckin' mind.''

''Yes. Well.'' Pentti closes his Mont Blanc and lays it on his desk.

''You have to *want* to be cured. Often delusions are less painful than the truth.''

I stare at him. My breath is ragged in my throat.

Somehow that last statement of his, more than anything else he has said or done, convinces me emotionally of what I had already decided, intellectually, was the case. Pentti, at his worst, was never trite. That triteness, now, smells of evasion. The anger rises in me like crystal meths.

But I don't want to do anything dumb. So, before I get too

carried away, I tuck my crutches under my armpits, open the door one-handed, and swing out into the reception area.

The actress is still complaining about how my appointment delayed hers for almost ten whole minutes and that wouldn't *ever* have happened if she was still Kerrie Courtland on *General Hospital*.

FIFTY

ONCE OUTSIDE, I swing down the block toward Broadway. The car that looks like Jackson Pollock puked on it is parked at a "NO STANDING" spot, engine running, keeping a large van with "Burning Spears" stickers from making deliveries.

I get in with difficulty, sliding my crutches in the back. I wish I'd reclaimed my Morgan.

"How'd it go?" Kaye asks.

I look at her. She has bandages on the fingers of her right hand. She wears a black sweater five sizes too big. Black tights and boots and new blue Ray⋅Bans. Her cheeks are pale and the dread-braids kinked under her usual beret. Her mouth is straight with tension, because the emotional twists from the last ten days have not worked out of her completely.

The sight of her settles the anger, and brings a different kind of agitation to my chest.

"I dunno," I say. "He denied the whole thing."

"Natch."

I shift my cast around till it's more comfortable. "It worries me."

She takes out her pack of Camels and lights one. "Now, what?"

"We wait." I move around again, so I can keep both eyes on the entrance to Pentti's building.

Sleet weeps down the windshield, melting the gray buildings together.

We don't wait long. The actress comes out ten minutes later, hunched against her anger. Five minutes or so after that, a man Pentti's size walks into the slush and hails a cab. I recognize his tuft of hair, his tennis racket, his compact build under a belted chamois coat.

"Go," I tell Kaye urgently, pointing at the cab.

"Just like *Copkiller*," she mutters, running a yellow light.

The cab turns south down Broadway. The traffic is fairly dense, but moving, so it's easy to keep two or three cars back without losing them. For a while I actually manage to enjoy the Christmas lights that have been strung across the avenue, the electric colors splashed on mounded, dirty snow. Shiny fruits and packages spill from Fairway's, the queue at Zabar's concertinas up the block.

Pentti's cab follows around Columbus Circle, takes Fifty-ninth eastbound. It turns right into Grand Army Plaza and pulls up outside the vast facade of the Plaza Hotel.

Kaye brakes sharply at the corner. "How'm I gonna park?" she complains. "The garages here are always full."

"I'll pay the ticket," I tell her, levering myself out, "my bank account's been unlocked."

"Where'll I meet you?"

"By the flowers."

She's a city kid, I reflect, swinging as fast as my crutches will go, she'll know what I mean.

The steps are a bitch on crutches, but a compassionate doorman opens the side entrance so I don't have to hop through the revolving doors.

Inside the hotel's east lobby I hike my Kmart scarf over my mouth and look around at the vast urn of flowers, the rows of boutiques and armchairs; Pentti is not there.

Fast through the portal into the arcade surrounding the Palm Court. I follow the crowd of gawkers looking sideways for celebrities in the tea area, and stand under the portrait of Eloise, doing my own gawking.

Expensive clothes shine from the sparkle of mirrors and chandeliers. The band medlies Andrew Lloyd Webber, reminding me of Kaye, dancing in Mrs. McCotter's living room. I note how, even after two minutes' absence, I miss her.

The tearoom is void of Pentti.

I hobble faster, around the Palm Court to the north lobby. He is standing, his yellow coat outlined against the gloomy entrance to the Edwardian Room. He laughs at something the maître d'hotel said. I turn quickly and crutch back to the main entrance.

Kaye is limping around the flowers, looking for me. Her eyebrows lift. I nod.

By the time we get back to the north lobby, Pentti has gone inside. The Edwardian Room maître d' sees us coming before we're past the Van Cleef and Arpels display. He stiffens; my corduroy jeans and brand-new gauchos constitute no major threat, but Kaye's getup, with its semiotics of Attitude, sets off big "WARNING" flashers in his head.

He walks toward us, brandishing menus like a 9 mm.

I pull the scarf down to talk.

"We're meeting someone," I tell him.

"I'm sorry," he begins. He looks at me, looks at Kaye, then at me again. His face clears the tiniest bit.

"I'm sorry, sir," he says, "whom did you say you were meeting?"

"Dr. Toivo Pentti," I tell him.

"Aha." His face clears further. "But you're not expected?"

"That's okay," I tell him grimly, "it's kind of a surprise."

"Right this way," the maître d' says, and struts into the pseudo-medieval gloom.

Kaye nudges me as we walk among tables isolated like atolls by their individual gold-shaded lamps. "He recognized you," she hisses. "That's how come we got in."

I shrug.

We pass a half-dozen atolls inhabited by middle-aged *WaBenzis,* robed Arabs, and diamond-sparkling women who may be their daughters.

One atoll, in the far right corner, is different.

The man has on a rollneck. The woman wears a silk dress that flares aqua around her shoulders. She has dark hair and indigo lipstick. Her fingers are set with many rings bearing opal stones in a setting of silver. The fingers of her right hand are twined around the fingers of my psychiatrist.

They don't spot us until Kaye and I are standing within the circle of illumination of their lamp.

Pentti looks up in the act of pouring liquid from a chilled silver pitcher, and his features shut like a sea anemone.

The woman's teak-colored skin is nicely set off by the paneling behind her. With her left hand she lifts a big bunch of keys hanging on a gold chain around her neck, then lets them drop, vaguely jangling, against her breasts.

A vague hint of Narcisse.

"Hello, Rosie," I say softly.

Her nostrils flare in and out with each breath.

The maître d'hôtel's antennae are working as efficiently as ever. He pauses in the act of placing extra menus.

"This *is* your party?" he asks Pentti.

My shrink continues to stare at me.

"Sir?"

"No," Pentti says quietly. "They are not welcome here."

"It's okay," I tell the flunky. "We'll leave in a second." I disengage from my crutches and lean on the table, hunching down close to Rose Obregon. Her eyes are dark, and she narrows her eyelids as if to protect the sanctity of that darkness.

"How did you know we were here?" Pentti asks.

I ignore him, still staring at Rosie. Her shutoff is good; I can read nothing in that gaze. And I can think of absolutely nothing else to say. Except this.

"Larissa Love—my wife." My voice is creaky with tension. "Stefan Zeng, my friend. And Derek, an' Mrs. McCotter, an' Brian. *You* killed 'em, Rosie; you killed 'em all."

"You're talking nonsense," Pentti says sharply, "cheap drama. You said it yourself—nothing will hold up in court."

"Sure." I don't take my eyes off Rose. "I just hope, now you're sitting in Tyrone's seat, you think the killing was worth it?"

"I killed nobody," she says. Her voice is clear and strong. She puts her hands together as if in prayer.

"Don't talk to him," Pentti urges.

"But you caused them to die," I tell her. "You wanted to bring down Tyrone. You wanted to make him think it was me doing it. When he started killing people to frame me, you did nothing to stop it.''

Rose rolls her eyes heavenward.

''This man is one of my patients,'' Pentti explains to the maître d'.

''Sir,'' the flunky interrupts. ''It would be best if—''

''Yeah, yeah.'' I shake his arm off. ''We're going.''

''We're *going*?'' Kaye asks incredulously, turning to stare at me.

I shrug, and saddle up my crutches again. I really need crutches now. It's not just my leg; I feel like energy has been flowing out of every limb and muscle since the VR lab, and for the last week or so I've been operating purely on the desire to understand; and now it's finally over, the last drops of fuel expended, the last question answered, I have nothing at all left to run on.

I pause to look once more at Rose and Pentti. I see their eyes widen in shock, Rose just beginning to duck as a shimmering slurp of sweet chilled cocktail engulfs her face and soaks the flimsy bodice of her dress.

Kaye puts down the empty silver pitcher and says, ''Cool,'' in a satisfied voice.

With the assistance of three waiters and a security guard we leave the Edwardian Room a lot faster than we came in.

Kaye leads me around the Pulitzer Fountain to Fifty-eighth Street. Her jaw is set angrily; she didn't like being manhandled by waiters. Her car is parked outside the Paris Cinema. Two tickets are jammed under the wipers. She bends down to unlock the door.

''You know,'' I begin excitedly, ''I bet Rose was Pentti's patient, to begin with at least—''

An arm grabs me around the waist, while something cold and metallic pokes into the bone just under my right ear.

''Get in the *cah,* bahstahd,'' a man's voice growls.

I freeze. Two dark-skinned men have walked up behind Kaye. Now she's walking backward between them, toward a black van with a ''Burning Spears'' sticker on the bumper. I want to scream ''No no *not again* I am so goddam *sick* of this!''

I keep my mouth shut. Kaye could get hurt if I yell.

The man beside me guides me to the side door. I sigh, toss in the crutches, and crawl after, feeling as incompetent as always in these situations.

The black men shut the door, keeping small .38s pointing at our bellies where we sit on the floor among heaps of empty Burger King boxes.

The van peels out, up Fifty-eighth to Fifth; after that, right and right again, west down Fifty-seventh. A tape deck plays Peter Tosh: "He's a steppin' razor, he's '*dangerous*'." One of our abductors stares tensely out the back window as we stop-go through midtown traffic. Another lights a joint. The sweet smell of ganja pervades the van's dim interior.

Judging by the stops and gos we must have turned onto Tenth Avenue and run as far as Thirtieth Street when a hatch opens in the grille separating us from the driver's area. A thin face surrounded by a large woolen snood peers through. A bloodshot eye focuses downward, on my head.

"You owe me twenty thousan dallah, rasclout," the face says. "What 'appen, you *fohget*?"

"Hello, Cosmo," I say wearily.

"Yah, Cosmo, mahn." He reaches out with one hand and a henchman places the joint in it. "Get you outta Riker's Island, you become fee-aymous, yah mahn, beeg Ree-ahlity-Gee-ate mahn, you fahget 'bout you friends." He takes a deep toke.

"That's not the way it happened," I tell him. "They froze my money."

"Dat's what you lawyah say." Cosmo spits, freeing his tongue of a dope-stem. "Heem a *rasclout*."

"Maybe. I'll pay you the dough."

"You bet you weel, cockroach. Where you bank?"

I direct him downtown. Kaye stares at me through the cabin's gloom. She takes off her Ray Bans and rubs her eyes.

When we get to the bank Cosmo makes a lot of superfluous threats about Kaye, and I go inside and seek out a vice president I've been doing business with ever since Larissa and I bought the town house on Perry Street.

It takes time; bankers hate dealing in cash because, in the most basic sense, liquid money denies their reason for existing. Still, between my savings and Gaynor's golden handshake I have a lot of shekels stashed with this bank. At length they agree to hand over two cashier's checks, each for 9,999 dollars, both made out to Cosmo Trelawney.

I go back to the van. The driver takes off immediately and speeds paranoically west, down Washington Street as far as Vandam. He pulls into an alley near the corner of King Street. Cosmo pokes his head through the grille again. I hand the checks to the payee.

"Dees don' mee-ake twenny tousan.'"

I fish in my pocket. A henchman lifts his trey-eight suggestively. I pull out my wallet with care and hand Cosmo two dollar bills.

"Nineteen thousand nine hundred ninety-eight. Here's two bucks, which makes twenty grand. The SEC investigates any transfers of ten thousand or more. I thought, maybe you'd rather they didn't?"

Cosmo examines the watermarks on the checks against the windshield. Finally he grunts.

"Arright."

"*Jee-*zuss," Kaye bursts out suddenly. Her Ray-Bans are back on and she looks at me, angry as a blue-eyed angel. "You don't have to pay him *anything*! He's a fuckin' *kidnapper*!"

"He got me out of Riker's," I remind her.

"He's a crook!"

"Her father's a cop," I explain to Cosmo, who examines her as if she were a particularly weird bird in the Central Park aviary.

"I was a crook, yah mahn," Cosmo tells her. "But on *heem* side."

One of his henchmen slides open the door of the van.

Kaye doesn't move.

"So there's no right or wrong anymore," she says quietly. She's not talking to the Rastamen but to me. "There's just, what—more or less *real*?"

"I guess," I tell her, shrugging.

The henchman gets out, beckoning us with the spliff in one hand and my crutches in the other. We clamber carefully out of the van. The alley is a narrow opening between a garage and an ancient warehouse. It's empty except for stacked oil drums, bits of packing crate, assorted garbage, scabs of unmelted snow. From an open window in the warehouse, some-one is playing Clam Fetish.

The henchman hands me my crutches and gets back in. The van door slams, the engine revs. Cosmo, eyes squinted suspiciously, is still examining his checks. We have to press against the warehouse wall so the van can back out.

The Rastamen screech into traffic, and disappear down-town.

The smell of ganja lingers briefly in the cold air.

Kaye turns toward me.

"So," she says. "Is that it?"

"Not quite."

"Oh, God," she sighs. "Now what?"

Above our heads Clam Fetish has segued into a thumping shifta-rap beat. I listen.

> *"The fix is in,*
> *They dealt me out,*
> *Even the barman's been paid off—*
> *Shit! Piss!*
> *I can't get a drink.*
> *Roach in the kitchen,*
> *Jis' in the sink."*

It's not anything faintly lyrical; not the sad chord progres-sions of "Cruel Edward"; nor is it the sweet Schubert we heard on the barge in Brooklyn.

But it's full of raw strength, and life, and change, and a pattern based on rhythm. It's the kind of rhythm that keeps this dark and violent burg alive.

> *"Piss! Shit!*
> *It's all fuckin' hype,*
> *The circle's closed, babe,*
> *Can't get in."*

I reach over and, using only thumb and forefinger, remove the Ray Bans from her face. The impulse rises stronger inside me. It's not just sex, though that's part of it; it's a general desire for life, and a specific need for Kaye, who in all her complexity and change is as vital and alive as the fractal city around us.

"Take your clothes off," I tell her.

She looks at me without expression.

"Here?"

"Here."

She continues to look in my eyes for a beat or two. Then her mouth curves; one peak, and finally two.

Our clothes drop like autumn leaves to lie untended around our ankles, among the slushy trash.

And we're dancing naked in the middle of New York.

ABOUT THE AUTHOR

GEORGE FOY is a writer and journalist. He has published five novels, including *Challenge* and *Asia Rip*. He has worked as a commercial fisherman, a vacuum-molding machine operator, and a paralegal in New York City law firms. He has traveled into Soviet-occupied Afghanistan with an arms-smuggling caravan, acted on network television, and participated in the creation of a CD-ROM game. He lives with his wife, daughter, and cat in New York City and Cape Cod.

Turn the page for a special preview of *Contraband* by George Foy. George Foy follows *The Shift* with the thrilling novel of the near future from one of science fiction's brightest new talents.

Don't miss *Contraband* on sale in April 1997 from Bantam Spectra Books.

The pilot had been on the run for almost twenty years before anyone realized, much less did anything about it.

The first murmur of pursuit came faint and abstract as the sound of strangers whispering in a forgotten language in another room.

It happened on an autumn Sunday in a village eighty-five miles up the Rio Chingado, in the corner of South America where Brazil, Colombia, and Peru are stitched together by rivers.

The pilot was sitting, waiting for cargo, on the porch of a tin-roofed hut. The hut hung over the river on long thin stilts. It smelled of coffee and minerals and rot. The hut belonged to the Brazilian, who always sat in the corner behind the weighing table. If you came in without knowing, you might not see the Brazilian, so still was he, so much a part of the jungle gloom inside this corrupted structure.

A board of green wood linked the hut to the riverbank. The Cayman came down the plank like a ballet star, toeing delicately in soft gaucho boots. He peered behind the weighing table, noting the shine of metal and how it was reflected in the Brazilian's eyes, apparently without reference to light.

"T'ree tolas," he said. With one hand he lifted a cellophane bag against the window, against the canopy of fattened trees overhanging the river.

The Cayman's other hand gripped a two-foot-long glass jar. It was an old-fashioned specimen bottle with a bell-shaped end, of a type that might have been used one hundred years earlier for experiments concerning phrenology and the seat of intelligence. Behind a ceramic stopper, the glass was full of long and curled silver. Two copper wires twisted out of the ceramic. "No fuck con migo, man," the Cayman went on, "dis t'ree at *least.*"

The Cayman was fat and gray; fever had leached color from his skin the way rain leached the forest's meager topsoil when the lumbermen had been and gone. His eyelids had folds so that when he blinked, three different cowls had to be moved in sequence to cover and uncover his pupils. A grimy mauve waistcoat failed to close over his large belly. Sweat dripped from his bellybutton, darkening his loose pants. It looked like he had pissed himself.

The Brazilian was thin and taut as piano wire. He kept on spooning gold dust from a small gourd to an even smaller bronze scale. Kerosene lamps wrestled the jade gloom. The gold took this light, broke and yellowed it, played it against the brass weights. Smoke from the steam pumps of the emerald mines upstream formed parentheses around the hut. The tin roof cooled the air's vapor, condensing it into water that dripped steadily on the floor.

Clouds rubbed bruise-marks into the jungle shade. A gunboat churned grayly upriver, radar turning in circular, arachnid alert.

The Cayman spat into the river and picked his way over soft planks, through the riverside door, to the porch at the shack's far end.

The pilot did not look up. He stuck the second finger of his left hand in a mug of *tinto*. He squinted through black glasses toward his float-jet where it crouched warily among the tendrils of smoke and the coiled black muscles of the river, rocking slightly in the gunboat's wake.

The Cayman leaned forward, almost touching the pilot's ear with his lips.

"Bokon Taylay. He look for *nosotros,*" the Cayman whispered.

The pilot lifted his finger out of the coffee. The movement pulled sweat from every pore in his body. The boil in the pulp of his finger was plummy and taut. He stuck it in an adjoining cup of *cachaca* rum, and winced.

"Go away, Fawcett," he muttered.

Upriver on the same side, an ancient paddlewheeler lay half awash, braided to the bank with vines. Indios had slung hammocks from brass fittings in the saloon. Even from the hut you could hear their guitars rub, like rough tools scraping music from the substance of the jungle itself.

In the trees overhead, bearded monkeys flung papaya rinds at each other. The trees' roots were lean, and white from lack of sun. They touched the fallen rinds and closed on them, seeking food.

"My last two cargoes, Bokon take."

"You're breakin' my heart."

"Bokon Taylay, he get everybody now. *Tu sabes?* He know de code. He know de *dance.*"

"I told ya. No."

The Cayman smiled sadly. No man trades for love, he thought. It was as close to an article of faith as he possessed. He shifted the glass jar from left hand to right, and reversed the procedure for his bag of gold.

"Fifteen tolas," he said. A tola was a wafer of gold, 3.75 troy ounces in weight. "Is K-Y, man. For dis you run only twelve bale of jisi. Next run, you bring Deutschmark. Or maybe you wan' jive wi' my *pescado*?"

"Your fish don't bother me."

"Escucha me." The Cayman leaned close. "Listen." The jungle had rotted his insides first and his breath smelled like mulch.

"If you don' help, my cargoes no run. If cargoes no run, my Indios no manjay."

"I got too much weight already." The pilot spoke too loud. He did not want to think about the Indians. "An' I'm down with a tai-lo, for this run. So forget it."

A raindrop the size of a walnut cracked into the water. A gun coughed from the Brazilian side of the Chingado. A soldier came out of the frontier post and stared through night-vision goggles over the dark water. It was two in the afternoon.

"Dey sell their M-2s. Can't buy bullets. Already dey go back to blowpipes." The tone was full of hurt, but the Cayman's face was rejigging itself in different directions—a curious sequence where the eyelids slid up, one after the other, and large cheek muscles hauled plates of fat out and up to reveal sharp teeth—a smile. His pupils narrowed. He jammed the bag of dust in a pocket of his waistcoat. The pilot dropped his right hand toward the switchblade in his boot, but the Cayman was quicker. He grabbed the glass jar with both hands and shook it very hard in front of the pilot's face, the wires almost touching his nose.

The jar exploded in a convulsion of finned and rounded silver, turning, twisting, folding. In the vortex of spasms you could catch a freeze-frame of Horror; its ratchet mouth and chainsaw teeth and psycho eyes.

The pilot backed away from the electric eel and the sparking wires that conducted its fury. His chair tilted. The doubled pressure under the back legs finally tore the soggy fibers of the deck planks, and the legs broke through. The pilot toppled backwards, without hope or possibility of saving himself; fingers spreading in a prayer for flight, he rolled straight over the edge of the deck, into the arterial river.

The Chingado was hot as blood, thick as gruel, the color of double-strong espresso. As the water closed over his head and leaked through his lips the pilot thought he could taste the whole history of its run; the flatness of Cordillera snow, the grit of stolen soil. Lime of murdered Indians, of poisoned jaguars. In his mouth he knew the death of peasant squatters who wound up tied hand and foot in the Chingado's middle stretch. He knew the quickness of alligators and blue piranhas and coral snakes, and the tiny silver fish that swim up your asshole and wedge themselves with hypo spines against the pink coruscations of your tripes.

He shot out of the water faster than a panicked porpoise. At the top of his arc he wrapped both arms around one of the hut supports. With elbows and knees he tried shinnying up the pole toward the broken deck. Algae grew green, inch-thick on the support, and for every upward thrust the pilot lost almost as much ground as he'd gained, so that at the end of two minutes his ankles still hung in the umber water.

The Cayman and the Brazilian stared over the edge of the deck, watching the pilot struggle among the fumes of mingled rivers. The Brazilian was laughing so hard he vibrated like an instrument and had to be held up by the fat man.

The clouds released their water. The opposite bank disappeared behind metallic folds of rain.

On the paddlewheeler, the guitars had stopped, or maybe it was just that the noise of rain overpowered their soft rhythms.

In the forest behind the paddlewheeler an Indio wadded a dart, and lifted his blowpipe toward the invisible sun. The Indio belonged to a tribe that thought they were parrots. He wore yellow feathers around his neck to protect himself from humans.

"I will radio to Chico Fong," the Cayman shouted. "He will *make* you take my jisi."

"Rot your balls," the pilot screamed. "You did this on purpose; you knew I *hate* getting my duds wet, ah you *scum!*"

But the pilot's anger was largely chemical, and soon faded. When it was gone, he hung onto his pole, wondering when the two would get over their giggling long enough to throw him a rope. He wondered, also, how to prevent the Cayman from getting in touch with Chico.

Wondered who in hell "Bokon Taylay" was.

It was his last trip to the Chingado, the pilot decided. He hated places with no horizon.

The Indio's dart found its mark.

A baby monkey fell with no sound while its mother screamed from above.

"The airplane is doubtless only a machine; but what a fine instrument for analysis!"

Antoine de Saint Exupery
Citadelle

A chapter called "Sit On My Interface" in the 14th edition of the *Freetrader's Almanac and Cookbook* (Charras Press, Boulder, Colorado)—better known as the "Smuggler's Bible"—includes the following advice:

The freetrader should always jive on the boundary layer between earth, air, water, and space. Interface like a beach, a storm-front, a dewpoint; this is the space where different kinds of waves meet, flirt—and zoom-zoom into craziness, because it is the nature of a wave to believe it is unique. This is the space where matter splits from form, because the FORM of a wave is what holds it together. The weird trips of turbulence or surf offer the same opportunities for chaos and catastrophe as a human frontier. Chaos and catastrophe are the freetrader's homeboys, because the instruments of the Man can ride only one wave of reality at a time. . . .

Practical applications of boundary-layer travel are numerous, especially if you want to evade visual and electronic surveillance in heavy crisis situations. They include dewpoint (fog), surf (small boat landings), saline layers and SOFAR (submarine operations), the Great Red Spot of Jupiter (radio transmissions), storm fronts (aviation, marine). . . ."

The pilot folded his hard-copy of the Smuggler's Bible and stowed it in his chartcase with one hand while with the other he touched the control column, feeling the autopilot adjust as it kept his aircraft hurtling over the western Atlantic, dead in the lane where night and water stretched invisible fingers toward each other and danced briefly, like shy kids in white gloves, wherever wind rubbed, and fog precipitated, and waves built—never quite mingling.

In the narrow windscreen, at forty-five feet of altitude and 320 knots of speed, the effect was hallucinating; worm after parallel, broken worm of white spume ripping out of the blue-black nothing of time unspent and distance-not-traveled, strobing almost quicker than the mind could grasp between dark sea and invisible night, to vanish one splinter of a second later under the nose-antenna of the jet.

The deflectors barely managed to keep his windscreen clear of salt spray. The squirts of rain-repellent only smeared around salt left on the glass. That same spray must be soaking the turbine blades of his two Pratt and Whitneys. He would have to take the crate in for overhaul as soon as he got back to Newark.

The pilot switched off the chartlight. The Smuggler's Bible came in CD-ROM form but you could not fool around with LCDs and keyboard at this speed and altitude. Luckily Charras still printed hard-copy for Darkworld use—for places, in what was once called the "Third World," or the Third-World-like areas of richer countries, where freetraders tended to end up. He had taken a risk reading hard-copy at this altitude but the Smuggler's Bible, if you ignored its weird pseudo-religious side, was full of vital info. It carried timetables for satellites, navigational listings for the Air Almanac, and microcharts of air routes with plastic magnifying pages attached. Also, the "Interface" chapter ended with a list of the Bureau of Nationalization's Synthetic Aperture and phased-array radar frequencies. The Synthetic Aperture radar was mounted on modified AWACS that BON was flying on the Exuma-Brownsville axis. Phased-array was what the new high-endurance cutters were carrying. Therefore the risk was necessary.

Only S.A. and phased-array radar stood a chance of touching a jet this low, and even that was a small threat.

The real danger lay in this kind of flying; the dearth of altitude protecting him from normal radar left him no margin for error if something fucked up. And his reaction time was dragging.

He'd been flying for thirteen hours, with one break to refuel at Duncan Town, in the Jumentos. It had not been much of a rest. He'd had to keep the engines whining while the plane floated at a broken dock; playing guard at the door while the Santa Martans and Guyanans aimed lusting eyes at his plane.

They were dangerous, these Santa Martans and Guyanans of Duncan Town; men with razor smiles, falsely loose gaits, and eight generations worth of natural selection in the Caribbean piracy industry coursing through their veins. In cooperation with the Organisatsya they recently had taken over all the coke and smack traffic in the Northeast. They'd achieved this by blowing away their opponents, as well as their opponents' families and third cousins and casual acquaintances and hairdressers, spreading carnage among the ports and airfields with Ingrams and M-16s and Roland anti-tank weapons. Thus the square-up smugglers—the ones who ran grass and gold and memory and stayed away from blow and Downtown—the square-ups kept a wary eye on them in case they got greedy for the rest. And so it was that the pilot had fought to stay alert for a total of an hour and twenty minutes while the dangerous men smoked spliffs around patched and leaky hoses full of warm Jet-A; while the moist tradewind blew salt, crab skeletons and bat guano into the delicate spinning whiskers of his turbines.

The pilot's eyes flicked automatically back and forth between the windscreen and his crucial sets of data; horizontal attitude indicator, gyro, vertical-velocity (windscreen); satnav, engine pressure ratio, first-stage compressor r.p.m. (windscreen); fuel flow, airspeed, counter-measures readout—and back to the windscreen to resume the cycle.

The pilot felt like the sheer torque of this work had altered him into a weird organism, half-blood, half-capacitor, specialized in the feedback between flight and darkness.

The autopilot was coupled to a Sperry Terrain-Following-Radar, which was how it could handle the plane this low—but the TFR, liberated from a mothballed B-52, was old. Even with new TFR you were supposed to be right there, because if the unit malfunctioned, even briefly, you would have maybe half a second to correct the error before the waves smashed plane and pilot to a million separate pieces.

Anyway he needed the discipline of sheepdogging the auto, to stay alert. The boil he'd got on the Rio Chingado had abscessed, he could feel his body temperature rising; and while his specialized hands and eyes could cope with reflexive supervision, the resulting fever made his mind wander.

Sometimes he saw shapes rushing out of the night; snowy mountains, lace curtains, buildings of wedged glass that had no place in this part of the Atlantic. At other times the illusions were more disturbing, and the forms of extinct birds, striking fists, and choirs of blonde women clad only in turquoise ribbons, had he actually been flying, would have affected the soft touch of his hands, putting him perilously close to the snapping spume beneath him or the questing electronic waves above.

The pilot, looking for solid images, checked his reflection in the side window. The features were strangely young; upturned nose, freckles; faraway and permanent grin crammed angular and Norman-Rockwell-ish into the leather World War I flying helmet that he'd modified to take audio from the counter-measures pak. It was the face of a slingshot sniper, an apple thief, someone who trafficked in firecrackers and baseball cards. A boy who stuck moths down girls' blouses and filled his pockets with string or the dried skins of tree frogs. Even the glitter of headache, the blackened eye-sockets of fatigue could not put age on him.

The pilot winced. He did not care to look fifteen. It made clients think maybe they could get away with things.

(Like Poop-face Provenzano had gotten away with things)

The pilot checked the plane's trim, reflexively, while the memory jimmied its way into the front of his brain.

The thing with Poop-face happened in the days before the pilot learned to fly, when he had quit Trout River Voke because he was so goddam sick of being young, and in school, and in upstate New York. All he'd wanted to do in those days was go fast. The destination didn't matter, it was speed alone that counted.

The pilot checked his throttle settings as the images flooded in.

He'd spent days following the downhill speed-skiing circuit, training to be one of those human bullets in stretch kevlar suits locked onto ten-foot boards.

He'd watched hours of Sunday television to catch the scant coverage of luge, or motorcycle rallies, or Open Offshore Superboat racing in the deceptively smooth swells off Florida.

Superboats, the young pilot had decided, were the best. The V-hulls were huge, sharp, dangerous as the water they moved upon. They mounted two, three, sometimes four turbocharged engines of up to eighteen-hundred-horsepower apiece. They thundered over the ocean at speeds close to 150 m.p.h. and spent as much time in the air between waves as on the water. Their drivers wore oxygen equipment to filter out the engine gases, and watercooled suits; they sat in airtight one-piece titanium ejection pods built for fighters. The pods were supposed to protect them in case the boat flipped, or burned, or sank. In practice, the pods just broke up, melted or went to the bottom with the rest of the boat.

One day the pilot told his parents he was going to South Florida to work on the superboat circuit and become, eventually, a racer.

"What part of Florida?" his father asked.

"It's a circuit, Papi," the young pilot answered. "Lauderdale, Miami, the Everglades. Key West."

His father reflected a moment.

"You got the Apalachicola Northern Railroad, the Seaboard Coast, the Florida East Coast," said Roman Marak. Roman had worked on railroads all his life, and tended to define issues by what trains ran, or had run, in the area. "Also, you will be near Cuba, the Bahamas, Jamaica, if you get into trouble."

Even at that time Roman Marak was fairly certain his son would wind up with uniformed men at his heels.

"I'll pack your swimsuit," his mother said.

So young Josef Marak—he was seventeen then—collected his savings from the Oneida County Savings Bank, and an Amtrak ticket from his father, and boarded a train going south.

He showed up in Everglades City eight days before the Everglades International Open Ocean Superboat Challenge Cup. For five days he was abused, laughed at and sometimes propositioned by overweight, loud, foul-talking men in greasy overalls. For five nights he slept under a tarp in a mechanic's pit that smelled of oil, whiskey and semen, in that order. On the sixth day Cal Bigbee—the biggest, loudest, foulest-talking man of them all—took pity on the Yankee kid with the funny accent and hired him on a temporary basis as coffeeboy and grease-monkey for the *Miss Slew/Rebel Beer* hydroplane racing team.

The pilot was good with his hands. More importantly, he loved machinery; loved the way it rumbled, interlocked, even "thought" in that honest gleaming step-by-step way machines had. The tight tolerances of superblower flanges rang like crystal in his brain. He adjusted them carefully, sensually, by feel, like playing an instrument. The clean balance of nitrated clutches, the smooth conjunctions of lubricant seemed to him the poetry of matter itself, the push-and-pull of atoms translated to heat and steel specifically for the religious devotions of man. After nine months on the circuit he could fine-tune the fuel injection of a fourteen-hundred-horsepower Statkus-Chevy as well as Cal Bigbee. After fourteen months Cal let him ride as driver, then throttleman on the *Miss Slew*.

"V-hull racing," Cal used to tell him reassuringly, "it's just like handlin' a woman. Y'all got to go so fast you're ready to explode with every cross-wave. But at the same time y'all got to go just slow enough that she don't blow up on you—keep her turbo and water temp and oil pressure just south of red-line the whole way."

On his third race the pilot pushed *Miss Slew* at an average speed of 139.74 m.p.h. over a 115-mile course. He won the heat on a red-hot bearing that burned the boat to the waterline ten minutes after he crossed the finish line.

Cal Bigbee knocked him off the dock by way of firing him. Poop-face Provenzano found him sitting on the dock that same night, drinking Rebel beer, nursing his bruises. Listening to the pelicans splash and croak.

Poop-face had no nose to speak of. He was weedy and dressed in K-mart "Windjammer" shorts and a safari jacket he thought made him look like Gregory Peck but in fact made him look like what he was, which was a geek.

"You wanna drive superboats?" Poop-face asked him.

"Who's gonna hire me?" the pilot asked sadly. Rebel beer was making him morose. "After I burned Cal's boat."

"Might know some people," Poop-face offered.

"Nah," the pilot answered. "I'm thinking of learnin' to fly. I'm sick of fuckin' with machines only spend half their time in the air."

"Fifteen thousand dollars a run," Poop-face said softly.

"Sens'?" The pilot had been around South Florida long enough to know what was going on.

"Hunnert bales of Guajira."

Fifteen thousand bucks would pay for flying school, qualify him on small jets, maybe leave a little left over, the pilot thought.

"For fifteen grand, maybe I could fuck around a little while longer," he told Poop-face.

Poop-face showed him the craft. It was a former circuit tunnel-boat, a catamaran-planer with twin turbo-charged Lycomings, rigged for single-handing. The pilot found out later what everyone on the waterfront knew all along, namely that the boat was so old it had two chances in five of surviving the 320-mile round trip to Mangrove Cay. Also the going rate was $25,000 for a hundred-bale run where the cargo would bring in close to a million dollars on the street. However in the beginning the pilot did not know any better and in due course he drove the boat carefully through the loud warm waters to Andros, and then back in a screaming, spine-telescoping rocket-ride over the odd-shaped swells and the startled dolphins, trying to keep the craft somewhere near stable at 95 m.p.h., skimming her like a fiberglas frisbee from the cracking slope of one wave to the ragged crest of the next; betting on luck and reflexes and good night-vision, waiting for the engines to rip out of their cracked supports or crush the craft like a Christmas ornament against the cement sea; looking for cutters and the slow boats of Customs under the great devil's temple of the tropical night—

A hint of green and white in the corner of one eye and the pilot stabs down with his right foot, yanks the control column back and right with the left hand while his right mashes the thrust levers forward for maximum power, the ancient Citation-C slewing to the right in a 375-knot banking climb that brings it over the deck of a light Panamanian crude carrier with a good twelve feet to spare.

The tanker was gone—smeared yellow decklights, bow wave, rusting pump-system lost under the plane's right wing.